Sarah Mason grew up in Cornwall but now lives in Cheltenham with her husband and children. Her first novel, *Playing James*, won the Romantic Novel of the Year Award 2003. Visit her website at www.sarah-mason.co.uk.

D0063137

Also by Sarah Mason

Playing James
The Party Season
High Society

Sea Fever

SARAH MASON

sphere

SPHERE

First published in Great Britain as a paperback original in 2007 by Sphere

Copyright © Sarah Mason 2007

The moral right of the author has been asserted.

A CIP catalogue record for this book
is available from the British Library.

ISBN 978-0-7515-3598-3

Papers used by Sphere are natural, recyclable products made from
wood grown in sustainable forests and certified in accordance with
the rules of the Forest Stewardship Council.

Typeset in BerkeleyOS-Medium by Palimpsest Book Production Limited,
Grangemouth, Stirlingshire
Printed and bound in Great Britain by Clays Ltd, St Ives plc
Paper supplied by Hellefoss AS, Norway

Sphere
An imprint of
Little, Brown Book Group
Brettenham House
Lancaster Place
London WC2E 7EN

A Member of the Hachette Livre Group of Companies

www.littlebrown.co.uk

For Toby

Acknowledgements

Sea Fever was a difficult and long book to write so there is a huge debt of thanks. The America's Cup sailors are very much a closed-off community so I am very grateful to anyone who helped me gain access to them and their world. All the people below deserve my thanks but there were some who went out of their way for me. In particular, I have to thank Bob Fisher who was unstintingly generous with his time and advice. He truly is an authority and, I have to add at this point, any mistakes are of my own making and I only took his advice insofar as to suit my plot. My fiction should not reflect on him or his expertise. Also Tom Schnackenburg, who was wonderfully friendly and never minded being called even when so much was going on in his own life. Matt Sheahan was happy to talk to me for hours on end and also deserves a special thank you. Ben Ainslie was amazingly helpful and even managed to find time to take me sailing for the day (for which I also have to thank the Team Volvo for Life), and had to put up with me wittering on about my new Sebago shoes for half an hour.

I also have to thank: David Atkinson, Barbara at Shosaloza, Christine Belanger, Vanessa Bellamy, Mark Beretta, Andrew Biggs, Amy Bradley-Watson, Peter De Savary, Mike Desmond, Louise Dier, Guillermo Garcia Román, Andy Green, Mo Griffiths, Julian Hocken, Bob Holt, Alice l'Anson Widdows, John Longley, Margaret at Villa Rothsay, Antony Matusch, Daphne Morgan

Barnicoat, Hayley Pattison, Sarah Rees at Team Volvo for Life, Robin Richardson, Dawn Riley, Nick Rogers, Peter Rusch, Leslie Ryan, Jenny and Greg Searle, Katie Strachan, Peta Stuart-Hunt, Bruno Troublé, Ian Walker.

On a personal note, there were many people who helped me with the constant pressure on time and schedule that such a book demands, which was particularly hard with one little one and a pregnancy. I need to thank my mother and her uncomplaining help with childcare. Also Sue and Brian, Tasha and Laurence, Christopher and Katie Cornwell and Lisa King for making my family life so comfortable and lavishing love on my little ones as though they were their own. I am so grateful for their support.

The lion's share of the gratitude does have to go to my husband who never complained (and only very occasionally raised his eyes to heaven) at the extra home duties. More importantly he was the biggest source of emotional support, incredibly loyal and always had confidence in me. He was encouraging when things were going well and comforting when they were going badly. I can honestly say that this book would not have been written without him.

I also have to thank Gina Smith, my wonderful PA; I could not have done without her kindness and good humour. She is now retired and living in Cyprus. I miss her greatly. I had to do a certain amount of work just after having my second child and Ele Stronge, my maternity nurse, certainly went beyond the call of duty and was such a pleasure to have around. Thank you.

I thank everyone at Little, Brown who has worked so hard in producing this book in such a short time, but mostly my editor, Jo Dickinson, who championed my cause throughout, even though the book was running terribly late. She worked unstintingly hard and made lots of suggestions on plot and character. I also have to thank Alison Lindsay for her work, and bothering to traipse all the way out to Valencia to see what all the fuss was about, Louise Davies and Richenda Todd for being wonderful and friendly editors, taking up the difficult mantle of the book whilst Jo was on maternity leave, and also Kerry Chapple and Emma Stonex for helping with some of the research. Thank you also to Tara Lawrence for giving up her free time and for being an invaluable sounding board and friend.

Great Britain did indeed challenge in the 2003 America's Cup held in Auckland (although not in the 2007 Cup in Valencia) and it was the first challenge in over twenty-five years. I do have to stress that *Sea Fever* is completely a work of fiction and none of my characters is supposed to resemble any of that crew or indeed any crew or organisation within the America's Cup. With such a wonderfully colourful past history there are many stories and anecdotes surrounding the Cup, but if an incident or a part of dialogue is acted or spoken by a character in this book then is it not meant to portray the original subject. All boat names are also fictional. Most of the action sequences were taken from real-life events and again are not supposed to portray the original crew.

Whilst going to press, I hear that Great Britain are planning to challenge for the America's Cup in 2009/2011 and I wish them the best of luck.

Character List

Fabian Beaufort	Troubled and ostracised young sailor.
David Beaufort	Fabian's missing father.
Elizabeth Beaufort	Fabian's snobby mother.
Rosie Beaufort	Fabian and Milly's little girl.
Franco Berlini	The owner of the Italian syndicate.
Jason Bryant	Callous helmsman who likes to win.
Beatrice Burman	Rafe's aunt. Also known as *Bee*. In her early fifties but a goddess by anyone's standards. She loves life and enjoys it to the full.
Carla	Local Spanish lady who caters for the syndicate and firmly believes in the crew and the restorative powers of buns and coffee.
Corposant	Henry Luter's sumptuous yacht where he lives with Saffron during the Cup. It is moored in the America's Cup marina.
Consuela	Saffron Luter's maid.
Milly Dantry	Sweet waitress working on the Isle of Wight during Cowes Week.
Bill Dantry	Her kind father.
Griff Dow	A sail maker and passionate devotee of the America's Cup.
Excalibur	The British challenge's awe-inspiring boat.

Marco Fraternelli	The skipper of the Italian syndicate.
Hattie Frobisher	Sweet PR girl, in charge of all the PR for the British syndicate.
Jane	Henry Luter's beady personal assistant. As thin as she is mean.
Tim Jenkins	Efficient and capable shore manager of the British syndicate.
Laura	The meteorologist for the British syndicate. Her nerves and inaccuracy at the start give her the nickname of *Fog*.
Rafe Louvel	Enigmatic loner who is loath to compete.
Tom Louvel	His father, also a wanderer.
Daisy Louvel	Rafe's long-dead mother.
Henry Luter	Ruthless billionaire, determined to win the Cup which ever way he can.
Saffron Luter	His beautiful trophy wife.
Sir Edward Lamb	A retired veteran persuaded to return to the Cup to coach. A slight hypochondriac.
John MacGregor	Also known as *Mack*. One of the most celebrated sailors of his generation. Highly respected until the 2003 America's Cup after which his capabilities are cast under shadow.
Josie MacGregor	Mack's ex-wife.
Colin Montague	Main sponsor of Mack and then the British challenge. A rich industrialist and a good sort of bloke.
Ava Montague	His wayward and Bohemian daughter. A talented artist in her own right but forever in the shadow of her father's name.
Luca Morenzo	The bowman of the Italian crew. Beautiful too.
Mucky Ducky	The tug-like hospitality boat of the British syndicate which also doubles up as

	coaching boat and tow.
Neville	The young apprentice boat designer on the design team of *Excalibur*. Generally attributed with her design.
Erica Pencarrow	Known by everyone as *Inky*. A very talented sailor, ahead of her time. Constantly battles to get ahead.
James Pencarrow	Inky's highly competitive father who is disbelieving of Inky and her ambitions.
Mary Pencarrow	Inky's mild mother.
Pipgin	Custard's dog. A red setter.
Mr and Mrs Rochester and Alicia Rochester	Ghastly friends of Elizabeth Beaufort. Put up Fabian during Cowes Week on their yacht.
Salty	Bee's annoying dog. Well known for his love of food and trouble.
Slayer	The number-two boat in the British challenge, crewed by the second crew.
Will Stanmore	Also known as *Custard*. Friendly sailor, well respected on the match-racing circuit. Good friend of Inky.
Rob Thornton	Friend of Fabian's, killed whilst sailing together.

It is the world's oldest sporting trophy.
During its one-hundred-and-fifty-four-year history,
Great Britain has yet to win the America's Cup.

Prologue

Inky was first round the mark on the makeshift race course, ignoring the shouts of her brothers in the boat behind and unseeing of the beautiful scenery around her. The golden, solid sands of the beaches, the dull blue-grey of the sea combed lightly with white and the promise of the ocean lying just outside of the mouth of the bay. All she cared about right now was beating her brothers.

'HOIST THE SPINNAKER!' she yelled at her ever-patient godfather who also happened to be one of the most famous match racers on the planet. A tall, aggressive, dark-haired Scot, he was generally acknowledged to be a formidable talent on any water. He had a wide, sensuous but expressive mouth which could instantly laugh or curl into a terrifying scowl.

'POLE!' he shouted back as the spinnaker pole clipped into place. The beautiful white sail puffed out like a cloud in front of them. He climbed back across the deck to his eleven-year-old charge and smiled indulgently at her. 'Now what?'

'Em . . . ' Inky peered around, trying to assess her brothers' progress behind them. 'Are they going to try and cover me?' she asked hesitantly. Inky had salt water in her blood. She and her three older brothers came from the stormy north coast of Cornwall.

'That's right,' said her godfather. 'They're going to try and take your wind and then overtake us.' Inky hadn't mistaken the competitive edge to the brotherly teasing and already she could hear the tell-tale flapping of her own spinnaker's edges as the other boat started to hunt them down. Ignoring the Mohawk yells coming from the other boat, he went on, 'You need to try and shake them off us.'

'Then we gybe?'

He nodded. 'You give the orders.' He leapt over the coils of line to the bow of the boat again. The art of match racing was still relatively new to Inky, mainly because her family were keen offshore sailors, but John MacGregor – her celebrated godfather – was slowly introducing her to the field. She had found that she looked forward to Mack's visits more than ever before, if that were possible

'GYBING!' Inky yelled. Mack smoothly lowered the spinnaker, reset the pole and then powered the sail into her new set as Inky turned the boat through the wind. She peered anxiously behind, watching her brothers effortlessly follow them in a perfect gybe, but she knew that their nonchalance had an edge to it as they were desperate to claim her godfather's attention. They didn't seem to have lost any time out of their gybe and were as closely on her tail as before. 'GYBING!' she yelled again. But no matter how many times she gybed, she simply couldn't lose them until eventually the boys claimed her wind and steamed past her to take the finish line.

Doubly competitive wherever her brothers were concerned, Inky Pencarrow was furious at being beaten, especially in front of Mack – though her brothers only deigned to sail with her when he visited anyway. But she especially didn't want Mack to think that she was useless; her sailing had little enough attention at home as it was. Her three brothers had all been sent away to school and excelled within the school's prominent sailing squad. They were given opportunities that Inky could only dream about. She had stayed in their native Cornwall, content at the village school because during the summer she could escape as soon as the bell went and jump on her bicycle, straight down to Rock village where she could take out a little Laser dinghy into the Camel estuary. Her greatest fear was that her father would carry out his oft-repeated threat to send her away to a school without sailing facilities. It was only her and her mother's pleading which had thus far kept her at home.

'Never mind, squirt,' said her brothers, patting her head once they had all landed on the pontoon. 'Better luck next time.'

'Can we race again tomorrow?' asked Inky eagerly.

'Mack won't be on board with you tomorrow. I'm not sure you'll be worthy competition. Besides, match racing isn't really our thing.'

'Let me try!' pleaded Inky.

'These boats are absolutely archaic.'

'Or let me sail with you?'

'You're not heavy enough. One puff of wind would take you out.'

'I'm heavy enough for match racing!' said Inky indignantly, tossing the blue-black hair that had inspired her name. 'It's much harder than you think.' Inky found her recent introduction to this more aggressive style of yachting absolutely addictive. The concept was simple. Two boats and a finish line. But the techniques required great ingenuity and resourcefulness, perfect reflexes, timing which could not be a millisecond out and the ability to think one step ahead. It was never a matter of just racing for the line and the fastest boat won. You had to put yourself between the finish line and the competitor and do anything to stay there. A bit like a game of British Bulldog except you were running for the line at the same time.

'Keep practising, squirt.' They turned their attention to Mack who had just appeared at her shoulder. 'We've got these fantastic boats at school, Mack. Charlie is going to take one across the Channel. Will you come and see them sometime?'

Mack laughed but seemed to refuse to be distracted from Inky. 'I think you should take Inky out again tomorrow. You

3

need to keep on top of her otherwise one day she'll be beating the lot of you.'

Her brothers all wanted to be professional sailors, much to the bursting pride of their father who had been a highly respected helmsman, now retired. Inky also wanted to be a professional sailor but it was a secret ambition because she knew her father wanted her to follow a more traditional, more *womanly* profession.

The boys were diverted by their mother delicately picking her way down the pontoon carrying a picnic basket and, ever hungry – like Labradors – they made for the food.

'Do you want to have lunch on my boat?' Mack asked Inky.

'Yes, please,' said Inky with relief. Whenever Inky was with Mack in a public place, people were forever stopping and asking him for his autograph or talking to him about boats. She had also noticed rather beadily that women in particular liked to toss their hair and smile a lot at him. At least if they had lunch on his boat she could have him to herself for a little while longer. Once they went home, Inky's father James would claim his attention and Inky wouldn't be able to ask him all the questions she had been saving up for months.

John MacGregor was Inky's father's oldest friend. They knew each other from the days they had spent together in the British youth squad. Whereas James Pencarrow won a respectable bronze medal dinghy sailing at the 1976 Olympic Games, John MacGregor walked away with the gold and once again (just to show it wasn't a fluke) four years later. But he then started experimenting with offshore and match racing, and for a long time his critics (and he had a few – his gruff straight-talking style, which didn't suffer fools easily, had ruffled a few feathers over the years) gleefully predicted his downfall. But every time Mack would prove them wrong by beating a record or winning a race until they were all but silenced. Inky often wondered whether, if her father could have foreseen Mack's almost meteoric rise to iconic status, he would have still asked him to be her godfather.

But James always tactlessly pointed out that when she was born was the only time Mack was in the country.

Mack watched Inky's mother Mary walk back up the pontoon. 'What are you looking at, Mack?' asked Inky, already biting into a banana.

'Your mother.'

Inky focused on someone usually quite invisible to her eleven-year-old eyes. 'Yes,' she said critically. 'She really shouldn't be wearing those shoes on the pontoon. We keep telling her.'

Mack laughed. 'I was thinking how little she's changed from when I first met her all those years ago.'

'What? Mum?'

'She used to be quite the socialite, you know. Admired wherever she went.'

But Inky had already eagerly jumped into the launch which would take them out to Mack's boat. 'She's such a beautiful boat,' she sighed on the short journey out to the mooring, not able to take her eyes off her. To Inky it looked as though *Wild Thing* had been tied down to her mooring to prevent her from getting away. They thanked the launch driver before clambering aboard and arranging their lunch in front of them. 'Why did you sail *Wild Thing* over?' Inky asked unwrapping her peanut butter and banana sandwiches and apple and watercress rolls.

'You know I'm going to be away for a while.'

'Doing the America's Cup,' prompted Inky. 'I wanted to come to America to see you but Dad said you didn't need any distractions.'

Mack smiled. 'Well, I thought you might like to use her for the summer.' She would need help but Mack would make it clear whom he was lending it to.

Inky's jaw dropped open. 'Me? Sail *Wild Thing*?' Her mind raced with delight as to what her brothers might say. 'Why?' was all she could manage to say.

'I don't need to see you winning to see how good you might be.'

Inky beamed at him. 'You think that I might be good one day?'

'I do.'

'I wish you would tell Dad that.'

'I do. Often.'

'He's always talking about sending me away to school. He thinks I need more of an education.'

'What do you think?'

'I think I would die. My mother wants me to stay here too but I don't think it's because of the sailing thing. I think it's because she doesn't want to be left alone.' Inky wondered if she should have said such a thing but Mack didn't look at all shocked.

'Maybe you should consider joining the national youth squad.'

'I would love to!' exclaimed Inky, her eyes shining. 'But Dad or Mum would have to drive me to places.'

'I'll talk to your father.'

Inky thought she might expire with happiness. The prospect of sailing *Wild Thing* all summer and joining the youth squad seemed almost too much to bear. 'Tell me about the America's Cup again. I got a book out of the library about the boats.' The America's Cup boats which Mack was so passionate about were not little dinghies. The masts scraped the sky at 110 feet high and they weighed nearly twenty-five tonnes. They were mean-ingless statistics on the page but when Inky talked to Mack they came to life as elegant and fierce war machines which were perfectly honed, yet so interbred they were useless for any other purpose except the race they were born to compete in. 'I would love to compete in the America's Cup one day,' she sighed. 'That's the best match racing ever, isn't it?'

'I think so and it's an obsession for some of the richest, most powerful and most eccentric characters in the world,' admitted Mack. 'But I'm afraid there are no women in the Cup. Maybe there will be by the time you grow up,' he added hastily.

'Would you win a lot of money if you won the Cup?' asked Inky.

'Nothing. No money. Nothing except the Cup itself and the right to set the rules and venue for the next one. It's a bit bizarre. Like giving the Olympic Games to the country who wins the most medals. But one of things you must understand is that it is not designed to be a fair contest. Whoever wins the Cup can set the rules.'

Inky absorbed this for a second. Her next question was on a more personal note. 'And will Auntie Josie be going with you to America?' Josie was Mack's wife. They had been married for about five years and she was terribly glamorous – or so Inky thought anyway. Her mother must have thought so too because she was always asking her about her clothes and about the cities she had visited. Inky knew that something funny was going on between Mack and Josie because she had overheard her parents talking.

'No, she won't,' said Mack shortly. 'I don't know what your parents have told you, Inky, but I'm afraid that Auntie Josie and I aren't . . . '

'Married any more?'

'Well, I suppose that's exactly right. Or won't be soon anyway.'

'Why not?'

Mack paused for a moment and put down his sandwich. 'You know that you said that you thought you would die if your father sent you away to school and from the water?' Inky nodded. 'Well, that's how I feel about sailing too. And Aunt Josie wants me to feel differently about it.'

'What do you mean, differently?'

'I think she would like me to love sailing a little less and her a little more.'

'But you can't help the way you feel!' said Inky indignantly.

'No, I can't. But when you love something like we do, Inky, it sometimes has a great cost to it. Maybe that's something your father is trying to protect you against. But you and I both know that there's nothing you can do about it. Stopping doing something you love would be as alien a concept as chopping off your arm.'

Mack waited until Inky had gone to bed that night before broaching the subject of her sailing with James. He watched in silence as Inky's beautiful mother, with her apron neatly tied in a bow behind her back, speared the lamb joint with more rosemary picked from her much beloved garden. Mary Pencarrow was constantly out there wrestling the elements and almost taking on the sea itself as she tried to introduce plants and bulbs which time and again failed to survive the wind or the constant pervasion of salt. It amazed Mack afresh how out of place Mary seemed on the rough and ragged coast of Cornwall instead of in her native and beloved London. It was still like seeing a sleek thoroughbred in a stable of ponies, even though it had been eighteen years since Inky's father had surprised everyone and married her within months of meeting her at a fashionable London party, the sort he usually so determinedly avoided. Their attraction to each other was undeniable but many of their family and friends thought it would be short-lived as James Pencarrow immediately whisked his new bride down to the remote family house on the north coast of Cornwall that he had recently inherited after his own father's death. But Mary's love for her new husband had overcome her love for her old cosmopolitan city life. At least until recently, anyway.

She had had four children in quick succession and was thrilled when her fourth child was a long-awaited girl. She dressed her slavishly in gingham frills and pastel florals, waiting and hoping for the day when she could chat to her about fashion and tea parties, nail varnish and Delia, only to find that her little girl spent more and more time on boats with her brothers and father. As soon as Inky found a voice she demanded to be dressed in the same clothes as her brothers and if her mother refused, patiently holding out gorgeous embroidered Capri pants, then she would run out into the sand dunes in her knickers.

Mary Pencarrow had long since come to terms with this and although she was inordinately proud of her daughter, she did long for just a glimmer of femininity from her, if only to give them something to talk about. Only she still called her Erica, although Inky actually suited her far better, with her blue-black hair and creamy, pale complexion, so reminiscent of fresh ink on thick parchment.

Mack jumped up to help her as Mary started to lay the table for supper. 'Mack, sit down. I'll do this. You talk to James.' She inclined her head firmly towards her husband as though reading Mack's mind. Mack smiled slightly at her. As someone about to be divorced he was ultra sensitive to others' unhappiness, but she was such a private person that he could only tread warily around hers. He stared at her for a moment, wondering how she had become involved in this obsessive world of boats, tides and wind with language and customs of its own – as if a coven of witches had ensnared a unicorn. He shook his head and tried to concentrate on Inky.

'I think Inky should be thinking about joining the youth squad,' he said to James who was sitting in the armchair next to the Aga, trying to find an article for Mack in one of his yachting magazines. Mary didn't react; she carried on setting the table slowly.

James sighed and laid down the magazine. 'Not this old chestnut again, Mack.'

'She's talented,' insisted Mack.

'It's pointless. I don't want you building up her hopes only for her to have them dashed. She thinks she can do everything that the boys can do. Look at that stupid stunt she pulled last week.' On the strongest spring tide of the season the boys would attach ropes to the buoys and water-ski behind them on the tide. James had expressly forbidden Inky from copying them but she had ignored him nonetheless, promptly fallen off and been swept out to sea. The lifeboat had to pick her up. 'We nearly died of worry. She shouldn't be trying stupid tricks.'

'But you didn't punish the boys for doing the same thing?'

'They didn't get swept out to sea. It's about time that Inky realised she's not just like the boys and she can't do anything she likes.'

'What do you mean?'

'It may have escaped your notice, Mack, but Inky is a girl. And that has its limitations.'

'But I don't think it's Inky's limitation. I know that I'm not around as much as I would like for her but Inky is the closest thing to having my own child, James . . . '

'I know that and it's wonderful that you take your responsibilities so seriously but Inky isn't going to be a great sailor. Women and sailing are incompatible. The sooner she learns that then the less of a disappointment it will be for her. She should spend her time more constructively. God knows her mother would like her to . . . ' He gestured his head towards Mary who didn't meet his eye.

'Constructively? What do you mean, constructively?'

'I don't know! Doing more womanly pursuits! Things that will stand her in good stead later on. You're simply encouraging her by lending her that boat for the summer.'

'You think I should have lent it to one of the boys,' said Mack quietly.

'They are actually going to have careers in sailing. Whereas Inky . . . '

'Whereas Inky what?'

'I'm just trying to protect her, Mack. I want her to have other options.'

'This is 1995, James. Not 1895. Why can't you . . . '

Inky, from the landing, didn't hear what he was about to say as one of her brothers came out of his bedroom. She drowned herself in the shadows until he passed and then scurried back into her room with her father's words still ringing in her ears. Pulling the covers over her head, she thought about what she had just heard. She might only be eleven years old, but it was old enough to realise that her mother wasn't terribly happy and yet too young to know why. This pursuit of womanly things (and her mother was the most feminine woman she knew) hadn't seemed to have brought her much happiness. It felt as though her own sex had betrayed her. Inky desperately wanted to sail like her brothers. She wanted the same freedom. And she would get it, whatever it took, whatever her father said.

'I must go down to the sea again . . .'
John Masefield, 'Sea Fever'

PART ONE

Chapter 1

Eight years later.

The Spanish boat, *Guerrero*, stormed in from the other side of the start box snarling with aggression. They were arrogant and insistent – a crew on the knife edge of perfection. As if stamping on an accelerator, Mack turned his boat, *Firebird*, into the wind and placed himself on a collision course with them. The two respective bowmen, oblivious to the bad weather, dipped in and out of each other's views as they called the distance between them. The five-minute gun had just gone, indicating the time left until the start of the race. Mack and his competitor were going through the vital pre-start battle. It was an elaborate game of cat and mouse where you were alternately the hunter and the hunted.

The boats were aimed head on. For all the money spent on her, *Firebird* was a difficult boat to control even after the countless hours spent practising and racing; Mack still couldn't get a real feel for her. It was like flying a plane simply on instruments. The two boats charged to within a few feet of one another before Mack threw *Firebird* into a tack. *Guerrero* matched him with a complementary one and the boats circled, waiting for the other to make an error. The crew could hardly hear themselves think above the frenzied shouts of the helmsman, the squeal of tortured lines, the thunder of sails as the boom slammed back and forth over the deck.

Again and again the boats drove at each other, battling for supremacy until the water was simply a bubbling, boiling mass. Again and again the better manoeuvrability of the Spanish boat would force Mack over, apparently holding him by the neck – but every time he wriggled free. On this last tack, he coiled back towards *Guerrero* and the two yachts charged to within half a foot of each other.

'Christ,' snapped the boat designer who was watching from one of the support launches. 'Was that necessary? Those are fucking three-million-pound boats they are playing chicken with.'

For the first time, the skippers were close enough to see each other properly. Mack eyed the Spanish skipper thoughtfully, then took the opportunity to wheel round and come up on the right-of-way starboard side. He practically nudged their stern, forcing them off their line. But suddenly: 'He's on our tail, Mack! Get him off us!' called his tactician and, wheeling round, Mack saw that *Guerrero* had circled sharply and popped up behind them. As in a dogfight, whoever is on the tail of the opposing boat can control them. Mack dived into the spectator boats, desperately trying to wipe him off. He saw a small opportunity to lose him, made as though he was about to tack and at the last second he swung the opposite way round the committee boat in a turn so tight and unexpected that he could see the whites of his opponents' startled eyes. *Guerrero* thankfully didn't follow suit.

Mack's navigator started the one-minute countdown to the actual start. 'Sixty . . . fifty, forty-nine, forty-eight . . . '

As though thinking ten moves ahead in a chess game, Mack glanced round. He started to run for the line, relying on his instinctive judgement of time on distance.

'You're not going to make it, Mack,' snapped Henry Luter, seeing what he was trying to do, for *Guerrero* had suddenly wheeled round and was making her approach for the line from the opposite end. The problem was that Henry Luter's advice was never to be relied on, a fundamental flaw for a strategist. Not least because he had absolutely no judge of time on distance.

The numbers echoed in the background, 'Thirty . . . twenty-nine . . . twenty-eight . . . '

'I fucking well am. I NEED MORE SPEED!'

'They're trying to cross our bow! This is going to be close, Mack!' yelled his bowman over his microphone – he was standing at the bow to watch the distance.

'Fucking hell,' Mack muttered. Instinctively he looked up to the mainsail to make sure it was trimmed hard enough and they were going as fast as they could.

The count went on. 'Nineteen . . . eighteen . . . seventeen . . . sixteen . . . ' His crew looked over to him, willing him to stop the other boat in its tracks, and then back to their bowman who was the only one who could see properly. 'They might make it,' the bowman muttered to himself. But in the last few seconds, the skipper of *Guerrero* obviously decided they couldn't and the bow literally whooshed past *Firebird*'s stern as he ducked behind. Mack's crew started to breathe again. The starting gun went and they hit the line running, ahead of *Guerrero*.

Inky Pencarrow hated having to sit on the reserve bench. She was watching the British crew race the mighty Spanish during the thirty-first America's Cup. They were 3–1 down in a best of seven series, and it was looking increasingly as if even their legendary helmsman, John 'Mack' MacGregor, couldn't save them. She was on the sumptuous yacht belonging to Henry Luter, who also insisted on taking the position of strategist on *Firebird*. Luter was the millionaire financing the syndicate behind the British challenge, and his boat, *Corposant*, was by far the largest and most ostentatious in the spectator fleet. The weather was awful and the guests were enjoying (what they could of) a lunch of oysters placed in a shooter of Bloody Mary followed by soft shelled crabs and salad all accompanied by ice-cold champagne – Henry Luter was generous only when he could pass the whole thing on expenses. The corporate helicopter delivering more guests to the watery dais momentarily drowned out the voice of the on-board commentator who was struggling to clarify some of the more complicated rules of the America's Cup.

At present he was just explaining the pre-start. 'On the first gun there is a five-minute countdown to the actual start, the boats enter from opposite ends and wrestle for the optimum position to start from, but woe and betide them if they are over the line when the actual starting gun fires. They will have to circle and restart. What you have just witnessed was an amazing display of time-on-distance judgement by our legendary helmsman John MacGregor. He has to know how long it will take the boat to get to the start line with the present wind speed, direction and current. Some of the most talented match racers in the world still get it wrong and it is disaster when they do. The pre-start is the biggest cat fight of them all, ladies and gentlemen, and will probably win or lose the race for them . . . ' said the commentator.

Inky sighed and stared after the two America's Cup yachts. They looked like no other boat. They were monstrous things, scarily narrow with barely any room for the seventeen-strong crew to move but with a mast that reached over thirty metres into the sky. The boats carried such powerful loads that they were as dangerous as standing inside an industrial machine because they were also built to be as light as possible, which meant they often broke. They were the most beautiful things that Inky had ever seen.

Inky's best friend, Will Stanmore, more popularly known as Custard, appeared by her side. He always reminded Inky of a Labrador, with his blond mane and exuberant love-me demeanour. His looks were actually very average but his personality beamed through every pore and he had a stunning, genuine smile which could work its magic on the sternest race official. 'There you are! I've been waiting outside the Ladies for the last ten minutes.'

'You could have used the Gents, Custard. No one would have minded.'

'Looking for you, you arse.'

'It was a good start,' sighed Inky gesturing her head towards the yachts. *Corposant* started her engines and prepared to follow them up the course.

'I know. I was watching the screen. But even Mack might not be able to fight his way out of this one.' Custard looked nervously over his shoulder in case Henry Luter's ever-present, beady personal assistant, Jane, might hear, and lowered his voice. 'First British entry in the Cup for over fifteen years and Henry Luter is the syndicate head. Fucking awful luck. Why couldn't we have had a different billionaire?' he joked.

'He runs the syndicate like one of his companies,' grumbled Inky.

'You heard about poor old Joe? First he knew about getting fired was a plane ticket pushed under his door last night. Christ, it's like musical chairs.' The comings and goings of their syndicate had entertained the America's Cup fraternity, who were well seasoned in the antics of eccentric billionaires, all summer long.

'Yeah, I heard. Lucky that you keep your room in such a mess. You wouldn't notice if a plane ticket was pushed under your door.'

'I know,' said Custard cheerfully. 'I've probably been fired six times already and they can't work out why I keep on turning up.'

'Luter would have been better off spending his millions on some good PR rather than an over-technical boat which no one can sail.' Luter had in fact used more computer power on the boat design than was used to crack the human genome.

'I keep wondering, why hasn't Mack left?'

Inky shrugged. 'I don't know. Same reason why you haven't, I suppose.'

'Regular cash and Kiwi crumpet?'

'No, idiot. Mack says it's the first chance that most of us have ever had to sail for our country in the Cup.'

'Inky, we're in the second crew. We're not going to get the chance to sail for our country.'

'At least you know it's because one of Luter's cronies is in your position. The America's Cup is positively archaic. I don't know why I bother,' she grumbled, thinking of Tracy Edwards' and Ellen MacArthur's pioneering path through off-shore sailing – much to her father's astonishment.

Custard put his arm around her. 'There's always next time.'

'As long as Luter isn't in charge.'

'So you're not going to join the next challenge?'

'Not Henry Luter's, no I'm not.'

'He's not going to stop until he's got his paws on the Cup. We could always join another syndicate.'

'Marvellous. Then I could sit on the second crew for them,' grumbled Inky. A woman was a rarity in the America's Cup. She was like a duckling amongst crocodiles. But the fact was that Inky couldn't be sure whether it was her abilities or her breasts which had kept her off the first boat.

'Let's go inside and chat up prospective syndicate heads for the next Cup. Try to persuade them that a mere fifty million for a challenge would be a very shrewd tax dodge.'

'It's so cheap I don't know why more people don't do it,' said Inky, parroting Luter's favourite joke. Custard laughed.

Henry Luter's personal assistant, a thin, pale girl who made herself look more than her twenty-five years of age by dragging back her hair and wearing no make-up on her bony face, crept up on them. 'What are you two doing out here?' Jane hissed. 'We pay you to entertain the guests, not to gossip.' Of course, they were there to entertain the guests; Custard, by virtue of the fact he was extremely personable and Inky because Luter liked to show off how marvellously equal-opportunist he was.

'It's an exciting race,' protested Custard who actually hadn't taken his eyes off the two boats in front of them. 'Look, Mack's starting a tacking duel.'

Back on the boats, conversation had been scarce. After starting behind, *Guerrero* had sailed out to the left-hand side of the course, hoping to find some breeze which Mack had missed. Mack, knowing that his crew work was sloppier than *Guerrero*'s, had also gone out to the left side. If the Spanish were to gain on them then at least Mack could cover them by placing his boat between them and the wind. They would be forced to use his second-hand air. It was like being offered the dregs of someone else's fuel tank on a Formula One race track. The Spanish boat had caught up enough to try and overtake *Firebird* but every time they made to stamp on the accelerator and overtake, Mack would swerve in front of them and block them. The only way to pass would be to tack and tack again until *Firebird* made a mistake. This was known as a tacking duel.

'TACKING!' yelled Mack as *Guerrero* threw yet another tack at them. Every time a boat tacks it puts enormous stress not only on the boat but also on the crew. He's hoping either the boat or the crew will break, Mack thought to himself, glancing at the Spanish skipper as *Firebird*'s massive mainsail swung across the deck again. For the first time in the series, he felt some nerves. *Firebird*'s grinders were crouched over their pedestals in the middle of the boat, ready for another tack. But they looked at odds with the fiery corporate orange they were wearing. They looked tired and their eyes already had that haunted look of failure. All of Henry Luter's screamed threats, on and offshore, had failed to motivate them. It was as if they were watching their own obituary.

'Mack, they're gaining on us,' snapped Luter. 'Fucking well do something. Don't just lie there and let them shit all over us.'

Mack ignored him. It was too late in the competition to explain to Luter how the crew actually worked. 'TACKING!' Mack yelled as *Guerrero* threw another tack. The Spanish skipper had obviously noticed the tiredness of their grinders – he was barely giving them four breaths between forcing them to tack again.

The sea was bitchy and acting up and, combined with the wash of the spectator boats, was making the boat hard to control, like a particularly lively toddler. The noise on the boat was deafening as the waves bashed into them from all sides.

Mack eyed the first mark of the course up ahead. It would be tight to hold them until then. Even though *Guerrero* was wallowing in their second-hand air, she was still faster and Mack was having trouble holding her. But just as Mack was thinking these thoughts, there came a cry which meant an almost certain loss in an America's Cup race.

'MAN OVERBOARD!'

'Jesus, where?' Mack muttered, frantically looking round for a bobbing head between the waves. He stared at the crew expecting an immediate damage report from whoever witnessed it and made the call, but as though guilty by association, they shifted their eyes.

A whistle from the umpire's boat and the showing of *Firebird*'s identifying flag indicated a penalty.

'Who was it?' asked Henry Luter.

'Bowman,' Mack muttered, seeing the empty position up ahead. That in itself was no surprise. The bowman is the most exposed of all the crew on a boat with a minimum of working surfaces and no safety rails. In this sea it was also acting like a bucking bronco. Nevertheless for a bowman to lose his footing was a rarity.

Mack left Luter muttering death threats as he spun the wheel through to make the obligatory 270-degree penalty turn. He wished he knew what exactly had happened but the man overboard cry was so sudden and unexpected that Mack couldn't even identify which crew member it had come from.

None of that mattered right now. One of *Firebird*'s support launches was picking up the bowman whilst Mack took the yacht through its penalty turn and *Guerrero* stormed past them towards the mark. They were already rounding it and breaking out their spinnaker by the time Mack was headed back on course with the embarrassed bowman back on board.

'COME ON!' Mack yelled at his crew. 'I WANT A PERFECT SET! WE CAN STILL BEAT THEM!'

The crew bustled round, getting ready for rounding the mark.

'CODE SIX SPINNAKER!' yelled Mack's tactician. The sewer man hauled it up from the sewer on to the deck. The genoa was getting ready to be lowered and be replaced by the spinnaker which the trimmers would form to a perfect aerofoil. And all of this had to happen in under eight seconds.

'*Guerrero* has six boat lengths on us,' announced Mack's tactician. 'Let's try and catch her in our wind shadow.' Once the boats have rounded the mark and are going downwind, the trailing boat can creep up and punch the air out of the leading boat's spinnaker by stealing their wind.

'Get ready to tack,' growled Mack. 'TACKING!'

Mack managed to extract rare moments of brilliance even from the most disgruntled of crews. They rounded the mark in a perfect set and in under eight seconds. The huge white spinnaker puffed into place and opened its giant wings in front of him. The wind was still big though and Mack frowned to himself.

'That spinnaker looks too big,' he said to his tactician. 'Are you sure we should—'

Mack didn't get to finish his sentence. The next moment *Firebird* punched through the middle of one big wave and then buried herself deep into the back of the next. The mast couldn't stand the extra tonnes of pressure, a rigging fitting broke and the mast, along with any last hopes of the 2003 America's Cup, came tumbling down.

The wake party, as they are so euphemistically called, certainly had a funereal air. It was being held in the vast hangar used to house the yachts; *Firebird*, forlorn under her tarpaulin skirt, stood close by on her enormous cradle.

Mack was standing by the door chatting to some of the crew. People who read of his exploits and adventures often dismissed them as overblown: it wasn't until you walked into his presence and felt the force of his personality that you instantly knew all those things must be true. In his late forties, he was not traditionally handsome but terribly attractive in a rugged sort of way.

As one journalist so aptly put it, 'If you were in any sort of trouble and the odds were completely against you then this is the only man you would wish to have at your side.'

His easy manner and the way he listened attentively masked any hint of the enormous row he had just had with Henry Luter. Luter had managed to keep his temper after the race until they'd hit the shore and their compound.

Then: 'What the fuck was that all about?' Luter had roared. He was only one footstep into the room. 'How could you fuck it up like that? Why the fuck do I pay you so much money?'

Mack hadn't explained whose fault it was. He didn't work like that. He would never apportion blame. A crew worked together and if one of them made a mistake then it was up to everyone else to cover their backs. It was just one of many philosophies that he and Henry Luter differed on.

'You pay me to shape your crew.'

'Shape my crew? What on earth are you talking about? I pay you to drive the fucking boat. Nothing more, nothing less.'

'One doesn't come without the other. Crews do not work independently of one another. They can't. They all rely on each other. They all rely on each other for their safety and even their lives. Everybody on that boat hated each other so much that I don't think they would lift a finger to save another crew member. You've got them into such a state of turmoil that all they are intent on is not getting blamed.'

'*I've* got them into that state? *I* have?' Henry had said in a fury.

'By swapping them around so much. By making them take responsibility for *your* mistakes. By creating politics so corrupt that you would make a small African coup look good. By just generally treating people like shit.'

Mack had turned on his heel and made to walk out.

'Don't think I'm going to ask you to helm the boat for my next Cup challenge,' Henry had yelled after him.

'Nothing could induce me to accept,' Mack had said softly.

But none of that showed on his face as he talked to Custard.

'Bad luck today,' said Custard.

'Even if we hadn't lost the mast, I think the Spanish still would have won.'

'Dismasting always tends to slow the boat down a bit.'

'Yeah, I've noticed that.'

'Luter has asked me to stay on for his next challenge in 2007,' said Custard. 'I don't know if I'll bother, I doubt I'll get on the first boat. What about you?'

'I doubt I would make it to the first boat either,' said Mack grimly. 'No, I won't be staying on.'

'I'm definitely not staying then. God knows what mad fucker he would get to helm it.'

'What Henry Luter doesn't know is that the America's Cup is about people. And if you fail to understand that then you have already lost. What are you going to do next?'

'I don't know. Go back on the World Match Racing Tour with Inky, I suppose. You?'

'I don't know. Maybe something different.'

Custard looked at him curiously. 'But you'll go back to match racing, won't you? You're addicted!'

'Not incurably,' said Mack lightly. He was thinking about the recent negative headlines which had blamed him for the British crew's patchy performance. Maybe he had been in this game too long. He was tired and thought it was time for a rest.

'Maybe you should get yourself a woman if you're going to have some time off. That's why you don't have one now, isn't it?' Custard nudged him.

'Not all of us, Custard, have the energy to go out with women at night and then sail all day.'

'But you would like a woman, wouldn't you?' Custard insisted.

'Why are you so desperate to get me married off?'

'Mack, I only have your happiness at heart,' said Custard piously. 'That and the fact Inky and I think we would win a lot more money on the match racing circuit without you around.'

'I've already tried it and it didn't really work out. The woman went and the sailing didn't. It would take one hell of a woman for me to do that again.'

'I could introduce you to a few. Some of my racer chasers are desperate to meet you. They wax lyrical about your strong jaw and distinguished looks.' Mack did look pretty good for his age. In fact he was one of those men who grew better looking with age. 'It's very annoying.'

'Thanks, Custard, but I'll pass.'

'I'll miss the odd occasions we got to sail together. That temper of yours is nasty though. That must be why you're so successful. The sea just opens up before you.'

'I only shouted at you on that particular occasion because you took the helm for five minutes and rammed the committee boat so hard that they had to spend the whole night taking turns bailing it out.'

'That's why I'm not a helmsman.'

'Custard, you can be an absolute knob but I'll miss sailing with you too.'

They smiled at each other and paused for a second, their eyes following Henry Luter as he moved around the room. 'There goes a man who still uses the rabbit, hole, tree method to tie a bowline,' commented Custard.

Chapter 2

Fabian Beaufort met Milly Dantry at the grand old age of twenty-four at the start of Skandia Cowes Week 2004, towards the end of a very beautiful summer.

It was still early when Fabian left the Rochesters' boat that morning. He hadn't slept well last night: dreams of Rob had haunted him. He woke up sweating and reached for the bedside light, waiting for his surroundings to assert themselves: the photo of his father tucked into the mirror, the pile of loose change and the racing programmes. After a few minutes he got up and found a solitary cigarette. He wondered about writing another letter to Rob's parents but knew it was futile. Instead he went up on deck, breathed the cool night air and thought about his father.

Although the sun had been up for barely an hour, the crews were already on deck, sorting and repairing equipment. Fabian walked along one of the pontoons looking for a boat called *Moonshine*. A mate had called and tipped him off about a crew space. He was desperate to get off the Rochester boat. The Rochesters were vague friends of his mother's and after he'd snogged Alicia, the Rochester daughter, at a party in London she had issued the invitation for Cowes Week. It had seemed a highly attractive offer at the time but in the cold light of day she was a much less desirable prospect and, like a bitch on heat, constantly trying to get him into bed. He'd had to pretend he was a really deep sleeper, unable to hear the soft tapping at his cabin door in the night. In the old days he would have just shagged her but at the moment he had other things on his mind.

The early morning sun was already glinting off the water, and the cool ocean breeze caught the boats, eliciting a furious round of clinking as the halyards and masts collided. Fabian loved this time of day. It reminded him of sleeping on the family yacht on one of his many fishing trips with his father.

He called up to someone on one of the decks and was pointed in the direction of *Moonshine*. He found her at the end of the pontoon. She was a beautiful boat, unsullied by the litter of sponsors' names running along her hull, and he felt a stir of excitement. What lines! How he would love to get to know her.

'Hello?' he called. And again. 'Hello?' He could see people were up. There were various jobs half done across the deck.

A head popped up and then someone came up from below deck. By the time the figure was standing in front of him, all Fabian's hopes had died.

'Well, well, well. If it isn't Fabian Beaufort.'

The voice belonged to Jason Bryant, a fair-haired, good-looking sailor with pale blue eyes whose cold intensity belied his ambition. They had been on rival boats in the Volvo Round the World Race. He was rather talented and also rather unpleasant. Fabian disliked him intensely.

'Jason. How are you?' muttered Fabian.

'What the fuck are you doing here, Beaufort?'

'Just came to see a friend. That's all,' he said, backing off.

'I hear you don't have many of those nowadays. Someone on this boat?'

'Maybe. I'll come back later.'

Fabian turned on his heel, but he could almost feel the slow smile start to appear on Jason's face. 'You're here because you heard that we need to fill a crew space, aren't you, Beaufort? Bit down on our luck, are we? I hear your dad has done a runner too,' he called after Fabian. 'You'd be the last person we would ever choose. Most of our people want to *live.*'

Milly Dantry wasn't a sailor by trade. Milly was a waitress. Each year she saved up her holiday from her waitress job in Whitstable and travelled down to Cowes for two weeks to cover the regatta, the Round the Island race and the Fastnet too, earning nearly three times as much as she did at home, which was just as well because working for Mr Sawman at the Crabclaw Café was not a great deal of fun. He insisted that all the female staff wore short black mini-skirts, then put them to work with the assiduity that a mine owner putting pit ponies down the mine would raise his eyebrows at. Still, Milly was desperately trying to save up for fashion college and every little helped. Money was still very tight at home and although waitressing would not be her natural choice of career, at least it paid the bills.

The restaurant was open bright and early for breakfast. Since the race course wasn't set until the morning of the race, when the wind speed and direction could be measured, some of the more serious sailors liked to gather their crew over breakfast to discuss tactics. Other sailors, who had been up until the early hours of the morning drinking and dancing at the yacht haven's concerts and then tipping themselves into their bunks whilst narrowly missing falling overboard, preferred to get takeaway bacon baguettes from Tiffins. Then, of course, they had to try and keep them down.

Milly was late and, apologising madly, she scrambled to dump her bag in the staffroom and get into her horrible apron. Despite the earliness of the hour, the little restaurant was heaving and the smell of bacon and eggs and fresh bread filled the air. Although fruit, muesli and yoghurt were on the menu there was a firm and decidedly male feeling that winning crews never went to sea on fruit, muesli and yoghurt. The talk was of the racing the day before.

'God, that weather. Four boats dismasted and umpteen collisions.'

'Did you hear one of the skippers lost his thumb? They took him to hospital but he refused to let them operate because he didn't want to miss the rest of the regatta.'

'I nearly collided with the King of Spain *and* the Aga Khan yesterday,' someone else boasted.

Milly took an order for the usual round of fried breakfasts while half listening to the crew conversation on table nine.

'I've asked Fabian Beaufort to be our bowman,' announced one man who seemed to be the skipper. The Gaggia spluttered boiling water over tea bags at the counter.

'Beaufort? Why the hell have you asked him? We're not that desperate.'

'Beaufort is a bloody talented sailor and we're lucky to get him.'

Another man snorted. 'Only because none of the professional crews will have him. He probably needs the cash now too.'

'How come?'

'Family money has gone kaput. His father has disappeared.'

'Old Pa Beaufort has disappeared?'

'God, where have you been? Everyone's talking about it! He's gone bankrupt. No one knows where he is. Just went in the night and left the family absolutely penniless. Rumour has it that Fabian's trial put him over the edge.'

'God, how awful. He was a really decent bloke. Pity the mother didn't disappear too.'

'Well, now Fabian's absolutely penniless. Sold his Porsche to keep hold of the family yacht but even that went too.'

'That's a bad run of luck.'

One man snorted. 'Luck has nothing to do with it. How do you know he won't be stoned out of his mind?'

'I heard it took four of them to throw him out at the Royal Corinthian Ball and now they won't have him back through their doors,' added someone else.

'He'll be fine,' snapped the skipper back. 'And he's our best chance to beat *Gipsy*.'

'Well, let's hope he doesn't turn up drunk and drown the bloody lot of us.'

'Or, worse than that, lose the bloody race for us.'

'Shut it. He's here.'

Milly was just taking their tea over to them and looked around with interest for this Fabian character. He came out of the fog of bodies and it was all she could do not to stand in front of him and stare with an open mouth. As it was she rushed back to the counter and snatched glances at him whenever she could. Milly didn't think she had seen anyone so arresting in all of her life. The very image of him branded itself on her mind like a scar. He was languidly shaking hands with everyone at the table as they stood to greet him. He had clearly been sailing in fairer climes because he was tanned. Not to a smooth café au lait colour of the continent but to the polished beige of an English cup of tea. His dark blond hair was flecked with the ice of white blond from the sun. His smooth rose-pink lips sat in a square jaw. He could only be described as beautiful rather than handsome but there was no denying the slightly predatory look in his blue eyes.

Milly walked apprehensively over to him and cleared her throat. 'Em, can I get you anything? To eat or drink?' she added hastily as the amused eyes swung towards her. She drank in his smell: freshly showered flesh and a faint sprinkling of aftershave. His strong forearms rested on the table, naked of a watch and any other adornment, only the little white hairs bleached by the sun.

'I'm not sure you'll have my usual tipple but please can you get me a bacon sandwich and an espresso? Thank you.' For a moment his eyes lingered on hers.

As Milly scurried off with his order, his gaze briefly followed her. He liked the kindness in her eyes. He had seen her yesterday as well being sweet to an old man who had spilt his tea. She had cleaned it up patiently, and stayed to listen as he rambled on about Cowes Week whilst the café owner swore at her in the background. Although it was something he had never appreciated before, indeed never had any use for, kindness was something which was certainly thin on the ground for him at the moment. He was aware of the whispered comments and the gossipy exchanged glances, at such odds to the looks of admiration that his looks and talent normally elicited, and the experience of having to scrabble around for an amateur crew place whilst his peers breakfasted in one of the corporate tents was truly humbling. He wondered fleetingly if this waitress would still be kind if she knew anything about him. He turned back to all the talk of racing.

Milly got up early the next morning to try to persuade her vibrant, slippery mass of hair into some semblance of style. She had a lovely olive, velvety skin and treacly, mahogany hair, for which she thanked her beauty fairy every day. Her straight, even features gave her a certain fresh-faced charm, and her chocolate eyes and wide, genuine, magical smile made even the toughest customer melt. When they shared out their tips at the end of the shift, Milly always had the most. She stood out amongst the rest of the waitresses as she was always wearing something different. The old sewing machine at home whirred away as she turned high street fashion into haute couture. Despite her limited budget she always looked chic and carried off the cheapest of trinkets with enviable style. She wasn't terribly vain but she did have an instinctive need to make herself look as nice as possible, and the possibility of seeing Fabian Beaufort again made her want to make the effort. She thought about him, remembering how the room had become more animated when he arrived as people surreptitiously pointed him out to their companions. Milly didn't know why. Had that crew said he was a druggie? They certainly didn't want him on the boat anyway. She shrugged to herself. She didn't know why she was even thinking about him. He was the embodiment of all those spoilt kids from London who wouldn't pause to give her the time of day.

Things went rapidly downhill once she got to work. Milly was reduced to tears by Mr Sawman when she accidentally scalded one of the other waiters. Then, halfway through the breakfast shift, she picked up a plate far hotter than it should have been, tried to dump it back on the counter and missed. She ducked down to pick up the broken pieces and scattered pieces of bacon whilst sucking on her burnt finger.

'Milly, what the fuck is going on?' hissed a voice in her ear. She straightened up to find Mr Sawman staring furiously at her.

'I'm . . . I'm sorry. It was hot and I missed the . . .'

'This is a café, Milly. Things are hot. That's part of your job.' He was trying to keep his voice even and low but Milly could see from his eyes that he really wanted to let rip on her. 'What the fuck is wrong with you today? Daydreaming about boys?'

'It was really hot. I'm sorry.'

'Get this mess cleared up now and I'm deducting the cost of all this from your wages. You can forget your tips for today as well.'

Milly was startled when a drawling voice interrupted.

'I don't think that's very fair.'

Milly was already quite red but she turned positively puce when she saw the owner of the voice. 'It's fine, honestly,' she stammered.

'No, it's not fine,' said Fabian. 'It wasn't her fault at all. You've been shitty to everyone all week. You haven't even asked her if she's hurt herself.'

'You don't tell me what to do with my staff. Besides, I know who you are and I don't want you in here,' replied Mr Sawman with a sneer.

'Fabian!' called someone from the door. 'We're going!'

'Get your stuff,' said Fabian, glancing at Milly.

'Eh?' said Milly, open-mouthed. She knew it wasn't quite the appropriate response but she couldn't help herself.

'The boat I'm staying on needs a cook and they'll pay you better than this place. Get your stuff.'

Milly's mind raced. She didn't particularly want to give up her job here but she was thrilled by his gesture and didn't feel she could let him down in front of all these people. It was like being proposed to on TV or something. She just couldn't say no. Wordlessly she scurried into the staffroom, seized her bag and ran back.

No one had moved. Fabian grabbed her hand and pulled her away. He wasn't quite sure why he'd done what he just did. All he knew was that he was sick of being pushed about himself and couldn't bear to see it happen to his kind waitress too.

'Did you hurt yourself?' he asked as they threaded their way through the crowds.

'No,' said Milly, knowing that to a sailor you had to lose your finger before it counted as hurting yourself.

'Can you cook?'

'Em, the basics. Shepherd's pie, that sort of thing.'

He nodded briskly. Already dozens of boats were wending their way out to sea in readiness for a day's racing.

'If you go and wait at the Royal Yacht Squadron's landing, I'll get someone to come and pick you up.' And then he hopped on to the bow of a boat. 'What's your name?' he called.

'Milly.'

It wasn't until she had walked round to the Royal Yacht Squadron (the long way so she didn't have to walk back past the restaurant) and leant on the railing by the imposing stone landing that Milly started to think about what she had just done. She'd given up a perfectly good job and let lots of people down, because the rest of the staff would have to try and make up for her absence today. She bit her lip anxiously, looking into the water. And all for what? Because she fancied someone? This Fabian probably hadn't got a job for her after all. She wandered dispiritedly past the landing stage, all the time keeping an eye out for a likely-looking boat coming to collect her. The turreted building of the Royal Yacht Squadron, half covered with bottle-green ivy, stood imposingly before her. A young man was watching her suspiciously from the guard house at the entrance; any moment she expected a fruity naval voice to demand to know what she was doing. She extracted an old copy of *Vogue* from her bag and tried to concentrate but the images kept blurring so in the end she simply walked up and down until she saw a smart navy blue launch gently weaving in and out of the bobbing yachts. It was definitely coming over to the landing stage. She walked quickly towards the wrought-iron gates as the boat made to pull alongside.

'Are you Milly?' called a tall, dark-haired man with an upper-class voice. He pronounced her name 'Mill-ay'. A small boy leapt on to the stone platform as soon as they reached it, holding a rope which he tied off.

'Yes!' Milly called from behind the gates, relief flooding through her.

'Fabian said he'd got us a new cook.'

'That's me!' she said joyfully. She would be earning money for the rest of the week and Fabian hadn't let her down.

'I'm starving,' pronounced the small boy.

'John! Get these bloody gates open!' yelled the man. The young man from the guard house scurried out, bearing keys and stumbling apologies.

'Glad Fabian found somebody.' Milly slipped through the gates as soon as they were opened and climbed gingerly aboard. 'I'm Philip Rochester by the way and this is Tom.'

'Nice to meet you. I'm Milly Dantry.' She didn't know whether to shake hands or not but none was proffered.

'Can you do me some bacon and eggs when we get back?' asked the boy. 'I'm racing in an hour.'

'Of course,' said Milly. At that moment she would have made the whole fleet bacon and eggs, and with fried bread too.

Chapter 3

The next morning Milly was in the Rochesters' galley, panicking. The weather was a little rougher and the yacht bobbed around on its moorings but she was getting used to the soft undulations. She still hadn't seen Fabian – from what she could gather at the breakfast table he had left early to meet with another boat he was crewing for.

Although Mr Rochester had offered her much more money than she could have possibly earned at the café for the rest of the week, they were being very sketchy about hours. Milly was worried she would miss her last bus back to her digs tonight as they were hosting a drinks party on the yacht and then a buffet afterwards for a select few. Mrs Rochester wanted her to prepare some canapés as well, which filled her with absolute dread. Fabian obviously hadn't told them she wasn't a real cook. Did crisps count as canapés?

But her day became more and more fraught. Alicia, the Rochester's beautiful daughter, rose from her bed and demanded boiled eggs, then Mr Rochester invited several of his cronies back to talk about their race strategy and she had to make them all packed lunch from two tins of red salmon which she found in the cupboard along with the potato salad she'd made for the buffet. She also had to make lunch for the rest of the crew, which took her by surprise, but they told her kindly that they hadn't liked to ask her yesterday as it was her first day. Mrs

Rochester and her friends then expected to be served tea on deck while watching the racing crews coming home, and Alicia and her friends went below deck to her bedroom to try on dresses for tonight's drinks party and summoned Milly to serve them tea there. Milly hadn't actually been into the cabins yet – they were situated at the bow of the boat – and she had to be pointed in the right direction by one of the crew.

She balanced the second tea tray on her hip and knocked on the door.

'Come in!'

Milly stepped over the lip into a spacious cabin. A double bed took up the middle of the room but the main focus was an enormous wardrobe which took up the whole of one wall. With all its doors flung open, it spewed the contents on to the bed and over chairs. One girl was posing in front of a full-length mirror in a beautiful halter-neck dress made entirely of tiny silver droplets. Milly would have given anything to spend just an hour in this room with that wardrobe, but the thought quickly left her as four girls immediately stopped and stared at her. Milly felt a flush start up her neck. 'Where would you like the tray?' she asked quietly.

'Here on the bed.' Alicia got up. She was very pretty in a baby-doll kind of way. Milly thought that since Fabian clearly wasn't related to the Rochesters he must be going out with Alicia. Lucky, lucky Alicia. Milly went to place the tray where she had been sitting, which was the only spare bit of space since clothes littered the rest of the bed.

'Careful! Mind my dresses!' snapped Alicia. 'They cost thousands.'

Milly placed the tray as gently as she could on the bed, all the while feeling the sly looks being passed between the girls behind her back. 'I hear Fabian found you in a café, is that so?' Alicia asked as Milly turned to go.

'That's right.'

'Clever old Fabian.'

Milly made to leave.

'When Fabian comes back, will you send him straight down?' Alicia called after her amidst the giggles.

'Yes. Of course.' Milly clicked the door shut on a life she could only dream of. The clothes were what made Milly envious. She had had her heart set on a fashion course in London but when her mother was killed in a car accident just before her GCSEs all of that changed. Milly had had to leave school early, and before taking those all-important exams, to help her father who was so stricken with grief that he was unable to work. She'd thought her heart might break. She had adored her mother, who was sweet and kind, just like her. She missed the easy chat, shopping for clothes together, the simple pleasure taken in so-and-so's engagement or promotion. She spent her summers serving spoilt kids from London talking loudly about their foreign holidays whilst leaving tiny tips. She watched her excited friends disappear off to university, giving her huge bear hugs and promising to write whilst she worked at her exams between her waitress shifts. But she had finally been granted a place at a college in London, starting this September. Although she was sad to leave her father, who was delighted for her, she couldn't wait for September to come. To earn her living surrounded by clothes and couture was the very stuff dreams were made of.

By the time she had got back to the galley and surveyed the mess, Milly was starting to feel a little less favourably about Fabian. It was all very well for him, she thought as she slammed the fridge door, playing the knight in shining armour, but he had taken her away from a perfectly good job and delivered her to the evil stepfamily. She was Cinderella in reverse. He'd probably forgotten all about her now. What on earth was she going to give to forty guests as canapés tonight? Not to mention the buffet afterwards. She looked at her watch. It was four-thirty and a wave of panic overcame her. She'd never make it.

'Milly?' said Tom appearing in the doorway. 'Is there anything to eat?'

'I'm not sure, Tom. Will some rich tea biscuits do?' She wasn't even sure about them. She couldn't remember whether she had given them all to Mrs Rochester's guests.

'But I'm starving! I've been racing all day!'

Tears started to well up and she sat down heavily on a stool. The restaurant wouldn't give her back her job now and she didn't know what she'd do after they'd fired her here.

'Are you all right, Milly?' Tom asked nervously.

It was all too much. The tears started to roll down her face. Tom came and stood gravely next to her, solemnly handing her a tea towel. 'Please don't cry, Milly. I like rich tea biscuits. I really do. I like you too.'

She smiled and blew her nose on an illustration of a reef knot. Her mascara mottled the previously white cloth. 'It's not you, Tom. It's just . . . '

'Tom, have you been making Milly cry?' asked a voice from the doorway. Milly and Tom started and looked up to see Fabian leaning in the doorway with his Oakley sunglasses pushed on top of his head.

'No, Fabian. I really do like rich tea biscuits. Milly thinks I don't.'

Fabian frowned. 'Milly's crying because you don't like rich tea biscuits? What are you doing down here, Tom?'

'I've been racing. I was hungry . . . '

Fabian immediately bustled over to the fridge. 'Well, let's get you something to eat then. How about some cheese and crackers?'

Milly groaned inwardly to herself. Why couldn't she have thought of cheese and crackers? Fabian was going to think she was useless.

After Fabian had pulled a big chunk of Cheddar out of the fridge and found some crackers in the cupboard, he sent a more cheerful and relieved Tom on his way and then pulled up a stool to join Milly. 'What's up?' he asked simply.

Milly twisted the tea towel through her fingers. 'There's a drinks party tonight and a buffet and I don't know how to make canapés. I'd made a potato salad for the buffet but Mr Rochester had that for lunch. I don't know what to do because I'm not really a cook, you know. I'm a waitress.'

He studied her without saying anything. She dried her eyes and awkwardly got up. She supposed she really needed to get on. One of the crew would have to run her ashore. 'Oh by the way,' she said. 'Alicia said you can go straight down to her cabin.'

He went to the doorway. 'Are you coming?'

'To see Alicia?' she said in confusion.

'No, to the shops,' he replied to her surprised face. 'Come on.'

Travelling with Fabian in the motor launch was really rather thrilling. They were stared at and pointed to by all the yachts as they weaved their way slowly through. Fabian didn't show off with elaborate zigzagging or speed and Milly felt a slight shiver when she realised that Fabian probably didn't need to prove his virility that way. Milly noticed that some of the sunbathing women smiled and waved but the men just looked and muttered. One man shouted out aggressively, 'Go home, Beaufort. You're not welcome here.' Milly looked across at Fabian curiously, wondering if he was going to react. Even though his face was impassive and he looked straight ahead of him, a tic was going slightly in one cheek. She wondered again about this constant antipathy towards him and how he could stand it.

'How did you do today?' asked Milly, trying to make some conversation.

'Awful. Fucking skipper was useless.' He didn't take his eyes from the water.

'Were you the bowman?' She blushed as she remembered their first meeting.

'Yes.' He slowed the boat down even more as they came to a mêlée of bobbing Laser dinghies. Against the size and weight of the Rochesters' yacht, they looked like little toy boats. 'Do you sail?' Fabian asked.

'A bit of dinghy sailing. Like these,' she pointed at the Lasers. 'But not really now. My dad used to have a boat. Before my mother died.'

Fabian looked over at her but he didn't look embarrassed or try to change the subject quickly. 'When did she die?'

'Six years ago.'

'I'm sorry. You must miss her.'

Milly had to bite on her lip hard, looking out over the Solent to stop her eyes filling with tears again. Stop it, she told herself firmly, for God's sake stop it. He's going to think that all you do is cry.

'Are you related to the Rochesters?' she asked quickly.

Fabian gave a mirthless laugh. 'No.'

It must be as she thought, Fabian was going out with Alicia. Milly jumped as a cannon went off to signify the start of a race.

'Someone accidentally left the loading baton in one year and it was fired through some poor sod's mainsail,' said Fabian gesturing towards the nearby cannons. 'One minute you're waiting to start the race and the next your sail's on fire with a huge hole in it.'

Milly giggled. She looked around her. 'Are you allowed to moor here?'

'No,' he said, tying the dinghy up.

They didn't speak again until Fabian had collected a trolley in the supermarket.

'How many are there tonight?'

'Em, forty for drinks and fifteen for supper.'

Fabian started to chuck things randomly into the trolley. In went several packets of smoked salmon, some quail's eggs, blinis, lumpfish roe and soured cream, then some pâté, chutney and melba toasts, some huge king prawns that were the size of eggs and sweet chilli sauce.

'I don't think you're going to have time to make anything complicated for the buffet.'

'What about some baked potatoes?' Milly seized a couple of huge bags and bunged them in the trolley and then ran back to the fridge section to get some bacon and cheese to stuff them with. When she got back, Fabian was buying four freshly roasted chickens from the deli counter. She paid with a wad of notes Mr Rochester had left her with this morning and firmly pocketed the receipt to show him.

Carrying four bags each, they weaved their way back through the dense crowds.

'Thank you,' said Milly awkwardly. 'Thanks for helping, Fabian.' She used his name shyly, almost as though it was a caress.

He shrugged. 'I know you'd have managed but I feel I got you into this.'

'Most men wouldn't have a clue what to feed people.'

'I did the Whitbread Round the World Race – well, it's the Volvo now. Makes you think a bit more about food.' He looked over to her and smiled. 'Not that we had quail's eggs and smoked salmon. Far from it. I lost about a stone.'

Milly privately thought it sounded an extreme sort of diet. 'How did you do?'

'I learnt a lot. My skipper was pretty amazing. I did it just to learn from him. He knew how to get everything he could out of the boat and from his crew. There was a point in the race when we were sailing at more than thirty knots and the boat was literally slicing the ocean apart. I've never been so scared.'

Since Fabian was grinning with delight, Milly presumed that being scared was something he actively enjoyed.

It was a beautiful evening. The yachts moored all around them hummed with life. People dressed in ball dresses and black tie were sitting out on the decks sipping cocktails; strains of Billie Holiday carried across the water and collided with the booming beat of R&B. The hum of motor launches as persistent as wasps moved in and out of the moorings, delivering glamorous people to the yacht clubs on shore and even more glamorous people to the Rochesters'.

Although Milly tried her best to keep her mind on the job that evening, she found herself constantly looking for Fabian as she circulated with food. Her eyes were forever drawn to him. She watched him chatting, his wary air at odds with his earlier sangfroid. She noticed that he avoided the older guests (who muttered behind his back) and spoke to the younger ones (who were clearly fascinated by him).

Milly absent-mindedly proffered her tray to a group of three over made-up, gaudy women who all looked like Ivana Trump. They were nudging each other and looking over at Fabian like vultures.

'Alicia Rochester more or less told me that she was seeing Fabian Beaufort, the lucky thing.'

'I don't care what they say about him, he is simply delicious. I would have him for breakfast, lunch and dinner.'

They grabbed canapés from Milly with liver-spotted, old crone hands without even pausing to look at her. Milly decided they looked more like the three witches from *Macbeth*.

'You know the old adage, "Never do the crew"? Well, Fabian always does. I always wished he would make a pass at me.'

Milly moved away, only to be confronted by Alicia in the middle of a group of glamorous young people laughing loudly.

'Fabian?' Alicia was pouting. She had clearly had too much to drink. 'Fabian!' she said again when he didn't respond.

'Yes?' he said. He didn't seem all that keen to talk to her, Milly noticed.

'Do you think I ought to get my boobs done?' She pressed her chest into his face.

'Well, I don't know.' He looked at her breasts.

'Do you think they're too small?' She had her hands on her hips and paraded her chest like an overanxious cockerel. God, any minute she was going to take her top off, thought Milly.

'Well . . . ' drawled Fabian, eyes still fixed. 'Why don't you get one done and see how you feel?' he said to shouts of laughter from the whole group.

He looked across to Milly, but she had already escaped downstairs before anyone noticed her grinning too. But once back down in her habitual galley she caught a distorted glance of her clothes in the aluminium fridge door and the smile faded from her face. Despite the laughter, Alicia still had unlimited access to Fabian whereas she was bound by this waitress's uniform. It didn't seem to be a fair position to be fighting from. She knew that she was becoming fascinated by him. It was as though everything centred on Fabian. He stood still whilst everyone and everything revolved around him.

She slowly chewed on her bottom lip and thought how defensive he seemed this evening, as though always waiting for the next line of attack, unsure what direction it would come from. It worried her that he could have so much ill feeling directed towards him. She wondered what awful things he could have done for the whole community to be practically ignoring him. She wondered if it was true that he was penniless and lost all his money. But above all, she wondered what she could do to make it better.

Chapter 4

The next morning Milly met her friend Amy from the restaurant for an early cup of tea on the yacht haven. Amy had been texting her since her departure.

'Tell me everything!' said Amy excitedly. 'Mr Sawman was furious when you walked out like that! Absolutely furious! I thought he was going to have some sort of coronary! It was marvellous! Well worth waiting all your tables for the rest of the decade, you old bag. So tell me all about this Fabian Beaufort. He is absolutely gorgeous. Mr Sawman has received about twenty applications for your job immediately after you left, all from green-eyed female customers hoping Mr Beaufort might come and rescue them from a life of drudgery.'

'He's lovely,' sighed Milly. 'Just lovely.'

She smiled dreamily at her friend who was now looking at her dubiously. 'Milly, please tell me you don't actually *like* him. He doesn't have the best of reputations. He'll eat you up and then spit you out.'

'What have you heard?'

'Lots of gossip. If they're not talking about the racing or sailing, they are talking about Fabian Beaufort. Most of the women seem secretly pleased that he's around and talk about his beautiful bum but the men all seem to hate him – they won't even talk to him.'

'What sort of gossip?'

'Like the fact he is seriously into drink and drugs. That he has shagged every vaguely attractive blonde in every corner of the globe. And he was so bombed up that he left someone to die out in the Caribbean.'

'Is that it?'

'That's not enough? Someone *died*. He left them to *die*.'

The words slowly sank into Milly's consciousness. She realised with a shock that she was so anxious to brush over any of Fabian's indiscretions that she could have dismissed this altogether without actually thinking about it. But it couldn't be dismissed. Certainly most of the sailing community felt it couldn't. Fabian was responsible for someone's death.

'Do you know how it happened?'

'Does it make a difference?'

'Maybe.'

'I'm not sure how even you could put a positive spin on this one.'

Milly was silent for a moment. 'Do you know anything else?'

'Not much. Something went on with his family, I don't know what. Rumour has it that he's seeing someone on the boat he's staying on.'

'Alicia,' mumbled Milly.

'Besides, he is a serious sailor. You know what that means.'

Milly did know what that meant. She'd been coming to Cowes long enough. That meant he only had one mistress. The sea. And she was a bitchy, demanding mistress. There was never any room for anyone else. Milly looked so crestfallen that Amy put a hand out to touch her. 'You're too sweet for him. But if you must shag him, and I only say must, please make him wear a condom and then walk away and don't look back.'

Milly left her friend wishing that all Amy had told her could have killed her desire for Fabian. But even after all she had just heard about him, perversely, she still wanted him. Maybe she could just sleep with him and then walk away. Maybe that would satisfy this longing for him and put an end to it? Then Milly shook herself crossly. What on earth made her think that Fabian would want to sleep with her? They came from such different backgrounds. His was public school – she could tell by his voice – skiing holidays and girls with wardrobes the size of a room. Hers was hanging around with mates on the beach and scrabbling down the back of the sofa to find enough money for a pint of cider. Milly suddenly wished she was back with Amy waiting tables at the café. She wished that she had never set eyes on Fabian Beaufort. The sun went behind the clouds and she shivered slightly.

Half an hour later Milly was busy frying eggs for everyone up on deck. Actually, she was only frying eggs for two of them because Alicia wanted an egg white omelette (Milly had never made one before. She hoped that the recipe was as obvious as its name) and Mrs Rochester wanted poached eggs. Thank God the men were easy. She had found a double-yolked egg which she was carefully handling for Tom as she knew he'd be thrilled. She had been surprised to see Alicia up but apparently she too was going racing today and was carefully dressed in tiny shorts and a vest top with a Henri Lloyd sailing top tied casually around her waist.

A shadow fell across the stove and when she looked up and saw Fabian she immediately took back her wish never to have met him. She didn't think it was fair that his hair should have so many colours of the sun or that he should seem to care so little about it. 'Hello,' he said simply.

'Hello.'

'Double-yolker,' he stated. Milly first thought this might be some sort of technical sailing term but he gestured his head towards the egg pan. 'Lucky.'

She smiled at him. 'I'm saving it for Tom.'

'He'll like it. Do you want to come sailing with me today?'

Milly looked at him in some confusion. 'Aren't you racing?' she asked to buy herself some time. 'With Alicia?' She cursed herself. She hadn't meant to mention her.

'God no!' he said with some amusement. 'She'll smack her head on the boom, lose her sunglasses whilst all the time moaning that the sail is casting a shadow over her legs. No, I'm not racing today. With or without Alicia.'

'But I've got to work.'

'Not this evening. They're all going to the Royal Yacht Squadron Ball.'

'OK,' she said finally. 'As long as the family don't need me.'

'I'll pick you up at six.'

And with that he was gone, obscurely pleased that she had accepted. Not that he'd imagined she would refuse.

Born to an impossibly beautiful mother and an entrepreneurial father, Fabian had inherited his looks from one and his sailing talent from the other. But despite his advantages, as an only child Fabian had been very lonely. His mother adored him, rather than straightforwardly loving him, and looked to him to provide everything that her life was missing, his father being frequently absent from the family home and utterly focused on building his vast fortune. The one thing that brought Fabian and his father together was sailing, and from an early age Fabian had loved to escape the cosseted, perfumed presence of his doting mother. He and his father would leave London together on a Friday night and travel down to their house in Hamble where their yacht *Ragamuffin* was berthed. Elizabeth always refused to accompany them and secretly the men preferred it that way. No one to tell them off for eating Nutella sandwiches for lunch or nag them about table manners. David Beaufort left his all-consuming work behind him and became Fabian's exclusive property. The rest of the world ceased to exist. Fabian's best memories of his father were standing beside him with a rod in his hand, fishing for mackerel off the back of the boat, the wind caressing their skin, alone on the ocean and content in the silence of each other's company.

Fabian had never found that sort of peace anywhere else – until recently. To his surprise, he found it in Milly's presence.

After leaving Harrow, Fabian had wanted nothing more than to prove himself as a sailor. He applied to become a crew member on the Volvo Ocean Race, the famous race which started as a bet in a yacht club bar and was now the greatest ocean race in the world. The main draw for him was the skipper on one of the boats, who was a sailing legend.

After a gruelling few days of assault courses and team-building exercises, the interviews began. As soon as Fabian walked into the room, the skipper thought, This boy won't last the course. He has no experience of when things go wrong. Things have only ever gone right for him.

'Why do you want to do this race?' he asked him.

'I want to win. I want to win the Volvo.'

'And what happens when we don't win? What happens when we're the last in the fleet?'

'Then we push our way to the front.'

The skipper tried a different tack. 'What if one of your crew mates doesn't work as hard as you? He can't pull his weight?'

'Then he shouldn't be on the boat,' said Fabian fiercely.

'But what if he is?' he persisted.

'Then I'll push him.'

'Or help him?' suggested the skipper.

Fabian looked at him curiously. 'Whatever gets results.'

The skipper wavered and then mentally scratched him off the list. He asked a few more questions before terminating the interview. Fabian thanked him but as he got up to leave, feeling he hadn't quite made the right impression, he turned back. 'At the start, you asked me why I wanted to do this race. I actually want to do it because I've never been really pushed before. I want to know where my limits are and I reckon the only place left to really find them is on the ocean.'

'What if you reach your limits?'

'Then I'll go beyond them because I'll have no choice. That's the beauty of the ocean, isn't it? The only victory is that you get to emerge alive. I want to know what that feels like.'

His new skipper surveyed him for a few seconds. 'You can call me Mack, by the way.' John MacGregor's mouth stretched into a smile. 'Welcome aboard.'

They came second in the race. The yachting press named Fabian as *the* one to watch and he looked set for an enormously successful career. Fabian decided he would have a small holiday and sail the *Mandarin,* a present from his father, to the Caribbean, meet some mates and party for a while. But intoxicated by this hedonistic lifestyle, a few weeks turned into a long summer of wild beach parties, sex and drugs. Reassured by his son that he would be entering local regattas to continue his sailing career, his worried father continued to wire transfer money out. Never pausing to consider the next day let alone the following week, Fabian raced in Antigua Race Week, carnival-ed in Trinidad and smoked cigars in Havana. Although Fabian was true to his word, what his father didn't know was that as his notoriety spread, race organisers started to refuse him permission to race as he invariably turned up pissed or stoned or both.

Then Rob Thornton died.

It was half past six by the time Fabian wandered down to the galley to collect Milly, who had been agonising for the last forty minutes over what exactly 'I'll pick you up at six' meant. Was it really a date or did he just need someone to sail with? And even if it was a date, should she really be going out with him? From all the gossip he hardly seemed to be the sort of person who'd be looking for a relationship. But then she couldn't bear the thought of not going out with him. She decided to try and keep the whole thing as low-key as possible because she had a nasty feeling that Alicia wouldn't take too kindly to it.

Luckily she had brought a little cardigan with her today, so whilst the rest of the family got ready for the ball, she untucked her floral shirt, undid the buttons as far as she dared and slung the short grey cardigan over the top. She wasn't sure that her black skirt was quite the sailing thing but at least she had on her best flip-flops from last summer which she had stuck black and white buttons on. She had a quick peek down the front of her blouse and then felt enormously presumptuous. This wasn't even an official date. But thank God she was wearing her nice black bra with hot-pink ribbon. Of course, she had no intention of sleeping with him.

'Are you ready?' he asked, appearing suddenly behind her.

Relief flooded through Milly and she quickly clamped her hands down by her sides. 'Em, yes. Am I OK like this? I mean, for sailing.'

'I'll try not to tip you in.'

They walked together to the stern.

'I had to bring the boat right in because they'll be using the launch later,' he said.

'Oh! Is she yours?' exclaimed Milly as the little Laser came into sight, tied on to the bigger yacht with a single rope and bobbing in the water. She looked like a tiny cygnet following her giant mother.

'No, I borrowed her from a mate. I still have a few left,' he said wryly. 'You said you'd sailed dinghies before.'

Milly looked at him in alarm. 'A while ago.'

'You'll remember. You never forget.' He handed her a life-jacket.

She clambered down the ladder to the little landing stage. Instinctively knowing that Fabian would despise women who made a fuss, she pulled the little boat in close and then hopped in. 'Are you coming?' she asked cheekily.

He grinned at her, untied the painter and leapt deftly in.

There were a few boats out and about, enjoying the last dregs of the warm, salty air, but they were soon a pinprick on the horizon. The burning heat of the sun had been replaced by a pleasant, drowsy warmth. Fabian had put Milly in charge of the tiller and she sat happily at the back taking great gulps of the breeze, peering, weaving and leaning as the boom swung back and forth and Fabian managed the tacking. He ducked under the boom, raised and lowered the centreboard and leant out over the water as easily and unconsciously as a fashion designer would drape cloth over a model's body, and slowly they tacked in vast zigzags towards the beautiful, squat red and white striped lighthouse sitting forebodingly in front of spiking, chalky cliffs which rose out of the water like the teeth of some abandoned sea monster.

When the Needles lighthouse at last loomed in front of them like a vast moon, Fabian decided to turn the boat into the wind and drop the sea anchor. After taking a few minutes to check that they weren't drifting, he seemed to relax a little and turned towards her. There wasn't much room in the dinghy, barely enough for two bodies to be comfortable, but with equilibrium restored they sat facing each other. Without speaking Fabian leant to the bow of the boat and from underneath a picnic rug whipped out a bottle of champagne.

The clichéd gesture, which made Milly fleetingly wonder how often he had done this, was thankfully tempered by Fabian saying, 'I nicked it from old Pa Rochester's cellars. He won't miss it.'

'Why aren't you going to the Ball tonight?' asked Milly. It hadn't escaped her notice that Fabian hadn't gone to anything this week and Cowes Week was crammed with social events: balls, cocktail parties, concerts and receptions.

'I wouldn't be particularly welcome. The Royal Yacht Squadron have blacklisted me,' he said, expertly twisting off the foil and wire cage. 'Everybody who is anybody is going,' he said mockingly and eased the cork out with a muted pop.

'Why wouldn't you be welcome?' said Milly quietly, holding her breath.

He took a moment as he poured some champagne into the cups and they both watched the bubbles disperse. She handed his cup back to him after he wedged the bottle between his feet but neither of them drank.

'I left someone,' he said quietly. 'I left someone when I shouldn't have done. I don't really want to talk about it. You most likely wouldn't want to know me.'

'I doubt that,' said Milly evenly. She had to know what happened. They couldn't go any further until he told her. She could feel the struggle within him, but even with the little she knew about him, she was sure he would be honest. He wasn't scared of being disliked. 'Was it an accident?'

Fabian looked at her for the first time since the start of the conversation. 'What have you heard?'

'That someone died.'

Fabian nodded. 'Yes,' he said slowly. 'Someone died.'

He looked into the water for what seemed like a long time, debating whether to tell her or not. She was independent, not part of his insular world where everyone seemed to have already made up their minds, and he also felt as though she was the sort of person you could truly say anything to and they would find the good in it. At the moment he needed all the comfort he could get and Milly was pure sugar syrup. 'Look,' he said eventually. 'I'll tell you but only because you might hear an even worse version from someone else – but then you probably already have.' He paused. 'I was sailing with a mate. Rob Thornton. We were out in the Grenadines and both pretty tanked up. We'd been drinking a lot and doing some coke at a party on someone's yacht and then all decided to have a race to another island in the middle of the night. Rob didn't really want to go but I persuaded him. So four yachts went out. Rob and I went out on his and I went to the bow to check the wind direction. I think I was gone about five minutes and when I got back Rob had disappeared. He'd fallen overboard, he must have stumbled or something. We weren't wearing life-jackets and he drowned. His body was washed up on a beach a few days later.' Fabian concentrated on looking at a distant yacht.

'I'm so sorry,' she murmured. 'How awful.'

Her words barely registered; he was reliving the full horror and that feeling of stomach-draining responsibility for what he had done.

'I tried go back for him. I managed to go about and I tried to search the area, but the boat wasn't really designed to sail single-handed. I probably could have done it if I'd been sober. And then I couldn't get the radio to work. It was broken and Rob hadn't got it fixed.' He looked at her this time for her reaction, for her verdict. His slate-blue eyes were those of someone who had been repeatedly kicked. All he could see in Milly was gentleness and sympathy. He carried on, everything coming out in a splurge, anxious for her to know the worst. 'At the inquest, they returned a verdict of accidental death but the judge came down really hard on me. Said that if he had his way we would all go to jail, we were just spoilt rich kids playing pranks. Of course, the papers picked up on this and the reports came back to England.' He shrugged slightly, trying to recover his nonchalance. For a second he was heartily glad that they were on a boat and Milly wouldn't be able to leave.

But Milly put out a hand to touch him. 'Fabian, it doesn't sound as though it was really your fault.'

'You don't understand, Milly. Rob really didn't want to go. I called him a pussy and pulled him out of his chair. He knew he wasn't capable. I forced him. It's my fault he's dead. Everyone knows I forced him.'

'It sounds like an awful accident to me,' said Milly firmly.

'Then I found out that my father had gone bankrupt and disappeared. Some people thought that my trial was somehow responsible for the bankruptcy and gossip fuels gossip, so almost everyone now thinks I'm the devil incarnate.'

'And you've lost your father too,' murmured Milly.

'I've been no saint,' Fabian snapped suddenly. He wanted her to know the truth, but he didn't want her sympathy because it wasn't deserved. He felt bitterly ashamed that he had been out in the Caribbean, contributing to his father's bankruptcy, whilst his father had been struggling back here in England.

'There seems to be so much talk about you . . . ' Milly hesitated. 'It's very brave of you to come to Cowes.'

Fabian shrugged. Of course he was tempted to disappear away from the crowd but he had his pride. 'I'd rather they said it to my face. Besides, if I'm around at least it stops them openly gossiping.' He didn't want to mention what they were saying about his father at the moment but it hadn't escaped his notice that his father hadn't stayed to face out *his* detractors.

'People are very judgemental.'

Fabian shrugged. 'Rob's parents are prominent sailors. There's a lot of sympathy for them and I suppose they feel better with someone to blame. I thought the least I could do was to take that blame.'

'Does it bother you? The hostility? I don't think I could take it if it were me. I think I would simply go home.'

'This *is* home for me. Besides I've never particularly cared for other people's opinions.' That was true. But he had been shocked by the depth of ill feeling directed at him. It wasn't caused simply by sympathy for Rob's parents: he hadn't realised just how many people he had pissed off on the way up. They were now enjoying seeing him on the way down: scorned women, blokes he'd won races against or taken girlfriends off. There were few in the sailing community he hadn't annoyed in one way or another. It made him feel humble: a sensation he wasn't particularly enjoying.

They both sat in silence for a second and then sipped at the champagne without any of the customary toasts. It was bizarre, he thought, after all that had happened he felt far more comfortable in the company of his waitress (as he thought of her) than with any of his peers. He simply wouldn't be able to speak to any of his friends like this, which confused him. He had extracted more comfort and pleasure from a girl he barely knew, whom he'd literally picked up in a café, than the people he grew up with and spent his day-to-day life with. And she was gorgeous, to boot. 'Do you want to go back?' he asked, just in case. 'You have to be up early tomorrow,' he said feeling strangely responsible for her.

'No.'

'But are you getting cold?' he asked, noticing that Milly was shivering now in the cooler evening air.

'A little.'

He pulled the picnic rug from the bow and handed it to her. She wrapped it around her shoulders.

'When did you start sailing?' asked Milly.

'As soon as I was old enough to pull the jib sheet. About five, I think. My dad and I used to go out all the time, in all weathers. I think it irritated the hell out of my mum. What about you?'

'Sunday afternoon sailors. It's practically compulsory in Whitstable. But we had to sell the boat after my mum died and then my father kind of lost interest.'

'Are you just working here for Cowes Week?'

'It's good money. A friend introduced me to it. I've done the last three years and this is my last one. I've saved enough to go to college in September.'

He filled up her cup. 'What are you going to do at college?'

'A fashion course. I'm not always dressed like this,' she said defensively. 'These are my work clothes.'

'You look great. Original.'

Milly grinned back at him in wordless thanks. 'How do you know the Rochesters?'

'Friends of the family. On my mother's side. That's the only reason they're prepared to put up with me. That and the fact they'll do anything dear Alicia asks of them. They're pretty unbearable but I'm on the water most of the time and at least it's my board and lodgings. How did your mum die?' he asked suddenly.

'Car accident. A drink-driver shot the lights. I was just starting my GCSEs. That's why I'm so late going to college. I failed them all.' She raised a small smile.

'That's tough.'

'Yes. It was.'

'Have you got a boyfriend back in Whitstable, Milly?' asked Fabian suddenly.

'On and off. More off than on.'

Fabian nodded slowly.

'And you? What about Alicia?' she asked.

'Alicia? Is that what you thought?' He gave a wry laugh. 'There's nothing much between me and Alicia but I do have to deliver a boat next week.' His eyes met hers in tacit understanding. He hoped she understood that he was married to the job. The passion he had for the water was hard to explain to anyone who didn't share it – although it seemed the only thing he had in common with other sailors at the moment. He found it hard to explain why something so uncomfortable and punishing, which also could be dangerous and stressful, could be quite so addictive. Once you'd experienced the true pleasure of it, it was difficult to go back to any other form of life.

'I've got to take a boat to Malta as a favour for a mate and after that, I don't know . . . ' He shrugged. 'Funnily enough, nobody particularly wants to pay me to be on their crew for racing. I tried to get on the Fastnet.'

'Have you done it before?' Even Milly had heard of Rolex Fastnet. It was an epic 600-mile offshore race often described as the sailing equivalent to climbing Everest.

'A couple of times with my father. He did the 1979 race as well. You know, the one with all the bad weather.'

'Lots of people died that year, didn't they?'

'Yes. My mother was pregnant with me and my father always said that during that storm all he could think about was getting safely home for us. He loved that race. He said the finest sight in all the world was the view of the lighthouse on Fastnet Rock.' But Fabian didn't want to talk about his father any more so he quickly leant forward and kissed her. Milly could taste salt and champagne. The warmth of his mouth was in delicious contrast to the elements. Milly wished she could stay kissing him forever.

Later, Fabian was to agree that he thought Milly's bra was very pretty indeed.

Chapter 5

The next morning whilst Milly was dancing on a cloud of euphoria, Fabian was quiet, brooding and reticent. He decided that beating the hell out of somebody on the water was the only cure for his ills and so immediately dashed out without saying goodbye to try and find an amateur boat he could crew on. Although it wouldn't be the professional standard he was used to, some sailing was better than no sailing.

Last night with Milly was the first time he had spoken about his father for a while and now it was as though the floodgates had been opened and he could think of nothing else.

After Rob's death Fabian had expected to hear something from his father, or even for him to fly out for the inquest, but to his bafflement there was no support from his parents.

Then one day, not long after, he turned up in Bridgetown in Barbados to collect his latest bank transfer and found it hadn't arrived. The next day, it still hadn't turned up. Nor the next one. So he called home (something he had been avoiding for a while because of the usual diatribes and lectures) and found out from his sobbing mother, who had been trying to get hold of him for weeks, that not only had his father gone bust and left them with nothing but also he had disappeared off the face of the earth. After trying to raise some cash from his local so-called friends, who were suddenly very reluctant to put their hands in their pockets, Fabian sold the *Mandarin* for a plane ticket home.

Now, Fabian stomped along the marina, for once not noticing the nudges and whispers as unwelcome thoughts crowded into his mind. He felt he must have let his father down terribly for him to disappear like that and it weighed on his mind. He cringed when he thought of some of his excesses. If only he, Fabian, had been in England and could have somehow helped him. He wondered about his father's secret life as well. What he hadn't told Milly was that the police were trying to trace him and implied he had been involved in some sort of fraud. When he'd first arrived home, Fabian had been absolutely convinced that his father would try and contact them somehow. He slowed down as he approached the end of the marina, unseeing of all the boats before him. He had been so convinced that his father would contact him that he'd failed to count the months of silence. The terrible thought struck him that maybe his father was dead.

He felt terribly disorientated suddenly. He had no money; nobody wanted to know him or give him a job. He couldn't remember what his old life was based on but he did know what he wanted to do. Sail professionally and find his father. He clung on to these two things like a drowning man.

He returned at teatime in a much better temper, dosed up on the powerful medicine of sunshine, water and a substantial win. He crept up behind Milly as she was setting out the tea tray and silently encircled his arms around her. She closed her eyes momentarily and allowed herself the delicious sensation of breathing his scent and melting into him. She felt giddy with relief.

'What's for tea?' he whispered, breathing in the scent of her hair. Sweetness and baking mixed with some sort of vanilla fragrance. She really was delicious with that huge non-judgemental smile. To his surprise he had found himself grinning today when he thought about her.

Milly smiled. 'Scones. How was the racing?'

'Marvellous. I feel better. Do you want to go out tonight?'

'I think I have to work. Mrs Rochester is having some friends over for supper.'

'God, is she? I'll have to go out. I don't think I can bear a blow-by-blow account of my-night-with-the-stars-at-the-Royal-Yacht-Squadron-Ball.'

Milly giggled. It was nice to be excluded together. Maybe they weren't so different, after all.

'You'll have to finish sometime. Come and spend the night with me.'

'Where?'

'A mate said he was spending all his time with an American stewardess. His yacht is free. It's small and he says it's not very comfortable but it's ours if we want it.'

'I don't know.' Milly turned back to arranging her scones on the tray.

Fabian kissed the back of her neck and her insides turned to liquid. 'We don't have that long together,' he whispered persuasively.

He was right, thought Milly, fighting her instincts, for at heart she was a relationship girl. Last night had been the most delicious of her life and she had to make the most of this affair. 'OK,' she said.

The yacht was called the *Coweslip*.

'She's a bit small,' said Fabian bowing his head under the eaves.

'She's perfect,' breathed Milly looking round at the tiny bunk and one-ringed cooker and kettle. 'Like a little doll's house.'

'She's ours for the rest of the week.'

Milly dumped her bag on the bunk.

'Mr Rochester said that Prince Philip of Sweden was here for the week,' she paused mischievously, 'but unfortunately couldn't make it to the Rochesters' for lunch. I nearly fainted from the relief.'

'You make wonderful tuna pittas. He would have been thrilled,' said Fabian seriously. Then he started talking about the new British challenge for the America's Cup. 'I wish I could be in it,' he said wistfully. 'My old skipper on the Volvo, John MacGregor, helmed the last America's Cup.'

'Is he here for Cowes Week?'

'No, he's not. We've lost touch a bit and I think he's decided to step down from racing for a while. Maybe even retire, I heard.'

'Who's the man leading the bid, Henry . . . ?'

'Luter.'

'Yes, Luter. The Rochesters were talking about him. Apparently they know him.'

'That doesn't surprise me because he's an absolute wanker by all accounts,' said Fabian a bit more cheerfully. 'But did you know that the original America's Cup started right here, in Cowes? Actually on these waters. Between a Yank boat *America* and some British yachts. They raced around the island just like the other day. Needless to say we lost. Hence it's called the *America*'s Cup.'

'Oh! I always thought it started in America.' Milly smiled at the animation that lit up his face and felt quite weak at the knees with wanting him so much. She wondered why he affected her like this. Probably because he felt like chocolate after a diet of salad. He was from a different world. To be honest, she was simply powerless to do anything else: his beauty had overwhelmed her. And she had seen his kindness to Tom. He wasn't all bad. 'Do you think we'll win it?'

'I don't know. Luter fucked up last time but he might have learnt something. God, I remember when the Cup was first won from the United States after more than a century. It was 1983. My father was so excited that he got me up in the middle of the night to watch the final race.'

Milly could tell from the way he talked about his father that Fabian clearly adored him. But it bothered her that he talked about him in the same way as she talked about her mother. As though he were dead. She longed to ask more about him but didn't want to ruin the mood. She wondered if he missed his

61

father as much as she missed her mother. She still treasured one of her mother's jumpers, hoping for some faint reminder of jasmine, vanilla-scented soap and her mother's warm skin every time she buried her head in its folds. She wondered if Fabian had kept any of his father's clothes. She went over to her bag to unpack her few things. Fabian came up behind her and, edging her cardigan off, dropped a long, leisurely kiss on her bare shoulder. 'Are you wearing that bra from yesterday?' he murmured.

'Yes, I am.'

'I think I need to check it's as pretty as I remember it.'

His warm hands slid down from her shoulders and tugged the vest top over her head. He turned her round. 'Ah, yes, it is,' he said solemnly.

Milly giggled and Fabian stopped her by kissing her fully now, his arms encircling her back. In one swift movement he moved them away and whipped off his own T-shirt. Milly wasn't terribly experienced; she'd only had two local boyfriends in Whitstable, and she suddenly realised what a beautiful body he had. A muscled, broad chest, so defined from all the sailing.

Their torsos were flesh on flesh now; Milly's heart was beating so fast she was surprised he didn't feel it coming out of her chest. He kissed her on and on until she thought she might faint from longing. She could feel his erection pressing into her stomach as he pulled her closer in to him.

'Milly?' he said a few minutes later. 'I really and truly am not trying to pressure you but can we go to bed? I think if I stoop any more my neck will break.'

Milly grinned and pulled him down on to the narrow bunk.

Jason Bryant tripped along the pontoon feeling on top of the world. His Oakleys were shoved on top of his head and the Dubarry boots came to mid-calf on his long, long legs; he wore his combat shorts fashionably low on his hips like a gunslinger and he was aware of the girls' admiring looks wherever he went.

But for all his suave appearance Jason Bryant was nothing more than a thug whose motto was 'win at all costs'. He had an over-aggressive nature which was usually satisfied by thrashing his competitors on the water by day and taking their women off them by night. Losing at anything provoked him into a vast fury.

Today he had every reason to swagger. He already had three substantial wins at Cowes Week and things were set to look even better. He had been summoned for a meeting with Henry Luter to talk about a place on the crew for the 2007 America's Cup.

Once at Henry Luter's sailing base, where the British side of the new challenge for the America's Cup would be operated from, he idly flirted with the receptionist. She spent most of her time being chatted up by avaricious sailors and leaving all the lights flashing on her switchboard, which infuriated the shore manager, but this time she didn't care. This particular sailor was worth any potential ticking-off.

He stopped as soon as he saw Henry Luter sweep out of one of the meeting rooms through the reception area. Luter's personal assistant gestured Jason to follow them and he ended up in an office which overlooked a Solent buzzing with nautical traffic. Henry Luter was seated at a vast desk; Jason was no expert but he knew the art which hung on the wall behind him was price-less and the blatant display of sailing trophies in a cabinet was the sign of man who liked to win – very much like himself. Another wall of the office was entirely given over to photos of Luter meeting the rich and famous. An especially prominent one pictured him shaking hands with the Queen and another one with the Aga Khan.

Luter noticed Bryant looking at it. 'We sail together,' he said on the strength of one outing. Luter came from a lowly family, and connections with the rich and famous were important to him. Painfully clever and yet socially inept, he started repairing computer boards in his parents' garage at the age of fifteen in lieu of a social life. By the age of twenty-four, Henry was the managing director of a computer software company specialising in anti-virus programmes. The more unscrupulous of his competitors suggested that Henry wrote the virus programmes merely to sell the anti-virus, a charge that Henry denied a little too strenuously. By his mid-thirties he was the biggest player in computing since Bill Gates and had conquered all of Europe.

He gestured his hand towards the window. 'Picked up this piece of land from a bankrupt boatyard. It's worth twice what I paid for it,' he couldn't resist boasting. 'What do you think of the view?'

'Great.'

'Sit down.' It was more of a command rather than a request. Someone came in with a tray of coffee for Luter but nothing was offered to Jason.

Luter inspected the coffee tray carefully before speaking. 'You've been on top of your game these last couple of years.'

'Just achieving my potential.'

'How do you feel about the America's Cup?'

'Greatest sailing competition in the world.'

'Yes it is and I'm going to win it. You helmed the second boat for the Swedish syndicate in the last Cup, didn't you?'

'Yes. I learnt a hell of a lot. But the only boat I would want to helm this time would be the first boat.'

There was a pause as Henry Luter got up and walked round his desk to stare out of the window. Jason wondered whether he'd pushed his luck.

'Well, Mr Bryant,' said Luter eventually, 'you might get the chance to do just that. But there would be a couple of ground rules we would need to establish first. I take the position of strategist and get to have final say on the crew. The boat design is my decision alone and I am spokesman and skipper for the crew. I'm not one of those syndicate owners whose job is simply to keep the cheque book dry.'

Jason paused. Sailing was littered with men like Luter. Rich businessmen who had taken up sailing to escape the pressure of their work, but then, naturally competitive, became addicted to the winning. Henry Luter had the whiff of a ruthless assassin about him though. A man who would stop at nothing to win. The America's Cup was considered to be the holy grail of sailing and that would be the very reason Henry Luter wanted it. It was one of the things that made the America's Cup fascinating: it was competed for by a group of men who never lost, yet this time all but one of them would lose.

Jason thought about the offer. A helmsman would usually pick his own crew and have some influence on the boat design. But he thought he could handle Henry Luter. His ambition got the better of him: the helm of the first boat on an America's Cup crew! He could already imagine the headlines.

'That would be fine,' he said shortly. 'What would be the package?'

'A hundred and twenty grand a year plus a bonus every time you win during the Cup.'

Jason liked the prospect of a bonus. It made crews super-aggressive.

'Of course we would pay for all your living expenses whilst you were out in Spain as well. Your contract would start next year out in Valencia.' The Cup was being defended there as the 2003 Cup had been won in the name of the Royal Valencia Yacht Club. 'I also would expect a letter of resignation from yourself up front which I can then invoke if I ever see the need.'

Jason had heard of Luter's request from other sailors. It meant Luter always got his own way – he could simply rustle it in his pocket if he had any opposition – and it also removed the possibility of him ever being sued for wrongful dismissal but Jason Bryant wasn't scared of it. 'Fine. So are all the rumours and press reports true, John MacGregor won't be on the boat?'

'Mr MacGregor and I chose to part company during the last Cup.'

'His experience would be useful though. In a different position of course.' God, how he would love that. Taking the helm away from John MacGregor and then still having him in his crew, taking his commands.

Luter had also clearly thought about the benefits of having Mack on board. 'I don't think he would want any position other than helm. He's an arrogant fucker. He's on the way out anyway. He's completely lost his nerve. Hasn't been able to sail competitively since we left Auckland. Taken up some sad charity case. I hear that he used to be a teacher of yours.'

'When I was in the youth squad,' said Jason quickly. 'A few years ago now. There's no love lost between us. He's getting old and needs to retire.'

'He cost me the Cup last time. I trust it won't happen again.' Luter got up suddenly, thus indicating the interview was at an end. 'You need to come in and sign confidentiality agreements next week but we'll save the actual contract until after a few try-outs on the boat next year and make a press announcement then. By the way, I saw you talking to our receptionist on your way in.' Jason stiffened, expecting a lecture. 'We don't have many women on the base in Spain. What do you think about that?'

'It's the way I like it.' Bryant paused, wondering if he could risk the next comment. He decided to try it. 'Women are only good at two things. Neither of them is sailing.'

'I couldn't agree more.' Luter pressed the intercom suddenly and spoke down it. 'Send my wife in to me,' he snapped to the responding voice.

They waited in silence. Luter hadn't dismissed him so Bryant stayed put. He was curious anyway to see Luter's new wife. Luter recently stunned the gossip pages by ditching his wife of eleven years (whose obsession with social mountaineering had pushed him into sailing and he had been instantly hooked) and marrying a young penniless socialite and Bryant had a feeling that Luter wanted to show him a trophy. Luter didn't want someone to sleep with him because they claimed to find him attractive (which he wasn't); he wanted them to sleep with him because he was powerful and rich. For him, it was simply a measure of how far he had come.

Within a couple of minutes the door opened and admitted a beautiful woman so sleek and scented that Bryant's senses reeled. She was like an orchid in a box. She didn't even look at Bryant but immediately went to Luter who was standing now by the window. He was slightly shorter than her even though she wore flats. He fingered her.

It was a surreal moment. Jason Bryant felt almost like a voyeur, and yet he thought Luter wanted it that way. 'See yourself out, Bryant,' he said.

Chapter 6

The next few days were the happiest Milly could remember. Everything was simply perfect. The weather was wonderful. She moved her stuff from her lodgings and woke up every morning in Fabian's arms having spent most of the night awake and talking after they had made love. Milly loved those hours best – lying sated in Fabian's arms in the early hours of the morning and chatting intimately about anything and everything: Milly's moles and Fabian's scars, childhood pets, favourite sweets, driving tests, and boats Fabian had loved, until sleep overtook them and they drifted off still lying entwined together. Sometimes Milly hoped that they would come adrift from their mooring in the middle of the night and simply float off into the ocean together. She was fooling herself thinking that she could cope with a simple fling, but she brushed aside her doubts and enjoyed it whilst she could.

It was surprising that the Rochesters didn't twig at all. Fabian was rarely on board, but when he was Milly made sure she didn't even look at him. Not only because Alicia was watching him hungrily agog but she knew that if she so much as cast him a glance, the whole world would be able to see how she felt. She was absolutely smitten.

When she was clearing away at one meal, studiously ignoring Fabian, she felt a warm hand slip up her skirt as he innocently carried on his conversation about wind conditions. It started to caress the inside of her thigh as she desperately loaded dishes on to her tray. Her one consolation was that Fabian was unable to get up for the next ten minutes.

The only blip was the day that Milly watched Fabian racing. As part of a lunch party, the Rochester yacht motored out to watch all the men competing in the Solent. Milly had no problems picking out the gleam of Fabian's hair at the bow of his boat. It was all she could do not to stand and stare with her mouth open – she had no idea racing would be so demanding nor, frankly, so dangerous. It was a blustery day and it looked as though he was riding a wild horse, with waves washing over him as he struggled to attach spinnaker poles and take down sails. Every time the boat buried its bow head first into a wave Milly held her breath, sure that it would come back up again without Fabian on board. She obviously spent too long looking at his boat because Alicia was now starting to watch *her* suspiciously.

'Is that Beaufort chap still staying with you?' asked a guest, an impossibly hearty ex-major, as Milly came back on deck with pudding. 'Bad business about his father.'

'David Beaufort was a fine man.'

'So we all thought. They say that business with Fabian and poor Rob Thornton must have sent him over the edge. Are they going to press charges on Fabian for possession?'

Milly placed the pecan pie on the table in slow motion. 'I'll cut it, Mother,' said Alicia sharply. 'You can go, Milly.'

'At the lunch party today they were all talking about your father as though he were dead,' said Milly as soon as they were alone that evening.

Fabian sat up suddenly and threw his legs over the side of the bunk. He stared sullenly at the wooden slats of the floor. 'They all think he is.'

'Why?'

'I don't know where he is,' snapped Fabian. 'Nobody knows.

I was still in the Caribbean when he disappeared. The first I knew was when my mum told me he'd gone and there was no money. I came home to the police crawling all over the house and his business and talking about fraud. But he's not dead. He can't be.'

'Oh, Fabian,' murmured Milly. 'How awful for you.'

Fabian slumped back. 'I leave my mobile on the whole time for him but he hasn't called. I don't know where he is or how to start looking for him. I miss him,' he said simply. 'I never missed him whilst I was away but knowing you might never see someone again feels quite different.' He smiled at Milly. 'But you know about that.'

He was grieving for him, she knew that. The difference was that he was grieving without sympathy cards or condolences or a funeral service. She nodded but waited for him to continue.

'He's another reason why I need to keep on sailing. At least he'll know where to find me.'

'I'm sure he will come and find you. Maybe he's just waiting for things to calm down a bit. Is it very serious? The fraud charges, I mean?' she asked tentatively.

'I don't know. I really don't know. One of his business partners said that he had been moving money around a lot to cover losses in one company. I think he hoped that he would be able to move the money back and no one would be any the wiser. I can't make up my mind whether he was being truly dishonest or just desperate and stupid. I just wish I had been here. He would certainly be arrested if he came back. I've got bad blood, they all say.'

'And all the money?'

'All gone.' He shook his head sadly. 'All the houses are up for sale. The cars have already gone and *Ragamuffin* was sold last week. I don't care about the money but it's funny how much you take for granted when it's around. I always thought I'd be able to choose what sailing I wanted to do when I wanted to do it. Now I'm relying on it and nobody will have me on their boat. I don't know how I'm going to get my mother through all this either.'

Milly put her arms around him and leant her head on his back. Fabian touched one of her arms. 'Thank God for you this week, Milly. You're the only thing that's kept me sane. If circumstances had been different . . . ' he trailed off.

Milly smiled but said nothing. She knew fully well that if circumstances had been different Fabian would not have glanced twice at the resident cook.

Milly couldn't help but raise a grin at the scene before her. She had come ashore to do some shopping and found the town remarkably busy because most of the racing crews had licked their fingers, not felt even a ghost of wind and decided to give up on a bad job and head inshore for some more traditional refreshment, not to mention huge water pistol fights.

This was the last day of Cowes Week. They'd had a wonderful week together. Milly couldn't believe so much could have happened. Her days were simply full of Fabian and it seemed unbelievable that soon there would be nothing but a void. Tomorrow Fabian was travelling back to Southampton where he would take charge of the yacht he had to sail to Malta. Milly wished he would ask her to go with him. It made no difference to her that he was penniless and in disgrace, or even that he had such an appalling track record. She understood what it was like to have your world turned upside down. But he had made absolutely no mention of what would happen after Cowes Week was over. She had an inkling that the Rochesters might ask her to stay on and cook for them as they were planning to take the yacht down the English Channel and visit some friends at Falmouth in Cornwall. She'd overheard Mrs Rochester whispering fiercely to Alicia this morning, 'Do you want to cook yourself, you stupid girl?' They both promptly shut up when she came into view.

Milly had no idea what she might do. After such a glorious week here she was loath to return to Whitstable. The idea of returning home and pretending the entire affair had never happened was too depressing. That was as far as she could go to admitting how much she was falling in love with Fabian. She decided that if the Rochester family offered her some more work then she would take it. At least that way she could earn some more money and Fabian would know where to find her.

Fabian and Milly stayed awake very late on their last night together, unwilling to let sleep claim their last few hours. Milly watched the minutes tick by with a strange intensity and thought she had never been so happy nor so miserable in her entire life.

Fabian also felt strangely bereft. Until now he'd been used to only the most cursory of love affairs; Milly was far from his usual stereotype but her gentle nature and uncomplicated sweetness were a tonic to his soul. As comforting as a hot bath after a drenching. She would be hard to let go.

In the morning she woke to find Fabian packing his bag. The *Coweslip* already looked strangely deserted. She sat up on the bunk. 'Take me with you,' she blurted out and then bit her lip. She really hadn't meant to ask but she had to try.

Fabian didn't stop packing. God, it was so tempting: just him and Milly taking off somewhere. But slowly reality reasserted itself. He needed a job and he needed to find his father. *He* was the one who needed to stay put. 'I can't,' he said eventually when he'd finished. 'I truly can't.' He came to sit next to her. They sat in silence for a moment. 'I really am bad news at the moment, Milly.'

'I don't care about that.'

'But I do. Everything is such a mess. I'm a mess. I need to get back into sailing and I need to find my father. The rest is immaterial. You can't come with me, Milly, because if I spent another week with you then I wouldn't be able to let *you* go. And that really wouldn't be fair on you. You deserve someone who can look after you.' He honestly meant it. There wasn't a lot he had done in his lifetime that he had felt proud of and for once he was trying to be truly unselfish.

'I can look after myself. I want you. And I want to help.'

Fabian slowly shook his head, kissed her and said goodbye. After he'd left, Milly flopped back into bed and cried until she thought her heart would break.

Chapter 7

A few weeks later Milly stared in total disbelief at the little blue line in front of her. She absolutely couldn't believe it. There it was, just as it had been earlier this morning, defiant in its existence.

A sharp knocking on the door brought her to suddenly. One of the other crew members wanted to get in and so she gathered up the paper, box and plastic bits and with stumbling apologies exited and hurried back to her tiny cabin. She stood trembling, her mind full of tumbling thoughts. She had to get back to cooking supper for the family but she couldn't move.

The Rochester yacht was moored just off the coast of Falmouth. Friends of theirs had a huge mansion overlooking the river and a motor launch seemed to hum constantly between the two, transporting Alicia and the hordes of glamorous friends or Mr and Mrs Rochester on their way to various drinks parties. Milly hadn't been able to stop thinking about Fabian. Time and again she went to the yacht atlas and looked up where Malta was. She roamed up the river on various ferry trips and wondered what he was doing. But that was all before the little blue line. Such an innocuous announcement to the start of a life.

By the end of the day she had decided that whatever she resolved to do, Fabian should at least know about it. But she wanted to make a decision before she spoke to him. Milly stayed awake long into the night. She had always dreamt about having children but none of them involved her being a single mother at the age of twenty-two. Each time she thought about having the child, she wondered how on earth she would support herself or take up her place at college, but each time she thought about getting rid of the baby then she knew she couldn't. This was Fabian's child, a man she had now admitted she was desperately in love with, and a little piece of him was living inside her.

After a few sleepless nights, Milly made her decision. She would keep the baby. She was used to setbacks in her life and she would manage. She would simply postpone her place at fashion college and go another time. But, she promised herself, she *would* go.

Waking at six the next morning, Milly called Fabian's mobile. She didn't know if he would be back from Malta yet but a sleepy voice answered.

'Fabian?'

'Yes?'

'It's Milly. Milly from Cowes.'

There was a pause as Fabian struggled to come into consciousness. 'Milly?'

'I'm really sorry to call you, Fabian. I know it's early but I'm afraid I've got some news.'

Fabian's mind immediately went to his father. 'What's happened?'

'I'm pregnant.'

This time the pause was so long. Milly thought the phone had cut out and said, 'Fabian? Are you still there?'

'I'm still here,' he said in a strange voice. 'How can that be? We were using condoms. Are you sure?'

'Yes. I'm sure.'

'No, I mean, are you sure it's mine? I'm sorry, I don't mean to be crass but was there someone before . . . ?'

Milly bit her lip. She supposed it was only fair that he should ask. 'Yes, I'm sure it's yours. I don't know how it happened.'

'What are you going to do?'

'I want to have the baby.'

'Are you sure about that?'

'Yes,' she said firmly. 'I'm only calling to tell you. I don't want anything from you but it would be nice if you did decide that you want to play a part in the child's life.' There was another pause. 'Look, you need to get used to the idea so why don't we talk again tomorrow?'

'Yes,' said Fabian. 'I'll call you.' And then the phone went dead.

The rest of the day was spent in a blind panic, completely convinced that she had said all the wrong things and that Fabian would immediately change his mobile phone number and she would never hear from him again.

Her sharp, blue eyes never far from Milly's face, Alicia had also picked up something was wrong and gave her a particularly hard time that day, sending dishes back because she imagined they were cold. So Milly was relieved when Fabian woke her at six-thirty the next morning and said he wanted to come down so that they could talk things over. She agreed to meet him at the National Maritime Museum in Falmouth the next day.

The next morning she arrived at the museum café early and eagerly looked around for Fabian. He was ordering coffee at the counter and she nervously went up behind him.

'Fabian?' she said quietly.

He spun round and smiled at her and her stomach dropped through the floor. She had forgotten just how beautiful he was. The picture of him in her mind had been fading like a negative in the sunlight. 'Would you like some coffee?'

Her nose involuntarily wrinkled. 'Er, no, thanks. Some tea would be nice.' Fabian paid and took the tray to the nearest table in silence.

'How was your trip?' she asked nervously. It seemed strangely formal, sitting opposite him after their time together in Cowes.

'It was good. Gave me a lot of time to think. I'd just got back when you called.'

'Do the Rochesters know you're here?'

'God, no! I was hoping to completely avoid them. How has work been? I was surprised you stayed on with them.'

'I thought the money might come in handy . . . ' There was a pause.

'So . . . ' he said. 'You want to keep the baby?'

'Yes, I do.'

'OK,' he said finally. 'It's your decision and I'll help financially.'

Milly opened her mouth to thank him, utterly relieved that she wasn't to be abandoned. She had been remembering all the stories about Fabian rather than her experience of him. Ever since she had left the café at his request he seemed to have taken some sort of responsibility for her. But then she was swamped with dreadful disappointment that he hadn't offered more. She tried to get a handle on her emotions – and on reality. Had she really been expecting him to ask her to marry him? No, not marriage, said a little voice within her, but surely something more . . . 'Please don't worry about the money now. I mean, I might need some in the future but I've decided to go to college another year and I have all the money I saved to live on for a while. Of course, I'm going to try and work right up to the birth . . . '

'Are you going to be able to get a job? I mean, you'll have to say you're pregnant.'

Milly frowned. 'Well, I don't know a lot about how maternity pay works but I'll find out. I might be able to stay on with the Rochesters.'

'He certainly won't pay you any maternity pay.'

'I'll manage,' said Milly brightly, trying not to let the problems overwhelm her.

Fabian decided to stay on a few days in Falmouth and booked in at the local youth hostel. Luckily the Rochesters were dining out a lot so many of her evenings were free; they were both very short of cash so they made do with fish and chips. After a couple of days, Milly was even brave enough to buy some folic acid and a book about pregnancy from the local bookstore.

On the third day, they arranged to meet on the main quayside at Falmouth and Milly was late. Fabian spent the time watching a father and his young toddler run up and down the quayside, the toddler squealing with joy every time the father almost caught him.

'God, sorry! Are you OK?' Milly said, rushing up with her bag slung over her shoulder. 'What shall we go and do? I wondered if we should catch a ferry—'

'Milly, I need to talk to you.'

Milly's heart sank. 'OK,' she said evenly, sitting back down on the bench, her heart going like a piston.

Fabian sat down next to her. He wouldn't look at her properly. 'I've got to leave today. The bloke I took that yacht to Malta for wants me to do something else. A long haul this time.'

'But that's great! I mean I'm sorry that you have to go but—'

'Milly, that's not just it. I've been thinking about you and the baby . . . Things have changed a lot for me over the last couple of months . . . It's just that children have never really featured on my agenda. With my work I'm never really in one place for any stretch of time. I didn't plan on this. I didn't plan on a child.'

'Nor did I.'

'Kids are such a commitment,' he muttered. 'I can't be committed like that. I have too many of my own problems at the moment. Look, I do want to contribute financially where I can and when I can but I really can't take on anything more than that. I won't be able to see the child regularly so it might be better if I'm not involved at all. I have to get back to Southampton. This bloke wants me to leave tomorrow if the weather's all right. I'll be away for some time.' Fabian got up. 'I'll call you.'

'Call me? Is that it? You'll call me?' she spluttered with rage. 'You're walking away just like your father did. You simply can't take the responsibility, can you? I can't walk away, Fabian. Did you think about that?'

'There are other options,' he muttered.

'Sure, there is always the easy way. But that will just have to remain the difference between you and me.'

Fabian's face was stricken, but he was still avoiding her eye. 'I'm sorry.'

What could she say to change his mind? She couldn't think – she was stunned. She was also furious. He had made a promise, a commitment to her and the baby. What gave him the right to walk away when she couldn't?

Without another word, Fabian put his hand on her shoulder and turned on his heel to leave.

Milly couldn't remember the journey back to the Rochester boat but somehow she made it back to her cabin. Her mind was reeling. How would she manage? Could she work? Should she live with her father? She started to panic. She simply didn't know what to do next. When Fabian was around it had felt as though they could find the answers together; now she just felt lost. She decided she couldn't keep the news to herself any longer.

She called Amy and poured her heart out to her. She had been talking for about three quarters of an hour when a knock on the door and a disembodied voice informed her that the family wanted her on deck. She said she would call Amy back, dried her eyes and made her way up.

Mr Rochester immediately strode over to her. 'You're pregnant,' he hissed, thrusting his purple face so close to Milly that she flinched.

How had he found out? She looked around and caught Alicia's eye. Alicia dropped her gaze innocently but not before Milly sensed a flash of triumph. She must have been listening at her door. She turned back to Mr Rochester. 'Yes, I'm pregnant but I don't really see what it's to do with you,' she said quietly.

'It has everything to do with me, girl, if it goes on whilst you're on my yacht. I will NOT have crew members sleeping with each other. So who is the father? Who? Or do you not know yourself?'

'I know perfectly well, thank you,' said Milly quietly.

There was a silence.

'Right then, if you're not going to tell me then we'll just get the whole of the male crew up here and we'll stay here until one of them confesses.'

'It's not one of the crew.'

'What? A local boy? We haven't been here long enough for one of them to get their leg over.'

Milly winced at his crudeness. 'No, it's not a local boy, either. Can I go now?'

'If you're not going to tell me who it is than you can go. You can go and pack your things and leave here and never come back.'

'I don't think you can fire me for being pregnant,' said Milly bravely.

Mr Rochester opened his mouth to bark something else but Mrs Rochester put a warning hand on his arm.

'Beaufort!' boomed Mr Rochester suddenly, looking at a figure over Milly's shoulder. 'What a pleasant surprise!'

Milly spun round and saw Fabian who had silently cat-footed on to the deck during this performance.

'What's going on?' asked Fabian softly.

'Just a small domestic dispute with one of the staff. What on earth are you doing here in Falmouth, Fabian dear boy? How is your lovely mother?'

'What sort of dispute?'

'An unplanned pregnancy, unfortunately. We can't have that sort of thing going on amongst the crew. You can go now,' he said fiercely turning back to Milly. 'We can pay you until the end of the month and then you will have to leave.' Mr Rochester went forward to greet Fabian but Fabian stopped him in his tracks.

'I am the father of Milly's child,' he announced, clear as a bell.

There was shocked silence. Mr Rochester looked completely flabbergasted, his arms dropped to his sides, Mrs Rochester's eyes jerked from face to face as though at an exciting tennis match and Alicia stared at Milly with ill-disguised fury. Milly felt a terrible hysterical urge to giggle.

'But I thought you and Alicia . . . ' spluttered Rochester.

'Your daughter is a spoilt and silly brat. She is the last person I would be with.'

Fabian walked over to Milly. 'Look, I know I've said this to you before and I know it didn't work out so well but . . . ' He shrugged and then met her eye. 'Get your stuff.'

Chapter 8

In summer the following year, whilst Fabian and Milly were coping with the staggering demands of a newborn baby, Inky Pencarrow was travelling to Falmouth from Daymer Bay to collect a new sail for the family boat. She was inordinately pleased to be home in Cornwall. The sea seeped into every nook and cranny of Cornish life, the land was cupped in its hands and their past was inextricably linked. Even religion respectfully bowed its head in deference to the more ancient cousin. Mermaids were carved into the church pews and prayers said to 'spare our men'. Inky adored Cornwall and felt at home here like no other place.

At the boatyard which the family used for all its boating supplies, old Dan was pleased to see her. The Pencarrows were an old Cornish family whose name peppered the annals of sailing and racing history and thus, in his opinion, they were like royalty.

'Back home, Inky?' he greeted her.

'Back home, Dan.' She stepped out of the old Volvo estate (more room for sails). 'How are you?'

'Keeping fit, keeping fit. South-easterly today,' he said, looking up at the sky. 'Ten knots if you're lucky. Your pa said that you've been match racing.'

'Bermuda. The King Edward Gold Cup.' Inky had been racing on the World Match Racing Tour circuit which travelled all over the world, match racing other professionals, and there was big prize money to be won. She had battled for the Danish Open in Copenhagen, lost her bowman overboard in the St Moritz Match Race in Switzerland (at which his ever helpful crewmates crowded over the side yelling, 'Swim, Beano, swim!'), clashed with the Italians in the Brazil Sailing Cup in Angra dos Reis and won the Toscana Elba Cup in Italy.

'How d'you do?'

'Came third.' Inky's nonchalance hid her annoyance at coming third. It had been a close semi-final and she had lost to none other than Jason Bryant – a sailor she had a great deal of history with and a none-too-friendly rivalry. She had worked hard over the last couple of years, since she had finished the America's Cup in Auckland, to come even close to her male adversaries. Whilst a woman on the World Match Racing Tour is not an anomaly she is certainly a rarity and certain skippers were taking it very personally when she beat them. She was finding it hard to topple Jason Bryant, however; he was on dazzling form at the moment. 'I'm lucky that Mack has taken some time out on that youth sailing scheme. Otherwise I might have come fourth!'

'John MacGregor? Is that what he's doing now? Thought I hadn't seen him round these parts for a while. Thought he'd retired since I hadn't seen him in the headlines either.'

'Mack? Retire? Never!' said Inky staunchly. Since losing in Auckland, Mack had decided to take some time out from match racing and put something back into the sport by teaching under-privileged youngsters on a youth sailing scheme. His critics said that his loss in Auckland had finally put him out of the big league. His supporters muttered about how he was just having a break after all the stress he'd been under.

'Still, I expect that coming third was still big prize money!'

Inky grinned at Dan's innate nosiness. 'Enough to keep me off the streets for a bit.'

'*And* you did the America's Cup. You're in the big time now, so you are, girl. Won't be talking to the likes of us soon.'

'I only made the second crew, Dan.'

'Most important bit, that. The sparring partner. Got to have somebody to race against in all those long days of practice and there ain't no point if you're not any good. I hear your brothers are doing handsome too. Your pa is fit to burst.' The OSTAR, the Fastnet, the Volvo, the Vendée. The boys were certainly covering themselves in glory. And Inky was pleased for them, she really was.

'They're doing well,' she acknowledged.

'But you're the one who was in the America's Cup.' They started slowly to walk towards the sail loft.

'I just like match racing, Dan. The boys prefer offshore racing. I'm not joining Henry Luter's new challenge though.'

''Tis a shame that he's such a bugger. That Cup is a world unto itself, it is that,' Dan shook his head to himself in wonderment. 'You've done us proud though, Inky.'

I wish my father thought so, Inky thought to herself. Jason Bryant's gloating was bad enough. On the pontoon after the race they had to make a show of sportsmanship. A huge crowd had gathered to watch them come in. Bryant had already been thrown in by his crew and by the time she reached him, he had stripped to the waist.

'Congratulations,' she had said through tight lips. 'You could always have a new career in bumper cars.'

'Only if you're in the neighbouring car.'

They shook hands with strained smiles and Jason pulled her towards him. 'However hard you try you're never going to beat me,' he'd whispered in her ear. 'Now run along like a good girl, I'm sure Daddy will kiss it better.'

Daddy, in actual fact, was bloody furious.

'They were forced errors!' he had yelled down the phone after staying up most of the night to watch the match on cable TV. Inky was lying on her hotel bed. She was feeling so miserable that she had eaten the extortionately priced nuts and chocolate out of the mini-bar.

'The wind shifted.'

'You should have seen that coming! Bloody Bryant is insufferable enough as it is; there's a rumour going round that Luter has asked him to join his new challenge. I suggest you think about following suit, it's the only chance you'll get to sail in the America's Cup.'

'Even if Luter would hire me again, I wouldn't get on the first boat. They'd only ever have me on the second. And if it's true about Jason Bryant then there is no way he would have me on the first boat either.'

'But no other syndicate has asked you to join their challenge, have they? This might be the only chance you get and if that's the second boat then so be it. Maybe that's the best you'll ever do.'

'I'm not joining their challenge because I want to be on the first boat and Henry Luter is never going to have a woman on the first boat,' she had said through gritted teeth.

'And by losing that semi-final you have just handed them the perfect excuse on a plate.' And with this he had slammed down the receiver.

When Inky got home, her mother was busy taking a casserole dish out of the Aga. When Mary Pencarrow had first arrived in Cornwall, she had tried to cook sophisticated dishes for her James, longing for them both to sit down at the table every evening and have a proper conversation, but she had long since given up this ideal as all that the men in her life seemed to want was hot, hearty food they could bolt down before going back to sanding down a boat or arguing over a yachting article. Mary was delightfully delicate with pale, paper-like skin and thick dark hair – both of which Inky had inherited. One of her earlier suitors, who had ardently courted her before she left London, had compared her with an extremely rare and beautiful flower that would perish without constant warmth and care. At the time she'd thought his words were overly sentimental but now she wondered if he had been right.

She was still a beautiful woman. Just a few lines ringed her eyes and although she had toned down her clothes somewhat since leaving London, she was still always immaculately turned out. 'What? Going to the opera, Mum?' the boys would joke when she appeared in the morning. 'Visiting Liz at Buck House?'

Mary had to develop her own survival techniques and her garden became a private passion. So she would don a large hat (tied firmly down with a Hermès scarf against the persistent sea breeze) and make her way into the garden where she would wrestle with the elements and the salt. Her old suitor's words became her mantra as she strove to protect her flowers against the sea and the constant pervasion of salt that could be neither seen nor felt, only detected in the havoc it wrought. Sometimes when Mary lay awake listening to the waves thrashing outside, sounding as though they were trying to get into the house, she felt like screaming. The sea had taken her husband and all of her children into its thrall, what else did it want?

None of her family realised how she really felt and she was too scared to let them know. Scared because she doubted whether any of them would particularly care and she loved them all so desperately that she didn't want to find out that this was true. She simply wouldn't be able to bear it.

'Erica, dear. There you are,' she said gently, and delicately closed the oven door. 'Do you want some of this? I thought you might have missed lunch today.'

'Thanks, Mum, but I'm not particularly hungry. I got a sandwich in Falmouth.'

'It doesn't matter,' said Mary quickly. 'There'll be plenty left for Mack when he arrives later.'

'What time did he say he'd get here?'

'About nine, I think.'

'At least I'll get to see him before I leave.' Inky was flying out to Malaysia tomorrow for a World Match Racing Tour event. 'How did he sound?' Despite her staunch outward loyalty to him, Inky did worry that all the stress of the last America's Cup in Auckland had really taken its toll on him.

'Fine,' said Mary firmly. But old, she added privately to herself. She too was worried about him.

'Where's Dad?' asked Inky eagerly.

'Checking the Volvo website. I think he wanted to see where your brother Charlie has got to.' Mary desperately hoped he would come out to speak to Inky soon.

Inky threw herself down in the armchair next to the Aga and used her foot to scratch their black Labrador, Nelson. It hadn't escaped her mother's notice that over the last few years Inky had tried to de-sex herself completely, as though by denying the things which made her a woman she could pretend it didn't make a difference. She told her mother that her long, blue-black hair was getting in the way, and so she adopted a short bob. She said she couldn't wear any make-up because her mascara ran in the water. Mostly it didn't make a difference because nothing could take away from her long, long legs and her natural blush. She moved with a certain fluidity, lithe and sinuous; every movement of her exceeding slimness was curiously graceful and infinitely more attractive than the manicured and saccharine beauty of the sailing groupies who tried so hard to emulate it.

Mary had noticed such changes in Inky since her return from Auckland and she desperately wished Inky would talk to her about it, but despite numerous efforts, Inky simply clammed up. The day when Inky cut off all her hair almost broke her heart.

'Where's Charlie?' asked Inky as soon as her father came in.

'Made another hundred and five miles since yesterday!' he said cheerfully. 'They'll be rounding Cape Horn this time tomorrow if the weather keeps up! He sent a three-line email saying that they were having freeze-dried ice cream tonight to celebrate someone's birthday and that he's just sold his last razor for a chocolate bar! God, I wish I were with him! Will you try to get back for his homecoming, Inky?'

'I'll try, but I don't know where I'll be on the match tour. I was thinking perhaps you and Mum could come out for one of the events?' Inky said quietly, concentrating on Nelson's ears.

'Hmm, we'll see. It depends what your brothers are up to.'

Mary looked at James impatiently. He was still punishing her for coming third in the Bermuda Gold Cup. Mary was inordinately proud of all her children and even if she did wish that Inky could spend a bit more time at home, she would always support her in whatever she chose to do. 'I would love to come out for one of your events, darling,' said Mary.

'Would you?' Inky looked eagerly at each of her parents and Mary realised that this was only an attractive proposition if James were accompanying her.

'Mary, you hate watching sailing,' commented James.

'I like watching Erica.'

Mary looked at her daughter slumped back in the chair and trying hard to mask her disappointment, and then at her husband poring over the globe in the corner of the room. 'Erica, could you take Nelson out for his night walk?' she asked, determined to give her husband a good talking-to.

Inky took Nelson out into the sand dunes and then on to the beach. It was getting dark but she and Nelson knew every rock, stone and pool on this beach. The dog star was there, waiting patiently for her and she wondered what stars she would be looking at tomorrow. It was a glassy night and the moon shone brightly on the spire of St Enodoc church, a little oasis sunken in the dunes accessible only on foot. Leaving Nelson to have a sniff around, she lay on top of one of the dunes and looked at the sky.

This estuary was the place where she and her brothers had raced their boats up and down all summer, where they'd fished for mackerel out at sea and watched for dolphins. It was where her father had constantly favoured the boys over her, making her even more determined to win. Memories darted into her head like silver-backed fish flashing in the sunlight. She remembered racing with Mack up the estuary with her brothers behind her and water skiing behind the buoys on the tide. She remembered being dreadfully jealous of her brothers when her father, carrying on the family tradition, gave each of his sons a twenty-pound note following their sixteenth birthday, and then instructed them to take the boat and not return for three weeks of the summer holidays. She remembered waiting with bated breath on her sixteenth birthday, desperate for the adventure and laden with plans as to where she would go, only to be told that it was too dangerous for a girl. Her brothers had patted her head and laughed at her. That wasn't the first or the last time that she wished she had been born a boy. The best summer of her life was when Mack lent her *Wild Thing*.

'Inky!' Her name was being called out very softly. She sat up suddenly and squinted around. She could just about make out the shape of a man coming towards her and she instantly recognised him.

'Mack!' she said in delight.

'Don't get up!' he called. 'I'll come to you.'

Panting slightly with the effort of walking through the soft sand dunes, he plonked himself beside her and roughly kissed her cheek.

'When did you arrive?'

'Just now. Your mother said you were out walking Nelson and I fancied some air after all that time in the car.'

'How are you?'

'Fine. All the better for seeing you. How was Bermuda?'

'Came third. Bryant beat me.'

'He's on good form.'

'You taught him everything he knows,' said Inky quickly, thinking about the rumours of Mack's loss of form. She could only pray that it was temporary. It didn't bear thinking about. It would be like seeing a lion stripped of his mane and teeth.

'Talking of Bryant, I heard on the radio on the way down that Henry Luter has made him the helmsman for the new challenge in 2007.'

'What?'

'You didn't know?'

'I haven't listened to the news today and I've no service on my mobile here.' Her racing pals would have been trying to call her all day to discuss the news. Inky stared at Mack in horror. 'Jason Bryant? Helming in the America's Cup? Dammit.' She slammed her hands down into the sand, burying them deep, and then getting up suddenly she started to pace. 'Bloody hell! There was a rumour going round. No wonder he was so bloody cocky in Bermuda. He knew already. I wondered why he kept shooting me strange looks.' She spat the words out vehemently.

'He always had the same ambitions as you. Even when you were both in the youth squad. You were both outstanding back then. Nothing between you in terms of talent.'

'And yet he's helming an America's Cup boat.'

'He's had better sponsorship, better crew, better boats. This has nothing to do with talent.'

'What's happened, Mack? Two years ago we were in Auckland, doing the America's Cup and now neither of us is doing anything.' Mack flinched but she was too upset to notice. She fell silent and dug one of her feet deep into the sand. She wanted to brood.

Mack, always sensitive to her needs, got up. 'I'm starving,' he said lightly. 'Think I'll just go and have some of that supper your mother made.'

Whilst Mack walked back across the dunes, Inky started to think about Jason Bryant. She felt sick with envy that he should have such an opportunity. In the years after they had both left the youth squad Inky had seen Jason Bryant accelerate away from her. Before the days when the World Match Racing Tour would pay all her expenses, Inky struggled to get herself a regular crew. She tried to accept the inevitability of this, after all, centuries' worth of social history lay behind it, but it was frustrating. Bryant had moved on to grade one and two events which had prize monies to be won whilst she was still trying to get her foot on the ladder.

He never failed to rub her nose in these facts at every opportunity. And he took special pleasure in flaunting his sexuality. Inky was never very sure why; she presumed that it was some sort of alpha male display of virility. It was not for nothing that Jason Bryant was known as the Stud of the South – with his slender hips and short blond hair he pulled a different groupie every night. She would often turn up on the race course to hear Bryant boasting about his last night's conquest deliberately within her hearing. One time, she got up to leave without even bothering to eat breakfast.

'What's the matter, Pencarrow?' he called after her. 'Still a virgin, are we?'

Inky was no virgin but she had carefully kept her love affairs clear of the sailing circuit for fear of a reputation and any additional distractions. But the affairs were always short-lived because she was never in one place long enough for them to mean anything.

The one area she did outclass Bryant in was on the race startline. Inky was fast becoming one of the best at that cryptic dance known as the pre-start. She could pin down her competitor within ten moves and lock them down until she claimed the side of the course she wanted. She took fiendish delight in pushing Jason Bryant as far as she could and derived immense satisfaction whenever she felt he was slightly ruffled and panicky as they made their endless circles in the start box, making her moves more and more audacious. But Bryant would use his greater physical strength to his advantage and often would reverse the damage that her superior start had caused and go on to win the race.

Eventually she had been able to turn professional and was invited to enter the World Match Racing Tour only a year after

Bryant, which was testament not only to her talent but to the amount of work she had put in.

But now Jason Bryant was one step ahead of her again. He was to helm an America's Cup boat. She was going to have to live with him beating her for a little while longer.

After Inky had left for Malaysia the following day, Mack decided to stay an extra night. Mack and James Pencarrow were sitting in the kitchen having finished a very satisfying meal of steak stewed in Guinness with a mound of fluffy, buttery mashed potato. 'Mary, that was wonderful,' said Mack, sitting back. 'I feel replete.'

Mary smiled and got up to remove the plates and then said she would take Nelson out for his nightly walk. Once she had left, Mack turned the conversation back to sailing. 'I suppose since the news about Bryant taking the helm for Henry Luter's new challenge for the Cup, Inky definitely won't be joining them.'

'She thinks she'll only end up on the second boat again. Besides, she said that if you weren't doing it then she definitely wouldn't. Said it would be unbearable.'

Mack kept his silence. He didn't need to articulate his well-known feelings about Henry Luter.

'So she's back on the World Match Racing Tour circuit at the moment and probably ever more shall remain so.'

'Well, she can always come down and work with me if she wants some time out. My new sponsor is nothing like Henry Luter.'

'We wouldn't want to burden you, Mack.'

'Burden me?' said Mack in genuine surprise. 'Inky is one of the best sailors I know. You know how much regard I have for her talent.'

'Now, you're just being kind,' muttered James. 'How is the . . . er, charity work?'

'Rewarding. One day one of these kids will be beating everyone.'

'Any plans to come back to the racing world?' asked James tentatively.

'Not at the moment. Why do you ask?' said Mack wickedly. He was well aware what the people and the newspapers had been saying about him. 'Henry Luter has put me off match racing for a while.'

'Maybe it would be better to get back on the horse.'

'And silence the critics?'

'I'm just saying you don't want to lose your edge by being out of the game too long. You're going to miss the next America's Cup at this rate.'

'Would that be so terrible?'

James looked as though it would be the worst thing in the world but he murmured, 'No . . . no. Not at all.'

He thinks I've lost my nerve, thought Mack. He carried on regardless, 'I don't think you realise how bad things were down in Auckland.'

'Mack, I know. I really do. But in this game you can't take a break because you lose momentum and . . .'

'I'm not talking about me, you arse. I'm talking about Inky. She had a really tough time in Auckland, you know. Luter wouldn't have her on the boat. Said women were unlucky. Stupidest thing I've ever heard.' He leant forward. 'She was the only woman on the crew but I never heard her complain once. She didn't even tell anyone that I was her godfather. On the first day that she walked in, they wouldn't let her into the common room because they thought she was one of the girl-friends. She had to put up with all the chauvinism, the jibes, the practical jokes. Christ, Luter wouldn't even give her a female changing room. She had to get changed in the shore manager's office. She could have done with a bit more support.'

'She's used to all that by now,' James said dismissively and changed the subject. 'By the way, you must come down to the club tomorrow, Mack.'

'The club?'

'At Rock.'

'Oh, I don't know, James. You know I don't like that whole local club thing. Get the flag up and meet for toddy at eighteen hundred hours.'

'Rock's not like that,' protested James Pencarrow. 'Besides I don't want you to come down to the actual club anyway, you'll only upset the locals. I want you to come and look at someone.'

'Who?' said Mack suspiciously.

'Someone special.'

'Loopy special?'

'No, just special.'

'I've got to get back to London to see my sponsor.'

'I promise it will be worth your while.'

James Pencarrow watched Mack's face change. The eyes grew a little sharper and more interested and then finally revealed open-mouthed wonder. They had taken James's rib out of the estuary to watch a sailboat cruising along at an insolent speed up the craggy coastline.

'He's one of the tutors,' said James. 'I saw him for the first time a couple of weeks ago. The sailing school have taken him on for the summer.'

'Who is he? Which yacht club is he from?'

James shrugged. 'No one knows. His name is Rafe but no one knows where he's come from. He's been taking people out on their boats all week. I tried to book a lesson with him just to have a chat but he's completely full. In the evenings he coaches the youngsters.' He got back into the driving seat, clipping on the ripcord as he went and started to chase the boat as it went whipping up the coastline. Terns dived for fish, puffins nested on the rocky outcrops, there was even a pod of dolphins to be seen if you were vigilant but Mack had eyes for nothing but the line of the boat in front of him.

Never had he seen such a natural talent. The man knew exactly where the breeze was coming from and the best line to take for the maximum speed. He made tiny adjustments with the sail angles to keep the boat's power at the optimum. He was on a knife edge between the most she could produce and disaster but the boat seemed to come alive under his touch, she danced along, stroked into a frenzy. He was an absolute joy to watch.

'Let's go back,' muttered Mack. 'I've seen enough.'

He felt an almost unbearable stab of envy, but it was the first time he felt really, in-his-gut excited about something since Auckland. He watched as the dark figure came away from behind the wheel and handed over to a second man whom Mack presumed was the owner. Immediately the boat slowed up and her sparkle died with him.

They waited for him to come back from his lesson. Mack hung around with his hands in his pockets and head down trying to avoid being recognised for the best part of an hour and wondered about the young man that he had just seen.

The boat finally returned. 'Rafe?' said James stepping forward as he jumped on to the pontoon. 'We haven't met but I really want to introduce you to someone . . . '

'My God!' interrupted the owner of the boat, barging through the ranks. 'Didn't you used to be John MacGregor?'

James Pencarrow neatly side-stepped him and took his arm, thinking briefly about the time when Mack would be practically mobbed. 'Now, Stuart, you have never told me where you got your boat rigged and I am really most interested . . . ' He dragged him off up the pontoon.

Mack proffered a hand. The young man in front of him was olive-skinned with generous features, his black eyes set deep into his face giving the illusion of pools of night. His hair was dark and glossy, wet from the spray. There was a sleek animal feel to him: the most striking feature about him was the way he moved, completely at ease with himself. He wore beige combat shorts and a T-shirt and boat shoes with no socks: the mark of a true sailor, as the salt water reacts with wool.

'My name is John MacGregor.'

'Rafe. Rafe Louvel.' They shook hands.

'Have you got a moment?'

'Yes. It's my lunch hour.'

'Can I buy you a sandwich?'

The young man look at him steadily. Mack got a fleeting sense of a foreigner struggling to translate but it could be that he was just weighing him up. 'Yes, of course. Thank you.'

Sitting in the Blue Tomato Café minutes later, Rafe ordered a steak ciabatta and a bottle of beer and Mack gestured the same.

'Do you sail?' asked Rafe politely.

It was like asking Ellen MacArthur if she'd ever set foot in a boat.

'In a manner of speaking,' said Mack with a smile. 'In fact that's what I wanted to talk to you about.'

'Why? Do you need a lesson?'

'No, but some of the crew I sail with might. Tell me a bit about your background, Rafe. Where are you from?'

'Where from? I'm not really from anywhere.'

'Well, then, where did you grow up?'

'On the sea. My father and I lived on a boat.'

Mack leant forward, his interest quickened. 'On a boat? Where was your mum?'

'She died.'

'I'm sorry.'

Rafe took a swig from his beer bottle. 'We moved around. So I'm not really from anywhere. British by birth though.'

Mack bit his lip. There was so much he wanted to ask him. How was he educated? When did his mother die? Where exactly did they move about?

'Your dad is British?'

Rafe nodded quickly. 'This is the first time I've been back though since we left . . . ' That would explain, thought Mack, why he was so out of touch with sailing affairs. Rafe was looking around at the other tables with a degree of boredom so Mack went on to explain his charity work down at Hamble and future plans – giving no-hope kids the chance to become winning yachtsmen – although Rafe wasn't reacting quite as he would have hoped.

'So I was watching you out on the water and it looked like you might have some talent. Maybe you'd like to come to our base and do some sailing sometime?'

'Where's the base?'

Mack looked at him in astonishment. Nobody ever asked where the base was. If John MacGregor's base was in the Outer Hebrides eager crew would just get into a row boat and start paddling. If he weren't so sure this blasé attitude was unconscious then he would have felt annoyed.

'In Hamble.'

'Where's that?'

'South coast.'

'Is that anywhere near . . .' Rafe leant to one side and extracted a dog-eared nylon wallet from his back pocket. '. . . Lymington?' He pronounced it Lie-mington.

'Em, not far. About half an hour.'

'Well, then yes. I'll come and sail with you. My aunt lives at Lie-mington and I think I would quite like to meet her.'

Once outside Rafe glanced over at the sun and thought he might be a bit late for the start of the afternoon session. It wouldn't matter anyway, most of the pupils seemed to want to spend the first hour standing around, smoking cigarettes, talking in loud voices about who they'd managed to shag behind the RNLI last night. He was unaware that they were actually trying to impress their young, rather strange new instructor who in their opinion was the epitome of cool.

It had been a big decision for him to return to England, one he had put off for many years as he was happy in the company of his father on the boat, sailing around the world, only staying in one port long enough to pick up some work before moving on. But things were subtly changing on board his father's boat. He was aware of a desire to return to the country of his birth whereas his father wouldn't even consider visiting. 'Too cold,' Tom Louvel would say and shiver. Rafe suspected he couldn't actually cope with all the memories, but they were his memories and not Rafe's. Tension had mounted, making the boat feel uncomfortably cramped, until Rafe resolved to take a holiday in England and return to his father maybe in the winter. Tom had dropped him off in France. They had shaken hands and said goodbye cheerfully, but both knew that things were changing irrevocably.

He hadn't particularly intended to end up in Cornwall but he had hitched a lift from France over to Falmouth where he had picked up some work on a fishing boat for a couple of months. One day the fishing boat rescued a floundering novice sailor who had sailed too far out of the estuary and away from the sailing school. Rafe sailed the boat back for him whilst the novice sat shivering on the fishing boat. The sailing school, having sent a boat out after their novice, found Rafe bringing back their boat as easily as a dolphin cuts through water, and poached him. After taking the RYA exams necessary in order to teach, which were as easy as falling off the proverbial log, Rafe decided to come to north Cornwall to a vacant post in Rock.

As the principal tutor Rafe had hoped that the work might bring him a sense of satisfaction but he found himself increasingly irked by the adolescents yanking and grinding the boats, not realising that their technique was akin to trying to get a car to top speed in first gear. Most of his pupils were spending the summer at the family second home and were from places with names like Hertfordshire and Gloucestershire, which sounded to Rafe like some exotic local dialect. Some of them were nice kids with a genuine love for the water but most were unbelievably spoilt. Armed with the latest gear (Sebago boat shoes with the laces trendily tied into corkscrews, Airwalk shorts, White Stuff sweatshirts and sunglasses from Oakley – a few had noted Rafe's tatty pair of Ripcurls and swapped their allegiance but unbeknown to them Rafe only wore them because an eighty-year-old American had left them at the sailing school) they strutted from party to party by night and boat to boat during the day and were disrespectful to the ocean and society alike. Rafe despised them for he knew such arrogance on the water was a danger not only to themselves but to anyone they sailed with. The ocean enjoyed exploiting weaknesses.

The afternoon session passed without incident and afterwards the owner of the sailing school hailed him. 'Rafe!' he called. 'Do you want supper tomorrow night? Missus made me promise to ask you.'

Rafe smiled. He really enjoyed visiting real homes. They fascinated and attracted him in equal measure.

'Love to, Bob. Do you know what we're having just so I can be prepared this time?'

'Yeah, I should have said toad-in-the-hole didn't mean actual toads. I'll let you know. My wife is taking it on herself to educate you in British cuisine.'

Bob's wife adored having Rafe over to supper. He had such beautiful manners. These were not purely through education. He had a deep respect for women, they meant all good things to him: comfort food, sweet-smelling clothes and a reminder of his mother.

'How are you getting on with *Love Monkey*?' Rafe was staying on Bob's boat.

'She's a lovely boat. I've fixed a couple of things, if that's OK. By the way, could I have a couple of days off at some point? A bloke asked me today to sail with him and I wanted to go and visit my aunt.'

'Of course. You're due some holiday anyway.'

As Bob strolled back up the path it suddenly occurred to him that everyone had been talking about seeing John MacGregor down here today and that might be the 'bloke' Rafe was referring to. He chuckled to himself. They would be a good match.

Rafe ignored the frantically beckoning hands waving from the pub whose youthful occupants had spilt out on to the pavement, squealing and shouting up to the people on the balcony above them. The girls wore short canvas mini-skirts which just covered their crotch and vest tops of various hues; at least half of them were on their mobiles. All of them behaved as though a fox had entered the chicken coop as soon as Rafe was around.

Instead he bought a pasty and went back to *Love Monkey*. He lay in the cockpit with a roll-up and a glass of bourbon and watched the sky streaked with vermilion and plum. He wondered what his father was doing right now and what stars he was looking at. He missed his father but knew it had been time to move on. After all, they couldn't have lived with each other on that boat for ever. If he ever got his own boat, maybe they could meet up and sail around together. The night – velvety, tinged with a touch of ice – drew in as he mused and his old friends, Sirius, Leo and the Pleiades appeared one by one. He smiled at them in greeting. In the distance he could hear the strains of music from the pub which drifted and then accelerated across the water.

Rafe Louvel was three years old when his mother, Daisy, died. He went from a house full of love to one of bewildering grief in a matter of months as the voracious disease took hold. After she died, his father couldn't bear to stay in England, forever associated with white coats, the smell of disinfectant and false hopes, and so he sold everything, bought a bigger boat and he and Rafe set off one early morning down the English Channel.

People presumed Rafe was stupid because he was unfamiliar with the country and his education was patchy in many places but he was far from it. His father had insisted on various tutors to educate him. He could speak six different languages and through his tutors' various passions he knew everything about the Impressionists, the Spanish Inquisition and Mussolini. His knowledge of marine life was second to none. But his first language wasn't really that of words. The term Mother Nature has an ancient meaning: it had been a mother to Rafe at a time when he sorely needed her. The tides were his clock, the dolphins and gannets were his playmates and the stars his comfort blanket.

Now, at the age of twenty-two, his talents were so highly tuned and instincts so in rhythm with the sea that he found it utterly disorientating to be anywhere else. After too long on land a screeching and jarring would start up inside him and the only way to still it was to slip anchor once more.

He could also tell exactly when the breeze would start and in what direction by the behaviour of birds, the smell of the air, the colour of the sky, the pressure he felt in his joints and the condition of the seas. He could predict storms accurately. This gift wasn't something that Rafe neglected or ignored; he nurtured it as much as he could by learning to interpret all the signs he was offered. After all, his and his father's lives often depended on it. It wasn't surprising that when he landed in England he felt as though he'd been plumped down where no one spoke his language.

Suddenly there was a lap-lap of water and a knocking at the end of the boat. Rafe jerked his head up and squinted in the gloom.

'Gabby?' It was Bob's daughter. 'What are you doing here?' He got up and grabbed the proffered line of her little rowing boat. 'Is everything OK?'

'Just thought I'd pop over,' she said, panting slightly, throwing a leg over the stern and climbing aboard. She was very attractive with thick brown hair cascading down her back in waves. 'Make sure you're OK. Dad said you sleep out here every night.'

Rafe shrugged and tethered the line. 'Can't seem to get used to a proper bed.'

'I brought you some beer.' She leant over into her wooden boat and extracted two bottles.

'Em, thanks,' said Rafe as she handed him one. 'Do your parents know you're out here?'

'No.'

'I'm not sure they'd be very happy.'

She tossed her hair and crossed her legs. 'I can do what I want. I'm sixteen years old. Beyond the age of consent.'

Rafe smiled slightly and took the caps off the beer on one of the metal fixings. He was prepared to indulge her for a while.

'People say you've always lived out at sea. Did you go to school?'

'No.'

'No school?' she squealed in delight.

'I had tutors.' He shivered slightly.

'Are you cold?'

'A bit. I suppose this is a bad summer for you?'

Gabby looked surprised. 'This is the nicest summer we can remember for ages.'

'Oh. I think the British weather might be an acquired taste. I'm used to a bit more heat.' He looked out towards the horizon. 'I wouldn't stay out here too long. The wind's going to pick up soon and you might not be able to get back.'

'How can you tell?'

Rafe looked at her in puzzlement; he would have thought it was obvious to anyone. 'I can feel it. You've got about thirty-five minutes.'

Gabby looked at her watch in bemusement. 'How are you liking Cornwall?'

'It's beautiful. The sea feels different though.'

Gabby looked puzzled. 'Different how?'

Had Gabby been a little older, he might have haltingly explained that the Mediterranean felt like a flirtatious woman; her rages were swift and spiteful but she was immediately contrite about them. The Atlantic felt more male. His temper was slow to come but when it did, it was as though it was from God himself. But words didn't always come easily to him so he simply smiled and said, 'Just different. Your dad said you were going away at the weekend. Where are you off to?'

'London.'

'Really? That's the capital, isn't it? I've never been.'

Gabby's mouth dropped open. 'You've never been to London?' she said in astonishment. 'That doesn't bother you?'

'Should it?'

'Em, well.' She slumped a little. 'I don't know. So you really don't know England at all? Where do you spend all your time?'

'Mediterranean, Caribbean, Mexico sometimes. African coast. All over really. I suppose I'm most at home in the Med.'

Gabby bit her lip. London was no longer sounding the quintessence of cool. To cover her embarrassment, she poked her head down into the cabin, reached out and picked up a leather-bound notebook.

'What's this?'

'That's precious,' he said sharply. He was across the deck in one stride and took it from her. 'It was my mother's,' he said softly. 'She left me a diary.'

Gabby leant clumsily over as though about to kiss him. She smelt wonderful and Rafe could feel his senses reeling. It would be so easy. He moved his head away. 'I think you should be getting back to shore now, Gabby. The wind will be picking up soon and your folks will be wondering where you are.'

Chapter 9

Rafe had arranged to visit his long-lost aunt and Mack at the same time, two weekends later. Rafe was nervous at meeting his Aunt Beatrice. She was his only living relative and her address had been burning a hole in his pocket since he had arrived in England. His excuse for not meeting up with her (and indeed not even telling her that he was in England) was that he wanted to take everything just one step at a time, but in reality he was worried that he might not like her. That the mental picture he had of her, pieced together from letters and pictures and the occasional painfully extracted memory from his father, would not match up to the actuality. What if he didn't like his own mother's sister? What would that say about his mother? Would she be like his mother? How could he know? It was only Mack's persistence that forced him to act. Rafe had never met anyone as tenacious as Mack. He kept being dragged to the telephone at the sailing club to take calls from him. (None of the sailing staff would dare tell the great man himself to call back; they even sent a RIB after a boat one time with a minion hanging over the side on a borrowed mobile phone.) Mack's doggedness wore him down and after much haranguing, Rafe agreed to visit.

'Do you drive?' Mack asked Rafe on one of their near daily phone calls.

'No.'

'Well, I'll come and pick you up from your aunt then.'

'I can catch a taxi.'

'Don't be stupid. Besides this way we can talk on the way. Give me the address.'

And so the plans were set and there was no backing out. Rafe had a few pictures of his Aunt Beatrice and his mother but they had been taken twenty years ago so he had no real idea what she looked like. His father was terrible at keeping in touch but whenever he did call and tell her where they were, a parcel and a letter would immediately arrive. The parcel always contained unusual treats: books and jelly beans, honeycombs and chocolates from a strange shop called Rococo.

After he'd paid the taxi which had brought him from the station, he nervously pressed the bell. Immediately the door was thrown open.

'I was looking out for you!' the woman gasped and gathered him into a huge hug. 'Rafe! It is so wonderful to see you!' She pulled apart from him suddenly. 'Let me look at you.' Her eyes filled with tears. 'You look like her. You have her eyes, you have Daisy's eyes.'

If Rafe had been expecting baggy cardigans and slippers then he would have been sorely disappointed because the woman standing before him could only be described as a goddess. She wore a low-cut blouse, through which could be glimpsed a lacy bra, a pencil skirt and fabulously impractical shoes. Yet it wasn't just her clothes which set her apart. She wasn't beautiful, and she was a few pounds overweight (because she loved food as she loved life), but there was simply something magical about her. Sex appeal has to do with energy, an undercurrent of vitality, and Bee obviously had bags of the stuff. Even the taxi driver was taking an inordinately long time to pull away whilst all the time gawping out of the window at her.

A dog jumped around him, completely ignoring his aunt's admonishments to 'get down'. Rafe smiled at her uncertainly and put down his bag in the hall. His aunt hadn't much aged from the pictures he had. She described herself as being in her early fifties; the vagueness wasn't due to vanity but merely because she couldn't actually remember.

'Come in, please come in.'

A few minutes later he sat in her sitting room. Already the warmth of her presence was making him feel more at ease. The room was comfortable and homely. Huge oriental lamps littered the floor and a beautiful grandfather clock ticked reassuringly. A wall full of books held classics such as Henry James and D. H. Lawrence. He got up and walked over to a table and picked up a framed photograph of his mother. It was one he had never seen before and he stared at it for a long time.

'What shall I call you?' he asked, replacing it on the table as she came back with two glasses of iced tea. They sat down.

'Anything you like. Everyone calls me Bee.'

'Bee then. You didn't mention you had a dog in your letters.' He stroked its head.

'We haven't been together long. I went out for a bag of ice and came back with Salty. He's terribly badly behaved and constantly getting into a ruckus with well-behaved Labradors who are then called on whistles whilst I have to run after him swearing.'

'I like him.'

'He has character.'

Much like you, thought Rafe, looking into her lined, perceptive eyes. 'Do you read a lot?' he gestured to the books, his heart sinking a little at a die-hard literate.

'Some of them. They were Arthur's.' She had been devastated to lose her darling husband a few years before but she firmly believed that life was for living and Arthur wouldn't be terribly impressed if she just moped around. 'The bigger ones are awfully useful for propping up tables.'

Rafe grinned at her. What a relief. He was going to like his Aunt Bee. But his happiness was flooded with great sadness as he suddenly realised, if his Aunt Bee was anything to judge by, how much he would have liked his mother too. As if he'd stepped off a cliff and found the ground whipped away from under his feet, he felt a huge chasm open up inside him. How was it possible to miss someone so much when he hadn't even known her?

After tea, Bee produced a huge photo album. It was the first time Rafe had ever seen a photograph of himself as a baby. He turned the page to find a picture of his mother holding him in her arms and smiling happily into the camera. He stared at it for a long time and Bee found that her eyes were filling with tears. 'That's me and her,' he said still staring at the picture. It wasn't so much a question but an affirmation of reality.

Turning the pages he found page after page of family pictures like a treasure chest and was delighted to learn about his grandparents and cousins. It took him by surprise to find out he had a whole past here in England without actually having been here. Soon, Bee was roaring with laughter at the fashions the two sisters were dressed in and telling hilarious anecdotes as the pictures prompted her memory. 'After that party we were both locked out without a key. It was past midnight when we got home and we knew your grandfather would be furious! So we shimmied along the flat roof of the house where a window was always wedged open for our cat but only part way because of burglars. Your mother was slimmer than me so she got through with no problem but I got stuck with my legs and bottom waving madly outside! Your mother had to go back outside and push me in!'

Rafe grinned, relishing every word. It was so wonderful to hear his mother talked about. His father had shared so little of his memories with him that it sometimes had felt as though he was the only evidence that she had actually ever lived.

'Does your father talk about Daisy much?' Aunt Bee asked, touching on the very point he had been thinking about. She was lying back on the sofa, feeling exhausted by so much emotion.

'Now and then. I think it hurts too much to remember some-times. Besides there aren't many reminders really, our life bears no resemblance to anything you've described.'

Of course. Bee had been puzzling over why he had felt so disconnected from all of them. It was because he couldn't recognise anything she had spoken about. 'I miss all of you,' she said simply. She couldn't tell Rafe what a huge blow it had been after losing her beloved sister to lose Rafe and his father Tom as well. The pain dulled over time, especially after her own marriage and the arrival of her longed-for children, who were now grown up and living away, but she was still sad for all the time they had missed together. She wondered how the strangely detached young man sitting before her would have differed if he had stayed in England. 'How's your father?' she asked.

'He's fine. Seeing a nice lady called Loulou.' Rafe frowned to himself. 'At least I think he is, they might have finished by now.'

'He wasn't tempted to come home too?'

'It's a way of life for us now. It's difficult for us to stay in one place for long.'

Bee had always suspected that Rafe's father's love for her sister was the only thing that had kept him on land anyway. As soon as the illness had been diagnosed, she'd thought he might take Rafe away after the worst happened. She understood his reasons and maybe even admired their way of life but it upset her to think that Rafe had never toasted marshmallows or made angels in the snow or any of the other hundreds of things unique to childhood. She'd always tried to think of those things when making up a parcel for him.

Rafe must have seen some sadness in her expression. 'Please don't feel sorry for me. I've spent my life in a place I love.'

'So dangerous,' mumbled Bee. 'I was always worried for you. Especially crossing the Atlantic so much. But I suppose if you take away the crossing of oceans and the climbing of mountains you tame mankind. Tom was never to be tamed. How long are you back for?' she asked tentatively.

'For a while, I hope. I'll be down at the sailing school in Rock for the summer.'

'You'll visit?'

'Of course.' Rafe would bring her his mother's diary next time.

'Do you think you might take a job with John MacGregor? That's who you're here to see, isn't it?'

'Yes. I don't know. I don't know anything about the man.'

'He's pretty famous. An amazing sailor by all accounts. You can't live in Lymington and not pick up the odd fact about the sailing world. He helmed the last British America's Cup challenge. Hasn't he had a nervous breakdown or something?'

When Mack turned up a day later to the address Rafe had given him, he wondered what sort of woman this aunt was as he looked round the extravagant sitting room and spotted a cigarette lighter posing as a mini pineapple.

He followed Rafe through to the kitchen where he was getting them some juice. In the fridge he could see a tower of face creams, strawberries and some hummus. Rafe handed him a glass. 'Where's your aunt?'

'Em, I think she said she was going to yoga.'

Mack frowned. This all felt far too like the high maintenance of his ex-wife; he wasn't sure he would like this aunt. 'Are you ready? Then let's go.'

They walked out to Mack's extremely comfortable car. A Mercedes convertible. 'I won it a couple of years ago in a regatta,' he said almost apologetically to Rafe by way of explanation for the fact that he thought it made him look like a pimp.

'Can you put your seat belt on please?' he said as the car beeped at him. 'Bloody thing tells me off about everything. Anyway how is your aunt? Was this the first time you've met her?'

'Since we left England, yes. She used to send us letters when we were in port. They were always like a next chapter in a book – a really funny book, I loved them.' The car started beeping again. 'What's wrong now?' asked Rafe.

'We're low on fuel.'

'It's a bit of a nag, isn't it?'

'Dreadful. I keep expecting it to produce tissues every time I sniff. Are you planning on staying in England a while?'

'I haven't made any plans either way. I was going to wait and see what happens. Something usually comes up.'

'The weather might be a bit of shock for you.'

'So I've been hearing. Apparently this is a good summer. We used to meet loads of other English people in ports and they were always going on about the weather.'

'You'll start going on about it soon.'

Rafe grinned. 'I hope so. I don't feel very English at the moment. Is your base close to here?'

'Not far.'

'What sort of thing did you want to do this weekend?'

'Oh, introduce you to a few people, do a bit of sailing. That sort of thing.'

Any last nagging doubts Mack might have had about Rafe's abilities were soon put to rest when he sailed with him. They took out one of the charity project's yachts. The boat was sturdy and tough, built for the forces of the Atlantic, but Rafe sailed her as though she were made of gossamer. He was utterly calm: many sailors' behaviour changes when they are actually sailing because of the stress but Rafe was entirely relaxed on the ocean.

'We've all got to go to a big black-tie charity bash tonight. Sponsor event,' said Mack over an extremely late lunch.

'Who's your sponsor?'

'A man called Colin Montague. Rich industrialist – but with a conscience. We've known each other for years. But I've never really taken major sponsorship before. I used to just rely on lots of smaller product deals and prize money.'

'And what changed your mind?'

Mack looked at him sharply, wondering what he'd heard. 'I

thought it was time to take a break. I'd just finished the America's Cup in Auckland and . . . '

'And?'

'Then Colin approached me with this charity idea. I've enjoyed putting something back. Some of these kids have real talent.'

'Do you miss the competition?'

Mack paused a moment too long. 'No. Not at all. Do you want to come tonight? Get to know everyone a bit better?'

'I haven't anything to wear,' said Rafe devouring a cheese roll in two bites.

'Oh, but you have, Cinderella. I hired you a suit with mine in London yesterday.'

'That was presumptuous.'

'Yes, wasn't it? Tell me about your childhood. Did you ever get off the boat? Travel inland?'

'I've never been away from the water. We used to stay in harbours for a while, get some work and then simply move on. It depended on the girlfriend my dad was seeing at the time.'

Mack took another bite of his sandwich but never moved his eyes off Rafe's face. 'And where would you go?'

'Probably over to the Caribbean in the winter and back to the Mediterranean for the summer.'

'How many times have you crossed the Atlantic?'

'I don't know. Twenty or thirty.'

'Which route did you take?'

'Usually the I65.' This was a latitude position, named like a highway because it was so busy.

'Did you do any sailing competitions?'

'When we needed some cash I used to do the local regattas.'

There was so much more that Mack wanted to ask but Rafe suddenly interrupted. 'Mack, can I ask a question of my own?'

'Of course!' Mack hoped he'd piqued his interest in the work they did here.

Rafe leant forward and extracted a dog-eared letter from his back pocket. 'This Inland . . . em . . . '

'Revenue,' finished Mack, noticing the familiar insignia of the letter.

'Yes. Them. Why do you think they want to come and see me? The sailing club wanted my National Insurance number or something so I filled in some forms.'

Mack took the letter and read it quickly. 'Rafe, you put as your address, "*Love Monkey*, moored off Rock."'

'That's the name of the boat I'm staying on.'

'Hmmm. I shouldn't think the Inland Revenue get to see that very much.'

When they were all suited and booted – five of them were going in all, two more of Mack's sailors and the shore manager – which seemed to take ages because Mack had to tie everyone's bow tie, they all looked proudly handsome apart from Mack who was looking gloomily handsome as he hated these black-tie things. Either old crones thrust their sons at him, telling him they'd been sailing since they were three, or the old crones thrust themselves at him and told him how brave they thought he was. Whichever way, it was his idea of hell.

'So, what happens at these events?' asked Rafe climbing into the car.

'We all get hideously drunk,' said one of the sailors from the back.

'Oh, I can do that,' said Rafe brightly.

'No, we do not.' Mack shot a glare into the mirror. 'We talk politely to our sponsors, and anyone else they want us to butter up, and draw the raffle.'

'I'm not drawing the raffle,' said the other sailor. 'I still haven't got over that time when that old bird pulled down her top and yelled, "You win me, Mack!" Her boobs were all crepey.'

'That's what greatness brings you.'

'What's a raffle?' asked Rafe.

'You pay money for tickets and then win things that you often wouldn't pay for.'

'Does greatness bring you cynicism too?'

'No, that just comes with old age.'

The ball was being held in the ballroom of a huge impersonal hotel. Telling Rafe that they would be back shortly, Mack and his crew soon got sucked into their corporate duties and left him and the shore manager at the bar.

'Cocktail?' he proffered.

'Beer, please,' said Rafe quickly. He turned his back on the bar and, leaning back, surveyed the room. The black be-suited backs seethed in front of him, with flashes of ball dresses of vermilion and azure like brilliant birds of paradise. The noise level was deafening and reminded Rafe of a flock of loud herring gulls. To one side, the tables were waiting for occupation, silver gleaming, rolls carefully placed on side plates.

Rafe had really enjoyed his day sailing but he couldn't help wondering why on earth he had agreed to come this evening. He was good with people but it was never long before he was wishing for the solace of his own company again. Besides, it wasn't as though he was seriously thinking about joining Mack's project.

He spotted a woman between the suits and stirred slightly. The lucidity of her skin was in stark contrast to those around her, the colour of palest, anaemic cream against a backdrop of synthetic orange tans. She was wearing a dress of such delicate beige and gold it was as though Rumpelstiltskin himself had spun it; it melted into her pale flesh. It was slashed to the waist and held there by a snarling gold serpent brooch, curled defensively around her tummy button. She moved though the throng gracefully like a cat, nodding and smiling occasionally. She wore no jewellery whatsoever; her feet were encased in one-strap sandals.

'Who's that?' he leant over and asked the shore manager.

He looked over. 'That? That's Ava Montague. She's Colin Montague's daughter. Colin Montague is our main sponsor so I would back off if I were you. She goes out with rock stars one minute and then serious writers the next. Doesn't care about convention, that one. Pretty unpredictable. See her in all the papers one day and then she disappears off the face of the earth only to reappear with a bang. I hear she's talented though. Set to become a great artist.' The shore manager waited for a response but Rafe was too mesmerised. He shrugged and turned back to the bar.

Rafe stared on, absolutely entranced by her. It was as though he had been fasting but wasn't aware of it until this moment. It was not only her beauty but her grace that fascinated him and reminded him painfully of someone at the same time, like the ghost of a perfume passed under his nose. Her gait was purposeful and measured and yet she almost vibrated with life. He felt as though she was the only point of reference in the room. All needles point north. As if drawn by his longing, she glanced over at him and still he stared. Had he been brought up in proper society then he would have known to look away. He also would have known trouble when he saw it.

She had stopped to talk to a small group now but looked over at Rafe occasionally who, having received his beer, was still not bothering to take his eyes off her. Frowning a little, she excused herself from the group and made her way over.

'Do we know each other?' She was even more stunning now in close up. The sleeves wrapped delicate wrists. She had a beautiful heart-shaped face with protruding cheekbones highlighted by softly luminescent rose blusher. Her blonde hair was tied back loosely in a sort of 1940s snood.

'No.'

'You're staring.'

'I'm sorry but you're beautiful.'

She registered slight surprise and a smile started across her lips. 'Then I suppose you're forgiven. That's a nice suit.'

It was Rafe's first time in black tie and it went well on him. He couldn't work out why everyone else was wearing the same though. 'Thank you.'

'Is it Armani?'

'I don't know who lent it to me. Mack picked it up in London.'

He didn't know who Armani was and she smiled widely at the novelty. 'I don't recognise you.'

'I'm not from around here.'

'But you're here with John MacGregor, I take it. My father is his illustrious sponsor. Are you a sailor?'

'Of sorts.' It was such a way of life for him that Rafe didn't really think of himself as a sailor.

'Can I have a drink?'

'Of course!' Rafe spun round to the bar and felt for his wallet. 'What would you like?'

'Champagne, please. It's a free bar, you don't need to pay.'

'What's your name?' he asked.

'Ava. My father adored Ava Gardner. And yours?'

'Rafe.'

'Short for Raphael? You are rather angelic-looking in a dark kind of way.'

'Short for nothing.'

'So why are you here with John MacGregor? He doesn't interest himself in many people.' He handed her a glass of champagne and took hold of a fresh, cold bottle of beer.

'He would like me to sail with him.'

She looked at him appraisingly and took a sip from her glass. 'You must have some talent.'

Rafe shrugged. 'A lifetime on the water.'

'From what I can gather, you can spend many lifetimes on the water and still be without talent. I'm afraid I don't sail but I do a good line in lying on deck in a bikini.'

She had a dazzling way of looking sideways at him and speaking with a slight smile on her face as though she was a cat playing with a delectable mouse. Rafe had to lean very deliberately on his arms to stop himself reaching out for her. He wanted to possess her. 'That sounds good,' he said slowly. 'Besides I've heard enough sailing talk for one day. I thought it was supposed to be a physical sport. For people who sail for a living, they certainly manage to talk a lot.'

When Mack came back to check on his young guest, he found he was being well looked after. 'Good evening, Ava. How are you?'

'John, how nice to see you.' She clearly didn't mean it. 'I'm just fine.' There was some slight antipathy in the air and Rafe wondered what it was about.

'Rafe, dear boy, I am sorry for leaving you alone for so long.'

'I'm enjoying myself, Mack.'

'I can see that. I want to introduce you to my sponsors.'

'I'll introduce him to my dad later, John,' interrupted Ava. 'Don't worry, I know you have corporate duties tonight.'

Mack looked as though he would rather do anything else but leave them alone but he found that he simply didn't have any choice.

At dinner Ava made absolutely sure that they were sitting together by rearranging all the place names which left the local yacht club commodore's wife absolutely seething as she was now sitting next to the club bore. Ava turned her chair completely towards Rafe and ignored the person on the other side. Rafe still couldn't take his eyes off her. Her blue eyes had been dramatically made up with black eyeliner and sooty, smudged eyeshadow but her lips were left bare. She was thrilling in her contrasts and contradictions.

'So, if you don't sail, what do you do?' Rafe asked taking his roll, smearing it with butter and handing it to her.

'Thank you. I make trouble. That's what my father tells me anyway. But in reality, I paint.'

'Paint?'

'Yes. Pictures. Portraits mainly.'

'Are you any good?'

'My tutors seem to think so. You would make a marvellous subject; will you sit for me?'

'Perhaps. What does your father do?'

'Daddy? Oh, he manufactures things.'

'Things?'

'You know, cars, matches, dog food.'

'And your mother?'

'Lots of charity work we're told. Repeatedly. I don't see her much. We tend to be up at conflicting times of day. What about your folks?'

'My mum is dead and my father has gone off again.'

'Gone off again?'

'Yes. Back to the Med, I presume. We've both got mobile phones now . . . ' Rafe produced his proudly from his inside pocket. He peered and fiddled with it. 'I expect he'll call me when he reaches harbour.' Ava enjoyed his obvious delight at the novelty. He was so gorgeous and different to anyone she had ever met before.

'So when you said a lifetime on the water . . . ?'

'We lived on a sailboat. We moved around.'

'What about friends?'

'I had a few mates at our regular stops and it's surprising how many other boat people you keep on bumping into.'

'And girlfriends? A girl in every port?'

Rafe took a swig of beer. 'Something like that.'

'What made you decide to come back to England?'

'I don't know really. It just felt like time. Besides it could get a bit crowded on the boat with my dad's girlfriend and whoever I was seeing. We used to have a system of putting one shoe out on the deck to show the boat was occupied but then we used to have to sprint back from wherever we were to get back first.'

Ava laughed. 'Did you always get back first?'

'I think my girlfriends were fitter.' Rafe grinned.

'Did your dad have many girlfriends?'

'A couple.'

'Did that upset you? Seeing your dad with another woman?'

'It was a relief to see him smile again.' He moved to one side

117

to let the waitress remove the untouched starter plates. 'What about you? Boyfriends?'

'Numerous but none of note.'

'Anyone now?'

'No.'

'Good.'

'So apart from girlfriends, what did you do to entertain yourself? No television, I presume?'

'No television. I used to play a lot of cards.'

'Really?'

'I play mean poker. I could strip you bare in three hands.' His eyes ran over her dress.

'In one if you don't count my shoes.'

They managed to eat some of their main course but got up to dance as soon as the music came on. They were the only ones on the floor but they barely noticed. Their lack of self-consciousness and eyes only for each other soon started tongues wagging.

Ava watched Rafe's naturally undulating hips. She wanted him. She was instinctively drawn to people who were different, like someone finding something valuable in a curio shop. 'Shall we go?' she whispered in his ear.

'Who is that?' asked Colin Montague watching Rafe and his youngest daughter dancing.

'That's what we all want to know,' answered Mack grimly. This clearly was not the time to introduce Rafe to his primary sponsor.

Ava was leading the young man by the hand towards the cloakrooms and the exit.

'Dammit. She promised me she would stay out of trouble tonight.' Colin slammed his fist down on the table. 'Where did I go wrong with her, Mack? The other two are happily working in the company and have been for years but not Ava, oh no.' Ava was the youngest of three sisters and whilst the rest of the family lived quietly in the country, Ava lived in the family Knightsbridge flat and rarely made it out of the gossip pages.

'She's your favourite, isn't she?' said Mack quietly.

'I would never admit that to anyone else but you but yes, she is. God simply isn't very fair sometimes. She has more talent and looks than the rest of the family put together.'

'Beautiful and reckless,' said Mack quietly, thinking of another evening such as this when a drunk Ava had tried to insist Mack came home with her. 'A fatal combination.'

'She's like a cuckoo who's found her way into our nest. I can't tame her.'

'Would you want to?'

Colin put his head in his hands. 'Sometimes I really think that I would. The problem with Ava is that she's one of those people to whom life comes easy. She thinks everyone else is just making heavy weather of it all. I only say this because I wasn't one of those people.'

'She can very charming and people automatically do what she wants. And yet she likes those who stand up to her.'

'I think she unconsciously looks for people to feed her talent. She often goes through a creative explosion afterwards.'

Mack looked after Ava and Rafe. 'Well, she might well have found one.'

Ava claimed the car from the valet parking: a fabulous new Bentley which looked to Rafe just like Mack's new car.

'Is this yours?' he asked.

'No, my dad's. He'll take a taxi.'

'Mack wanted me to meet him. Should we have said goodbye?'

'Christ, no. Mack will be furious,' she said happily.

'Where are we going?'

'We have a house here. Our boat house we call it.'

'Will your dad be back later?'

'He'll be here for hours yet. He has to talk shop. Literally.'

They didn't say anything for the journey. Ava didn't take her eyes from the road as she drove fast down the motorway, overtaking cars on the inside, and from there into country lanes which whistled by in a blur. Rafe didn't take his eyes from her. Ava could just feel his hand delicately moving along her leg, finding the slit of the dress and dextrously creeping a few centimetres at a time up towards her groin until she thought she would scream with frustration. Then he suddenly stopped and started circling his fingers around her ribcage, all in perfect silence.

She roared into a gravel drive.

'This is your boat house?' he asked in amazement and as though the last twenty minutes never happened.

Ava glanced up. 'Yes.'

Rafe peered up through the car windscreen. A stunning white-washed house on stilts soared up before him. 'It's wonderful.'

Ava put a hand up to his face and pulled it towards her. 'Enough talking,' she said. 'As someone who sails for a living, you shouldn't talk so much.'

Rafe had been fully intending to take her by the hand and find the nearest bedroom but he couldn't even manage that. He climbed over into the driver's seat on top of her and kissed her, his tongue urgently finding hers. Ava roughly pulled her dress up and opened her legs to accommodate him. Finding bare Ava a few seconds later, he really couldn't help himself; he fumbled with his flies and then thrust into her.

He didn't last very long. 'Christ, sorry,' he mumbled, kissing her eyes and cheekbones. 'You're too beautiful.'

'With manners like that you may come and come again,' she said slightly mockingly.

'Let's go to bed.'

A few hours later, Ava really did think that whatever Rafe's education might have been lacking, she was clearly in expert hands.

Rafe was wondering how he could ever let her go.

Chapter 10

Whohen Ava surfaced the following morning, she found her father waiting for her, grimly drinking black coffee in the kitchen and reading the paper.

She wrapped her Chinese robe more tightly round her as she had been expecting to be alone. 'Morning, Dad,' she said breezily, smelling the tension but knowing her best way was to brazen it out.

'Morning.' There was a pause as she turned her back on him and busied herself with the infusion of green tea. 'Did you enjoy yourself last night?'

'Very much so.'

'Is he still here?' he said quietly.

She still had her back to him but she paused in what she was doing. 'No. He went home.'

'Where's home?'

'I don't know. He mentioned an aunt or something.'

'Or something?'

She turned and looked at him steadily. 'Your point being?'

'You don't know him!' shouted Colin suddenly losing his temper.

'Of course I know him. I knew him the moment I set eyes on him.'

'Don't be flippant,' he snapped misunderstanding her meaning. 'Knowing someone for approximately three hours before you bring them home and sleep with them doesn't add up to very much.'

'I didn't sleep with him after three hours,' replied Ava coldly. Her father's heart lifted a little. 'It was at least four before we had sex and even then we didn't make it to the house.' She stalked out, leaving the little poisoned dagger still in his heart.

Unlike Ava, Rafe did feel some qualms over their escapade. He called Mack to apologise and thank him for the day.

'She is my sponsor's daughter.'

'It wouldn't have mattered if she were the commodore's daughter,' said Rafe simply. 'We still would have gone home together.'

Mack sighed. He could scarcely be blamed for any of his charges' conduct; sailors were a fairly rapacious lot when it came to the opposite sex but they were expected to behave when it came to sponsors.

'If you come to work for me then you can't keep picking up random girls at sponsor events.'

'Ava was far from random and I haven't decided whether I'm coming to work for you yet.'

Ava didn't bother going to bed the next night; she painted until the dawn delicately peered through her windows, changing the light she had been working under, which fascinated her for another hour. She had finished a still life that she had been stumped by for days before moving on to an abstract painting of greys, whites and blacks and a pair of dusky eyes. A rare feeling of satisfaction – so infrequent in an artist's life – came over her. Smiling to herself, she thought her new muse must have inspired her and how much she would like to see him again.

She slept for a few hours and then requisitioned the company jet. Telling her father she was flying to Paris to see an art dealer, which didn't fool him for a second, she flew down to Newquay airport and from there took a taxi to Rock. She had never been to Cornwall before and she wondered where all the shops were. It seemed fairly bleak to her.

'How do you manage?' she asked Rafe when he arrived back from a sailing lesson to find her waiting on the pontoon, a positively strange and thrilling sight in Alberta Ferretti, a large hat pulled over one eye, bright plum lipstick and platform shoes. No wonder she was getting some fascinated looks. All Ava could see was Boden and boat shoes.

'Manage?'

'In such a backwater.'

Both were oblivious to the frantic chunters of the boat owners around them listening to their conversation. 'I've spent my whole life in places like this,' said Rafe honestly with a shrug of his shoulders. 'First time I got in a train was a couple of days ago.'

'Well, you'll only travel by plane from now on. Don't tell me you haven't been in one of those either?' she said in reply to Rafe's hesitancy. He shook his head and she laughed in delight. Amazing that he could have travelled so far without setting foot in a plane.

Since he didn't have another lesson for a couple of hours, he took her to the pub and bought them both a pint of lager. They found a couple of chairs and he leant forward with both elbows on his knees and took her hand and kissed it.

'I haven't been able to walk properly, the inside of my legs hurt so much,' she whispered.

'Lucky for you. I haven't been able to sail properly because the muscles in my arse hurt so much.' Ava giggled. 'Was your father furious?'

'Yes. Any repercussions your end?'

Rafe shrugged and leant back without letting go of her hand. 'Mack wasn't all that pleased.'

Ava was secretly delighted. She adored provoking a reaction. 'Really? What did he say?'

'That I shouldn't be sleeping with the sponsor's daughter.'

Ava wasn't interested in any reference to her father. 'Oh, Mack can be so bloody righteous sometimes. Are you going to work for him?'

'Maybe. I haven't decided yet. How long have I got you for?'

'Until tomorrow morning.' She gave a shiver of delight; his eyes had that drunk and hazy look of lust. And to the sound of breaking hearts resounding all round Rock, as his female fan club looked on helplessly, he replaced their drinks on the table and leant forward to kiss her.

Rafe taught sailing until late and then on his return took *Love Monkey* off her mooring and down the estuary. It was easier for Ava to sit at the stern and steer whilst he trimmed the sails. It was still light, at the end of one of those long, summer days which time doesn't seem to intrude on. Ava, who had been complaining that Cornwall seemed terribly chocolate-boxy, began to think a little more favourably of the scene. The air caressed them within the protection of the land and yet as soon as they made the open sea, it became more aggressive and Ava was forced to pull off her hat and don one of Rafe's sweatshirts.

'Now, I *would* like to paint this,' she sighed, staring at the sea crashing over the severe rocks, filling the air with spray.

'We haven't long because of the tide,' said Rafe, jumping down into the cockpit. 'The wind is about to turn too.'

'How do you know?'

'You can see it if you care to look.' He came and sat next to her and pointed to what looked like the shadow of a dark cloud chasing over the water. 'That's a wind shift. Our speed will pick up as it hits the sails. Watch it . . . In five . . . four . . . three . . . two . . . one . . . ' The little boat suddenly accelerated through the water. 'See also when the waves are closer together.' He pointed over to their right. This was harder for Ava to see. 'It's easy in these sorts of conditions. The wind is invisible and untouchable and yet it's all a sailor has.'

It fell dark as they returned up the estuary and when they

had moored, they made love outside on the deck under the stars. By the time they had finished the moon was well up. Ava rolled off Rafe and settled down next to him in the small cockpit with a sigh, heaving her legs over the side so the casual passer-by, if there could be such a thing, would have seen four feet in a row and not much else. After a moment she leant over and pulled up the champagne which had been cooling in the water. Rafe popped it open. 'Thanks for bringing this.'

'No problem.' Ava went into the cabin to find some glasses, completely unconscious of her nakedness, and re-emerged a few moments later with two plastic beakers in different colours.

She snuggled back down in the crook of his arm. 'The stars are bright tonight.'

'That's Sirius, the dog star over there. The bright, almost blue one. The Romans used to believe that the heat of the star added to the heat of the sun. That's why really hot days are called dog days.'

'You know peculiar stuff, don't you?'

'I don't know, do I?'

'Do you want to go for a swim?'

'Sure.'

Rafe lazily watched Ava stand up, the moon reflecting off her pale, pale body to make her look almost ethereal. There were people still on the beach having barbecues around camp fires, the murmur of their voices reaching them across the water, but Ava didn't even pause to look at them. She went to the side of the boat and dived into the inky pool of moon with the smallest of splashes. Rafe grinned to himself and walked over to the side to watch her surface.

'It's wonderful!' she called smoothing her hair back.

'Not too cold?'

'Come and find out.'

Much later they lay on his bunk below deck, lying head to toe in a mêlée of limbs as Ava was propped up at the other end of bunk and attempting to draw Rafe in her sketchpad which she never left home without. Her hair, tangled now with the wind, was loose and a thin crust of sea salt had dried around her hair line and under her eyes. Rafe didn't think he had ever seen anyone so desirable and his stomach twisted with longing.

Sensing his eyes on her, Ava looked up and smiled. 'What did you think when you first saw me?'

'That I had never known hunger before. What about you?'

Ava reflected for a moment. 'How much I wanted to draw you but I don't think I would have captured that look. I thought it was slightly feral but now I don't know.' She paused as she looked now but then, her interest suddenly whetted, said, 'I heard one of your pupils talking to you about Oasis this afternoon and you not knowing who they were. Does it bother you?'

'Who? Oasis?'

'No! Not knowing about things other people know about.'

Rafe shrugged and rolled on to his stomach. 'Not particularly. Makes it harder to connect but I wouldn't trade my childhood for anything.'

'Not even your mother?' asked Ava softly.

'Maybe her.'

'Is this your boat?' she asked absently. Her tongue stuck out slightly in the effort to get a likeness.

'No, not mine. Owner of the sailing club. My dad's gone off in ours. But I suppose that's not mine either.'

'Brought a lot of girls back here?'

'A couple. Been to many sailing balls with your dad?'

'A couple,' she acknowledged.

'How did your dad react then?'

'Not so badly. But I don't think it was so blatant and I don't think he liked the look of you.'

'That's fair enough. If I was your father then I wouldn't like the look of me.'

'I like the look of you.'

'Where did you get that dress you wore that evening?'

She lay down her pad and looked at him differently from the last ten minutes. He wasn't a subject to be drawn any more. 'Gucci.'

'Don't wear it again,' he said seriously. 'There wasn't a man in the room who didn't want you.'

She dragged herself over to him and looked down into his eyes. 'Even Mack?' she said in delight.

'Even Mack.'

'Then I won't wear it again,' she promised of a six-thousand-pound dress with just one outing to its name.

They paused and smiled slightly at each other. 'I think I've seen Gucci,' said Rafe. 'On Capri. Funny little shop.'

'Tell me where you've been.'

'Lots of islands.'

'You like your islands?'

'All men of the sea like their islands. It makes us feel contained. I suppose because our boats are just little islands really and that's what we're used to.'

'Tell me about your islands.'

So he told her about Elba and Menorca, Sicily and Malta. He spoke of volcanoes and olive groves, fishing boats and white-washed villages which gleamed in the sun.

The poor pilot of the Montague company jet was certainly busy that summer. If he wasn't running Colin Montague all over Europe then he was down at Newquay as Ava travelled up and down to visit Rafe, startling the residents of Rock who believed themselves to be so terribly cosmopolitan as she waltzed on by in Moschino and Miu Miu. The girls in their mini-skirts and flip-flops tossed their hair and muttered, knowing they were outclassed.

The observers watched, amazed at how long the affair was lasting. Maybe it was because Rafe refused to run after her, or maybe because she was enchanted with her new muse who gave her so much inspiration. The observers whispered, waiting for a crack to affect the foundation. Surely Ava would want her whims indulged? Or Rafe would tire of her turbulent moods? In truth, they did not bother him: he was used to Mediterranean women who were as tempestuous as they were lovely. He was used to quick tempers and passionate rows followed by ardent love-making. So the observers waited in vain for each row to be the last, and one by one they were silenced. The volatile couple seemed as much in love as ever. Maybe this time it would work . . .

Chapter 11

One dark autumn evening in late 2005, with the echoes of fireworks reverberating around the streets of London, Fabian Beaufort finally plucked up the courage to collect his father's things from the Royal Ocean Racing Club. He had left it so long because it was another admission that his father simply wasn't coming back. What made it particularly poignant was the fact that the RORC was where David Beaufort had been most at home. The club was tucked away in a cul-de-sac of Regency houses in St James's Place, a few yards from the bustling traffic of Piccadilly and a stone's throw from Fortnum and Mason (where his father would insist Fabian buy Patum Peperium to bring to the club with him because he said it tasted better from there). Fabian had many memories of a Friday night on the tiles, falling out of some strange girl's bed and then going along to the club to find his father shielded behind a huge paper in one of the old worn leather armchairs surrounded by wooden panels, books on sailing and the echoes of great adventures.

Fabian was sure that if his father were to return to England, this would be where he would make for and so he had kept the club updated with his every contact detail.

After the club secretary's sixth call to him he could put off his visit no longer. It was about five o'clock by the time he reached the club. The secretary had bustled off to collect the pile and he stood uncomfortably at the bottom of the stairs pretending to read an article which detailed Henry Luter's soon to be launched 2007 America's Cup campaign out in Valencia.

'Fabian Beaufort?' asked a strong voice from the top of the stairs.

Fabian looked up sharply. The club was full of old ghosts for him and he felt on edge.

'Mack . . . ? Mack, is that you?' he asked disbelievingly, his voice starting to fill with pleasure as he stared at his old skipper from the Volvo Ocean Race. His lasting memories of this man were with a wild beard and longish hair plastered to his face with the rain, a little at odds with the clean-shaven man in chinos and jacket in front of him.

'Good to see you, Fabian.' They warmly shook hands.

The club's secretary bustled out with the pile of belongings in a Fortnum's bag. She smiled at Mack as she handed it over to Fabian. 'I've included a picture which he loved.' Fabian glanced down to see a framed picture at the top of the bag. 'It's from the 1981 Fastnet Race. David with the rest of the crew.'

'Thank you. That's very kind.'

'Come and have a drink,' said Mack.

'I'm not sure . . . ' Fabian glanced towards the top of the stairs. The sailing fraternity still made him feel unwelcome.

'You're with me,' said Mack firmly and led the way up to the bar.

Their drinks were free because, as Fabian established, Mack was there to run a seminar about the Fastnet race which was organised by the club. They settled in two comfortable armchairs by the window.

'What time's your talk?' asked Fabian.

'Not for another hour. But I just got in this afternoon from an Atlantic crossing and haven't been to bed so thought it was best to come straight here. At least if I drop off here they just have to give me a nudge.' The trace of Scottish accent broadened with fatigue in his deep, lyrical voice.

'How was the crossing?'

'A bit rough. Which was good because it was a training exercise for my youth crew. It's one thing to sit in an office and ask them to make decisions but quite another when the sea is like a washing machine set on cold rinse and tumble. There's some talent in the squad which is nice to see, reminds me of you when we first sailed together. But tell me how you're getting on, who are you sailing with now? I haven't heard anything of you since that awful accident with Rob Thornton.'

'Unfortunately I'm not sailing professionally at all. A few amateur crews but nothing that pays.'

Mack frowned. 'How come?'

'Well, it would appear there aren't many of the sailing community that I haven't pissed off in one way or another. I've tried to get work everywhere but the answer is always the same. The local club won't even let me coach the juniors.'

'My dear boy, I didn't realise things had got so bad,' said Mack in concern. 'I'm afraid I've been out of touch a little since Auckland.'

'You heard about my dad?' Mack nodded. 'Well, people seem to think the court case when Rob died sent him into bankruptcy so they seem to hold that against me too.' Fabian looked at his hands. 'I don't mind. I mean, I kind of think it is my fault. I should have been here instead of messing about on the other side of the world.' He paused. 'I'm living with someone. We have a little girl,' Fabian added on quickly as though to indicate the seriousness of the relationship. He didn't mention his ambiguity about it or that the only thing he felt certain of was the love he felt when his little girl stared at him with her beautiful blue eyes.

'Really?' said Mack disbelievingly, disproportionately shocked at this. 'How's fatherhood suiting you?'

Fabian grinned. 'It's grown on me.'

'Where are you living?'

'Outside of Hamble.'

'So what are you doing to live?'

'Shifts at the local pub. Some work at a boatyard whenever I can get it.'

'Money tight?'

'You could say that. Milly's home-made wine ran out last week. I didn't know whether to be pleased or not,' he joked. For all his faults, there wasn't much room in Fabian's character for self-pity.

'Been hitting the bottle hard?'

'No. I haven't been drinking properly since Rob died. Nor the drugs, don't think I ever will again,' he continued lest Mack thought he'd become a complete dropout. 'Not that we have the money anyway.'

'Quite a change of direction then. Why didn't you call me?'

Fabian looked away embarrassed. 'I thought about it but you were off the racing scene. I did look for you at Cowes Week last year and . . . '

'The rot had already set in?'

'Something like that,' Fabian mumbled. 'I was embarrassed too. Thought I'd let you down.'

'I did hear some talk about you but I just dismissed it. After all, you can't do the Volvo with someone and not know the best of them and the worst of them. You certainly have your faults but some of that stuff just didn't sound like you. I'm sorry, I didn't know the gossip would gain such momentum.'

Mack remembered their time on the boat together in the Volvo Ocean Race. One incident during the Southern Ocean leg particularly stuck in his head. Mack and Fabian were on watch at night together and the navigator had just told them an iceberg was coming up on the starboard side. They were just about to bear away from it when he told them there was another iceberg to port. For one heart-stopping moment they both looked at the spinnaker, realised how fast they were going, and then looked back at each other. 'Through the middle?' Fabian had asked.

'Through the middle,' repeated Mack.

'What if . . . ?' But Fabian didn't finish. He didn't really need to voice the fear that the navigator had picked up just one iceberg. One very large one.

Mack had shaken his head. Neither said another word; they both knew that they might be taking their sleeping crew mates to a certain death. But what Mack remembered most about the incident was that Fabian never breathed a word of it to the rest of the crew. It was true when Mack said he knew the best of Fabian and the worst of him. When you sail round the world with someone in such conditions, it sets your relationship in stone.

One of the bar staff brought over a plate of sandwiches. Mack proffered the plate to Fabian and then took one himself. 'So nice to have some real food. I've had more nutritionally balanced, protein-enhanced energy bars than I care to mention in the last week. Why don't you come and work with me?' he added on casually.

'Work with you?'

'We could do with someone with your talent. You'd be a huge asset to the team. It's rewarding work and our sponsor, Colin Montague, is a wonderful man. What do you say?'

Mack didn't need an answer. The huge grin spreading across Fabian's face said it all.

The simplicity of Fabian's bald statement to Mack didn't betray his doubts about staying with Milly. He was besieged by them. It was just over a year since he had left her at Falmouth docks. He had determinedly walked away, convinced he had made the right decision. He liked Milly but there was no way he was going to throw his life away for the sake of a short-lived affair. But with every step that he took, his father came more and more strongly to his mind and he found himself sitting at the bus station staring into a styrofoam cup of builder's tea as the buses came and went without him. He thought about not knowing his own child, being a mere shadowy presence in his or her life. Being such a stranger to his own father would have been unbearable. He wondered what his father would say. He certainly wouldn't think he should abandon Milly. Fabian also thought about Milly. How terrifying the prospect of being a single parent must be, especially without money and support. He couldn't leave. He wouldn't be able to live with himself.

When he and Milly left the Rochester yacht, they went to a bed and breakfast for the night. 'You realise,' joked Fabian, 'what a bad deal this is for you? You might start wishing that you were back with the Rochesters.'

The only place he could think of ultimately taking Milly was home to his mother and wisely Fabian took his mobile phone outside to call her. He remembered the phone call well.

'Where did you meet this girl?' she asked hysterically. 'Who are her parents?'

'We met on the Rochester yacht.' Fabian hesitated for a second. 'She was the cook.'

'The cook? THE COOK? You mean she was staff? Dear God, Fabian. She obviously saw you coming. She probably planned the whole thing.'

'I'm not quite the bankable asset you think I am, Mum,' said Fabian dryly.

'Well, I will be calling Philip Rochester and asking what sort of staff he employs.'

'I wouldn't bother. I doubt they'll want anything to do with us.'

'Fabian, I desperately need all my friends because of my current *situation*. Did you not once think of me in all this?'

'No, I didn't.'

'Well, I know what you think of your mother now. Wasn't the silly girl using any birth control or I suppose that was her plan?'

'*We* were using condoms and they don't work all of the time,' said Fabian, knowing the flagrant use of the word condom would ruffle her.

'How do you know the baby is yours?'

'Because Milly told me so.'

'And you're taking her word for it?' she asked, furious that Fabian was sticking up for this girl. 'She's probably slept with half the crew.'

There was silence on the other end of the phone. Fabian didn't want a fight; he just needed somewhere to come home to.

'Mum, I want to bring her home.'

'Very well,' she said after a pause. After all, she could control the situation better if he was under her roof.

The first meeting between Milly and Elizabeth Beaufort was not a success. After grilling Milly about her parents and upbringing, she asked if they had considered all the options.

'What options are those, Mum?' asked Fabian quietly.

Elizabeth hadn't counted on actually having to spell them out. 'You're both so young. Fabian, you are barely twenty-four. Have you considered whether you really want this baby?'

Fabian put out a hand to touch Milly. A show of solidarity was vital otherwise his mother might sniff out his weakness and exploit it. 'We really want this baby,' he said firmly. Milly said nothing but looked absolutely petrified.

'Well, you realise that the odds aren't really in your favour,' Elizabeth snapped back. She hadn't meant to lose her temper but they were being absolutely infuriating. 'You scarcely know one another and you're far too young to have a baby. You haven't any money or any prospects or even anywhere to live. You simply will not last the distance.' She swept regally to her feet without giving them time to answer. 'I'll show you to Fabian's room, Milly, because I suppose it is a little late to consider singles. Mrs Bradshaw has changed all the sheets.'

It wasn't the first or last time that Fabian wanted to just get in a boat and sail far away. He had been reading bits of Milly's pregnancy book which warned of miscarriage in the first twelve weeks and he was ashamed to find himself praying for it.

The meeting with Milly's father went slightly better. Elizabeth didn't offer so Milly and Fabian borrowed the housekeeper's car (whom Elizabeth still kept on despite the looming bankruptcy orders) and drove down to see him at Whitstable. Milly thought it would be a good idea for her to go in first to explain the situation and then for Fabian to meet her father. So Fabian walked down to the seafront and, like a needle facing north, made straight for the sailing club. There Milly and her father found him, three quarters of an hour later, chatting to one of the older members about the joys of canted keels. He leapt up in embarrassment, feeling that he had forgotten himself, as soon as he saw Milly walking down the boardwalk with an older man, slightly stooped and balding. A patched old cardigan was wrapped round his thin frame. Fabian went forward to meet them and as he shook hands with the quiet, gentle man, he saw his eyes were full of tears.

'Hello, Fabian. It's nice to meet you,' he said kindly.

'Nice to meet you too, Mr Dantry,' said Fabian.

'Please call me Bill.'

'Bill, then.' They stopped shaking hands and the three of them fell into line and started to walk slowly along the seafront. Bill Dantry put his arm affectionately around Milly, but whether this was a protective motion or the last gesture of ownership it was hard to tell.

'So, Fabian, Milly tells me that you're a sailor.' This wasn't said in the accusing, direct fashion that Fabian had been expecting but more chattily.

'Yes, but I'm planning to get more regular shore-based work until the baby comes.'

'That's good. Where are you two planning to live?'

'Where I can get some work. Probably Lymington or Southampton.'

'Not too far then. I can still come on day trips to see my grandchild.' He gave Milly's shoulder a little squeeze and she smiled thankfully at him. 'Let's go back to the workshop. I think I might have a bottle of champagne somewhere,' said Mr Dantry. 'I think this could justify an early closing, don't you?'

Fabian felt vastly relieved at his own reception and equally regretful at his mother's treatment of Milly. He would never ask Milly what she had said to her father to aid his welcome. In fact she had told her father many things but in Bill Dantry's mind there was only one thing she had told him about Fabian which mattered. She loved him.

They quickly found a place to live. A small, blue-painted house called Bramble Cottage, twenty minutes away from the coast with a small garden for the baby and a garage to over-winter a future boat in. It was going cheap because the owner's father used to live there and hadn't touched the place in terms of decoration; the sitting room still had 1960s swirling green wallpaper but Milly thought she would enjoy painting it all. It was also perfect because it only had two bedrooms which put to rest any sneaking worries that Elizabeth might have to move in with them when the family house was sold.

Between Milly's temping work and Fabian's shifts at the local pub, they had enough money to stay at Bramble Cottage. The first winter was a struggle. Fabian was still looking for sailing work but in the meantime took whatever jobs he could. Milly remembered him returning home the first time he had got paid at the local pub. She was up a ladder stripping wallpaper.

'Should you be up that ladder?' he'd asked as he'd walked in.

'Only way to keep warm,' said Milly, who was dressed in all the jumpers they owned. 'I'd finished all the bits I could reach. How much did you get?' she asked in excitement, starting to climb down the ladder. Perhaps they could splurge on some maternity clothes after the bills.

'A hundred and fifty quid,' said Fabian in disgust.

Milly slowed down and stepped carefully from the last rung on to the bare floor. 'But you were expecting a lot more, weren't you?'

'Apparently I have to pay tax and National Insurance.'

Milly stared at him in surprise. 'Didn't you know that?'

'It's my first job. How would I know that?'

'That's fine,' said Milly quickly, thinking her maternity clothes were out the window. They'd be lucky to pay the bills. 'Brilliant in fact. One hundred and fifty quid! A veritable fortune!'

Fabian could be hard to live with. He was terribly proud and although riddled with misgivings about Rob and his father, he never doubted his own talent so frustration at his situation frequently spilt over. He'd never before had to rely on other people's goodwill or care about their opinions. But he was painfully aware of his responsibilities and never shirked any work which came their way. He cut wood in the winter, pulled up onions and cleared guttering. But he couldn't get used to being without money.

As far as money went, Milly, in contrast, was endlessly creative. She became a connoisseur of charity shops, combing them for clothes for her and the baby. The old sewing machine was brought from Whitstable and night after night it would whirr away as she recut her clothes and added crochet trims or ribbon hems. She sewed French knots into baby hats and big appliqué daisies on to her own skirts. Fabian absolutely refused to have anything from a charity shop and stuck steadfastly to his designer classics which were getting gradually worn out. At Christmas and birthdays Milly happily produced home-made cards and pots of seeds sprouted in the dilapidated greenhouse whereas Fabian would be furious at having to scrabble around the car to find enough change to buy a pint of milk.

When a woman is about to have a child she desperately needs her mother around. Milly never missed her own mother more than those long evenings at the cottage alone, feeling the baby moving inside her. There were a hundred things she suddenly wanted to ask her about her own pregnancy and birth which she had never thought to ask before. Elizabeth Beaufort could have filled that gap in a small way but she was so wrapped up in the wrongs she thought had been wrought on her that it was surprising she had noticed Milly was pregnant at all. Whilst Bill Dantry came often to visit and gave them a second-hand car as a moving-in present, Elizabeth merely pointed out that the windows of their new home needed cleaning and that it was a pity they were so small. One good thing was that when the bailiffs had removed every item of value from the Beaufort house they had left seemingly worthless things like cutlery and potato mashers, and they had come on temporary loan to Fabian and Milly.

On her last visit before the baby was born, Elizabeth had turned up with a porcelain loo-roll holder for the bathroom because they didn't have one and then demanded ten pounds for it. When Fabian had got back in the car for the short run to the station and she murmured, 'Fabric seats, how quaint,' he could take it no longer. He thrust gears about for a few minutes before he could trust himself to speak.

'Look, Mum, you may not have noticed but we have our own problems here,' he said firmly. 'I really am sorry that my father left. I really am sorry that you don't have any money. But have you stopped to think for a moment if you're responsible for any of it? Do you think my father would have just disappeared like that if you were the sort of woman who would listen to his problems? Offer him a friendly ear? Why do you think he left you behind? I think he would have stayed here and fought if he thought just for a second that any of it was worth fighting for.'

'Your father was a thief and a fraud.'

'I think he was in a mess and needed some help.'

'Well, where were you when he needed you? Spending his money on coke and girls, that's where.'

'You don't need to remind me,' he'd said between gritted teeth. 'I think about it every day.'

'So do I.'

'Why can't you count your blessings?'

'There are no blessings.'

'You have a grandchild on the way.'

'Do you really call that a blessing?'

'Yes, I do.'

'You tell me that when she's run off with the milkman and you're in some dreary bedsit posting child support cheques every month.'

'If you really think that about Milly then we've been wasting our time on you. You're not welcome at our house until you change your attitude. At least towards Milly and the baby.'

'What on earth do you see in the girl?'

'Milly? She's fun and never complains. Unlike some.'

'I can't imagine why you are so determined to keep on this ridiculous path.'

'You forget that my father didn't stand by you. Would you wish me to do the same thing to Milly?'

They had arrived at the station and without another word Elizabeth had got out of the car with her overnight bag, slamming the door hard behind her.

Fabian had sunk into the seat and put his head in his hands. This was getting harder and harder. He wasn't sure why the righteous path seemed to have such good press. There wasn't anything nice about it. Despite his words to his mother, he never stopped doubting his decision to stay with Milly. She was easy to be with but he wasn't sure that he loved her. If only he had been left to make his own decision without the complicated addition of the baby. But he knew what that decision would have been. Every day he looked for a reason to leave and a reason to stay. One day he had even got so far as packing his bag but when he came face to face with Milly's twenty-week scan picture, tucked into the frame of the dressing-table mirror, and remembered all over again that his father had left when he shouldn't have, he slowly replaced his things.

It didn't help that his mother so obviously thought that Milly and her family were socially beneath him. Although he truly didn't believe in all that, he couldn't help but feel infected by it. He had taken to watching Milly for any minute imperfection in her character. Instead of admiring the way she chatted with the postman or made soup for an ill neighbour he became irritated with her. He'd even picked her up on a small point of etiquette one day then immediately hated himself for it.

It had taken a taxi hooting behind him for him to come out of his reverie.

Milly, ever hopeful of some sort of reconciliation, wrote to Elizabeth often and sent her a picture of her twenty-week scan. Fabian still occasionally wrote to Rob Thornton's parents. Neither of them received a reply. 'At least we can save on presents,' said Fabian, trying to make a joke of it.

In May the following year, Milly gave birth to a little girl. In the months leading up to Milly's due date, Fabian had grown more and more apprehensive (particularly when they'd had to buy baby equipment so expensive he was convinced it should convert into a small light aircraft too). He was certain he would hate the baby and be a dreadful father. Feeling appallingly out of his depth, he was present at the birth but as soon as Rosie Molly Beaufort opened her beautiful blue eyes, he was enchanted. He was absolutely dumbstruck that he and Milly could produce anything so perfect. In a complete role reversal it was now he who pored over the textbooks to monitor Rosie's different stages. Endlessly patient, he changed nappies, cleared up sick and played with her. This enchantment grew day by day as she started to be able to communicate more. Her first smile was at him and he was sure her first word would be 'dada'.

When he left Mack at the RORC that night, he raced to catch the first train home, hoping that Rosie wouldn't already be in bed by the time he arrived back. He deliberately hadn't called Milly to tell her the news as he wanted to tell her face to face.

Picking up their battered VW Polo from the station car park

and resisting the urge to race someone off the lights (he had to remember that he was a grown-up father now and didn't own a Porsche any more), he stopped impulsively to buy them all fish and chips. Once home with his arms full of food and his own father's things he couldn't reach his keys and so leant on the doorbell. Milly opened the door with Rosie in her arms.

'Darling! Thank goodness you're back! Are you OK? I was starting to get worried.'

'I'm fine,' he said grinning.

The three of them shuffled their way towards the kitchen as Fabian told his news.

Milly's eyes immediately filled with tears. 'How wonderful! A proper job! I can't believe it!' Putting Rosie in her carrycot, she went over and hugged Fabian tightly.

Fabian scooped Rosie up as well.

'Daddy's going sailing again,' he whispered to her.

Milly lay awake that night. She smiled to herself in the dark. Fabian was going back to something he adored. It had been hard watching him fight his addiction; it was like seeing a wild animal caged. Sometimes she almost felt something pacing the room at night whilst he slept. Pacing, pacing, pacing.

But the smile died on her face when she wondered what this new job with John MacGregor might mean for her family. She had always felt that she had Fabian on a temporary loan. He had never mentioned marriage and never talked about the future. Milly was too scared of rocking the boat to mention it herself. She felt as though she had made a deal with the devil and only the bad things which had happened to him had kept him tied to her. Now that all might change.

The week after being taken on by Mack, Fabian went along to his father's old boatyard which he had avoided ever since he had returned from the Caribbean. He had been too proud to go there and ask for some work but now he was thinking about buying a small second-hand dinghy that he could teach Rosie the rudiments of sailing in when she was older (he was too excited at the idea of it to wait) and couldn't think of anywhere better to go. They had managed all the boats that the Beaufort family had ever bought and Fabian knew that his father had trusted the owner implicitly. The owner was working on a boat and instantly came over to shake Fabian's hand as soon as he recognised him. After they had exchanged pleasantries, he asked after things at home.

'I left you a couple of messages to say how sorry I was about everything. It broke my heart to sell *Ragamuffin*. She was a beautiful boat. I got the best price I could for her. I still think about your dad. Any word from him?'

Fabian shook his head slowly. 'Nothing at all. Nobody has a clue where he is.'

They went on to talk about a possible Mirror dinghy that Fabian could buy and when their business had been concluded they walked together back to Fabian's car. There was a small silence. The owner seemed to be struggling with something as Fabian took the keys out of his pocket.

'You know, Fabian, your dad came in here a few weeks before he . . . disappeared. Wanted to know if there were any boats for sale. Naturally I was curious because he already had *Ragamuffin* at the time. Said he wanted a *sea*worthy vessel.' He looked at Fabian sharply. 'I pointed him in the direction of a man.'

Fabian stared at him. 'A seaworthy vessel?'

'Capable of crossing oceans.'

'Crossing oceans?' This sank in for a moment. 'Why didn't you come and tell me?'

'He made me swear I would tell no one. Known each other for years, we have. Besides, I didn't want to draw attention to myself. I left you a couple of messages but I didn't know what else to do. Didn't want no one else asking any questions, see? This way I could pretend that he never asked. Besides I didn't know whether he wanted you or your mum to know.'

'What man did you point him in the direction of?'

The owner hesitated. 'I'll write it down for you, but take care, Fabian. We don't want other people poking their noses in. This man wouldn't have known who your father was. He probably just bought the boat for cash.'

He crossed the yard over to his office and Fabian paced around the car with his heart feeling as though it might leap out of his chest. His father had bought a boat. A boat capable of crossing oceans. This must mean he was alive. His mind filled with questions as he pictured his father laying plans. He had wondered about this in the past but as he watched *Ragamuffin* being sold, he had wiped the thought from his mind. Why hadn't this occurred to him? If he wanted to escape then of course his father would take a boat. A piece of paper was thrust into his hand and he stared at it disbelievingly. It might be his first step to finding his dad.

Chapter 12

Henry Luter's personal assistant, Jane, watched her boss's face as she carefully told him the news.

'How many people know about this?' he asked when she had finished.

'They're not releasing the news until next week.'

'Good work, Jane.' He must be pleased. Words of praise were rare indeed. They were currently standing in Henry Luter's office overlooking the Solent. Two high spots of colour in Luter's cheek told how excited he was. 'The question is . . . ' he said slowly, 'am I more likely to get my hands on the Cup that way?'

It was no coincidence that Henry Luter's passion for sailing coincided with him moving up ten places on the richest list. Worth over ten billion pounds, he was starting to find the boardroom battles flavourless and was looking around for a new arena in which to flex his muscles. Yacht racing was by its very nature extremely competitive and the list of men who challenge for the America's Cup read like a roster of power. At last this was an arena where his natural aggression could be celebrated, not hidden under handshakes and false smiles. '*Have no God but self . . . * ' one man said about the America's Cup billionaires.

Henry Luter's ambition marked a basic insecurity. Eight million pounds was not enough so he had to earn more. His wife wasn't pretty enough so he had to get himself a beauty. Winning the odd yacht race didn't make him the best so he wanted to win the America's Cup. And the more he played the game, the more desperate he became to win. Entering the America's Cup also admitted him to a very exclusive little club. He was utterly addicted.

'The only problem would be . . . ' said Jane slowly, 'how the press would perceive it.'

'Fucking leeches. I do all of this,' he gestured his hand piously around the office, 'for this country to win the America's Cup and all they do is criticise.' Luter was quite deaf and blind to his blatant hypocrisy. 'They would all deserve it.'

'The official launch of our campaign isn't until next month; if we do it before that then it wouldn't look too bad. How would the America's Cup community feel?'

'They wouldn't give a shit. Most ungentlemanly sport there is. It's bare-knuckle fighting, the rules of the street apply and that's why thugs like me like it. We understand it.'

'What about the members of the syndicate?'

'I would certainly take Jason Bryant with me. He would do anything that would bring him closer to winning the Cup.' He clasped his hands behind his back and looked out over the Solent. Suddenly he seemed to make up his mind. 'Make the arrangements, Jane.'

Rafe's Aunt Bee was a common sight on the coast near Lymington. Every morning, she and Salty would get into their little motor boat and phut-phut a mile up the coast to buy their bread and milk from the local shop. Of course she could have just as easily got into her car to do so but she liked doing it this way. In winter she would dress the part in navy cords and a cream fisherman's jumper complete with yellow macintosh hat and waterproofs and whatever the weather (although she wouldn't go out beyond a force 5) would find her, with Salty leaning out as far as he could over the bow and barking at seagulls, wending their way towards sustenance.

When the Rock sailing school had closed up for the winter, Rafe had agreed (under much duress) to move temporarily to Ava's flat. London hadn't really suited Rafe. The Underground system was beyond him and he was forever getting lost. He couldn't understand how people could live in such proximity to one another and yet barricade themselves so firmly behind car windows, double glazing and central heating away from the elements. It also had never occurred to him that he would miss the sea as much as he did, like only noticing oxygen when you struggle to breathe. So, much to Ava's chagrin, as she had enjoyed having him on site, he decided to take the job with Mack and took up residence with his Aunt Bee instead.

Rafe and Ava's relationship settled into as much of a pattern as there ever could be, albeit a stormy one. Ava had since returned to art school which made her much more tempestuous. She would flip into terrible rages if a piece of work wasn't going well or a teacher made an unfair criticism. She seemed to thrive on them: her creative energy would be redoubled. Things would be thrown against the walls: perfume bottles, vases and once even an unopened bottle of whisky. Rafe would either shrug his shoulders and keep out of the way or try to laugh her out of it, infuriatingly catching things as they were thrown and even taking a swig from the bottle of whisky on the second time she tried it which made her laugh. Whatever she did though, it never affected Rafe's actions or attitudes. He would never compromise. She supposed it had something to do with the way he was brought up; he simply saw things in terms of black and white. But ironically it was one of the things Ava admired about him: she liked people to do what she wanted, but she was attracted to those who wouldn't.

Another factor that possibly gave the affair even more momentum was Colin Montague's abject disapproval, which Ava secretly revelled in. He didn't want Ava seeing anyone who worked under his sponsorship. Full stop. And Rafe, since he was working with Mack, was now under Colin Montague's sponsorship. This only confirmed the disapproval he had felt since the night they first met. But if Rafe wasn't impressing Colin Montague then he was certainly making an impression on his sailing colleagues.

On this particular bleak winter day, Bee came back from her usual morning shop and found Rafe just surfacing from his bed.

'Darling! You're up!' She was thrilled to have her nephew back after all these years, and to have someone in the house now her own two sons were happily living in London. She was also enjoying getting to know Rafe. 'What can I make you for breakfast? Eggs? Is Ava here too?' Bee accepted Ava for Rafe's sake but she was wary of her. She felt that she was charming to her only because she was Rafe's aunt, not actually because she liked her.

Rafe went forward to collect Bee's shopping bags and then carefully put them on the table. 'No, she had to meet her tutor today so she went back to London.'

Bee loved the way he said London. Like a foreigner struggling with strange consonants. 'Shame. What time are you due at work?'

Rafe yawned. 'Late today. Not until ten. Mack wants to do all the drills in the dark tonight. I really need to find that watch Mack gave me. He keeps asking me the time.'

Bee put some eggs on to boil. Rafe knew not to talk to her during this vital period because the only way she could time them was by singing three verses of 'Onward Christian Soldiers' (which made her feel much better, she told Rafe, about not going to church every Sunday). He set about making some toast.

'Mack has set up some interviews with the local yachting magazine,' commented Rafe as the last verse came to a close.

'Really?' said Bee with interest. 'Gosh, how exciting! I shall become quite the celebrity as the aunt of the famous sailor!'

'Who, me?' said Rafe dubiously.

'Ava will be pleased.'

'Why do you say that?'

'Well . . . ' said Bee, wishing she hadn't said that quite so impulsively, 'I think Ava thinks you have a tremendous amount of talent. I mean everybody at your work says so, don't they? I think she would just like you to have a bit more recognition. Sit down, the eggs are getting cold.'

'Mack is collecting me today,' he said when the eggs were safely in their cups. 'You said you wanted to meet him; will you be around?'

Rafe had been working with Mack for over a month now and Bee had yet to meet him.

'Yes!' she said. 'Lovely!'

Rafe's eyes travelled briefly over her outfit. As soon as she had got home, Bee had changed into her normal attire: something hopelessly impractical. A flowery wrap-around dress, a baby cardigan in the softest moss green, little Boho slippers, and bangles which jangled, announcing her arrival like an ice cream van. He did wonder how she would get along with the forthright Mack.

The doorbell rang half an hour later. Bee invited Mack in for coffee thinking that he didn't look much like his photographs. He had an almost larger-than-life presence.

'Such a pleasure to meet you,' she said. Mack looked at her doubtfully. He couldn't bear gushing women. 'Rafe talks so much about you,' she chattered as she busied around getting coffee. 'Of course I'm such a dolt with all things sailing. Salty and I do have a little boat but we're no good at anything else. I spent ten minutes talking with Rafe about gerberas the other night. I thought they were bizarre things to have on boats and I kept picturing sweet little pots of flowers everywhere until it turned out that a gerber is a sort of knife. It is a strange profession.'

Mack didn't know what to say. He hated people taking the piss out of sailing even as innocuously as Bee. Rafe sighed to himself and wondered why he thought it was ever a good idea to introduce them. Bee didn't help matters by asking him exactly how a sail worked and if he could think of an analogy to do with hair dryers then that would help.

Chapter 13

If her family and friends were surprised at the longevity of Ava's relationship, then all of Rafe's colleagues were more so. Soon it was being whispered that Rafe was not only possessed of uncanny sailing skills but he was also the man who had tamed Ava Montague.

Down at the Hamble base, Rafe was busy working on one of the boats. One of the youth scheme youngsters called Jack was watching him whilst wet-sanding the hull. Mack insisted on a strict programme of maintenance; he believed that if the sailors took the pleasure of sailing the boat then they should also take the responsibility of maintaining it.

'What does this do?' Jack asked tentatively as he sanded. They were all a bit in awe of Rafe. Some of them could barely get a sentence out in his presence without stammering.

'Makes the boat go faster through the water.'

'Do you know how to fix anything?' he asked.

'Had to really. My dad and I never had much cash. Couldn't afford anyone else to fix them.' Rafe grinned at him. 'The problem is that I don't know much about new technology. Mack is sending me on an electronics course.'

'That was amazing this morning. When the sail got stuck,' muttered Jack. Rafe had free-climbed the mast to clear a snagged sail.

'Mack wasn't too pleased. I should have been wearing a

harness. I've done it a million times before,' he added on hastily, just in case Jack took it into his head to climb masts without a safety harness.

'Don't you ever wear shoes?' asked Jack. He had been dying to ask this ever since he'd arrived at the base.

'Not usually on a boat. Force of habit. My Aunt Bee is buying me some of those sock things. It must be getting cold enough to snow.'

'Snow?'

'Yes, it's freezing, isn't it?'

'Er, not really,' said Jack doubtfully, not sure whether he should disagree with him and rethinking his position on whether or not it was cool to live with your aunt.

Rafe was well liked by everyone. He was respected by the others sailors for his undoubted skill and boat handling and by the youngsters on the scheme because he treated everyone exactly the same and was also extremely unassuming. Once, they were sailing in bad conditions, the wind battered the boat and they all had to shout to make themselves heard above the noise. 'What force is this?' yelled one of the sailors, desperate to know for posterity. 'A force nine? Ten?'

'I don't know,' yelled Rafe back. 'It's pretty windy though.'

Mack was also extremely relieved to see his lack of compromise being applied to his work since Rafe's motivation had once concerned him. But once Rafe committed to something, he was absolutely single-minded and nothing could sway him from his course.

Much to Mack's annoyance (as he disliked distractions to the sailors) Ava was a regular visitor at the base. She could be inclined towards jealousy and she liked to turn up unannounced just in case Rafe and one of his female co-workers might be getting close. 'I don't know why she worries,' murmured the shore manager to whom her behaviour hadn't gone unnoticed. 'I've never seen a man so much in love.'

Ava turned up this afternoon, just before Rafe's scheduled

152

interview with the local sailing magazine. Jack and Rafe were still working on one of the boats.

She called Rafe's name softly at the door of the vast hangar and Jack looked on as Rafe moved forward to meet her. She was wearing a wrap dress hand-painted with peacock feathers over skinny jeans, and huge, chunky, jewelled earrings in peacock hues of greens and blues. Her hair was up and she'd made up her eyes in dramatic green. She looked kittenish. He kissed her just above her jaw line, breathing in her signature Shalimar.

'Did I forget something?' he asked. 'I only left you this morning.'

'I know. I missed you.' She'd actually only just got up. Ava found it hard to keep up with Rafe's incredible stamina. After a lifetime at sea where sometimes he would have no sleep for five days in a row, he would think nothing of being with Ava until five in the morning and then driving down to the base for first light.

'Your scent is still on my skin. I've been able to smell you all day.' He smiled, astonished all over again at her beauty and at how much he loved her.

She squeezed his hand. 'Haven't you got a journalist coming to interview you?'

'Yes, I think she's just arrived.'

'Do you think I might be able to listen in?'

He looked surprised. 'If you want to. She's waiting in the common room.'

'Aren't you going to change?'

Rafe looked down at his three-quarter-length combats, a couple of T-shirts and bare feet (which were very cold). 'No.'

Any dismay that the journalist might have felt at a stranger sitting in on the interview was soon dismissed when she realised who she was looking at.

'Ava Montague!' she said with delight. 'I was going to ask Rafe about you. Word has it that you're stepping out together.'

Ava smiled and nodded. 'Do you mind if I sit in? I won't interrupt.'

'Of course not.'

Ava was as good as her word. She didn't butt in once for the entire interview.

Rafe took the journalist for a tour of the base after the interview. She studied the dark, impassive face as they went around, feeling faintly in love with him, and tried not to look at Ava. The chemistry between them was such that it was hard to see them together and not imagine them in bed.

'Have you thought about doing the Olympics or the America's Cup?' she asked.

'God forbid!' drawled Ava as she ran a finger down the white hull of a boat sitting in her cradle. 'Rafe has no interest in anything competitive, have you, darling?'

Rafe didn't even look at her. 'I haven't been in England long enough to think about anything like that.'

'But you have British nationality? You could compete for your country if you wanted to?'

'Yes, I am British by birth but I have never really felt the need to compete.' His voice was low and quiet, the deep-set eyes stared down at her and the journalist shivered slightly. 'I just don't feel I have anything to prove. I'm enjoying working with Mack though, and will probably do so for a while.'

They went out on to one of the pontoons. In the distance they could see Mack on the water with another two boats. 'Off the record, do you think Mack will ever race again? Did he lose his nerve after the America's Cup in Auckland?'

'I didn't know Mack before that but it strikes me that it would take a lot for Mack to lose his nerve,' said Rafe firmly.

'What's he like to work with?'

'He's unbearably bossy,' said Ava.

'He's great,' said Rafe firmly. 'Very inspiring. He could lead all his crew into hell and they would follow him.'

'My father adores him,' commented Ava. 'I think a little too much sometimes.'

'Ava!' said Rafe warningly. Ava raised her eyebrows. 'This is off the record, darling. That means it will go no further.' She made a cosy face at the journalist. She was clearly spoiling for a fight.

Rafe wound everything up pretty quickly and saw the journalist back to her car. She looked after him wistfully and wondered how long he and Ava Montague would last. They were obviously going to have the most humongous row by the way he was tightly gripping her elbow. With any luck he might be back on the market soon, she thought hopefully and started the car.

Rafe was furious with Ava. She was being deliberately provocative.

'Why didn't you mention the fact that you've crossed the Atlantic so many times before?' she got out before he could say anything.

'She didn't ask me.'

'And you said you haven't got any real plans,' she snapped.

'Why are you so annoyed? I haven't any real plans.'

'Why don't you do the America's Cup? There's a lot in the press about Henry Luter's new America's Cup challenge. Why don't you do that instead?

Rafe tried to contain his impatience. Ava was slightly obsessed with the press. 'So you can show off to everyone?'

'It's incredibly glamorous.'

'And competitive.'

'I like a bit of competition. A friend of mine used to go out with Jason Bryant, the helmsman. He's staggeringly successful.'

'I don't like competition.'

'People will think you have no ambition.'

'Why are other people's opinions so important to you? Who cares what people think? I only gave the interview because Mack wanted me to.'

But Ava was just getting started. 'It was the same when we had dinner with my parents. You told them you didn't have a clue what you were going to do in the future. You must understand that all my family are achievers. They're not impressed by a lack of goals.'

'They'll have to take me as I am. What's this about?'

'Nothing. Everything,' she said in confusion. 'My father thinks you're unfocused.'

'What on? Money?'

'You have so much talent. Everyone says so. I hate to see it going to waste.'

'Who says it's going to waste? Just because it's not plastered across the media? I know what I've got and furthermore I use it. And I use it on something I love. That's not going to waste.'

Ava was suddenly contrite. 'I'm sorry. I'm being a bitch. I'm surrounded by people who think it matters and I let them influence me.'

Rafe hugged her. 'Don't,' he whispered into her hair. 'They all seem desperate to crowbar us apart. Don't let them. Don't show them a gap.'

It was amazing, thought Ava as she walked away, with his lack of experience within society, just how much insight Rafe sometimes showed.

A few days later Rafe decided to make a most uncharacteristic visit to London to surprise Ava. They hadn't seen each other since the row and the atmosphere on the telephone had been decidedly chilly ever since. Lately it seemed that the outside world was starting to dent their love. No matter how they hid themselves away, it was merely a phone call or a door buzzer away. Often a friend would come round with news of a fabulous new gallery opening that everyone was at whilst Ava was down in Hamble with Rafe or some gossip from the in-crowd that Ava would have normally been party to. It always made Ava very restless.

To pass the time on the train Rafe read a discarded newspaper, which ironically included a huge article about Henry Luter's new British challenge for the America's Cup. At about four o'clock he managed to emerge from the right tube station (Knightsbridge, though the charm of the area was completely lost on him). He dived into Baker and Spice en route to Ava's flat to pick up some macaroons which he knew she adored and with delight he spotted the back of her head as soon as he walked through the door. She was sitting by herself at a table with remnants of tea. He was just about to walk up and surprise her when he decided it might be more fun to call her on the mobile and then saunter up whilst they were talking. He ducked out of the shop and peered through the window at her whilst taking his phone out of his pocket at the same time.

Rafe grinned to himself as he dialled, but the smile died on his lips as he watched a man emerge from the loos and go back to Ava's table. As he went towards the chair opposite her, he dragged a hand across her shoulders which she grabbed and kissed. They kept on holding hands as he sat down.

Rafe watched as Ava's free hand dipped towards her bag and extracted her mobile. It seemed to be moving in slow motion.

'Hello?' the voice echoed. Looking down at his hands, Rafe realised that he must have pressed the call button.

He slowly put the phone up to his ear and said, 'Hello?'

'Rafe,' she said stiltedly.

'Where are you?' he asked.

There was the slightest pause. 'In the flat. Painting the most dreary still life. Are we still meeting this evening?'

'Of course.' His voice sounded disembodied.

'Are you all right? You sound strange.'

'I'm fine. I have to go, Mack is calling me. I'll see you later.'

He had turned away from the window whilst they'd been talking because he couldn't bear to watch her telling lies but now he turned back to see them paying the bill and gathering their things. He hung back, time enough for them to kiss each

157

other goodbye and go their separate ways. After a moment Rafe followed Ava back to her flat. He was in a daze, his mind just a jumble. Ava was seeing someone else. He sat on the stairs trying to make sense of it. Trying to pinpoint a time or an occasion when things had changed for her. Although, if he thought back over her recent behaviour, it was certain that things *had* changed.

He let himself in with his key and paused for a second to look round, desperately trying to see if anything was different, as if there should be some physical marking of the event. He could see through to the huge sitting room, full of light with the easel next to the window and against the wall leant piles of canvases of work. He could see her moving around. She had been painting at least, he reflected, her old painting smock, which she had just put back on, was covered with fresh splodges. He moved into the doorway.

She was clearly shocked to see him. 'Rafe! What on earth are you doing here? I just spoke to you on the phone.'

'I came to surprise you,' he said slowly. 'But it was me who got the surprise. I saw you, Ava. Who is he?'

Ava paled visibly but said lightly, 'Who do you mean?'

'The man you were with. In the bakery. You kissed him goodbye. Who is he?'

Ava looked down and busied herself by preparing her brushes. 'It was no one,' she said shortly.

He came over to the easel. Her latest picture of some apples and a skull lay there half finished. What's left of me, he thought.

'Have you slept with him?'

She bit her lip and started to mix some paint.

'Have you slept with him?' said Rafe, his voice starting to rise.

'Yes. No. I don't know.'

'What do you mean? You either have or you haven't. Which is it?'

'Please. Let me explain.'

'Yes or no?'

'I have slept with him. But I didn't mean to,' she said in a very small voice. 'There is an explanation.'

'How do you mean, you didn't mean to sleep with him? You can't accidentally sleep with someone.'

Ava came over to him and tried to touch his hand and Rafe jerked it away. It didn't even feel like it was his hand. He felt as though he was completely disconnected, as though they were discussing a piece of fiction or rehearsing lines for a play. 'It was late. I was drunk. You were supposed to be here but got caught up with Mack. I meant to turn him out but he was persistent and I ended up sleeping with him. I was seduced, I suppose.'

'Seduced? When was this?'

'Last week.'

'After our row,' Rafe stated dully.

'It was just once and you were supposed to be here!' she said hysterically.

'Who is he?'

'Jason Bryant.'

'Jason Bryant? The America's Cup helmsman? Mr Staggeringly Successful? You have to be kidding! You're so fucking predictable. It's been more than once, hasn't it?'

Ava stared fixedly at her painting. Her silence spoke volumes.

'Why him? WHY HIM? Tell me! And you'd better spell it out because I am really struggling to understand.'

She tilted her chin defiantly. 'You're too scared to compete like him.'

'Scared?' he stared at her disbelievingly. 'You think the reason I don't compete is because I'm scared?'

'What else can it be? You have all this much-talked-about talent but you fail to show it.'

'I don't compete because I don't need to.'

'That's bullshit. Jason says if you have talent then the only way to validate it is to show the world you have it.'

'I wasn't going far enough for you, was I? I was never going to get your picture on the front of a magazine. Not like an America's Cup helmsman.'

'Look, Rafe, it's not easy being the daughter of Colin Montague. I am more than that but all anybody sees is him. They look at me and they see my father.'

'What do you think Jason Bryant saw? The real you or a quick fuck?'

'SHUT UP, RAFE!' she screamed, suddenly losing her temper. 'Life is so simple to you, isn't it? You don't know the rules.'

'You used to like that about me. I looked at you and saw only you.'

'People are saying that I'm dropping off the scene. I used to be going places. *You're* making me drop off the scene.'

'Listening to other people again? You really need to make up your own mind. You're sacrificing all we had just for that?'

'You may not want success, but I do because I deserve it. I refuse to be dragged down with you.'

'Oh, I'm not going to drag you anywhere,' said Rafe softly and made to walk out but suddenly Ava was all over him.

She clung to his back and started to cry. 'I was confused,' she sobbed. 'I just don't know what I want. I don't know who to listen to.' For a second Rafe was defeated. He didn't know how to cope with tears and pleas. But then she said something which made up his mind. She said, 'Forgive me.'

'Forgive you?' Rafe's voice was incredulous. 'Ava, can't you see this changes everything? This isn't about forgiveness. You have broken something.'

'No, please no. We could fix it. I know we could,' she pleaded. The tears were pouring down her face now.

'It would never fit back together again. Not properly.' His voice was dull.

Ava let go, searching his face. There was no softness, no chink. She knew at once that one of the things she really loved about him, his lack of compromise, was the thing that was going to keep them apart.

He turned to go and she caught hold of his arm. 'Please don't go,' she begged. 'Please. I do love you. I really do.'

And he loved her. He loved her more than he'd loved anyone. But Ava was right when she said she had been seduced. Not just by Jason Bryant but by everything he represented.

Chapter 14

'*Billionaire Abandons the British America's Cup Challenge,*' screamed the headline. Mack stopped short, retraced his steps and bought a paper. He strode quickly to the Royal Ocean Racing Club, the headline filling his mind. It just didn't make sense. He sat down in the club library to read the article.

Henry Luter, the telecommunications and software billionaire, today expressed his heartfelt apologies that he could no longer continue to fund the British effort in the 2007 America's Cup to be held in Valencia. He said in a statement today, 'Myself, my family and members of the syndicate suffered terribly at the hands of the press during the Cup in Auckland in 2003. Although I desperately wanted to carry on the British challenge for the Cup, I didn't feel I could subject my family or my syndicate to those levels of criticism again.'

Mack lowered the paper and looked around in disbelief. The same headline was spread across the room. Every single member seemed to have a copy. He thought of the crew of young sailors who now would not get the opportunity to compete in the biggest sailing contest in the world. Sailing's holy grail.

'Bloody awful, isn't it?' commented the man next to him.

'Yes, it is,' murmured Mack.

'I don't know what's happening out there but there's rumours that the Spanish syndicate owner is in a lot of financial trouble too.' The Spanish were the defenders of the Cup and thus were hosting the whole event. 'With them in so much trouble, they don't know if the Cup will even be able to go ahead. Maybe that's another reason why Luter decided to pull out. I feel sorry for the people he left behind. Poor sods. I waited my whole life to sail for my country in the America's Cup. This was only the second chance to do it in over eighteen years and now it's all been taken away from them.'

'Not yet,' said Mack. 'Not quite yet.'

Mack placed his first call to Colin Montague. His secretary put him through.

'Mack! You're not calling to cancel dinner tonight, are you?'

'No, no. Just wondered if you'd seen the headlines today. About the America's Cup.'

'Yes. Looks awful.'

'Have you ever thought about sponsoring an America's Cup challenge?' said Mack casually.

There was a long pause on the other end of the phone. 'I sponsor people, Mack. Not causes. That's how we got involved, do you remember? Because I believed in *you*, not specifically in what you were doing.'

'Maybe it's something you should look at.'

'The America's Cup? Are you mad? Haven't you had enough of the America's Cup?'

'I don't particularly like the politics around the America's Cup. I don't like the glamour, the ritzy tittle-tattle and the rest of that crap but if you cut through all of that then you still have the greatest sailing competition in the world.'

'I knew it wouldn't be long,' muttered Colin.

'What do you mean?'

'I knew you wouldn't be able to stay away from racing for very long. I could see you were getting itchy feet.'

'Come on, Colin! Doesn't it make you mad? To see Henry Luter abandon the challenge at the last minute? To see all those people's dreams of competing in the Cup thrown away?'

'You can't resist it, can you? You love a fight and if there isn't a wall for your back to go up against then you'll go miles out of your way to find one.'

Mack grinned and told Colin he had some other calls to make but perhaps they could discuss the matter of brickwork further at dinner.

Mack and Colin had dinner in the grill room at the Savoy. Colin ordered some magnificent Margaux. Mack didn't know whether to take that as a good sign or not.

'So what's it going to take to convince you?' was Mack's opening gambit.

'Why are *you* so convinced?'

'Because I think it can be done, that's why. Of course I couldn't possibly work under Henry Luter but you're a completely different matter.'

'Thank you,' said Colin dryly.

'Haven't you ever wanted to do it?'

'It's not that, Mack,' sighed Colin. 'Of course it's crossed my mind! But I've never pretended to be anything but an old-fashioned millionaire. Running a Cup campaign is usually reserved for billionaires. I don't have the sort of money needed for an America's Cup challenge.'

'I reckon we could do the whole thing for under thirty million.'

'How come?'

'Henry Luter has abandoned his British base out in Valencia. Could we use that?'

'No, he wouldn't let us have anything. And what about staff?'

'I could gather enough staff together to satisfy even you.'

'Which yacht club would we challenge through?'

'Same one as Luter used. They're pissed off. We'll get a lot of support from them.'

'And boat design?'

Mack smacked Colin's shoulder in his excitement. 'You have plenty of contacts!'

'Have we enough time?'

'Deadlines for entries are in a month. Would your company think about putting up the money? As a corporate venture?'

'Maybe the directors would go for it, I don't know. It's probably cheap for the exposure they'll gain in bailing out the British effort, not to mention the international exposure. But it is a well-known fact that experience goes a long way in the Cup. Only with experience can you tell where to cut corners. Otherwise you have to chuck money at it. We won't win on a first effort.'

'A lot of the staff were in Auckland in 2003. They have experience.'

'Why did Luter abandon the challenge? I don't believe all that too-much-criticism press release for a second.'

Mack hesitated. 'I've heard a rumour that the Spanish syndicate may be in financial trouble. I made a few calls and apparently it's true. The Spanish government are desperately looking for a private individual to fund the campaign if the present syndicate owner goes belly up. Billionaires are a little thin on the ground at the moment and I think Henry Luter has stepped forward to help out. Obviously that's hugely appealing to Luter as the defender of the Cup has a distinct advantage and only has to run one set of races. The final ones. They don't have to make their way through the series racing all the challengers. It would be a huge embarrassment for the Spanish if they had to call off the Cup until they found a new sponsor but they've told Luter it has to be a nationalistic effort. It'll be announced in the press later in the week.'

'And those are the people we'll be competing against,' said Colin grimly. 'What about our plans?'

'The charity work can carry on without me for a while! This

is the America's Cup, Colin! In my match racing days I thought of nothing else.'

'I suppose you would be the man to carry a challenge. It's wonderful to see you so enthusiastic. But why can't we look at this properly and put a bid in for 2009? Why is this so important to you?'

'Because of all those young sailors who might never get a chance to sail in the America's Cup for their country again, because Luter is a shit who needs putting in his place, because someone needs to fly the flag and . . . and because everyone tells me it can't be done.'

'That's it, isn't it? You pig-headed swine. It's because they told you it couldn't be done and nobody tells John MacGregor that.' Colin laughed, shaking his head at him. Then he thought for a moment, growing more serious. 'I hate it when people tell me that too. What about a crew?'

'I've got some ideas.'

'Mack, you get me a crew that I approve of and I will put your idea forward to the board. Deal?'

'Deal.'

Mack thought about nothing else for the next twenty hours straight. Colin Montague was right when he said Mack had been getting itchy feet. Mack just hadn't realised how itchy they were until he started scratching. The standards in America's Cup boats were unimaginably high. You have boats which are near impossible to handle, a crew who has to react in split seconds and engineer shapes on sails the size of Boeing 747 wings.

The first person he tried to track down was Inky. She was back in Cornwall for a few days. She came to the phone. 'Inky? It's Mack.'

'Mack! How are you? Have you read about what that shit Luter has been up to? Thank Christ I didn't join his challenge—'

'Actually that's what I'm calling about,' Mack interrupted.

'Colin Montague might be resurrecting the British challenge. I would helm the boat . . . ' he paused. 'And I would want you to come in as tactician.'

There was a small lull before Inky let out a scream of joy. Mack had to hold the receiver away from his ear.

'What on earth is going on?' Mack could hear Inky's mother in the background.

'Mack wants me as tactician on a new British America's Cup challenge! Where's Dad? I have to tell him.' Inky rushed off oblivious to the fact that she had left Mack on the other end. Dammit. He was going to ask her where he might be able to get hold of Custard.

James Pencarrow came on the line. 'Mack? Is this true?'

'Perfectly.'

'How splendid!' He lowered his voice suddenly. 'You're not just doing this because you're her godfather, are you?'

'You really think I would put Inky on a multi-million-pound boat, up against the cream of match racing with the world watching her, just because I'm her godfather?'

Fabian had just got back from the base in Hamble. He had been working with Mack for just over a month now and was loving every second of it. He had been giving his little girl her supper whilst Milly filled in some forms when the call came through from Mack. Milly couldn't get any sense out of him for ages. 'The America's Cup,' he kept saying. 'The America's Cup. I can't believe it. The America's Cup. God, I wish my father was around to hear this.' Eventually he managed to spit the whole thing out and after giving her a euphoric kiss, Milly could hear him dancing back into the kitchen and saying to Rosie, 'We might be going to live in Spain for a while!' Milly looked down at the application forms for her fashion course, due to start the following September. 'Milly!' Fabian yelled from the kitchen. 'What's Spanish for "boat"?'

* * *

Mack decided to call and see Rafe in person as he would be his most difficult recruit. Since his split with Ava, Mack had not been able to convince him to come to work nor could any of the other members of his crew. His previous commitment to his work had evaporated in the face of his depression.

Rafe couldn't care less about the British America's Cup challenge problems. His Aunt Bee had told him about it, trying to encourage him to take an interest in something, but it was fruitless. Nothing could have prepared him for how he would feel at the end of his relationship with Ava. He was shocked that it hurt so much. He had never been in so much pain.

If only, thought his aunt, it was fixable. He had refused to take any of Ava's calls, or see her, and eventually she had given up. Bee watched him pace like a bear with toothache or lie on the sofa and watch the flies bang exhaustedly against a window. If only she could put a big Elastoplast over his heart. 'How is he?' Mack asked Bee when she answered the door.

'No different since your last visit,' she said shortly. Bee and Mack had slightly different ideas about Rafe. Bee thought he should be left to get over this in his own time whilst Mack thought the only cure was to get back on to the water and the thing he loved. Bee wondered if his solution was conveniently self-serving. The last time he visited he had also brought the unwelcome news that Ava was now officially seeing Jason Bryant. It had been plastered all over the gossip columns.

'Are you going out?' he said hopefully, looking at her dress and heels, which actually meant nothing as it was her everyday attire.

'Yes. I'll be leaving shortly.'

Mack walked through to the sitting room. Rafe looked terrible with black circles under his eyes; Mack noticed that he had lost weight.

'Rafe, I want to speak to you about a new project.'

'That sounds exciting!' said Bee, following him back into the room, damn her. 'What is this project?' she asked, since Rafe wasn't looking that interested.

'The America's Cup. We might have a chance to sail in it. Colin Montague's company may back a new British effort.'

'Does Colin Montague want me to sail in it?' asked Rafe.

'I don't know,' said Mack after a pause. 'I have to put a crew together for him to approve. But I don't think he will object. No one doubts you, Rafe.'

Rafe looked at him steadily. 'What will it consist of?'

'Out to Valencia in Spain to live and train. The Cup is in eighteen months' time. I want you with us not just because you're a wonderful sailor but you also know the Med. Local knowledge will be very important.'

There was a silence as Rafe looked down at his hands.

'You'll be going up against crews from across the world. The absolute cream of the cream of the match racing world. You might go up against Jason Bryant.'

Rafe looked up sharply. 'Jason Bryant?'

'The defenders of the Cup need some financial help. We think that Henry Luter is going to step into the breach. Jason Bryant will probably helm for him. So Ava would be there. Watching you.' It was cheap psychology but Mack didn't care.

'I'll think about it.'

'Call me tomorrow.'

Aunt Bee was less than enamoured. 'What a disgusting thing to do,' she hissed as they stood on the doorstep. 'You're using him. Using him for your own means. Have you thought what might be best for Rafe and not your stupid challenge?'

'I think he needs to start sailing again.'

'That's very convenient for you.'

'The America's Cup is as good a place to start as any.'

'You really think so? This whole ghastly scenario being played out in front of the world? And what happens when he doesn't beat this Jason Bryant?'

'I don't think we need to think that far ahead.'

'I don't think that you chose to think at all,' she said abruptly. Maybe, thought Mack feeling a little ashamed, I'm already starting to let the America's Cup affect me. I'm behaving as though nothing else matters. This is one of the reasons I'd been avoiding it. This single-minded fanaticism. Ironically the extreme focus was also the thing he was relishing. He hadn't been aware how much he had actually missed the thrill of putting a crew together combined with the possibility of winning with them. It was like taking a new lover. The America's Cup still had him enthralled after all this time.

Rafe went for a walk after Mack had left. He walked for hours even though it was raining, thinking about Ava and Jason Bryant, Mack and the America's Cup. Despite his refusal to see her he didn't think he could bear the thought of *not* seeing Ava again – perversely, she was the main reason for him staying put at the moment – but he despised the thought of actually doing something he had railed so hard against. Things had changed too much for him just to go back to his old life at the moment, and yet he hated his current state of apathy. At least something might shift if he took up Mack's offer; for a person like Rafe to be static was unbearable. The possibility of going head to head with Jason Bryant, who he'd grown to hate, put the seal on it and he went to the nearest payphone and called Mack. It was raining hard now, the raindrops clattering noisily on top of the phone box. He dialled Mack's mobile and he answered on the third ring.

'Hello?'

'Mack, it's Rafe. I'm calling to let you know that I'm going to take that position for the America's Cup.'

'My dear boy! That's absolutely marvellous . . . '

But Rafe gently put the receiver down and then went to the nearest bar and got quietly drunk. People looked with interest at the beautiful young man who was so obviously bereft. At closing time, the barman leant over and asked if someone had died.

Rafe managed a smile. 'Only myself.'

He emptied his pockets to pay for his bill and then left.

* * *

Mack was utterly delighted that Inky and Rafe were on board, but he knew his choice of them as afterguard, the brains of the boat, was highly provocative – so he approached the most highly respected sailor he knew to coach the crew. He had an Olympic gold medal, was thrice World Match Racing Champion and was a Cup veteran from the 1983 campaign; he was a knight of the realm to boot for inventing a new keel. The only problem had been that Sir Edward Lamb was retired. But if there was anyone silver-tongued enough to entice him back to the fray, that person was Mack. The promise of Valenciano sunshine and booze decided him.

Mack kicked off his meeting with the Isle of Wight yacht club through whom Colin would be challenging with the news that he had appointed Sir Edward as the crew's coach.

'He's agreed to do it?' said Richard Foss-Morgan, the club commodore. He was a frightful old fossil who had been enormously vocal when Henry Luter had deserted the challenge, chuntering about the dangers of letting in members who 'weren't quite gentlemen' with plenty of reminiscing about the old days. 'But that's marvellous.'

'Henry Luter had already offered him the same position with his syndicate and Sir Edward turned him down.' Sir Edward had actually been a little more forthright. 'Jumped-up little pipsqueak. He should be tried for treason' was one of the more polite comments he had made about Luter.

'And Colin Montague has agreed to fund the syndicate?'

'He has. His board of directors have approved twenty-five million. It was dependent on my choice of crew. He has officially entered the Cup and his challenge dossier has been accepted by the Spanish.'

'And the crew is?'

Mack told them. Old Foss-Morgan flushed so purple Mack thought he was having a heart attack. He nearly went and rolled him off his chair into the recovery position.

It was a full minute before Foss-Morgan recovered his powers of speech. 'You're inviting a girl, an ex-druggie and someone no one has ever heard of before to represent our country at the most coveted trophy in sailing? Bigger than the World Match Racing Championships, bigger than the Olympics? We're supposed to be one of the most talented sailing nations in the world!' he roared.

'And we have never won the America's Cup,' Mack pointed out quietly.

'This is turning into some sort of pantomime. We'll be the laughing stock. I don't think you're being very serious about this. The America's Cup is all about the team. If you haven't got it right, it will corrode from the inside out.'

Mack leant across the table. 'Believe me, gentlemen, I am deadly serious about this. You have my full commitment. But I have to do things my way.' Mack wasn't lying about his commitment. He hadn't thought about anything else apart from the America's Cup since he had sat in the RORC library and read that newspaper article. He was aware that he was picking up the phone at midnight, expecting people to answer, whereas he wouldn't have dreamt of treating any of his youth scheme crew that way. He was also aware how much he had missed the challenge of racing and the sheer adrenalin rush of the America's Cup.

'Fabian Beaufort is too old to be the bowman,' interjected someone else. The bowman on an America's Cup boat was the most physically stressful position. You had to have the balance of a ballet dancer, the agility of a gymnast and the strength of a rock climber.

'He's too old,' another voice agreed. 'What is he? Twenty-four?'

'Fabian is twenty-five.'

'And no one will sail with him.'

'Fabian is my bowman. He comes with me.'

'Erica Pencarrow,' stated the chairman. 'But I think the family's name far surpasses her abilities. She's your god-daughter, isn't she?'

Mack ignored the jibe. 'Inky is enormously talented. Her record on the match racing circuit is exemplary.'

'That isn't the problem. She could be a Dennis Connor reincarnated; it is how the rest of the crew will deal with her. It upsets the balance having a woman on board. The crew don't knit together as well.'

'They'll learn,' said Mack grimly. 'Besides, she has valuable Cup experience. She was on the last campaign.'

'And what about this Ralph man?'

'Rafe. Most talented sailor I know. I've worked with him.'

'Why haven't we heard of him?'

'He's been abroad.'

'Competing?'

Mack paused for a second and then shook his head.

'So apart from yourself, there are no big names on the boat.' Foss-Morgan had been planning to quiz Mack about his own motivation since Mack had been out of match racing for so long, but now he was faced with the intense Scotsman with his iron jaw and expressive eyes, he had no doubt about his passion or his dedication. It was as though he could find no challenge on land equal to him so he had taken to the sea.

'In my experience the rock star sailors, as they are so euphemistically called, create more problems than they are worth. If there are too many personalities on the boat, they argue, they're rude and they never work as a team. I have to do this my way with my choice of crew.' Mack then went on to talk about his shore crew and how involved they all would be in the process of winning this battle. 'It's like taking a massive army on to the front line. They are all involved in the success of the challenge. For the sail man, the fight is in every inch of every sail he makes. For the maintenance man, it is in every fixing he checks and screw he tightens. For the weather man, it's in every moment they spend checking the weather. The commitment stretches right down to the caterers and the cleaners. You have to instil pride in each and every one of them. Their role in the winning of the Cup is as vital as mine.'

Gradually, one by one, Mack won them over. His enthusiasm spoke volumes. By the end of the meeting everyone in the room was as fired up as Mack himself was. If Henry Luter's philosophy was to shout and threaten his syndicate until he got results, then Mack's was to inspire the team until each member wanted to lay down their lives for him. Perhaps, just perhaps, this was possible.

A few days later it was made known that Henry Luter had come to the rescue of the host Valencia Yacht Club and the America's Cup. Since the dramatic bankruptcy of their syndicate chief (with a few accusations of foul play to boot), the yacht club was highly embarrassed and the whole of the America's Cup community up in arms at the prospect of the Cup not going ahead. After all, deposits had been paid (and at a million euros per syndicate this was no small amount) and millions and millions of pounds spent on challenges. Everyone was relieved Henry Luter had stepped forward to fund the defence of the Cup. He had a few conditions however. He wanted to choose his own crew and Phoenix – the name of his corporation – was to be the name and principal sponsor of the boat. The Spanish gladly agreed.

Mack read the account in the paper and grimaced. Henry Luter must be very pleased with himself. Behind all the excitement of Mack's plans, there was one key motive that he hadn't actually mentioned to anyone. He wanted to wipe the smile off Henry Luter's face. And when they came head to head on the race course, he would take enormous pleasure in doing just that.

It felt good to be back.

PART TWO

Chapter 15

M ack marched into the crew's seven o'clock morning meeting. Despite the earliness of the hour and the fact it was January, it was quite mild in Valencia, which partly compensated for the fact that the crew had to be up at five every morning to go to the gym. They had been here only a week and had fifteen months until the America's Cup. And there was no chance, thought Mack, of them peaking too soon.

His newest appointment, Laura, was busy trying to fill the crew in on the day's weather. Most of the other meteorologists had already been out here for at least six months analysing the weather on what was the most intensely studied piece of water on the planet. Mack hoped Laura was up to it.

At the moment she was trying to speak above the hum of conversation, paper aeroplanes being chucked at her and the odd wolf whistle and catcall. Sir Edward, who had a much less combative form of leadership than Mack, was ineffectively trying to shush them. Yesterday had been the third day on the trot that she'd got it wrong and the natives were getting restless. Mack hoped it was just new-on-the-job nerves. Whereas the ace meteorologist in the New Zealand team was nicknamed 'Clouds', his crew had taken to calling Laura 'Fog'.

'ALL RIGHT!' shouted Mack above the din. 'THAT IS ENOUGH!'

The noise petered out and Mack made a motion for her to continue.

'And . . . and the humidity stays the same as yesterday at forty-five per cent. The wind looks as though it might . . . er . . . might remain pretty steady at twelve knots . . . '

'Why don't you carry all the wrong sails out to the boat next time, Laura?' called out a voice from the back. Mack shot a look over his shoulder.

Laura raised her voice slightly. 'But there will be, er . . . the odd gust of no more than fifteen knots. Em . . . and that's all.'

'What does your crystal ball say, Rafe?' someone called out. 'You're supposed to be the wind god. You tell us.'

Rafe looked languidly out from his dark eyes. He didn't rise.

Once out on the water, when the shout went up that they were nearing the practice course, Ho, the sewer man, started hustling the sailors off his piles of sails. They were all lying on them, resting until it was time to start sailing. The boat was always towed out to the course because, of course, it had no engine. 'Come on, everyone!' he roared. 'Get out of my sewer! I want to get the sails sorted.' Ho was a giant of a man, with a thick-set neck and long dangling arms; Mack half expected him to drag his knuckles along the deck. He went by the nickname Ho because of his well-spoken voice and naval background, which made everyone expect him to say *What ho!* Of course he never did.

Inky pulled herself up still giggling about something Custard had said to her, to be greeted with the unsmiling face of Golly, one of the grinders who bench-pressed 120kg in the gym and spent their lives hoisting the huge sails. Women were considered unlucky on boats, even on an America's Cup yacht that was on the cutting edge of technology, and Golly resented her being there. Bananas were also considered unlucky. Inky wondered if any of the men would faint clean away if she ever dared to eat one on board.

'Are you two shagging or something?'

'No, but wouldn't you like to?' said Custard, putting an arm round Inky's shoulder and giving her a tight squeeze. Inky could have kissed him. 'We've just sailed together a lot.'

'Well, I haven't,' snapped Golly which pretty much translated to, 'I don't trust you.'

'I've sailed with Inky,' vouched Dougie, one of the sail trimmers. 'She'll run rings around you.'

'I doubt it,' retorted Golly. His bad temper was mostly attributable to nerves. They were all edgy. The excitement and privilege of being chosen to sail in the America's Cup had given way to sheer terror since their arrival in Valencia when they realised what they would be up against. It was easy to dream of holding that silver ewer back in the relative cold of England but now they were actually out here and could see the other bases with their professional-looking crews and boats, those dreams were quickly fading and giving way to the blind hope they just might get the boat around the course.

The sailors were split into social camps according to who had sailed together before. Golly, Flipper and Rump, the three grinders, had all been on a Volvo boat together. Rafe and Fabian had been together briefly on the youth challenge but Fabian was pretty much known to everyone anyway (Custard, for one, had lost plenty of girls to him). Mack had sailed with Sammy the navigator, an ex-RAF pilot, in Auckland. Sammy had refused to join Henry Luter again, because as he said, 'I'd already been through two years of hell; why would I voluntarily sign up to it again?' They had been extremely lucky to get him as he was just about to join another challenge.

Getting ready to sail, the boat was a hive of activity. Everyone checked their positions and equipment, applied sun cream and attached their few personal possessions to the side of the boat with masking tape. They would be racing against the second boat up the course today. Their official America's Cup boat was currently being designed but they would build two of the same design and one of them would become the sparring boat, crewed by the second crew, and a standard against which they could measure themselves. Until then they had borrowed two old America's Cup yachts from a redundant Chinese challenge and called them simply *First Boat* and *Second Boat*. It was a concept that even Golly was able to grasp.

'All right, heads up!' Mack called to the rest of the crew. 'We're up against *Second Boat* today.' Mack didn't really need to mention this; the crew were very much aware that there was a second crew who was just waiting to step into their shoes. 'We're going to start and then continue up the first leg. As you are probably aware we are on *First Boat*. She slips through the water fractionally quicker than *Second Boat* so we might drift on to her if they manage to lock us down. Which, needless to say, would mean a penalty turn. So I'm going to make the start soft and loping, keep us moving and nail them before they have chance to nail us. Any questions?'

Mack paused before marching down to where the mainsail was based.

'HOIST THE MAINSAIL.' Golly and Flipper got to work grinding the sail up the mast. The huge mainsail snagged halfway up and Mack cursed. It hovered uncertainly in the wind. 'FREE IT!' he yelled irritably. In a crew which was working well he wouldn't have to say anything. 'For fuck's sake, free it!'

Custard shinned up the mast and freed it to continue on its journey. It took a good few seconds.

'LOCKED!' shouted Golly as it softly clunked into place.

Mack felt the power of the vast sail as they were sucked immediately into the wind. He made some circles and then they sailed away, glancing back towards *Second Boat*, who was still hauling the mainsail into place.

'Who's counting down?' Mack asked, referring to the pre-start countdown. There was a pause as Dougie looked at Inky. Golly looked at Custard and Rafe looked at the horizon.

'I'm counting down,' said Sammy hastily.

'Fine.'

After the gun Mack shied away until Sammy began the one-minute countdown whilst the other boat did a couple of circles. Just as they came out of the last one, in one beautiful and forceful move, Mack tacked hard back and came in underneath them, pinned them hard and held tight as they sailed, seemingly locked together, all the way towards the buoy which signalled the end of the start line.

'Ten . . . nine . . . eight,' called Sammy.

On the current course *First Boat* would cross the start line but *Second Boat* could only miss it altogether. They had no choice but to gybe round and come in behind Mack.

The starting gun went and Mack crossed the line barely a second behind it with *Second Boat* another six seconds behind her.

Dougie and Inky looked at each other in relief. At least today they had crossed the start line. Yesterday they rammed the starting buoy.

The boats sailed on, still apparently locked together. *Second Boat* was constantly trying to inch up on them but could not pass as they were wallowing in *First Boat*'s air.

Mack debated the choice of spinnaker with Inky and Rafe. 'Code two or code three?' he asked.

Inky thought code three would be best but she was distracted by Dougie, who was trying to unjam a sheet. Rafe didn't seem to be connecting properly and was being completely indecisive. There was a little too much wind for one and not quite enough for the other.

Mack made up his own mind. 'Code two spinnaker!' he shouted and the order was passed down to Ho in the sewer as they made ready to round the mark.

The rounding of the mark was a tightly choreographed operation which involved every single member of the crew, each one preferably knowing exactly what they were doing. This was known as a set and a perfect one would be complete in under eight seconds.

The pantomime started with Ho heaving the spinnaker sail up on deck only to find it was the wrong way up so Sparky, the midbowman, had to grapple with it in order to find the top and clip on the halyard, which lost them at least five seconds. Ho then hoisted the five thousand square feet of sail into the air, helped by the mastman, Jonny, but as their fitness wasn't quite up to scratch yet it took them twice as long as it should.

Whilst this was all happening, Dougie had rushed forward to jam the genoa but was late and then struggled to get the bottom of the spinnaker to Fabian in time. Golly and Flipper were already grinding the spinnaker pole up but Fabian did manage to grab it in time and shin up the pole, although he nearly put his shoulder out in the process.

Someone had to haul down the genoa but Dougie and Germ were trimming the spinnaker and everyone expected someone else to do it. 'GET THAT SAIL DOWN!' yelled Mack when he realised what was happening. Jonny and Sparky hustled forward, colliding together in their effort like something out of Laurel and Hardy.

All this took place amongst the persistent spray as the boat heeled sharply to one side, the thunderous flapping of sails, the spaghetti heap of lines on the deck, the shouting of commands and the boat's relentless chatting.

Mack watched the whole episode with his hand clasped to his forehead. 'How long was that?' he quietly asked Sammy, his navigator.

'Twenty-three seconds,' he said looking at the stopwatch.

'Dear God, help me.'

A new drama with the spinnaker was literally unfolding as they spoke. Unfortunately, as the huge sail pinged open the straps which held it, Mack realised that they had made the wrong choice. The wind was too strong for it. He was just about to open his mouth to shout for another sail change when he saw the tiniest of rips appear.

'Get it down! We need the code three spinnaker!' he yelled.

They were already dropping speed and *Second Boat* was hard on their heels.

Within a second the rip was opening out in front of their eyes. When a spinnaker tears it can drop over the side and drag the boat or get wrapped round the keel.

The bow of the boat was a pandemonium of activity. Already the tear was splitting the sail in two, and Mack watched as the last inch of cloth gave way to separate the two halves. This would be disaster in a real race because if any part of the boat were to touch their competitor (including ripped sails) then it would mean a penalty.

'GET IT DOWN! GET THE FUCKING THING DOWN!' roared Mack again as the whole crew had a mass panic. 'GET ME ANOTHER SPINNAKER! CODE THREE!'

Ho didn't have the sewer in as good an order as he would like and wasted valuable seconds searching for the code three spinnaker. Pond, the pitman, thinking he could help, dived down the hatch into the sewer and nearly floored Ho who was just dragging the code three on to the deck.

The rest of the crew were fumbling fingers, trying to get the top half of the sail down and then wrestle the bottom half away as well. Flipper, waiting before he hauled the pole up again, started to hum tunelessly – a nervous habit of his.

This was all too much for the normally mild-mannered Dougie. 'SHUT UP!' he yelled at Flipper. 'JUST SHUT THE FUCK UP!

Flipper's best mate, Golly, left his grinding pedestal and with a heart-stopping growl, threw himself at Dougie and had him by the throat within a couple of minutes, yelling something about an apology.

Inky, who was highly protective of Dougie, gave Golly an almighty shove. Fabian thought Golly wouldn't hesitate in lamping Inky and ran forward to help her. Custard dived in with a Mohawk shriek. Pond was yelling furiously because everyone was trampling on his lines and Sparky looked around to find that he was trying to raise the spinnaker single-handedly.

Mack ran the entire length of the boat to split them up. When he couldn't, he pushed them all over the side.

'So that went well,' said Sir Edward. It was Sir Edward's first day with the challenge. He wasn't impressed so far. Mack had left Inky nervously in charge of the boat and he and Sir Edward were on board the launch, *Mucky Ducky* to discuss the morning. (A tatty, almost tug-like boat, *Mucky Ducky* would double up as the tow, coaching base and hospitality boat.) Of course, they had started a little earlier than scheduled because a sulky, soaking-wet crew were presently changing.

'Flipper started humming. Sounded like "She'll be coming round the mountain". I think Dougie thought he was taking the piss. We lost a twenty-thousand-pound spinnaker too. All in all a good morning's work,' said Mack in disgust.

'I think Fabian could be good. It's no place for the faint-hearted, but he looks as though he can handle himself,' said Sir Edward. 'Are you sure about him, by the way? I heard rumours about him back in England . . . '

'I'll vouch for Fabian,' said Mack firmly.

'Where did you find the sewer man? In the jungle?'

'He will be good,' smiled Mack. 'Just needs to get organised.' Ho was strong and capable, vital for the man responsible for dragging the sails out of the sewer and on to the deck. 'He just wants to get into the fray. Loves the competition.'

'Who is the mainsheet trimmer?' asked Sir Edward, pointing further along the boat.

'Will Stanmore. Goes by the nickname of Custard. He sailed in the Auckland campaign with Inky, kept off the first boat by one of Luter's cronies. I've not sailed with him before but come up against him on the circuit.'

'He's talented.'

'He has the most superior sail-handling skills that I have ever seen.'

'Luter's loss is our gain. The other two trimmers look good too.'

'Dougie and Germ. Dougie is here on Inky's recommendation. She's sailed with him a lot.'

'Who's the pitman?'

'Pond. He's very solid and reliable. Calms everyone down. The grinders are left behind from Luter's challenge. They refused to go with him.'

'That was brave considering they had no guarantee of the challenge being resurrected,' commented Sir Edward.

'Golly, Flipper and Rump – they're like sticks of rock. If you broke them in half they would have GREAT BRITAIN running through them from top to bottom. They have very little respect for the opposition. Almost not bright enough for that. They just want to go out and pulverise them.'

'And those two?' asked Sir Edward. 'The traveller and the runner?'

'Cherry and Bandit. Both Olympians. They just get their heads down and do the job.'

'And who's the afterguard?'

'Inky will be taking the position of tactician with Rafe as the strategist. I thought that would be the best position for him as the wind caller.'

'Are you sure he's got the talent?'

'Apart from being a gifted sailor, he knows exactly where the wind is and when it's going to come. I've seen him stand on shore and tell me exactly when the breeze is going to appear almost down to the minute. It's a rare power,' said Mack shortly. 'Wait and see.' Mack sincerely hoped Rafe would recover form. He was distinctly lacklustre. It seemed as though Ava had infected everything. It was Rafe's appointment that had caused most upset amongst the crew. The most important thing in the afterguard of an America's Cup boat was experience, of which Rafe had none and on his current form no one could see why he was on the boat.

'The crew hear you talking about what a huge privilege it is to be sailing for their country and then it looks as if you've picked a nobody. They already want the second-crew man to replace him. What are you going to do to integrate him?'

'These are people who don't communicate through language. Only actions will win you a right to be on the boat. When things get tough, they'll watch what you do and then they'll decide. They'll come to appreciate Rafe.'

'I only hope he's not the pinprick that turns septic and into blood poisoning. Mind you, he's not the only one. I've noticed that they don't like taking orders from Inky and they don't trust Fabian. An acrimonious crew can never win the America's Cup. They have to be like jackstraws. Take them one by one and you can snap them. Take them all together and they are unbreakable. You need to find the glue to stick them. How do you think the crew have taken to Inky?'

'They are wary but they'll grow to respect her because of her experience.'

Sir Edward watched them all silently for a moment. 'There's no cohesion though, is there? Could you have got it wrong?' he added gently. Despite Mack's sometimes instantaneous selections, he usually had an uncanny ability for selecting compatible people. 'After all, you had to put the crew together in such a short time and you were under a huge amount of pressure.'

Only Sir Edward could have posed such a question. Mack wasn't offended – or surprised. 'Give them time,' he said shortly.

Time is one thing we haven't got, thought Sir Edward to himself. He wondered whether Mack had let the scale of the challenge cloud his thinking. There was a first time for everything.

'How's Colin Montague?'

'Quiet. Which is slightly worrying.'

'Especially in contrast to the other syndicate heads who poke their noses in.'

'Exactly. He's not even flying out for the design meeting.'

'How's the new boat design coming along?' Although they had the two boats to practise in, the rules of the Cup said they had to have their own boat, designed and built in their own country.

'The designers are flying out today.' There was a pause. 'I really hope that there are no hovering cameras. Ducking the crew wouldn't be a great start to the PR campaign. Talking of PR, I've got to appoint someone to head the PR team. The niece of a friend of mine is flying out for an interview at lunchtime.'

'You're flying her out?'

'I'm going to give her the job unless I hate her on sight. Her uncle said she was good. Works for a high-flying ad company in the city but her family are sailors. Speaks a bit of Spanish and just needs bringing out of herself. Daughter of a vicar.'

Sir Edward nodded. 'So you thought you would break her in gently by chucking her in with the most debauched group of professionals there ever was, in the biggest capitalist exhibition of the world.'

'Now don't be negative. If I had my way, we wouldn't be bothering with PR at all. But as Colin Montague pointed out, his company are plunging twenty-five million into the project, so it would quite nice if the team had some sort of positive image. Besides, she's good at her job and she's sailed.'

Whilst they were waiting for the niece who, Sir Edward gathered, was called Hattie, Mack got back into *First Boat* and made the crew take the spinnaker up and down thirty times in a row to see if they could get the thing up in eight seconds flat. They couldn't.

He clambered wearily back into Sir Edward's launch and watched the RIB coming ever closer. He could see the head of what he could only describe as a dolly bird: shining hair with bright red lipstick and a pair of huge Jackie O sunglasses. He gave a groan. God, he hated PR girls.

The foredeck crew, lying exhausted on the deck, pulled themselves up on to their elbows and, shielding their eyes against the sun, looked hopefully at the approaching RIB.

'Need any help with the interview, Mack?' called one of the grinders. 'I do shorthand.'

Another reason to hate PR girls. The crew were so pumped up from the gym and adrenalin with no time free to let off steam that girls were a huge distraction. It was like waving steak in front of lions who had only been allowed chickpeas.

The girl had impractical heels on and a funny sort of skirt which she carefully hitched up around her knees in order to clamber into the launch. The whole crew were now gathered on one side of the boat, which was heeling sharply with their weight, and staring absolutely agog. At that moment she missed the step over into the other boat and fell bodily into Mack's launch with her legs trailing in the water. Mack grabbed whatever bits of material he could and heaved her over the edge, inadvertently flashing her knickers to the crew who couldn't quite believe their luck and erupted into a cacophony of applause and whooping.

'Are you all right?' he panted.

'Oh, my goodness . . . oh, dear . . . ' A frantic hand checked for her sunglasses and the small bag she was carrying but then she let out a wail. 'Oh, I've lost my shoe!'

Mack sighed and put on what he hoped was his kind voice. 'So you must be Hattie?'

'Em, yes. How do you do?' She put out a hand with a formality Mack found a bit strange when he had just dragged her into the boat by her pants. Christ, he probably gave her a wedgie.

'John MacGregor. You can call me Mack.'

'My uncle talks about you a lot. It's a pleasure to meet you.'

'Have you been following what's been happening with the challenge?'

'Avidly. All my family have. And that's why I want to do this so badly because it's going to be such a wonderful challenge to turn this around and create some good PR for you all.' She flushed bright red for the second time that day. 'Not that you haven't been . . . you know . . . or . . . '

'It's all right, Hattie. I'm quite aware of what the papers have been saying.' Since news of Colin Montague's challenge had been officially announced, there had been a plethora of articles about them. Was Mack up to the task? Did Colin Montague have enough money to see it through? Had the new crew enough experience? A recent publication had even compared Mack with his present crew to 'Michael Schumacher driving a Robin Reliant around the race track'. 'You know you would have to recruit and head up a whole team here in Valencia. Can you manage that?'

'Absolutely.'

Mack dispensed with the chit-chat. 'Well then, consider yourself employed.'

'Oh, thank you,' she said going quite pink with pleasure. 'Are you sure? I mean don't you want to ask me any more questions?'

'You come highly recommended and I've read your references,' said Mack firmly. 'You'll have quite a job on your hands. We'll expect you to handle all the press. You need to put a positive spin on all the recent happenings, by the way. We need to distance ourselves completely from Henry Luter. A challenge needs to be feared, not pitied, and we don't want to look as though we're picking up the pieces from him. You will also need to drum up some sponsorship. We're a bit short on cash.'

'How short?'

'I reckon we'll need about another five million. Of course, you can also get things in lieu. You know, clothing, drinks, etc. Some free stuff to take some burden off the bills.'

Hattie went slightly pale, but her voice was steady as she replied, 'Of course.'

'When can you start?'

'Well, my company doesn't usually let anyone work out their notice period . . . '

'So immediately then?' Hattie blinked. He was extremely forthright. 'The shore manager, Tim Jenkins, will show you around.'

'Her father is going to have a fit when he finds out she's going to be in a hundred-strong male syndicate. I feel quite sorry for him,' commented Sir Edward as they watched Hattie being whizzed back to shore and after he'd promised to keep an eye out for her shoe. 'Especially now the crew have just nicknamed her "Red Pants".'

Hattie's appearance unintentionally made the tow home much more cheerful than it would have been otherwise but the crew still didn't waste much time saying goodbye to each other, not only because they didn't like each other much but also because their base was none too comfortable. In contrast to Henry Luter and the Spanish defenders' plush headquarters, which sat almost directly across the America's Cup harbour with a purpose-built PR centre and chefs making fresh sushi, their base consisted of the containers which had delivered all their equipment. Once they had been unloaded, they had temporarily become a kitchen, shower, massage room and admin centre. Soon they would build a changing room and small gym for the crew, a common room, a sail loft and the admin offices.

Fabian made his way back to the hotel where Mack had temporarily settled the whole team until proper accommodation could be found. The hotel staff didn't take much notice of him or any of the crew, as a formal uniform had yet to be decided upon and they didn't look anything like a sports team representing their country. If anyone cared to look closely (which they didn't), they did at least share a common look of Oakleys pushed to the top of their heads, calloused hands, sun-bleached hair and a deep tan.

Fabian was the first home as he was keen to catch Rosie before she went to bed. Being included in the newly formed British Challenge had given him a huge amount of kudos and the first two people he had thought of were Rob Thornton and his father. He wondered what they would think of his recent appointment. He felt vaguely guilty about it. Somehow it didn't feel fair to Rob. But he was doing his best to shake off this feeling and was determined to prove all the gossip about him wrong. He had written to Rob's parents to tell them about the news but, as before, had received no reply. He tried not to think about Henry Luter's posh base looming across the harbour. Not because theirs was so basic but simply the sight of Luter's corporate logo and his crew's smart uniforms made him feel sick to the stomach. He couldn't imagine ever being ready to race them around an America's Cup course.

Rosie was still up when Fabian reached the hotel.

'Everything OK?' he asked Milly as he swung a joyful Rosie into the air.

'Fine,' she said, determined not to mention her difficulties with the language or with filling in Fabian's tax return over the Internet, or the fact she had paced the streets most of the day with a baby trying to look for the same formula brand they had in England. All this and the only person she had spoken to in English was Rosie who also stared uncomprehendingly at her. She felt like bursting into tears. She hadn't mentioned her fashion course since Fabian had been included on the crew. Fabian had been so excited that she doubted he would have listened anyway. Watching him with his beloved daughter now, Milly's feelings of insecurity and transience grew. How long would it be before she was left behind?

Bee, a few doors down, felt like bursting into tears too. She could have done with a large gin and tonic instead of a biscuit. When Rafe had told her that he was joining the new British America's Cup Challenge, Bee had immediately offered to come out to Spain with him, to which Rafe had somewhat bemusedly agreed. 'After all, darling, we're only just getting to know one another and it sounds like such a wonderful adventure! Please let me come!'

She didn't really want to go to Spain at all. All she knew was that her beloved sister would have wanted her to and she had become terribly fond of Rafe during his short stay in England.

Rafe's awful apathy over Ava had been replaced by a single-minded determination and she wasn't sure which extreme concerned her the most. His new desire to beat Jason Bryant to a pulp on the race course, combined with the fact that Ava would probably be around *and* Rafe was racing in her father's syndicate, seemed to Bee a recipe for disaster. Even though Rafe had said that Colin Montague was indifferent to his presence on the crew, Bee had noticed that they hadn't actually seen each other yet. The only positive thing was that Rafe didn't seem as overawed as the rest of the crew at the challenge before them.

She sincerely hoped that Rafe would in time see the futility of his actions and then she could flick two fingers at that ogre John MacGregor and this stupid America's Cup thing and they could both return to England.

However, at the moment she felt very homesick and disorientated. She was terribly upset at having to put Salty in the aircraft hold, she'd had to sublet her gorgeous cottage and said tearful goodbyes to her own two children to come to a strange, foreign city where she didn't speak the language and where she was going to be for a very long time. 'What a wonderful adventure!' all her friends had exclaimed when she told them. 'We shall all come and visit.' But right now it didn't feel like a grand adventure at all. The rooms smelt slightly, didn't have air-conditioning and she didn't like the look at all of the dock area where the Cup was based. She had told Rafe that she'd always wanted to live in Spain, was sick of the English weather and adored sangria. All of which were lies.

She frowned. Moping wasn't going to help. It was her idea to come and she'd better make the best of it. She unpacked her bath cap, found her duty-free gin and phoned her children, which made her feel much better. After all, with the lure of weekend flights and fiesta, she would probably see more of them than she did back at home.

* * *

Further down the hall, Custard was lying on the bed, staring at the ceiling and wondering why on earth he had agreed to join the challenge. It was like being asked to star in a Broadway show but moments before you are about to go on, you feel sick to the stomach and wonder what on earth you are doing.

It wasn't long before Inky barged in. 'I'm bored. What are you doing?'

'What do I look like I'm doing?'

Inky ignored him and plonked herself down on the bed. 'That was dreadful today, wasn't it?'

'Fucking awful.'

'I thought I'd died and gone to heaven being picked for the crew but now I wonder if I was sent to hell instead. I'm scared stupid.'

'Me too.'

'What's my father going to say when we lose every race straight?'

'He's going to say, "Bloody women drivers."'

Inky grinned at him and felt a bit better. Custard was absolutely adorable. He came from a middle-class family, and had had a straightforward upbringing on the coast of Dorset. His parents, seeing he had a gift for sailing, enrolled him in the local sailing school and he had gradually worked his way up the ranks. Meeting Inky often at match-racing events, he started to crew for her. He had absolutely no hang-ups about her being female, he simply saw that she was an exceptional sailor. He was tall and brown-haired with a very agreeable face and a slightly crooked nose where the boom had smashed into his face at the age of seven. He found life endlessly amusing and looked for the joke in everything. Some people say a glass is half full, some people say it is half empty and Custard always asked, 'Are you drinking that?' Many girls had been in love with him but he hadn't as yet fallen for anyone.

'Do you think Mack really has lost the plot? I mean, what if the newspapers are right? What if Mack has lost his edge?'

'Then we're buggered. Come on, we've been in worse situations together. Let's do what we always do.'

'Stuff them all and win anyway?'

'No! Go down the pub.'

While the crew had been making their way to the hotel, Mack and Sir Edward had gone straight into a design meeting for the new boat. As Mack shook their hands, one of the designers said, 'I hope you don't mind but we brought along our new apprentice. Young Neville will be working on some aspects of the design.' Mack gave him a brisk nod.

'Clearly we're short of time,' Mack started, 'so I would rather we didn't waste it. We need a boat which is a dream to sail and goes like a rocket. We've got about three million to spend.'

'Peanuts,' muttered one of the men.

'You'll need the latest technology in carbon fibre to make it as light as possible. That'll be expensive,' said the other designer. 'The problem is,' he added for Neville's sake, 'because all the boats are closely guarded secrets, you have no idea how competitive they are until they actually start to race one another which isn't for another fifteen months.'

'Any ideas?' asked Mack. 'We're slightly short on time too so we'll need it quickly.'

'We'll have to fall back on old designs and modify them,' said one to the other. 'That will cut down on tank testing and computer time.'

'But are we going to get a fast boat?'

One of them shrugged. 'Fast boats cost more money than we have.'

'They have skirts, don't they?' piped up Neville. 'All the boats wear skirts so no one can see what's underneath.'

'Neville! Let's talk about this later, shall we?' said one of the designers pertly.

'No, let's hear what the boy has to say,' said Mack. Sir Edward sincerely hoped, for Neville's sake, that whatever he was about to say was intelligent.

'I've been reading about *Australia II*'s winged keel back in 1983 and a sort of idea came to me.'

'Do you want to run this past us first, Neville?' interrupted one of the designers.

'I want to hear it now,' said Mack. 'What is it?'

When Neville finished outlining his design idea Mack was quite flabbergasted. It was audacious and it was cheeky. He liked it. And it was just about within the rules and within the budget.

Chapter 16

'What's this?' Mack roared into Hattie's office flapping a piece of paper in her face. 'What the hell is this?'

'What's what?' said Hattie calmly, barely looking up from her laptop. She was getting used to Mack's kinetics, scattering people in his wake.

'THIS! This summons of yours.'

Hattie took the piece of paper from him and peered at it. 'It's hardly a summons. I've managed to get you a press interview. That tells you the date and time they want you and then a little bit about the sort of questions they'll ask you and what you should reply.'

'But I don't want a press interview. I hate press interviews.'

'I can't get any sponsorship without publicity.'

'Why do I have to do it? Why can't Inky or Rafe or even Golly do it?'

Hattie looked at him beadily. 'Because you're the skipper. People want to talk to you. And the only way you can sail your boat is if you have enough money to do so and . . .'

'All right, all right, I'll do it. When and where is it?'

'It's all on the piece of paper.' She handed the offending memo back to him.

He made to march out but Hattie called after him. 'And please don't do that look you do when you think the other person is an idiot.'

'But the other person usually is an idiot.'

'Is that why you do it with me so much?'

'Yes.'

'Well, don't do it with any journalists.'

Hattie was to have an exhausting spring. With no time to even fly back to England to collect her belongings, she'd had to ask her mother to pack them up for her. She couldn't remember if she'd done all her washing before she left, which was terribly embarrassing.

Starting at the Montague Challenge had been completely intimidating, especially under the command of John MacGregor, whose reputation had preceded him but by no means eclipsed him. 'You'll find him an exacting man. He expects high standards and doesn't suffer fools,' said her uncle on the phone when she had called to tell him her news. 'But anyone who has worked with him would walk through fire for him.'

Hattie hadn't been convinced that she would walk through fire for anyone but within a week she too had fallen under his spell.

Mack had already called her in to ask if she had recruited anyone else for her PR team yet. There was absolutely no shortage of candidates, all wanting to live in Spain for a while and mix with the glamorous America's Cup crowd.

'I've been through lots of CVs, interviewed everyone by phone and narrowed them down to a handful. Can I fly them out for interviews?'

Mack shook his head. 'No money and no time. You'll have to find another way of picking them.'

'Fine, I'll pick them by star sign then,' Hattie said cheekily.

Mack stared at her for a second and then laughed suddenly. 'Perfect. You and I are going to get on fine, Hattie.'

Mack and money weren't Hattie's only problems. Her first PR efforts had produced a journalist who flew out to Valencia to talk to the crew and then published an article about 'Rafe Louvel, the prima donna who insists on having his own private balcony'.

Quite annoyed that her first attempt had backfired, she sought out this Rafe and found him at breakfast time in the makeshift canteen drinking coffee away from the rest of the crew. Most of them weren't speaking to each other anyway; the animosity was quite apparent.

Rafe fixed Hattie with dark, watchful eyes as she pulled up a seat and she found herself uncomfortably under scrutiny. Despite his stillness, there was something restless about him. He reminded her of a predator, something quite feral, watching his prey.

'It's Hattie, isn't it?' he asked.

'Yes. Now, I don't know if you've seen this . . . '

'May I get you some coffee?'

Hattie blinked slightly. The manners were slightly at odds with the aura he projected. Like a lion in a dinner jacket. 'No. No, thank you. I've come to talk to you about this article.' She waved the offending piece crossly in front of his face. 'Have you seen it?'

Most of the crew had seen it because relatives and friends had sent it out from England. The idea that the already tight finances were having to pay for Rafe's foibles added fuel to the already disgruntled crew's dissatisfaction with their wind caller. It wasn't Mack's method to swap crew members about but the second boat's man in Rafe's position was feeling highly hopeful.

'No.'

'Oh,' said Hattie a bit taken back.

'May I?' He gently took the piece from her and started to read. When he'd finished, he quietly put the piece back in front of her.

'Is that true?' she demanded. 'Did you say to him that you had to have a private balcony?'

'I think he asked me if it was difficult to adjust to life ashore and what was sleeping in a real bed like and I said that I didn't know because I prefer to sleep out on the balcony.'

'Well, you have to understand that . . . Sorry? You sleep out on the balcony?'

'Apart from a short time in Lymington, this is the first time I've really slept on land for any amount of time. I can't really get used to it. It feels better sleeping outside,' he said simply. He didn't like hotels, breathing the second-hand air of the previous occupants: malevolent businessmen and their discontented mistresses. 'I wanted to come and sleep on the launch but Mack thought it was better for all the crew to stay together. Do you want me to move rooms?'

'Em, no. No, don't do that. It's just that the press think you're being self-important.'

'Oh. What do you think?'

'It doesn't really matter what I think.'

'Doesn't it? I would have thought it was the only thing that mattered.'

Hattie walked away from the meeting feeling utterly nonplussed.

Whilst Mack inspired near hero worship in all of his crew, he certainly didn't elicit any from Beatrice Burman who was currently on her way down to the challenge's offices to tear a strip off him. She popped her head round the door of Hattie's makeshift office.

'Hello, Hattie! Have you seen Mack?' Salty barged straight in and stuck his head in the wastepaper basket.

'No, but I would jolly well like to see him. It's impossible to drum up PR when I'm told not to make a fuss about anything. Mack doesn't want me to say anything derogatory about Henry Luter to the press which is jolly hard when I have spent the whole day trying to get some sponsorship for the challenge only to be told that they were sponsoring the old Luter challenge and under the terms of their contract they can't sponsor anyone else. Then our sail company called and told us they couldn't make sails for us any more because they're found they're still technically under contract to Henry Luter. I think he is . . . beastly.' Hattie went quite pink.

'He certainly doesn't seem a very nice man,' admitted Bee,

coming fully into the container. She liked Hattie. Despite her very prim upbringing (and she *did* look exactly like a vicar's daughter, Bee could never quite work out why), she had a strong streak of cheekiness and humour. She was a pretty girl but lacked Bee's strong sense of Bohemian style – she was fond of what Bee could only describe as frocks. The word *beastly* sounded utterly natural coming from her.

'It's not as though he's even using their sponsorship with his new challenge but his staff have been calling round all the British sponsors reminding them of their commitment.'

'So no sponsors yet?'

'Well, I found a drink company who promised to send us their product throughout the Cup.'

'That sounds promising.'

'Mack didn't really specify what sort of drink. I didn't realise he meant for the crew to have some.'

'What sort of drink is it?'

'Whisky.' Hattie hung her head. 'He was quite cross and told me when it arrives to send it into his office. He and Sir Edward would drink it.'

'Hattie, your first sponsor! You should be very proud!'

'Do you think so?'

'I think that sounds marvellous!' said Bee beaming at her and feeling quite cross with Mack for making her feel bad. He was such an ogre. 'Are you settling in OK?'

'Fine. I haven't really seen my hotel room yet but I'm sure it will be very nice when I finally get there.'

Bee laughed. 'Let me know if you need anything. I can always bring you down a sandwich or something. In fact I might have a pain au chocolat from breakfast,' she said, frantically rummaging in her bag.

'Ooh, yummy, thank you. I was feeling peckish. Just don't let Carla catch you.'

'Carla?'

'Haven't you met her yet? She's the local lady we've taken on to take care of all the crew catering. She and Sir Edward are already coming to blows.'

'Really?'

'She won't let him have any coffee unless he has an espresso and drinks it standing up because it's better for his digestion. He wants a cappuccino and, as he puts it, preferably lying down.'

Bee laughed. 'She sounds quite a character.'

'Hey, Red Pants!' called Custard poking his head around the door.

'Please don't call me that, Custard.'

'Oh come on, Hattie! I can't tell you how much that little incident cheered us all up. It did wonders for the old morale. We didn't stop grinning for the whole day.'

'I'm very glad to hear it.' Despite herself a small smile escaped.

'I'm here because it's taking for ever to walk anywhere in the America's Cup village. Found any bicycles for us yet?'

Custard was to regret his request when their transport finally materialised. At least it made a local paper notice them – but only to poke fun of their lack of uniform and deriding their choice of pink bicycles. Hattie repeated until she too was pink in the face that she couldn't get any other colour at such short notice and the shop was trying to get rid of them cheaply ('I don't bloody blame them,' said Dougie) besides it was such a cheerful colour and she had much better things to do than paint them all black. The only consolation for the team was the arrival of Mack's Mercedes. Each week Hattie organised a raffle for use of the pimp-mobile (as it was known) and boy, did they fight hard for it.

The same magazine who was due to interview Mack later that week was currently interviewing Henry Luter on his super-yacht, *Corposant*, which was moored in the America's Cup harbour.

'There aren't many people who have enough money to mount an America's Cup challenge,' the journalist started. 'You must be proud to be part of a very elite club now, Mr Luter.'

'Yes, I am.'

'Have you been bringing your corporate strategies to the running of your challenge as many syndicate heads have done before you?'

'I'm worth over ten billion pounds. It would be foolish not to have brought my strategies to the syndicate.'

'And how have they manifested themselves?' asked the reporter, who was well briefed on Henry Luter corporate strategies. She was tempted to add, 'You've obviously done the part where you fire everyone in sight until only the liars and the ruthless are left standing?'

'I believe in not letting anyone become complacent. Everyone has been constantly up against their opposite number on the second boat and there have never been any confirmed positions on the crew.'

'Not even your own?' she asked slyly.

'Not even my own position of strategist has been secured,' replied Luter shortly.

'As you know, the defender of the Cup has a great advantage over the challengers. What do you say about the rumours that the only reason you ditched the British challenge was so you could bail out the Spanish challenge and have more chance of winning the Cup?'

'Rubbish. Absolute rubbish. And I didn't *ditch* the British challenge. We had made only loose plans to enter the Cup. But when I heard about the desperate plight of the Spanish hosts, which put the whole event in jeopardy, then I felt I should step in and help out.'

'And you want to win?'

'I didn't personally invest fifty million pounds just to be a good loser.'

'Do you practise with your crew every day?'

'I have business commitments and various other appointments like today,' Henry swept his hand in front of him. 'But I know that *Phoenix* have been out practising today and I will join them later in the week.'

'And what about the current British challenge under Colin Montague? John MacGregor is at the helm. How do you feel about them?'

'I wish them the best of luck,' said Luter heartily. 'And let the best man win.'

The reporter took the interview to a more personal note. 'Will your new wife continue to stay with you down here in Valencia or will she be returning to one of the other ten Luter abodes?'

'No, my wife, Saffron, will continue to stay with me on *Corposant* and support me throughout. As long as there are enough shops.'

Henry Luter had married Saffron two years earlier. His dependable old boot of a first wife, who was a bit plain but had contacts in the army and navy world that Luter had found invaluable when he was first starting out in business, had been thrown out of her own house by a locksmith. Whilst Henry and Saffron were on the company jet bound for the Caribbean, a fax had arrived for the current Mrs Luter announcing her dismissal. She was given one hour to pack. She could take all of her personal wardrobe (because as the fax bitchily pointed out, the new Mrs Luter-to-be was not her size) but nothing else, and the butler would be watching her. Everyone was astonished – not that Henry Luter had taken up with a younger, more beautiful woman (his affairs had been oft documented), but that he had decided to marry her. He clearly thought his wife needed upgrading too.

'Is it true that you proposed to your wife within a few days of knowing her and she got on a jet with you that night, leaving everything she owned behind?' asked the reporter, looking at Luter's wolfish face, weak jaw, receding hairline and short bullish legs. *Not* a good-looking man. Nothing would be worth sleeping with that every night, she thought to herself. But then she remembered the golf ball-sized diamond she had seen on Saffron Luter's finger yesterday and reconsidered.

Luter chose to ignore the question. He smiled at the reporter. 'Let's talk about the design for my new boat, shall we?'

After the reporter had left, Luter summoned Jason Bryant to *Corposant*. Whilst he was waiting for him, he sent Saffron's maid Consuela to fetch her.

Saffron was sitting in front of the mirror and staring at her beautiful reflection. In the two years she and Henry had been married her life had changed beyond all recognition – which was precisely what she had wanted. Her appallingly middle-classed parents, who would insist on calling her Judith, had been quite bewildered when she declared her intention to go and find her fortune in London in the form of a rich husband. She knew she had just swapped one controlling man for another but dismissed the thought rapidly. She wouldn't be able to look like this with a cut and a perm four times a year at the local salon. It had all been worth it, she thought, tossing her head at herself in the mirror. The months of planning to get invites to the right events. The scrimping and saving for make-up and dresses whilst living in a rackety bedsit in Camden. And then finally the golden ticket. An invitation to the charity ball in the city. She had done her homework and had her eyes set on the prize. Henry Luter. One of the richest men in Britain. She needed to escape properly. To the frantic chunters of the guests around her, Saffron monopolised Luter for the evening. And he adored her blatancy. Yes, she had been right to want all this. No one could touch her now. Consuela tapped her on the shoulder and told her that Henry was waiting for her.

'I want you to wear that red Yves Saint Laurent dress tonight,' said Henry by way of greeting. They were dining with a few sponsors.

'But I was going to wear the green one from the new designer I found. He was sweet, he has a tiny shop now but—'

'No one will know who the hell he is. Wear the red one. All

the men have to want you but know that I'm the one who gets to fuck you. Don't make trouble, Saffron. You know what happens when you make trouble.'

Saffron fell silent as Luter went over to the salon table where the newspapers were laid out.

'The English papers have arrived. Have you seen this? Ha!' He thrust a rather cruel cartoon of Mack holding a collection box and rattling it outside Buckingham Palace's gates. 'That will teach the arrogant shit not to fuck with me. I'm going to break them. Every single one of them. Did he really think he could beat me? He's fielding a crew of nobodies. He hasn't got a chance. I hear they can't get any sponsorship!' he continued gleefully. 'We put everyone under contract so they can't sponsor anyone else. Colin Montague hasn't got enough money to see this through.'

He put his hand over her breast and didn't bother to remove it when Jason Bryant came in.

'How was practice today?' he asked shortly. Saffron tried to move away but his other hand at the back of her neck held on tightly.

'Fine. I'm not sure about that new mainsail. It doesn't seem as good—'

Luter dismissed it with an impatient motion. 'I paid thousands for that sail. It's got to be better than the one we had. It stays.'

'We saw John MacGregor's challenge today. They were practising not far from us.'

'And?'

A smile crept over Bryant's face. 'They are really not getting it together at all. Fabian Beaufort is their bowman and he was knocked overboard. They found him clinging to a line off the boat about five minutes later. They really are crap.'

Luter smiled too. 'People don't even know they exist.'

The Phoenix Challenge's finely oiled PR team made sure the Spanish people knew exactly who they were. Their personally monogrammed cars were everywhere and the Phoenix Challenge's motif was appearing all over town in stickers and posters on lamp-posts, billboards and pavements. Jason, of course, relished the exposure.

On the walk from *Corposant* back to the Phoenix base, Jason Bryant spotted Inky on her way back to the hotel.

'Hey, Pencarrow!' he yelled at her. 'We saw you practising today!' He ran to catch up with her, but Inky carried on walking. 'There must be more imaginative ways to drown your bowman than just chucking him over the side,' he commented coming alongside her.

'I wish I could drown you,' muttered Inky.

'Poor old Fabian. Does he know you all dislike him that much?'

'It was a simple accident, Jason. Could happen to anyone.'

Jason made a fake choking noise. 'An accident? You mean to say that Beaufort was knocked overboard?' he laughed. 'You mean you're still practising man-overboard procedures? Fucking hell, Pencarrow, we'll probably lap you on the course next year,' he said and strode off.

'You won't be bloody laughing next year!' Inky called after him with a lot more confidence than she was feeling.

Chapter 17

'I have been trying to get hold of you all day. What the hell is this all about?' yelled James Pencarrow down the phone.

Inky held the receiver slightly away from her ear and said gingerly, 'What's that, Dad?' She had just stepped out of the shower after a very long day. She sat down and started to towel dry her hair.

'This headline!' he said furiously shaking the paper in front of him as though Inky could see it.

'What does it say?'

'It says, "LAMBS TO THE SLAUGHTER".'

'Is it the *Local Farming Times*?'

'Don't get cheeky with me. It's a report about your performance. It says:

Colin Montague's bid for the America's Cup doesn't seem to be going well. His skipper, John MacGregor, has put his well-deserved reputation on the line with his choice of crew. Some would go so far as to say that he was being irresponsible to the British cause by indulging this whim. A peer of MacGregor was quoted yesterday, 'John can never resist a load of lame ducks but he is representing his country now and should have taken the very best with him.' A spy in Valencia who has seen both Colin Montague's and the defenders of the America's Cup, Henry

Luter's team in practice said, 'How many ways are there to say that the Phoenix Challenge are faster?'

'What the hell is going on? Are you sailing backwards?'

'We're a late challenge, Dad. The crew are just getting used to each other. What did you expect?'

'I expected better.'

Inky stiffened but tried not to take it personally. Sometimes her father was so desperate to slaughter the competition that he forgot who exactly was competing.

'It's not the America's Cup yet,' she tried to say lightly. 'Mack is leading the crew, surely that is good enough for you? Mack picked me.'

'Yes,' said her father darkly. 'I have been wondering about that.'

'What do you mean by that?'

'I'm worried about Mack,' her father confided. 'I'm worried that he's not a bit . . . you know.'

'Mad? Deluded?' snapped Inky.

'Well, the Cup in Auckland did take its toll on him. He's not as young as he used to be.'

'And you think he proved this by choosing me, don't you? My God! I thought you'd be proud that I'd been chosen for the America's Cup.'

'You only have to look at the papers, Inky, to know this is an embarrassment.'

'For you?'

'For the country,' snarled James.

'Oh, well, if it's just for the country. Look, Dad, we're doing our best which clearly isn't good enough for you but I'm afraid it's all I can do. Now if you will excuse me, Custard and I have to go out drinking.'

She calmly replaced the receiver and then sat staring at it for a minute. She was so tired of craving her father's good opinion, but she couldn't help it. The more he denied it the more she wanted it. She sometimes wondered if she had got involved in this whole America's Cup thing just to please him. 'Well, you cocked up on that one,' she said out loud to herself.

Custard and Inky were sitting in a small bar on the dockside much frequented by America's Cup sailors. Inky had dressed hurriedly in a pair of barely there beige shorts (her gorgeous long legs getting lots of admiring glances – attention Inky was completely unaware of) and a Montague Challenge T-shirt. She had slicked back her still-wet hair and her skin was a nutty brown despite the fact it was only spring. The crew had been out in Valencia for three months now. Her lips had no need of lipstick and the light bounced off the top of her cheekbones. The old-fashioned jukebox was playing The Corrs.

'Practice, practice, practice,' moaned Custard. 'What if we spend all this time practising and then next year, when we start the America's Cup, we find out we're crap and we're on the next plane home?'

'I can tell you we're crap right now.' Inky told Custard about the headline.

'Is it true that Mack used to teach Jason Bryant?' Custard shifted round so he was facing out on the room and leant both elbows back on the bar.

'Bryant and I were in the same youth squad taught by Mack.'

'I never knew that. You told me you were in the same squad as Bryant but—'

'I don't usually mention that we were taught by Mack. People always think I got a leg up because he's my godfather. Either that or a leg over with someone else.'

'Mack must be pissed off about coming up against Bryant. If we ever get that far.' They would have to race every other challenge in order to face Bryant and his crew who, as the defenders of the Cup, were guaranteed a place in the final races. 'He's a man of few words, isn't he? Most of them are "fuck".'

Inky grinned. 'But Mack never bears grudges and he always

apologises afterwards if he's gone too far.'

'He was being absolutely charming the other day with the old bloke Jack who maintains all the equipment. He'd been working late so Mack went and made him a sandwich.'

'Do you remember how Luter used to treat all the shore crew in Auckland like shit? Apparently he used to make Jack go and clean his car – and Jack's got an engineering degree.'

'What's the story with this Rafe character?' The crew were still deeply suspicious of Rafe. They hadn't even given him a nickname, such was the extent of their distrust.

Inky shrugged and took another swig. 'Mack said he was talented. He finds the wind.'

'Well, I've yet to see this so-called gift.'

'Fabian said he was a bit out of the running at the moment because of a love affair.'

'A woman?' said Custard in disgust.

'I don't know about his talent but experience is more important on an America's Cup boat. Rafe doesn't know the rules and he might lose us the race on that.'

'I think you have to be in with a chance of winning it first. At least you seem to be having a better time.'

'It's not as hostile as Auckland but still no one trusts me. Whenever I give an instruction, they always look over at Mack to see if he objects to it.'

'We're rubbish, aren't we?' said Custard gloomily.

'Yes, we are and it's nothing to do with any of your voodoo nonsense.'

Custard looked deeply offended. He was the most superstitious of all the crew. 'You wouldn't say that if my granddad was here. I swear that the day we had a banana on board the boat we didn't catch a thing. The moment I threw it overboard, we were overrun by mackerel.'

Inky ignored him. 'Do you know where the rest of the crew are tonight?'

'As long as they're not here, I don't care.'

Inky glanced round as one of her favourite songs came on the jukebox. 'Better Together', by Jack Johnson. One of the Italian crew stood by the jukebox. The flamboyant Italians, who had a long, proud and passionate history with the Cup, were often here, good-naturedly fighting with the locals over the football results. They were proving to be very popular and beautifully dressed in their instantly recognisable dark red and black designer uniforms. It looked as though even their calluses were manicured.

'He's been looking at you all evening,' commented Custard.

'Who has?'

'He has.'

Inky took a better look. His dark olive skin and short black hair were very attractive and his eyes were watchful and coolly appraising. She liked the look of him.

'Do you know who he is?'

'I think he's the Italian bowman. I can't remember his name.'

'He wasn't in Auckland though, was he?'

'I don't think so.'

Inky looked back to find him looking straight at her, with a faint smile playing around his lips. She hastily looked away.

'What is wrong with you?' demanded Custard. 'He's a good-looking bloke, isn't he? Go over and talk to him.'

'I don't know, Custard. I'm not sure I want to get involved with anyone right now.'

'Too late now, they're going,' said Custard in exasperation.

Inky looked over to see the whole Italian crew departing. The Italian shot one last look in her direction. Inky didn't know whether to feel relieved or upset at him leaving.

'Well, you blew it there,' said Custard. 'Besides, what's wrong with a one-night stand?'

'They might be OK for you but I want a relationship.'

'That's just a euphemism for a series of one-night stands, isn't it?'

'That is such a bloke thing to say. One day, Custard, love is going to punch you straight between the eyes and you'll be seeing so many stars that you won't know what hit you.'

Custard laughed. 'I'd like to see the woman who could do that to me.'

Inky was being besieged by all things Italian. After not really registering the team on her radar at all she suddenly seemed to be falling over one of their crew at least once a day. Last night she ate pizza and then dreamt about their bowman. Their bases were positioned next door to each other around the harbour and the crew had started to shout 'Ciao bella!' at her and blow kisses, often leaping to the barbed-wire fences to try and kiss her hand as though they were in a prisoner of war movie (they behaved like this to all the women; Inky much preferred it to the restrained Englishness of her own crew). Their bowman, however, wasn't as effusive as the rest of them. He merely smiled and waved at her but there was no doubt that his eyes lingered and Inky found herself applying the odd dab of lip gloss and mascara in the morning. Then her father called to tell her there had been a huge magazine article about the Italian crew detailing how wonderful they were and how strong a contender for the America's Cup. Could the bowman truly be interested in her, when she practically had to punch her way through the hordes of glamorous groupies waiting at the Italian compound gates?

'Has anyone mentioned dating outside the syndicate to you?' she whispered to Dougie during their morning briefing.

'No, why?'

'Oh, no reason. I was just wondering what the official position was.'

'Who are you thinking of dating?'

'No one.'

212

'Inky, are you dating someone?' whispered Fabian who was sitting behind them and listening in.

'No! I'm not!'

'What's this?' Custard's ears pricked up.

'Inky's dating someone but won't say who.'

'Why didn't you tell me?'

'I'm not dating anyone!'

'It's not the Italian?' All eyes went to Custard.

'IS ANYBODY LISTENING TO ME?' bellowed Sir Edward.

To add to Inky's embarrassment, they followed the Italians out of the harbour for that day's practice amidst lots of oop-laas from the rest of the crew. Marvellous, she thought, the only time the crew had shared a joke together and it was decidedly on her. She dived down below into the sewer as soon as she could and found herself the best position. Ho eyed her speculatively. He didn't like anyone messing up what he saw as his sails. Custard came down and sat beside her. Inky pinched him hard.

'Ow! What was that for?'

Now that all the syndicates were assembled in Valencia, Louis Vuitton, the main sponsor of the America's Cup, started their usual whirl of social events. They sent out invitations for a party to welcome everyone to Valencia. This was greeted with howls of derision from the crew (as far as they were concerned they had to spend over twelve hours a day in each other's company and any moment more seemed like absolute torture) which increased in volume when they learnt that it was strictly crew only – no partners allowed – and Henry Luter's crew, as the defenders of the Cup, would be the guests of honour.

By contrast Inky felt on top of the world. Whilst the rest of the crew were dreading the party and pleading with Mack not to make them go, Inky was hugely excited. It was a chance to see *her* Italian outside of the syndicate. Maybe too much time in the gym was making her delirious: it had been a while since she had fancied a man like this. She had never been so fit. Her clothes were starting to hang off her to the extent that Carla, despairing, began to make gallons of rice pudding for her to eat. Her stomach was like a washboard and her arms strong and lean. She bounced with energy and today she was positively in orbit.

She leapt into the common room which had just finished being built and started to forage through the pile of magazines that Hattie had just put there. She wanted to find the article about the Italian crew that her father had told her about again.

Custard was lying in a chair with a Spanish newspaper over his head. 'Inky, I know that's you and you haven't said a word yet,' he groaned. 'No one else could be quite so irritating. Why are you so full of energy? The rest of us are tired, you know.'

'Are you coming to the party tonight?'

'No.'

'Awww come on, Custard. It could be fun.'

'It doesn't sound like a lot of fun.'

'For me?'

'OK. I'll come for you.'

'Thank you,' said Inky, beaming. 'Anyway, Mack said he would take you all off the boat if you didn't go.'

'I know but let's pretend I'm doing it for you.' Custard got up and went towards the showers. 'By the way, the article about the Italian crew is in *Time* magazine at the bottom. I presume that's what you're looking for.'

Inky ignored his smirking and immediately rifled through the pile until she came to the US mag. She went to the nearest chair, sat cross-legged and flicked through the magazine until she found the feature. A huge five-page spread. Ahh, there he was with the rest of his crew. She bit her lip and smiled down at him. God, she really must get a grip, she was being completely pathetic. She read the text. Luca Morenzo, bowman. There was little detail about Luca except to describe him as 'the enigmatic lynchpin of the crew'. The article was very complimentary generally, emphasising how the 'Latin Rascals' had stolen the show. She flipped back to his photograph and stared at him for a while longer before following Custard to go and take a shower.

Back at the hotel, she was busy looking through her wardrobe trying to make a final decision on what she should wear tonight when a knock came at the door. Inky tentatively opened it to Bee.

'Oh, it's you,' moaned Inky. 'Thank God. I thought it was that terrible Fiona Hargreaves. She's convinced I'm shagging her husband, who must be the ugliest bloke on the shore crew, and keeps dropping by to check he's not here.'

'Well, it's your own fault for being so pretty. I can't stand her either. Always complaining. And she's certainly not making any friends by being so thin and then telling everyone how much cake she's eaten.'

'Come in, come in.'

'I was just too excited to wait for Rafe to get home, I simply had to come and tell someone.'

'What is it?'

'You know I've been looking round for somewhere more permanent for us all to live? Well, I think I might have found the perfect place!'

'Where is it?'

'Down on the waterfront.'

'Really?' said Inky doubtfully.

'Don't look like that. There's a huge amount of restoration going on down there and there's this absolutely gorgeous, crumbling old apartment block practically on the beach.'

Inky looked at her dubiously. Bee was the only person she knew who could use 'gorgeous' and 'crumbling' in the same sentence.

'They're doing it up a bit but, Inky, it has lemon and orange trees in the garden, which is admittedly a little overgrown, and wrought-iron balconies. It's called Casa Fortuna which I think is a good omen, don't you? I'm going to talk to Mack about it.' She looked at Inky excitedly and then suddenly clocked Inky's dressing gown. 'Oh! Are you going anywhere?'

'I'm trying to get ready for this party.'

'Of course!' said Bee following her into the bedroom. 'I'd forgotten that it was tonight. How exciting! What are you going to wear?'

Inky indicated a simple trouser suit which was hanging on the wardrobe door.

Bee wrinkled her nose. 'Darling, it's very nice for a lunch or something but this is a party! Have you got anything else?' She went over to the wardrobe and started bustling through the contents, emerging a few minutes later with a skimpy little black dress in chiffon held up by a couple of shoestring straps.

'Look! It will show off your long, fabulous legs to perfection.'

'I can't wear that!'

'Then why did you buy it?'

'I don't know. I must have been drunk. I bought it out of my winnings when we'd been match racing in Japan.'

'It's fabulous! You have to wear it! How were you thinking of doing your hair?'

Inky looked at her doubtfully. 'Like this?' she said pointing at her head.

Bee tut-tutted and hustled Inky towards her dressing table and sat her down.

Bee slicked Inky's hair back, leaving a few longer locks framing her face. 'You have the most beautiful hair, you know. Such a fabulous almost blue-black colour. You really are quite beautiful.'

Inky blushed and then peeped into the mirror. 'I do look nice!' she said in surprise. 'I was going to get my hair cut next week as well, I thought it was getting too long!'

'Don't do that! Leave it to grow a bit. Now, what shoes do you have?'

Inky pointed to pair of black slingbacks that she had been planning to wear with the trouser suit.

'Not sexy enough for this dress. What size are you?'

'Six.'

'Same as me,' said Bee happily. 'Back in a mo!'

Inky walked over to the boat house where the crew were meeting. Hattie had laid down the law at the morning meeting. 'If you're planning on drinking less than three pints then you go in official kit.'

'Three pints of what?' called someone from the back.

Hattie had ignored the voice. 'But if any of you are planning to get completely wasted then you go in your own clothes. I'm not having this syndicate's reputation blighted by drunken behaviour.'

'What are you going in, Hattie? Your nightie?' Fabian had shouted.

Feeling self-conscious Inky tugged at her skirt, her face hot as she approached the group. They fell silent and stared as she entered. Inky thought a few of them looked on the verge of a coronary. Oh God, thought Mack bleakly. How on earth am I supposed to police that? As her godfather he felt *in loco parentis* but there were some things that were simply out of his control.

Custard was the first to speak. 'Bloody hell, Inky!' he stumbled.

'Do I look OK?' she asked suddenly anxious, seeing that most of the crew were in T-shirts, that she was horribly overdressed.

'You look bloody fantastic! Too fantastic! The whole Italian crew will be on their knees! I think you should wear that on the boat. Everyone would be so busy looking at you we could just slip over the start line and be halfway down the course before they noticed.'

Despite their backchat this morning, the crew weren't really

217

enthused by the idea of this party and so had all turned up in their Montague Challenge polo shirts apart from Inky. 'So are you planning to get wasted, Inky?' asked Jonny gesturing at her mufti and proffering a beer.

Inky came and sat down next to him, shaking her head at the beer. 'No, I just wanted to feel like a woman.'

'I would love to feel a woman,' said Custard. 'Promise you'll introduce me to plenty, Inky.'

'I don't know any.'

'Then Hattie will have to. You must know all the PR totty, Hattie?' he called out to her as she entered the room.

'I wouldn't subject any of them to the likes of you,' she snorted and sat down next to Rafe.

Inky needn't have worried about being overdressed. The party's hosts were, after all, Louis Vuitton. 'Come on, Inky!' said Sparky as she had stopped to look round for Luca. 'You're holding everyone up. It's like the bloody desert in here.'

Sparky led the crew over to the bar. Inky finally caught sight of the Italian crew over to one side of the vast dance floor. She eyed them for a while whilst everyone had drinks and thrashed out that day's sailing. She was just about to suggest that it would only be polite if they went and said hello to their closest neighbours when Custard said, 'Come and dance, Inky.'

But Inky couldn't take her eyes off the Italian group. One of them was obviously re-enacting a scene from the boat today to roars of laughter. Luca was at the back, grinning at the antics of his crew mates. His eyes met hers and her stomach nearly fell through the floor. He nodded at her, still grinning. She hastily looked away.

'Come on, Inky,' pleaded Custard. 'Do you want me to die an old and lonely bachelor?'

'Oh, OK.'

Custard grabbed her hand. 'We have to dance over to that group,' he said pointing to a female-rich area.

Inky indulged him for a short while, then tried to steer him back towards the Italians. Every time she got close, however, either Fabian or Dougie would swoop down on her and drag her off somewhere else. Again and again she would try to manoeuvre closer, on one occasion just as Luca was seeming to edge towards her, but then Dougie arrived at her elbow with two fresh Moët et Chandon sip bottles and suddenly attached himself like a limpet to her side.

'Dougie!' she said in complete frustration. 'What is it now?' Poor Dougie. He was a kind of God on the water: decisive, quick and concentrated. But he was the complete opposite on land.

'I was going to talk to that girl but I think that's her boyfriend who's just turned up.'

Inky peered over to where he was pointing. 'I don't think so, Dougie. Looks more like her boss to me.'

'Do you think so?'

'I'm absolutely positive,' said Inky who wasn't positive at all. 'Go and talk to her.'

'Maybe I'll just go to the loo first,' Dougie mumbled and shot off.

Inky couldn't see any of the Italians now and with a sinking heart wondered if they had all decided to have an early night and go home. She dispiritedly started to follow Dougie upstairs to the loos to retouch her make-up which she was sure must be sliding off her face after her exertions with Custard on the dance floor.

She literally bumped into Luca coming out.

'Oh! Excuse me!' she said and then realised who he was.

He seemed undecided whether to talk to her or not, then bowed slightly. 'Your name?'

'Inky,' she said.

He screwed his eyes up at her and she suddenly deflated, thinking how useless the whole thing was. He didn't understand English.

'As in ink. In a pen,' she flailed around.

'I know perfectly,' he said. 'But they tell me your name is Erica.'

She grinned with relief. 'My brothers called me Inky when I was little.'

'It likes you. Your hair is the colour of ink. Was that why they call you that?'

'Yes. And because I didn't like doing homework very much at school. And they used to call me Irritating Inky.'

He laughed. His teeth were so white in contrast to the darkness of his skin.

'What is your name?' She would be damned before she admitted she knew it.

'Luca. Luca Morenzo. Would you like to come and have a drink?'

Inky smiled. 'Thank you.'

He waited for her whilst she went into the loo and feverishly checked her reflection. She hastily applied some lip gloss from the little evening bag which Bee had lent her. She didn't need too much make-up; she was bright-eyed and still flushed from dancing.

'Does your syndicate allow it?' he asked as she emerged. They started to wander back downstairs towards the loud noise of the party.

'Allow what?'

'You speaking with other syndicates? With me?'

'Of course!'

'I hear the defenders of the Cup will not allow it for their crew. The Phoenix Challenge. But of course, Henry Luter is English! Do you know him?'

'Henry Luter? I worked on his previous challenge in the last Cup.'

'You are a, what do they say? A veteran of the Cup?'

'This my second. And you?'

'Only my first. A virgin.' He smiled at her and held open the door back into the main room. Inky felt her stomach disappear. His manner was so friendly and easy that she felt she had known him for years.

They walked towards the bar where he got them two more sip bottles of champagne and then asked if she would prefer to go outside where it was quieter.

Luca and Inky wandered out on to the veranda of the old house. Inky had been so busy looking for Luca when they arrived that she had failed to notice how fabulous their surroundings were. The party was being held, in true Louis Vuitton style, in a magnificent old colonial house, with crumbling façades and huge windows. Out on the veranda, the geraniums were still flowering in huge pots. The reds and oranges clashed spectacularly. Most people were still dancing so they were quite alone outside.

Inky looked over the balustrade whilst Luca leant beside her. 'You speak wonderful English, where did you learn?'

'I come from the Amalfi coast in Italy. Lots of tourists and lots of English girlfriends.' His eyes glinted wickedly and Inky laughed.

'And the Cup? Have you always wanted to do it?'

'All my life. I want to be one of the crew who will finally bring the America's Cup to Italy. What about you?'

'Same,' she sighed. 'I mean, I don't want to bring the Cup to Italy,' she said quickly as he laughed. 'But I have always dreamt of competing in it.'

'Is this your dream come true? You are the only woman here, are you not?'

'I want to win it too,' said Inky firmly and took a sip of champagne.

'Ambitious and beautiful.' He smiled slightly and bowed his head. Inky could feel her competitiveness rising in her throat. He was patronising her. But then the Montague Challenge weren't considered a real threat for the Cup.

He might have discerned her feeling because he said quickly, 'We have a great deal of respect for your skipper. John MacGregor. He is a great sailor.'

'He's a great man too,' said Inky loyally.

'You come from a family of sailors?'

'Yes. My brothers are all offshore sailors though. When we were young they used to take our boat and sail it round Britain by themselves in their summer holidays. I was never allowed to go.'

'I think that would make you cross.' She liked the way his eyes creased when he smiled. Such dark eyes, with the colour and gloss of treacle.

'Very. Tell me about Italy. You said you come from the Amalfi coast?'

'Yes, have you been?' Inky shook her head. 'Most beautiful place in the world. To me, anyway. My family live the next village on from Positano. It is so beautiful that the artists came first and then the tourists followed. It is nothing but mountains and the sea. The mountains are so high you feel as though you are walking with the gods.'

'It sounds wonderful,' breathed Inky.

'It is. But difficult to live there. The tourists make it possible. Before they came, three quarters of us emigrated.'

'But not your family?'

Luca smiled. 'We stay. That's why I make a good bowman. What about you? Where do you come from?' He took another sip of drink.

'A place in England called Cornwall. It's very beautiful there as well.' Inky paused, wondering how to describe such a place to him. 'It's full of magic. It's so isolated, the families are ancient. You can't call yourself Cornish until your family has been there for more than five generations.'

'And your family?'

'We've been there longer than that. Not my mother though. My mother is from London.'

'Does she like it?'

Nobody had ever asked this before and Inky opened her mouth to say that she liked it very much but then suddenly realised this might not be true. 'I don't know,' she said honestly.

'Haven't you asked her?'

'No.' She paused slightly, embarrassed by this seeming lack of connection to her mother and slightly shocked too. 'Have you a big family?' she asked quickly to change the subject.

'Lots of brothers and sisters.'

'Do they all still live on the Amalfi?'

'We are a typical Italian family. We all live very close to each other. Blood is blood.' There was a pause and Inky felt him look her over appraisingly. 'You have lost weight since you arrive,' he stated.

'The gym. Mack insists that we are frighteningly fit.'

'My mama would have a fit if she saw you. She would think you are all bones. She hates the idea of the gym. "Luca!" she says.' He put on an exaggerated Italian accent. '"Luca! Why you go to the gym? You sail-a the boat, you make-a the love, you climb-a the steps! You do not need to go!"'

Inky laughed in delight. 'So you think I am too thin?'

'*I* think you are perfect.' After he said this, he shifted awkwardly. 'I'm sorry. I should not have said that.'

Inky's smile died slightly. 'Why?'

'I think we have been getting carried away because nothing is possible.'

'How do you mean?'

'We cannot see each other. I mean, I don't know if you would want—'

Inky cut across him. 'Why? Do you have a girlfriend already?'

He looked at her in surprise. 'No, I am single. I mean we cannot have girlfriend and boyfriend because of the Cup. My team want to win the America's Cup. We do not think of anything else. You would distract me.'

'How do you know I don't just want to sleep with you?' said Inky defensively. She didn't.

Luca looked surprised. 'I don't. But either way you would distract me. None of us needs distractions.'

Nothing like that had crossed Inky's mind and she turned away feeling bitterly disappointed and also ashamed, in a way, that she couldn't hide her feelings. 'I think I should be getting home,' she said gruffly, suddenly desperate to get away.

Luca caught hold of her hand. 'Inky, please don't go. I have liked talking to you. I'm sorry. We all make sacrifices for the Cup.'

Inky pulled her hand roughly away. The zealotry of the Cup struck her afresh. 'Does anyone think of anything else?'

Inky was furious as she walked home. Furious with Luca and furious with herself. His words implied that she wasn't serious enough about the Cup. Maybe she wasn't fit to be there. She had let down the crew and let down herself. She looked at her black chiffon dress in disgust. This was where feminist trappings got you. In all sorts of trouble. And the worst hit of all was a little voice which kept suggesting that if she really had been so attractive then Luca just wouldn't have been able to resist sleeping with her. No, the bottom line was that he didn't fancy her enough, which meant she had failed not only as a sailor but also as a woman.

Whilst Inky was stomping home, the rest of her crew were propping up the bar and wondering where she was. Over the course of the evening they had somehow managed to end up back to back with Luter's Phoenix crew who were looking incredibly smart in their tailor-made blazers and ties whilst they were a mismatch of jeans and chinos with Montague Challenge polo shirts. They could overhear several languages in the group. Because Henry Luter had come in at the last moment to take over the challenge there were many nationalities on the boat. Luter didn't care where he bought his talent in from. Jason Bryant kept looking over at them until eventually he came over. He wasn't popular with any of Mack's crew. Nearly all of them had crossed swords with him over the advancement of his career, and learnt the hard way that nobody stood in the way of Jason Bryant's ambition.

'Where's Inky?' he said swaying slightly. 'I need to put her straight on a few finer points of sailing that she might have missed out on from our youth squad days.'

'You're drunk, Bryant. Go home,' said Mack.

'No, no. I want to . . . ' His words trailed off as he clocked Mack. 'Mack! My dear old teacher! I thought you might have retired! Have you lost anyone else overboard? Or is that where Inky has gone? Have you lost Inky in the drinky?'

This was all too much for Rafe. He had been incredibly restrained all evening but now he pushed his way to the front and confronted Bryant.

Bryant peered at him. 'Ah, my predecessor! Ava sends her love. We were just saying in bed the other night—'

He didn't manage to tell them what because Rafe, without saying a word, punched him square in the face.

'Jesus!' said Mack staring at Bryant on the floor. He'd gone down like a sack of potatoes. Mack hastily stepped between the two crews, sensing an imminent punch-up.

'A private matter,' Mack said loudly. 'Girlfriend trouble.' He dragged Rafe away while physically pushing the rest of the crew to the other side of the room. One of the Phoenix crew was helping Jason Bryant to his feet and looking bemusedly after Rafe.

'Rafe,' Mack said shortly. 'You're going home. I'll walk you. Everyone else, finish your drinks and then go home. And stay out of trouble. I mean it.' He gave them all a piercing look.

As soon as Mack and Rafe left, the crew headed straight back for the bar (in deference to Mack's words choosing the opposite side to Phoenix), all talking loudly about what had just happened.

'That was fucking marvellous!' said Pond. 'Jason Bryant was the bloke who took Rafe's woman off him, wasn't he?'

'God, still waters run deep, don't they? Who would have guessed Rafe would do that?' said Custard.

Rafe and Mack walked in silence for a moment.

'Sorry, Mack,' said Rafe eventually.

'You're not sounding terribly sorry.'

'I'm sorry for embarrassing you and the syndicate.'

'But not sorry for hitting Jason Bryant?'

'God, no. Only wish I'd hit him harder. Hurt my hand enough as it is.'

'He's going to have a hell of a black eye in the morning.'

'Good.'

'Rafe, you can't smack Jason Bryant every time you meet him. We can't have you in the syndicate if you're going to do that. Besides, I know Jason Bryant, more is the pity, and I assure you that he will not take this lying down, so to speak. You'll be walking home one evening past a dark alley and then you'll find yourself with a broken leg, which won't be good news for any of us.'

'I promise I won't hit him again. Well, not unless he hits me first anyway. This was just something I had to get out of my system.'

'Fair enough. But is this entire America's Cup about Ava?'

'It's about winning.'

'Winning Ava back or winning the Cup?' persisted Mack.

'I don't know what it was at the start. I didn't want her back and yet it felt as though I couldn't live without her. It used to be about Ava but now I would like to win the Cup as well. The ironic thing is that I can't seem even to wind call. It's like I'm impotent.'

They walked in silence for a moment. Mack was thinking of the conversation that he'd had recently with the commodore of the yacht club. The commodore had been hearing about Rafe's lack of form and was demanding that he be taken off the boat and the second-crew man move up.

'Look, Mack. I know I'm not pulling my weight at the moment.' Rafe had worked hard at overcoming his problem; he hated being so affected by her. He wanted to be over her. But it was like sleeping sickness, the harder he worked the more it seemed to overcome him. He was like a seer who had lost his sight.

Mack looked at him steadily, weighing up the situation.

226

Eventually he said, 'Rafe, I know how brilliant you can be, you have absolutely nothing to prove to me.'

'I think I'm just having some difficulty in getting my confidence back.'

'It will come,' said Mack with certainty, privately hoping that it would be sooner rather than later.

Chapter 18

At the crew meeting the morning after the party, only Fabian noticed Inky creeping in at the back wearing a pair of dark glasses. Everyone else still seemed engrossed by the Rafe–Jason Bryant story. There were fewer frosty faces than usual when Rafe walked in. Out of sympathy for his cause and the fact that the Phoenix Challenge were so generally despised, good feeling for Rafe was running high.

Fabian, observing this, was amazed at what tiny things could rip a crew apart and how an unrelated thing, such as this, could start to pull them back together. It did help, he thought, that Jason Bryant was so dislikeable. A wry smile crossed his handsome face every time an image of Bryant's surprise as Rafe hit him came into his head.

His mobile went and he looked at the number. Frowning he took it to the back. Milly knew better than to call him at work.

'Everything OK?' he answered.

'It's Rosie. She's got a temperature and she's really listless. I'm worried.'

'She was OK last night.'

'I know but she didn't look well this morning and didn't have any breakfast.' Fabian had always left before Rosie got up.

'Perhaps you'd better take her to the doctor.'

'Can you come back?'

Fabian frowned. 'Why? She's OK though, isn't she?'

'Yes. I mean she doesn't have a rash or anything but her temperature is really high and I don't speak Spanish as well as you . . . '

'Well, it's really difficult here . . . Why don't you take her to the doctor and I'll come back straight after the outing.'

'OK, I'll call you later.' Milly sounded reluctant but rang off.

Fabian got sucked into his duties. The wind was quite light that day and when they gybed two of the spinnakers got snagged on the mast, so both had to be taken to the sail loft for repairs on their return. Then, after the debrief meeting, there was boat maintenance to do. Fabian had asked Custard to take over but Custard had been sent off with a winch that needed repairing. Fabian kept trying Milly on her mobile but with no success. It was late when eventually he managed to get away. He borrowed one of the challenge's pink bicycles and rushed back to the hotel.

'How is she?' he asked panting slightly as he let himself into their room. Milly was standing by the window. 'What did the doctor say?'

'She's fine. Just a bug. But no thanks to you,' snapped Milly.

'Where is she?'

'Sleeping.'

Fabian went to the adjoining door which led into Rosie's room and peeped round. He could see Rosie bundled underneath her blankets and hear her breathing. He gently shut the door and went back to Milly.

'I'm sorry. I couldn't get away.'

'Couldn't get away? Why wouldn't Mack let you?'

'I didn't ask him.'

'Why didn't you ask him?'

'Come on, Milly! She's OK, isn't she?'

'But you didn't know that! She could have been dying for all you knew!'

'But she's not! I thought you would call me if there was any real problem.'

229

'On your mobile which doesn't work out at sea?'

'But this is my job and the reason we're out in Spain in the first place.'

'I was scared, Fabian. She had a high fever and was all floppy. I didn't know what to do, I don't know how anything works in this bloody country.'

'Milly, I just can't drop everything as soon as Rosie gets a temperature.'

'I would have hoped your family would be your priority,' said Milly icily. 'Or are you too much like your father to care?'

Fabian stared at her and felt the blood draining from his head. He turned around and walked out of the room and out of the hotel. How dare she accuse him of being like his father? Didn't he, Fabian, stay when he could have left? Surely she knew how much he adored Rosie? He would never do anything to hurt her. But for all his indignation, a faint residue of guilt remained. Maybe he should have tried harder to get home. Milly was right, he didn't really know that Rosie was all right. Were there truly similarities between him and his father? Did his father love him as much as he loved the little bundle he had cradled? Would he have been able to leave if he had? Since joining the challenge, Fabian had been so busy that he had spent precious little time thinking about his father, something he reproached himself for now. He had been so excited when he'd learnt about his father buying another boat. He should have done something more with the information he had found out.

He had been walking blindly until then but now, slowing down and registering where he was, he redirected his footsteps towards the harbour. All manner of questions suddenly filled his mind. If his father had just taken off somewhere, how would he get around without his passport? The police had found it when they came to the house to ask questions. Where would he go first? Would he stay in Europe or immediately sail the Atlantic? Guilt flooded him again at his inaction. Well, he was going to do something now.

He had found out the type and class of boat that his father had purchased; now he looked through all the records at the Valencia yacht harbour (which was in a completely different place to the America's Cup harbour) on the off chance that his father might have visited. Although this was a terribly long shot, it made Fabian feel better. Then to keep his mind further off Milly and the row, he decided to go back to the base. The shore crew and the sail makers were still working away as he walked through to the offices and signed on to one of the syndicate computers. Racking his brains to think of ways to trace a missing person and boat, he entered various combinations of such in a search engine. For hours he looked for boat movements across the Atlantic. Then he wondered if his father might have sold the boat again to cover his tracks, and started to look for boats for sale. He looked in the sailing chat rooms to see if he might have left Fabian an obscure message there and he ransacked his memory to find some clue of where to look. The sheer amount of information and possibilities overwhelmed him.

Eventually he was forced to admit defeat. He didn't know what had happened to his father and had to entertain the thought that he might never know. Exhausted, he trudged home to a sleeping Milly and Rosie.

The next morning as everyone filed out of the morning meeting, Fabian glimpsed Rafe ahead of him. Suddenly he knew who might have some answers for him. Last night he had given up – perhaps he shouldn't have done. He caught Rafe up.

'Rafe! Can I ask you something?'

'Of course.' Rafe smiled at him and Fabian suddenly didn't know where to start so he plunged straight in.

'Em, would I be able to sail round Europe without a passport?'

Rafe looked slightly surprised. 'Yeah, it would be pretty easy. Your passport is rarely checked. Especially if you avoided the bigger ports and stuck to the small ones. You could always say you'd lost it somehow and were making your way up the coast to the nearest embassy. Why? Have you lost yours?'

'Not exactly. So it would be pretty easy to get yourself lost in the Med?'

'If you don't want to be found.' Rafe shrugged. 'Pretty easy to get yourself lost anywhere on a boat. It leaves no trail, no footprint to say you've been there. There are no roads to follow, no distinct paths. You can appear one day and then disappear into the night and nobody will ever know you've been. Sometimes it can make you doubt your own existence.'

'How safe is it in winter?' Fabian couldn't help asking. 'If you were a solo sailor?'

'Em, well that depends obviously on how good you are and how cautious you are. White squalls can strike without any warning at all.'

Fabian had gone quite pale, which prompted Rafe to ask, 'Are you OK? Is there anything I can do to help?'

'No,' he mumbled. 'But thanks.' Rafe hadn't said anything that he didn't know himself – if he were honest. But it wasn't something he had wanted to be honest about. He shook his head. Work. He had to concentrate. He forced the conversation to the back of his mind.

Later, after practice, the crew were gossiping about Jason Bryant and Rafe again as they left the boat and started to wander back towards their hangar. So distracted were they that Fabian was the first to notice it. He could only stand in front of the base with an open mouth. Mack practically bumped into the back of him.

'HATTIE!' bellowed Mack as soon as he too clocked the change. 'HATTIE, GET OUT HERE!' He'd left her in sole charge of a team of painters who were decorating the base that day.

She poked her head out of one of the windows. 'Oh! You're all back! We weren't expecting—'

'What are you trying to do to us, woman?! Come out here now!' he yelled.

The head disappeared and re-emerged a few minutes later in front of the hangar. 'What on earth is . . . ?'

Mack gestured behind her and then as she turned the smile slowly died on her face. 'Oh, no,' she whispered. She turned back to Mack. 'Mack, I didn't ask for this. You have to believe me. I can't believe it, but how . . . ?'

'What colour did you ask for?'

'Red. I asked for red. I couldn't remember the word, so I spoke in French. Rouge, I asked for rouge.'

'They must have thought you said *rosa*. *Rosa* means pink.'

'I can change it, I can make them take all the paint . . . '

'No. Besides the fact that it will cost money, we'll be the laughing stock with such a mistake. Not that we're taken terribly seriously anyway. The whole of the America's Cup has seen our pink boat-shed by now. We'll just have to pretend this is how we wanted it to be all the way along,' he said between gritted teeth. He stalked into the hangar with the crew following gloomily behind them.

'Great,' muttered Fabian. 'Now if we lean any of our bicycles up against the boat shed, we'll never find them again.'

Fabian wasn't the only one who was faint with disgust when Colin Montague (very taken with the whole concept) proposed changing their polo shirts to shocking pink and pairing them with beige chinos as the crew uniform. None of the crew would speak to Hattie for a week.

Chapter 19

Hattie was excited. This was one of her most successful projects so far and she was determined to enjoy it. She practically danced into the crew common room to tell them all the news.

'Now, you know that the BBC have been having a competition to name our new boat, which I think you'll all agree was marvellous news . . . '

'Don't they also have competitions to name guide dogs?' asked Fabian.

'And . . . ' said Hattie, ignoring Fabian. 'Not only do we have a winning entry but Princess Anne has also agreed to come to name the boat!' She looked excitedly round the group for their reaction. She thought she might have heard Custard say 'what a wank', but then decided she must have been mistaken.

'What's the name of the boat?' asked Inky.

'I'll read you the winning entry. It's from a Joshua Cornwell, aged nine. "I think the British boat should be called *Excalibur* because I think the British team are going to pull the sword from the stone and win the America's Cup."'

'I hope he's not holding his breath,' muttered Fabian.

Their new boat was arriving on a huge container ship next week. Mack wanted her named and in the water as quickly as possible so the princess agreed to fly out the following Saturday for the naming ceremony. Her visit was causing a terrible kerfuffle at the base. Some of the wives had been roped in to help Carla with the tea and for some reason everything had become terribly English. (As Carla had said to her husband in bed that night, 'One whiff of royalty and it's talk of cucumber sandwiches all the way. They're all as mad as snakes. Why would you put cucumber in a sandwich? I should think the princess is sick of English anyway and would like a good paella and some Valenciano orange juice.') The wives, however, were not to be distracted. It might be hotter than the desert but they were going to lay on a tea that would make their little corner of England proud. Salmon sandwiches with dill mayonnaise, Victoria sponge with raspberry jam and cream, fresh scones with real Cornish clotted cream which Inky's mother had mailed to Colin Montague's secretary for him to bring with him, gingerbread and lemon icing. Carla was terribly bad-tempered throughout and was heard to remark more than once, 'What would I know? I am simple Spanish woman.' So the sailors were sucking up to her like mad, drinking shot after shot of her gut-wrenching coffee and trying to smile at the same time. God, we'll all have nervous twitches from the caffeine by the time the princess tips up. She's going to think we've all got Tourette's, thought Mack.

Hattie insisted the *Excalibur* crew wear their best uniform of long beige shorts and freshly pressed pink polo shirts. (She called each crew member the night before to remind them to iron them and called Custard twice.) She had great trouble lining everyone up on the dock. Inky didn't want to stand on the side of the Italian syndicate. Custard didn't want to stand near the perimeter fence because there was a racer chaser he'd slept with hanging about and he didn't want to see her. But when he'd relocated next to Inky and made a joke about it, she hissed, 'She must have been attractive enough for you to sleep with but then you dump her. You're a bloody disgrace.' And then he didn't want to stand next to her either.

Eventually Hattie squeezed him in between Fabian and Rafe who were gossiping madly about an errant wife, 'And she was naked on the bed and at that point he came back with the nuts.'

'Oh, I hadn't heard about the nuts.'

'What nuts?' said Custard slotting straight in. Hattie gave one last lingering look at Rafe and went to speak to Inky.

'God, I really feel like some chocolate, don't you?' she remarked. 'I hate this rule where the syndicate can't have chocolate. Colin should at least install a vending machine in the ladies' loo,' she added jokily.

'Chocolate?' snapped Inky. 'Why would I want to eat chocolate?'

Hattie was taken aback. 'Em, no reason. I just thought . . . '

'And why should we have a vending machine in the ladies' loos?'

'Well, because, you know, women like to eat . . . '

Inky stalked off (which was irritating in itself because now she would have to slot her into place again). Hattie blinked after her and edged up to Mack.

'If you don't mind me saying, I think Inky seems more edgy than usual.'

'Definitely more sensitive,' commented Mack. He despised talking about anyone behind their back but he was desperate to know why she was so unhappy. Her behaviour had changed since the Louis Vuitton party. She arrived at work earlier than anyone else and left later. She practically bolted every time he tried to corner her for a chat.

'Why would she be so upset about chocolate? As though I was trying to poison her or something.' Hattie looked upset.

'She doesn't want to be singled out. She wants to think she's just like the rest of the crew.'

'But she isn't,' Hattie whispered in bafflement. 'Actually, I was going to ask her if she wanted to wear a skirt for the ceremony.'

'I don't think the skirt would be a good suggestion,' sighed Mack. 'But thank you for thinking of it.'

The naming ceremony went smoothly enough. The crew looked extremely smart in their new pink uniforms, albeit a little sulky.

(At least they now had a mutual hatred of something.) However, they couldn't help but feel a swell of excitement at the boat before them. She was profoundly beautiful, with sleek, clean lines and a smart white hull. Her name *Excalibur* was printed in swirling black letters. At last, here was the boat that all their dreams were based on. She was built for one purpose and one purpose only. To win the America's Cup.

They all felt a little choked when the princess said, 'I name this boat *Excalibur*. May God bless her and all who sail on her.'

The wives ran around afterwards, loading the trestle tables with food and drink and curtseying whenever they could. There was one slightly awkward moment when the princess asked if they had any mugs for the tea rather than the dainty, rose-patterned china. And she had to fly out quite soon afterwards but the food was greatly appreciated by all the press.

Hattie had been extremely busy persuading and arranging for all the British yachting press to come to the boat naming, not to mention potential sponsors whom she hoped would be wooed by the occasion. The next day she had arranged to take out most of them on the *Mucky Ducky* to watch the British sailors in action, which would also be the first time they would sail *Excalibur*. Everyone was tremendously excited about the new boat. Neville and the rest of the designers were out for the launch. Neville was looking about twelve, sporting a rather sassy new pair of sunglasses and making a huge fuss about the boat's skirt and the new keel which MUST NOT be seen. The press was already whispering about the 'rocket boat' whose keel had been skirted from the moment she had been cast. Even the painters had been forced to work inside the skirt so her secrets could not be revealed.

Mack would have preferred a week alone with the new boat rather than showcase her immediately to the world but he understood what a great press opportunity it was and superstition dictated that she couldn't be out in the water before she was named. As helmsman, he was under the greatest pressure out of all the crew and wanted to show them and *Excalibur* off at their best – especially since his latest press article was entitled, 'Has John MacGregor finally lost the plot?' It was with some trepidation that they prepared for that day's sailing.

'As you all know, Colin Montague is joining us today,' Mack said in the wind-up of his skipper talk to the crew. 'Can we try and limit the language a bit?'

'What fucking language?' called a voice.

'I did mean you, Custard. And also the death threats, the fights and the name calling.'

'And that's just you, Inky,' said Fabian.

'Just for today. Tomorrow you can go back to all of that. I think *Excalibur* will be a wonderful boat. But you will have to know her blindfolded. You have to learn her language. Every groan, creak and whisper means something. Even the key in which the wind hums through the sail has meaning. This is like beginning a love affair with a girl who speaks no English. Or boy,' he added with a smile, his eye falling on Inky. 'She's yours. Treat her well.'

Mack glanced out to where *Excalibur* was being prepared to go into the water, her skirt still firmly wrapped around her. The shore crew had been up all night making sure she would be ready. Her keel had been sanded and polished since dawn, one of the shore crew was hosing down her gleaming white deck and someone else was threading lines which had been soaked for hours to remove carbon dust. She looked proud and beautiful with a regality (utterly appropriate given her naming yesterday by a princess) that was at odds with the brutality and ferocity of the battles to be fought with her. Mack hoped she would live up to her name.

Colin Montague was deposited on *Excalibur* just before the tow line was cast off. Mack had suggested Colin should become *Excalibur*'s very first eighteenth man.

'What exactly is that?' asked Colin.

'It's a strictly non-participating position in the back of the boat, put in place so that syndicate owners could experience the thrill of racing without actually being in the crew. You don't always have to take up the position. Luter normally flogs it for thousands of pounds to one of his business cronies.'

Colin sat in the ice cream scoop at the back of the boat and was told by Mack that for his own safety he was not to move. The boat felt completely different to anything else that Colin had ever been in. She was gloriously complicated and yet stripped to nothing. Two huge steering wheels dominated the stern of the boat, which was where the afterguard lived and breathed. In the centre was the cockpit, absolutely stuffed with handles and pedestals, where the grinders' muscles would scream with pain. The most cruelly exposed of all the crew was Fabian, working at the constant mercy of breaking seas, using only his knees to grip the forestay. He once described it as like climbing a ladder whilst riding on a rollercoaster. Colin thanked the good Lord that he was in the comparative safety of the eighteenth man's position. He didn't feel as though he could really ask for a lifejacket while the crew, running up and down the equivalent of a bucking bronco, weren't wearing them.

After one of the RIBs had been to each boat and collected the debris from lunch and the crew had a last-minute pee over the side (Colin was too nervous), Mack asked the grinders to take up the mainsail. It rose slowly from the deck, the grinders pumping for all they were worth. And suddenly the air caught it and *Excalibur* was sucked into the wind. She heeled sharply and Colin slid down the side, and without anything to grasp, just dipped his toes in the water.

Excalibur and *Slayer* (*Excalibur*'s identical twin, created for her to spar with and crewed by the second crew; Sir Edward was sailing her today) were at opposite ends of the starting box and set on a collision course for each other. They came to within inches of the other boat.

'TACKING!' Mack shouted. Roaring with belligerence, Golly

and Flipper wound the winches for all they were worth. A good grinder can turn the handles nearly four times per second and they were certainly in that sphere. They exalted in the challenge. Custard and Dougie, pumped with adrenalin, trimmed the sails as they swung round, their eyes anxiously scanning the canvas. And *Excalibur* swivelled on a sixpence. Colin could have reached out and touched *Slayer* as he whizzed by her. The designers on board *Mucky Ducky* and out in Valencia for the launch winced.

Round and round the two boats went, the respective bowmen shouting out the distance between them. 'Let's go for a double tack,' said Inky.

'Let the grinders know. Three-second gap.'

Word was passed on down to Golly and Flipper.

'TACK!' shouted Mack again. Golly and Flipper wound in the genoa. The sails were set and Sir Edward eyed them thoughtfully from *Slayer*'s helm.

Without another instruction from Mack, Custard quickly flipped the mainsail back across the deck. They took *Slayer* by surprise and held her on the inside and away from the line until the starting gun was fired.

Colin was struck by the noise of *Excalibur*. He remembered vividly his first trip aboard an America's Cup-class boat. It seemed impossible that a boat could bear such stresses; each time one of the sails was trimmed the enormous pressure caused a bang of such fearful ferocity that he immediately expected major equipment failure. The lines carrying loads up to the weight of a double-decker bus were slowly eased by hand and they screamed and whined like souls in torment.

This was Colin's first visit to Valencia, business commitments having kept him in England. Mack had been slightly concerned at his apparent indifference. He wouldn't have to be any longer. By the time they had finished the race, two hours later, Colin was well and truly hooked.

For the tow home Colin came out of the eighteenth man

position to join the exhausted crew on deck. He felt stiff but alive with energy. Mack spoke to him for the first time in over two hours. 'How was it?' he asked.

'Amazing! Absolutely amazing!' Colin said, eyes gleaming. He collapsed down on the deck, next to Mack. 'She's a wonderful boat! How did you like her?'

'Wonderful. Need to get used to the steering but wonderful. The designers have done a fine job. Look, we have visitors.' Mack pointed.

Colin looked. 'Who is it?'

'*Corposant*. Henry Luter's yacht.' The huge super-yacht had sneaked up on their shoulder. The rules of the Cup stated that they weren't allowed within a certain distance, to guard against espionage, but they were close enough to see Luter on deck, leaning over the rail, smoking a cigar and watching them.

'Probably trying to psych us out.'

Further down *Excalibur*, Inky and Custard were watching too.

'What a wanker,' commented Custard.

'Who's that just joined him?'

Custard squinted at the figure. 'Must be his new wife. Didn't you read about it? I think her name is . . . em, it's a spice . . . ' He tried to remember the article. It must have been about eighteen months ago that it came out. He'd been interested to read about his old boss and had felt more than a faint stirring of lust when he'd looked at Luter's wife's beautiful photograph.

'Cinnamon? Paprika?'

'Saffron, idiot. Her name is Saffron.'

Inky took another look at her. 'Yes, I remember reading that he'd got remarried now.'

'She's beautiful.'

'Yes, stunning, isn't she?'

'Wonder what she's doing with Luter?'

'His kind eyes probably.'

Custard laughed but didn't take her eyes off her. Her blonde hair was tied loosely back and she was wearing a full white dress which the breeze caught slightly through the rails. She stood a slight distance away from Luter.

'I think she's too thin,' commented Inky.

'Hark who's talking.'

'I'm not thin. I'm slim. There is a world of difference. Besides I eat loads and she looks as though she might gulp down a couple of painkillers with some coffee for the day.'

Custard could see what she meant. There was a nervous look about her. Like she was a young, frightened horse about to bolt. He was intrigued by her. 'She looks different though, don't you think? A bit like an ordinary girl who's been dressed up for the day. Like a doll.'

Inky was bored of the discussion. 'God, Custard, it's like talking to a girlfriend. What is it with you today?' She smacked him and started to talk excitedly about *Excalibur*.

Custard joined in but his thoughts were still with Saffron Luter.

Inky called home that night to tell her parents about *Excalibur*. Her mother answered the phone. 'Darling!' she said, her voice filling with pleasure. 'How nice to hear from you! How are you? How is Valencia?'

Inky indulged her mother briefly, answering all her questions whilst all the time bursting to get to the point of the call.

'Mum,' she said in the end. 'Is Dad there? I've got something really important to tell him.'

Mary tried not to sound disappointed when she said, 'Of course, darling. I'll just get him.'

The gruff tones of James Pencarrow came on the phone. 'Inky? How was the boat launch? It was today, wasn't it?'

'That's what I called to tell you, Dad! *Excalibur* is the most amazing boat . . . '

Chapter 20

With the America's Cup less than a year away, Mack knew that the requests for press interviews with the crew would start soon. So he insisted that all of the crew go along to Hattie and take one-on-one media training. Hattie had been thrilled, not so much at putting a reticent crew through their paces but at the prospect of legitimately spending time alone with one particular crew member. After a difficult session with Custard, who either joked around or frowned and said he didn't really get it (and in the end they decided it was best for him not to say anything at all), she waited anxiously for her next and last appointment of the day, frenziedly pinching her cheeks and checking her hair in the mirror.

Rafe popped his head round the door. 'Are you ready for me, Hattie?'

Hattie bit her lip. 'Absolutely.' She had been discovering things about Rafe's life which intrigued her and those dark eyes had been popping rather too frequently into her thoughts lately.

After she had rather shyly taught him some interview techniques and they'd talked about the messages she needed him to get over to the media, Hattie noticed Rafe was starting to look more and more out of the window. Granted this wasn't a particularly enthralling subject but . . .

'Sorry, Hattie. The wind's doing something interesting. Have we got much more to do or would you mind if we finished this up on the RIB?'

Hattie was about to say they were nearly finished anyway but then said instead, 'Of course we can finish this up on the RIB.'

As Rafe gave her a careful hand in, Hattie blushed at the memory of when he first saw her, legs apart, knickers flashing, astride a giant inflatable. 'What are you going to look at?' she asked hastily to cover her embarrassment.

'I just wanted to see how this felt actually out at sea. See if there are any patterns.'

'Couldn't you talk to Laura the meteorologist?'

Rafe smiled and glanced across at her as he started the engine. 'I never have a clue what she's talking about.'

They travelled slowly out of the harbour, obeying the stringent speed limits until they hit the open sea and then Rafe opened the throttle. Hattie found herself hanging on to the side for grim death, bouncing along and wishing she'd worn her sports bra.

Eventually they slowed down and Rafe stopped the engine. The silence was almost deafening. They were completely alone and the shore was only just visible in the distance. The sea had looked so calm from shore but the boat bobbed viciously around. Rafe stood at the bow and looked out over the water. It was almost a full ten minutes before Hattie said again, 'What are you looking at?'

'The wind shifts.' He came and sat down next to her, completely at ease with the motion of the boat. 'I'm trying to learn as much as I can about this piece of water.'

'Is it different from anywhere else?'

'Of course. I've been going down every day to speak to the local fishermen as they come off their boats. It strikes me that they would know more than anyone. Do you know about match racing, Hattie?'

She blushed. 'Not much. My family sail but none of them match race.'

'I didn't know much before we started. But the more I do it, the more I think I like it. In fact I'm starting to love it. The yachts may only be ten metres apart but it's as though they are in different parts of the world. Just that short distance apart and they are subject to different currents, wind and wave patterns. The wind is the most important factor of all. It's my job to tell Mack where to find it and I'm being singularly crap at it. One day I can do it, the next I can't. It used to come as naturally to me as breathing and I never questioned it.'

'It will come back,' said Hattie urgently. 'It will.' Stories of Rafe's brushes with brilliance which then disappeared completely the next day had been circulating.

He smiled at her. He couldn't explain to her how he used to be able to feel the wind's erratic mood changes, shifting thrusts and climbing vortices. He couldn't tell her that the sleep he once welcomed now contained constant images of a white curved body diving into the water. 'It feels as though someone has cut the ground away from me.'

Hattie didn't know what to say. She knew about Ava through the crew's gossip but felt ill-equipped to say anything.

'At least it feels better to be sailing, but I really want to succeed at match racing. It's so frustrating not to be better at it.' He paused a moment and obviously decided to move the conversation away from him because he asked, 'How are you settling in to Valencia?' It was a shame because she could have stayed talking about him for ever. It was a rare insight.

'I like it. At least I think I do. I haven't been able to see much of it yet.'

'Mack's working you hard?'

'No harder than the crew. And you? Do you like it here?'

'It feels more like home to me. I'm more used to the Mediterranean.' It was true. Everything seemed familiar to him, the adverts for soap powder, the smells of cooking, the layout of the supermarkets.

'My father says it's not a real sailor's sea. Is that true?'

Rafe looked surprised. 'The Mediterranean is the sea of winds.

The air you are feeling on your face now must have come straight from Palermo.' He paused.

'Tell me more,' said Hattie.

'About the wind?' Hattie nodded. 'Well, the gregale is a really ferocious wind. It comes from Greece but meets nothing until Malta. Which makes it impossible sometimes to get into the harbour there. Once Churchill and Roosevelt tried to meet in secret off the coast of Malta. The gregale kept them out at sea for five days and they nearly called off the meeting. Imagine a wind being able to affect the outcome of a war.' Hattie smiled. 'Then there are the desert winds which are called the sirocco and can bring sand from the Sahara all the way to Italy. In Sicily more than three days of sirocco can be used to excuse crimes of passion.'

They sat in silence for a second. 'How are you settling in to the hotel now? Do you still sleep out on the balcony?'

'Yes. I think they're getting used to it. The maid used to bring all my bedding in every morning and remake the bed but now she just makes it up out there. How are you getting on?'

'Fine, never have enough plug adapters, but fine!'

Rafe grinned. 'I don't own anything to plug in.'

'How are you getting on with the crew?' Hattie was curious to hear.

'OK. I've never really sailed with strangers before. I'm used to just doing something without communication. When sailing with my dad, we became so used to one another that we didn't really have to speak any more. I suppose that's what we're aiming for but in the meantime we have to say everything out loud. It slows everything up. It's harder than I thought it would be . . . I suppose we ought to be getting back. Mack might be wondering where his RIB has gone,' said Rafe.

'I suppose,' said Hattie in a small voice. 'Thank you for bringing me. It's been so interesting.'

Rafe smiled at her and Hattie felt her stomach drop, her eyes fixed on that full sensuous mouth. 'You're welcome to come out with me any time, Hattie.'

Rafe was an intensely private person but he couldn't have explained how he was feeling to anyone even if he wanted to. The only person who had some sort of inkling was his Aunt Bee, but there was a limited amount she could do for him. There were days where she couldn't even reach out and touch him. Outwardly he looked unaffected: he was good-natured and smiling with the crew, taking all their banter with good spirit; he played with the syndicate children and he was co-operative with Hattie when the rest of the crew really couldn't be bothered.

But inside, he felt as though his heart had been irreparably broken. Just as he thought he had swept all the pieces up, he would find another one, nestling in the dust under the sofa. Everywhere he went, he was reminded of Ava. The colours of a sunset reminded him of a dress she loved. The patterns in the sky of one of her paintings. He was starting to question his own motivation in coming to Valencia. He hadn't stopped wanting her back but logically he knew that nothing would change the fact she had been unfaithful to him. Someone once said that love was blind, but they didn't say it was also deaf, dumb and desensitised as well. He couldn't reason with himself.

One night, he was so desperate that he called Ava's mobile, prepared to hang up if she answered, simply to hear her voice on the answering service message. Instead of Ava's voice, Jason Bryant's slightly mocking tones came through. 'If you want Ava Montague then you'll just have to wait your turn . . .'

Rafe hung up. He has to put his mark on everything, thought Rafe bitterly. Almost like he's branding her.

It didn't help that the Phoenix Challenge was so high profile. Their PR team had made sure that everyone knew Jason Bryant was the man leading them to victory. They had even gone to the expense of plastering billboards with Bryant's picture and the caption: 'The America's Cup. Spain won't be left without it'. There didn't seem to be a day that went past without one of the Phoenix syndicate cars whizzing by, mocking them on their pink bicycles, or an article in the press, carefully leaked, where they reported on the latest technology the team were using direct from Henry Luter's development department. Everywhere Rafe looked they seemed to be jeering at him and he was sure they would never beat *Phoenix*.

Things were made much worse by the fact that he had never been in one place for so long. When he signed up for the challenge, it hadn't occurred to him it would be such a problem but as time ticked on, he became ever more restless, fighting urges that were put in place the moment his father set sail down the English Channel and away from England. Before he could have followed those urges and similarly sailed away but now something stopped him and it wasn't just that he knew his issues with Ava weren't resolved and would never be if he left Valencia. His father's solution was always to move on to the next port; Rafe was no longer sure whether it was his solution (although they were from dramatically different backgrounds; maybe he had more in common with Fabian than at first appeared). Ironically the one thing that helped Rafe was the one benefit from staying put – a growing friendship with the rest of the *Excalibur* crew. Slowly the crew were beginning to trust one another and unite. A fascination with match racing also put its seal on him.

Because they were in training, late nights and drinking were strictly banned so he took out his frustration in the gym and as such was becoming wickedly lean and toned. He had always been of medium build and height but now had filled out dramatically, putting on about a stone in muscle.

Sir Edward came to talk to Mack in the gym one day. He watched Rafe for a few minutes pummelling a punch bag as if he would like to kill it.

'How's Rafe's form?' he asked.

Mack glanced over to Rafe. 'Patchy,' he said quietly. 'But he's trying.'

Unfortunately, thought Sir Edward to himself, no one has won the America's Cup by simply trying. 'How are the electronics lessons going?'

'Good.'

'Have he and Colin Montague spoken yet?'

'No, not yet.'

'Will it be a problem? I mean when the racing starts, Colin will be out here a lot more. How does he feel about Jason Bryant and Ava?'

'Colin hasn't said but I do know that he and Ava aren't speaking. He doesn't even know if she's over here with Bryant or back in England. She hasn't told any of the family.'

'Might be worth him trying to find out.'

'Yes, I see what you mean,' puffed Mack slowly, pushing an arm press, loaded with weights.

'We don't want Rafe any more disrupted.'

'I'll get Hattie to remind me when Colin is visiting next.'

'I'm sure she will,' said Sir Edward dryly.

Something in his tone made Mack look up. 'What do you mean?'

Sir Edward realised that Mack hadn't noticed Hattie's slight crush on Rafe. 'Nothing,' he said hastily. 'Do you need to press so many weights? You might give yourself a hernia. I think I'm going to have to sit down. You're making me feel quite exhausted.'

'Have you tried not concentrating?' asked Fabian whilst they were waiting for Mack at their morning briefing. 'Maybe wind-calling is like some subconscious thing where it won't work if you try too hard.'

'I've tried everything,' said Rafe, broodingly watching a fly at the window. He was developing a real hatred for flies. There were no flies out at sea.

'What about just not thinking about Ava?'

Rafe fixed him with a look. 'Have you ever been in love, Fabian?'

'Of course!' blustered Fabian. 'Tons of times. That's when you can't stop wanting to shag someone, isn't it? Doesn't last long though . . . '

'I think you might be talking about something else,' said Rafe. 'Have you tried—'

'For God's sake!' exploded Inky. 'Why don't you suggest that he tries dressing up as a rain cloud whilst we all dance round naked eating salt and vinegar crisps? It might come back if you stop bloody talking about it. And I don't know how you can be so fatuous, Fabian,' she viciously spat out the f's, 'saying you've never been in love when you have a child with someone. You're all abominable.' She stormed off to get some coffee from the back of the room.

'What's she talking about? I said I'd been in love tons of times. What's eating her?' said Fabian.

'I think it might be a matter of who's not. Man trouble,' said Custard darkly, who had just joined them.

'She needs to stop behaving like one.'

'I think this is more of the Latin variety.'

'Must be difficult for her,' said Rafe who had the benefit of an outsider's point of view. 'After all, the America's Cup is a man's game. Created by men, evolved by men and played by men. Must be difficult to know where that puts her.'

The others stared at him as if he were mad. 'Anyway,' said Custard. 'I think we should try the salt and vinegar crisp thing, I love them and it might just work.'

Everyone witnessing Fabian's flippancy that morning would have been surprised to know that he had a heavy heart. The past has a funny way of rearing its head when you least expect it. He had been looking in one of their many cases, which Milly hadn't unpacked due to their lack of space, for his old copy of Sir Francis Chichester's *The Lonely Sea and Sky*. He was sure he had been reading it before they left and he wanted to lend it to Dougie. Dougie had never been offshore racing so he thought it would be a good book to start from, before the days of satellite navigation and hourly weather reports, when you just set off with a fair wind, some charts and your velvet smoking jacket. Fabian was just thinking how much he would have liked to have belonged to that era when he came across his father's watch. He had fallen back on his haunches, feeling as if all the air had been punched out of him. Since his foray on the computer and his conversation with Rafe, the realisation that he might never find his father had been slowly setting.

He carried the watch over to Milly, all thoughts of Dougie's book forgotten.

'What's that?' asked Milly who had just read *The Hungry Caterpillar* three times in a row to Rosie.

'My dad's watch.'

'Oh.' Milly put a hand out to touch him.

'Why would he leave it behind?'

'I think he left it for you.'

'Something for me to have, you mean?'

'Yes.'

'As though he'd died,' murmured Fabian still looking at it.

'How do you mean?'

'I mean it's something that you would leave to your son in your will. I think I've started to think of him like that. Every time I look at Rosie I simply think how much he would have loved her. As though he were dead.'

'How long ago is it now?'

'He disappeared just before I met you, so it must be two years now.'

'Two years,' said Milly in wonderment. 'Can it really be that long? So much has happened.'

'Why hasn't he contacted me?'

'I don't know,' said Milly simply. There was a pause and then she added softly. 'Do you still leave your mobile on for him?'

'I changed provider last month,' said Fabian bleakly. 'He won't have the new number. I used to leave it on all the time, hoping that he'd call. It's been more than two years. He's been killed sailing that yacht. He's dead. He must be.'

And to that Milly didn't have any answers because she privately thought that he must be too. She went forward and gently kissed him on the cheek, then moving down to his mouth, kissed him again. She could feel how tense he was but suddenly he relaxed against her and pushed his hands into her hair and kissed her back hard.

'I love it when you wear your hair down,' he murmured starting to kiss round her eyes.

'Too much of it,' mumbled Milly back.

'Can we go to bed?'

'Of course,' she said and took him by the hand to lead him to the bed. Usually Fabian took the initiative but this time Milly sensed he needed looking after and sat down next to him, gently removing each article of clothing one by one. She dropped kisses on his shoulder as she went and then, pushing him back on the bed, straddled him.

They made love that night as when they had first met and Milly, snuggling into the crook of his arm, thought she should be at her happiest. After all, between the demands of the Cup and family life, nights like these were rare. But instead she was filled with foreboding. Fabian had only made love to her like that because he was in pain and needed comfort. Once again she was overcome with fear that he was only hers in adversity.

The next morning, Milly, feeling terribly down, answered the door to Bee. 'I was just popping to the shops,' said Bee. 'Do you need anything?'

'A new life?'

'I'm not sure I can get one of those but what about some bottled water?'

Milly laughed and said that bottled water would do very nicely. 'Come in. Sorry for the mess. It's not the ideal place for children here.'

'Never mind, we'll be moving to the new apartments soon and that will be a lot better.'

'I hope so. Rosie has a new trick of waiting until I go for a pee and then running hell for leather for the balcony. We always have the balcony doors open because the new air-conditioning seems to have a mind of its own. I'm having to barricade her in the loo with me.'

'Let's go and have some lunch out,' said Bee. 'Forget washing and chores for the day, Bring Rosie and let's go and out and have some nice food and wine.'

After Milly had changed Rosie twice (the second time because she immediately spilt juice down herelf) into a gorgeous sundress she had made, they met outside the hotel and set off along the seafront to one of the many restaurants on the Paseo de Neptuno. Bee was looking lovely in a pink strappy dress with a huge hat and espadrilles.

'You're so brown,' sighed Milly. 'I'm absolutely milk white apart from little bits.' Milly was wearing a mini-skirt with a stripy top and a huge brooch.

'Been sunbathing. I unfortunately have a book-shaped shadow over my tummy though.'

'Are you reading a lot?'

'No. Just dozing off with it. You go to the beach with Rosie though, don't you?'

'I know but I spend so much time making endless sand-castles and then persuading her not to eat them that I never seem to be able to get my top off.'

'I love Rosie's dress.'

'I made it. Does it look a bit homespun?'

'No! It looks wonderful!' She looked at Milly in amazement. 'You are so talented! It's just beautiful.'

'Do you want to sit outside?' asked Milly to cover her embar-rassment.

'Yes, please.'

'Thank God. I daren't let Rosie walk through any restaurant.

She squeezes everybody's bread roll as she goes past.'

Bee laughed. 'It's so blissful being outside. There's such a wonderful breeze coming off the sea. Rafe says it's the *poniente* winds.'

The waiter presented them with menus and fussed over Rosie. 'Let's have a jug of *agua de Valencia* to start with,' she said and he set off for the bar. 'I'm getting quite addicted to the stuff.' It was a potent cocktail of fresh orange juice, Cava and spirits.

'I love the way the Spanish make you feel so welcome with children.'

'I know. One thing I don't miss about darling England. But it must be hard for you with Rosie under school age?'

'A bit but I would be even more worried about sending her to school here with the language barrier if she were older.'

'I know poor Ann Jenkins is getting quite desperate. Her little boy Stuart is dyslexic so she's having awful trouble finding a suitable school.' Bee had become a bit of a matriarch to all the wives since they had arrived – because she was so sympathetic and truly listened to them – and her door seemed permanently ajar making it easy to pop by and say hello. 'Do you think we should all do some language classes or something?'

'That would be fun! Something for all us Excalibur widows to do on the long evenings. I can't wait until we move into our new apartments. Things are so cramped, I say one thing to Fabian whilst we're in bed and Rosie could answer me from next door. Are you thinking you might be staying a bit longer then?'

'Rafe seems settled.' Bee took a huge slug of her drink. 'I don't suppose he really needs me here but I can't help thinking my sister would have wanted me to stick around for him. Besides, it's wonderful to be together with him after all these years and I am enjoying it out here now.'

'What was Ava like?' asked Milly shyly.

'Beautiful. Headstrong. Inclined to look at what a person could do for her rather than the person themselves. I think she thought that Rafe was going to be the next big thing. But he never wanted that.'

'Jason Bryant seems a strange contrast from what Fabian has told me about him. I mean Rafe is so sweet with Rosie and so kind.'

'Jason Bryant is the next big thing though, isn't he? Henry Luter's rock star.'

The waiter came back for their order and another roll for Rosie whom Milly had been feeding like a little bird. 'I'll have the mussels, *gracias*,' said Bee whilst Milly still perused the menu. 'This is my treat,' she urged. 'Have anything you like.' Milly chose a paella.

'How is Fabian coping with all the pressure?' asked Bee when the waiter had gone.

Milly was about to say he was fine but her tongue had been loosened by a couple of glasses and Bee's eyes were so kind that instead she said, 'I'm so worried, Bee.'

Bee touched her hand. 'What about?'

Milly looked over to Rosie who was content, jabbering to her dolly in her own special language. 'Well, Fabian and I haven't been together for very long and this America's Cup is all so new and everyone is so glamorous that I can't help thinking he might have his head turned. He's so beautiful,' she mumbled.

'He is that,' sighed Bee, a fervent admirer of beauty in other people. She hastily glanced at Milly, wondering if it was the wrong thing to say, but Milly hadn't noticed.

'I can't think why he wouldn't stray.'

'Why would he?' queried Bee. She had heard mutterings from the other wives about Fabian's past but not being overly prone to gossip had never enquired any further.

So between some pasta arriving for Rosie, which Milly cut up very small, a bottle of white wine and the mussels and paella, Milly told Bee their story, leaving out any pertinent bits about his father.

'How does Fabian feel about Rob now? I mean, has he recovered?'

'He often talks about him and he's tried writing to Rob's parents.

He says he feels guilty about the chance he has been given.'

'He shouldn't. From what Rafe has told me Fabian deserves to be on that boat. Is he ever tempted by the drink and the drugs any more?'

'Well, he drinks a bit. I mean, with the rest of the crew, but never really to excess. And he has never done drugs since Rob died. I think it put him off them for good.' Milly paused. 'I absolutely dread *Excalibur* being successful and yet want it so much for Fabian at the same time. I see the groupies swarming all over the other syndicates and I don't know if Fabian will want to stay once he starts being successful and getting the taste of money again. I . . . I wouldn't blame him, you know. I don't really feel as though he belongs to me anyway. And it's not terribly thrilling for him to come home to me and Rosie. The other night he got back and my fringe was stuck together because Rosie had put peanut butter on my hairbrush and Rosie was so pleased to see him that she had a wee on the carpet.' She smiled but felt quite desperate underneath. 'I love him so much, you see. I just want to keep my family together.'

'I think you underestimate yourself and the appeal of family life to Fabian. I don't know him very well but it strikes me that he takes his family very seriously.' Bee patted her hand reassuringly.

'Takes Rosie very seriously anyway.' Milly shook herself slightly. 'I'm sorry. I shouldn't dump on you.'

'Of course you should. We've only got each other out here.'

'We really ought to do more all together. I mean, all the wives. After all, we're out here for a long time.'

'We'll do those language classes,' said Bee firmly. 'I'll sign everyone up. The men will have to babysit for us for a change.'

'It would be helpful to have someone local who could help us when we move into the new apartments,' said Milly. 'Fabian wants broadband connected and I simply do not have a clue who to call about it. Could you go and ask Mack about that?'

'Why me?'

'Oh, Bee, you're so good at that sort of thing. Everyone loves you.'

'I'm not sure Mack does. We don't particularly get on. We're too different.' Bee snorted. 'Can I take your leftovers for Salty?' she said pointing at Milly's plate. 'He adores paella.'

Chapter 21

Bee decided to take the bull by the horns and go down that afternoon to see Mack. They usually finished sailing for the day by five. Once at the syndicate she took the short cut through the sail loft and, merely pausing to nod at Rafe who was helping to recut a sail, went to the back of the boatshed where Mack was normally based. Bee poked her head round the door of the office. 'Hello! Have you seen Mack?' she asked Tim Jenkins.

'Em, I think he's on the *Mucky Ducky*, Bee. He said he can't get any peace here. You know Colin Montague is out here for the King of Spain's visit tomorrow.'

'Oh, I forgot! Rafe did mention that. I won't bother Mack today then. It was nothing urgent.'

'No, he's not in a meeting or anything. He won't mind. Thanks for lending Susan that book, by the way. She's desperately trying to finish it so she can get it back to you.'

'Oh, no rush. I wasn't reading it anyway, it was just propping up my bedside table because one of the legs was broken. I've slotted in D.H. Lawrence now. He's doing it *much* better.'

She left Tim thinking what an exceptionally nice lady she was. Sexy too. Always dressed in completely inappropriate clothing though. You got the impression that she'd never even set eyes on an anorak and if she did she might cut holes in it and make Salty wear it.

She bent down and knocked on the window of *Mucky Ducky*,

which was bobbing up and down in the water. Mack, who was working at one of the tables covered in papers, glanced up. He got up and started to move towards the hatch. A second later his head popped through.

'Bee,' he said politely. 'What can I do for you?'

'Have you got a moment?'

'Certainly. But you can't come aboard in those.' Mack pointed at Bee's high heels.

Bee defiantly slipped them off her feet and held them in one hand whilst Mack came up on deck and gave her a hand aboard – not easy in a pencil skirt.

Bee felt at a disadvantage without her extra few inches and also slightly silly in her bare feet. She drew herself up to her full height and prepared for battle.

'What can I do for you?'

'Well, some of the wives and I feel that maybe a local person might be able to help us all settle in together when we move into Casa Fortuna. You know, help us get insurance or buy unusual things. I've been thinking about it a lot on the way down here and I know that the crew spend so much time together anyway but maybe we should start doing some social things together as well. Help everybody to relax – the partners too – and get to know each other. We've been out here now for more than six months and it's high time we all did something together.'

There was a pause and then Mack commented, 'You seem to have settled in nicely.' He'd dropped by for a drink with Rafe the other night (Bee had been out with one of the wives) and couldn't help but notice how homely Bee had made the place, shipping out her spotty Cath Kidston china from England and some books and belongings. 'Considering you're not staying long,' he added.

'Em, yes. Well.' He seemed to be laughing at her slightly. 'I'll stay as long as Rafe needs me here,' she commented shortly.

'Rafe seems to have settled in quite well. I think you could probably go home if you wanted to. I'm sure that he would hate to think that he was the only thing keeping you here in Valencia.'

Bee shuffled uncomfortably. Had this insufferable man who was now silently laughing at her been more approachable then she would have explained that she was actually starting to see why the Cup was so addictive and she thought she might like to stay and see how it all turned out. She was enjoying the dramas which unfolded like a soap opera in this legendary race day by day. Every morning she woke up with a sense of great excitement for the next instalment. Sir Edward often popped by for some tea and, after some pretend arm bending and some cake, kept her up to date with all the developments in their syndicate and the others. She adored hearing about the passionate Italians, the chaotic French and the friendly South Africans. She enjoyed the company of the wives and girlfriends with all the problems they brought to her friendly ear. Not to mention the fact that she loved being with Rafe and didn't think she could bear to leave him now.

Mack decided to save her face just as she opened her mouth to let a barrage of abuse escape. 'I think all your ideas sound great.'

'I know that . . . Sorry? What did you say?'

'I said I think you have some good ideas.'

'Oh,' she said, the wind thoroughly taken out of her sails. She'd had a huge speech planned about how Mack didn't care properly about the partners of the syndicate and how they were important too and now she couldn't say anything. Damn him. John MacGregor was really a thoroughly annoying man.

Colin Montague came along the pontoon and started to climb aboard the *Mucky Ducky*. 'Bee!' he exclaimed. 'How very nice to see you!'

Mack quickly outlined her idea to him. 'That sounds marvellous!' Colin beamed. 'Mack was just saying today that the staff need a bit of a break and of course we should get a local person to help you all. We've been so wrapped up in sails and boats that I should have thought about that. I'll get Tim on to it.'

The next day, Colin Montague came to find Bee.

'Tim might have already found someone to help you,' he said. 'She works part time at the local tourist office and speaks wonderful English. Her name is Maria.'

'That's marvellous news!' said Bee.

'And I've been thinking long and hard about your idea to integrate us all more socially and since Mack said that none of the syndicate has had any time off for a while, I wondered whether we should all take a trip up to Barcelona. Really kick things off in style.'

Milly was so pleased when she heard that Hattie had arranged air-conditioned coaches for everyone. The air-conditioning at the hotel had been playing up so much that she would have been delighted to simply drive around in one for the day. Everyone else was tremendously excited to be having a day out and talked enthusiastically about Gaudi's Temple and the Ramblas. Now the crew were more at ease with one another, a day out together didn't seem unbearable and there were even a few jokes and ribbings which would have been unthinkable a few months ago. They had become such a part of each other's lives that it was strange to see them with their other life partners. Ho looked at odds with his petite, blonde wife whom he so obviously adored, and Fabian looked strange with his little girl in his arms rather than a spinnaker pole.

Milly looked apprehensively across at Fabian who was sitting with Rosie on his knee pointing at things out of the window. They'd had a huge row last night. One of the wives had brought down a bin bag of clothes that her little girl, who was a year older than Rosie, had grown out of since they'd been in Valencia. Milly had very gratefully accepted them. Fabian had completely lost his rag when he found Rosie contentedly playing in what he called 'someone else's cast-offs'.

'We're not some fucking charity case,' he hissed at Milly after they had gone to bed.

'I know. But it was so kind of her to think of us and Rosie *did* need—'

'We can go and buy what Rosie needs.'

'Don't be such a snob, Fabian! Everybody passes on kids' clothes! It's nothing to do with affording it or not.'

'I'm not having people think the poor Beaufort child is down on her luck and needs looking after.'

'Why would they do that?'

'The Beaufort name is mud and I'm not having Rosie bear the brunt of it.'

'But I don't matter because I don't bear the Beaufort name,' Milly snapped, anger filling her voice.

Fabian stared at her. Milly never got angry. 'What are you talking about?'

'I'm good enough to bring up your child and play house for you but I'm not good enough to bear the precious Beaufort name, am I?'

Fabian opened his mouth to reply but at that point Rosie, hearing the raised voices, started to cry.

Milly got out of bed and, without another glance at Fabian, went to see to Rosie. She spent the night in the single bed next to her cot. The next morning she and Fabian didn't mention the row but stepped politely around one another. Sometimes she really wished she could see what Fabian was thinking.

She wouldn't have been any the wiser if she could, because Fabian's thoughts were very confused indeed. He was intoxicated with the sense of success that the Cup had brought him. It made him realise how long he had been out in the wilderness and how much he had missed his former life. Whereas he had been quite happy back in England to bite the bullet and make do with his reduced circumstance, he now felt constrained by Milly and Rosie. Things were shifting. The sailing fraternity seemed more willing now to move on from the tragedy of Rob's death; he felt more settled inside himself about it. Rosie wasn't a baby any more, which seemed to cast doubt on his decision to stay with Milly. Had she simply been the best option for him at the time? Had he been grieving for his father and simply vulnerable to her kindness? Was he too young to settle down and have the responsibilities of a young family? He couldn't separate anything out. The nature of the commitment required for the Cup tends to make the sailors withdrawn but with Fabian this was doubly apparent. He was aware how distant he was becoming from Milly and felt powerless to do anything about it. But it was like biting the hand which fed him. He needed her warm-heartedness and sweetness. He looked across at Milly who had now moved down the coach to speak to Flipper's wife and felt terribly ashamed of himself for having such disloyal thoughts, and for making such a fuss about the clothes – how trivial. He had been surprised at her outburst last night, he hadn't realised that getting married was so important to her.

Their first stop was Gaudi's Temple and the coach deposited them all outside. Milly clipped Rosie into her buggy and together they lifted her up the numerous steps to the cathedral. 'Sorry,' panted Milly. 'I should have put her in at the top.' She grinned at Fabian and he knew she had already forgiven and forgotten their row. He put his hand on the back of her neck with sudden affection.

'She's getting heavy. I don't want you to put your back out.'

They strolled hand in hand around the beautiful place, losing the rest of the crew in the vastness and straining their necks to look up at the top of the columns which represented trees in a forest. They tried to point out some details for Rosie and then laughed at themselves for their efforts. The things they were pointing at she wouldn't possibly be able to see.

'Isn't it amazing that Gaudi could plan such a thing? Knowing that he would never see it finished?' sighed Milly. 'That really is the work of a lifetime.'

'It is amazing. I can't think beyond next year,' said Fabian simply.

Rosie seemed to be getting hungry and told her parents so in no uncertain terms. There wasn't a café at the Temple so they told Hattie they would meet everyone back at the coach and then set off to find a place to eat.

They found a sweet little place just around the corner and tentatively asked if they could order something to eat for themselves and heat up some food for Rosie, even though it was still early. They placated Rosie with some breadsticks whilst they were waiting. Fabian reached for Rosie's rucksack to unpack her food.

'Jesus Christ! What the hell is that?' He jumped up and threw the rucksack on the floor.

'What?'

He peered tentatively at the rucksack. A little snout was poking out. 'That!' he pointed.

Milly laughed. 'Oh, that's Rosie's rat.'

'Her rat? She has a pet rat?'

'It's plastic. We found it at the supermarket, God knows why they were selling it, and she just wouldn't let go of it.'

'You bought her a plastic rat?' said Fabian, grinning. 'It nearly gave me a bloody heart attack.'

The waitress came for their order, smiling shyly at the laughing Fabian who was now falteringly trying to order coffee in Spanish. She was young and pretty and didn't even look at Milly or Rosie as she repeated words for him to copy. Milly tried not to mind that he was flirting with her.

'Who are you sending the postcards to?' Milly asked after the waitress had left. She pointed to the small bag Fabian had purchased at the Temple.

'Oh, maybe my mum or the Thorntons,' he said awkwardly.

'Still no reply?' she said needlessly.

'No. I don't really expect one. I just thought they might like a postcard.'

264

'Like Rob might send if he were here?'

'Something like that. I just feel that people are forgetting him. It's great that everyone is starting to forgive me and people are being so much more friendly. But I feel I have to remind them about him.'

'You mustn't feel guilty about your place on the crew. You're on *Excalibur* because you're exceptional.'

Fabian was silent a moment, then he admitted: 'Every time we go out I'm determined to do well, as if I might save Rob this time.'

A sudden shout of laughter distracted them and they both looked over at a table of young people, probably around their age, across the other side of the restaurant. They were clearly making the most of their weekend, larking about and kicking into huge jugs of beer and cocktails with the remnants of the weekend papers nearby. The girls had already spotted Fabian and looked back at them. Fabian smiled at the prettiest one.

The waitress brought their coffee and the heated-up toddler mash. Fabian and Milly scurried around Rosie, checking her nappy, blowing on her food, tying bibs and testing milk, pausing only for the occasional gulp of cooling coffee. Fabian shot the occasional glance over to the other table. He knew that being a father to Rosie was infinitely more precious but he couldn't help but envy their carefree and child-free state. Milly saw him watching. 'I was just remembering what it was like to have a long, boozy lunch followed by afternoon sex and a siesta,' he commented.

Milly grinned and spooned more stewed apple into Rosie. 'Or to leave the house without being weighed down by a tonne of baby paraphernalia.'

'And plans to rival the D-Day landings.'

'Before I go to sleep, I calculate how many hours I'm going to have to the nearest minute.'

Milly watched Fabian laugh but wondered if he came back

to her that day on the Rochester yacht only out of duty. She wondered if he chose to stay only because his father did not.

Whilst the rest of the *Excalibur* crew was enjoying themselves in Barcelona, Inky had used the time to take a quick flight back home. Her father had called the night before to tell her that her mother was ill.

'Ill with what?' asked Inky quickly.

'It's pneumonia.'

'Pneumonia?'

'She's out in all weathers in that stupid garden of hers. Caught her death of cold and now it's developed into pneumonia.'

'Will she be OK?'

'The doctor says so.'

'I'll come home.'

'No, don't do that . . . ' said her father, but not in a very convincing manner, which made up her mind for her. God, thought Inky. She must be ill.

'Everyone's going to Barcelona for a jolly tomorrow. I'll catch an early flight and be back for the team practice on Monday.'

Her father didn't argue with her.

Inky fretted all the way home. Bizarrely the one question which played over and over in her head was the one put there by Luca. Did her mother like Cornwall? Did she? She searched for one memory which would prove it. She found one of her mother waiting with a Thermos and dry clothes for her and the boys to come back into the harbour after a storm. When she looked closely at the memory her mother was pale and worried and didn't join in the voracious chatter about what a fabulous adventure it had been. She also remembered her when she received a letter or catalogue from London, how she would light up like a firefly. And then with a pang of guilt, also remembered how uninterested she had been.

Getting off the plane, she waited for her connection to

Newquay and then spent the taxi ride home desperately trying to get hold of her father on his mobile until she remembered that you weren't allowed them in hospitals. She was feeling increasingly panicky and wondered why on earth she hadn't asked her dad which hospital her mother was in. Her mother had never been ill before. She would just have to ask the taxi to wait and hope he'd left her a note at home.

She rushed into the kitchen at home and was surprised to find her father on his hands and knees. 'How is she?' she gasped.

'Thank God you're here, Inky,' said her father.

'Is it that bad?' she asked. 'Which hospital is she in?'

'Hospital? She's not in hospital. She's upstairs,' he said calmly, still ferreting around in a cupboard.

Inky visibly slowed down. 'Upstairs?'

'Yes. The doctor has put her on antibiotics.'

'So she's not dying?'

Her father looked up in surprise. 'No, she'll be fine.'

'But you said, "Thank God" . . . '

'I can't find any more dog biscuits for Nelson and your mother's asleep. Thought you might know where she keeps the new packs.'

After Inky had paid off the taxi and peeped in on her sleeping mother, she came back down to the kitchen. 'So she's going to be OK?' she said just to make sure.

'She's going to be fine,' he said in a surprised, no-fuss voice.

'But you asked me to come home.'

'I didn't! I said you shouldn't come home.'

'Yes but in a voice which clearly said I should.'

'Don't be ridiculous, Inky. What nonsense. Anyway I am glad you are home, your mother has never been ill before and it's been very difficult for me here. The bloody Aga never seems to cook anything properly; I have no idea how she has managed to feed us on that damn thing all these years. Everyone keeps calling me to ask how she is. I've got to take Nelson out twice a day and feed him as well as look after your mother. Could you look in the freezer and try to find some food we can actually cook?'

Inky stomped upstairs feeling furious with her father for dragging her home needlessly. Furious, that is, until she sat down next to her mother to wait for her to wake up. She studied her pale face, her dark hair puffed around her on the pillow, and felt pleased that she was able to come back for her. Although she knew Mary would be fine, she still felt shaken. What a cliché: not knowing what you have until you lose it. What would she do without her mother? What would this house become without her? It was only home to her because her mother was there, with her patience and Sunday roasts and the importance of going out with socks on.

Her mother started to stir and Inky put a hand out to touch her arm.

'Erica?' she murmured. 'Erica, is that you?'

'Yes, Mum, it's me. Inky . . . I mean Erica.'

She started to wake up more fully. Her eyes opened wide and she struggled to sit up. 'What are you doing here? Is everything all right? What's wrong?'

Inky smiled. 'Everything is fine. I came because Dad said you were ill.'

'You came because of me?'

'Yes.'

'Darling, you shouldn't have done that. What about the Cup and the crew?'

'It's fine. They're all off in Barcelona for the day. I came here instead.'

'But you missed Barcelona?'

'I don't mind. It's all a bit sunny out there anyway. I miss the weather here.'

'I told your father not to tell any of the children. You could do without me disrupting you.'

'You haven't disrupted me.'

'He hasn't called any of the boys as well?'

'No. I think they're all offshore anyway.' She didn't like to say to her mum that she thought the only reason her father had called her was because he wanted a hot meal. 'How are you feeling?'

'OK,' she said nodding firmly.

'How long did the doctor say it will take?'

'A couple of weeks of bed rest and antibiotics. That's all.'

'What on earth were you doing out in the garden to catch pneumonia?'

'Just weeding. I need to have something to do.'

'Why don't you go back up to London for a while? I mean, when you're better.'

'Maybe I will. But I like to be around when any of you come home.'

Inky noticed suddenly that the glass on her bedside table was empty and went into the bathroom to fill it up. 'Do you want the curtains open?' she asked on her way back. 'Or will that hurt your eyes?'

'No, that would be nice.'

Inky tugged them open, 'It's a shame that you haven't a view of the sea,' she commented looking down over the garden. 'You should have the bedroom at the front of the house.'

'Oh, I always thought this one was slightly bigger,' said Mary idly. 'So nice to use the curtains for once. When I first arrived here from London, I used to draw the curtains every night until your father pointed out that it was needless – there was no one around to look in.'

Inky suddenly wanted to ask her all manner of questions. She wanted to know about her life in London, who she was before she became just their mother. She wanted to know all sorts of things. But she noticed her mother's eyes were getting heavy again. 'I'll leave you,' she said drawing the covers up to her mother's chin.

*   *   *

Inky didn't waste her afternoon there. She went out and made several stops. When she got back her mother was sitting up in bed again and sipping tea.

'I've been to the library and got you some books and also some talking ones in case your eyes got tired.'

Her mother smiled in delight. 'Thank you!'

'I'm afraid I didn't know what you would like so I had to make some guesses,' Inky said awkwardly, feeling quite ashamed that she didn't know what her mother read. She'd had to ask the librarian what she thought Mary would like and was even more ashamed to find the librarian not only knew her mother but also treated her, Inky, like a long-lost friend because her mother had talked so much about her.

'And I got you a new nightdress and a funny sort of jumper thing that the lady in the shop said was a bed jacket – for when you're sitting up in bed.' She produced it out of the bag. 'It has ribbons on it,' she pointed out needlessly.

'Darling, it's beautiful.'

'And I also got some food for Dad and Nelson and I'm going to make you some chicken soup. Is that OK?'

'Lovely.'

She turned on her heel and made to go.

'But darling, don't spend all the time in the kitchen. I mean, I'd much rather you stayed and talked to me if that's OK with you.'

Inky put the bags down by the door. 'That's OK with me,' she said coming back in.

Chapter 22

Jason Bryant narrowed his eyes and shielded them against the sun as he focused on a scene unfolding across the harbour.

'What is it?' asked Henry Luter, stopping alongside him. It was a day of one of his rare practices with the crew.

'It's Excalibur. Have you noticed how furtive they are around their boat?'

'Everyone is furtive round their own boat.'

'But they are exceptionally jumpy.' It was absolutely de rigueur that every syndicate cloak the keel of their boat in a skirt to prevent prying eyes. Everyone was desperate to see what was under everyone else's skirt. 'One of the ropes of their skirt just got caught as the crane was lowering the boat into the water. All the crew were shouting at the driver to stop until Beaufort leapt up and cut the rope.'

'Beaufort? Is that the blond one?'

'Their bowman.'

'Did you see their keel?'

'No, it was too quick for me.'

'Who's their boat designer?'

'I don't know. No one special. Certainly not one of the famous designers.'

'You would need years of experience to create a great boat. It's nothing.'

'Maybe,' muttered Jason. 'Could we send someone over to take a look?'

'As long as they can't be traced to us.'

'Thou shalt not get caught. I owe one to the Excalibur camp anyway. I'd like to get even, though I'd prefer a more direct method.'

Luter looked sharply at him. 'Don't you dare put this syndicate at risk,' he snapped. 'If you have a debt to pay then there are other ways . . . '

'How do you mean?'

'I have a better idea.' They were interrupted by the sight of Saffron coming towards them. Luter liked her to come and wave them off from the pontoon when they left. 'We'll talk about this later.' They both watched Saffron's progress in silence and Jason glanced over to Luter expecting him to make some comment about her, some sort of explanation for her but he didn't seem to have noticed anything. To Jason, she looked decidedly ill.

The smile she gave them didn't stretch to her eyes. 'Have a good practice,' she said.

'Going out today?' asked Henry.

'I have no plans to.'

'Go shopping,' he instructed.

'I don't need anything. I thought I might help Consuela with—'

'You don't help anybody. Go to that underwear shop we both like.' Luter met Jason's eye with a smirk. 'Get something for tonight.'

Saffron looked away in embarrassment. Jason thought she was about to protest again but she bit her lip and gave a sharp nod instead. Still she didn't meet their eyes. Jason thought that any minute a gust of breeze might take her away.

Sir Edward Lamb was staring at his fresh fruit salad of kiwi, nectarine and raspberries and thinking he would like nothing more than to tuck into some bacon and eggs. And maybe some black pudding too. He narrowed his eyes and glared at Carla, their resident cook, who glared back at him.

'Pig and eggs is only Sundays, Mr Lamb. You know that,' she called out to him. 'There is rice pudding here, if you want.'

Sir Edward walked over to her and drew himself up to his full height. 'No English person eats rice pudding for breakfast, Carla.'

'Mr Mack tell me lots of carbohydrate. So I give lots of carbohydrate. You want some pasta?'

'No, I do not.'

'Well, you no important. Only my boys and girl important.' She beamed at Inky who came up for second helpings of rice pudding. 'The crew have to eat lots.'

The two trestle tables heaved with food. Besides the pasta and rice pudding, a huge fruit bowl piled with apples, pears and bananas, a bowl of fresh fruit salad, platters of meat, chicken and smoked fish and baskets of the bite-sized *xuxo* – little Spanish sugary croissants. Cartons of chocolate milk adorned the plastic tables where the crew sat on the makeshift garden furniture. They used to ask Carla to heat up great mugfuls for them until she found out they were adding their eye-watering espresso shots to make a sort of mocha latte and she soon put a stop to that.

Sir Edward dejectedly sniffed and then made his way to the crew meeting. All this America's Cup malarkey was very bad for his health. He was craving bacon and eggs when he used to be happy with porridge and stewed prunes (*so* good for you, full of antioxidants). He would sip aloe vera juice from his flask and contemplate his kidneys whilst that PR girl waffled on about her interviews.

When the crew of *Excalibur* and the crew of *Slayer* went out for their normal practice, their neighbours, the Italians, chased them down the canal out of the harbour. They wondered whether the Italians had noticed their skirt incident the other day but it appeared that the only skirt the Italians were interested in was

Inky. All the way out their tender was tooting the slower *Mucky Ducky* who was towing *Excalibur*. '*Ciao!*' They waved. '*Ciao bella!*' they called to Inky, who dived into the sewer as soon as she was able. 'I hope your crew are faster than your tow!' one of them yelled.

'God, they speak good English,' muttered Custard. 'I wish I knew some Italian. What's "wanker" in Italian, Rafe?'

'I don't know.'

'Great. You know how to ask for directions but you don't know anything useful.'

Once they hit open water, the Italians overtook them with much waving and good-natured jeering and went off in a different direction.

They spent the morning trying out new sail combinations with their sail maker Griff Dow on board *Mucky Ducky*, taking countless still shots of the sails, and one of the shore crew constantly videoing the action. Griff Dow had only been in Valencia a short while and was proving, thankfully, to be quite an asset to the team. Inadvertently Mack found that Luter had actually done them a favour by refusing to release their sail company from his contract, along with all his other suppliers. The sail company had been outraged at his heavy-handed treatment of the new UK challenge and, although they had stuck by the terms of their agreement with Luter, had promptly (but secretly) put Mack in touch with an ex-employee of theirs who had just set up by himself. They found out that Griff Dow was a passionate America's Cup aficionado. He was over the moon when Mack called to ask him to take over the project, revealing a private database he had been recording of every sail that every challenger and defender had been using since 1983.

As was their wont, at lunchtime they stopped for their debrief and to eat. The crew were all lying on the deck waiting for Carla to appear in the launch with food. Mack had decamped to the *Mucky Ducky* to talk to Griff, and Custard was the only one standing. He had his eyes cupped against the sun, watching the two Italian boats who had edged closer in the course of the day and were now just in view. He frowned.

'Custard! What are you looking at?'

He didn't answer even when they threw a tube of sunscreen at the back of his head. Inky went to stand next to him.

'What's up?'

'Something seems to be going on.'

Inky too sheltered her eyes and watched the Italian boats. On one of them there was a sort of panic going on. They couldn't make out much but people were running up and down the boat. And then they spotted, way up the mast, a small figure hanging, caught in the rigging. Inky's hand automatically went up to her mouth. 'Oh no,' she whispered. Custard quickly put his arm around her. Neither of them said anything but both of them knew that the bowman was the crew most often sent up the mast.

'This is no time for smooching,' called Sammy.

'Someone is hurt on the Italian boat. Scan the radio frequencies.'

Inky couldn't bear to look any longer and came to stand next to Dougie. Mack and Griff re-boarded the boat from *Mucky Ducky* just as he found a channel with a lot of babbling Italian voices. 'Rafe, you understand Italian, you listen.' Grabbing the radio, Inky shoved it at him.

Rafe listened for a few moments. 'Someone's hurt up the mast. They're trying to get him down.' Instantly all eyes swivelled over to the Italian boats.

'Who?' said Inky urgently. 'Who do they say it is?'

'They haven't mentioned a name yet.'

'I'll take one of the launches over,' said Mack. 'See if they need any help. Pond, come with me.'

As Mack and Pond zoomed off in one of the quicker RIBs, the crew took it in turns to borrow Sir Edward's binoculars and silently watched the drama. The one who had the binoculars kept a running commentary going for the rest of the crew.

Whoever the crew member was, he was certainly unconscious. Maybe even dead, thought Inky, but she couldn't voice it. The rest of the crew stood sympathetically round her. Inky hadn't confided in anyone since the Louis Vuitton party so no one had a clue what was going on but they could see how distressed she was.

Within a few minutes, Pond's voice crackled over their own radio frequency. 'Tommaso the midbowman has a broken arm and we are taking him to shore. All is well. Out.'

The crew's eyes went to Inky as tears started dropping one by one down her face so Sir Edward and Custard bustled her on to the *Mucky Ducky*. They sat in the cabin whilst Sir Edward went to get her a glass of water. Custard anxiously watched him go. He would have much rather gone and got the glass of water. He'd never really seen Inky upset before.

He put a tentative hand on Inky's knee but that seemed to make her cry even more, so he removed it. His sidekick seemed to be taking an inordinate amount of time over a glass of water so he thought he'd better try by himself. 'Em, Inky? I thought it was the bowman, Luca, that you liked?'

She nodded and relief flooded Custard. Ah, a simple misunderstanding then.

'But it was Tommaso the midbowman who was hurt!' he said triumphantly. 'Not something to be joyful about, I know, but it wasn't Luca.'

Still the tears flowed and Custard's mystification returned. Sir Edward came back with the glass of water and raised his eyebrows at Custard who shook his head a little.

'So if it was Luca you liked and Tommaso who is hurt,' Custard said slowly, more for Sir Edward's benefit than for Inky's (Sir Edward nodded eagerly), 'then what are you crying about?'

'Nothing,' came the muffled response.

'Oh.'

They sat in silence for a few minutes. 'Would you like some chocolate?' said Sir Edward kindly. 'We keep some in the fridge.'

Custard looked over in surprise at him. Chocolate was strictly forbidden for the crew whilst they were in training and it was news to him that some was kept on the *Mucky Ducky*. 'For emergencies,' said Sir Edward firmly to Custard.

'What emergencies would those be?'

'Yes, please,' said Inky.

Sir Edward made a 'see?' face and fetched the chocolate.

Snuffling somewhat, Inky took the bar and immediately consumed half of it. 'I'm sorry,' she said. 'I thought it was Luca, I thought he might even be dead and I realised that I like him so much. I really like him.'

'But at the Louis Vuitton party?' asked Custard gently. He had gathered something had happened there even though Inky had told everyone she had simply gone home early. Oh God, the tears were coming again.

'Have some more chocolate,' said Sir Edward urgently.

'He doesn't want a girlfriend,' said Inky between sobs and mouthfuls. 'He wants to concentrate on the Cup. Which made me think I wasn't concentrating enough on it.' She let out a wail. 'How can you have a relationship with this sort of life?'

'Don't ask me,' said Custard.

The two men looked at each other in alarm. This really wasn't their territory.

There was a knock at the door and Carla popped her head round. 'I have brought lunch.' Seeing Inky crying, she stopped for a moment in surprise but Sir Edward, sensing a woman's touch was needed, opened the door fully for her and she immediately crossed straight over to Inky, sat down beside her and gave her a big hug. 'There, there, what is wrong with Inky? Why she cry?'

As best she could, Inky told the whole sorry story with Carla's arm around her.

'Inky, you are beautiful. Very beautiful and he is very stupid.'

'But he didn't even try to sleep with me. I mean, it's one thing to say he wanted to and obviously I would have said no but he didn't even *try*.'

Custard and Sir Edward frowned at each other.

'Ah, men,' said Carla sighing. 'They think they do the right thing but they make the cock-up all the time.' She glared at the men present. 'He probably is trying to respect you. But what he don't realise is that women want men to at least try to sleep with them, otherwise it's an insult. He does like you, Inky. I am not blind. I know exactly who you talk about. He is the less – how you say? – loud of all the Italians. He hangs back a little. He has a mole on neck.'

'Yes! That's him!'

'Of course it's him. And how do I know? Because I see him look at you. He is always watching you. His eyes follow you when you leave. I can see you avoid him lately but he still watch you. He likes you very much.'

Inky smiled, feeling better. 'But then I think that if he isn't prepared to have a girlfriend, then what am I thinking? Am I taking this seriously enough?'

'Inky. You are the first in, you are the longest in the gym. I am very proud of you for being a woman. You don't need to be frightened of it.' Then Carla put her old, crooked, sun-spotted hand on top of Inky's young one and squeezed it. 'Besides, men can't concentrate on more than one thing at once. Now you go and show all those men why you so good.'

Within a few minutes Inky had washed her face and joined the others back on deck. When Mack and Pond returned from the shore and quickly gobbled the remainder of Carla's lunch, they gave the full story from the Italian boat. It turned out that a crane had collapsed on top of Tommaso's arm when he went up to repair something; he had managed to work the trapped arm loose but then lost consciousness with the pain. They splinted the arm, and then decided to speed the injured man to shore in Mack's faster RIB and have an ambulance meet him there rather than risk trying to winch him aboard a helicopter.

Oblivious to the goings-on since he'd been away, Mack

demanded they got back to practice as soon as the story had been told and several cheese rolls consumed. Inky was extremely glad of this approach; she couldn't bear for any more fuss to be made and was already embarrassed enough. God, she'd burst into tears in front of the crew. How could she? Would they all be muttering under their breath, 'Bloody women, that's why we don't have them on the boat'?

But Inky underestimated her abilities. She barked out orders with particular proficiency that afternoon and by the end of the day, the crew complained of being so tired that they couldn't even eat on the tow home. And she needn't have worried about losing any face because as they stepped off *Excalibur*, Mack commented within plain hearing of everyone, 'You were bloody fantastic today, Inky. Well done.' And when Sir Edward went over the mistakes from the day at the debrief, Inky's name did not feature once. After her shower she opened her locker to find Carla had placed a beautiful cake in there, decorated with fresh icing and lots of nuts. Inky smiled to herself and took it out, meaning to drop it into Bee later but then changed her mind and thought, just this once, that she might eat it herself.

Chapter 23

Whilst Inky had been taking her shower, the Italian skipper, Marco Fraternelli, came to pay the Montague Challenge a visit.

After repeated thanks for their intervention in the day's proceedings, he said to Mack, 'We will be practising again tomorrow and we wonder if you would like . . . what do you call it? A friend race?' To relieve the monotony of practice, occasionally one challenger will offer to race another – but never against the defender.

Mack thought about it for a second and then agreed. The Italians would absolutely thrash the British crew but at least, Mack thought, it would give them something to measure against and since there was nine months to go until the America's Cup then surely not too much damage could be done. After all, a lot can happen in nine months.

The crew had just got back from the gym and were settling down to breakfast when Mack announced that they would be racing *Baci* in a friendly race that morning. Then he disappeared to make ready for the day's briefing. Immediately plates were pushed to one side and the level of chatter increased dramatically.

'They are going to bloody thrash us,' said Dougie nervously.

'No, they're not,' howled Fabian and Custard in unison.

'No one can mention rabbits,' said Custard firmly. 'I must go and check if I brought my lucky pants.'

Whilst Custard was absent, talk turned to everyone's talisman and Dougie took the opportunity to ask Inky if she had got her lucky coin with her.

'It's in my locker. I'll get it.'

Custard buttonholed Inky in the locker room. 'Will you be OK today?' he said quietly.

Inky stopped in her tracks and said firmly, 'I can guarantee that no one on this boat wants to beat *Baci* more than I do, Custard.'

Both sides were determined to give the race the most official atmosphere that they could. A representative from the Italian challenge and Sir Edward had already met early in the morning to decide the course. It was also decided that both of them would be on-the-water umpires, doling out instant justice.

After Sir Edward's part in the briefing, it was Mack's turn to speak.

'This might be the first and last time we will have a chance to race another crew before the America's Cup itself. I want everyone to take it deadly seriously and whatever the outcome, to learn everything they can from it. The Italians are an incredibly competent challenge who many people think are in with a good chance to win the Cup. Everything has to be treated as though it is race day itself.'

The Italians left the dock just before them but today there was no friendly catcalling or camaraderie. The two crews steadfastly ignored one another. Inky did not even look to see if Luca was at the bow. As far as she was concerned, just for today, he didn't even exist. Custard unintentionally broke the tension by opening everyone's sandwich up and throwing the lettuce overboard because it was green and that was unlucky.

As the allotted race time drew near, the adrenalin on *Excalibur* was running high. The whole crew were already up on deck, checking over their equipment and applying sunscreen. It was peculiar to see another pair of America's Cup boats so close by. At exactly nine thirty-five, Mack gave the command to hoist the mainsail. Golly and Flipper grunted away, relishing the opportunity to flex their muscles properly, as the mainsail started to slowly rise like smoke from a garden bonfire. 'LOCKED!' shouted Golly as the huge sail locked into place at the top of the mast.

The two Italian boats were already doing the traditional practice run with their sparring boat in order to assess the conditions. They looked beautiful together and in very, very good shape. Mack looked over to Rafe. This would be a real test for him. He needed to perform when it mattered.

Mack and Sammy the navigator took their advice over the radio from Laura the meteorologist. 'The breeze is difficult,' commented Rafe. 'It's shifting all the time.'

With a few seconds to go until the starting gun, all radios were placed in a watertight canister and thrown overboard. Now there was silence on board *Excalibur*; everyone was watchful and the seconds ticked slowly by. Rafe didn't take his eyes from the horizon.

BANG! Sir Edward fired the five-minute pre-start gun and Sammy hit his stopwatch. *Excalibur* and *Baci* entered the starting box from opposite sides but Mack planned to keep his distance from the Italian boat until Sammy called three minutes and then he would lock into them. They made a couple of turns, the grinders' arms a blur as they moved the massive sails from one side to the other. Mack glanced over to his navigator whose eyes were glued to the computer screen in front of him; his normal perpetual outpourings of facts and figures from the instruments had suddenly ceased.

'What's the preference?' asked Mack, meaning between starting on the side of the committee boat or the port side.

'I was going to say port side but now I don't know,' said Sammy looking alarmed.

'You don't know?'

'Something's just gone wrong with the readouts.'

They both instinctively looked up at the mast where, right at the top, wind sensors were positioned giving readouts of wind strength and direction.

'Shit.'

'Four minutes,' said Sammy in answer to the inherent question.

Just our luck, thought Mack. Just as the gun goes. 'We'll send someone up.'

'Now?' said Inky.

'No, I don't want them to know anything is wrong, besides it's too dangerous.' On the ducking and weaving of the start line whoever went up would be whacked against the mainsail and probably knocked unconscious.

'Rafe, which side of the course do we want?'

'Committee boat,' he said without hesitation. Mack saw his tactician's face and knew it was the opposite to what she was going to suggest before the equipment broke. 'It's going to shift. A different wind stream is coming.'

'Three minutes, Mack. Time to go.'

Mack didn't ask any more questions but swooped and locked on to the Italian boat. They made a couple of predatory circles around one another but the faster manoeuvrability of *Excalibur* showed itself and the Italians decided to get out whilst they still could. They obviously didn't want to get locked down. Mack chased after them, snapping at their heels and daring them to engage. He could see Fabian standing on the bow, his body naturally leaning in and out with the whipping turns but his head taut with concentration and his hand counting the distance between them and the Italian boat.

They hit the one-minute mark and Sammy started to count down. 'Sixty . . . fifty-nine . . . fifty-eight . . . fifty-seven . . . '

'*Baci* is tacking,' said Rafe. Mack went ahead of her and then, seeing his opening, turned around and came back at her, forcing her to tack and head for the port end, leaving themselves with the committee boat end free. That was too easy, thought Mack as they tacked away and he swung around positioning himself to head for the line. And they weren't coming back either. They obviously wanted the port end.

'Which side, Rafe?'

'Committee boat,' stated Rafe once again. Normally he would ask for back-up confirmation from the rest of the afterguard but he could see that they thought they should be heading for the port end. The breeze was consistently coming from there. It was a show of Mack's leadership that everyone kept their opinions to themselves, only one startled glance back from Custard.

'Twenty . . . nineteen . . . eighteen . . . seventeen . . . '

Mack tacked hard to starboard and hit the line flying as far as possible away from *Baci* and prayed.

Inky and Custard were both equally good at fixing electronics but Mack decided to send Inky up the mast because she was lighter. She got ready quickly, strapping herself into the harness. In addition to the lethal gerber permanently strapped to her leg, she also took a variety of screwdrivers and other equipment and secured them around her waist. Custard and Golly started to hoist her up the ninety-five-foot mast, pausing at about sixty feet for her to unclip herself, hang on for grim death and re-clip to the next halyard. The rest of the crew, after whispered exchanges about what happened on the start line and why they were shooting off to the right whilst the Italians were shooting off to the left, seemingly faster than them, grimly shuffled round to balance the temporary loss of Custard and Golly, not daring to meet anyone else's eye. Despite the relatively calm conditions on the deck, it was fairly alarming from Inky's perspective. For every inch of movement on the deck, there are about twenty inches of movement at the top of the mast, hardly ideal conditions to try and fix a fiddly piece of electronics.

'Nine point eight, nine point eight, nine point nine . . . ' Sammy recited his vital monologue of boat speed.

'What's the Italian boat doing?'

'They're still on a port tack and she's faster than us.'

'Where's your wind shift, Rafe?' muttered Mack.

'About two minutes,' said Rafe calmly not taking his eyes from the horizon.

'Nine point eight, nine point seven. Bear up harder, Mack.'

They sailed for one minute and fifty seconds in tense silence apart from the muttered speed bearings of Sammy, and then suddenly Rafe said, 'Lifting out. Lifting out,' and the boat lifted. She lifted as though she had wings. She felt as though she was about to glide off the water into the air.

A slow smile spread across Mack's face. He could feel the relief across the boat.

'Tack the boat,' said Rafe. 'It's heading.'

Mack looked up to Inky. 'Hold on, Inky! We're going to tack!' he yelled up at her. She kept shouting back down to them but the wind and the sails whipped her words away. His must have reached her though because he watched her brace and then shouted, 'TACKING!'

Excalibur was striding along now, revelling in the wind and the conditions that she loved. They had already gained a few boat lengths on the Italians who were still languishing without breeze. Inky had indicated that she needed to be brought down and as soon as she hit the deck, she panted, 'I need a soldering iron. A wire has worked loose. I can't fix it.'

Mack paused and looked at her, hesitating. As skipper of the boat he had to do everything he could to get the equipment up and working but this was a crucial team decision. He needed to give the crew confidence. And he had to do it now, quickly, cleanly and unfalteringly.

'Don't worry, Inky. Rafe knows what he's doing.'

He didn't tell her that the real reasons were that he wouldn't risk her life by sending her up the mast in these windier conditions and that he doubted anyone could fix it with a soldering iron whilst swaying in a twenty-knot stiff breeze. He told them what they needed to hear and then looked to Rafe.

'Another lift coming in five . . . ' Rafe said.

Two hours and forty-three minutes later, the Italians had beaten the British by only a margin of forty-three seconds but Mack was inordinately pleased with a good day's work. The crew were very disappointed in the result but not only was their faith completely and finally restored in Rafe but his own faith was restored in himself.

Rafe wasn't quite sure what had happened out there, whether it was finally Mack's conviction that he would come good or the fact that the memory of Ava was receding. Whatever it was he wasn't about to question it. This definitive connection he had with the crew and the elements was the best he had felt for a long time and he knew it was back to stay. He looked around at them all and smiled. They had come a long way.

The two boats drew alongside each other to shout thanks. The Italians smiled and waved, gracious in victory and particularly full of praise for the 'bella donna' who had fearlessly gone up the mast. Inky couldn't help but cast a small look over at Luca, looking so incredibly brown and handsome in his crew uniform of black and red.

'The devil wears Prada,' she murmured to herself.

Chapter 24

Luca was waiting for her when she left the compound that evening. She went slowly up to him. 'The crew of *Excalibur*!' he said and bent his head slightly. She liked the way he pronounced *Excalibur*, like an exotic Arabic word

'Congratulations,' she said even though it choked her.

'Thank you.'

'How is your crew mate? The one who was hurt up the mast?'

'Tommaso. In hospital still. No America's Cup for him. The second-boat man moves up. You were very brave today. Up the mast.'

'No more than anyone else would have done.'

'I hear all my crew mates talk about it and I realise that I don't like them talking about you. So really you win.'

'I win?'

'Yes, you win. Will you come out with me tonight?'

'Tonight?'

'Yes.'

Inky paused. Torn between a desire to make him suffer a bit and an absolute lust to bite his arm off at the offer. Not to mention the fact that her ribs were killing her. 'I don't know,' she said cautiously.

'We go somewhere quiet.'

* * *

True to his word, Luca took her to a small, intimate restaurant and requested a table in the corner. He ordered them the three-cheese risotto and a bottle of wine. When Inky raised her eyebrows at this blatant flouting of the rules of a crew in training, Luca said, 'I think you have a saying about hanging.'

'Hanging?'

'Yes, might as well be hung for . . . ' He waggled his hands to make her finish.

Inky laughed, 'For a prince than a pauper.'

'*Si*. Are you very sore?'

Inky's ribs were incredibly painful; a huge bruise had come up on her thigh where she had tried to hold her torso away from the mast so her legs had swung into it instead, and her collarbone was so tender that she thought her head might drop off if she moved it too much. 'A bit.'

'When I go up the mast in the conditions like that, I sometimes can't walk for days.'

'OK then, I'm very sore.'

Luca put his hand over hers and left it there.

Afterwards they strolled through the gardens of the Turia river and, under a beautiful arch of sweet-smelling rose, Luca kissed her very gently.

'I couldn't stand all my crew talking about your beautiful legs. A couple wanted to come over and ask you out. I wanted to shout at them and I realised it was my fault that I couldn't. I'm sorry.'

'*I'm* sorry I'm so battered.' Inky sighed and gestured down to her legs covered up by a long, gypsy skirt.

'You're forgiven. My flatmate flew back to Naples for the night. His girlfriend gives him a, what do you call it? Bent ear?' Inky giggled. 'Will you come to mine?'

The Italian syndicate lived in a different part of the city – one Inky wasn't familiar with – and Luca's flat was typical of two men living together. She loved the fact that he clearly wasn't expecting her back this evening as he scurried round, picking clothes off the floor of his room and dumping them all on a chair which was already overladen. 'I sorry that it such a mess.' He looked at her apologetically and said it with such a typical Italian shrug that Inky could have leapt on him there and then.

She smiled. 'That's OK.'

'Coffee?'

'No.'

'Tea then?'

Inky slowly shook her head.

'How are your bruises?'

'Sore.'

'I be careful.'

Luca smiled and walked towards her. He kissed her again but this time his tongue and mouth were much more demanding. He stopped suddenly and taking her by the hand led her over to the bed. They collapsed on to it, a mêlée of limbs, with Luca kissing her neck and her face. He tore off her top and started to kiss her shoulders. Inky felt ignited with desire and, all injuries forgotten, started to peel off his T-shirt. She wasn't disappointed with what was underneath. 'Definitely a sex-pack,' she murmured. He went to undo her bra and they giggled as he fiddled about with no joy. Inky helped him and hoped he wouldn't be disappointed. 'Sorry,' she whispered, peeling the bra away and aware that she shouldn't be apologising for anything but had to nevertheless. 'I'm not exactly well endowed.'

'Endowed?' said Luca, frowning. 'What's that?'

'Big. I'm not exactly big.'

Luca's face cleared. '*Cara*, they are beautiful. *You* are beautiful.' She had petite, pert breasts with nipples the colour of hazelnuts. Luca went on to demonstrate exactly how beautiful he thought they were, covering them with kisses and sucking on them as though they were cherries. Inky thought she was going to explode with desire and started to undo his jeans, struggling to pull them down over his erection. Luca certainly had nothing to apologise for.

The next morning, Inky woke very early to bright light and to a very broad and brown back scattered with moles. Luca. Of course. She smiled to herself and then bit her lip. She hoped she hadn't blown things by sleeping with him on the first night and she wondered if Mack or Colin Montague would mind her seeing someone from another syndicate. Mack would probably immediately get on the phone to her father. A few minutes later she decided she didn't care about any of that as Luca woke up and languidly turned to face her. 'Good morning, *cara*,' he said sleepily. 'Come over here and wake me up.'

'That is a nasty bruise,' he said a while later after they had made love again. He was looking in horror at her ribcage whilst she was still straddling him. 'I sorry, I did not realise last night. Did I hurt you?'

'I didn't feel a thing. That's hormones for you.'

'I think you have beautiful breasts.' He leant back and put his arms behind his head.

Inky peered down at them. 'Do you really? Jason Bryant used to call me Mrs Beeton – she's a famous cook – when we were in youth squad together. Because he said my breasts were the size of drop scones. I had to tell my father it was because he thought I was as good a cook as her.'

'Jason Bryant? The Phoenix helmsman?'

'Yes.'

'He has seen your breasts? You sleep with him?'

Inky grinned. 'No!'

'He probably want to sleep with you.'

'I don't think so.'

'How can anyone be with you and not want to sleep with you?'

Inky smiled widely at him. 'Believe me, Jason Bryant does not want to sleep with me.' She frowned to herself. 'I'm not quite sure why, because he's slept with most girls. You'd probably be more upset if he *hadn't*. But I think it's because we always compete against each other.'

'If I see this Jason Bryant I will tell him that you have beautiful breasts.'

'Thank you. I like your place. We're about to move into digs on the Malvarossa beach.'

'Dig? What is a dig? I thought a dig was to do with spades.'

Inky laughed. 'Sorry. It's slang. It means lodging. How did you get that scar?' she asked pointing to his back.

He smiled ruefully. 'My harness failed and I fell from the spinnaker pole. Caught my back on the bow on the way down. What about this?' He pointed to a long, thin scar down Inky's hip.

'My father's Laser dinghy. I capsized and cut myself on something. I don't know what.'

'Sailing is no sport for gentlemen.'

'Nothing gentle about it.'

'I forget to ask you if you sail today?'

'We sail every day but once a month we get a day off.'

'Today?'

Inky smiled and slowly nodded. 'You?'

'We never sail on a Sunday. The gods, they smile on us. What shall we do?'

By the time they had got up, eaten some of the strange Spanish bread, toasted and with marmalade (which surprised Inky as she always thought of marmalade as very English but as Luca pointed out there were more oranges in Europe than England) and Luca had dragged Inky back to bed as he said she looked far too sexy in one of his shirts, it was about midday before they appeared outside the apartment. Inky was wearing a pair of Luca's jeans, held up by a belt (which belonged to his flatmate who was a grinder) wrapped twice round her waist, a striped blue shirt of Luca's and Bee's strappy stilettos which were still on loan to her. She felt gloriously sybaritic. Luca offered to run her back to her 'digs' first but Inky didn't want to break the mood with whatever might await her.

'Where shall we go?' she asked.

'I thought we could go down to the cathedral. There supposedly resides the other holy grail.'

'The other holy grail? I thought the America's Cup was the only one?' questioned Inky.

'The cup of Christ. I haven't been to visit yet and it seems appropriate.'

After they had visited the cathedral, reading the history of the grail which Inky reworded for Luca because they didn't have the leaflet in Italian and looking with wonderment at the small-handled gold cup, they wandered around the old part of Valencia. Luca held her hand all the way round. They paused only for lunch where Luca insisted on feeding her the most delicious *fideua*, noodles fried with garlic and rockfish. 'The noodles are boiled first in fish stock for the taste of the sea,' explained Luca. 'The fishermen here still make it on their boats.'

'Maybe not like this,' said Inky, her mouth full of the delicious concoction.

'Maybe not,' agreed Luca. 'Have you managed to see anything of Spain since you got here?'

'My syndicate all went to Barcelona but I went back to England to visit my mother. She was ill.'

Luca looked concerned. 'Ah, *cara,* how horrible for you. It is dreadful when the mama is ill. Is she OK now?'

'Yes, she's fine. I called her before our race.'

'Is she coming out for the racing?'

'I hope so. I think she'd like Valencia.'

They had fabulous orange and coconut *millefeuille* with *garrapinadas* – caramelised almonds – for pudding.

'How do you know all this?' asked Inky.

'We have been here in Valencia longer than you. Would you like to do something else I've just discovered?'

'What's that?' asked Inky, quite hoping he meant sex with her.

'Horse riding on the beach. You'll have to go in bare feet,' he said looking at her lethal stilettos.

It wasn't as good but nearly as exhilarating. 'Will you come back and spend the night with me?' he asked after they had dismounted. Inky thought she would never walk properly again – and not just because of the saddle. She ruefully shook her head. 'I have to be up at five. And I think Mack will be waiting for me.'

'Who is Mack?' demanded Luca fiercely.

'John MacGregor. My godfather and our skipper.'

'The famous John MacGregor is your godfather? Ahhh. I thought this "Mack" was boyfriend but now I see he is worse.'

Inky laughed. 'Much worse, I'm afraid.'

'Give me your mobile number,' he commanded. 'I call you.'

And with that Inky had to be satisfied. After all, she was sleeping with the enemy now.

The following few weeks were a revelation for Inky. Although their time was spent strictly with their own syndicates, she and Luca spent every other spare moment together, usually sloping off to bed. Inky was delighted with the effect she seemed to have on him; he found her absolutely irresistible and was completely unselfish in bed. 'You see, it's your own fault,' he would say ruefully. 'I say that you will distract me.' And although he loved having sex with her, he also never demanded it, content simply to share a bath or rub her shoulders if she was too tired.

When they weren't in bed together, they would discuss sailing. Nothing specific about either syndicate – Inky certainly never forgot that she would be sailing against him – but just general talk about the conditions in Valencia and their past sailing careers. Inky noticed that their relationship and the way they spoke to each other would subtly change as they had such conversations. It became more spirited and less soothing. She could feel the ambition rising in her throat as she spoke and could only imagine he felt the same way. After all, the sailors who do the America's Cup were talented and determined. Not much could keep them down.

Everyone at the syndicate was delighted for her, although some of them were a little wary of the fact that Luca was one of the enemy. The real change in Inky was apparent in her sailing. As her confidence in herself increased, her sailing became sharper and her commands had such an air of authority that the crew no longer looked to Mack before obeying them. She was also much happier on the boat and had taken to accepting (to a small degree) various concessions to the fact that she was a woman. So much so that the phrase 'Because she's a girl' was being jokingly applied to everything.

'Thank God, you've finally accepted you don't actually have a dick,' said Custard one day after Inky had finally agreed that she would like to pee in the loo on the *Mucky Ducky*, which had been on offer all along, rather than balance precariously off the side of the boat. 'I was getting really bored having to stand in front of you all the time. You can be really stubborn sometimes, you know. This is obviously what love does to you. Either that or don't you want us to see the Italian flag tattooed on your bum?'

Inky threw her bread roll at him which he infuriatingly caught and started to eat.

'It will happen to you one day, Custard. You'll see.'

'I bloody hope not.' He spluttered crumbs. 'Look how soppy you are over him. When we went out for that drink the other night you just gazed at him all evening.'

Mack was particularly pleased to see Inky so happy. 'Hey you!' he said coming into the canteen early one morning to find Inky there already. 'What a pleasure to find my god-daughter here. Or is Luca here too?' He pretended to peer under the table.

Inky laughed. 'I'm not that bad!' she protested.

'It's great to see you though. I haven't had any proper time with you for ages.'

'You're not counting all the hours you spend shouting at me on the boat?'

'No, that's strictly professional.'

'But you're OK about me seeing Luca? I mean him being from another syndicate.'

'Of course! I trust you, Inky. As your godfather I'm glad to see you happy and as your skipper I just hope he doesn't keep you up too late.'

'And what about you, Mack? Any Cupids on the horizon for you?'

'Just because you're in love you're trying to drag every other poor bugger down with you, are you?'

'No! I just want to see you happy too.'

'And where do you think I'd find time for any love affair? I'm too busy shouting at all of you for that.' Inky grinned at his back as he went off to ask Carla for an extra-strong espresso.

By complete contrast, her own father seemed enraged. It didn't help that no one told him. Mack presumed that Inky would tell him and was too busy with syndicate business anyway and Inky was actually delaying telling her parents (or so she told herself) until she was sure this was more than a brief fling. Inky usually called her father during the week to ask about some technical point which had come up or a complicated move which needed honing, and when she hadn't called for a couple of weeks, James Pencarrow called her.

Luca picked up the phone. ''ello?'

'Hello?'

''ello?'

'Who's that?' demanded James.

'It is Luca,' said Luca in surprise. 'Do you want to speak to Inky?'

'Yes.' His tone was icy cold. 'Tell her it's her father on the phone.'

He could hear Luca calling in the background. '*Cara!* It's your papa!'

'Who was that?' James demanded as soon as Inky came on the line. 'And why was he calling you *cara*?'

'Well, *cara* in Italian means . . . '

'I know what *cara* means, Inky,' he said stonily. 'What I want to know is why was he calling you that?'

'We're seeing each other.'

'Oh yes? And how long has this been going on?'

'A few weeks.'

'No one thought to tell your mother or me?'

'I said a few weeks, Dad. Not a few months. And I will, with pleasure, tell my mother if you care to put her on.'

Her dad ignored her. 'Where did you meet him?'

'He's the bowman on the Italian challenge.'

'Another syndicate?' he asked in horror. 'Have you told Mack about this?'

'Of course I have.'

'But he hasn't called me!'

'Probably because I am well over the age of twenty-one.'

'I just hope you will not forget you are in a major competition called the America's Cup.'

'I never forget about the America's Cup and nor does Luca. Don't you want to know anything else about him?'

'I want to know if he's affecting your sailing. You can't afford for him to impact your performance. Something like this is often the difference between winning and losing.'

'I wasn't aware that you expected us to win,' said Inky dryly.

Her father spluttered down the phone. 'I suppose he is keeping you up late and distracting you?'

'He is just as serious about the America's Cup as I am.'

'Well, you better make sure this Luca isn't trying to wriggle secrets out of you. How do you know he isn't simply using you for that?'

'Because no one could find me attractive without some sort of ulterior motive?'

'I didn't say that. But you have to bear in mind . . . '

'Actually Luca is taking me home to Italy to meet his mother next month,' interrupted Inky coldly. 'Do you think she's in on it too?'

She was so furious that she put the phone down on him.

Chapter 25

A few weeks later both the Italian and British crews had four, much anticipated days off whilst Valencia celebrated one of their saint days, and Luca took Inky home to Italy. This wasn't specifically to meet his mother as she so casually said to her father but because he wanted to show her the Amalfi coast. Most of Excalibur used the time to move into Casa Fortuna. Tim Jenkins and Mack had been won over by the blue flash of the Mediterranean and the mountains in the distance and turned a blind eye to the crumbling façade. Tim had moved quickly to sign the lease on the flats. Bee and Rafe moved into an apartment on the first floor. Custard and Dougie had an apartment on the same floor. Inky was one floor up and then Fabian and Milly with Rosie, and Mack were the floor above that. Everyone was thrilled to feel settled at last and also – since they had been spread over several hotels – to all feel part of a little British colony.

Inky merely dumped her belongings in the new apartment and then took a taxi to the airport. Luca insisted that the only way to see the Amalfi coast for the first time was from the water so after they had landed at Naples, they took a death-defying taxi journey down to the docks during which the traffic lights seemed to be purely for decorative purposes, no one ever indicated and scooters swooped in and out of the traffic. She passed the startling sight of three girls on a scooter, none of them wearing helmets and two of them holding out a pizza box like a waiter whilst the other was on a mobile. 'See Naples and die,' she quoted to herself. 'And that's exactly what's going to happen.' Inky supposed it was the effect of living forever in the shadow of Vesuvius which made them so hot-headed. Luca wasn't helping matters by leaning forward and chatting casually to the taxi driver when Inky would have really preferred to let the driver concentrate. She gladly left the taxi at the docks where Luca's brother, Gennaro, was waiting with a small motor boat.

'Gennaro doesn't speak much English,' Luca explained to Inky who had greeted Gennaro gladly whilst he chatted away to her in Italian and heaved the luggage on board. It took them a while to be free from the commercial shipping area of the docks, the massive container ships and the cranes but they were soon on open water and despite it being October, Inky felt the warm wind of the Mediterranean sea on her face.

'What island is that?' Inky shouted over the noise of the boat and pointed at a mountainous crag rising steeply out of the sea.

'Capri,' yelled Luca back. 'We'll visit next time.'

It make Inky dizzy every time he talked in terms of their future.

Inky was so busy gazing in awe at the beautiful island that she didn't look at anything else and didn't notice them rounding the peninsula until Luca nudged her. She glanced forward and the sight nearly took her breath away. The Amalfi coast in all its splendour lay before her, the surprise made even more intense by her expectations of something similar to Cornwall. Luca had said it was rocky with lots of cliffs but this was nothing compared with reality.

Vast mountains reared out of the water. Sheer rock faces dotted with brittle greenery. Crumbling pastel-coloured villas were built into the nooks and crannies, seemingly piled on top of one another.

Luca had been watching her. 'It is beautiful, no?'

'It is beautiful, yes! Stunning! You said cliffs, I just didn't believe . . . ' Her words trailed off as she had to crane her neck as far as she could to glimpse the peaks, some of them shrouded in mist. 'It feels as though the whole world has been flooded and it's only us and these mountains left.'

Luca laughed. 'Yes! There is a famous saying here, it is: "There is only the sun, the moon and Amalfi." People think it is because we are arrogant but it's because it feels as though there is only us left here.'

Inky drank in every sight. The tiny, one-room fortresses on baby capes, the grottos and caves carved into the cliffs by watery sculptors, the gulls swooping and diving, flashes of colour spilling over from balconies.

'Where is that?' she shouted, pointing across to a big cluster of houses. Taking advantage of the gap between two of the mountains there was a small town of villas piled higgledy-piggledy, looking like a cluster of pastel barnacles clinging to a rock. The gleaming mosaic dome of a church stood out at the bottom of the pile.

'Positano! We're the next village along.'

It seemed as though the whole village was aware of her arrival. Firstly everyone from the restaurant at the bottom of the village where they moored the boat came out to greet Luca and firmly shake his hand. They chatted non-stop to Inky, seemingly oblivious to the fact that she didn't understand a word. They climbed a few flights of stone steps which had been carved into the cliff and then into narrow zigzagging alleyways which occasionally opened out to overlook carefully laid terraces of lemon and pomegranate trees.

'I thought you only called your mother yesterday,' whispered Inky between greetings. Luca hadn't wanted a fuss about bringing a girlfriend home and so casually announced it the day before. Gennaro had long since disappeared out of sight with their luggage.

'I did but how do you say? News travels quickly.'

Luca had told Inky that his mother ran a little shop, so she had been expecting the Italian version of a Spar or corner shop or suchlike. As soon as she stepped into the beaded entrance she realised her mistake. In England this could only be described as an upmarket delicatessen. Whole hams and lines of chillis hung from the ceiling, huge wheels of Parmesan were piled up in the corner, the cool counter was rammed with cheeses, olives, marinating tomatoes and aubergines, pesto the colour of emeralds and fresh pasta of all descriptions. And Luca's mother was standing in the corner, arms crossed, looking absolutely formidable in every sense of the word. She was a huge woman, dressed in a hideously patterned wraparound dress, her black hair flecked with grey and pulled back tightly into a bun. No make-up adorned her unsmiling face.

'Mama!' cried Luca. '*Come sta?*'

He gave her a huge hug and her face momentarily softened but reverted back to a mask as soon as he released her.

Luca led her by the hand over to Inky. 'Mama, this is Inky.' Inky realised he was speaking in English for her sake and she flashed him a thankful smile.

Inky stepped forward to say hello and Mama's eyes wandered down her, stopping firmly on her hips.

The next day she woke at six. The bright sunshine had pierced through the shuttered windows and lit the room in a dull light. Inky was sleeping in a narrow wooden bed in a tiny box room, painted simply in white with cool tiled floors and a huge crucifix nailed above the bed. She remembered that she was on holiday and stretched out luxuriously like a cat. She only wished that Luca was lying next to her. The next moment, she had fallen asleep again. When she eventually woke up again she washed in the little hand basin as best as she could, then wandered downstairs to be greeted by a wonderful smell of baking filling the house. She tentatively pushed the door to the kitchen open, quite hoping that Luca would be up already, but she found only Mama in the kitchen. She smiled brightly. 'Something smells good.'

'Bread,' said Mama shortly. 'It ready soon.'

'Lovely.'

'Do you cook?'

'Em, I would like to. Perhaps if I had more time . . . '

'We have time here.'

That wasn't exactly what Inky meant. She had envisaged her short holiday on the Amalfi coast strolling hand in hand with Luca, not sweating in a small kitchen.

Inky smiled again and changed the subject. 'You speak good English.'

'We have to. The tourists. They are the reason we are able to live here. Without them it is too hard.'

'Really?'

'The Amalfi is not a hospitable place. It is beautiful, yes, but to live is difficult. My family have always lived here but many left during the war for America as it was too hard. We live between the sea and the mountains.'

Inky nodded. 'You must be proud of Luca and his sailing.'

'Very proud. Luca says that you are sailor too?'

'Yes,' said Inky expecting a similar sort of your-parents-must-be-proud reaction but Mama just snorted.

'Luca's team, they will win that silver cup.'

'We all hope we will win the Cup,' said Inky diplomatically. Luca came in.

'Ahhh, you are awake!' he said and came over to drop a kiss on the top of her head. 'I have been out to look at the boat. I thought we might take her up the coast today!'

'Lovely!' said Inky.

'Let's have some breakfast first. Mama! We need food!'

Somewhat to Inky's surprise, Mama gladly acquiesced to this order as though she expected to be ordered around by her son. She wondered where Luca's father was; nobody had mentioned him so far, nor had she seen sight nor sound of him.

'Where's your father?' she whispered to Luca.

'Papa? Working. He starts early. He and my aunt own a restaurant. We'll stop for lunch there.'

Inky didn't really know what to expect from the town of Amalfi. She and Luca put their mobile phones, wallets and Inky's camera into one of the America's Cup waterproof canisters which Luca had taken from *Baci* and swam out through warm turquoise waters to the boat, pushing the canister in front of them as they went. The water felt like velvet. They pulled themselves out and lay on the back of the boat for a while to dry off whilst Luca whispered in her ear and told her all the things he would like to do to her if only they had half the chance. Inky had her eyes half closed and looked dreamily through the shadows of her eyelashes into the sky. She could still see the very tips of the mountains shrouded in cloud from this angle.

They set off for Amalfi under motor. 'We will sail tomorrow,' said Luca, 'but to get the wind you have to come away from the mountains and I want you to see the coastline.'

And it was indeed a beautiful coastline. Inky sat up on the bow of the boat and admired it. The mountains were rocky and inhospitable but there were crumbling villas in the most unlikely places. A mere crack or small plateau and someone had wedged a tenacious dwelling into it. Outcrops jutted into the ocean, the sea sculpturing them into arches and statues. The odd gnarled and twisted trunk of an olive tree. Mostly all the houses were gathered together as though sheltering for cover, with the odd mosaic or ochre dome of a yellow church.

'The Amalfi was an important trading post in the sixteenth century. All the trade ships carrying silks and spices stopped here from the Middle East,' yelled Luca over the noise of the engine. Inky could see that there were distinct Moorish influences: the houses were a mixture of Baroque and Arabic; they twisted together verandas and vines, arches and balconies.

They berthed in the small harbour at Amalfi.

'You have a berth here?' asked Inky.

'My father's. For the restaurant. The only way you can get to his restaurant is by boat.'

They wandered hand in hand through the streets of Amalfi,

pausing at the dramatic duomo where every inch was covered with mosaic and frescos, ornate carvings and columns with gold altars and heavy marbles, a far cry from Cornwall's granite walls and wooden pews.

'St Andrew, the first disciple, is buried here. Amalfians are dedicated to him. Every year they use the liquid his bones produce to heal the sick,' said Luca. Inky sincerely hoped she would never get sick.

They walked back down the mountain of steps, passing carts selling fresh lemonade and piled with big, fat, imperfect lemons, and then turned into a back street to find some coffee. Occasionally people stopped and said hello to Luca, greeting him with huge bear hugs and flamboyant kisses before exploding into effusive Italian.

'Are you famous?' asked Inky.

Luca shrugged and grinned. 'They are proud of me. Proud that Amalfi could produce an America's Cup sailor. Italians love the Cup.'

'What would you like?' asked Luca at the coffee shop. 'Espresso?'

'No, cappuccino please.'

'They will laugh at you. Cappuccino is for tourists.'

'I like cappuccino,' said Inky.

They settled at one of the standing tables. Inky already knew from Valencia that coffee had to be drunk standing up because it was better for the digestion.

'The sea feels different here,' she said. 'Different from Valencia.'

'No beaches,' he said. 'We just dive straight into the ocean.'

'Maybe that's it,' she agreed.

'Must be difficult coming from your sea in England to sail in ours.'

'Rafe is used to it. He was brought up on the Mediterranean.'

'Rafe?'

'Our strategist.' Luca was nodding but Inky was suddenly aware they were straying into syndicate secrets and changed the subject.

'You know your mother is convinced that you will win the Cup?'

'Of course we win the Cup. How can you doubt it?'

'You'll have to get past me first,' said Inky, unable to keep the competitive note from creeping into her voice.

'*Cara*, if you fix me with those eyes then how the whole of the ocean not fail to bow down before you?'

Luca's father was a wiry man who looked like Luca. He would be a runner bean next to Mama. Inky couldn't quite imagine them in bed together. He was extremely pleased to see Inky but couldn't spend much time with them as he was busy in the restaurant which was built on stilts overlooking a small bay. They had dropped anchor in the bay and then swum ashore. After several courses and the promise of several more, Inky sincerely hoped that she wouldn't have to swim back again because surely she would sink. They had huge slices of tomatoes and torn basil leaves to start, dripping with olive oil, then small, battered fish which the fishermen had delivered twenty minutes before, followed by tomato pasta with clams, and round, firm pears with cheese and fresh walnuts. The promise of cake and coffee and the inevitable limoncello was yet to come. Despite the inaccessibility of the restaurant, it was surprising how many locals it packed in. Huge gossiping families who all took it enormously personally if a baby was crying and took turns to soothe them. Luca's aunt, whom everyone else seemed to call Nonna, was carrying a small, visiting child on her hip and feeding her jellies and the huge, tough fishermen were cooing over her. Luca and Inky sat side by side staring out to sea, with Inky resting her head on his shoulder, dozy with all the food and alcohol.

Luca nudged her head with his shoulder. 'Don't go to sleep, *cara*. We have the house to ourselves this afternoon. Mama always makes her visits in the afternoon.'

Inky suddenly felt a lot more energetic and practically dragged him out of the restaurant to the boat.

Luca made love to her that afternoon with a tenderness and sweetness which belied only a few days of this sunshine. She lay naked on Luca's bed. Luca had just got up to start getting dressed.

'Are you never allowed to sleep with your girlfriends here?' asked Inky. She hadn't really thought about sleeping arrangements before they came out here but she certainly hadn't expected for them to be so strictly separated.

Luca looked vaguely shifty. 'Well, we are Catholics. No sex before marriage.'

'Ahh.'

'And I suppose they are a bit more serious about you because you are not Italian.'

'Is that a problem?'

'Not to me.'

'But to Mama?' Inky persisted.

'Maybe to Mama,' admitted Luca struggling to pull on his boxer shorts without falling over and inadvertently flashing the whole of the street.

'The sun, the moon and Amalfi,' said Inky giggling.

'Why you laugh?' demanded Luca.

But his words stayed with Inky and this was the real reason why she allowed herself to be railroaded into cooking lessons with Mama. 'I can be Italian,' she told herself fiercely. She also got the impression that they didn't really approve of the fact that she had a career, especially not as a sailor. It seemed in conflict with the family's idea that women were for the home.

So early on Monday morning she turned off the alarm on her mobile and stole downstairs to the kitchen where she knew that Mama got up early to start the cooking for the day before disappearing to her shop.

Mama looked up in surprise. '*Buongiorno, Inky. E una giornata stupenda, no?*' Isn't it a beautiful day?

Inky got the general gist as she had been picking up Italian words from Luca all summer and nodded. 'I am here, Mama, to learn to cook. Teach me.'

Mama looked even more surprised. 'I am cooking *sfogliatelle* for Luca. He loves them as a boy.'

'What are they?'

'Pastries.' And with that Inky had to be satisfied. Finding an apron, she got to work with Mama coaxing and cajoling and seeming like she was almost enjoying herself.

'How much do I add?' she asked of the cinnamon.

'A pinch is too much – no more than a whisper. As the French would say *un soupçon*, a suspicion, a ghost. You must suspect it is there but not be sure.' Inky looked at her with bafflement and then added a tiny pinch.

Mama was equally as infuriating as to how long the little oyster-shaped pastries should be cooked for. 'Until they are done.'

'But when is that?' insisted Inky.

'Until the smell of them makes you so hungry that you cannot stand it any longer.'

Inky was childishly pleased to present them to Luca who took wild, euphoric mouthfuls. Mama had already departed to tend to the shop. 'You know, Luca,' said Inky thoughtfully. 'I think your Mama cooks as we sail. I think it's inherent in her and hard to explain to other people.'

Luca laughed at her and reached for another *sfogliatelle*.

And so Inky left the Amalfi coast with much more than she had brought there. She and Mama had cooked together in the kitchen, joined later in the day by one of Luca's sisters and his aunt, and Inky had enjoyed the homely feel. She enjoyed the sound of chatter and laughter, the occasional sip of *vino santo*, the company of the women who would speak to her in pidgin English. For the first time she was actually enjoying something which women did and was actually enjoying the segregation too (although she still wasn't too keen on the segregation of Luca and herself at night). It made her think of her mother at home, slaving in the kitchen whilst she and her brothers were out on their boats, only pausing to grab something from her on their way through the kitchen. They didn't even bother to sit down and eat with her. She must have been very lonely. Inky's long nights alone only gave her the chance to think more about her home life and why she had kicked up so much against these womanly pursuits before.

It seemed strange to Inky that these families could live in such close proximity to the sea yet ignore it so flagrantly: like a huge friendly monster which would surely go away if they didn't pet it or feed it. Such a contrast to Cornwall where the sea seemed to pervade every inch of people's lives, admittedly in a much less benign version than the Mediterranean; it demanded that its power be constantly seen and felt.

This had been playing on Inky's mind all evening as she lit the candles in the old ship's lanterns to protect against the persistent sirocco and returned to the kitchen to help Mama stuff *calzones* with grapes and rosemary.

'Pass the *rosmarino*, Inky,' said Mama pointing.

'Rosemary,' sighed Inky. 'My mother's garden is full of rosemary bushes.'

'Rose of the sea.'

'Of course!' said Inky. 'I hadn't thought where the name came from before.'

She had an unexpected image of her mother. Her beautiful, serene mother, dragged down from London by her father and always living in fear of the sea in case it took one of her children from her. Living in fear of something she hated and had no affinity for. She suddenly understood why her parents' bedroom faced away from the sea. How many years had her mother put up with it? And how much comfort had her own children given back to her? Her eyes filled in sorrow for her. Even her precious garden was filled with the rose of the sea.

'Inky!' said Mama. 'The *rosmarino*, please.'

Chapter 26

Milly hadn't been idle for the last few months in Valencia. She had been making friends, learning the lingo and was generally thought of as marvellous in the Excalibur camp. She had also managed to set up a little business, although it wasn't very profitable because she mostly refused payment or just took very little when her clients insisted. But it kept her creative fingers busy and alive. It had started one day when one of the shore crew's wives commented on a suede bag that Milly had over her shoulder. Milly had glanced down. 'Oh, I found it in a charity shop and just took an old belt buckle and some ribbon and tarted it up.' She smiled at the wife who was looking at her incredulously.

'You *did* that?'

'Yes.'

'If I got a bag could you do the same thing for me? Would you mind?'

'No, I'd love to!' said Milly with real enthusiasm.

She asked her father to send out her mother's old sewing machine and, as word of mouth spread, buried herself updating dress and skirts, re-fashioning jackets, adding embroidery to create something unique. She was much happier to be doing something as often Fabian would come home so tired that he would fall asleep in his food; this way at least Milly had something to occupy her on the long evenings alone.

Her talents particularly came into use when the British ambassador for Spain gave a reception for all the British sailors taking part in the America's Cup at his summer residence in the hills outside Valencia. The stiff white invitations had clearly stated '. . . *and partner*' when they had arrived a month previously and all the wives were thrilled at being asked somewhere posh, trooping in and out of Milly and Fabian's apartment with new dresses to be altered and old dresses and shoes to be transformed.

Bee, whilst glad to help with the lending of bags and jewellery, was expecting to stay at home that evening. Rafe wasn't planning to take anyone but she had insisted that she would rather stay at home because she hadn't wanted him to feel he had to take her everywhere. But Custard bounded in a few days before shouting, 'Mrs Bee, Mrs Bee! Get your glad rags on! Rafe says that he's taking Hattie to this diplomatic wank on Saturday. So will you come with me? I don't want to go by myself. Besides I can't think of anyone I would rather go with and we can cause a scandal by smooching over the caviar.'

Laughing, Bee disengaged herself from him and assured him that if she did come there would be no smooching over anything. 'We'll have to get Milly to smarten you up though,' she said. 'Make you a fitting escort!' Just fleetingly, she wondered whom Mack was taking.

Once everyone was kitted out to their – and Milly's – satisfaction it was with happy hearts that the crew and partners of Excalibur set off for Sir David Bassington's humble little holiday home. Sir David had sent huge people-carriers for them all and Bee found herself squashed in the back between the two huge grinders, Flipper and Rump, with no room whatsoever for her bottom. Custard pulled her out. 'You can't sit there, go and sit up the front with Mack.'

'No, no. I'm fine. Really.'

'No, I absolutely insist. You'll crease that beautiful skirt.'

It was a beautiful skirt and it was getting creased but Bee still went up to the front rather reluctantly. She had been alarmed to find herself beetling around Valencia yesterday like a woman possessed to find the perfect outfit for this evening. In the end, she had settled on an expensive but totally gorgeous coral chiffon skirt with tons of layers peeping out, and a wrap-around top. She finished the whole thing off with a dramatic coral choker and ring. Her newly washed hair was piled on top of her head and she looked a million dollars.

'Em, hello,' she greeted Mack, who was already in conversation with the driver. 'I've been ordered up here because the grinders are taking up too much room.'

'Of course! I'll shift up. In fact do you want me to move back there and you can have the front seat to yourself?'

'No, no. Not at all. I don't think there'll be enough room for you anyway.'

'OK.' Mack moved up obligingly and they set off on their way.

'So do they always have these sort of parties for the crew?'

'Yes, well, we're here in the country for such a long time, and we're getting closer to the Cup now. I suppose they see us as sort of ambassadors as well. I'm not expecting a lot of attention though because we're not high profile and we're definitely not expected to win.'

He looked over at her thoughtfully. Bee hoped he might be approving of her appearance but apparently he was thinking of something else. 'I thought Rafe had asked Hattie?'

'I came with Custard,' said Bee hastily. 'He asked me last week.' Custard had told her that Mack was going alone.

'Custard?'

'Yes, in a friendly sort of way though, of course.'

'Of course.'

'He said he couldn't find a girl.' Bee hoped she wasn't supplying too much information in her effort to convince him that she and Custard weren't having some sort of crazy affair.

'He could have taken his pick from all the girls hanging around outside the compound.'

'Maybe he didn't want that sort of girl.' God, why did she say that? She probably just sounded like a mad prude now.

'Maybe.'

'Inky seems happy,' she commented. 'It's nice to see her so relaxed.'

'Yes, it is,' Mack replied gruffly.

'I was in her apartment the other day and answered the phone to her mum. She sounds a nice lady.' Bee knew that Inky was Mack's god-daughter and thus must know the family.

'She's lovely,' said Mack with a note of warmth in his voice.

'Do they look alike?'

'Very. Mary – that's Inky's mum – is more delicate-looking though.'

'But still with that dramatic hair and skin?'

'Yes.'

'She must be stunning,' sighed Bee.

'Do you like Luca?' he asked suddenly. 'Have you met him?'

'Yes,' she said in surprise. 'We usually bump into each other on the stairs. He's very polite. Always offers to carry my shopping for me and so handsome! I can certainly see what Inky sees in him from that point of view . . .'

'But?' prompted Mack.

'But what?'

'You sounded as though you had a but at the end of that.'

'Did I? Well, maybe I'm just a little worried. He's so proper round me. Really treats women like women, do you know? I adore it but I have a feeling that Inky won't. Things may get difficult when the racing starts, that's all.'

Mack felt impressed at her insight. 'You care about her, don't you?'

'Of course! I care about all of them.'

Mack was suddenly grateful and an unfamiliar feeling of solidarity flooded over him. He was so used to being a loner that it felt strange. He really felt as though he could rely on this woman. She would look out for things that he couldn't see.

'Thank you,' he said.

They travelled in silence for a while. They were starting to come into the real countryside now and the driver wound his window halfway down.

'Too windy?' he asked Bee in heavily accented English.

'No,' she breathed. 'Just perfect.'

She could smell tantalising whiffs of pine and jasmine on the warm air, occasional juniper and thyme. The landscape gave way to fields, obviously tended but separated by old hewn stone walls and paths. Odd copses of trees were dotted around consisting of olive, walnut, oak and yew, a peculiar scratchy undergrowth of sarsaparilla, honeysuckle, and juniper.

'Beautiful, isn't it?' said Mack quietly.

'And there up on the hill is the Torre del Matarrana,' said the driver. 'The ambassador named it after the local river. *Torre* comes from a Latin word meaning castle or palace.'

Mack and Bee both swivelled their heads to where he was pointing. A huge castellated building stood there. It had the air and elegance of a palace.

As they swept up the driveway, the dusty brittleness of the countryside gave way to lush manicured lawns and flowerbeds. They drew to a stop and were hustled into an enormous stone-flagged hall which buzzed with conversation. They stood awkwardly on the perimeter for a second.

Custard gestured to a huge candlestick mounted on the wall next to him. 'If I pulled this, do you think we would disappear down a trap door like Scooby Doo?' he whispered, and Bee giggled.

Next moment an impeccably dressed man came towards them with open arms. 'Welcome!' he cried. 'Welcome to Spain! Welcome to Valencia!'

Mack introduced himself and shook hands.

'David Bassington, how do you do? And this is your crew, I take it? Marvellous! Now, come through and let's get you all a drink. I took the liberty of inviting the defenders of the Cup too! I thought you would like to meet them, especially as Henry Luter is English.'

'Henry Luter?' queried Mack.

'I can't tell you what a good turn he did us by bailing out the Spanish challenge. We thought what a marvellous opportunity to have you all under one roof so everyone can get to know each other. After all, you might be competing against each other soon enough!'

It was lucky that the ambassador had his back to the crew as he led the way because Mack's face was a sight to behold.

Bee was trying to look as appalled as the rest of the crew but was secretly quite thrilled that she would get the chance to meet such a legendary figure. Until she thought of Rafe, that is. Because presumably if Henry Luter's Phoenix Challenge was here then that would mean Jason Bryant and Ava. She glanced back through the throngs, dodging her head and trying to catch a glimpse of Rafe. She suddenly felt desperately sorry for him. These last few months he had almost been back to his old self; she knew his miraculous sailing abilities had newly been restored to a pre-Ava level. The wound had closed over and she could only hope that it wouldn't be wrenched open again.

'She might not be here,' murmured Mack, reading her thoughts, into her ear.

'I hope not,' she whispered back.

Luckily the vast airy drawing room they were shown into was teeming with people, spilling out on to the lawn through three huge French doors at the end of the room. The ambassador said he had more guests to greet and he would be back later for a chat but in the meantime they would be well looked after.

'Some alcohol would make this easier,' said Mack to Bee.

'Do you think that would be wise? I mean I don't think Rafe should drink a lot. It might spark off some sort of . . . '

'Not for Rafe. For us.'

314

'Oh.'

Mack entered the crowd gathered round a white-tableclothed table and emerged with two glasses of champagne.

'What are you going to do about Henry Luter?' asked Bee, her head still straining for a glimpse of Rafe, who was at the back of the group.

'Ignore him.'

'Should we try to keep Rafe and Ava apart?'

'We can try but I think Rafe will either want to see her or won't. Christ, I wouldn't have agreed to come to this thing if I'd known. I should have asked.'

'You weren't to know,' said Bee comfortingly. 'Do you think Colin Montague knew Ava might be here?' she asked hesitantly.

'No, I don't think so. They're still not speaking. He has no idea where she is from one day to the next. And Ava's never been close to her mother. I know when the racing starts we're going to have to come face to face with her on a daily basis, not least on the race course. All the Louis Vuitton parties for one.'

'But that's not for a while.'

'Exactly. He's just starting to get his confidence back on the water and I thought by the time we started to race . . . ' Mack shrugged.

'That he would be unaffected by her.'

It was such a glorious evening that most people were drifting out on to the lawn. The façade of the ancient house took on a sienna and ochre hue and the views stretched out at their feet with the beauty of the valley to one side and the olive and orange groves to the other.

Custard appeared at Bee's elbow. He'd managed to requisition a bottle of champagne from somewhere and a bowl of olives.

'Come on, Mrs Bee. Let's go and spit olive stones at the opposition's necks.'

On the lawn she positioned herself with her back to the views and was busy chatting to some of the crew wives whilst keeping one eye on Rafe who was in another group to her left and the other on the French doors which spilt out more and more guests.

Ava and Jason Bryant appeared at the top of the steps. Ava looked heartbreakingly beautiful, wearing a simple Alice Temperley strappy dress in cream and exquisitely embroidered black. Her skin was almost the same colour as the dress and she looked as delicate as the orchid which was cradled in her hair. One lone curl had escaped and was lying on her shoulder. Jason walked with an exaggerated swagger. He clearly knew he was with the most stunning girl in the room.

Bee tore her eyes away from them to look at Rafe. He was staring at Ava with an intensity which told Bee instantly that he couldn't have got over her. Bee sighed. Rafe and Ava always looked completely amazing together. Their dark and light looks were in dramatic contrast. Like heaven and hell. Her eye was caught also by Hattie, standing directly behind Rafe, and staring at Ava with a strange sort of awe. Bee frowned to herself and wondered if she had been missing something.

Ava hadn't spotted any of them; she descended the steps and was soon sucked into the vortex and disappeared. Bee excused herself and wandered over to Rafe's side. He looked pale and shocked. That haunted look which he had almost lost over the last couple of months had returned. Bee suddenly hated Mack and his stupid challenge.

'Are you all right, darling?' she asked in a low voice.

Rafe didn't look at her. 'I'm fine,' he said shortly.

'Do you want to go?'

'No. I don't.' He downed his glass of champagne in one go and then marched into the house.

Hattie found Rafe slumped in one of the ambassador's extremely comfortable sofa chairs, beautifully upholstered in Osborne and Little print.

'Are you OK?' she asked awkwardly, perching on the neighbouring chair.

He was staring ahead, eyes seemingly fixed on nothing. 'Fine,' he snapped.

Hattie bit her lip and folded her hands in her lap which she always did when she was nonplussed. 'I . . . I saw that Ava Montague was here . . . '

He got up suddenly and dived into the mass of people. Hattie was undecided for a second but then followed him. She scooted to a halt when she found Ava and Rafe staring at each other.

'I heard you were doing the Cup,' Ava said.

'Yes.'

'How . . . how are you? I've been wondering about you.'

'Have you?' His tone was unfriendly.

Hattie didn't know what to do. They were oblivious to her anyway.

'You didn't return any of my calls.'

'It didn't stop you going out with Bryant. Still with him?'

'What's wrong with Jason?'

'He's all wrong for you. He's a vicious thug.'

'Look who's talking. That was a blinder of a black eye you gave him. I didn't see him retaliate.'

'Not yet.'

'Jason is handsome and successful, in fact he's the best in the world at what he does. Why wouldn't I pick him?' she said in a trembling voice.

'He defected.'

'He goes where there are the greatest opportunities.'

'Why? Couldn't he get the Cup for himself? What about loyalty?'

'Loyalty can't get in the way of ambition.'

'I thought we were talking about Jason Bryant, Ava. Not about us,' said Rafe sardonically. 'Are you trying to piss off your father? Because you're doing it spectacularly well. If Daddy didn't like

317

the look of me then he sure as hell won't like the look of Jason Bryant.'

Her eyes flickered. 'He won't speak to me. Look, I'm sorry about everything. I thought that you would . . . ' She shrugged.

'What? Forgive you? Turn a blind eye when someone else caught yours? I don't work like that, Ava. I can't work like that and I thought you felt the same way.'

'I did.' She bit her lip hard and looked down.

Hattie, alarmed by the sudden intimacy of the conversation and feeling slightly voyeuristic, started to back away. Her movement caught Ava's eye. Her head snapped up.

'I see that you haven't wasted much time. Who's your little friend here?'

Rafe noticed Hattie for the first time and, with sudden kindness prompted by the panic in her eyes, caught hold of her elbow. He turned to go and then leant back impulsively. 'I wouldn't be too sure about Bryant being the best in the world by the way. Stick around and watch.'

Hattie stumbled slightly as Rafe moved her quickly through the throng. She glanced back to find Ava glaring at her. Beautiful, bewitching Ava. How could she even possibly start to compete with her for Rafe? Their love affair clearly reached depths which she could only guess at. She tried to gather herself by smoothing down her Monsoon dress (which she had considered to be the height of sophistication until she saw Ava's) but it was no good. She gave a sob, wrenched her arm away from Rafe and ran off.

Hattie wasn't the only one who was upset. She cannoned into a woman coming out of the loos and, pausing only a second to apologise, left her to pick up her bag, the contents of which had spilt all over the floor. Custard was just coming out of the Gents and hurried over.

'Here, let me help you.' He started to gather lipsticks and eyebrow pencils, diplomatically leaving the tampons for her to pick up. It wasn't until he glanced up that he recognised the person they all belonged to.

'Mrs Luter!' he exclaimed in surprise, recognising her from her photograph and their sighting from *Excalibur*. He peered more closely at her, wondering if he'd made a mistake. The figure before him had only a passing resemblance to the woman he remembered. 'It is Mrs Luter, isn't it? Henry Luter's wife?'

He held out his hand when she nodded feebly. 'My name is Custard, I mean Will. Will Stanmore. I was in Auckland on your husband's last challenge.'

Saffron looked vaguely at him and shook his hand. 'How do you do,' she murmured. Her hand was small and weak in his.

'We probably shouldn't be chatting,' he said cheerfully. 'Or we'll be accused of fraternising . . . ' Saffron's eyes filled with tears. 'Mrs Luter, what on earth is the matter?' He helped her up. 'Come round here, out of the way.' He guided her round the corner and into a chair leaning against the wall and then sprinted off into the loos to emerge with a wad of loo paper. 'Here.'

Tears filled her eyes again at his kindness and they dropped down her cheek one by one. Custard knelt next to her and just patted her knee now and then. This felt much more comfortable than that time Inky had cried on board *Mucky Ducky*: he wasn't sure why. He didn't feel awkward or panicky, he simply wanted to comfort her. Saffron looked vastly different from how he remembered her. Now she was a lot thinner for one thing, her clothes were just falling off her; her face had no colour nor her hair any shine and the light had gone out of her eyes. It was as though she had been a sleek, thoroughbred racehorse, prancing with life and spirit and now she was just a broken wreck about to be carted off to the knacker's yard. Maybe she was ill.

'God, I'm sorry,' she said eventually. 'You must think I'm an idiot.'

'No, no. Not at all. Can I get you something? A brandy or some water? Paella?'

319

She smiled. 'No, I'm fine.'

They sat for a moment in silence until she said. 'Are you with our challenge this time as well?'

Goes to show, he thought, how much time she spends down at the team base. 'No, I'm with Excalibur.'

'Of course,' she said slowly. 'That's why you said we shouldn't be talking, isn't it?' It wasn't really a question; she wasn't concentrating. She was gripping the chair arms hard as though trying to convince herself of their reality.

'Are you OK, Mrs Luter? Is there anything I can do for you?'

She looked at him again and smiled. 'No. There's nothing anybody can do for me.'

Oh God, she must have cancer or something, thought Custard. She started searching around in her bag. Custard realised he was still holding something in his hand and opened it out to look.

'Are you looking for this?' He proffered a pill bottle towards her.

She scooped it hastily out of his hand. 'Just for my nerves,' she mumbled. For her nerves? How old can she be? thought Custard. Twenty-four? Twenty-five?

'You know, doctors can do things all the time. They thought my Aunt Peggy was on her last legs but she went on to live another twenty . . .'

'Oh no. I'm not ill,' she said. 'It's just that . . . ' Suddenly she was still and lifted her head to listen, like an animal taking a respite and then hearing the sound of the hunters.

'That's Henry. I have to go.' She rose quickly. 'Thank you. You've been kind.'

'You're welcome,' he said to her retreating back. He stood for a moment staring after her. She was still beautiful despite the erosion, but he hadn't realised just how fragile.

Oblivious to all the upset going on around her, Inky was having a lovely evening. She was revelling in the attention *her* new dress had brought her. The dress was completely backless and the top seam just caressed the top of her bottom. The front was just two strips of material which covered her breasts and tied behind her neck. The rest of it dropped to her knees in black crumpled taffeta. She felt pretty sexy and the rest of the crew thought so too; they were proud of her and wanted to show her off.

They hadn't noticed that they had drifted near Jason Bryant's chattering crowd. He had his back to them so he couldn't have seen them. The crew were just beseeching Inky to pick up a napkin in the wild hope that her dress would slip in some way when Bryant started to loudly proclaim to his group, 'I know that no one has heard of them but they're the new British challenge. All completely useless of course since Phoenix took the best. They were so desperate they even had to have a woman on the team; it's a pity she's not black and got one leg and then they'd be the most PC crew . . . '

The next few moments were such a blur of scuffling that Inky couldn't work out which men from Excalibur were trying to get to Jason to wring his neck and which crew members were trying to hold them back. The only one they missed was the lithe, relatively small Dougie. He was now apoplectic with rage, prodding Jason's chest and yelling at the top of his voice. 'TAKE THAT BACK, YOU BASTARD. YOU JUST WANT TO FUCK HER, DON'T YOU? THAT'S WHAT THIS IS ALL ABOUT . . . ' Mack had been standing only a short way away and sprinted over to Dougie and dragged him off. 'That's enough,' he hissed into his ear, thrusting him back amidst the Excalibur group who were all still tangled up together and looking murderous, ready to pounce at another word from Bryant. 'Save it for the water. That means all of you.' He looked from one man to the other.

Henry Luter appeared out of nowhere. 'John MacGregor,' he drawled. 'Every time one of your crew meets mine, they try to hit them.'

'They're provocative.'

'That's a term you apply to women, not to grown men. At

least mine can keep their tempers. You need to get your house in order and get your staff under control.'

'They are not my staff. They are my crew.'

'More is the pity for you. Well, if you pay peanuts . . . '

'This crew wasn't put together with a pay packet in mind.'

'Clearly they weren't put together with anything in mind. You need to stop playing with schoolgirls and has-beens. Not sure if we can't put you under that category now.'

'To famously quote a skipper, better to be a has-been than a never-was.'

'I own the Cup now, Mack, and don't you forget it. You will never be in a position to lay one finger on it.'

'We haven't even started yet.'

'You're one team we wouldn't worry about beating.'

The ambassador hurried over. 'Is there a problem? Is everyone all right?'

'Yes, sir, we're all fine. There's no problem. Just a few tempers boiling over with a rival team.'

'Of course,' said Sir David. He still looked fairly horrified.

'All the men have been training too hard. We won't embarrass you any longer.'

Slowly he rounded them up and hustled them all away. Inky got the last laugh, as with her hands on her hips, she did a slow turn in front of Bryant, giving a small smile and, for those quick enough to catch it, an imperceptible V-sign.

By the time they had rounded up all the Excalibur crew, the people-carriers were at the front of the house. Rafe had to be extracted from the bar and Custard was found at the last moment emerging from the direction of the loos. Amidst further apologies to the ambassador, they made their excuses and left.

Mack let rip all the way back about what an embarrassment it was for the team and how they had let everyone down, including Colin Montague. After his diatribe, he looked back at his forlorn crew members. Hattie was quietly crying in the back and Bee was looking worried. He reflected this perhaps wasn't the most successful evening ever. But there was one thing he was exceptionally pleased about.

Excalibur wouldn't have stood up for each other like this six months earlier.

Chapter 27

Hattie was feeling pretty low. Ever since that night at the diplomatic party, images of Rafe and Ava had haunted her. She had felt so disgustingly middle class and ordinary next to Ava. They were all going home for the holidays soon and she could bet Ava wasn't stressing about Christmas presents.

Just a few months ago she had been longing for the week off to spend within her family's comforting embrace. But now she couldn't bear the idea of being away from Rafe. Having seen Rafe and Ava together, she realised her hopes were futile. Being a stoical sort of girl (and coming from a long line of the best sort of stiff-upper-lippers), she forced herself to take a long, hard look at the situation. She was quite sure he harboured no special feelings for her. He was very kind and clearly enjoyed her company but she was fooling herself if it was anything more than that.

She still couldn't help doing one tiny thing for him though and caught him before practice one day. 'Rafe! Hi! I've, er, loaded my iPod with some music for you. You said you didn't know any British music, so I thought I'd give you a quick résumé of the last ten years.'

Rafe looked down at the tiny piece of equipment and his face lit up. 'Thanks, Hattie! Are you sure you don't need it for the moment?'

Hattie stood on one foot. 'Well, I don't really have the time, the challenge keeps me pretty busy. You just press this and then this . . . ' She demonstrated, knowing Rafe's understanding of electronics was basic.

'That's kind, really kind,' said Rafe after observing.

Hattie went bright red. 'My pleasure.'

For the next few weeks, Rafe spent the tow out to the race waters listening to The Strokes, the Kaiser Chiefs, Coldplay and Jamie Cullum on Hattie's iPod. And because she couldn't resist inserting a small love note for him, she had put The Beautiful South's 'Dream a Little Dream of Me' in the middle.

'Where did Rafe get that iPod?' asked Custard one day. 'I thought he and technology didn't get on.'

Fabian looked over to Rafe lying on a pile of sails, his foot tapping away to something. 'It's Hattie's. She did it for him. She loaded all the songs for him so he could catch up a bit on Brit culture.'

'Hattie? What did she load it with? *Songs of Praise*?'

'Oh, I don't know. I think our Hattie is a bit of a dark horse. Probably all Sex Pistols and The Prodigy. I also think she's got a bit of a crush on our wind caller.'

'She's up against Ava. One completely gorgeous woman.' Custard paused and dwelled on their comparative good looks for a second. 'She'd have been better off spending her time painting our sodding bicycles,' he muttered before flopping back on his sails for another doze. And it seemed only seconds before Ho was yelling at them all to get out of his sewer because he wanted to make sure all his sails were sorted.

There seemed to be so much to talk about after the diplomatic party that it took the crew a while to work their way round to any gossip concerning Rafe and Ava. Word had it the two of them had a bit of a showdown and the crew started to get worried that she would affect his sailing again. 'Was that the first time he's seen Ava since the break-up?' Golly asked Fabian. 'Has he said anything to you?' Jonny asked Inky. 'How does he feel about her?' Custard asked Mack.

The whole of the crew felt very personally involved in all of this. Fifteen enormously tough men, four of them able to bench-press 120kg in the gym and one who'd sailed around the world with a fractured elbow, were now all whispering and wondering and desperately trying to get in touch with their more sensitive side, which most of them hadn't seen for decades. Mack knew this wasn't merely because they didn't want to lose in the competition but that they were starting to look after one of their own.

None of them wanted to mention it directly to him, afraid that if they dabbled with something they didn't understand they might make it worse. It frightened them – which made them realise just how quietly confident they had been becoming and how much they had been relying on Rafe for that extra bit of magic. So they watched and waited, muttering amongst themselves, and if Rafe was surprised that the crew were constantly asking if he was OK or if they could get him anything then he didn't show it.

It seemed amazing that a crew which started off as not being able to stand more than one second than was absolutely necessary in each other's company now weren't really comfortable any place else. They gave the impression of one huge old married couple, who had been together for years, constantly finishing off each other's sentences and pre-empting each other's stories. On the boat, only a nod or a look would communicate a wealth of information.

This morning, on their last outing before they broke for Christmas, they were pulling off the docks with Rafe at the helm when a passing American sailor yelled at him, 'Drive it like you stole it, dude!'

Rafe looked at the rest of the crew in bafflement. 'What does that mean? How can he think I've managed to steal this boat?'

'Rafe. You are *so* English. That is such an English thing to say,' said Custard. 'I don't give a fuck what anyone says, it's like it says on your passport. You're English. You're going to turn into Victor Meldrew in twenty years' time.'

Rafe thought this was a nice thing to say and wondered who Victor Meldrew was and which yacht club he belonged to.

Rafe's wind-calling skills were seemingly unaffected by his meeting with Ava and the crew started to relax again. Although he spent hours trying to explain to the rest of them, some of whom had a good eye for the dark puddles of water and close ripples which meant the wind was coming, it was all to no avail because no one else was so masterful at understanding the signs of nature. To some it was a matter of interpretation, to Rafe it was already in his language. He could even predict the appearance of white squalls accurately. Although he used a lot of instinct, he also relied on more local knowledge. He still often went down to speak to the local fishermen and harbour staff, his Spanish holding him in good stead. Sometimes he made Fabian borrow Mack's Merc and drive him up into the hills where he would look at the sea through binoculars. He would always look for signs from the shore as well, plumes of smoke and drifting umbrellas.

'Where did you learn to speak Spanish?' Dougie asked Rafe later that day basking in the last rays of sun on the deck as they were towed home, disbelieving of the fact that within twenty-four hours they would all be at their respective homes shivering by the radiators for Christmas. No one went down into the sewer for the tow home because all the sails were so wet and the atmosphere so fuggy from Ho's exertions that it was like being in a Chinese laundry. Except smellier.

'My dad saw a Spanish lady for a while when we were in Cadiz. Margarita. She was lovely. Beautiful too. Taught me Spanish, Picasso, a little bit of piano and flamenco.'

'What was Cadiz like?' asked Inky.

'We actually met Margarita a bit further up the coast at Sanlucar; they have huge beach parties there. They barbecue shellfish marinated in manzanilla sherry and the gypsies exercise their horses on the beach. But Cadiz is a twisting, secret labyrinth. History seeps from it. It is as much Africa as it is Spain.'

'Sod Cadiz. Tell us more about Margarita. Was she a babe?

Come on, Rafe. You must have been tempted.' Custard propped himself up on his elbow and shaded his eyes against the sun.

'I was seven.'

'Still.' Custard flopped back down on the deck. 'Sorry, I've been far too long without a woman.'

'I need to pee,' sighed Inky.

'*Mucky Ducky* has gone on ahead. You'll have to hold it,' said Custard.

'Don't bother.'

Although she now normally peed in the posh loo on the *Mucky Ducky*, she was so comfortable with everyone that she just went off the side like everyone else if the launch wasn't around. The clothing people had made all her polo shirts with extra long shirt-tails so she didn't moon the whole of the Mediterranean. If there were boats nearby some of the crew always offered to stand in front of her.

'Careful, Inky!' called Custard after her. 'Some of us haven't had any sex for so long we might rugby-tackle you to the deck at the sight of you in flagrante.'

'I'll take my chances.'

'I'm not quite at the stage where the sight of Inky peeing is a big turn on,' grumbled Jonny. 'I'll worry when it is.'

'I'm so tired I don't think I can lift my hand to my mouth to eat a bun,' said Custard.

Carla had zoomed out on the launch with tea and buns for the tow home. Dougie was tucking into a couple of them. 'I wouldn't dare to tell Carla this but the Spanish really can't make buns, can they? I dream of Chelsea buns. I'm going straight to a bakery when I get home.'

'The first thing I'm going to do when I get home is find me a girl,' commented Custard, who was still thinking about Rafe's Margarita. 'I might deign to say hello to my mum and dad and Pipgin first who are so graciously having me for Christmas but then I'm going to find me a girl. Pipgin is flying back with me on the third.'

'And who is Pipgin?' asked Rafe.

'My red setter. He was staying with my folks but Bee offered to have him with Salty during the day and I'll have him back at night.'

'Custard, you secretly just want to settle down, take your dog for walks, eat Sunday roasts and play with your children, don't you?' said Inky, laughing at him.

'Of course. That's why I'm on this bloody boat in Spain, sweating my guts out with you lot.'

'The lady doth protest too much,' said Inky flopping back on the deck.

Custard ignored her. 'Maybe Sir Edward would let Pipgin and Salty come on the *Mucky Ducky* occasionally.'

'Er, maybe,' said Rafe doubtfully, thinking that maybe Sir Edward would but Mack definitely wouldn't.

'Bought any Christmas presents yet?' Dougie asked Custard.

'I'm going to get all of mine at the airport. A bottle of Baileys and some mints goes a long way in my family.'

They were coming up to the docks now and Custard could see the huge spectre of *Corposant* berthed at the super-yacht marina. He wondered fleetingly what Saffron Luter would be doing for Christmas. Whenever he thought about her it was always within the context of a luxurious life. Staff and cars to take her everywhere and shopping trips around the world. But for Christmas would there be turkey and crackers and a tree? Would she and Henry Luter exchange gifts on Christmas morning? He doubted it.

Chapter 28

Even the most dedicated of the America's Cup teams went home for Christmas. Inky suspected this was more to do with the fact that the Spanish waters were slightly less hospitable in the winter and they didn't want to risk the boats with the increased danger of white squalls rather than any great religious affirmation, but she was glad of the chance to return home anyway. Whilst the Mediterranean was not the toothless, placid sea portrayed in the postcards, it was still a completely different creature to her Atlantic. It was like dealing with a flighty young girl when all she understood was the wisdom and strength of the father. She missed his sombre grey on days when you couldn't tell the sea from the sky. She missed the crashing waves, the coal-black mussels clinging to the rocks and the icy sting of the spray. She would miss Luca but she was glad to be going home.

Rafe's Aunt Bee had decided to join her daughter skiing in St Anton for Christmas. She was planning to drive there, stopping for various nights along the way. She had asked Rafe to join them but Rafe desisted, not least on the grounds that he wasn't sure he could stand four days cooped up in a car with Salty in the back. He had been trying to get hold of his father who was in the Caribbean to ask if he could come and visit but a stranger eventually answered his mobile and said it had been left in a bar in St Barts and where could it be posted? At this point Inky stepped in and insisted he come back with her to

Cornwall. They flew into Bristol airport and a delighted James Pencarrow picked them up. He always felt that he had discovered Rafe and thus had some sort of special responsibility towards him. Anyone could be forgiven for thinking that he was more pleased to see Rafe than Inky.

'Your mother is so excited,' he told Inky as they waited for the barrier to come up on the airport car park. 'She has been scurrying about all week, trying to get everything ready.'

'Is she up to it?' asked Inky worriedly. 'Surely she should be relaxing a bit more?'

'I have told her so.'

Her father seemed to have forgotten completely about their dreadful row concerning Luca although he studiously avoided the subject. Inky wondered whether Mack might have had a hand in this. 'I hope she hasn't been working too hard. We'd just settle for some chicken and a couple of sprouts. Just a change from Spanish food.'

'Sprouts? What are sprouts?' asked Rafe.

'Brussel sprouts.'

'Never heard of them.'

Inky sighed. It was easy to forget that Rafe wasn't quite English. 'The boys home?' she asked.

'Everyone except Charlie, of course. Charlie,' he explained proudly to Rafe, 'is my eldest son. He's doing the Volvo.'

'Really? We tried to follow the fleet across the Atlantic once,' said Rafe. 'But we lost sight of them within half a day. Those boats really shift.' They went on to discuss sails and the fabulousness of having Christmas with ten other smelly men and a freeze-dried turkey.

Mary Pencarrow had spent the best part of the morning rushing around Truro buying stocking presents for Rafe. All the children and James had one every year and there would be anarchy if they ever stopped the tradition. She couldn't bear for Rafe to have to sit and watch the stockings being opened without actually having one himself. The thought didn't occur that she did exactly that every year because nobody actually went to the bother of doing a stocking for her. She bought a Rick Tomlinson sailing calendar, a little book about sailing myths and sayings, and a box of nougat. She also bought a toothbrush and some chocolate coins because that's what the other children always had. She wandered rather aimlessly around Marks and Spencer with a basket looking at the tie racks and golf accessories. She picked up and put back some boxer shorts because it seemed rather presumptuous and then put back the three pack of socks as well because she suddenly remembered that Inky said he didn't wear any, eventually walking out empty-handed. She looked at her watch and cursed herself for wasting half an hour when she had so much to do back at home. Tomorrow was Christmas Eve and she had to make all the stuffing and sauces for the turkey and finish wrapping all the presents for James's mother who, every year, sent her some money and asked her to buy presents for all the family. She was exhausted but she so loved having everyone together for Christmas and wanted to make everything nice for them that she really didn't mind. She would have gift-wrapped a Farr 40 and pushed it up the hill herself if she'd had to.

Rafe and Inky arrived just as she was hiding the carrier bags behind the armchair in the kitchen. She straightened up and greeted her daughter with a huge hug. 'You've let your hair grow!' she said in delight. 'How come?'

'Oh, no reason. Just thought it looked nicer.'

'It does! You look more beautiful than ever!'

Mary turned her attention to Rafe. God, he was striking-looking and with a strange brooding feel about him as though he was a panther ready to pounce. She got a feeling he didn't unbend easily. She shot a glance back at Inky who already had her head in the fridge looking for one of her inevitable yoghurts.

She didn't get the chance to speak with Inky until later when James had taken Rafe out to the garage to show him his boat.

'Darling, he is dishy.'

Inky was fiddling with Nelson the Labrador's ears and thought that only her mother – or possibly Hattie – could get away with using the word *dishy*. 'Who? Rafe?'

'Yes, Rafe.'

'Hands off, Ma!' said Inky with a grin. 'His heart belongs to another. Although I'm afraid the feeling is not returned.'

'Who?'

'Ava Montague, Colin Montague's daughter. Do you remember I pointed her out?'

'Yes, in one of your *Tatler* magazines.'

'Oh I remember. Beautiful girl.' Mary walked over to the Aga and leant against the rail, wiping her hands on a teacloth drying there. 'What happened?'

Inky shrugged. 'I didn't know him back then. It was before he joined the challenge. But I think that's why he joined. Because Ava is now going out with Jason Bryant.'

'No!'

'Yes! Rumour has it that Mack convinced him to join by telling him he could beat the arse off Bryant.'

'Have you asked Mack?'

'Yes, but you know Mack. He won't tell me anything and it's useless me asking because I'm always the last one to know in case anyone accuses him of favouring his god-daughter. So he wouldn't confirm or deny.'

'So Ava went from Rafe to Jason Bryant? I wonder why? I mean Jason is a nice-looking boy . . . ' Inky shifted uncomfortably in her seat; she didn't like talk of Bryant in favourable terms. 'But there is something slightly unsettling about Rafe. Something almost feral, don't you think?' She looked keenly at Inky who had realised to her surprise that she was really enjoying this chinwag with her mum. Normally she would want to be with the men talking about boats and tactics.

'Mack hasn't met anyone?'

'No!'

333

Mary frowned. 'That's funny . . . because when I called to thank him for the wonderful flowers he sent me when I was ill, he left me with the distinct impression he liked someone.'

'Where on earth would he have had the chance to meet anyone?'

'I don't know. Maybe I was imagining it.'

'Have you managed to get up to London recently?' asked Inky.

'No, darling. You know how your father despises it.'

'You could go by yourself. Or I'll come when I'm back. I'm sure Dad could manage for a couple of days by himself. Do him good.'

Mary stared at her daughter. 'Maybe it would.' She smiled suddenly. 'Now, darling. Tell me all about your beautiful Italian.'

Inky grinned and snuggled down in her chair.

On Christmas Eve the whole family made the ritual trip to St Enodoc church for the carol service by walking across the golf course to the tiny granite church folded amongst the sand dunes. It used to be completely covered in sand and the vicar had to be lowered by rope through the roof in order to hold the annual service to justify it being kept open. But the church and the graveyard had since been restored and Mary Pencarrow regularly walked up for a Sunday service by herself. The stout, cool stone of the church with its small mullioned windows and redolence of history gave her a real sense of a stronghold against the sea, the relentless sound of which she could still hear in the distance with the seagulls weaving overhead. She often dropped to her knees in those little pews and prayed for her family and her marriage. But today was a much more cheerful affair for her. Her family were with her and although she could still hear the waves crashing and the wind howling, at least the cheerful carols nearly drowned them out.

After the service she rushed back across the golf course, her head buried into the fug of hats and scarves around her shoulders, leaving Inky, James and the boys to make small talk with the vicar and the locals. It had become somewhat of a tradition for them to host a small outdoor cinema on Christmas Eve where they would gather all the outdoor heaters and sun loungers they could muster, pile the latter high with blankets, duvets and pillows and project a Christmas movie on to the side of the house. This year it was *It's a Wonderful Life*. Mary would be too busy making sure everyone had enough mulled wine and serving piping-hot sausage rolls from the oven to watch any major part of it but she often wondered if she hadn't been born if the effects would have been quite so dramatic as for George Bailey.

'Are you all right, Rafe?' she asked as he came into the kitchen.

He glanced up. 'I'm fine, thanks. Everyone is following.'

'Not too cold?'

Rafe grinned. 'A bit. I'm not used to it.'

Mary moved instinctively to the kettle to make tea for them all at the mention of cold. 'Did you enjoy the service?'

'Very much. I haven't been inside a church very often.'

Mary looked at him keenly, she had noticed he was barely singing the carols.

'Last time was for my mother's funeral but I really don't remember that,' he said without a trace of embarrassment.

'Do you miss her?'

'I don't think I remember her enough to miss her but there's always a space where she used to be.'

'I'm sorry.' She wondered about his childhood without Christmas carols, teatime cake and years of playing the shepherd in the nativity play.

He looked up as though reading her mind. 'Don't be. I truly am more comfortable at sea. It's as though . . . ' he struggled with the words, 'as though I wasn't really built for the land.' Or the trouble which came hand in hand with it, he thought, thinking of Ava. 'Can I help you with anything? In the kitchen?'

Mary stared at him in surprise. 'Really?'

'Of course.'

'Well, could you put all these on baking trays?' she asked,

pointing at the home-made sausage rolls. 'Where were you last Christmas?' she asked as they both busied themselves with their chores.

'With my aunt.' He paused in his work. 'I had just broken up with a girl,' he admitted. 'It was a pretty rough time.' He didn't know why he had just told her that. He was usually such a private person but there was something about Mary Pencarrow which made her very easy to talk to.

'Was that Ava Montague? Inky told me about her,' she added quickly.

'Yes. It was Ava.'

'I get *Tatler* sent to me and I've been reading about her new exhibition in London. She's an impressive artist.'

Rafe nodded slowly. 'I didn't know she got her own exhibition. It's what she always wanted.'

'And have you seen her since you broke up?' It was automatic for Mary to take a maternal role and ask such questions and she felt instinctively protective of Rafe, maybe because he had no mother.

'She's going out with Jason Bryant, the helmsman for the Phoenix Challenge. So I have seen her in Valencia.'

There was a pause as Mary made him a mug of tea. 'I can tell it was a bad break-up,' she said with her back still to him.

'I thought I'd never recover,' he said simply. 'I'm finding it easier now though. The crew help a lot and I finally seem to have been able to connect back to my sailing. For a while I thought I had lost that too.'

'And what brought it back?'

'I think it was stronger than she was.'

On Christmas morning, everyone was up early to open their stockings. There was much laughter and good-natured ribbing. Mary sat with some tea and watched her family open their presents, delighted at their pleasure. But she felt utterly overwhelmed when Inky quietly went upstairs and came back down with a small stocking of presents she had prepared in Valencia for her. Duty-free moisturising cream, earrings and a bracelet from a street market, some Valenciano orange liqueur, washing-up gloves trimmed with jewels and some packets of seeds.

'I'm afraid they're Spanish plants,' said Inky pointing at the packets.

'I love trying to make plants grow here.' She thanked Inky profusely and reluctantly then got up to go through to the kitchen to start lunch.

Inky followed her. Without saying a word, she flipped on the radio to listen to the carols, opened one of the lower Aga doors to heat up the kitchen and poured her mother and herself a large glass of champagne. She sat down at the table. 'Do you want me to do the sprouts?'

Mary looked at her in surprise. 'We can do them together.' She showed her how to take the leaves off and make a small cross at the base.

They sat and chatted about inanities, listened to carols and sipped their champagne until Mary reached over and touched Inky's hand. 'Darling,' she said. 'I think this might be my nicest Christmas ever.'

'You will come out to Valencia, won't you?' said Inky, suddenly aware of the intimacy.

'Nothing could keep me away.'

It was with some small guilty satisfaction that Mary noticed Inky never once, in the whole of her stay, asked her father the same question.

Custard was right when he thought that Saffron Luter's Christmas wouldn't involve crackers, turkey or a tree. Saffron glanced over the mound of status symbols littering the cabin – Chanel clothes, Fendi and Balenciaga bags, La Perla underwear, the mounds of make-up from Dior – and wondered dispiritedly what to wear. Henry had decided that they were going out for Christmas lunch. He left this decision until the last moment every year, insisting

337

that his chef prepare everything for a sumptuous Christmas lunch just in case he wanted to stay in. 'At least,' thought Saffron, 'the staff will eat well this year.' She wished she was staying with them.

Her husband yelling 'Saffron!' outside the door made her jump. He tried the handle crossly and Saffron leapt forward to unlock the door.

Henry Luter came into the cabin. 'Why was the door locked?'

'Habit. Sorry,' she muttered.

'Don't do it again. This is my boat. Don't you forget it. Why isn't Consuela getting you dressed?'

'I thought I could do it myself,' mumbled Saffron. 'After all it is Christmas Day and maybe . . . ' But Henry wasn't listening to her, he had already strode over to the call bell and pressed it.

'Wear the necklace,' he commanded. He had presented Saffron with a beautiful emerald necklace last night. She knew this hadn't been because he wanted to please or spoil her but because he liked to show off his wealth and she was the perfect showcase. 'I'll be in my study. Come up when you're ready.'

After he left, Consuela had come in. While her maid rubbed moisturiser into her shoulders and back Saffron sat at her dressing table and stared at her reflection.

'Are you not spending Christmas with your family, Consuela?' she asked.

'Oh, I would like to, madam, but it is not easy to get time off.' She didn't meet Saffron's eye.

'You have a little boy and a girl, don't you?' she asked.

'Yes! I have sent them gifts. What about your family, madam?' she asked.

'I don't have any family. Not any more.'

She didn't know if it was the mention of Consuela's children or her own family that made her eyes fill with tears. Consuela quickly passed her a tissue which reminded her of Custard and his sympathy to her. It was a small beacon which had flared, but had been extinguished as quickly as it had started. Nobody could help her now. Especially not someone who probably didn't even remember their meeting.

When she was ready Saffron went to see Henry in his study. Even on Christmas Day he worked. She knocked gently and slipped in, knowing better than to say anything. She always thought that his study looked like the underground headquarters of some evil regime. It was crammed with technology of every description. He was on the telephone and waved her into a chair. She sat patiently and waited, looking uninterestedly around the room. A vast see-through fridge sat in one corner with cans of Coke arranged pedantically in pairs. Saffron remembered the day when she had helped herself to a can and Henry had screamed abuse at her until she ran off in tears. His butler had calmly explained that Mr Luter could not have unevenly matched pairs of cans in his fridge. You always had to take two cans out and either drink both or throw one away. She'd never touched anything of his again.

Eventually Henry came off the phone. 'Stand up,' he commanded. 'Turn around.' He looked her up and down. 'You'll do. Now come here.'

Saffron's stomach sank. 'But, Henry, have we got time?'

'There's always time.'

'But I've just got ready. I'll have to go and shower again.'

'Why do you always have to shower after sex?'

Saffron didn't answer, but she thought it was a bit rich that a virtual obsessive compulsive should pick on her only habit.

'You'll just have to call Consuela again,' he'd snapped. 'You sound like you're protesting.'

'No, I was just worried . . . '

'Come here now.'

Saffron went to shut the door. 'Leave it open,' he commanded. He liked the staff to hear them. Custard's kindness did indeed seem a very long way away.

PART THREE

Chapter 29

The round robin heats of the America's Cup were to start in April, the final series in late June. Now there were just a few days to go until the first heat and Fabian couldn't believe that the time had gone so quickly. It seemed like yesterday when they were all piling off the planes from England, after Christmas. He remembered the journey well, for the flight path into Valencia approached over the sea and the Cup stadium: where the battles would be acted out; where the Cup's motto would be fulfilled. *No habrá segundo*. There can be no second. Fabian was lost in a reverie as the air hostess came round checking seat belts for landing.

'I've been meaning to ask you since we left England,' she said shyly. 'Are you an America's Cup sailor?'

Fabian came to with a start. She was exceptionally pretty. 'Yes, I am.'

'Which team are you with?'

'Excalibur. The British crew.'

'I'll look out for you.'

'Why don't you come and watch?' Fabian said although he suddenly became aware of Milly listening on the other side of him.

'Maybe I will.'

When they landed they were delighted to bump into Ho and his wife, and then Sparky and Germ. They were all back together again and immediately reestablished their routines.

For those months of practice after Christmas, it felt as though *Excalibur* couldn't go anywhere in the Mediterranean without falling over another America's Cup team. The Italians were testing new spinnakers; Fabian spotted a new helmsman heading up the Germans (it seemed very late to be changing any of the crew) and the French just seemed to spend their time coming in and out of the harbour. On *Excalibur* some of the time they were buzzed up, high on adrenalin and desperate to get into the fray; at other times they were quiet – scared that their best wouldn't be good enough. The week before the battle was the worst, worried that their dream would be crushed underfoot within a matter of days. *No habrá segundo*.

Most of the crew's families were arriving in Valencia at the weekend. They knew if Great Britain was knocked out in the early rounds then this might be the only chance they got to see them race so they were coming in their droves – which was fairly depressing for the crew, who knew perfectly well what they were thinking.

Mack decided to give them all the last weekend off. They hadn't had a break since Christmas and the tension was finally getting to them. Words were no longer merely spoken on the boat, they were either whispered or shouted. Fabian lost his rag so badly that he was not only awarded Most Obnoxious Crew of the Week hat but no one would answer him unless he said 'have a nice day' at the end of all his questions. He only hoped he could hold it together once the racing began.

On the morning of their first race, Mack was up and dressed and cycling down to the *Excalibur* base by five a.m. He had been too worried about the weather reports to sleep and wondered if Laura was back from checking the weather buoys.

He said good morning to the security guard, who formally stopped him at the gates of the compound and checked his pass, then passed through the sail loft where a couple of the machinists lay snoring on top of a pile of sails. Griff Dow was also there, fast asleep. He'd probably been working until at least three or four in the morning and, as the heats approached, he'd given up going back to his apartment at all, merely snatching a few hours' kip at the base before watching the crew to reassess all the sails in action.

Mack walked past *Excalibur*, putting a reassuring hand out to touch her. She didn't give the impression so much of slumbering under her rug of tarpaulin as merely waiting. Finally he reached the offices and poked his head into one to find Laura, poring over charts and hard at work.

'What's it looking like, Laura?'

'Tricky. Full of holes.'

'Which sails?'

'I haven't finished yet but plan for medium winds. They recut the number three spinnaker during the night.'

'I'll check on it.'

But as he left her to go and wake Griff, he took pity on him and decided to give him another twenty minutes whilst he had some coffee and thought about the day. They must treat today like any other. Routine was vital for the crew. Inky nearly lost the plot last week because Carla, who normally put a blob of raspberry jam in the middle of the rice pudding, had changed it to strawberry. Inky threw down her bowl and spoon in disgust and stormed out. Carla quietly went away and bought every jar of raspberry jam the supermarket had to offer after Mack explained that sailors, being a superstitious lot, would need everything exactly the same every day until they left Valencia. Carla had taken this very much to heart and was already in her makeshift kitchen where she prepared daily miracles on the rough concrete floor, with one trestle table, a set of rings attached to a gas bottle and a lonely fridge, which for some reason stood out in the middle by itself trailing wires.

'Coffee, Mr Mack?' asked Carla.

'Please.'

She quietly went about making her eyelid-punching brew. They might not like it but she had always done it.

'A big day, Carla.'

'Yes, Mr Mack. I know.'

'It will be better once we start racing though. Relax into it.'

'We watch you.' Tim Jenkins with his usual consummate efficiency had a television set up in one corner and as many beanbags and chairs as the challenge could afford, so that all the shore crew could watch the action. 'I make lots of buns for everyone. The beautiful Mrs Bee say she come and help.'

Mack smiled and thought how wonderful that sounded. If only the beautiful Mrs Bee could come and help him. For a second he was surprised at himself. He gave his head a shake. The pressure must be getting to him.

Back at the apartments Bee too had woken early. She wondered if Mack had already gone to the base. Certainly none of the crew would be up yet and she didn't want to disturb Rafe by moving around in the apartment so maybe she would just walk down and see if anyone was there.

Bee said a cheery good morning to security and then walked through the sail loft. She found Mack in the common room, standing at the window, staring out to the water beyond the harbour where the sun was making its slow ascent. Staring at the lonely acres of the America's Cup course which within a few hours would echo with the shouts of victory and the crack of dreams.

'Morning!' she said tentatively, with just her head round the door.

He jerked round in surprise. 'Bee! You're here early! Anything wrong?'

'No, just couldn't sleep.'

'Can I get you some tea?'

'I'll make it.' She walked over to the kettle and flipped it on to boil. 'Did you sleep?' she asked.

'Sporadically.'

'You're racing the Americans today and then . . . '

'And the French tomorrow. We'll race each of the other syndicates in the round robins until we have a sort of league table. The results of the races don't count for anything except our place in the draw.'

'Are you worried about the Americans?'

Mack shrugged. 'We don't know. That's one of the challenges of the America's Cup. You never know what the other boat will be like until the racing begins. You can only guess. The Americans have always had a huge presence in the Cup though. I don't think they've missed one and they always have a lot of supporters. Whereas we . . . '

'Do you think that's important?'

'Hugely. There's a lot of psychology involved in the Cup. The sailors need to know that people are rooting for them. And if they win today it will be a huge boost for them.'

'Sir Edward said at least all the families are coming out to watch.'

'Probably because they think it will be the only chance they'll get to see us race.' He smiled ruefully.

Bee was aware of his time. 'I must go. You have work to do.'

He smiled at her as she rinsed her mug in the sink. 'I'm usually here at this time, by the way. I mean, if you can't sleep again and need some tea.'

Bee paused at the door and smiled back. 'I'll remember,' she said.

It was a glorious April morning and by the time the crew had gone for their customary run along the beach, the docks were already teeming with people. Security was really tight to get into the America's Cup village, along the lines of airport security, with metal detectors and X-ray machines, and the queues to get in were enormous. Not everyone would be able to watch the action from the water but a huge plasma screen television with live commentary was mounted inside the village for the public to watch. Sir Edward would be out on the water in *Mucky Ducky* along with a randomly chosen family of the crew (today it was Sparky's family) and Colin Montague was going to be taking up the position of eighteenth man on *Excalibur*.

Breakfast was a very subdued affair, unlike the raucous event it had become over the last six months. Fabian sat staring at his porridge, looking as though it might bite him. Inky was trying to wade through a bowl of rice pudding whilst Carla looked over at her with concern. Rafe, however, seemed relatively unperturbed by the atmosphere and was eating toast whilst chatting to the grinders who were cheerfully working their way through their second plate of eggs. Ho kept going to the window to check the weather but then seeing all the people teeming outside in the village had to run to the loos. Mack thanked God for the calmness of Custard, who was cracking his usual jokes. 'I think,' Custard announced, 'that everyone should fart at the same time on the boat to give us a bit of extra propulsion. Carla! You must start giving us all baked beans in the morning.'

Mack looked down the table at this little group, now laughing at Custard's antics, and thought how far they had come from the bedraggled band who arrived a mere fifteen months earlier.

Mack kept his usual team talk short and sweet. 'Today is the day when we find out how competitive we are. We will find out if all our work over the last fifteen months has been in vain and discover if *Excalibur* is everything that we hope she is.

'As you know we are up against the American boat, *Valiant*. She has an enormously experienced crew on board and is rumoured to be a fast boat. We will have a hard time beating her. But,' continued Mack quietly, 'the good thing about today is that I am not asking you to do any more than you have been doing every day. This is what we have been training for.' He looked briefly up to one of the stencilled quotes around the room, *Train so hard that war is easy*. 'Just bring *Excalibur* home.'

He looked over to Laura, who was desperately nervous and

constantly sipping from a bottle of Evian. Mack didn't need to tell her that whatever information she gave could win or lose the race for them. There was none of the usual high-spirited catcalling which usually accompanied her report this morning. Everyone was deadly serious. Laura gave her report of medium to strong winds, with wind directions, humidity and pressure.

Wives were waiting with the shore crew when they walked out. They had all become so close that every single one moved forward to kiss everyone and wish them good luck. Bee came face to face with Mack. Her heart was beating in her throat and she felt suddenly shy, unsure whether to kiss him or not.

He kissed her quickly on the cheek. 'Good luck,' she whispered, unable to think of anything more original to say. He just looked at her and nodded.

Together the crew walked out on to the dock. There weren't crowds of people waiting for them at the perimeter fence, unlike the rest of the syndicates whose fences buckled under the weight of their supporters but there were staunch fans. One man playing the bagpipes caught their eye and Inky and Custard grinned at each other and waved at him.

As the crew made their way over to *Excalibur,* who was already waiting in the water, Mack hung back to have a word with Colin Montague.

'What do you think, Mack?' Colin murmured, out of hearing of the crew who were now busy loading the sails.

'*Excalibur* goes well in these conditions. But the American crew have experience and a good boat. It would mean a huge amount to the crew if we won, give them a lot of confidence. God, talk about being thrown in at the deep end . . . ' Just for a second, Mack remembered that article 'Has John MacGregor finally lost the plot?'

'I've got faith in you. In all of you. Just do your best. Good luck.'

Colin left Mack with his crew.

* * *

349

Slayer left the dock at the same time as *Excalibur* and was towed out in parallel. A huge parade of mostly American and Spanish spectators followed in their boats, a rag-tag flotilla of RIBs, yachts, launches, police boats and press boats. The crew scrambled down into the sewer where a few of them talked in low, subdued voices, but most were content in their own silence. All too soon Mack was rousing them ready to race. They came up on deck to find themselves staring at the official America's Cup course.

Luckily there was no time to consider how petrifying it all looked, as *Slayer* was preparing to warm up with them and take *Excalibur* up the first leg of the course. Mack radioed across to the helm of *Slayer* to tell him which sails he wanted him to use. They raced together for a good twenty minutes before Mack decided that *Excalibur* wasn't going quite as well as she should and called for a different sail. All the time Laura was radioing in new weather reports. The Americans were warming up nearby, absorbing the good wishes from the crowds, looking relaxed and at ease. For most of their crew it wasn't their first America's Cup and probably wouldn't be their last. Mack ignored them. The *Excalibur* crew, however, were almost transfixed by the sight of the spectator fleet. It was a veritable armada after such a long time on empty seas. Mack hoped it wouldn't distract them.

As the committee boat hoisted the course signals, which was a precursor to the race start, *Mucky Ducky* came alongside to pick up any rubbish and excess belongings and deposit a silent and nervous Colin Montague on board into the eighteenth man position. With a few minutes to go until the start gun, they received their last weather report but from now on it would be radio silence. Custard packed the radios into the waterproof canister and threw it overboard for the chase boat to pick up. They were by themselves for the moment they had simultaneously longed for and dreaded.

There was a lull before the start gun fired on the first race of the 2007 America's Cup.

Chapter 30

Mack was expecting a better fight on the start line. It started aggressively enough with a hawkish charge from *Valiant*. She came at *Excalibur*, snapping with hostility and put herself on a head-on collision course. Fabian, at the bow of the boat, counted down the distance closing between them, 'One hundred metres,' he said down his radio mike, whilst indicating with his hand as well. 'Fifty . . . '

'Thirty . . . ' said Fabian, thinking this was getting too close; only seconds separated them from a head-on collision. He had just called twenty metres when Mack suddenly swung low and hard, gathering speed before turning upwind back towards them. The boats circled and circled, the two helmsmen flinging themselves at the wheel, barely able to hear themselves shout above the noise of screaming sails, the groan of winches, the cracking of the genoa as it whipped across the deck, and the shouting of the trimmers as they yelled for speed. Their speed decreased down to just a few knots and they broke away from each other with the grinders gasping for breath.

As Mack bore away to give *Excalibur* some breathing space he could feel *Valiant* already starting to growl at his heels. He ducked and dived but she simply moved better in these conditions. She seemed to come out of nowhere as she locked on to *Excalibur's* stern and, now in control, proceeded to try and drive them away from the start line. Inky acted as his eyes and ears, facing backwards towards *Valiant* and directly into the face of their bowman. She proceeded to accurately call the distances.

'Overlap to leeward, Mack,' she called. 'She's in close.'

Knowing it was their opponents' responsibility to give *Excalibur* enough space to turn, Mack wheeled the boat over towards them. He seemed to take *Valiant* by surprise. Inky would never know if it was the fault of the helmsman or the very surprised bowman inaccurately calling the distance between them, but *Valiant*'s bow clipped them as they turned.

'She's hit us!' called Inky whilst Rafe simultaneously broke out the protest flag. 'We're protesting that, *Valiant*!' she called out to them.

Within seconds the jury boat indicated a penalty against the Americans. *Valiant* seemed undeterred and followed *Excalibur* into a tack, but they must have been shaken by the incident because when Rafe started to call the time down to the starting gun, *Valiant* one of their grinders made a mistake on the port winch which left them floundering for pace.

'We're leaving *Valiant* behind,' said Inky. 'Drive for the line, Mack, drive for it now.'

The starting gun fired and Mack crossed the line a few seconds behind it.

'Damage report, please.'

Inky clambered past a very dazed Colin Montague in the eighteenth man position, with whom she wasn't allowed to communicate, and bent over the back of the stern. 'Just a small clip,' she called back. 'It won't affect us.'

'*Valiant* is six seconds behind us,' said Sammy. 'And heading on a port tack.'

Almost as though they were embarrassed, *Valiant* was now heading away from *Excalibur*, way out to the right-hand side of the course. By the time the two boats re-converged and rounded the mark, *Valiant* was just in the lead.

'Cover her,' snapped Inky.

They placed themselves between the wind and *Valiant*,

covering her as best they could, but although they could see the wind being punched out of *Valiant*'s spinnaker, they never had quite enough speed to overtake her. They trailed *Valiant* all the way up to the next mark, the crew frustrated and anxious.

The Americans were having a bad day. They reached the mark a mere few seconds ahead of *Excalibur* but as they rounded it, they fluffed the spinnaker drop and before anyone could react, part of the dropped sail started to flop into the water.

With their own spinnaker obscuring their view, *Excalibur* heard the American's shouts of panic first.

'They're trawling! They're trawling!' said Rafe, hoarse with shouted instructions.

Barely feet behind them, Mack was in a shit-awful situation. He knew that *Valiant*'s dropped spinnaker would act as a huge fishing net and drag her round. *Excalibur*'s crew were busy with their own spinnaker drop and it was still his responsibility to keep clear of *Valiant*. His mind raced, trying to calculate which side they'd dropped the spinnaker on, but because of the mark, Mack had no room to go to starboard, so he barked short orders and banked to port, simply having to hope it was the right decision.

Please get our spinnaker in, don't fuck it up, he prayed silently, watching Ho and Fabian gather the huge sail in, hand over hand, unwilling to break their concentration by shouting at them.

But it seemed that the gods were determined not to favour either side. No sooner had their own spinnaker been unceremoniously shoved into the sewer than the call came from Rafe, 'The Yanks are cutting theirs away!' They obviously didn't want to risk a dismasting. It took merely two sweeps of the lethal knife strapped to their bowman's thigh to dispose of the twenty-thousand-pound sail. The now free floating sail headed straight under *Excalibur*'s hull and wrapped itself around their keel.

Mack immediately felt *Excalibur* stutter and pull up.

'Fabian!' he yelled. 'Get it free!'

But Fabian and Ho were already running up the boat with

Rafe running down to join them. Everyone available hurtled to the toerails, trying to glimpse the white sail which was now strangling *Excalibur*. Sammy stayed with Mack and broke out the protest flag. *Valiant* might not be liable for a penalty, but it wouldn't matter if they were given ten; if *Excalibur* couldn't get themselves free of the spinnaker then they would never catch them.

'It's here!' yelled Fabian as he dived into the water, grabbing on to the guilty spinnaker as he went. *Excalibur* had slowed down to a mere few knots and he hung on to the white spinnaker, yanking it away and yet clinging on for dear life as it was his only link with the boat.

'Hang on, for fuck's sake!' yelled Mack. If he let go and floated away, it would mean a penalty for *Excalibur* as he would officially become 'man overboard'.

Fabian had both feet on the side of *Excalibur* and was pulling at the sail frenziedly. In the meantime, Inky was being hung like a monkey upside down over the side and was lowered to clip a rope on to Fabian's harness so that when the sail eventually came free, they would still have hold of Fabian. As many hands as possible were hanging over the side, grasping and pulling. It seemed like for ever before Fabian eventually called, 'It's coming!' and hand over hand he was able to pull it until, seemingly harmless, it started to float away. Golly and Ho pulled Fabian back on to the deck, who lay there gasping for breath whilst the rest of the crew ran back to their stations and concentrated on *Excalibur* getting back up to full speed.

'Talk to me, Rafe, talk to me,' muttered Mack. 'Tell me where the wind is.'

'It's where *Valiant* is. Follow her course,' said Rafe regretfully.

'Inky?' questioned Mack.

'*Valiant* still has to perform their first penalty.' No penalty had been awarded to *Valiant* for their lost spinnaker as no rules had been broken and *Valiant* had gained valuable ground whilst *Excalibur* was struggling with her trawling spinnaker. 'We might be able to overtake her. You need to get the numbers up,' she said referring to Sammy's speed monologue.

Mack looked anxiously down at his trimmers. He didn't want to break their concentration. He looked up at the sails to see they were set as well as they could be. He looked everywhere for that extra ounce of speed. *Excalibur* had no more to give. All he could do was meet every wind shift as perfectly as he could. *Valiant* was seven boat lengths ahead and a mere fifty metres from the finish line as she started to perform her penalty turn. The spectators were on the edge of their seats. All on board *Mucky Ducky* held their breath, whilst back on shore their families were shouting themselves hoarse.

As *Valiant* came out of her penalty turn, the bowman of *Excalibur* – so blond that he could have been born on the sun – grinned and waved as he crossed the line first.

Pandemonium broke out on board *Mucky Ducky*. Sir Edward sank into a chair and put his head into his hands. 'This will kill me,' he said. 'I think this will literally kill me.'

Everyone on *Excalibur* was jumping up and down and hugging each other, buoyed up with the adrenalin of the last few hours. The photographers went mad at the sight of Colin Montague, rising from his position as eighteenth man, gleefully grinning and unveiling a T-shirt which read 'British sailors do it for England' and shouting good-naturedly to the press boats, 'Has John MacGregor finally lost the plot indeed!'

Chapter 31

In the crush and swell of well-wishers and everyone trying to leave the post-race press conference at the same time, most of the crew became separated from each other. Caught up in the tide of people, they simply went with the flow. Custard was grabbed from behind by a very emotional British woman and had just finished disentangling himself when he came face to face with a hopeful-looking Saffron Luter. In the primrose yellow of her sundress she looked wan and pale against the vibrancy of the scene.

'You won,' she said simply.

Custard smiled. 'Yes.'

She bit her lip anxiously.

'How are you?' he said. 'I've been wondering.'

'I'm fine.'

A particularly strong wave from the crowd pushed them together. 'Meet me,' Custard was appalled to find himself whispering in her ear.

'I can't.'

'Please.'

She hesitated. 'Where?'

'The Casa America's Cup tonight at six.' And then the crowd simply swept them apart, leaving the image of her staring after him burnt into his eyes.

Stupid, he told himself, wandering back to the compound, people smiling and clapping him on the back as he went. Stupid,

stupid. What on earth was he doing tangling with a married woman? And the wife of Henry Luter no less? They were just starting an America's Cup competition, he didn't need any distractions. It was simply the reaction to being on such a high. But how on earth could he get hold of her to tell her that they couldn't meet up? He had no contact details for her, no one he could trust to leave a message for her. In the end, he resolved to go along there himself, take her out for a cup of coffee and then firmly deposit her back in the super-yacht marina where she belonged.

The museum of the America's Cup or Casa America's Cup was a short ride around the marina. When Custard left at five to six on one of the pink bicycles, the shore staff were cheerfully wet-sanding *Excalibur* to make her hull slice faster through the water. *Excalibur* sat patiently in her cradle, enduring all the work on her merely so that she could get out and race again tomorrow.

Once at the Casa, Custard took one of the audio devices and started to walk through the museum. He had watched Sir Peter Blake's victory in 1995 twice before Saffron arrived.

'Sorry,' she gasped as she eventually slid through the door. She had changed: now she was wearing a little white shift dress and carried a small handbag with a scarf tied around the handle. She wore a huge straw hat and big glasses, which just emphasised her desire to remain anonymous.

'Come on.'

'Where are we going?'

'To a bar.' It was fabulously air-conditioned in the museum but the mosquitoes were hell.

Custard led the way to a hotel on the beach front. The smell of sautéed garlic lazily drifted across the warm air.

'I'm sorry I was late,' Saffron said when they were eventually sitting on the hotel veranda with two *horchatas*, a milk-like drink made from a fruit similar to a hazelnut.

'How come?'

'I just couldn't get away,' she said, pleating the tablecloth in front of her. The truth was that Henry had refused to let her go until she lied and told him that she was picking up a new dress, which, of course, came under the heading of official duties. She didn't know what she would tell him when she returned empty-handed: perhaps that the shop had shut early or it wasn't ready.

'Did you watch the racing today?' asked Custard for something to say. Why on earth had he asked her to come?

'Em, yes. We watch all the racing from the yacht. Henry likes to make sure that the . . . ' Her words trailed off as she remembered who she was speaking to. She bit her lip.

'Afraid that syndicate secrets will spill out?' asked Custard with a grin.

Saffron smiled and relaxed slightly. She nodded.

'We couldn't be two more unlikely people, could we? I'm literally in the Montague camp and so you must be the Capulets.'

'Hardly Romeo and Juliet though.'

'I should bloody hope not,' snorted Custard. 'I've no plans to poison myself or run myself through with a sword or whatever the silly sod did.'

Saffron smiled properly and Custard, out of the blue, saw a glimmer of her former self, as if a light had briefly flickered on inside her and cast shadows around a room normally in darkness. He suddenly knew why he had asked her out here today.

'You must be tired after your race.'

'I was but not any more.'

'Do you have to be up early tomorrow?'

'About six. Usual time. What about you?'

'Henry likes me to get up at the same time as him so he has someone to have breakfast with. So about the same as you.'

'I always thought of you as lying in the lap of luxury and surfacing for hot chocolate and cream at eleven.'

'Some hope. And Henry likes me thin so that's the hot chocolate out. All part of the job description, I suppose. Have you thought of me a lot?' she asked coyly.

'More than I should. I was worried about you, I guess.' He put his hand out and covered hers as he saw her face fall. 'But that's not the only reason,' he said softly.

She reluctantly pulled her hand away. 'I'm sorry. So many people around.'

'Famous face.'

'Not for the right reasons.'

'All part of the job description?'

'You could say that.'

'What is the job description?'

'I don't know. Trophy wife of Henry Luter? Would that fit? Paid to look good and act the part.'

'Are you paid well?'

'Paid too well.'

There was a pause in their conversation. 'Thank you for looking after me the last time we met. I was a bit of a wreck. Nobody had been kind to me for a while.'

'You're welcome.'

Saffron looked at her watch. Diamond-encrusted, Custard noticed. On anyone else he would say they weren't real. 'I have to go. They'll be wondering where I've got to.'

'That's fine. I have to see my folks off and then have dinner with the crew.'

She grinned suddenly pleased. 'Did your parents come to see you race?'

'Never missed one. Can I see you again?'

'I'd like that. But are you sure you don't want to be concentrating on the racing?'

'Without wishing to sound smug, women aren't the only ones who are any good at multi-tasking. Besides, I'm afraid you might get on that ocean liner of yours after the racing, disappear into the sunset and I'll never see you again.'

He could still feel her hand in his long after she disappeared from sight.

Chapter 32

The crew supper was a tradition which had started just after Christmas. No one knew quite how but it was always on a Thursday night at Bee's apartment (probably because she was such a natural hostess and she clearly adored having everyone). Over time everyone had come to look forward to the evenings tremendously. Despite it being during the long weeks of racing the round robins, they decided to keep them going, as all their routines were important and also because the last time Custard was at Bee's apartment doing his washing, he had let it slip Mack's birthday was coming up.

'When?' asked Bee.

'Next Thursday, I think Hattie said. She obviously has been looking through the personnel files. I hope she has mine marked down for a big fat cake.' Custard idly fed Salty and Pipgin some of his sandwich.

'We ought to do something.'

'Should we?' said Custard in surprise. 'We didn't last year.'

'What about at the crew supper? Make it into a birthday party for him.'

'OK. Have you any instant coffee? I don't think I can face another ball-breaking espresso shot. Carla at the compound pretends she can't understand us when we ask for a cappuccino.'

And so Mack was duly informed there would be a crew supper as usual. No one mentioned that it was a birthday party especially for him as they felt sure that he wouldn't turn up if he knew. Colin Montague had to fly home immediately after the race (which Bee silently thanked the gods for as she was sure there would be a strained atmosphere between him and Rafe – they still hadn't talked properly) but he arranged for a case of champagne to be delivered.

'Happy Birthday!' they all chorused as Mack turned up a bit late and unchanged from the boat shed. He looked about him in shock and surprise and then grinned suddenly. 'You buggers.' Someone thrust a glass of champagne in his hand. The crew had bought Mack a T-shirt saying 'The beatings will continue until morale improves' and some wrinkle cream. Bee had hastily gathered as much information as she could from everyone and made Mack all his favourite things from home as her sort of present. Tongue firmly in cheek, she was serving everyone little bits of Marmite toast with cheese on the top as a canapé.

'Cheese and Marmite!' said Mack grinning. 'My favourite! How did you . . . ?'

Bee just smiled and moved on.

'Mack!' yelled Custard coming up to him with a glass of Bollinger in one hand and several canapés in the other. 'A reporter asked me today what it felt like to be in one of the youngest crews of the America's Cup.'

'Are we the youngest crew in the Cup?' asked Dougie, butting in.

'Apparently so! I told him that Mack must push the old stats up a bit because he's ancient.'

'God, the press go on so much about our crew being too young.'

'Talking of youth, where's Inky?' said her godfather.

'Talking on the phone to Luca.' Custard raised his eyes to heaven. 'Young love,' he sighed. 'I think he phoned to congratulate her.'

Custard grabbed Bee as she was passing and insisted she put down her canapés. 'Have some champagne,' he urged. 'Where's your glass?'

'I keep putting it down somewhere.'

'You must have glasses of champagne littering the apartment. Do you have one in the loo so you can have a quick swig as you're having a wee? I'll get you another fresh glass.'

Mack shifted his weight awkwardly. He felt tongue-tied now that he and Bee had been left alone. He wondered fleetingly why this should be – it had never happened between them before. He rarely cared what people thought of him but maybe he was lost for words simply because he *had* come to care what she thought of him. He had also been wrong-footed by all the effort she had made just for his birthday.

'Thanks for all this,' he gestured all around.

'The Bollinger is a present from our illustrious sponsor in honour of your birthday and very appropriate for your first win today. Maybe he was thinking it would be a consolation if you didn't.'

'Very kind. I'll call him. We'll have to go back to Moet next week,' he sighed in a life-is-hard way.

'I was speaking with someone from Louis Vuitton last week,' (Louis Vuitton owned Moët et Chandon and thus it sometimes felt as though it were on tap) 'and they told me you simply have to pronounce the "t" on Moët.'

'Really? All these years . . .'

'I know! I simply cannot wait to get back to England and start to be terribly pretentious about the whole thing. It will bankrupt me having to serve Moet all night simply so I can show off about it. Get down, Salty! Sorry he is so overexcited,' apologised Bee as she shooed an unrepentant Salty away. 'He's getting terribly fat. Little Rosie Beaufort keeps feeding him biscuits and he gets invited to all the syndicate children's parties and then causes mayhem with the sandwiches. I despair of him.'

'I'll miss him when we all leave,' said Mack. He was aware he was grinning foolishly at her. God, he must get a grip on himself. Maybe he shouldn't be drinking champagne. Seeing her here, queen of her own domain, made him appreciate her charm even more. Earlier, she had been floating around making everyone feel at ease, reassuring anyone if their drink spilt on the carpet that it wouldn't possibly show, teasing the crew, involving all their wives and just generally making everyone feel terrific. She ought to be available on prescription.

'You must be on top of the world,' commented Bee, misinterpreting his grin. 'After your win today. I didn't realise how glamorous all this Cup business would be. All those beautiful women and their designer clothes. It made me feel quite drab. I shall make more of an effort for your next race. Mind you, I was fretting so much for you all this morning I simply didn't notice what I was getting dressed in. I can't imagine what it must have been like for all of you. Even Sir Edward didn't pop in for breakfast this morning.' Bee had taken to giving him a little pre-breakfast snackette of bacon which he ate principally to piss Carla off. Mack always took the moral high ground of muesli but was secretly annoyed because he would have liked to pop in for breakfast bacon too.

'By the way, have you been OK here in the apartment? Milly says there's been a man hanging around outside Casa Fortuna and she's a bit worried. A couple of others have spotted him too.'

'Someone hanging around outside here?' Bee queried.

'Yes. She says she's noticed him a couple of times. So I think we might start employing a doorman. There are always people sniffing about at the base but we need to up our security at home too. The espionage is rife.' Everyone seemed more alert to this rather more murky aspect of the Cup lately. A huge story had blown up about a designer who had been newly employed by a syndicate and turned up with a few too many secrets on his laptop. The America's Cup committee were currently considering how to penalise them. 'I'm glad Rafe is with you at night but let me know if you see anything suspicious during the day. Hattie also told me yesterday that someone has been taking advantage of the fact that Henry Luter has been opening accounts all over town. He's been using a passable American accent in the video hire shop, pretending to be the American mastman from the Phoenix Challenge and then not returning them, making Phoenix fork out a fortune in fees.'

'What's that?' asked Custard returning with a full glass for Bee.

'Someone called from Phoenix Challenge and said their video hire account is being used. Funnily enough, they were pointing the finger at us. Do you know anything about that Custard?'

'No, not me. I couldn't do an American accent.'

Mack didn't think Custard had even caught the bit about accents. 'If I ever officially learn who it is then I will have to do something about it,' he said sternly.

'Of course. Dreadful. Whoever it is should be severely repri-manded.'

Later on they all pretended not to hear Custard's extremely good impression of George Bush.

Chapter 33

Excalibur stormed through the round robin series. They raced each syndicate in turn apart from Henry Luter, who, as the defender of the Cup, had the privilege of not competing until the final (a dubious privilege, in Mack's view, as they didn't get their teeth sharpened). Excalibur had easy wins against most of the syndicates but lost to the Italians and the New Zealanders who were both well tipped to win the Cup. At the end of the series they had determined their place in the draw and their next match would be a series of seven races against the French. Mack was repeatedly asked if *Excalibur* had some sort of revolutionary design but he remained tight-lipped. The one story he didn't need to embellish and which seemed to take on a life of its own was Rafe.

Since the racing had started and people were able to witness first hand his abilities, rumours had started to whip around about *Excalibur*'s diffident strategist and slowly all the competitors started to fear him. They could not fathom his connection to the sea. He seemed to smell the wind, they whispered. It was eerie.

Rafe was standing on their pontoon finishing off an interview with a deeply impressed journalist who was planning to entitle his article 'The Wind Caller', the name sometimes given to Rafe's position on the boat. Rafe was staring out to sea as the shore crew made the boat ready for that day's practice, marching sails back and forward to *Excalibur*.

'What sort of conditions are you hoping for for the race series with the French?'

Rafe found this a peculiar sort of question. He frowned. 'We'll sail in whatever conditions we have on the day. It's going to be windy today though.'

'How do you know? Can you feel it?' the journalist asked, deeply empathetic.

'No, that girl's dress has just blown over her head.' He pointed to a struggling figure on the super-yacht marina.

The more Rafe shrank back from the hype, the more he fuelled it and Hattie was being ferocious about protecting him from the publicity he hated so much.

In order to escape the fuss, most mornings he would leave Casa Fortuna early and go and visit his local fishermen friends who had been so helpful when he first arrived in Valencia. That simple half an hour came as such a relief to him. Some days he would sit and chat with them and other days he would wordlessly help them with their catch. Their world, so far removed from the America's Cup madness, soothed him.

One morning as he was walking back from the fishing harbour he turned a corner and bumped into Jason Bryant. His fists clenched involuntarily, but, not wanting to start something which might affect his crew, he ignored him.

'Well, well, well. If it isn't the mysterious wind caller everyone's talking about.'

Rafe made to walk past but Bryant blocked his path.

'Fancy yourself as something special, do you?'

'Not really.'

'Don't I owe you something, Louvel?' Jason pretended to look puzzled. 'Isn't there a small debt outstanding?'

Rafe shrugged. 'Hit me if you want but I doubt it will help.'

'Oh, I think it might.'

'Playing you up, is she?'

Jason Bryant looked startled. 'Who?' Rafe could tell by the

feebleness of his response that he had hit a nerve. It was a shot in the dark but had obviously found its mark.

'Ava. She likes rows. You have to know how to handle her. Maybe you don't.'

Bryant laughed harshly. 'And you did?'

Rafe shrugged. 'Perhaps.'

'She's seeing me now.'

'But for how long?'

'As long as I say.'

'I think you'll find Ava is a law unto herself.' Rafe made to walk past him again.

'You're all fucking Pencarrow anyway,' Bryant suddenly blurted out. 'If she isn't a dyke.'

Rafe stopped and frowned. 'Inky?' Bryant was staring at him with an intensity which betrayed his interest in the answer. Rafe wasn't about to give him the satisfaction. 'She could take her pick not only of any of us but of any of the syndicates. And I think she already has.' This time Rafe managed to push past him and walk away.

Saffron and Custard met the following week at a local hotel so horrifically tatty that he didn't think there could be a chance that any of the America's Cup fraternity would be there. It wasn't the sort of establishment where you had to sign in nor where porters took your bags, which was lucky because Custard only had a bottle of gin for Saffron and apple juice for him in there. He was almost expecting to ask them to pay by the hour.

'I'm sorry,' he whispered as he grappled with the door into the room. 'I didn't want us to be recognised.'

He had nearly asked her to come to his apartment in Casa Fortuna but he didn't know what any of the Montague Challenge would do if they came upon a Capulet actually inside the building. Probably faint clean away from the shock.

'It's OK,' whispered Saffron back, her eyes glistening. 'You'd pay millions in Manhattan for a designer to do this to your apartment. At least the sheets look clean.'

'I didn't bring you here to . . . '

'I know.'

'There just didn't seem to be anywhere to get any privacy.'

'I know.'

There was a silence as they both sat down on the bed, unsure as to what might happen next.

'Have things been pretty awful?' asked Custard. 'I mean, since I saw you at the party.'

'Yes,' said Saffron. 'Things have been pretty awful.'

'Tell me.'

'It's hard to know where to start . . . ' said Saffron. 'You don't want to listen to my problems.'

'I want to know about you.'

'So does everyone else, apparently. Henry wants me to give interviews all the time. I hate them.'

'Why?' said Custard in surprise, and then didn't know why he should be surprised. He'd realised that Saffron Luter didn't actually quite fit the mould.

'I don't know. The way they write about me. "Saffron Luter lies back on her luxury sofa and eats grapes, admiring her perfect French manicure." It's such a load of rubbish. I suppose it's my middle-class roots,' she joked but then suddenly sobered. 'Henry likes me on show.'

'Why don't you just say no?'

'You don't say no to Henry.'

'Really? Why not?'

She looked wary. 'You just don't. He won't even let me garden, I wanted to pot some plants for the deck,' she said quickly, probably to stop Custard asking any more. 'I think this particular manicure would look a lot better with a bit of dirt under my nails.'

'He wants to win, doesn't he?'

'Over everyone. This Cup obsesses him. I don't know where he'll stop. I don't think anyone will win against him. Not because he's better than everyone else but simply because he's not going to let them.'

'But the best crew will win, they must,' protested Custard.

'No. You have no idea what he is really like. He once took a slight at a man at a drinks party who called him a "short little man with a superiority complex". A year later that man came to Henry to beg for money. He had systematically broken him. He never forgets or forgives.'

'How did you come to marry him?'

Saffron shrugged and looked sad. 'I thought he was the answer.'

'The answer to what?'

Saffron got up and went to look out of the window. She changed the subject. 'Do you come from a big family?'

'A brother and a sister. Ton of cousins and a fair smattering of aunts. You?'

'Only child. Not many relations. I would love to belong to a big family. Tell me about them, Christmas must have been amazing.'

Custard smiled. He liked the thought of this wonderful girl thinking about families. 'Do you want children?' he asked. He could picture her with a baby on her hip. It seemed a more natural image than the painted, coiffured woman before him.

'I did. But with Henry,' she added, 'I wouldn't want them. He doesn't want children anyway.'

'Why do you stay?'

'I'm not brave enough to leave.'

'I think it takes more courage to stay than to leave.'

Saffron shook her head. 'Fear of the unknown. At least I know what I'm dealing with.'

Custard stared at her. She fascinated him; she was such a curious mix. She was beautiful and yet so down to earth. Unspeakably glamorous and yet wanted to talk about his family. She seemed to have a terribly low opinion of herself but cared about other people.

'What are you thinking of?' she asked him.

'I was thinking of that story of a beautiful bird which was too frightened to fly out of the open cage door.'

'You think the cage door is open?' she asked with amusement. 'I don't think Henry would be that remiss.'

'Luter might not necessarily be able to see it.'

Saffron wasn't completely sure what they were talking about any more. 'It's complicated,' she said eventually. 'Henry does have things that I need.'

'Money?' asked Custard in puzzlement. This was at odds to his image of her.

'No, not money.' She paused. 'Protection.'

Chapter 34

Inky was getting ready in her apartment at Casa Fortuna. Hearing a knock at the door, and presuming it was her mother coming from her hotel (where she insisted on staying to preserve Inky's privacy) to say hello, she yelled 'Come in! It's open!'

She finished her make-up and then went through to the sitting room to find Luca sitting with his legs up on the coffee table, a bunch of purple tulips thrown casually to one side and insolently opening a bottle of Moët. He looked tremendously excited. She immediately felt her tiredness tumbling away from her.

'Luca! You won?' she said in response to the air of exhilaration about him.

'Yes! We won! We probably lose tomorrow but we win today! But, *cara,* you win too.'

She grinned. 'Yes, I win too.'

'I saw you. With the spinnaker pole. Very brave.' In the race before last, Fabian had got something hooked over the spinnaker pole and Inky was the only one who had seen it and raced up the boat to help him. Not so used to the bow, she was smashed against the spinnaker pole several times before she got her balance.

'Thank you. Not easy being at the bow. I don't know how you do it.'

'Thank *you*. And if you beat the French and then the Germans then you will face either us or the Australians. Which would you prefer?'

Inky fetched some glasses from the kitchen. 'It doesn't matter. We'll have to face you both in time to win the America's Cup.'

'Ahh, the confidence of a winner. Brave *and* beautiful. Are your parents coming out for the race?'

'My mum is already here, my dad is arriving tomorrow. Are yours coming out?'

'Yes. But not until after the next round. None of our crew's families are coming until then.' He said this with some pride. It was a show of confidence that he knew the Italian challenge would make it through. Unfortunately the Excalibur families still had no such conviction.

'Your papa will not be very pleased to see me.' He handed her a glass of champagne.

Inky laughed. 'Your mama will not be very pleased to see me.'

'She would if you said you would give up racing and come and bear me babies on the Amalfi coast.'

Inky smiled. 'And what would I do instead of race?'

'Raise the children. Bake for me. Help mama in the shop.'

It sounded quite attractive at the moment but Inky knew as soon as the starting gun fired and the first shot of adrenalin surged through her veins, she wouldn't be able to contemplate ever doing anything else. She didn't respond.

'We have not seen much of each other over the last few weeks. For that I am sorry.'

'That's OK. We've both been busy.'

'I hope when all this is over we can see more of each other.'

'I hope so too.'

'I hope things can go back to normal.'

'Whatever that is.'

'Have you thought what you are doing after the Cup?'

'I can't think beyond it,' said Inky honestly. It was true. The event was of such a magnitude and they had been so long preparing for it that everything else seemed immaterial. 'What about you?'

Luca shrugged. 'I don't know. Get ready for the next one, I suppose.'

They sipped in silence for a second. 'Luca, what happens if we race each other?' asked Inky. The way the draw fell currently, either could lose and drop out of the competition before that happened.

'One will win and the other will lose,' he said calmly. Actually this wasn't the question Inky really wanted to ask. She wanted to ask, what will happen if *you* lose? But this obviously was not how Luca was thinking at all. She could tell he thought that he would win. She left it. There was a silence.

'How are the preparations with *Excalibur*?' he asked eventually.

'We're fine,' she said guardedly. This was awful, they were like two tigers pacing around each other in a cage. Too aware of the competition and what was at stake. Both felt they were being sized up for supper. 'How about *Baci*?'

'We're good. But none of us dares put our jackets down. People keep stealing them.' The Italian crew clothing was fast becoming the most coveted item in Valencia. Inky laughed but as always felt a mixed stab of pride and envy when she heard about the extent of their popularity. The groupies were having an absolute ball, proudly walking round with *Baci* jackets and T-shirts as proof they'd slept with one of the Italian crew.

'Have you heard how things are with the Phoenix Challenge?'

'I hear story about Jason Bryant losing his temper,' said Luca.

'What happened?'

'He was so furious that he kicked one of the grinders and when the grinder ask why he kick him, he say, "No reason. Just pass it on."'

'Jason Bryant is not very nice.'

'I think he like you. I see him look at you.'

'Doubtless thinking how much he would like to drown me. I don't trust Bryant or Luter.'

'*Cara*, what can Luter do to you?'

'You don't know him.'

He pulled her back on the sofa. Inky could smell the racing on him. If it weren't for that smell, a peculiar and yet unmistakable odour of adrenalin, oil, salt water and the high of an animal after a kill, Inky would have sworn he was just on the way somewhere for dinner because, like all the Italians, he was impeccably turned out. Their sail clothes were clearly designer made and highly pressed, Luca's face was clean-shaven with tousled hair, and his fingernails clean and short. She was tempted to ask whether they all had valets.

'Will you sleep with me to celebrate?'

'I don't think I want to celebrate an Italian victory but I'll sleep with you anyway. But do you race tomorrow or have a lay day?'

'Then we could have had a lay day too.' He sighed, 'No, we race.'

'And will sex help or hinder?' said Inky teasingly.

'Does it matter to you?'

'I suppose I need to know whether I'm contributing towards an Italian or Kiwi victory.'

'Contributing?'

'I do a lot for charity.'

He laughed and pulled her towards him. She winced.

'What's wrong?'

'Bruises. From the spinnaker pole.'

'Show me,' he instructed.

Inky pulled up her top to show him some richly purple ribs. 'Match my flowers,' she said awkwardly, aware that they were none too attractive.

She needn't have worried. 'No matter,' said Luca cheerfully. 'I will work round them.' He took their glasses and put them on the table and then started to gently kiss her hand, working his way up from the palm to her wrist to her forearm. His lips were soft and dry and Inky felt herself starting to melt. But unable to let the Cup leave her for a second, Inky weighed up the pros and cons of having sex before a major race – they were racing the French tomorrow in the first of what would be a best of seven series. It would deplete Luca but leave her relaxed and able to sleep. She smiled at him and leant forward to kiss him. She had to admit it was one of the wonderful things about being a woman.

Chapter 35

At least, Hattie reflected, the headlines were getting better. Today, only one of the articles was slightly snide. It was in one of the more gossipy papers and they had somehow managed to get hold of the information that all the afterguard, who quite literally drive the boat, were a little less successful on land. Rafe couldn't drive, Mack drove in bare feet and Inky only passed her test on the fifth attempt. Their resident Mercedes (Mack's pimpmobile) was covered in scratches from being driven on the wrong side of the road and together this little group of people would be driving a boat worth over three million pounds. The other article was a massive spread on Fabian – it would seem the world had forgiven him (and almost forgotten about Rob's death) and he was now the darling of the centre spread. There was a sort of rags-to-riches angle, except in Fabian's case it was playboy to success story. They even managed to glamorise his father's disappearance. Hattie had frowned as the article went on to talk about his groupies who apparently stood at the compound gate simply for a glimpse of him. Hattie hoped Fabian hadn't been letting the success go to his head and been messing around with girls. She adored Milly.

Hattie looked idly at Colin Montague who was sitting next to Mack at the front of the usual early morning meeting and wondered what else she could persuade them to do to attract the headlines. It would be simply marvellous if Mack could lose his temper at one of the press conferences and punch someone.

Her eyes wandered back to rest on Rafe who was sitting in the front row of the meeting with his legs stretched out in front of him and his hands clasped behind his head. She hoped that he would enjoy the surprise she had organised for him later. She stared longingly at his hands. God, they were beautiful. She would be the luckiest girl in the world to stroll hand in hand with him. She willed the thoughts away. She *mustn't* think of him like that. They were simply friends. Involuntarily her mind started to show her images of Rafe's hands travelling over Ava's body. She tried to close her eyes against them.

Mack's voice broke into her thoughts. 'Hattie?' he questioned again.

She opened her eyes to find the room staring at her. Rafe had unclasped his hands and was looking over his shoulder at her.

'Sorry. Yes?'

'Time for your update.'

'Of course!' She leapt up in a hurry, red with embarrassment, and came to the front. 'Em, several newspapers have requested interviews after the racing next week and the BBC would like a live interview to camera. I have suggested Fabian as the bowman . . . '

'Why is that, Hattie?' yelled Jonny. 'Is it because he is so bee-yoo-tee-ful?'

'No, it's because you're all so ugly,' said Hattie. Rafe grinned.

'Fabian, you're going to be the pin-up of women everywhere,' said Flipper, fluttering his eyelids at him.

'And I imagine a few men too,' drawled Custard.

'Ha, ha. Very funny,' said Fabian.

'Can we *please* stick to the point?' said Sir Edward.

'Happy Birthday!' they all chorused as Rafe came into the common room that night after the usual showers.

He grinned. 'What's all this?' he said as a drink was shoved in his hand.

Custard's mouth was bulging with canapés of *jamon* and figs. 'Birthday party for you. You kept that date very quiet from us.'

'We never usually celebrate,' he said, but Custard could tell he was pleased.

Carla thrust a tray under their noses. 'It was Hattie, she find out it your birthday from Bee and organise it all,' she commented.

Rafe glanced over to Hattie chatting to Pond on the other side of the room. 'I'll thank her.'

'What, no buns, Carla?' asked Fabian.

'What is wrong with my buns?'

'Nothing, nothing,' said Fabian hastily. 'I was simply looking forward to having one.'

'I shall make some specially for you,' beamed Carla.

'Lovely. That will be just lovely.'

'Carla, this ham is seriously good,' said Custard, grabbing another three canapés. 'Did you kill it with your bare hands or just give it one of your looks?'

Later on Rafe excused himself from Sir Edward who was starting on a long diatribe of the history of his colon and made his way over to Hattie.

'Thank you,' he said.

'You're welcome. By the way, we have a table booked for nine o'clock at Albacar.'

'Fantastic. I had no idea, I wasn't expecting . . .'

'Everyone needs a fuss on their birthday,' said Hattie, looking shocked.

'I can't remember how long it's been since we've been allowed to drink.'

'Mack's birthday perhaps?'

'Oh yes. You're right. It feels like a lifetime ago.'

'Besides, Mack thought it would be good for all of us to let our hair down for a night. We won today and we don't race the French again for another two days.'

* * *

When they arrived at the restaurant, presents were piled up in front of Rafe's chair. Mack had given him a little book on amusing nautical stories, Bee had recreated one of their boxes from childhood, full of Fortnum chocolates, jelly beans and other goodies, Sir Edward had given him a gift pack of arnica ('for all those aches and bruises, dear boy'), and the rest of the crew had clubbed together to buy Rafe a new pair of Oakleys because his old ones were looking very tatty ('That's because they were an old pair someone left behind at the sailing school,' Rafe explained) and a blow-up doll. At the bottom of the pile was a small rectangular present, beautifully wrapped in black spotty paper and tied with raffia and a single, exquisitely dotted black guinea fowl feather. 'From me,' said Hattie quietly.

It was a very old leather-bound book on the winds of the Mediterranean. Rafe looked at it wonderingly and turned it over. 'Thanks, Hattie. I'll treasure it.'

Hattie was blushing. 'It was just from our conversation on the boat that day . . . ' she stammered.

'I remember. I remember perfectly.'

'I read a little bit before I wrapped it. It was talking all about Aeolus, the wind God.'

'He supposedly lives in a cave on the Aeolian islands.'

They smiled at each other.

'Are your parents coming out for any of the racing, Hattie?'

'They're going to try. They're both busy with work.'

'I'd like to meet them.'

'Would you?' Hattie took a gulp of wine to cover her embarrassment. Rafe looked at her appraisingly. She really was very pretty like that, with her shiny, wavy hair dropping over her face and her smear of red lipstick left on her wine glass. 'They'll probably come out with Dougie's parents. They all know each other.'

'What does Dougie's dad do, by the way? Every time one of the crew asks him, he changes the subject or just mumbles about his father's work commitments. They're all starting to think he's some sort of Mafia hood.'

'Do you really not know who he is?'

'No.'

'He's the Bishop of Southampton! He and my father have tea together!'

'Bloody hell! Dougie's Dad is a bishop.'

'What about your dad?'

'He hasn't turned up yet. I'm not sure where he was coming from but the weather has probably delayed him. I last spoke to him three weeks ago and he was in Egypt.'

'I think your lifestyle sounds fascinating,' sighed Hattie. 'Do you think you'll go back to it after the Cup?'

Rafe frowned. 'I don't know, actually. I haven't made any plans. Guess I'll see what turns up. Anyway, I think *your* lifestyle sounds fascinating. Tell me all about school. I can't imagine being with twenty other children in one room.'

They all left at the end of the evening fairly the worse for wear. Things had got pretty raucous. After carrying Rafe shoulder high round the restaurant, Custard nearly passed out from blowing up Rafe's blow-up doll all by himself and had to be revived with a jug of water and some brandy forced down his throat. Most of the crew were crying with laughter as Sir Edward initiated the emergency procedure. Jonny had requisitioned a mouth organ from Rafe's box of pressies from Bee and proceeded to announce everyone's sentences with it. Inky was desperately trying to explain how she could fail her driving test four times, including one time where she didn't see a round-about and drove straight over the top of it, making the examiner bang his head on the roof. Finally they staggered out, Rafe carrying what was left of his presents and walking with Fabian and Inky.

Hattie dashed out after them, giggling and carrying the dolly under one arm. 'Rafe! You'd better take this, I don't think the restaurant really wants it . . .'

She slowed down suddenly, the smile dying on her face. Rafe turned round to see what she was looking at.

Ava. Standing on the other side of the road. She crossed hesitantly over and stopped in front of Rafe. They stared at each other.

Fabian pulled on Inky's sleeve. 'Come *on*,' he hissed. Inky didn't want to come on at all. She felt massively protective towards Rafe and if that bitch was going to screw Rafe and, by consequence, the entire crew again then she wanted to stay around and tell her exactly what she thought of her. But Fabian was tugging persistently on her top and she was suddenly distracted by the sight of poor Hattie looking absolutely aghast. She went over and took her arm.

Hattie stumbled as she went past, catching Ava's eye who gave her a look of complete disdain. Why did she always have to look so stupid in front of her all the time? What on earth would she think of her carrying a blow-up doll underneath her arm?

Ava and Rafe were left alone standing underneath a street lamp.

'Someone's birthday?' she asked eying the gifts in Rafe's hands.

'Mine actually.'

'I'd forgotten. Of course, you were in May. Happy birthday.'

'Thank you.'

There was a pause.

'I've been thinking about you,' she said. 'I've been watching you too. You'll be in Valencia a little while yet.'

'Maybe long enough to race *Phoenix*. Congratulations on your exhibition by the way.'

'You read about that?' For a moment she looked abashed. 'That was mostly work I did when I was with you.'

'Really. Your new muse is not inspiring you? How is Jason, by the way?'

'Not containing his nerves very well. Things would be very different with you, I imagine.'

Rafe didn't reply.

'Who was the girl?'

'Which one?'

'She was with you at the ambassador's party.'

'Hattie. She does our marketing.'

'PR. How parochial. Home counties, private school, Mummy does good works. Of course, I forget that means nothing to you.'

'She's sweet,' said Rafe firmly.

'Sweet on you. I saw how she looked at you. Is she going to write a press release on how marvellous you are in bed?' She couldn't help herself. She knew it was catty but seeing Rafe with another woman – however innocently – had driven her into a whirlwind of jealousy. The vehemence of it had taken her by surprise.

'Don't be a bitch.' His stomach was churning. She was looking quite, quite beautiful. A clinging dress made of black lace, big heels and her eyes smudged with blues and greys. She looked wanton, heady with her own sex appeal. The unnatural light from the street lamp made her look like gossamer. Rafe didn't think she'd ever been more desirable. 'Were you waiting for me?'

'Yes.'

'How did you know where we were?'

'I went down to the base and smiled nicely at the security guard. Mack left all the details in case he needed to be contacted.'

'Bryant giving you the runaround?'

'No. But you have.'

'I have?'

'I dream about you.'

'We've only won one round, Ava. Hardly anything to be excited about,' said Rafe dryly, thinking about her obsession with the press and success.

'I dreamt about you before the racing started. Do you ever think about us?'

Rafe hesitated. His face was impassive but his dark, sooty eyes flickered.

Smelling weakness, Ava moved nearer to him, her face close to his neck. Rafe breathed in her scent: Shalimar, she'd once told him. His senses started to reel.

She ran a hand lightly down his side. 'You've put on muscle. It suits you. In fact the whole Mediterranean lifestyle seems to be suiting you.' It was true. Rafe was looking lean; his dark skin was coffee brown; he smelt of rapacious animal health. Passers-by, attracted by the intensity of the couple, looked at them strangely. 'Are you sleeping with her?'

'No.'

'But you'd like to?'

'I hardly think you're in a position to ask those questions any more.' He paused. 'Hattie's been very good to me and the rest of the crew too. I will not do anything to upset the challenge whilst we race.'

'You mean, you won't rock the boat?' said Ava mockingly. 'How about afterwards?'

'I don't know. Is your work suffering whilst you're with Bryant?' he asked. 'Is this what this is all about?'

He'd found a weak spot. 'No,' she said, slowly shaking her head. 'I mean, my work isn't as good as it used to be but I don't think that's because I'm with Bryant. I think it's because I'm *not* with you. And that's not the reason I want to get back with you. I think we could have been happy together. I just hope I haven't ruined it.'

She kissed him lightly on his jaw line and, unable to stop himself, he gathered her tightly into his arms and kissed her. The presents he had been carrying tumbled to the ground. Hattie's *Book of Winds* hit the ground first.

Fabian and Inky had argued all the way home from the restaurant whilst Hattie walked beside them in numb silence.

'Do you think she wants him back?' asked Inky.

'It looked like it.'

'We shouldn't have left them,' said Inky fiercely. 'She's only come back because we're winning. I've talked to Bee about her and she says she was always utterly obsessed about it.'

'That doesn't make sense. We've hardly won the America's Cup.'

'She affects him. It took him ages to get it together after she dumped him for Jason Bryant.'

'But he was fine after the ambassador's party,' Fabian pointed out and looked over at Hattie. 'Maybe he's over her,' he added kindly for Hattie's benefit.

'Let's hope you're right. I still say we should have dragged him home with us. We need him too much.'

'You can't interfere, Inky, in people's love lives.'

'Well, the America's Cup interferes with everything and everyone,' she said thinking regretfully of Luca. 'Since when were you such a champion of love? Where is Milly, anyway?'

'We couldn't get a babysitter. So she insisted I came.'

'She is far too nice for you,' said Inky firmly.

They'd arrived at Casa Fortuna and Inky fished out her keys to let them all in.

'Will you be OK, Hattie? Do you want to come and have some tea or something?'

'No. No, thank you. I'd rather be by myself.'

'Is there somewhere we can go?' whispered Ava.

'No,' said Rafe firmly. 'We're not going to sleep together.'

'Why not? I know you want to. I can *feel* you want to.' She rubbed her voracious body against his. He closed his eyes against the onslaught.

'We can't.'

'Your little PR girl playing on your mind?'

'Jason Bryant playing on yours?'

'Should he be?' asked Ava innocently.

'You're still going out together, aren't you? You can't have us both, Ava.'

'I want you.'

'You have to finish with Bryant then.'

Hattie didn't go straight to bed. She went down to the overgrown gardens behind Casa Fortuna and walked amongst the lemon and orange trees in her bare feet, glancing now and then up to Rafe's window, which was still in darkness. Even in the heaviness of the night, the smell of blossom was overpowering, and now she would for ever think of Rafe whenever she smelt it. She hadn't realised, despite all her lectures to herself and her stern reprimands, how useless the whole thing was. She hadn't realised how much hope she had been attaching to their casual little chats and encounters.

She had absolutely no right to be so unhappy, she told herself. Rafe had never suggested their friendship was anything more than it was. It was clear to her that she could never be in the same class as Ava. She was too beautiful, too sophisticated, too talented and clearly exuded some sort of salacious sexiness which she, Hattie, could never hope to emulate. Her feelings towards Rafe were simply an unfortunate crush, the sort you got as a teenager. As soon as the America's Cup was over, Rafe would be out of her life, she would never see him again and she would recover. The thought was designed to be comforting but it had the opposite effect. She thought she'd never been so miserable in all of her life and, sinking to her knees, she started to cry as if her heart might break.

She had no idea how long she was there for but eventually, wiping her eyes, she looked up again at Rafe's window. It was still in darkness.

Chapter 36

With their confidence on a high, *Excalibur* went on to score easy victories against the French and after that the Germans. After two years of preparing for the Cup, those teams simply had to pack their bags and go home. *Excalibur* was to face the Italian boat, *Baci*, in the next round.

'They have been doing some very intense racing,' said Sir Edward whilst discussing with Mack whether to give the crew some time off. 'The sword is well and truly sharpened. I think they need some time to relax. Go sightseeing with their families. That sort of thing.'

'Their families are more uptight than they are,' murmured Mack.

'Inky's family over?'

'They're going home tomorrow. Such is the amount of faith in us, all the families keep booking flights home thinking we'll have lost. I daresay they'll be back out when the series with the Italians starts. Why?'

'Just wondering about her and her Italian sailor. Luca, isn't it? The bowman? Could be a tricky situation. How is she going to feel about going up against him? She needs to distance herself. If her family were with her this week, they could keep her busy on the days off.'

'I'll talk to her mother,' murmured Mack.

'Good-looking woman, that,' said Sir Edward appreciatively.

'You would think she was paid staff the way her husband treats her sometimes.'

'She's not even paid. The family are prone to take her somewhat for granted. I'll sort it out. Now get along with you. I've got piles of things to go through.'

Sir Edward simultaneously got up and gave a shudder. 'Don't mention piles, dear boy, mine have been giving me dreadful gyp all morning.'

Mack was surprised to find that Mary Pencarrow didn't need any extra persuading to stay. She had already made up her mind to, despite frantic protesting by James that he still didn't know where the dog food was kept and how the hell was he going to be able to sort everything out in time for him to come back out to Valencia for the next round against Italy?

'You'll manage,' said Mary quite firmly and in a tone she normally reserved for the dog. 'Inky needs me here and she is far more important right now than you or Nelson. You've seen the sort of stress they are all under and I am staying here.'

'But we have a call scheduled with David next week, Mary.'

'Well, David will have to call in Valencia,' said her mother briskly. 'Inky is far more important.'

James frowned. He had never seen such defiance in his wife and wasn't quite sure how to handle it. Their little exchange was interrupted by Mack knocking at the hotel door. James was further surprised when Mack seemed to side with Mary.

'She's quite right,' he said after Mary told him her plans. 'I'm worried about Inky. I'm not sure how she is going to react when she sees Luca lined up against her on the start line. They are all very close to the edge and that could be just the sort of thing to tip her over. The crew can't do without her.'

'See? Come on. I'll pack for you,' said Mary. 'Mack, dear, I think you ought to go home and get some rest. You look tired. Are you eating?'

'Tonight, I'm being cooked for which I am greatly looking forward to.' He smiled and took his leave.

There had been horrific thunderstorms all day. The rain had bucketed down but it still felt terribly muggy. Inky returned to her apartment, which was looking spotless because her mother had spent the last few days, between races, scrubbing it from top to bottom and filling the fridge with delicious things to eat. She thought Inky was looking far too thin.

Inky was just lying on the sofa and debating whether she could actually be bothered to eat any of the things in the fridge. It was a Thursday which meant Bee would be having a supper party for the crew in her apartment but she was too tired to go. The adrenalin of yesterday's race had worn off and all she could feel were the various bruises where she had either knocked against the mast or bashed somewhere she couldn't even remember. If only she could lever herself off the sofa to go and take some arnica. A knock came at the door, followed by an even louder one seconds later.

'It's open!' she shouted irritably.

To her surprise, Luca sauntered in carrying a bottle of champagne. He sat down opposite her.

'What are you doing?' she asked stupidly, pulling herself into a sitting position.

'I'm here to celebrate.' His eyes glinted dangerously. This clearly was not his first drink of the evening. 'We both win, *cara*.'

'I thought we agreed not to see each other until after the racing.' They had spoken yesterday on the telephone with the euphoria of both syndicates burning in their ears. This was before Mack and she had spoken about it and agreed it would be much the best thing if she and Luca kept their distance.

'I thought that was silly. We will just ignore each other on the start line.'

'No, Luca. It's not silly. I need some distance from you. I need to concentrate.'

'Why? We shall race and we will win and then you and I will go back to normal.'

'Who will win?' asked Inky with an edge in her voice, painfully aware she was being childish.

'We will win, of course. Come on, *cara*! You do not think you will honestly beat us! You lost to us in the round robins!'

'And we're racing again.'

'I do not wish to, how do you say? Divide hairs. Let's have a drink.'

'Have you come here deliberately to wind me up?'

Luca shrugged. A typical Neopolitan shrug. 'I do not need to do that. We are simply the better crew. Remember that we beat you in the friend race that time *and* the round robins. You have come as far as you're going to go. Now don't be a bad sport.'

'I'm not being a bad sport. I am simply telling you that I need some space, and surely my needs are equally important as yours. But I can tell that you clearly don't think so.'

God knows what Luca was going to say next because at that moment, after a light tap on the door, in walked Mary Pencarrow.

'This is Luca, Mother,' snapped Inky. 'And he's just leaving.' With this she stalked into her bedroom and slammed the door.

'So nice to meet you . . . ' said Mary hesitantly.

Inky had another reason to feel harassed: that day's practice had certainly proved eventful. A broken spinnaker pole combined with atrocious weather had stressed everyone. The America's Cup boats were built as light as they can possibly be; they are strong enough to withstand a certain number of tacks and then they break. This made practice in bad weather harrowing: the crew weren't scared for themselves – they were well aware of the risks they ran – but they were terrified something might happen to the boat and make them drop out of the competition. On the tow home they were so exhausted that recriminations began to fly.

'It's all your fault, Rafe,' grumbled Fabian who often seemed to be in a bad mood these days. He was particularly cross about the spinnaker pole because it was on his part of the boat. 'You were eating a green apple earlier.'

'An apple?'

'Green is unlucky.'

'Surely food doesn't count. I ate it.'

'We'll have to remind Carla to take out all the cucumber in the sandwiches,' commented Inky, trying to defuse the row. Rafe and Fabian were still looking crossly at each other.

'Maybe you could throw me overboard. I feel a bit green after all those beers last night,' Custard interjected

'Don't tempt me,' snapped Fabian.

'Did you see that boat following us today?' asked Inky.

'Probably one of Luter's spies,' said Fabian.

'They weren't doing a very good job. It was never close enough for me to catch the name. Anyway it was a yacht.'

'Christ, don't look now,' said Custard looking over Rafe's shoulder.

Everyone looked.

'God, that's all we need,' moaned Inky.

Mack had already leapt up and gone to the side of the boat. One of Henry Luter's support boats had come alongside them with Henry Luter and Jason Bryant on board. They never deigned to travel back with their own crew. Mack was busy shouting at the launch driver who had come in very close, which was against the rules and could be considered espionage.

Jason Bryant leant out. 'Hey! *Excalibur*! Good practice? Did you manage to get your mainsail up? Or can you not get it up?' he yelled. The remark was apparently addressed to everyone but he was looking directly at Inky as he said it. He stared at her, eyes glinting with his demon king smile.

'Piss off, Bryant! You're just trying to look at our keel!' yelled Inky back.

'I'll look under your skirt any time, sweetheart. But you'd better be careful who's looking at your keel! Are you sure it's legal?'

Mack's tirade at the driver must have made some difference because at this point the launch started to pull away. Inky frowned as she watched the boat's wake. What on earth was he on about? She felt discomfited but soon forgot it as she was sucked back into the crew discussion of 'why Jason Bryant is such a prick'.

As it was a Thursday, Mack popped down to Bee's apartment to see if he could contribute anything for that evening's crew supper. He thought he must have walked into the wrong apartment because at least fifteen toddlers were running around screaming, with a few mothers, oblivious to the noise, standing by and chatting.

Eventually Bee emerged from the kitchen with a party hat on. 'Mack!' she said. 'How nice to see you!'

'What on earth is going on here?'

'One of the shore crew's little girl's birthday. She's three. Her mother just went into labour this morning and the poor father was looking so harassed that I said I would have her party here. He's just called me on the midlife support's telephone.'

'Do you mean midwife?'

'What did I say?'

'Midlife.'

'I meant midwife. I wonder what midlife support would come with? A box of tissues and some HRT strips probably. God, it sounds marvellous. Anyway, come into the kitchen and have some tea. There's some cake left too.'

Bee led the way and pulling down one of her pink spotty mugs poured him a cup from a teapot. 'I've just made it. Let me just go and get Salty and Pipgin. They are being an absolute nuisance.'

She went out and hauled the dogs back in by their collars. 'I'd bribe them with a Bonio to stay here,' she panted, 'but they are absolutely stuffed with cake. They have been taking it out of all the toddler's hands. You can't blame them really, children are such a perfect height for them. I haven't had a particularly good day all round,' she sighed.

'What happened?'

'It was silly really, you know how we seem to have a universal borrowing scheme for everything here. Well, it was still bucketing down at lunchtime, so I took one of the umbrellas from the hall, went shopping and after some coffee just mindlessly picked up any old umbrella from the umbrella stand thinking that I was still at Casa Fortuna. A Spanish man yelled at me so much for stealing his umbrella, I almost couldn't understand a word he was saying.'

'The bloody lout!' said Mack indignantly. 'Tell me where you were and I'll go straight down there and have a word with the owner.'

'It doesn't matter at all. Tell me your news. How are preparations going?'

'Broken spinnaker pole and a run-in with the Phoenix crew which is too tedious to mention. Colin has asked a psychologist to come in for a couple of days to see if the crew needed any help with the pressure but every time I'm yelling at somebody, the bugger keeps popping up and saying, "Are you feeling a little stressed, Mr MacGregor? Can I help you with that?" I'll probably be forced to biff him on the nose.'

Bee laughed.

'What are you making?' asked Mack, idly taking a piece of fluorescent yellow cake which looked as though it might have been the face of a dinosaur.

'Flambé bananas.'

'You are never happy unless it's soused in alcohol and set alight.'

'My dangerous puddings.' They smiled at each other. 'How's Fabian?'

'I don't know. Why?'

'Milly said he's going out a lot. Is Inky's lovely mother around?'

'Yes. She's staying with Inky for a bit.'

'Oh, I'm so glad. Especially with the Italian series coming up. Poor Inky must be really worried about it.'

'Everybody has been worried about Inky. Sir Edward has been secretly feeding her chocolate at the crew meeting, he thinks it a general cure for all feminine ills, and then Custard found him out and all I've heard this morning is Sir Edward yelling "NOBODY ELSE GETS ANY CHOCOLATE" all over the compound. Carla is looking as though the weight of the world is on her and every time she lays eyes on Inky and Hattie I think she's going to burst into tears . . . well, Hattie is worse than a wet weekend. The psychologist is having the time of his life.'

'I know Hattie is miserable. I feel so badly for her. I've tried to ask Rafe about Ava but he simply clams up. I have absolutely no idea what is going on.'

Rafe had a very trying day. Practice had been awful; they didn't have a spare spinnaker pole on board to use after it had broken, and the pesky psychologist had been following them everywhere asking them if they found that worrying. After taking the sails in need of attention into the sail loft, he looked up at the offices and saw the bent head of Hattie at her desk. He hadn't seen much of her lately and didn't know why. He thought he might feel a lot better if they could have one of their comforting chats.

'Hello, stranger,' he said popping his head round the office door.

'Rafe!' Hattie went pink.

'Have you got time for an ice cream? The rain has stopped. I thought we could wander up and get one.'

Hattie felt absolutely torn. It seemed ironic to her that before the racing she would have grabbed any excuse to see Rafe but their paths rarely legitimately crossed and now when she wanted to avoid him, she couldn't because he attracted so much interest from the press. On one hand she knew it would be bad for her to go, it was all quite, quite hopeless, but on the other, it was simply heavenly to see him and she could hardly keep on making excuses to avoid him.

'Of course. Do you want to take a bike?'

'No. Let's walk. I'd rather talk to you.'

They clattered down the stairs with Hattie surreptitiously pinching her cheeks and running her tongue over her teeth as she went. She still had no idea what happened that night between him and Ava. He hadn't mentioned it to her or, apparently, anyone else.

'Have you heard anything?' she had asked Inky tentatively this morning.

She shook her head. 'Not a thing. And you know Rafe, he has such an aura of privacy around him that it makes it difficult to ask. But his sailing doesn't seem to be affected,' she added cheerfully. 'He was calling the shifts yesterday as accurately as ever. It was like having that wind god on the boat with us. What's his name?'

'Aeolus,' Hattie had answered numbly.

'I haven't seen you for ages,' Rafe commented.

'I've been busy.'

'Busy doing what?' He smiled as he held the door open for her out of the compound. They started to walk along the dockside. Rafe made sure that he was walking on the outside of her. The rain had cleared the air temporarily and Hattie wished it could have had the same effect on her and Rafe.

'Well, obviously the coverage is starting to increase. So I spend a lot of time with the press. How was practice today?'

'Broken spinnaker pole. Then we came upon the Phoenix crew whose support boat made a great pretence of coming alongside and trying to see our keel. They then trailed behind us all the way home. Mack got so mad I thought he might try and leap in the boat and throttle the driver.'

'The keel is one secret we could do without getting out. How is Inky holding out when she's about to race Luca?'

'Getting sick of everyone asking. She only has to sneeze and sixteen voices all say, "Are you OK, Inky?"'

'And how are you getting on?'

'I'm fine. I want to get on and race, I don't much like this waiting business.'

'It must be difficult for you and A . . . Ava.' She felt that she absolutely had to mention it. It might be better if it was out in the open. 'Do you think you are going to get back together? I mean, it would be awful if the press got hold of it now.'

'Awful for who?' asked Rafe quietly.

'Awful for you and the syndicate,' Hattie quickly qualified it.

There was a long pause. They passed the perimeter of the South African syndicate. The doors of their shed were open and Hattie could see people working on their boat. They looked like ants, swarming over her.

'I don't know,' said Rafe eventually. 'She wants to get back together. But I really don't know. It's a bit confusing, to be honest. I don't know whether she came back to me because I've done exactly what she wanted me to do in the first place – join an America's Cup challenge – and I don't know whether I did that to get her back. And now so much has changed that I don't know if I want her back.'

'What's changed?'

'I have, I suppose. We had such a tempestuous relationship, always rowing, always making up. It took up so much energy. It took up so much *life*. There wasn't much time for anything else. Like a sort of addiction. But now I'm not sure I want that sort of relationship any more. Now I know it doesn't have to be like that.'

Hattie was dying to ask what he'd learnt to make him change his mind but instead she said, 'It must be hard for her, going out with Jason Bryant.' Why on earth was she sticking up for her? 'A real case of divided loyalties.'

Rafe's face hardened. 'Whatever happens between me and Ava, I want to make sure I get to race that little shit. I only hope Excalibur will make it that far.'

Chapter 37

Fabian put his head around the bedroom door. Milly was folding Rosie's clothes. 'Darling, I'm just popping out.'

'Where are you going?'

His eyes didn't quite meet hers. 'I'm just going for a drink with Custard.'

'But you race tomorrow.'

'We just need to wind down. I shan't be long.'

'Don't be,' she said lightly. She was getting quite nervous by herself. 'I saw that man again today.'

'Don't worry about him,' said Fabian soothingly. 'Mack has put a doorman on here now and no one can get in. People hang around the compound all the time.' He came fully into the room and pecked her on the cheek. 'I'll be back later.'

She smiled and then, standing stock-still in the middle of the room, waited until she heard the door click shut behind him. She quickly went to his chest of drawers and, hating herself, started to rifle through the top drawer. She didn't know what she was looking for. But she could feel the tight fingers of apprehension gripping her hard around the chest. In a peculiar way, to find nothing would be worse than finding something. At least that way her suspicions could be confirmed. She wasn't sure she could live with these stomach-churning doubts any more. She was quite sure she would go mad.

Milly couldn't think what else it could be. It had started a week ago. The secret texting and hastily finished phone calls. The going out for drinks without really saying where he was going, and coming back smelling of mints and a fragrance she couldn't quite put her finger on. (She'd even checked up on him the other night when he said he was going out with Dougie, and Dougie said he'd been in all night watching *Lethal Weapon*). She felt dreadfully underhand, like a cheap detective.

After going through the chest of drawers and finding nothing, she went over to the wastepaper basket and at the very bottom found a piece of paper carefully torn into eight pieces. It took her only a few seconds. The scribbled note said, 'Daphne. 8 p.m.'

Sinking to her knees, Milly started to cry.

Past ten that night Mack still hadn't made it back to Casa Fortuna. They started their race series with the Italians tomorrow and he was watching for the umpteenth time videos of the Italian skipper, pausing the tape to look closely at this move or that technique. Marco Fraternelli was only twenty-nine but had earned himself a good name on the World Match Racing Tour circuit. He seemed to follow a pattern: take control in the start box and then break right. Their boat also seemed faster in tacking duels. The whole base hummed with activity below him. The sail lofts buzzed as the machinists recut the sails under the ever watchful eye of Griff Dow; they would work through the night so they were ready for the next day's sailing. The shore crew were still working on *Excalibur*.

There was a knock at the door. It was Bee.

'I've brought you some sandwiches. I didn't know if you would have eaten.'

'Hmm? Oh, thanks, Bee. Made with nasty bread?'

She smiled, coming fully into the room, and plonked two huge baguettes on his desk. 'French bread from the nice bakery.'

Mack hungrily grabbed one and took a huge bite. Carla had actually stayed on and made them all an early supper but now they were all ravenous again. He leant back in his chair. God, it was delicious. Melted Brie, bacon and Bee's home-made pear chutney.

'How's everything going?' she asked.

'As well as possible,' he said between mouthfuls. 'Where's Rafe?'

'At home. I left him trying to read the first Harry Potter book which Hattie lent him but I'm not sure he's getting on very well. I think he's only ever read the back of cereal packets. His father is sailing over from Egypt. He should have been here two weeks ago for the start but got the dates mixed up. We're waiting for a call when his mobile phone comes into service.'

'Actually, Bee, I've been meaning to ask you if you would come out on the *Mucky Ducky* when the racing starts again and help Carla with some of the food. We've got quite a lot of the sponsors coming out to watch.'

'Of course! I'd love to!'

'Thanks.' He didn't add that her disarming chattiness would also ease the day for all of them. 'We haven't quite got round to telling her that none of us likes the bread so you'll have to make up some sort of English allergy and pretend we have to have it all from the French bakery.'

'You're all petrified of her, aren't you?'

'Absolutely.'

'I'll let you get on.' She gestured to the TV. 'I'm just going to distribute these.' She held up her bag of baguettes.

'Did you come down by yourself?'

'Yes.'

He rose to his feet. 'I'll get one of the shore crew to walk you back.'

'Please don't bother. I'm on one of the syndicate bicycles. I just pedal really fast and I'm a blur of pink to any potential muggers.'

'Hattie's making Colin go around on one of those motorised scooters with a cigar hanging out of his mouth. She says it will add to his eccentricity. I think he's really enjoying it actually. He's already been in three papers.'

Bee laughed and said she would see him later. After she had given out all her baguettes to some of the remaining *Excalibur* crew and shore crew, she had a quick look round for Custard. He hadn't been home a lot lately and she had thought that he would be here. She presumed he'd just been working harder. She shrugged and got on her bike for home.

Out of all the *Excalibur* crew, Custard was actually the only one properly enjoying his evening. Whilst Henry Luter was spending his every minute down at the Phoenix Challenge boat shed, Saffron was enjoying such an extra degree of freedom that she and Custard couldn't resist taking the opportunity to spend every single moment together.

'I'm sorry I'm so thin,' Saffron said, lying next to him in her incredibly sexy petticoat. It was all coffee and cream lace.

'Could do with a little bit of padding here and there but other than that you are perfect.' Custard gently moved his hand round her torso. She found his gentle unhurriedness such a turn-on after Henry. He slowly fingered each nipple and then his hand travelling slowly downwards and underneath her slip found the top of her panties. He lightly twanged them and Saffron laughed. She looked so beautiful to Custard. Her fair hair was lying spread out on the pillow and her eyes huge in her pale face. 'I love you with your hair down,' he said suddenly. 'You should always wear it that way.'

'I know, I hate having it up and so arranged, it feels so unnatural. But Henry insists.'

'Well, as long as you always wear it down with me. At least I know it's something that Henry doesn't have.'

She pulled herself on to her side and started to kiss Custard's chest. Being with someone so well formed only made her recent enforced sessions with Henry even more hideous – if that were possible. His feverish demands had no basis in desire, merely in control. She firmly put him out of her mind.

Slowly she started to kiss her way down Custard's chest. She adored the way he made her feel, which made her completely unselfish. All she wanted to do was give him pleasure.

'You don't have to . . . ' he murmured.

'I want to,' she whispered back.

'Was it OK?' asked Custard anxiously as he eased himself out of her half an hour later.

'Heavenly,' said Saffron truthfully. She particularly loved the way Custard wanted her so much.

'If you keep looking at me like that, I might have to leap on you again.'

She smiled as she lay back on his mismatched pillows with her hair fanned round her. She didn't bother to pull the green sheet back to cover her. It was so hot anyway. With Henry she always took a shower immediately after sex, scrubbing and scrubbing herself until she was red raw. She wanted Custard's scent to stay on her as long as possible.

'Why do they call you Custard?'

'Because I have a boat back home called *Crème Anglaise*. My dad is sailing it for the summer.'

'I prefer Will. I think I might call you Will.'

'What about your name? Is it really Saffron?' he asked astutely.

She blushed. 'No, it's not. Promise you won't laugh? It's really Judith.'

Custard smiled. 'Judith is not so bad.'

They were in Custard's flat in Casa Fortuna with all the curtains drawn, just a few candles for light and ignoring anyone knocking at the door. Pipgin lay panting at the bottom of the bed, which they had found slightly off-putting at first. Custard had left the window open in the bathroom to let some breeze in and the smell of orange blossom from the garden floated in with it. There was a perceptible haze of it in the air and the trees looked as though they were alive until you realised it was just the bees.

'The orange blossom is just wonderful.'

'The lady next door asked if she could lay some sheets out under the tree to catch all the blossom. Apparently they make tea from it. *Flor de azahara*. It helps you sleep. Mack asked for some for us all.'

Saffron's brow furrowed. 'I'm worried you're not getting enough sleep.'

'Oh, I wouldn't be sleeping,' Custard hastily assured her. 'None of us is. I'd much rather be with you than tossing and turning and dreaming about boats overtaking us.'

'I like your place.' Saffron looked around the room. In contrast to the minimalist style of the Luter houses where cushions were fluffed as your bottom left them, the room was full of personality, from the pile of kit on the floor to the photos propped on the chest of drawers. She adored it. Everything about Will just seemed to fit. She was realising it more and more. She had thought money and labels would be the answer. How was she supposed to know it would be mismatched sheets and a smelly red setter?

'Not terribly tidy, I'm afraid. It's even worse back in England. What time do you have to be back?'

Saffron looked at her watch. 'Twelve-thirty, I think. Henry hasn't been getting back before one a.m.'

'Hatching dastardly plans?'

'Something like that. I would tell you if I knew but Henry and I don't exactly talk about anything.'

Custard inwardly winced. The thought of Saffron and Henry in bed together continually taunted him. Those grasping hands all over her beautiful body.

'Have you told anyone at the challenge about me?' she asked.

'God, no. They would die of shock.' As it was Custard had had to smuggle her in this evening under a trilby hat and huge sunglasses. If she was seen coming into his flat, he was simply going to say that she was a terribly famous celebrity whom he couldn't possibly name. 'What about the staff on the *Corposant*?'

'I tell them that I'm having some dramatic beauty treatment

that I would rather my husband didn't know about. Besides, they probably all hate Henry too much to snitch on me. He told them all off for going through too many boxes of tissues the other day. Who is the pretty woman with the little girl I saw on the dock, by the way?'

Custard frowned for second. 'I think you might mean Milly. She's Fabian's, our bowman's, girlfriend,' he added hastily. He had lost an inordinate number of girls to Fabian over his lifetime and wasn't about to lose this one too. He didn't know if Fabian's wandering eye had been completely stilled.

'Yes, of course.' She was learning an awful lot about the Montague Challenge. When Henry was giving her a particularly torturous time by shouting at her or belittling her in front of his business cronies, she liked to be able to picture Custard with his crew mates so she always took a great deal of notice when she saw the pink crew colours around. Then as a shut-down technique she would conjure little scenes in her head of what they might be doing.

'Her little girl is sweet. She stuffs Pipgin full of biscuits. He adores her.'

Saffron stretched out a hand to stroke Pipgin who had leapt up at the sound of his name in conjunction with biscuits and trotted round to her side of the bed.

'I never expected you to like dogs.'

'I love them. I had a little Westie when I was a child. I wanted another one but Henry doesn't like them.' Custard opened his mouth to tell her he would let her have any dog she liked (provided of course that it got on with Pipgin) but then closed it again. He wasn't quite sure where this relationship was going. All he knew was that he was powerless to stop it.

'Tell me about your childhood, what did you dream about when you were a girl?' Custard had asked her about her childhood before but she was always quite reticent. He wanted to know everything about her including whatever it was she wasn't telling him.

'Escape. Money.' She smiled apologetically. 'Neither of which have brought me much happiness.'

'Didn't you think about modelling? I'm not just trying to flatter you . . . ' he added as she blushed. ' . . . You could have easily been a model – that would have brought you escape and money.'

'I didn't really think I was very pretty. I had an old-fashioned idea about an old-fashioned millionaire. I think I liked the idea of being looked after for a change.' She clammed up suddenly and started to pleat the sheet. She didn't want Custard to know too much about her childhood in case he went off her. And that was something she couldn't bear. The locked doors. Being constantly on her guard. Always sleeping lightly in case . . . It was her fault. 'Besides,' she gabbled, 'I'm too old for that sort of work now even if Henry would let me. But I would love to be busy.'

'Maybe escape and money meant different things to you back then,' said Custard idly playing with her hand. 'Maybe you were really dreaming about freedom.'

Saffron stared at him. Freedom. Of course. A huge smile lit up her face.

That was when she really started to fall in love.

Chapter 38

'They look formidable,' whispered Inky to Sparky who had gone a little pale. The crew of Excalibur were sitting in a darkened room watching video tapes of the Italian crew. They all had difficulty in eating any breakfast that morning. The only people to have cheerfully worked their way through porridge, eggs and then raisin toast were all the grinders, Rafe and Ho.

'Our crew work has to be faultless because it looks as though they have more manoeuvrability than us. Remember that the crew who wins is the crew who makes the fewest mistakes. So this is simply about going out there and doing the same thing that you have been doing day in and day out for the last eighteen months. Nothing more, nothing less. You need to focus and concentrate and not even look at what the other boat is doing. If we win then we will be one up.' Mack knew that winning the first race in a series was vital for the crew's confidence, especially against such a formidable opponent. 'Unfortunately we have light winds forecast for the day . . .'

On board the *Mucky Ducky*, Bee, Carla and Hattie were getting ready for the visitors. Bee was arranging the food whilst Carla bustled around her coffee machine which was the spare one from her brother's restaurant that she had heaved on board this morning by herself. Bee was convinced that they were listing to one side with the weight of it. 'You cannot have people on the boat for hours without proper coffee,' said Carla. 'They might die and who would you point the finger at? Me, of course!'

Carla had luckily acquiesced to Bee's bizarre bread request after Bee told her several people seemed to be allergic to something in Spanish bread. 'I'll look out for them,' said Carla darkly. 'Let us hope that they will not be allergic to anything else.' Carla had prepared some fabulous tapas dishes full of local delicacies which Pipgin and Salty were eying greedily. Carla eyed them back.

'If I wasn't so nervous about *Excalibur*,' said Bee whose tummy was churning with nerves, 'I think I would really enjoy today.' She started to help Hattie with the little welcome bags for the guests.

'I know,' sighed Hattie. 'I feel terribly sick so goodness knows how the crew are feeling. How was Rafe this morning?' she asked awkwardly.

'Fine, actually. He finally spoke to his father last night. He was so pleased that I think it took his mind off everything. I don't think Rafe really feels the nerves like everyone else though. The racing is the natural part for him, he's so calm on the water because I think he feels at home there. It's all the press conferences and attention afterwards that he gets nervous about.' She filled the welcome bags in turn with bottles of water, sunscreen and sea sickness tablets, all donated by British firms.

'I know. I try to protect him a bit from it but everyone is so interested in talking to him. What's his father like?'

'Like Rafe, except more worldly-wise. He did live in society whereas Rafe never has. Of course, I haven't seen him for years. He's trying to get back to see Rafe at the moment, so he should be arriving any day now. I'm so looking forward to seeing him. Who is in the eighteenth man position by the way?'

'Colin. He loves it so much that he doesn't seem to want to give anyone else a go. He says it's like a particularly wild roller-coaster ride. I've given him another T-shirt which he's wearing under his Excalibur one and I've told him to whip off the top one when we win.'

'What does it say?' asked Bee curiously.

'You'll see,' said Hattie. 'Well at least I hope you will, anyway.'

Bee was lucky enough to have the company of Sir Edward on board *Mucky Ducky* today. After they had settled the visitors, doled out refreshments and reassured a couple about the existence of sea legs, Bee went on deck to watch the proceedings. She was distracted by a panting Sir Edward dragging Salty out on to the deck by his collar. 'Just found him in the bin.'

'God, sorry.'

They leant against the railings and watched the final preparations on board *Excalibur*.

'The balance within the crew must be quite delicate,' commented Bee.

'Yes. Something you can't predict and something they have to grow into. A wonderful thing when it comes right.'

'Fabian is amazing, isn't he?' commented Bee, watching him dangling upside down from a spinnaker pole.

'I was dubious about him after that business with Rob Thornton. You heard about that?' Bee nodded. 'But he's proved them all wrong, I'm pleased for him. I thought he'd be some sort of beer-swilling druggie, but he's never given me a moment's concern on that score.'

Sir Edward excused himself but Bee stayed watching the crew and Fabian in particular. She noticed that he was continually looking out of the boat, as though searching round for someone. Suddenly his whole body, which had been so tense, relaxed. He'd obviously found the object of his affection. She followed his eyeline across to a group of boats but it could have been any of them. She looked at him again: he was waving subtly. Then he turned back to his task. Bee squinted at the boats once more, trying to make out their names but they were too far off. She knew that Fabian's mother hadn't arrived yet but it couldn't have been her any way, Fabian's manner was all wrong. He was really being quite furtive.

Just before the start, *Excalibur* was nose to nose with the Italians, circling aggressively, the crew unable to hear themselves think above the shout of commands and the chaos of activity. And now they were across the start line and sailing away from each other, the only noise being the lapping of waves.

'They're twenty-six seconds behind us and on a port tack,' reported Sammy. 'They think there's more wind out to the right.'

'Wind shift coming, five degrees. First knock for us,' said Rafe. 'Tack now, Mack.'

Mack yelled the instruction and eased the wheel round smoothly. There was furious activity in the powerhouse of the boat as the mainsail swung across the deck and the great *Excalibur* heeled to the other side. Her huge sails began to fill again with the wind.

Inky had her eyes constantly pinned on *Baci*. 'They're catching up,' she muttered. It was one of the ironies of match racing. Simply by being in a different part of the course, *Baci* was subject to different wind changes and shifts and could catch up. Inky thought fleetingly about Luca laughingly telling her of the Italian's crew practice of making a sacrifice to the wind gods whilst at the same time praying to the tiny crucifix they had propped on board. She wondered grimly which one was responding to them now.

By the first mark, the Italian crew seemed to have caught a couple of good shifts and were barely one length behind. 'They can't get into our water,' said Inky. 'You're clear.'

But as Mack yelled out the instructions to round the mark, a noise rang out like a gunshot and, simultaneously, Golly, howling with pain, tumbled to the deck. Fabian and Ho couldn't be spared from the spinnaker so Rafe ran forward to take over the winch control as Golly dragged himself out of the way.

'The winch has exploded. Only one side is working!' he yelled. They watched Flipper, the other grinder, wind in the genoa on just one winch. They were powerless to help. But he went at it like a man possessed and slowly but surely the giant sail moved. Ho and Fabian waited with the spinnaker which they couldn't set until this was completed and such was the laboured sluggishness of the set that it felt as though the Italians were literally on top of them. *Baci*'s spinnaker was up and set and they sped ahead as soon as they had clear water to do so. *Excalibur* was still turning through her circle. 'Come on, come on,' whispered Fabian, watching and poised for action. It took fifteen seconds longer than usual before their pure white spinnaker with Colin Montague's corporate logo burst into action.

'They've passed us,' whispered Inky in horror.

'Can I have an injury report?' called Mack to Rafe who was now free to tend to Golly. Flipper and Dougie were examining the damaged winch whilst Ho had dashed down to the sewer to look for a new winch part in the very limited supply of spare parts they carried.

Rafe was binding Golly's knee very tightly. 'Winch exploded,' he called. 'Ball bearings are in his knee.'

'I'm all right, Mack. No need to take me off,' called Golly. 'Just bind it tight,' he muttered to Rafe.

Mack was deliberating whether to send for the support boat and have Golly taken off – which would be within the rules – or if he was fit enough to be left on. No one was as fit as Golly.

'Could you still grind, Golly?'

'Don't need my knee to grind and I can stand.'

'What about the winch? Can it be fixed?'

'We're working on it,' said Flipper. The grinders practised for such an emergency on shore by timing each other to disassemble the winches. Rump already had the winch in bits on the floor and was trying to slot in a new part. 'The part is OK. We should be up and running again soon.'

'Sure you can grind?' Mack asked Golly again.

'I'm fine, leave me on.'

'How long on this bearing?' he asked Inky. If they gybed before the full power of the winches was restored, *Excalibur* would lose a lot of speed.

Inky appeared a little shocked. She clearly hadn't considered the possibility of losing. 'Inky?' he questioned again. 'How long?'

Rafe reappeared at Mack's elbow. 'Let's stay with this shift. *Baci* aren't going to get anything faster.'

'*Baci* are fifteen seconds ahead,' said Sammy.

Inky would never know whether those pesky wind gods were playing their tricks again but *Baci* never let the lead slip. They crossed the finish line ahead of the British boat and to the ecstatic celebrations of their syndicate.

At Excalibur's base camp, they all looked at each other in dismay. The camera, as though telepathic, focused in on Inky's rather shocked and pale face. Hattie and Milly held hands and stared at the television screen. 'I didn't know the Italians were that good. They've come back so well,' Milly whispered hollowly.

'We did have an injury,' said Hattie. Sir Edward had come back to shore in a RIB to collect a doctor who could treat Golly immediately after the race.

'I hope Golly is OK,' said Milly looking round for his wife but she had already left in the launch with the doctor.

'They would have taken him off if he was really bad.'

Milly sighed and glanced over at Rosie who was being well looked after by Carla. Cake was in the offing and Rosie became like a limpet as soon as cake appeared. Carla had probably found out by now how difficult it is to eat cake with a small child hanging off your leg.

The shore crew, and those who had to, disappeared off to make ready for *Excalibur*'s return. Everyone else flopped despondently down into chairs while Carla bustled round with Rosie in tow. 'Would you like tea?' she asked Milly and Hattie kindly. She knew the English were funny about their tea: it tended to comfort them. Even if someone had died, you always offered tea. But not with the teabag still in the cup. They were peculiar like that.

'Yes, please,' said Milly and Hattie automatically. 'But I ought to be sorting out the press conference,' Hattie added, hovering uncertainly.

'Stay for one cup,' urged Milly.

'OK.' She sank down on to an opposite beanbag. 'I'll take it with me.' She took in Milly's yellow broderie anglaise strappy top, which she'd matched with frayed denim hotpants and stripy wedges. She had a little sigh to herself. Milly always looked so avant-garde.

'Where's your dad, Milly?' she asked. They could have done with his kindly, cheerful presence right now.

'He's watching in the main enclosure. He's leaving tomorrow. Got to get back to do some work; he thinks his customers will have forgotten all about him!'

'But he'll be out again?'

'Yes, he wants to. Of course, we might not still be here.'

I might not still be here, she added silently to herself. Only the Italian race series had kept her from confronting Fabian. Since the night she had found out about Fabian's affair (she tortured herself with the thought that it was with a woman with a perfectly toned stomach – hers still stuck out a fraction, almost still moulded into a Rosie shape), her misery had set in a concrete fury. She knew he had thought about leaving before, she'd seen it in his eyes, but now she was thinking of leaving him. She was sick of the insecurity, she was sick of looking at other women and constantly worrying if he would leave her for them. Sick of listening to bright-eyed girls trying to snatch his attention, and him letting them. She was sick of it all. She and Rosie would be perfectly all right by themselves. If another woman wanted him then she was welcome to him. See how long she could put up with it all.

Hattie took her tea from Carla with grateful thanks and disappeared off to organise her press conference, leaving Milly brooding. She couldn't go and meet her father yet; she had to wait for the crew to return. She stared out at the busy scene of the *Excalibur* dock before her, unseeing. To make matters worse, Elizabeth Beaufort had announced her intention to come out and support Excalibur too. Milly was quite sure it was only since they had started winning and thus the precious Beaufort name wouldn't be further sullied.

She could see *Excalibur*'s mast in the distance as she was towed up the canal into the harbour. She finished the dregs of her tea and got up. Like most of the wives and support crew around her, she practised a smile. It was important that the crew never saw you low. You had to be continually upbeat for them. It certainly wasn't for Fabian's sake she was doing this today (he probably would take his share of the consolation, absorbing it like a sponge, and then disappear again anyway) but for the rest of the crew. It was a measure of her strength and it was exhausting.

Chapter 39

Whilst the crew of *Excalibur* were getting ready for their second race against the Italians, Saffron was sitting below deck of the *Corposant* giving an interview to *Hello!*. She looked at her watch anxiously. She had to be up on deck to watch the start.

'Don't worry, Mrs Luter,' said the interviewer reassuringly. 'We'll be through in plenty of time for you to watch the races with your husband. Doesn't matter if you miss the first bit, though, does it?'

It did to Saffron, and Custard's race was in forty-five minutes. She'd instructed the *Corposant* crew that she wanted to be on the race course to watch the first set of races and that the reporter and photographer were to be taken back to shore in the launch. Already she could hear the hum of the engines starting up.

The press made Saffron nervous. They were always asking awkward questions and trying to delve into things that she would rather remain hidden.

'Tell me about where you grew up, Mrs Luter,' Katie the reporter started. 'Was there a lot of money in your family?'

'No. There wasn't.'

'Holidays abroad? Treats and trips?'

'Not many.'

'Where exactly did you grow up?'

'In the country.'

'Whereabouts exactly?'

'Surrey.'

The journalist changed tack slightly. 'Did you go to university?'

'No. My parents didn't want me to go away.'

'You don't talk much about them.'

'There is nothing to tell. My father worked in an office and my mother was a housewife.'

'Then what sort of work did you do? That is, before you met Mr Luter.'

'I was in London. I worked there.'

'What as?'

'In a shop. I was a shop assistant.'

Katie knew she wasn't getting anywhere. A new tactic was required. She jumped to her feet. 'It's such a beautiful boat! Could you possibly show me around?'

'Of course,' said Saffron just longing for the whole ordeal to be over.

The journalist was incurably nosy anyway and took her time going from room to room. They finally got to the cabins. 'Gorgeous,' she breathed, looking round. She popped her head into the bathroom and looked longingly at the gold-plated taps.

'Did you decorate?'

'No. My husband knew exactly what he wanted and instructed a designer.'

'All the doors have locks on,' she said suddenly.

Saffron had tried to smile. 'I like my privacy.' She gestured for Katie to go out first and tried not to remember a long time ago when there weren't any locks on the door and she didn't dare to sleep.

They returned to the main saloon.

'Tell me, Mrs Luter, out of all your beautiful homes – those in France, Barbados and Aspen, to name a few – which do you prefer?'

Her mind was blank. 'Em, I actually like the *Corposant* best. I like being near the water.'

Katie looked admiringly round the luxurious sitting room lined with oak panels and leather sofas which would swallow you up whole. Saffron had been allowed no hand in decorating it. 'It is beautiful.' She leant forward and fingered the leaves of a huge vase of flowers, the only request of Saffron's that had been acceded to. 'It smells so gorgeous,' she murmured. 'What is it?'

'Orange blossom,' said Saffron faintly.

'Of course. So . . . ' Katie said more briskly, returning to her notes. 'It was a truly philanthropic gesture of your husband to come to the aid of the Spanish challenge after their finances fell through, wasn't it?'

Saffron didn't like to say Henry thought it was the only way he could get his hands on the Cup. It didn't sound terribly philanthropic. 'Henry felt terribly embarrassed for everyone and just wanted to help out,' she lied.

'Are you and Mr Luter planning on a family at any point in the future?'

Saffron opened her mouth and closed it again. She had fulfilled her brief so far; she had waxed on about how proud she was of Henry and his sailing, how happy she was being his trophy wife, she'd boasted of her jewels and clothes, but here was something she wasn't sure she could lie about. It wasn't until recently that she had started to dream of children. It hadn't really been on her agenda before and Henry had always made his position quite plain. No children. Why would you want to ruin something so perfect?

'We're . . . we're not considering a family right now because . . . why would you want to ruin something so perfect?' she parroted.

Katie smiled in perfect understanding. 'Absolutely. All that shouting and sticky fingers!'

Saffron forced herself to laugh, feeling quite sick.

'Oh, we're moving!' said Katie looking out of the window. 'Just a few more questions.' She glanced down to her notepad. 'Would it make your life complete if the well-tipped Phoenix Challenge were able to defend the America's Cup?'

'It would be a dream come true,' she lied. Now she was

beginning to hate herself. 'Shall we go up on deck?' At least Custard could see her that way. He liked to see her before each race. He said that she brought him luck. She half rose to her feet.

'Well, if you don't mind, I'd like a few of shots of you in this fabulous room. It would make more sense to do them now and the deck later on.' She signalled to the photographer.

Saffron sat back down again. The only thing which made sense to her was standing on *Excalibur* waiting for a glimpse of her.

The rest of the crew were trying to shield themselves from the intense media scrutiny and were all sitting down in Ho's sewer. Ordinarily they would take the opportunity to sleep on the tow out to the race waters but today nobody slept apart from Golly and Flipper whose skins were pure crocodile hide anyway. Inky lay on a pile of sails with her eyes closed so that no one would speak to her, trying to distance herself from a pair of dark, mocking, foreign eyes. Rafe was listening to the iPod, looking watchful, and Custard was up on deck as the only one to volunteer steering the boat on her tow out. Every now and then he would look back to the huge spectre of *Corposant* – easily the largest yacht in the spectator fleet – following behind them. He fingered the St Christopher Saffron had given him which hung around his neck and prayed for her to appear. But soon the huge Louis Vuitton buoys which marked out the race course and the various committee boats and umpire boats came into sight and still no sign of her. Custard, with one last puzzled look back at *Corposant*, went to stir the crew for action.

At last the reporter seemed to have asked all her questions. Saffron hustled them as quickly as she could out of the vast drawing room and on to deck. *Excalibur* would be starting to race within a quarter of an hour. They would be getting the sails up now. She looked quickly about as they emerged into strong sunlight, desperate for some orientation. Thankfully they seemed to be on the right side of the boat and there was *Excalibur*. She looked for Custard; even though the crew was all dressed in identical kit and of similar build, she didn't need binoculars. She was not only familiar with every inch of his body but knew the way he carried himself, the way he jerked his head up like he did now. She could even tell when he was arriving by the sound of his footsteps. She smiled broadly. A pulse leapt between her legs and she knew he had seen her.

'Mrs Luter,' sighed the reporter, looking round at the glamorous scene of yachts, bikinis and cocktails. 'You must be the luckiest woman in the world.'

Saffron grinned. 'At this very moment I think I am.'

Whilst Colin did get to display one of his T-shirts (RULE BRITANNIA) that day as *Excalibur* won the race – and the two after that, leaving them thinking the whole series might prove to be a walkover – they were sorely disappointed from then on. The light winds started to prevail for the Italians and *Excalibur* had to fight them every inch of the way only to be beaten by mere seconds in the subsequent two races. Both days long waits preceded the racing as the committee decided whether to call it off for the day, which the British crew would have preferred, but unfortunately just as they were on the cusp of what was considered not enough wind, it would pick up slightly.

The press began to moan about *Excalibur* following the all-too-familiar pattern in British sport of starting out well and then losing focus just as the smell of victory was wafting under their noses. There was a distinct suggestion that they had had it, accompanied by a lot of sighing, even though it was still 3–3 in a best of seven series. One last race would decide who would go on to race the mighty New Zealanders.

'Watch the crew,' murmured Sir Edward to Mack as they walked out of the boatshed that night. 'They're bubbling over with frustration which will translate into mistakes.' He didn't mention the despondency and lack of confidence expressed by the sponsors on the *Mucky Ducky*. A very depressed Mack for once didn't have an answer. He got on his bike and cycled back to Casa Fortuna. It was always such a relief to walk into that tiny English colony. He paused momentarily outside his own door before putting his keys back in his pocket and walking down two floors to Bee.

Henry Luter had not been idle over the last few days. He had been thinking about this line of action for a while and now it was time to enforce it. His first visit was to Franco Berlini, the head of the Italian syndicate.

The two men greeted each other warily and Franco led them into an office. He eyed Henry Luter's lawyer thoughtfully. 'Would you like some refreshments, gentlemen?' He didn't want to offer them anything. He disliked and distrusted Luter. They declined. 'So what can I do for you?'

Luter didn't waste any time. 'It would be awful if you lost against *Excalibur*.'

'What makes you think we might lose?'

'Maybe *Excalibur* has an unfair advantage.'

'What do you mean?' said Franco sharply. 'Like what?'

'Have you seen how secretive they are around their keel?'

Franco shrugged. 'We are all secretive about our keels.'

'I believe theirs was designed illegally.'

Franco Berlini leant forward. 'That is a serious allegation. I would hope you have the evidence to back it up.'

'I have. We have been making some enquiries and I think they used a foreign national to design their keel. During the tank testing, there was a French hydro- and aerodynamics expert staying at the facility who says he had some input into their design. As you know, the boat has to be designed and built solely in the challenging country.'

Franco stared at them. 'Is he willing to stand up and swear to this?'

'He is.'

'Why have you brought this to me? You should be making an official protest through the challenger's committee.'

'I thought it would be in your interest. If you protested it before your final race with *Excalibur*, then it doesn't matter if you win or lose that race. If you lose and they are disqualified, that would put you through to the next round to face the New Zealanders. If you win then it doesn't matter because you still go through to face the New Zealanders.'

'You want my club to protest it?'

Henry Luter shrugged. 'Well, it's not really an issue for us, Excalibur probably won't beat the New Zealanders anyway, but it would be a tragedy if all this . . . ' Luter waved his hand around the building, ' . . . were for nothing. The fact is that you might be racing an illegal boat. It's not my place to bring this to the protest room. They would wonder why an Englishman would make such an accusation about an English syndicate. I left England to help out the Spanish defenders. It would look like sour grapes and then the point might be lost amongst the politics.'

'Do you think John MacGregor knows about this?' growled Franco, his blood up.

'Undoubtedly. Why do you think they are so secretive about their keel? Because they know it's illegal. If I can feed you all the details then you can make the protest before your last race. It might take another race series before the outcome can be decided, but they'll be disqualified and you are back in the game.'

Franco got up and walked to the window which looked out over his syndicate compound. He decided not to mention a word of this to his crew. It might put them off. He would rather they won for themselves but if was true that *Excalibur* was an illegal boat that would explain a lot . . .

Chapter 40

'Inky is going to take the helm for the pre-start,' Mack announced at their morning meeting.

Inky's head jerked up and she stared at him absolutely aghast. 'Me? No, Mack. I . . .' she started. One glare from Mack silenced her.

'Now, as we have all heard from Laura, the weather report is challenging to say the least. I daresay Hattie's press release might describe it as thrilling but I would call it bloody dangerous . . .'

'Are you sure about Inky taking the helm?' whispered Sir Edward as they left the meeting following an ashen, silent Inky. 'This is the deciding race.'

'I know my crew,' said Mack shortly.

'Of course. Why do you need to do this?'

'She's slightly losing confidence. I can see it. There are milliseconds of hesitancy which we simply can't afford. I need to give her back her confidence. She needs to beat Luca personally.'

'But what if she, I don't know . . . doesn't want to win? Subconsciously I mean. And what if we don't win, for whatever reason?'

'I know Inky. She'll rise to the occasion.' Mack made to walk away but then paused and looked back. 'Inky doesn't know how to lose. She only knows how to win.'

* * *

As a complete contrast to the last few days of racing, the tow out to the race course was difficult in the pitching sea and eighteen-knot winds. Green water poured into the sewer, so much so that they had to close the hatch, leaving everyone in darkness. No one could sleep with the motion of the boat anyway so while some of the crew stayed below chatting in the gloom the rest donned their foul weather gear and went up on deck, Inky and Custard amongst them. The ocean was a mass of white wave crests all marching towards them. *Excalibur* was pitching so much that the tow rope would continually go slack and then suddenly tauten, giving the boat a huge yank. The weather meant the spectator fleet was smaller than usual, but the faithful few hundred struggled through the waves. The *Mucky Ducky* had just pulled alongside to deposit Mack on *Excalibur* and Inky could see two of *Excalibur*'s designers watching the boat and looking terribly anxious which petrified her even more. She gave Custard a nudge and gestured towards them. 'They're worried whether she's going to hold out,' he murmured.

'That's not your concern,' said Mack sharply who had just joined them. 'Let's talk about the pre-start, Inky. Laura says, and Rafe agrees, that there is no one side of the course which is preferable today. Marco Fraternelli and his crew might disagree and be prepared to fight for one side. If that seems to be the case then we'll fight them for it but keep them guessing about which side of the course we actually want. They know we have Rafe, so they'll always be thinking that we know something they don't. When he sees you at the helm, whatever his plans are at the moment, he'll want to duel. He won't want anyone saying he was too frightened to engage with you . . . '

The five-minute gun went and immediately the Italian boat came in from the right, snapping with aggression, and headed for *Excalibur* with full rights of way. For a second, a heart-stopping second, Inky froze, and *Excalibur* was sitting there, like a duck in the water, with the Italians shooting at her. All Inky remembered was freezing water dripping down her neck from her wet-weather gear and a startled glance back from the bandaged Golly that jolted her out of her reverie. She suddenly moved, heading *Excalibur* on a collision course with *Baci*. Mack let out a breath he didn't know he was holding. Some of his earlier words echoed in Inky's head, 'He likes to go low and deep and then punch upwards.' So she needed to keep him circling.

They spun round each other angrily. Inky could barely hear her own voice for the roar of orders from the Italian skipper. She was ready for him when he really came for her, trying to hold her away from the line, but she dodged under his stern. The water was combed white as the boats cut and thrust across it. The spray flying upwards made it difficult for everyone to see. Their foul-weather gear felt impeding, as though some of their senses were being cut off. Inky noticed that Rafe didn't wear anything apart from a light jacket, his hair plastered to his head, but he didn't seem to notice.

'Which side, Rafe?'

'It's full of holes. No benefit to either.'

'Mack?'

'They look like they want the left side, so let's go right and get a good start.'

Inky played along as *Baci* tried to drive *Excalibur* away from the left side with Sammy's numbers singing in her ears. But to *Baci*'s frustration they couldn't get properly on her tail to push her away.

They started to circle each other loosely. It was difficult conditions for both of their crews. Mack was taking up Inky's usual position of tactician and trying to find a weakness in their opponent. 'She's going,' he said suddenly, more out of pure intuition than surveillance. A few seconds later the squeal of *Baci*'s sails confirmed this as she charged towards them again but Mack's precious few seconds of anticipation gave them an advantage. Again Inky ducked behind and came up on *Baci*'s tail in prime driving position which, to the fury of the Italian crew, she took full advantage of and proceeded to mercilessly drive her away from the left-hand side of the start line.

Rafe started to count down the time to the start, 'Sixty . . . fifty . . . forty-nine . . . ' and with split-second judgement only worthy of the finest match racers in the world, Inky judged the point where *Baci* were the furthest she could get them away from the line and where she could make a perfect start from the right side. At that instant she turned away from them and started to run. Later they were to say that they couldn't split the start time from the second that *Excalibur*'s bow crossed the line.

There was a moment of smug silence from the whole of the crew and Mack stepped forward to take the helm from Inky. For the first time in that race, she allowed herself one glance back at *Baci*, where they were still languishing well behind the line, and at Luca. Mack broke the silence by announcing, 'And that was a lesson given by Inky Pencarrow on how to start a match race. Do you think Marco Fraternelli will remember it for the rest of his life or just the next few decades or so?'

'They're crossing . . . they're crossing . . . now,' said Sammy fifteen seconds later and pressed his stopwatch.

Watching Inky on the pre-start, Mack knew she had done a wonderful job steering *Excalibur* in these conditions. The waves crashed against her bow and the chop bounced her up and down.

'OK, Fabian?' Mack said into his tiny microphone, the accompanying earpiece of which was firmly in his bowman's ear. Fabian kept disappearing from eyeline and even now Mack could only see a thumb jerked upwards to say he was fine. 'Stay sharp, everyone,' he called out. 'Let's just get *Excalibur* round the course.'

They sailed hard up to the first mark but in fits and starts, the fierce chop under the boat making her swing about a lot. Mack would shout, 'Ease the mainsheet, Custard. Little more. Another half-centimetre. That's it.' Then *Excalibur* would surge forward for a while, only to plough through the next set of waves, which were up to Fabian's knees, and lose speed again. Sammy constantly recorded the distance of *Baci* behind them. Luckily they were holding them perfectly on speed but Mack was still wary.

'Any suggestions, Rafe?'

'I think it might flatten out but not for a while.'

They were approaching the mark now, 'Go for the code three spinnaker,' Mack shouted down to Ho. Ho heaved the sail on to the deck by himself – he would have taken on *Baci* single-handedly if he could – and within seconds it was clipped to the pole and hoisted. But one of the straps which held the sail in place was stuck; Inky ran forward to help them and for what seemed like hours, but in actuality it was just a few seconds, she, Fabian and Ho tried – and failed – to clear the hourglass-shaped sail. In the end it had to be dropped to the deck.

'Christ . . . ' muttered Mack as *Excalibur* lost momentum.

'*Baci* is gaining,' Sammy the navigator announced calmly.

By the time the spinnaker was re-hoisted, *Baci* had nearly caught them up. 'They're faster and closer to the wind,' commented Sammy.

Inky could hear their bow wave against the side of *Excalibur* and the sound of Italian voices getting louder. She didn't give them the satisfaction of turning round. Sammy, who was facing back towards them, kept talking all the time. 'They've gained three metres . . . point her a little higher, Mack . . . we've gained two back . . . just keep at this speed . . . they're edging ahead of us . . . '

On their current course, they weren't sailing directly to the next mark but at an angle to it, so at some point *Baci* would have to gybe to cross their bow in order to pass and get to the mark first. But they couldn't quite get far enough ahead of *Excalibur* to do it.

Inky had taken all of this in. 'Shall we gybe, Inky?' asked Mack.

'No, let's force them out to the lay line.' The lay line was an imaginary line beyond which they would lose time if they didn't tack for the mark. 'We can inflict more damage out there.'

Baci was desperately trying to get enough room to gybe to cross *Excalibur* but every time she gained a little, Mack gained it back.

Inky waited until the last second to give the instruction to gybe and then just as they had pushed *Baci* over the lay line they gybed and raced for the mark, reaching it seconds before the Italians. Fabian was already out on the spinnaker pole, preparing for it to be dropped, and just as they rounded the mark, he withdrew the pin which held the foot of the spinnaker and the enormous expanse of sail flopped down, now impotent. Fabian dropped down on the deck like a monkey and helped gather the enormous sail in arm over arm with Ho and Sparky. If any part of the sail fell into the water, it would drag *Excalibur* and lose them precious seconds.

Within moments the sail was safely in the sewer and the spinnaker pole unclipped.

'Rafe, any change?'

Rafe hesitated as he watched a small shift travelling across the water and driving the rain before it. 'Just small shifts. Nothing major.'

'We're just going to have to catch them better than *Baci*.'

The rain was falling in sheets now and the visibility was slowly decreasing. Shit, thought Mack. They might lose sight of *Baci* and then God knows what might happen. In an America's Cup race where you race against another team, not against time, it is torturous to be out of contact with the other yacht. Everything is raced in relation to them.

The same thing must have been playing on Inky's mind because she said, 'Let's put a loose cover on *Baci*.' At least that way, although they wouldn't impede on her wind, they could keep in the same area and impose a blanket cover if they wanted to. 'I don't particularly want to duel with them,' commented Inky. '*Baci* seems to be faster out of her tacks.'

'I agree,' said Mack. 'Let's stay on a loose cover.'

But whilst the rain and the visibility fell even more, *Baci* gained on them. *Excalibur* had no choice but to impose a close cover. *Baci* must have been aware of her better acceleration out of tacks because immediately she started a tacking duel with a quick succession of four tacks.

'TACK!' yelled Mack for the fifth time, and the sails swung across the deck. 'She's giving us no time to recover,' he muttered to Inky.

'They're gaining. She's going to have enough speed to over-take within three more tacks,' commented Inky.

Sammy had been making frantic calculations. 'We're nine hundred metres from the mark.'

'I can't see it yet.'

'Tack again,' said Inky whose job it was to watch the opposing boat.

'We might just make it,' said Mack. 'TACK!'

Rafe went to the grinding pedestals to tell them that the Italians would be overtaking them in three tacks and then proceeded to scream abuse at them. It must have had some effect because it took the Italians five tacks in all to overtake them.

'Let's tack away,' said Inky quietly. 'And then come back to leeward at the mark.'

Mack nodded and understood. There was absolutely no point in them tagging after the Italians all the way to the mark. They might as well try and take the element of surprise that the driving rain could afford them and come to leeward which gave them full right of way. Mack tacked away and was soon lost to the Italians in the rain.

Mack thanked God for Sammy. He flawlessly calculated their position, and *Baci* and the mark emerged concurrently out of the rain. He had put them in absolute prime position. Without the crippling tacks *Excalibur* had managed to gain some speed and a few inches on *Baci*. Their bow was only just overlapping *Baci*'s stern, now that they were on a parallel course, but that was all they needed to exercise their right of way. Fabian, at the bow, whilst constantly relaying the distance between the two boats, could hear frantic Italian voices. *Baci* had no choice but to give them clear water in which to round the mark. Fabian got the spinnaker pole ready.

But Mack passed the mark without turning and squeezed tighter, eliciting a flood of abuse from *Baci*, who wasn't able to turn until *Excalibur* did. The dark heads of the Italian afterguard were constantly spinning round to check their position. The spectator fleet suddenly loomed out of the rain.

After squinting for them on the horizon and losing them in the rain, the spectator fleet had decided to wait for them at the mark. The leaders were petrified to see the two beasts suddenly looming out of the mist. Mack pushed *Baci* into the fleet. *Excalibur* turned and Fabian simultaneously punched the spinnaker into the air but it was far too late for *Baci*. The Italian abuse turned to sheer panic as they yelled in English and Italian for the spectator fleet to stay absolutely still as they navigated their way through. Mack didn't hear the punch of their spinnaker for at least another twenty seconds and smiled to himself in satisfaction.

'*Baci* is trailing by twelve boat lengths,' said Sammy.

Baci were so far behind that they never had a chance to catch up. Mack kissed the steering wheel of *Excalibur*. They were through.

Chapter 41

Hattie pushed her way through the wet crowds of people who had been waiting for *Excalibur* on the dockside. Rain was dripping off the tips of her hair, her mascara slightly run on one side. The first person she came face to face with was Rafe. 'You won! You won!' she screamed and threw her arms around his neck. He lifted her off the ground in a huge hug, kissed her on the neck and then set her down before being swept away by an avalanche of well-wishers. People stampeded past her but Hattie stood rooted to the spot, hazily touching the place where he had kissed her.

She didn't have long before she had to pull herself together and herd the whole crew to the press conference. Inky was desperate to try and see Luca but every time she caught sight of their crew colours and tried to make her way over to them, she was swamped by yet more people. She had watched the limp and defeated figures over on the Italian boat and found it hard to rejoice with her crew. The victory for *Excalibur* was probably the end for her and Luca.

A huge crocodile of colours and people marched towards the press conference. Custard managed to catch up with Inky. 'Are you OK?' he panted when he finally did. He had guessed what she was thinking.

'I suppose. Just a bit sad.'

Custard squeezed her elbow. 'Think of all that pasta you'd have to have eaten.'

'But I like pasta,' protested Inky almost in tears.

'No, Inky. It wouldn't be good for you. What you need is a good dose of *custard*.'

It was the first time Inky had laughed in days and the clicking of the cameras increased tenfold at their shot of the day.

Eventually they were all seated at a massive trestle in the bandstand, which was in the middle of the America's Cup village and surrounded with microphones. The crew were glowing with confidence and had the omnipotent feel of a team reaching perfection. Luca was positioned at the other end from Inky. He wouldn't look at her.

'You're through to the next round, Mack. How does that feel?' shouted an English reporter from the middle of the excited crowd.

Mack grinned in response to the question. 'It feels wonderful. We couldn't be happier. The Italian crew have been worthy opponents.'

They directed a similar question to Marco Fraternelli, the skipper of the Italian crew. 'We are naturally disappointed. We were hoping to go a lot further in the competition. But we have a saying in Italy which says the greatness of your people depends only on the greatness of your enemies. John MacGregor and the crew of *Excalibur* have made us very great indeed.'

There was a ripple of applause. Mack went on to answer many questions; he matched the graciousness of the Italian's response.

At the end of the conference, Mack noticed that the skipper of the New Zealand boat *Black Heart* had come in silently to watch them. He was standing towards the back, leaning against one of the columns and looking very preoccupied. Mack made his way towards him. They eyed each other thoughtfully. 'You're next,' Mack whispered.

The headline the next day, 'WOMAN STEERS GREAT BRITISH BOAT TO VICTORY IN THE AMERICA'S CUP' (which Mack took in good part) was accompanied by a stunning photograph of Inky. The paper had captured her at the helm; some of her hair had escaped and lay in rain-whipped lashes across her face, which was intense with concentration. 'That really is gorgeous,' said her mother admiring it yet again. 'I'm going to write to them for the original. It will be wonderful to put in the hall.'

Their hall at home was dedicated to pictures of great moments from all their careers.

'Actually, sod the hall,' Mary said as an afterthought. 'I think I would like it on my bedside table.' She kissed Inky on the forehead. 'I'm so very proud of you.'

Inky smiled. She didn't know what was more shocking: for her mother to flout a family tradition, or to say the word 'sod', but she was too preoccupied to respond. The whole of the *Excalibur* crew had been invited to a party thrown by the Italians. Such wakes are an America's Cup tradition and it was a huge sign of respect for the British crew that they had been asked too. Inky didn't know whether she should go or not. She was lying on her sofa in a morass of indecision.

'Do you *want* to go?' asked her mother, putting down the newspaper and sitting on the coffee table opposite her.

'I just don't think Luca will want to see me.'

'But you don't know that.'

'I know he won't have liked losing very much.'

'No one likes losing very much.'

'I mean losing to me. Maybe I should leave him to come to terms with it for a while.'

James Pencarrow came bustling through the front door at that moment carrying bags of shopping. 'They didn't have any butter so we're going to have to—'

'James?' said Mary firmly.

He stopped in surprise. 'Yes?'

'Do you mind dreadfully going to another shop to find some butter?

'Now?'

'Yes. Now.'

James looked from one woman to the other, put down the shopping and disappeared without another word.

'If you could have chosen, would you rather have lost and kept Luca?'

Inky looked up at her mother in surprise. 'No,' she said bluntly. 'I wouldn't.'

'Then this is a scenario you wished for and let's hope that Luca is big enough to accept it, but either way I think you need to go and find out,' said Mary gently. 'Will Mack be going?'

'Yes, I think so.'

'So he'll be around if you need anyone. Why don't you go and get ready?'

This was the first time Inky had been inside the Italian base, even though they were neighbours, and she was surprised by how friendly it all seemed after the usual security checks at the gates by burly suited men wearing sunglasses. The inevitable dark-eyed children were running between groups of chattering people, someone had set up a barbecue outside and the smell of marinated meat drifted tantalisingly on the evening air. A toddler was lying on the floor having a screaming fit whilst being coaxed up by its mother and the Italians politely stepped over it merely increasing the volume of their conversations to compensate. Inky looked nervously round for Luca. She didn't need to look for long. He was sitting on a sunlounger and chatting very familiarly to a blonde woman wearing a mini-skirt and a vest top.

'Hello,' said Inky apprehensively. She had tried to look as feminine as possible tonight so as not to remind Luca of anything sailor-ish: a long, floral sundress with a pale blue shawl to cover her shoulders against the night air and trendy flip-flops embroidered with daisies that her mother had bought her as a present from Liberty's. She loved them.

Luca looked up. 'Inky! May we finish this later?' he added as an aside to the lady. He drew Inky away. 'A journalist,' he explained.

He seemed friendly and Inky relaxed slightly. 'Would you like some food and drink?'

'Please.'

They went to the makeshift bar, made from two trestle tables. Inky was served ice-cold prosecco whilst Luca took another beer. In silence they wandered over towards the barbecue where Luca piled their plates with spitting kebabs, potato and artichoke salad and chargrilled peppers slippery with olive oil. They found a quiet corner.

'Are your parents here?' asked Inky between mouthfuls. It was delicious.

'Somewhere. We will start to pack up the base tomorrow and then we will be returning to Italy.'

'I'm sorry,' said Inky honestly. She put down her fork.

Luca shrugged. 'That is the America's Cup. The winner takes all.'

His eyes followed Jason Bryant walking across the compound. 'What is he doing here?' asked Inky.

'I think he is friends with one of the trimmers. I think *Phoenix* will be a formidable crew. I have seen them in practice. You will have trouble beating them, if you get that far.'

'I am sorry you lost but I'm not sorry we won.'

'It is the end of all our dreams. Two years of hard training. You took it all away from us.' Luca's tone was harsh.

'There will be other America's Cups.'

'We have a strong syndicate this time. Maybe next time we won't be so strong. Maybe next time I won't be chosen.' He couldn't keep the disappointment out of his voice.

Inky opened her mouth to say something and then closed it. She knew that if she were in his position she would be feeling just the same. No words would console her. And he especially didn't want to be comforted by her.

'You said you could handle it if we won.'

Luca looked at her directly. 'I said that when I thought you would lose. I always thought that we would win.'

'So you can't handle it,' said Inky slowly.

'No. No, I don't think so.'

Inky looked at his dark eyes; his handsome face was twisted

with resentment. How different things would be if the situation had been reversed, but she could understand, she'd visited his home. There, Luca was king. The men provided and the women stayed home and looked after the house. It was a wonderful status quo when it worked but it didn't when the women went out to work and then beat the men in an America's Cup race. It amazed her that an attitude quite so primeval could still exist, but exist it did and there it was sitting on a sunlounger and staring at her with a peculiar mix of desire and bitterness.

'Inky, I am sorry.'

'Do you need some space?' He was so raw at the moment. Maybe when things calmed down . . .

'Yes, I need space.'

She steadily got up and placed her plate on a nearby table. She smiled at him. 'You can get hold of me if you want to. Goodbye, Luca.'

'Goodbye, Inky.'

She started to walk away. He was packing up to go back to Italy and she didn't know if she would ever see him again.

'Inky?'

She turned back hopefully. 'Yes?'

'Good luck.'

She smiled. 'Thank you.'

Someone caught her arm as she came towards the gates. To her surprise it was Jason Bryant.

'What are you doing here, Pencarrow?'

'Visiting a friend.' She cast her eyes back to the barbecue where Luca had returned to his sunlounger and had started talking again to the blonde journalist. Inky was shocked at how much it hurt. She forced her eyes back to Jason Bryant's face. 'What about you?'

'I'm seeing a friend as well. You won today.'

'Yes.'

They stared at each other defiantly. Jason Bryant dropped his eyes first. 'Do you want to come and have a drink?'

'So you can get me drunk and pump me for information?' said Inky suspiciously.

'How about if I drink two units for your every one?'

Inky looked at him dubiously and then curiosity got the better of her. 'OK.' Her eyes flipped back to Luca. 'But not here.'

They went to a nearby bar.

'What do you want to drink?'

Inky considered. After her encounter with Luca, she wanted something uncompromising, strong and honest. 'Whisky,' she replied. 'Straight up.'

'You always surprise me,' he muttered. 'I heard that you were going out with someone from the Italian syndicate. Was that the friend you were seeing?'

'Yes, it was,' she said, unwilling to commit herself further.

Inky perched herself on a bar stool and watched Jason order a whisky for her and a double whisky for himself at the bar. He pushed the glass in front of her when it arrived and raised his own. 'Double, see? I'm true to my word.'

'Won't Henry Luter fire you for fraternising with the enemy? You're banned from talking to members of other syndicates, aren't you?'

'It's not strictly forbidden but we do have to file a written report of our conversation. You realise that if you win against New Zealand you'll be facing us?' Excalibur were going to be facing the New Zealanders in nine days' time, the winner of whom would officially challenge for the America's Cup and take on Phoenix.

'I'm looking forward to it.'

'You're confident.'

'We're more than that.' She looked directly at him and smiled. She wondered if he was deliberately trying to psych her out and so changed the subject. 'How's Ava?'

Jason looked surprised, almost as though he wouldn't expect

her to know about them. He looked unenthusiastic and shrugged. 'She's difficult as always.'

'Maybe you're handling her wrong.' Careful, she said to herself. Don't put his back up. But Bryant had had too many drinks to notice, his defences were well and truly down.

'I don't know if there is a good way to handle her. She's yet to learn who the important one in the relationship is.'

'Not playing the America's Cup game?'

'Not even close. Why are you so interested?'

'I'm good friends with Rafe,' said Inky in puzzlement.

'Oh, I didn't realise,' he said stiffly. Obviously being friends with any of his crew was a new idea for Jason. 'He's getting quite the reputation, isn't he? Your wind caller.'

'He's amazing,' said Inky simply.

'No one is that good,' snaped Jason. 'Besides they say he's not British.'

'Oh, he's British all right.'

'You need to tell him to watch his back. I still owe him one.'

There was a pause. 'Another drink?' he gestured to her empty glass.

Inky hesitated. 'I need to be getting along. I need to meet my crew.'

Jason leant forward and put his hand over hers. 'Don't go,' he said simply.

Inky stared at him hard. Was this some sort of sick joke? Would the entire crew of *Phoenix* leap out in a second and laugh at her? But his eyes were sincere and almost hungry.

'Unless, of course, you have to get back to your friend at the Italian syndicate,' he mumbled.

Still, Inky didn't move her hand. She wondered about their relationship over the years. The antipathy bordering on hatred, the near psychotic need to beat one another. Did any of it have any basis in desire? She was raw with rejection from Luca and yet high on her achievements. It was a dangerous combination.

Chapter 42

The rest of the crew were meeting at a bar a mere half a mile away from where Inky and Jason Bryant sat. They had all dropped into the Italian wake, but feeling uncomfortable and unable to celebrate their win properly, they soon made their excuses and left. The absence of Inky had been duly commented on and Custard texted her to say, 'Where the fuck are you?' He would have been very surprised to find out the truth.

Earlier they had taken the hard-working shore crew some pizza and beers to celebrate their Italian win. Ordinarily they would be given the night off but the designers were concerned about *Excalibur* taking such a pounding and wanted a complete overhaul of her between the race series, and Griff Dow, the sails co-ordinator, was working desperately hard on their sails. So they had a brief impromptu party together before – somewhat guiltily – leaving them to their work.

Unusually, as he normally had a meeting to fly off to, Colin Montague had come out with them all. 'What do you want to drink?' Custard asked him.

'Thanks, Custard. I'll just have a beer,' said Colin. 'Any sort.'

'I would like a gin and tonic please,' said Sir Edward. For one lovely moment, Custard thought that request sounded quite easy. 'But can you ask them to make it with Bombay Sapphire and if they don't have that, then I'll have Gordons, but only if I must.' Custard started to walk off. 'I would like only a twist of lemon, dear boy. Not a wedge but a twist and preferably in a tall glass,' he called after him.

'Why is Griff so worried about the sails?' Colin asked Sir Edward.

'Everyone in the competition is only allowed forty-five sails to compete with, regardless of how many races they do and we've done more than most as our series have been long ones, so ours have had an awful lot of wear.'

'Of course.'

'Mack gets on well with Bee, doesn't he?' he said watching the crew do a line of tequila slammers.

'She soothes him.'

'I wish that bloody dog of hers soothed me. What's his name?'

'Salty. Pipgin is the red setter. He belongs to Custard. Bee doesn't let them come out if there are very important people on board *Mucky Ducky*. He and Pipgin sulk at home. Actually, he's never seen us lose,' he added on idly.

'Salty the dog has never seen us lose?'

'Not once.'

There was a silence as Colin contemplated this fact.

'He must be lucky. I want him on *Mucky Ducky* every time we race from now on.'

Sir Edward grinned to himself. 'Very well.'

Towards the end of the evening Colin buttonholed Rafe. He had deliberately left it until later when he thought Rafe might have ingested enough beer.

'I'm sorry we haven't had much time to talk to each other since the challenge began,' he started awkwardly.

'That's OK, Mr Montague. You've been busy.'

'Please call me Colin. I'm aware that we perhaps should have spoken about this a long time ago and I've been meaning to say for a while that I'm sorry about you and Ava. It was a bad business.'

'It was scarcely your fault. You didn't make her sleep with Jason Bryant,' said Rafe bluntly.

'No, I know. But I wish I had been more encouraging of your relationship at the time. I'm afraid I've always been a bit protective around Ava. I thought you seemed happy together.'

'We can't have been,' said Rafe. The beer was making him unbutton slightly. 'We can't have been happy together. Otherwise she wouldn't have slept with Jason Bryant.' He stared forthrightly at Colin Montague.

Colin shifted slightly. He was surprised at Rafe's self possession. Maybe he had underestimated him. 'I don't think happiness impacts on Ava though. She seems to have a different agenda.'

'Different to mine at any rate.'

'Which was?'

'Ava is too concerned at what everybody else thinks of her. How she is perceived. I don't particularly care about any of that. I loved her. Not because she was an artist or rich or your daughter or even beautiful. But because she was passionate and vibrant and unconventional.'

Colin looked at him sadly, aware that Ava might have missed a wonderful opportunity. 'I think it's her passion which gets her into trouble. She wants to taste too many things. She wants to experience so much. It's difficult for her to stand still. And people do talk down to her thinking she has her name in the paper simply because of me. I've seen it. It's difficult for someone with so much talent. I have,' Colin hurried on, 'made my feelings perfectly plain to her about Jason Bryant but as you probably know we're not really talking at the moment.'

He stared so wretchedly into his beer bottle that Rafe was prompted to say, 'I don't know how much longer they'll be going out together if it's any consolation.'

Colin's head jerked up. 'You've been in contact?'

'Yes.'

'Any chance that the two of you might get back together?'

There was a long silence. Rafe had clammed up again.

'Maybe,' Rafe eventually acquiesced and looked round for

438

Custard who was still texting on his mobile. Even Fabian was tapping away. Rafe wondered fleetingly who to. God, he needed another beer.

The last thing that Salty could be described as was soothing. Bee had forgotten to pull the curtains in the sitting room and as a consequence Salty had been up bright and early to bark at the birds in the garden. Then just as she was drifting back to sleep, she was woken again by an early call from a very sheepish Custard.

'Em, Bee? It's Custard.'

Bee struggled to get her eyes open. 'Hi, Custard,' she yawned. 'Couldn't you have come down and knocked on the door? Do you want me to bring Pipgin up?'

'Well, no, actually. I'm not at home.'

'Where are you? With an exciting mystery woman?'

'Not exactly. I'm with Rafe.' There was a small pause. 'And Dougie. But don't tell his father.'

'Rafe?' She had a quick look round the room as though that might confirm he hadn't come home.

'Yes, we're in prison.'

'WHAT?' Bee sat bolt upright in bed. 'In prison? How did you get there?'

'It was all Dougie's fault and . . . actually, Bee, I would love to tell you the whole story but they're making signs at me. Could you just come down and get us?'

'What's the address?'

Custard gave it to her. 'Oh and bring some cash.'

Bee got dressed, cursing them all the way and wondering what on earth Mack would have to say about it. She had to go upstairs and borrow a car from one of the shore crew and since it had been such a long time since she had driven, kept forgetting which side of the road to drive on. Thankfully the Valencianos aren't early risers on Sundays. She arrived to find three fairly sheepish young men and after some haranguing with the officials and a

bit of bail money which Bee was quite sure wasn't in any official capacity they were all free to go.

'So what exactly were you arrested for?' she hissed at Custard
who seemed to be the only one capable of speaking. The other
two wouldn't open their mouths in case they were sick.

'Being drunk and disorderly.'

'Where's Inky? You didn't involve her in all this, did you?'

'She never showed up last night. She probably kissed and
made up with Luca. Besides there was nothing to involve her
in. We are the completely innocent parties in all this.'

But Bee wasn't listening. She was already in the middle of a
hot rage. 'How could you do this?' she hissed as she led the
way out to the car. 'How could you risk everything the challenge has worked for? What would have happened if one of you
had broken his arm or something? What would the crew have
done then? Did you think about any of that?'

'It was a bit of a misunderstanding, Bee. Honestly. We all
went to get some late tapas but then couldn't get a cab from
the restaurant, no one would stop for us. And everyone else had
gone home so we decided to walk back. Dougie just sort of
stumbled and fell over and hit a car which set the alarm off and
the next thing we knew was that we were all being arrested.'

'Did they know who you were?'

'Ha! We didn't give our proper names,' Custard grinned at
her.

'Do you expect me to be pleased about that?'

'We didn't want the challenge to be involved so we didn't
call Mack this morning – he would be much more frightening
than you anyway – just in case they recognised him. They would
probably throw away the key if they realised they had almost
half the crew of *Excalibur* in there.'

'Mack is not going to be pleased when I tell him.'

'We could always not tell him?' Bee threw Custard a look.
'Aww, come on, Bee, I don't think they were taking us very seriously. The man in my cell tried to rob a bank.'

'That sounds quite serious to me.'

'In flip-flops.'

Bee didn't mean to laugh but she really couldn't help herself. 'By the way, where is Fabian? Isn't he with you? I met Milly in the hall and she said that he hadn't been home.'

They all looked shifty and looked at one another. 'He might be in my apartment,' said Custard.

'Why would he be in your apartment?'

'Because he forgot his keys?'

'Why didn't he knock at Milly's door or ask the doorman to let him in?' Bee stared at him. 'You don't know where he is, do you?'

Custard's brain simply wasn't working fast enough. It had been a long night. He gave in. 'Oh, OK. I don't know where he is.'

'Why would you try and cover up for him?'

'I'm not covering up for him.'

'Have you covered up for him before?' demanded Bee.

'I think there might be a girl,' he finally acquiesced. Rafe and Dougie rolled their eyes. 'Oh shut up, you two. She's pretty scary,' snapped Custard at them.

'How long have you been covering up for him?'

Custard shrugged. 'Once. Twice.'

'You think there's a girl or you know there's a girl?'

'Could we do this later, Aunt Bee? None of us are feeling too great,' said Rafe.

'No, we bloody can't. I'm not leaving time for you all to get your story straight.'

'We don't know the story. We don't ask too many questions.'

'I'm going to be sick,' said Dougie uttering his first words of the day and racing to the gutter.

After she had dropped all the men off at their respective apartments, Bee was at an absolute loss as to what to do. She felt ill at ease with this news about Fabian. She made a snap decision to visit Milly and gathered all she had in the fridge as an excuse.

'I've brought breakfast!' she said when Milly answered the door.

'How lovely!'

'Where's Rosie?'

'Morning nap. Come in, come in.'

Bee followed Milly through to the kitchen and dumped the strawberries and brioche on one of the counters. 'Where's Fabian?' she asked lightly. She felt she had to ask. It was too obvious otherwise.

'I don't know. He still hasn't come home.'

There was a silence as Bee went very deliberately to a drawer and extracted a knife to hull the strawberries with.

'I think he's having an affair, Bee,' Milly blurted out. 'You probably suspected as much . . . ' Milly's eyes filled with tears and Bee dropped her knife and went round to the other side of the counter in a flash. She put an arm around her and rocked her slightly. Milly could smell the fragrance on her clothes. She wanted it to be the same as her mother's jumper and for a second wished she had brought it to Valencia with her.

Milly sniffed. 'I'm fine, really I am. Bloody angry to be truthful. I've suspected for a while. Then I found a name. Daphne. His mother will be pleased. Sort of upper-class name she'd be proud of. He's probably with Daphne.'

'Have you asked him about it?'

'Not yet.'

'Why not?'

'I don't know really, because I feel so furious. I feel like saying, sod the bloody America's Cup and throwing a huge wobbly. But then I think about the stress they're all under and how it's only a few more weeks and I should hold my tongue. Not so much for Fabian – because believe me I could wring his neck – but more for the rest of the crew. I would never forgive myself if they lost simply because of me.'

'What do you think you're going to do?'

Milly looked surprised. 'I'm going to leave, of course. I'll take

442

Rosie and go back to Whitstable and take my fashion course somehow.'

'Oh God, I'm so sorry,' said Bee, feeling immeasurably sad.

'I'm fine,' insisted Milly. 'Really I am. It's just so peculiar trying to carry on as normal. Wives keep asking when we're going to have our second baby and I keep smiling and just say I don't know. He had the nerve to stay out all night last week and then told me he'd fallen asleep on a park bench or some such guff. And to top it all Fabian's awful mother is coming out to watch him.'

'Is she really awful?'

Milly gave her some choice examples of Elizabeth's behaviour.

'And when his mother is around, Fabian seems to become infected with this dreadful snobbery. I'll be glad to be shot of them all. It's going to be terrible.'

'Where will she stay?'

'His mother? Well, that's the other thing. She'll have to stay at a hotel because I've already told my dad he can stay with us, and anyway she sneers at the apartment.'

'Will that be a problem with Fabian's mum?'

'It will because she'll have to pay for it and then everything will be wrong. The bed will be too hard, the windows will be dirty, her view will be awful, there won't be enough running water and to top it all the television will be in Spanish.'

Bee laughed. 'Could she stay with me?'

'I wouldn't inflict her on you,' said Milly grimly. 'I'm trying to stay cheerful for Rosie's sake but it's so hard when you're eyeing all the luggage and trying to decide which bags you're going to take.' She tried to smile. 'At least my little business is going well. Some people think I can perform miracles though. One of the shore crew wives came down with a picture yesterday and said, "Can you make me look like this?" I felt like saying, only if you lose thirty pounds and have plastic surgery.' Milly tried to laugh but started to cry instead. Bee put her arms around her again. 'I'm so angry with him, Bee, because he's so stupid. I try desperately not to love him but every time I see him with Rosie or he makes me laugh with a stupid joke and starts grinning at it before he's even finished, I just can't help myself. I love him, Bee. That's the problem,' she sobbed into her shoulder. 'In spite of all of this, I still love him.'

Milly was absolutely right when she said that she thought Fabian was with Daphne.

Fabian woke up in a vast panic. He'd meant to go back home but he'd been so tired that he had simply fallen asleep where he lay. A rug had been thrown over him. He rubbed his eyes frantically and reached for his mobile, looking for messages. He heaved a sigh of relief. Milly hadn't called him.

He could smell sausages being cooked and slowly swung his legs over the front of the bed and stared at the floorboards, feeling terribly guilty. He was on a boat.

He padded through to the tiny galley and could see a tall figure bent over the stove. 'Morning,' he grunted.

A man spun round. He had thinning hair in which some silver was beginning to show, but was still luxuriantly blond. His face was tanned and clean-shaven with a few lines and wrinkles. He looked startlingly like Fabian.

PART FOUR

Chapter 43

F abian remembered the very first time he caught sight of his father. It was just before the racing series with the Italians. There was a yacht that had followed them out to their practice a couple of times. No one took much notice; there was often a lot of traffic around. But Fabian remembered the moment exactly. He had just attached the spinnaker pole and had leapt down back on to the bow. The boat caught his eye because there was a figure on the deck. The man had his back to the sun so his outline was in silhouette. Fabian wasn't quite sure what made the figure so familiar but as he stood with his hand cupped over his eyes, his crew mates' shouts in his ears, the memories started to stir and snuffle.

As soon as *Excalibur* had hit port, Fabian had jumped off and, oblivious to the cries of Inky and Custard, ran all the way to the yacht harbour. He stepped aboard *Daphne* and the tall, blond figure, who was very deliberately making tea at the stove, had broken down and wept. Moments later, Fabian was cradling him in his arms. 'Dad,' he kept saying as though to convince him of his existence.

They had eventually sat down for tea. 'I thought you were dead,' said Fabian.

He thought his father looked ashamed but he couldn't be sure. 'I'm sorry,' David Beaufort said eventually.

'Where have you been? I've been looking.'

'Europe for the first year and then to South America.'

'Just like that? What about your passport?'

His dad shrugged. 'Got round without it. No big ports. Just had to hope that I never needed the coastguard or anything.'

'How did you find me?'

'I read about you in a back copy of a yachting mag. I've been looking out for you, hoping to see your name and then there it was. I was so proud.' He put his hand over Fabian's but Fabian pulled his roughly away.

'I haven't seen you since Rob died,' he said abruptly.

'I was sorry about that.'

'Me too. I needed you.'

'It must have been hard.'

'Hard? It was fucking awful. No one would speak to me and then you disappear as well as the bankruptcy and somehow everyone thinks I'm responsible for that too. Like I pushed you over the edge or something. What happened?'

'I moved some money to cover a small loss in one of the companies. You know the small manufacturing company I had? The one which made building fixings? Well, it employed about five hundred people and it was simply having a bad time. Nothing wrong with the product or the market but just a run of bad luck. So I moved some money to cover its losses. And then one of the buildings collapsed and they found it was due to one of our metal beams, so they sued us. Suddenly no one wanted to trade with us, the company was about to go belly up and I had sunk one hell of a lot of money into it. Everything snowballed. Soon, I was moving money all over the place trying to shore everything up.'

'Why didn't you just go bankrupt?'

'It was fraudulent. I shouldn't have diverted that money in the first place. It wasn't my money.'

'You could have stayed. Stayed and gone to prison.'

His father nodded his head. 'Yes, I could have done. I sometimes wish I had. But once you start to run you simply can't stop. Your mum and I have never really been happy together,

448

you weren't around and I couldn't really think what I was doing there any more. There seemed like nothing to stay for.'

'The boatyard told me you had bought a boat.'

His father nodded. 'They did, did they? I'm glad. I couldn't work out how to get a message to you.'

'It was hardly a message, Dad,' snapped Fabian. 'You could have tried a bit harder. I kept my phone on for you all the time.'

'I thought they might be tracing the calls or something. I thought they would be watching if I contacted you or your mother. I couldn't risk it.'

'How long have you been back?'

'Since the start of the round robins.'

'That long? Why didn't you come and find me?'

'I was worried you wouldn't want to see me. I thought I'd just see how you got on first. It was wonderful to see you.' He paused. 'You're married?'

'No, but with someone.'

'Milly. You have a little girl called Rosie.'

Fabian looked up sharply. The penny dropped. 'You're the stranger hanging around Casa Fortuna.'

'I've been noticed, have I?'

'We thought you were a spy.'

'Not a very good one, evidently. Rosie's beautiful.'

'Yes, she is.'

'How old?'

'Just turned two . . . '

And so the tentative refamiliarising began. As the days passed, Fabian consumed his father. The emotions he experienced were far more complex than he ever expected. He was angry, elated, bemused and disorientated and he felt he needed a few days to reconcile all of that before he told Milly, but he still hadn't really been able to make sense of it all. In the end, he couldn't tell Milly because he felt ashamed that his own father had been out there for three years and not come and found him until now. What sort of father would that make him to Rosie? He was truly overwhelmed to have his father back – the love he felt for him had not diminished but the more he thought about it, the more he felt embarrassed by his family. They had behaved so appallingly. Milly's father had welcomed him and accepted him and tried his hardest. His mother had been a bitch and his father had run off. In a way he felt angry that David *wasn't* dead.

And now he had stayed out all night again. How on earth was he going to explain that to Milly? 'Why didn't you wake me?'

'I tried. You told me to piss off.'

'Oh. Sorry.'

'I'm making you a sausage sandwich. What are you going to say to Milly about where you've been?'

'I'll just have to say I fell asleep at the base. She'll never swallow the park bench story again. God, I hate lying to her. And you're going to have to stop hanging round Casa Fortuna, Dad.'

'Just want to see my granddaughter,' he replied gruffly.

Fabian sat down at the small table and watched his dad's back in silence for a few minutes.

'When are you going to tell her?' David asked without turning round.

'Soon,' said Fabian. 'She comes from a straightforward family, Dad. They're lovely . . . ' He was about to use the word 'honest' but then stopped himself. 'Uncomplicated people.'

'You mean her dad wouldn't think of leaving her,' he said gruffly.

'No,' said Fabian simply. 'He wouldn't.' He wasn't about to disguise the fact that he still felt angry with his father. David came over and placed a sausage sandwich in front of Fabian, who didn't touch it.

'I just feel my whole life has been a lie over the last three years. Don't you get it? I thought you were *dead*.'

'I'm sorry. I can't tell you how sorry. Your mother wasn't . . . well, she wasn't like Milly.'

'You don't know Milly.'

'I've been watching her and Rosie for a long time now. I can

450

see how good she is with her. I can see how much she loves her. I see Milly's kindness everywhere. She smiles at everyone in the shops. She gives change to the homeless but doesn't just toss it down, she always crouches down to speak to them. She is so friendly to everyone. If I had had a wife like Milly then we wouldn't be sitting here now. We would be back home, admittedly with me bankrupt and probably in jail. When I see who you have settled down with and what your life has become, it's the only thing that makes me pleased that I left.'

Fabian looked at him and wondered what had become of the man before him. At what point exactly had he started to despise his own life? The very life he had created. Fabian had been so used to relying on his father for so many things that it was strange to see him actually coveting the things Fabian had. The role reversal unnerved him. 'I have to get home,' he said wearily.

Chapter 44

F abian and Milly were the only ones who didn't welcome the
next day off. They trod wary circles around each other whilst
Custard, Rafe and Dougie spent all of Sunday nursing their hang-
overs and feeling very sorry for themselves. Even on Monday
things were a bit ropey at practice.

'What is wrong with you all?' roared Mack as they fluffed yet
another spinnaker drop. 'The only thing consistent on this boat
is my fucking swearing! The New Zealanders are going to tear
you apart! I don't mind a small celebration at the end of a series
but you're behaving as though you've won the Cup and I can
tell you that from where I'm standing there is no fucking chance
of that happening!'

'He's right about the swearing,' remarked Custard idly.

The tow home was not as much fun as it usually was. Inky
had been depressed and miserable since the end of the race
series with the Italians, Fabian was troubled and pensive whilst
Rafe was being uncommunicative as he was thinking about Ava.
Even Custard didn't brighten up proceedings with his usual jokes
as he seemed to be constantly texting on his mobile and feeding
one of Carla's buns to the seagulls.

'Who are you texting, Custard? Christ, you're as bad as Fabian,'
asked Inky eventually in irritation. 'We're all here.'

'Just someone from home.'

'In England?'

'They are *from* England,' he hedged. It was actually Saffron, who was sweetly jealous when a picture of Inky and Custard had appeared in that morning's papers laughing together just after the final race on Saturday.

'I wish you would stop feeding the seagulls. They are becoming such a nuisance.'

'Seagulls are the souls of dead sailors,' said Custard earnestly.

'Not your bloody great-granddad again,' groaned Inky.

'We're a very superstitious family and if you were a seagull then I'm positive you would appreciate one of Carla's buns.'

'I wouldn't be too sure about that. The only consolation is that they can't tell the difference between us and the other America's Cup boats and harass us all.'

'I'm sure my great-granddad is shitting on Jason Bryant's head right now. What is up with you anyway? Didn't you get enough Luca-love on Saturday?'

'Not exactly.'

The crew became increasingly uptight. 'It's not any fun any more,' Inky complained. 'Practice isn't fun any more. Nobody cracks any jokes. Everybody is so serious.'

'You know, Carla,' said Sir Edward thoughtfully one morning whilst drinking his early morning coffee. 'I think they're starting to entertain the possibility that they really are capable of winning the America's Cup. Not that that wasn't always the goal, but now they can almost taste it. Besides the fact they are nervous because the New Zealanders are mighty opponents. I just hope the crew don't frighten themselves with the thought of winning, do you know what I mean?'

Carla didn't know but she was very amused by the fact that Sir Edward was finally drinking coffee her way, by the shot and standing up. '*Si*, Mr Edward. More coffee?'

Mack came charging like a bull in the door. 'Some bugger has stolen my oilskin!' he roared. 'I'm going to be sailing in my pants soon! Dear God, help me!'

Since the Italians had left, the groupies had wasted no time in swapping their allegiance to the British crew. Now Excalibur clothing was the hottest thing in Valencia and as a consequence all nature of branded stuff seemed to be walking out of the base.

'My dear boy, you'll do yourself an injury,' murmured Sir Edward. 'Come and have some blueberries. They'll make you feel better.'

'They will not sodding well make me feel better. The only thing that would make me feel better is a large glass of whisky. This is bloody Custard's fault!' he continued without pausing for breath. 'He has been sleeping with a racer chaser again and she's probably wearing my oilskin!' He marched out again

'It's not good for him to have all those stress hormones running about his system,' commented Sir Edward.

'I don't think it Custard,' commented Carla. 'Custard is in love.'

'Custard is?' Sir Edward frowned. 'With a racer chaser?'

'I don't know with who but I see the signs. He got it bad.'

If Mack thought the day had started badly he certainly wasn't prepared for the news which came in later that day. Some Italian lawyers had clearly been logging overtime because the news came through at about nine a.m. Despite his shots of coffee Sir Edward was ashen when he came into Mack's office.

Mack glanced up. 'I'm coming! I know the crew are waiting! Just finishing up. Now, what do you want to . . . What's up? Not your hernia again?'

'The Italian team have lodged a protest. They're claiming our boat is illegal.'

Mack stared at him. 'How ridiculous! *Excalibur* was officially measured by the committee and found to be perfect. What on earth are they talking about?'

'It's not the measurements that concern them, apparently, it's the design. They're saying she's not a British design, that a foreign national helped to design her.'

'What nonsense,' he snorted. 'We can easily put them right on that.'

'I don't think it's that easy. When *Excalibur* was being tank tested at Woolston there was apparently a rather eminent French hydro- and aerodynamics expert staying there at the same time. They are saying that he made a few suggestions and thus played a part in the design. I'm afraid it looks quite serious.'

'It's not true, is it?'

Sir Edward lifted his hands. 'I don't know. I'll call Colin Montague. We need to get the lawyers working. There's a preliminary hearing during the week. God knows how much this is going to cost us.'

Mack sat heavily down, leant back in his chair and closed his eyes to think.

'You need to decide what to tell the crew,' Sir Edward continued. 'It's only a matter of time before this is leaked to the press and it will still be going on when they race the New Zealanders. Might be difficult for them to think they could be sailing what will be deemed an illegal boat and we'll all be thrown out of the competition. An important psychological angle.'

'I'll deal with it. What are the Italians hoping to achieve?'

'I suppose that we might get thrown out and then they would be back in the competition and racing the New Zealanders.'

'It doesn't make a lot of sense. I could believe that the Phoenix Challenge would do this but not the Italians. They must have filed this protest before the final race. Do you think the Italian crew knew?

'No, I don't. Maybe it's an elaborate ploy to force us to reveal our keel.'

'But that wouldn't benefit the Italians.'

'Maybe someone has put them up to it,' said Sir Edward grimly.

'Bloody hell! As if we didn't have enough already to cope with.'

Mack gathered the whole of the syndicate for an emergency meeting. They all shuffled in to the vast hangar of the Pink

Palacio, which was the only place where they would all fit, chattering madly to each other until one by one they fell silent, noticing that Colin Montague was standing up at the front with Mack. Whatever the meeting was about, it would have to be pretty serious to drag Colin back from England as he wasn't due to fly in until the racing series with the New Zealanders started.

Mack stepped forward. 'I'm sorry to drag you away from your work . . . '

'Why? Have you lost your shorts now, Mack?' yelled a voice from the back.

Mack smiled faintly. The lack of his usual grin worried people more than ever. 'Shut up!' someone shouted back.

'I'm going to let Colin tell you now why you're all here.'

Colin Montague took over. 'We wanted to tell you before you read it in the papers tomorrow. There is no easy way to say this so I'm just going to spit it out. *Excalibur* has been accused of being an illegal boat.'

There was a small silence and then the voices started to hum, until frantic shushing reduced them to silence again.

'I want to reassure you personally that there is absolutely no truth in this. *Excalibur* is *not* an illegal boat . . . '

Inky was the most perplexed out of everyone. After the meeting Mack had immediately dragged her up for a private word. He was quite sure she wouldn't but he wanted to check that Inky hadn't mentioned anything about *Excalibur*'s keel to Luca. Of course she hadn't but she quite understood that he had to close down every possible avenue.

She called Luca. 'Did you know about this?' she asked without even saying hello.

'I only just found out.'

'Why didn't you call me?'

'You have an illegal boat. Why do I call you about that?'

'*You* believe that *Excalibur* is illegal?'

Luca sighed. 'This is not a sailor's war, Inky.'

'Why would you accuse us of such a thing?'

'Because if it's true then *we* should be racing the New Zealanders. The only reason you won is because you have an illegal boat not—'

'Not what?' demanded Inky.

'Nothing.'

'You were going say not because we were a better crew, weren't you?'

Luca's silence said it all.

'God, Colin wasn't wrong when he said about reading it in the papers,' commented Custard in the common room the next day staring at a headline which read, 'GREAT BRITAIN ACCUSED OF CHEATING' and 'WILL THEY BE SENT HOME IN DISGRACE FROM THE AMERICA'S CUP?'

They had all been waiting for the papers' arrival from the airport. Colin and Sir Edward had debated whether it would be better to withhold them all but realised friends and family from back home would just send clippings or repeat hearsay down the phone, which would be worse.

Mack came in half an hour later. 'Have you all had your fill? Because this is the last time we are going to mention it. We're here to sail the boat and if you let any of this distract you then that's exactly what the opposition want you to do. Rest assured that Colin Montague has the finest lawyers on top of this and they will sort it out. Our job is to sail the perfectly legal *Excalibur*.'

He didn't mention he had been up all night on a conference call with a team of frantic lawyers who couldn't get hold of this French hydrodynamist for him to sign an affidavit. Or an equally concerned PR team who Colin had shipped in specially to deal with the negative publicity. He just told the crew what they needed to hear.

Chapter 45

Milly went to collect her father from the airport. The heat had hit him like a punch in the face as soon as he had stepped off the plane. 'What on earth is this all about?' he asked Milly as soon as he set eyes on her. 'It's causing a hell of a fuss back home. A reporter knocked at my door and I thought he was a delivery man and tried to sign his notepad because I thought it was a delivery docket. A reporter knocking at my door!' He dragged his suitcase towards the exit. 'Can you imagine such a thing! Where's Rosie?'

'With Bee.'

'I simply didn't know what to say to him.'

'What did you say?'

'Nothing at all. Pretended I was a bit loopy, which he thought anyway since I tried to sign his notepad.'

'First time they've even properly acknowledged we've got a crew in the America's Cup.'

'Nobody really understands what's going on. I mean you see a headline like "SENT HOME IN DISGRACE" and everyone thinks it's the crew who have been cheating, not some random comment from a boat designer over a year ago. How's Fabian doing with it all?'

Milly set her teeth. She had been finding it harder and harder not to have it out with Fabian, but when the keel issue arose and put the crew under even more pressure, she had resolved once again to hold her tongue. 'He's not sleeping much but I don't think any of them are. The first race with the New Zealanders is tomorrow. This business with the keel has to be sorted soon otherwise they're going to start losing the plot.'

The crew weren't the only ones not sleeping. Bee tossed and turned all night, worrying about Fabian and Milly. She wanted to shake Fabian until his teeth rattled for risking things as precious as Milly and Rosie. She tried desperately to think of what she could do to help but came to the same conclusion as Milly. She simply couldn't interfere without upsetting Fabian and consequently the whole crew. Bee remembered Mack's invitation for early morning tea and as soon as the sun started to rise she got dressed and cycled down to the base. As always, it was already busy with shore crew and the sail workers. Carla was at her station getting breakfast ready for the crew, deadly serious about the small but significant part she played in their lives. Bee found Mack in the common room, staring out to the sunlit course of the America's Cup, undisturbed for now except for the occasional swoop of a herring gull but which soon would be resonating with the noise of hundreds of boats and people like some gladiatorial coliseum, and they would be hungry for the sight of blood.

'Are you sleeping?' she asked as she came in, concerned to see his pale face and tired eyes. She went over to the kettle.

'All I dream about is the sight of *Black Heart* bearing down on us. I shout for more speed from the crew but it always overtakes us in the end.' He sounded quite hollow.

'The New Zealanders are a good crew.'

'Good enough to win the America's Cup twice already.'

'I know a better one. After all this fuss, when it comes down to it, it will be you and the crew and *Excalibur* with the sails and the wind and the water and all the things you know best. And the little I know about you, Mack, is that you don't like to lose. *Especially* with these allegations hanging over you.'

There was a pause as Mack slowly nodded.

'God, I wish I could do something for you,' she added fretfully.

'You already do, Bee.'

It was no real consolation to the crew that they seemed to roll right over the New Zealanders in that race. Mack had gone straight from the end of the race into a meeting about *Excalibur*'s potentially illegal design in which he stayed until late.

'Have you managed to track down the French hydrodynamic expert?' was his opening question.

Colin Montague's head lawyer hesitated. 'No.'

'Why not? I'm no legal expert but it would strike me that without him we don't really have a defence. He's the one saying that he played a part in our design.'

'We're tracking him down.'

'The preliminary hearing is the day after tomorrow.'

'We'll find him.'

'You need to try harder.'

'As we see it there are two possibilities. The first is that he really did have something to do with the design but for whatever reason has gone into hiding . . .'

'Or?'

'Or someone has paid for him not to appear until after the court case is over.'

'We're stuffed either way, aren't we?'

There was a small silence. They might as well have just leapt to their feet shouting 'YES! You are up the proverbial shit creek,' reflected Sir Edward to himself.

'This stinks to high heaven.'

'Fe, fi, fo, fum, I smell the blood of an Englishman,' said Sir Edward idly. 'I wonder if Henry Luter might be involved somewhere?'

'Sir Edward is right. I don't think the Italians have done this off their own bats. I wonder if Henry Luter might have taken evidence over to them and invited them to use it, so to speak.'

'Especially if it did look as though we were guilty. Anyone would leap at the chance of getting back into the Cup.'

'We still need to find the Frenchman,' said the head lawyer firmly.

After a few more minutes of discussion the lawyers departed. Hattie was waiting outside the door.

'Come in!' said Sir Edward.

Hattie placed the personal pile of syndicate post on top of the table. Even though it was addressed to individual members, it all still had to be opened and gone through, especially with the increased security risk over *Excalibur*, before it was passed on to the addressee.

'What startling piece of bad news do you have for us, Hattie?'

'I'm afraid I really do have a bit of bad news. Support for Excalibur is dropping. Everyone is so preoccupied with the keel issue. They're calling it "keelgate".'

'Mud sticks,' murmured Sir Edward.

'And Colin Montague's company share price is down as a result. The directors have been on the phone to me all afternoon. Most of the sponsors too. I'm surprised they haven't called you, Mack.'

'The difference is, Hattie, that I never answer my phone.'

'They want everything resolved quickly or they are threatening to pull the plug on the finances.'

Everyone sat up slightly. This put a different light on things.

'Have you spoken to Colin?'

'No, I can't get hold of him. He's been in a meeting all morning in Lisbon.'

'Well, we're doing everything in our power to resolve the keel problem.'

'What about if we send a sort of ambassador back to England? A spokesman or woman who could give interviews, reassure everyone and put the emphasis back on the real message of the challenge? It might make Colin Montague's board members a bit happier.'

'I'll go,' said Hattie quickly. 'I can manage that.'

'What about sending Bee with Hattie?' said Sir Edward. 'She's articulate and charming. She might be just the message we need.'

Mack said sharply, 'No. I need her here.'

All eyes came to rest on him.

'I mean, she's so good on the hospitality boat and with the sponsors. We can't do without her *and* Hattie.'

Sir Edward quickly changed the subject but his eyes lingered a little longer on Mack than everyone else.

Hattie got on a plane that night bound for England. It wasn't purely altruistic reasons that made her volunteer so quickly. She wanted to be away from Rafe. When she'd found a moment to open some of the crew's post, she'd found a letter from Ava to him. It was almost as though she had deliberately wanted Hattie to read it. Ava would have known that all their post would be opened and probably by Hattie too. Still the words haunted her.

My darling Rafe,
I haven't been able to stop thinking about you since our night together. I wanted you to know that I will be watching you whilst you race and will be praying that when all this is over we will be together again. Please carry this note close to your heart and as a talisman. I am yours eternally.
Ava.

Custard had come in just as she was reading it.

'What's that?' he'd asked, seeing the strange look on her face.

'A letter,' she'd said faintly.

Custard had marched round to her side of the desk and grabbed it out of her hand.

'Bloody hell!' he exclaimed when he'd finished reading it. Immediately he started to tear it up.

'You can't do that!' said Hattie, half rising to her feet.

'I bloody well can and you are not going to breathe one word about it. He doesn't need that bitch back in his life.'

She had felt relieved and guilty at the same time but when she passed the post out later, she hadn't said a word.

She had been so busy before she left, organising television, newspaper and radio interviews, that she had forced herself not to think about it. Everyone was passionately interested in the accusations of cheating thrown at the British team so coverage was not a problem (ironic considering how hard Hattie had to work initially to get a centimetre-worth of coverage in a local newspaper) but it was up to Hattie to get the facts across and put the emphasis back on the crew and how hard they were working to get *Excalibur* over the finish line. It wasn't until she had actually boarded the plane and snapped on her seat belt, with her emotional props of mobile phone and laptop temporarily denied to her, that she gave way to tears.

Chapter 46

'Dad!' exclaimed Rafe. 'You're here!'

In one single bound he was off the sofa and hugging his father. Tom Louvel was carrying ten mackerel he'd caught off the boat and a pair of shorts. He hugged his son, the fish bouncing off Rafe's back, but Rafe didn't particularly care.

'When did you get in?'

'Just now. I went to your base and they told me how to get here.'

'Why didn't you call? I'd have come down to the harbour and met you!'

'I wanted to surprise you and anyway I seem to have mislaid the phone again. It keeps running out of charge anyway. How are you? It's so good to see you!'

They hugged again.

'Where's your Aunt Beatrice?'

Just as he was saying this, Bee came to the doorway of the kitchen, wiping her hands on a tea towel to see what all the noise was about. She went quite pale when she saw who the visitor was. 'Tom! My God! How wonderful to see you!' She went forward to greet him. 'You look just the same.'

'*You* look just the same, Bee. I look a lot older.' He kissed her on both cheeks. 'I brought you some mackerel. Caught them this morning.'

Bee was overwhelmed. Memories flooded in, the strength of

which took her by surprise. She almost expected her long-dead sister to walk in after him. 'I am so glad you came,' she managed to say.

'Took long enough. Can't seem to manage the boat so well without Rafe.' He grinned at his son. 'You left a pair of shorts on board. Thought you might want them.' He proffered the clothing to Rafe.

'Thanks, Dad. It's been two years, but thanks.'

Bee bustled through to make them all some tea. Tom sat down.

'So the America's Cup!' he said. 'How amazing! I always knew you were good.'

'We might not be around to finish it. We've been accused of being an illegal boat.' Rafe filled his father in on the accusations.

'Bloody hell! You don't do things by halves, do you?'

'I hope it gets sorted out. I don't want to leave.' Rafe paused. 'So you think I've copped out? Sailing professionally?'

'Course not! I'm proud of you. Just because I bum around the world doesn't mean I should drag you down with me. It was about time you left the boat anyway. You were cramping my style.'

Rafe grinned at him. Bee reappeared with a tray. 'Kettle's just boiling. Daisy would have been so proud of him,' she said to Tom. His eyes flickered slightly.

'Yes,' he said softly. 'She would have been.'

Rafe looked from one to the other with interest. It was the first time he had ever seen them together and he was interested to see how they slotted back in. They shared so many years of history together that Rafe was never part of.

'Of course she would have been petrified too,' Bee chatted on. 'I am, every time I watch Rafe on one of those things.'

Rafe wanted to stay talking about his mother but Tom changed the subject. 'How are things with that girl?' Rafe had told him briefly about Ava on one of their short telephone conversations.

'Which girl?' asked Bee. 'Hattie?'

'Hattie?' said Rafe. 'What do you mean, Hattie?'

'Well, you keep asking when she's coming back, don't you?'

'Who's Hattie?' asked Tom. 'This girl was called something else.'

'Ava,' chorused Bee and Rafe.

Tom rubbed his hands together. 'Gosh, Ava *and* Hattie. Can we have some tea, Bee? Whilst my errant son tells me all about these hordes of women?'

Bee went off to get the teapot, pleased at this aspect of Tom's fathering. It seemed as though there wasn't much that he and Rafe couldn't talk about.

It was Mack's habit to occasionally drop in on Bee outside of the Thursday night crew suppers. He hovered uncertainly outside her door late that evening and heard the sound of voices chatting and Bee's occasional laugh and decided against knocking. He'd seen a handsome man at the base late this afternoon and had been told it was Rafe's dad who had been redirected here. He felt slightly peeved that Rafe's father was here at all. Maybe if her sister had loved him enough to marry him then Bee might feel the same attraction? But then he wondered why he felt so proprietorial about Bee. He cursed himself for being a grumpy old man and stomped upstairs to find himself a whisky.

Much to the surprise of the entire yachting world, Excalibur was sailing out of its skin and only lost one race to the New Zealanders. Some put this down to the supposed cutting-edge design of the New Zealanders' boat being difficult to sail and others said it was due to Excalibur's increased desire to win with the keelgate drama. Either way the atmosphere on the press boats was electric for potentially the last race of the series. Excalibur was currently at 3–1 up. If they won this race they would be through to the final match series and facing Henry Luter and *Phoenix*. But the issue of their possibly illegal keel might stop them. The crew were performing so well under the circumstances. But

Custard was irritating everyone by insisting that as many spiders be introduced on to the boat as possible because he thought they brought good luck.

Even the infamously busy Dougie's dad flew out to 'offer some support'. He showed up in full bishop kit and Mack, who wasn't the most religious of men, sincerely hoped he wasn't going to be annoying. Much to Mack's chagrin he insisted on blessing the crew before the race and gathered everyone in a circle around him. Here we go, thought Mack.

'O Lord,' started the prayer. 'You know how busy I must be this day. If I forget you, do not forget me . . . '

The bishop opened one eye and winked at Mack who suddenly decided he quite liked the codger after all. 'If you could do anything about the opposition then that would be greatly appreciated,' Mack murmured afterwards.

'I'm not sure what I can do but I'll have a chat.'

'Thanks.'

'Mack?' He turned around. 'When I left, the bookies had you as the outsiders to win. Prove them wrong.'

'I will.' Mack smiled, walked for a few paces and then turned back. 'Did you put any money on?'

'I didn't think that would be terribly fitting in my position . . . but I sent my wife in with a tenner. So important to have faith, don't you think?'

Unconsciously the British yachting journalists had grouped more tightly together than they normally would and today they were all sitting on the top deck of the boat, waiting for the start and talking in low voices about the 'keelgate' drama.

'The preliminary hearing merely confirmed the facts of the case. The worst thing is that we don't know the truth. They might well have an illegal design on their hands.'

'If someone suggests an idea and the designer incorporates that idea, it doesn't mean they are cheating.'

'But they can't even get hold of this French hydrodynamics

expert to confirm or deny anything, which doesn't bode terribly well.'

'And there has always been a suggestion that *Excalibur* might have a revolutionary design. They might have to unveil it.'

The Times journalist looked furtively over his shoulder. Because of the increased interest in the team, several non-sporting journalists had flown out to report on this new drama and they were responsible for the more sensational headlines at home. He could easily pick them out. Very English-looking and very bored-looking. One of them approached the group.

'Are you English?'

They all nodded, somewhat reluctantly.

'Thank God!' He looked terribly relieved. 'Can you tell me when this is all going to start? We've been here for ages. Someone said yacht racing was like watching grass grow and they weren't wrong.'

'We were waiting for the weather to settle. The eleven-minute gun is about to go,' one of them rejoined stiffly.

'What does that mean?'

'Eleven minutes before the start. At ten minutes there is another gun, and five minutes later both boats enter the start box and basically wrestle with each other for control.'

The man was still looking blank.

'Sit down,' said the *Guardian* correspondent kindly. 'Learn a thing or two. Did you call this yacht racing? Well, this is actually match racing, a completely different creature . . . '

At five minutes the gun fired again and immediately *Excalibur* and *Black Heart* came charging in from their corners like two prizefighters. The quicker manoeuvrability of *Black Heart* showed itself almost instantly and within a few circles they had *Excalibur* pinned hard.

'Jesus! Get them off us!' snarled Inky.

'I will,' muttered Mack. He ducked and dived but every time he tacked, *Black Heart* tacked on top of him and blocked his way. It was clear that they intended to do what Inky did to the Italians and herd *Excalibur* as far away from the line as possible before they broke for the line.

'Which side do we want, Rafe?'

'Breeze is stronger on the right but it's marginal. No great shakes if we start from the left and the chop from the spectator fleet will be less.'

'Mack will be trying to gain control by getting on the New Zealand boat's tail and then he can herd them in any direction he wants to.' All of the old media hands were pitching in and helping the journalist, whose name turned out to be Matt. He was from the *Mail*, which doesn't normally have a sailing correspondent. 'Usually away from the starting line. But always remember that whoever has the wind on their starboard side has right of way over an opponent whose bow is on their portside. They can basically charge their opponent and they have to move out of the way.'

Suddenly everyone was on their feet. 'Oooohhhh,' they all said; there were even a few claps of applause.

'What happened there?' asked Matt anxiously. There seemed to be an enormous kerfuffle on the water.

'John MacGregor. What a master. He left a tantalising gap between him and the committee boat and then just as *Black Heart* decided to take the lure and go for the gap, he closed it and *Black Heart* found themselves sandwiched there. A penalty for not keeping clear.'

'*Excalibur* is free to go but because *Black Heart* has a red penalty flag, they have to perform it now.'

Matt could see *Excalibur* racing up the course whilst *Black Heart* was spinning through its turn. The press boat started its engines and prepared to follow the race.

It had been a beautiful start and Inky couldn't help but smile. The New Zealanders deciding to go for the gap, Mack's quick instruction to tack and close it, *Black Heart's* panic when they realised that they didn't have right of way and literally had to stall the boat to bring it to a stop.

But the New Zealanders were a gutsy crew and it wasn't long before they seemed to be catching up. *Excalibur* had separated from the New Zealanders once across the start line in search of better breeze to the left-hand side of the course. For once it looked as though a foreign boat had gained on a wind shift over *Excalibur*.

'I think we should change the genoa. It's the wrong sail,' said Rafe.

Mack shouted down to Ho to change the genoa to the next sail up and immediately he was up on deck, single-handedly hauling the hefty sail behind him and glad of something to vent his frustration on.

'That's better,' said Mack, two minutes later when the new sail was in place. He had a felt a fraction of speed increase.

Rafe's and Inky's eyes were constantly on the black boat now on the far side of the course.

'Let's tack,' said Rafe quietly. 'The wind is shifting again and they're going to feel the benefit. Let's go and join them.' He sounded reluctant and looked uncomfortable. Mack glanced at him. 'The wind is fickle today. It feels light, shifty. I don't like it,' Rafe explained.

'TACKING!' yelled Mack. The whole crew burst into action and soon *Excalibur* was pointed towards the black boat. Now all eyes were on the boat in front.

'Let's slam-dunk them,' muttered Inky to Mack. Slam dunk is one of the most audacious moves in match racing. Mack would take *Excalibur* right to the bow of *Black Heart* and then tack on top of them, thereby punching all the wind from their sails. It would force them to stay behind as they would never recover enough power to overtake. Mack would have to take into account the current, waves, wind shifts, crew reactions and, most importantly, evasive action from *Black Heart*. And there would be about a twenty-centimetre margin for error.

'Rafe?' questioned Mack.

'There's a five-degree wind shift. We can catch them.'

Everyone seemed to sense what Mack was about to try and stiffened. Eyes were huge with the anticipation.

'Custard!' yelled Mack. 'I need more speed!'

'Aye, aye, Captain Kirk,' he yelled back.

'Talk to me, Sammy.'

'Speed is ten point six, ten point six, ten point seven. We need eleven, Mack, to reach them. That's good, Mack. We're up to ten point eight. You can afford to bear up another couple of degrees. We'll still reach them. That's it. We're on eleven. Stay on this bearing.'

Mack was unable to see the black boat; Inky was acting as his eyes and he was relying on her for the split-second timing of the manoeuvre, but he could hear *Black Heart*'s bow wave starting to slap against the hull so he knew they were getting close. 'Wait . . . wait . . . nearly there . . . ' Inky was saying. The whole crew was tensed for action. 'NOW!' she yelled. And Mack spun *Excalibur* to land bang on top of the New Zealanders.

'Well done, Inky,' said Mack quietly.

Mack sailed the next leg perfectly. He was on a sword edge of perfection, he and Custard were so in tune with each other that no words were necessary. The sails were as flawlessly full of wind as they could be. Custard's arms bulged with muscle and yet his hands tweaked the sails as delicately as a virtuoso on a Stradivarius. The whole crew was silent, ears as intent on *Excalibur* as a mother's on her newborn. They listened to the now familiar language, the melancholy howl of her rigging, the parting of the water as her hull sliced through, the song of her sails as she captured the air, alert for any sound of distress but nothing interrupted her chatter. The New Zealanders never recovered. Excalibur came home the clear winners by over three minutes.

They were through to the final round of the America's Cup.

*   *   *

After the race the crew just had their showers and went back to sit in the common room. It should have been a huge occasion, they should have been celebrating, but with the final hearing over the boat the day after tomorrow the whole future of the syndicate hung in the balance. No one was in the mood. No one even wanted to go home. They simply wanted to stay together. Carla stayed on and cooked them a late supper. Every now and then they would break into laughter only to sober up a few seconds later when they remembered the fate that hung over them.

'Inky!' One of the security guards poked his head around the door. 'Your Italian bloke is at the gate. Wants to see you. I didn't let him in because he didn't have a security pass.'

Inky frowned to herself. 'Luca? Luca is here?' she said in puzzlement.

'I didn't ask the name.'

To oop-laas from the crew and good natured catcalling, Inky went out of the common room and down to the compound gates. Sure enough, Luca was there waiting for her. Her footsteps slowed.

'Inky,' he called out quickly. 'I come to say I'm sorry about what I say on the phone.'

'Oh.'

'I don't think you won just because you have illegal keel.'

Inky frowned. This didn't sound like Luca. 'What changed your mind?'

'That's what I came to tell you. The gossip in the syndicate says that Henry Luter visited our syndicate head and gave him all the evidence.' He pushed his hand through the wires of the gate and squeezed her arm.

'Tell me everything,' said Inky.

Inky later returned, slightly stunned, to the common room and sitting down told the rest of the crew what Luca had just told her. 'I must go and tell Mack,' said Inky getting up.

'What were you and Jason Bryant talking about the Saturday

of the Italian wake?' blurted out Golly just as she was going. 'You were out drinking together.'

All eyes came to look at Inky.

'You and Jason Bryant?' said Custard slowly. 'But you said you were with Luca.'

'I never said anything of the sort,' said Inky quickly. 'You presumed I was with Luca.'

'You were looking pretty cosy,' interjected Golly.

'Luca and I have finished. I didn't want to tell you. I met Jason at the Italian wake, we had a drink together. I went home. Alone. That's all.'

'He had his hand over yours.'

'He wanted to sleep with me.' He had tried to get her to go home with him and, in truth, Inky had for one wild moment contemplated sleeping with him. She had been confused and amazed that all these years his hostility had simply masked his desire for her. But in the end it seemed like a too major betrayal of Excalibur.

There was an awkward silence. 'I KNEW IT!' Dougie leapt to his feet and punched his finger out in front of him. 'I knew he fancied you! Ha! I'm not so crap at this love stuff after all!'

There was a silence before Custard burst out laughing with everyone else gradually joining in. 'That's my girl!' he said jumping up and clapping her on the back. 'You turned down Jason Bryant! Bloody marvellous! This is one pot of ink he won't be dipping his nib into! Ha! She conquers them all!'

'I'm sorry, Inky,' said Golly over the ruckus. 'I'm really sorry. I didn't know what to think, and when you said Henry Luter was involved in this keel thing and you never openly mentioned that you'd seen Jason Bryant, I didn't really know what to think . . . ' he repeated.

Inky couldn't face the huge, gorilla-like man looking any more dejected so she said it was fine and gave him a hug whilst the crew chanted EX-CAL-I-BUR! in the background.

Bizarrely, it was the one thing that really cheered them up all night.

Chapter 47

The next morning Henry Luter gave a press conference. Ever keen to seize the limelight and psych out the opposition, he wanted to talk about some new technology on *Phoenix* which his company had just developed and would blow the opposition out of the water. Custard hadn't been able to see Saffron for the last week and it was driving him mad. Custard had been racing during the day, and at night, when Custard was free, Saffron was obliged to be having dinner on board *Corposant* with Henry. Despite a lifetime of racing to split seconds, Custard had never truly realised how long a minute, an hour or a day was before. The magazine interview with Saffron had appeared in *Hello!* last week to coincide with the final of the America's Cup and Custard had eagerly cut it out. The pictures of her had included some nice ones taken in *Corposant*'s panelled sitting room but the ones that he truly adored were taken up on deck with her looking out to sea with a slight smile playing on her lips, hair faintly blowing in the breeze. From the occasional messages he'd managed to elicit this week, she'd coyly admitted that she was looking at him whilst they were being taken. He put them in his wallet.

Today, Custard couldn't resist the opportunity to go along to the press conference; even though there wouldn't be much chance to speak to her, he would at least see her. Custard immediately spotted Saffron sitting at the end of the first row. Through the gap in the chair he could see that her top was just starting to rise up to show the bare flesh of the small of her back. It was all he could do not to go over there and kiss it. He thought he'd never seen anything so desirable in all of this life. As though burnt by his longing, Saffron glanced round. She stared at him for a second before snapping her head back towards her husband. A few moments later, she edged her bag on to her lap and extracted her mobile.

Whilst Henry Luter was waffling on, a text came through on Custard's mobile.

'*What u doing here?*'

'*Came 2 c u.*'

'*Have 2 speak 2 u.*'

'*I know. Missing u 2.*'

'*No. Have news.*'

Custard frowned at the back of her head and then sent the response, '*C u later?*'

'*Casa AC after.*'

He hung around until after the press conference was finished and then made his way along to the Casa America's Cup, the museum of the America's Cup where he and Saffron first met. Smiling faintly at the memory, he wandered around until Saffron entered, panting, about ten minutes later. He dragged her behind a screen and grabbed her small hand in his huge paws. 'God, I am missing you!'

Saffron looked over her shoulder. 'I haven't long, I'll be missed soon. I had to come and tell you.'

'Tell me what?'

'I overheard Henry on the phone just before we left. I couldn't make out all of the conversation but I think he's got something to do with your illegal boat allegations.'

'We know he has. Someone else told us. I haven't seen you to be able to tell you. What did you hear?'

'I just heard him mention *Excalibur* and then laugh and then say that he gave some information to the Italians. He

475

was also talking about someone with a foreign name . . . I don't know.'

'Maybe, there's this French hydrodynamics man . . . '

'It might have been a French name, I can't remember. I'm sorry, I don't know how much of that will help. I just wanted you to know what you might be up against.' She bit her lip and looked worried. 'You don't know what Henry can be like sometimes. I'll keep my ears open for you.'

'Please don't risk anything for us.'

She glanced over her shoulder. 'I have to go.' She kissed him briefly on the lips and then left.

'I love you,' he called softly after her. He wasn't sure if she heard or not.

Henry had gone out to practise with the crew of *Phoenix*. Saffron wasted no time. She went immediately into his office. She didn't know where to start. She tried looking through papers on his desk, careful to replace everything exactly. There was nothing there. She nervously opened his laptop. She glanced at the clock. He could be back any minute and she had no idea what she was looking for. Saffron took a deep breath and started to look through his files.

Later that afternoon Custard's mobile beeped. He went immediately to it. On the screen was a text from Saffron. It simply said a name and an address. In Avignon. It was for the French hydrodynamics expert. Custard closed his eyes and wondered what she did to get hold of this information.

Custard went straight to Mack and showed him the text from Saffron.

'How did you come by this information?' Mack asked.

'I truly cannot tell you that.'

'Custard, you have to say . . . '

'Please don't ask me.'

'How do we know if we can trust it?'

'Because you trust me and this is someone close to me.'

Mack looked at him in puzzlement. Custard was becoming more mysterious by the second. 'Very well,' he said finally.

Bee came down specially to the base to see Mack off to the hearing which was being held privately in a discreet room at the Valencia Yacht Club. Mack didn't know who was more uptight. 'Right,' she kept saying.

'Right what?'

'Nothing. Just right. Are you nervous?'

'No. Are you?'

'Of course not. It's all going to be fine. Just fine.' She patted him nervously. 'They're not going to send us home, are they?'

'No. No. Absolutely not.'

The whole of the challenger committee was present, along with a presiding judge, who was American in the name of impartiality, and representatives from each syndicate. Colin Montague had flown out for the trial, coming direct from the airport. With him were the team of lawyers who had been working so hard on the case. Mack thanked God that Colin Montague had never stinted on paying out for the best legal support even though he was having to pay for them personally as his board of directors refused to give any more money to Excalibur. ('Because why would we want to throw good money after bad?' one of them pointed out.) On the opposing side, there sat a very imposing team of lawyers in Prada suits and the head of the Italian syndicate. Mack was glad to see that the Italian skipper Marco Fraternelli wasn't there. Maybe he felt he couldn't lend his name to such an affair. Mack hadn't heard a thing since yesterday when he handed the name of the French hydrodynamics man over to Colin's head lawyer. He felt jumpy.

The judge opened proceedings. 'We are here today to decide if the Montague Challenge has broken the Protocol of the America's Cup by using a foreign national to help design their boat . . . '

* * *

The crew were all waiting behind the compound gate like prisoners, eagerly watching for the first sight of Mack's beaten-up Mercedes. They didn't talk much as there didn't seem much to say. Some of them feigned nonchalance by wandering away from the fence and kicking at little bunches of weed which occasionally grew up between the concrete but as soon as the cry went up, 'He's back!', they rushed to the fence and pinned their noses up to the wire.

They circled the car as he pulled in. It was deathly silent as Mack turned off the engine and opened the door with a quiet click.

Inky could bear it no longer. 'Well?'

Mack looked at them all. 'We do *not* have an illegal boat . . . '

They carried Mack shoulder high all round the compound. Now the whole syndicate and the families felt they really had something to celebrate. They wasted absolutely no time in cracking out the barbecue and hoofing it down to the supermarket for some beers for a party that they should have had when *Excalibur* arrived back on the docks after her last race. Slowly the immensity of their achievement began to dawn on them all. 'We're in the final match of the America's Cup,' they whispered to one another.

Mack managed to buttonhole Custard later on. 'Thanks,' he said quietly.

'I'll pass it on.'

'Sure you can't tell me where you got that information from?'

Slowly Custard shook his head.

'Well, whoever they were they certainly saved our bacon. From what Colin has told me, they found the Frenchman at that address you gave us. He won't admit to it but it's clear that Henry Luter paid him a lot of money to say he played a part in the design. He was scheduled to appear and testify against us but Colin Montague's lawyers got him to cave in and he signed the affidavit at the last minute instead. I should think he's made himself scarce. Henry Luter won't be too pleased.' He looked at Custard curiously. 'It must be someone in Luter's camp who gave you that address.'

'Not completely in his camp.'

'We'll face him on the water in six days' time.'

They stood in silence for a few seconds, Mack reflecting on all the stress and extra financial pressure that Henry Luter had caused the syndicate. Custard thinking of the distress he caused Saffron and wondering what lengths she had gone to to get that information.

'I'm going to fucking pulverise him,' said Mack.

Custard chinked his beer bottle against Mack's. 'Amen to that.'

Back at the Luter camp things weren't looking so rosy. When Henry Luter received a phone call to tell him the result of the hearing, he went apoplectic with rage. He smashed every piece of china he could reach, a blood vessel popping so hard out of his forehead that Jason Bryant thought it would explode. He couldn't speak with fury for a full minute.

'Fucking man. Fucking, fucking man. He said he would swear. He said he would do it.'

Jason presumed he was talking about the hearing and the French hydrodynamicist. Whilst he hadn't had much to do with the accusation, he would have been happy for Excalibur to be out of the picture.

Luter turned his attention to Bryant. 'It's all down to you now. I hope you're up to it.'

Bryant nodded. 'I'm up to it.'

Chapter 48

A very tired Hattie arrived back a few days later. She had stayed in England as long as she could to spread the good news of *Excalibur*'s trial result but then, desperately wanting to return to Valencia, she left Colin Montague's marketing team to continue the good work and packed her things.

She had caught an early flight and came straight to the base from the airport. The crew were just getting ready for their day's practice and they crowded round her, thrilled to see her and surprised by how much they had all missed her.

Custard gave her a big hug. 'It's a mixed blessing. Carla has just announced she's going to make some of her *special* buns for your arrival home.'

Hattie laughed. She looked shyly round for Rafe (even whilst repeating firmly to herself, 'Rafe's with Ava'), but, reticent as always, he was standing near the back and smiling slightly. Dougie caught Inky's eye as Hattie went towards Rafe and motioned for her to leave. The crew seemed to mysteriously melt away from them.

'See?' whispered Dougie to Inky as they went to get the sails ready. 'I'm getting so good at this love stuff.'

'I'm glad you're back,' Rafe said. 'I missed you.'

'Did you really?'

'Mack has given us the day off tomorrow. Can we go and do something?'

All Hattie's firm resolutions to keep her head down and simply concentrate on work until the end of the Cup fell away and she nodded.

Hattie went into a tailspin of panic. Rafe didn't really say what they were going to be doing and all her clothes were dirty from her trip to England and presently stuffed in her suitcase under her desk. Luckily, Mack was so thrilled with the result of the hearing and her work back in England, that he sent her home two hours early. 'But what about the press?' she had tentatively asked.

'Bugger the press, they've had the initial press release and now they can wait. You look shattered,' he said kindly. 'Go back to your apartment and get some rest.'

But Hattie had other ideas. She immediately hot-footed it down to the shops and invested in a beautiful, strappy floral dress which she thought she could wear with her jewelled flip-flops and a cream cardigan in case it got cold.

When they met outside Casa Fortuna the next morning, she found out that Rafe had requisitioned his father's boat for the day. Just as they were walking away, a man came rushing out of the doors. 'Rafe!' he called. 'Rafe!' Both of them spun round to find Tom sprinting towards them waving something. Hattie thought how much they looked alike. Of course, Tom didn't have the depth of Rafe's eyes or the fullness of his mouth but then she was very biased.

'The keys!' he said arriving in front of them. 'You forgot the keys. Hello, you must be Hattie.' He immediately turned to her. Rafe narrowed his eyes and wondered if he had let him forget on purpose.

Hattie was smiling widely, thrilled at meeting Rafe's father. 'Hello.'

'So nice to meet you. I have been hearing an awful lot about you.'

'Have you?'

'Yes, yes, Dad. Thanks for the keys,' said Rafe.

'Well, it's nice to meet you, Hattie. I'm sure we'll see each other again soon.'

'I hope so,' said Hattie, grinning. She thought she would like Rafe's dad.

Hattie had never been sailing with anyone other than her father, who usually became so overexcited that he shouted himself hoarse, so she was surprised how coolly and calmly Rafe took them out of the marina with nothing more than a few muttered instructions. Soon they were coming out of the industrial dock area of Valencia and then up the coast towards Sagunto.

'I can see Casa Fortuna!' Hattie shouted as they passed the long stretch of Malvarrosa beach.

Rafe grinned, cleated off the genoa and then sat down in the cockpit beside Hattie. The breeze was good and strong today and they flew along. 'Do you mind coming out sailing?' he asked. 'You must be sick of boats.'

'I haven't been sailing once since I got here!' said Hattie truthfully. 'It's wonderful to be out on the water and so much cooler.' She put on more sunscreen and handed the tube to Rafe.

'Do you want a lifejacket?'

Hattie shook her head. She felt perfectly safe with him. 'Do you ever wear one?' she asked curiously.

'Only if the weather is bad or during the night.'

She took the tiller whilst he unpacked some things. 'I didn't know what you'd like to eat, so I brought a selection.'

'You shouldn't have gone to so much trouble.'

'Don't give me too much credit. Aunt Bee did a lot of it.'

They had a breakfast picnic of fresh pineapple, smoked salmon on bagels and delicious croissants from the French bakery. Rafe went below deck and managed to brew some tea on the ancient stove.

'I've been reading your *Book of Winds* whilst you've been away,' he said.

'Really?'

'It's fascinating. Did you know that the south and north winds literally shaped Greek civilisation? When they set out to trade, they couldn't sail into the north wind they called the bora, so they went south instead to Africa.'

'You must lend it to me afterwards.'

'Of course. How was England, by the way? I haven't asked.'

'Chilly.'

'Did you see any friends or family?'

'Not enough time. I saw my parents once for breakfast but I was moving round a lot.'

Rafe got up to retrim the genoa. Hattie closed her eyes and let the sun soak into her skin whilst the breeze stroked her. It was a brilliant, sunny day. Just the sort of weather to ripen those famous Valenciano oranges. The air was salty and clean and Hattie felt marvellous.

They anchored in a small bay for lunch. It was deserted apart from a couple of children playing in the surf a long way up the beach. The murky industrial waters of Valencia port had given way to crystal-clear blue.

Rafe unpacked yet more delicious things. Bee had done them proud. A fresh tomato salad done Spanish-style mixed with olive oil and shavings of *bonito* (dried, salty tuna roe). Piles of delicious hams, tortilla made with juicy chorizo sausage, giant prawns and chilli sauce. To drink, there was a bottle of champagne and good old Valenciano orange juice to make Buck's Fizz. For pudding there was simply a bowl of the blackest, ripest cherries and Rafe and Hattie amused themselves by lazily lying opposite and spitting the stones at each other.

'Rafe.'

'Hattie.'

'This is what visitors must do when they come to Valencia.'

'If they have a boat.'

'No, I mean just relaxing.'

'You mean no America's Cup.'

'I can't remember life without it.' And I can't remember life without you, she thought.

There was the faintest pause. 'Nor can I. Do you want to swim?'
Hattie sat up. 'But I haven't brought a costume.'
'I'll have a look below. We often have one floating around.'
'How come?'
He grinned. 'Ex-girlfriend of me or my dad.'
He foraged in the cabin for a bit and then produced a polka dot
one-piece. Hattie tried it on and then couldn't stop giggling. The
last owner must have been at least a 40G cup next to Hattie's singularly modest 32B. She couldn't help but think if Ava had been here
she would have emerged in a sexy, white two-piece or something.
Rafe frowned when she reappeared from the cabin. 'God, I
don't think that can have been one of my girlfriends'. I think I
would remember.' He smiled at her, thinking how pretty she
was with her hair falling over her face, laughing in her too-big
costume. It was so easy to be with her.
'You'll have to promise not to look. The whole thing is going
to drop off me any second.'
'I promise.'
He went to the back of the boat and dived into the water.
Hattie followed him in and together they swam round the boat
and to a nearby cave to explore. Eventually, declaring himself tired,
Rafe swam to the back of the boat and hauled himself out on to
the little platform. The water ran like velvet off his body and Hattie
marvelled to herself that this beautiful, lean, dark-skinned creature was actually out here with her. She thought fleetingly again
of Ava. She'd like to be here with him too; Hattie knew just how
much. But she resolved firmly to put her out of her mind. Rafe
had chosen to spend the day with her. Anyway, Ava wouldn't
have been able to spend the day with him because of Jason Bryant,
a sly little voice in her head pointed out. But if Rafe had known
about Ava's letter, would he still be here? Hattie shook her head
firmly as though physically trying to dislodge the thoughts.
She swam round the boat by herself and then clambered out
on to the platform.
Making an excuse that she needed the loo, Hattie escaped

down below to see how much her mascara had run in the water. Feeling ridiculously happy and wishing the day would go on for ever, she grabbed her bag off one of the bunk beds and brought out her mascara and lipstick. She loosely towel-dried her hair and then went back on deck.

'So this is the boat you sailed with your father?' she asked shyly, wondering if that used to be Rafe's bed down below.

'Yes.' He looked round her briefly. 'I know every inch of her. Every scratch, every mark. I know the lap of the waves against the bow and the pitch of the wind in her sails. This is my childhood, I suppose.'

'How does it feel to be back on her?'

'Strange. I mean so much has happened since I left her. So much has changed.'

He means Ava, thought Hattie. 'It seems a nice life.'

'It was. But it wasn't always like this. We'd often spend some time in port and we'd work or I'd have a tutor. At night my dad and I would lie on the deck and he'd show me all the stars. When he had a steady girlfriend, she would come and cook for us. We had Dominique whilst we were around France. She used to clean out all the cupboards and tut at the amount of buckets we had. Margarita was from Spain and she taught me about Picasso. Sophia was Italian but we met her in Greece; she taught me to play poker and made the best bolognese I have ever tasted. I loved those times too. I loved the feel of having a woman around. I would often pretend that she was my mother and this is how it would have been.' He looked down at his arms, embarrassed to be talking so much. He'd never told anyone that.

'You must miss her.'

'Only when I realise what I actually missed.'

'Apple pie, pyjamas warming on the radiator, someone to draw a picture for.'

Rafe smiled and nodded. '*Your* mother?' he asked.

'Yes.'

*   *   *

They came back into the dock at about six o'clock. 'Would you like some supper?' Rafe asked as they folded the sails away together.

Hattie nodded eagerly. Anything to prolong this day with him.

Rafe took her down to the dockside where his old friends the fishermen had come in with their catch for the day. He sent Hattie to buy a couple of beers from the local shop and then plonked her in a tatty plastic chair. In the meantime he had paid for some fresh sardines and then proceeded to cook them on the fishermen's open barbecue.

Telling them he'd bring back the plates and forks later, he tipped most of the sardines on to Hattie's plate and together they wandered down on the beach together. Sitting cross-legged opposite one another, they guzzled their way through a huge pile of fish washed down with slugs of cool San Miguel beer.

'God, these are delicious. I've never had them this way.'

'Be good for you. You're losing weight.'

'Too much work. I wish every day could be like this.' Hattie pushed her bare feet into the sand which had the consistency of finely milled flour.

'So do I.'

'Do you?' asked Hattie shyly.

'What? Choosing between spending time eating and drinking with you or being with sixteen other sweaty men and getting shouted at by Mack?'

'Don't forget Inky.'

'Ah yes. She is the saving grace.' He paused. 'I'm afraid I haven't any coffee or chocolate to offer you. We might have some at Casa Fortuna. Do you want to come back?'

Hattie's heart started to beat like mad as she said that sounded very nice. 'But what about Bee and your dad?'

'They'll have to get their own. Besides, they mentioned something about going out to dinner anyway. You might have to put up with Salty and Pipgin.'

They got up and slowly started to walk back to the dock area.

486

'Doesn't Pipgin stay with Custard at night?' she asked.

'Custard keeps slightly bizarre hours, to be honest. I don't know what he gets up to and he won't say. The other evening he came in with his shirt all done up on the wrong buttons.'

'Maybe a racer chaser?'

'Maybe.'

After depositing their plates and forks back with the fishermen and expressing their profuse thanks, they made their way slowly back to Casa Fortuna. They turned on to the main boardwalk along the beach which was very wide and lined with restaurants. The sun was starting to set, spraying the whole area with warm, orange light. Children were roller-skating up and down; couples were strolling hand in hand. Diners were starting on their aperitifs, sitting outside under huge canopies. Hattie's hands hung loosely by her side. She had suddenly become terribly aware of them and couldn't remember what she did with them normally. Did she swing them or did they just hang? Occasionally they brushed against Rafe, and then he seemed to pick one up. He squeezed it and they walked together in silence.

Once at Casa Fortuna, he led the way through the lobby and they walked together up the few flights of stairs. Once outside his door, he tucked a strand of hair back behind her ear and then opened the door. For a second he was puzzled. Normally when Salty and Pipgin were home alone, they burst out to greet him.

But a few seconds later he understood why. A figure was standing in the sitting room, with the two dogs lying contently at her feet. For one confused moment, Hattie thought it must be Bee but then the figure turned around. It was Ava, looking stunning in jeans and high heels and a tiny top. She smiled at them both.

'How did you get in?' asked Rafe slowly.

'It would seem that your doorman is a bit of a sucker for a sob story. I recall you did the same thing to me once before, Rafe. Tit for tat, as they say.' She sauntered over to Hattie and looked her bitchily up and down. 'Although decidedly not in her case,' she drawled. 'Had a nice day?'

487

Hattie ran out of the door. A second later Rafe had caught up with her. 'Hattie, don't go. I'm sorry. I had no idea she would be there.'

'She wrote you a letter. I let Custard tear it up,' Hattie blurted out.

'When?'

'Just before I left for England. I'm sorry. I should have told you.'

'I'll come and talk to you later.'

She didn't want him to see her cry so she tried to smile and nod and then shut the door.

Half an hour later there was a knock on the door. Hattie flew off the bed and ran to the door, frantically wiping her tears as she went. But it wasn't Rafe at the door, it was Bee. Hattie's face visibly fell.

'I'm so sorry,' said Bee feeling terribly distressed for her. 'I just came to see if you were all right. We just got back.'

'Did Rafe send you?'

'No, no. He and Ava were there when we returned from dinner. They're . . . they're still talking.' Bee didn't want to say that they had disappeared into the bedroom. Hopefully just for some privacy. 'I'm so sorry,' she gabbled. 'It was my fault that Ava was there. She turned up earlier in the day and I told her you and Rafe were out together. I thought it would make it clear that you two were – I hoped – an item. I had no idea she would come back and wait for you.' She was too ashamed to admit that she had enjoyed telling Ava all that and so had unwittingly made the situation worse.

Hattie's heart sank. Ava must be desperate to have him. She wouldn't give up. She turned and walked back into the room, leaving Bee hovering uncertainly in the doorway. Eventually Bee followed her in and shut the door. She sat down on the sofa next to Hattie and took her hand.

Hattie started to cry again and leant her head on Bee's shoulder. 'I think I love him, Bee. I don't know what to do.'

Bee patted and consoled but couldn't say anything helpful because she didn't know what to do either.

Now that she had gained access to the bedroom, Ava was laying siege to Rafe.

'Where have you two been?' she started.

'Out on the boat,' said Rafe warily.

'Were you bringing her back here to fuck her?' The coarseness sat oddly on her beautiful lips.

'I didn't really have plans in mind,' he said dryly.

Ava went over to the window and looked out over the gardens. 'She's a pretty little thing. Not really your type though.'

'What is my type?'

'Me.'

'She's easy to be with.'

'Boring, you mean.'

'No. I mean pleasant.' Rafe sighed. He used to find these rows challenging but now they just made him feel drained.

'What do you want with her?'

'What do you mean?'

'What's your fascination with her?'

Rafe stared at her. She always spoke about love in terms of spells. Like some form of witchcraft. 'There's no fascination. I just like her,' he said firmly.

'She's your PR girl, isn't she? Was she responsible for all those headlines? The man from Atlantis stuff?'

'Hattie? No. That doesn't sound like Hattie.'

Ava changed tactics. 'Was that your dad who just brought Bee back?'

'Yes.' An introduction had seemed a little inappropriate.

'Interesting to see how you would grow old. Well, by the look of him.'

'He finally made it here.' Rafe sat down on the bed and Ava curled herself up next to him.

'Are you tempted to go back with him?'

Rafe hesitated. 'Yes. I am,' he said truthfully. 'But I won't.'

'And after the Cup?'

'I don't know. I can't think about it.'

'What if I came with you? We could see Rio and Trinidad, Le Touquet and Brighton.'

Rafe laughed in spite of himself. 'Brighton aside, you want to see Rio?'

'I've always wanted to carnival there. Have you been?'

'Yes. Once.' Rafe got a strong image of Ava with a hibiscus flower behind her ear, hips moving to the street music. A carnival would suit her. 'What about your painting?'

'I presume Rio would have canvas, wouldn't it? Imagine all that different light I could capture. I could do a study of light around the world. And I'm sure you could do with an on-board cook. I make a very mean trifle.'

'Trifles don't need cooking.'

'It's very individual.' Ava ran her finger lightly down Rafe's jaw. 'I might have finished with Jason.'

'Might have?'

'Yes, might have. Can we get back together? That's what you wanted last time we met, isn't it?'

'Was it?'

'That's what I came to tell you. About me and Jason. You notice that I am not remotely interested in the outcome of the Cup? I am here before the two of you have even raced. I just want to be with you. Of course, you can't see that girl again.'

'We work together, Ava,' said Rafe wearily.

'I'll get Daddy to fire her.'

'You'll do no such thing.'

'You and I were so good together.'

'Ava, we're in the middle of the America's Cup. I know you're making a point about the outcome being unimportant but can't all this wait until afterwards? It's only a short while now. I was a mess when we broke up last time. I can't afford for it to happen again.'

'Who said we would break up?'

Rafe sighed 'Let's not do this now.'

'I'm sorry about last time,' persisted Ava.

'I don't need you to be sorry, Ava,' he snapped. 'Why have you come back?'

'I made a mistake. This time away from you, I've realised that I only want to be with you. This time for good.'

'Do you think it's that easy? You can click your fingers and everything would be back to how it was?'

The contrite and kittenish Ava sat up, eyes gleaming. 'It would be wrong to waste something that wonderful,' she whispered, coiling towards him.

'You already did.'

Ava straddled Rafe, rubbing her groin slightly against his. 'Don't you want me, Rafe?' she whispered. 'Don't you want to be inside me?'

He gripped her hips hard, trying to stop the gyrations. Whatever happened, she always reduced him to a mess of need.

Chapter 49

Early the next morning Mack bumped into Rafe creeping into the compound carrying a large takeaway of frothy cappuccino. He raised his eyebrows. 'Have you some sort of death wish? Carla will kill you. Who are you taking to the ball tomorrow?'

Tomorrow was the evening of the Louis Vuitton Challengers' Ball, an absolutely sumptuous, invitation-only affair. An age-old tradition where all the challengers and the defender of the Cup gathered to celebrate before the final. 'No one. What about you?'

'Em, no one.' He had been planning on asking Bee but when Golly couldn't come because he was flying back to England for some physiotherapy on his knee it was absolutely insisted that his pair of tickets went to Bee in appreciation of all she had done for the challenge. So now she had her own set of tickets, and the last race series and illegal boat charges had naturally rather preoccupied him. He wondered whether it was too late. 'Who is your aunt taking with her?' he enquired, but not without a certain degree of awkwardness. 'I'm only asking because Louis Vuitton need to know for the place settings.'

'My dad, I think.'

Mack had been to plenty of events and balls by himself and wondered why it would be bothering him now that he was without a partner. Or was it just being without Bee that bothered him? 'Of course, of course. His name is Tom, isn't it?'

'Yes.'

'I'm looking forward to properly meeting him,' said Mack, who wasn't at all.

Hattie managed not to look at Rafe once whilst she was going over the interview schedule with the crew that morning. It had been two days since they spent the day together and she hadn't spoken to him once. He hadn't returned the night that he left her. He must have spent it with Ava. She was too proud to ask Bee what was going on – besides, she was sure that Bee wouldn't know. Rafe played his cards close to his chest. She knew that they had both been frantically busy. He hadn't a moment to spare between tuning *Excalibur* or being in the gym – the whole crew had redoubled their efforts there; anything to give them an edge. She didn't have any time either, between calming down journalists (who were getting hopelessly overexcited about the on-going battle between Henry Luter and Excalibur), crew members (who were verging on feverish), Colin Montague (who was the most uptight of all) and occasionally all three. But who was she kidding? He could have made time to see her if he had wanted to.

Since her visit back to England, Hattie had been reaping the rewards of increased media attention. Most of the journalists she had spoken to came flocking out to Valencia and were constantly calling her, wanting interviews or press releases. She was enjoying what Colin Montague called 'throwing him to the lions', as she insisted he trundle round the America's Cup village on his motorised scooter with a large cigar hanging out of his mouth and wearing various T-shirts saying BRITANNIA RULES THE WAVES and THE GREAT WHITE, referring to *Excalibur*'s hull. She'd even printed on to his T-shirt a very frivolous article from England about the crew's bottoms (and a cunning photographer had managed to take them all in a row on board *Excalibur*) and how teams with gorgeous bottoms never managed to win anything, along with the immortal quote, 'judging the evidence, Colin Montague must be very worried indeed.' With his easy charm and laid-back manner, he was an instant hit with the press and his share price was slowly climbing back again.

So much free stuff was coming in for the *Excalibur* crew that Hattie was forced to give most of it away to the shore crew. Carla was regularly going home wearing a new baseball cap or trainers or a beautiful scarf some Paris designer had sent down for Inky, none of which Inky was interested in. She got the feeling that Inky was throwing herself back into her work after the departure of Luca.

In retaliation Henry Luter had upped his publicity campaign and everywhere *Excalibur*'s crew went, there were billboard posters of Phoenix, every TV channel they turned on was a Spanish-subtitled interview with Henry Luter.

None of this particularly bothered Rafe. He was bemused rather than in awe of it. Only this morning, people waving programmes in front of their faces had been waiting for them as they arrived at the base. Custard had gone through ahead of him, signing as many as he could before disappearing through the compound gates.

'What were you doing?' Rafe asked curiously when he caught up with him.

Custard looked at him in surprise. 'Autographs, of course. Signing my name.' He laughed. 'You've never seen that before?'

'No. I thought you only signed cheques with your name.'

'I keep signing Custard. Not the coolest image in the world.'

'That's a bit strange. To sign your name like that, I mean.'

Custard clapped him on the back. 'When I look at the world through your eyes, mate, everything seems a bit strange.'

Rafe had indeed been busy since that night with Ava and Hattie, or had kept himself so. The truth was that he had studiously avoided Hattie all week (and felt faintly justified when he remembered she hadn't told him about Ava's letter). He shuddered as he remembered Ava laying siege to him that night.

'We could remove ourselves from reality,' she had whispered in his ear. 'Go far away from my father and England. I could paint and you could sail and nothing need interrupt us again. You said once that you had never known hunger until you met me. You could be sated.'

She had kissed him then, seizing his face delicately between her hands. Her hair was falling over his face. He breathed in her fragrance and kissed her back, reluctantly at first and then harder. He seized her hips and pushed them down. Slowly she pushed him back until she was lying on top of him. She moved her hands underneath his T-shirt, caressing his chest. 'I want you. Please, Rafe,' she whispered.

Reality was niggling at him. He managed to half sit up, 'Wouldn't we just be removing ourselves from our problems? If we simply went away.'

'Isn't that the best way? It would just be the two of us. Without my father or Mack or anybody.'

'Rather than face them? They wouldn't go away. And I don't think you could be out of the limelight for that long. Maybe a small while whilst you put together some work but not for long. Soon you would want to come back and exhibit it.'

'So we could pop back to England for a while.'

'And you wouldn't miss the parties, the gossip, the in-scene?'

'We could stay for a couple of months and then set off again. You could visit your Aunt Bee and I'd stay in London.'

'I don't think you would want to leave.'

'Well, you might want to do another Cup again. I could fly back and forth as I do now.'

'Ava,' said Rafe wearily, 'we're kidding ourselves.'

'No, Rafe. We've *been* kidding ourselves. That we could be apart. We belong together. We should be together.'

'I need to think about it. I think you should go.'

'Why? Because if I stay you know that you'll sleep with me?'

'Yes,' said Rafe simply.

He had then seen her out, not without a small smile of triumph on her face. He had slumped down in a chair in the sitting room where his father was innocently reading a book from Bee's bookcase. Rafe had only ever seen him with a book of tide tables in his hand.

'So that was Ava?' remarked Tom. 'Beautiful woman.'

They stared at each other in silence for a second before Tom went back to his book and Rafe stared out of the window. Just having his father there made everything feel easier, it took him back to the rhythm of an earlier time. He wondered about all Ava had said. He wondered if he wanted to go back to his old life of wandering and exile. He had gone from spending all his time within a crew of two to a crew of seventeen. He had become less self-sufficient and more dependent. He liked the competition too, the adrenalin rush of the matches, the perfect combination of challenge from sea and man. He thought he quite liked it all.

He felt ashamed that he had treated Hattie so badly but the truth was that he really couldn't make up his mind and he didn't want to mess her about any further until he had. It didn't help that he was about to face Jason Bryant daily on the race course. Wasn't he, after all, the only reason that Rafe came to Valencia?

At the Dantry/Beaufort household, things weren't very harmonious either. The theme for the Challengers' Ball was 'fairy tale' and Milly had been roped into helping with almost every costume. The pressure had stepped up somewhat since Excalibur had grasped the very important role of official challenger to the America's Cup. They would be very much in the public eye, and now even wives who refused initially to go in costume suddenly wanted the grandest, most flamboyant one there. Thankfully it took Milly's mind off everything that was going on at home. She was loving every minute of it.

The day of the ball seemed to start innocuously enough. A steady stream of fairy-tale costume traffic started at about eight o'clock with Pond. The characters would disappear into the bedroom with Milly and then reappear and parade in front of her dad who would whoop and clap with joy at Milly's creations.

She had just produced a very sexy Goldilocks with Ho's petite blonde wife. Custard dashed in to try on his costume but kept yawning throughout.

'Custard, what on earth have you been doing?' said Milly eventually. 'I know you were in last night because when I walked past your door I could hear music.'

'God, sorry Milly. I was reading a fascinating book.'

'About what?'

'The life of cod.'

Fabian had a late start that morning. They had all been given the day off because of the ball and he was now mooching around the breakfast table and hiding behind a Spanish newspaper. Milly knew that there was no way he was able to read it. She tossed the odd look at him, wondering what he was thinking about behind it. She felt like a single mother whilst still having to look after a non-existent husband. They were treading on egg shells. One moment he seemed on top of the world, bringing her flowers and chocolates and the next he was snapping with the stress. Milly had on more than one occasion bitten her tongue and then fed the chocolates to Salty.

At about ten o'clock, Elizabeth wafted in on a cloud of perfume. She planted a kiss on Fabian's mute head. 'Morning, darling!'

She managed to nod vaguely to Milly's dad Bill and completely ignored Milly and Rosie. 'I simply had to have a lie-in this morning. I still have not got over that dreadful plane journey.' Elizabeth hadn't quite recovered from the shock of having to travel by a low-cost airline. 'I had to jostle for my seat and when I managed to get an exit seat, did you know I wasn't allowed to have a *single* thing on my lap?' She looked around the room willing them to grasp the awfulness of it. 'I mean, I was only carrying a croissant and a copy of *Vogue*. Did they think I was going to kill someone with it?'

Bill and Milly met eyes. The first time she had related the story, Milly had whispered, 'She could kill someone with a lot less than that,' and Bill had to bite his lip to stop himself smiling again.

Milly's next 'client', Inky, appeared at the door and again she disappeared into the bedroom for her to try on her costume. When she came out, Milly's dad clapped.

'Inky, you look beautiful,' he said, smiling delightedly. 'The most beautiful ugly ducking I've ever seen. Or rather swan.'

Milly looked at the top of Fabian's head pleadingly. If only he could look up and say something. If only he could see all the work and effort she had put into everyone's costumes. But there was no response. She followed Inky back into the bedroom and helped her out of the ghost-grey dress which gave way to a train of white feathers. 'Thank you, Milly,' said Inky, beaming. 'I absolutely love it.'

'It was a pleasure. Really it was. Is Luca going to be there?'

'I hope so. I mean it's all over between us but I would like to see him.'

Milly squeezed her hand. 'Your parents must be so proud of you.'

Inky grinned. 'I think they are. My mother especially. She's been trying to learn swear words in Spanish all week so she can yell at the other crew during the racing which is *so* unlike my mother. I don't know what can have got into her!'

'A little bit of you, by the sound of it.'

After Inky had left, Milly sank down on the floor for a welcome few minutes to read a book with Rosie whilst her father went to make coffee for them all. 'Nanny read?' she whispered to Milly.

'Why don't you go and ask?'

Rosie got up and went over to Elizabeth. 'Nanny?' she said, tugging at her sleeve.

'Dear, I really think you should call me Grandmother. Could you do that?'

Rosie looked slightly confused. 'But she's always called you nanny, ever since she was little,' Milly jumped in.

Elizabeth raised her eyebrows. 'I always think that Nanny sounds slightly common.'

'But it was easier for her to pronounce.'

'Still, better to get rid of these nasty habits early. Don't you think, Fabian? Fabian?'

Fabian lowered his newspaper somewhat reluctantly.

'I think Nanny sounds far too provincial and common. What do you think?'

Milly looked at him, willing him to stick up for her. Please, she thought silently, please say something. Fabian looked from one to the other of them with a vague, preoccupied look in his eyes. 'Whatever's easiest,' he said, and raised the paper again. Elizabeth smiled smugly.

To be truthful, Fabian hadn't even heard what his mother was saying, he was too anxious and churned up inside. He wished his mother had stayed in England. He was more nervous about the racing than he had ever been in his life. Despite his recent good press he hadn't forgotten the past. He felt that it was his opportunity once and for all to rehabilitate himself in the eyes of the world. He was ambivalent about his mother being there as it kept him away from his father. He hadn't seen David for two days and he was shocked to find how unsettled that made him.

That last time they'd sat on *Daphne* drinking beer. 'Mum is coming out to watch me race,' commented Fabian.

David Beaufort had started to peel the label off his beer. 'Then I ought to go. Besides there's going to be more of the sailing fraternity there. It's only a matter of time before someone recognises me.'

Fabian had nodded. 'You'll miss the final match.' It was a statement of fact more than a question.

'I'll stop off somewhere and watch on TV.'

There was a silence as they both sipped from their bottles. 'I could always fly out and meet you in a port somewhere after all this is over.'

'Do you want to?'

'Of course.'

'You have my mobile number.'

'I'll use a pay phone. I'd better go,' Fabian stood up. 'Milly will be wondering where I've got to.'

'You'll bring her when you visit?'

'Rosie too.'

David stood up and silently they'd hugged one another. 'It seems hard,' said his dad, 'that I should have to go so soon. As soon as we find each other, we lose each other again.'

Fabian had nodded. 'But I know you'll be watching when it counts. Besides, I have Milly and Rosie now.'

He had left his father and looked back once to wave, full of regret now rather than anger. He felt desperately sorry for him because he didn't have a Milly or a Rosie.

At the Challengers' Ball huge squeals of delight greeted the arrival of each costume, and old friends fell on each other. Thanks to Milly's efforts the crew of *Excalibur* looked marvellous, not least Milly herself who looked quite absurdly sexy as a rakish Tinkerbell, with fairy wings and thigh-high leather boots.

The design team of *Excalibur* looked rather dashing too, even Neville who had come as some sort of knight. Soon he was surrounded by adoring females as the creator of *Excalibur*'s revolutionary keel. 'I hear that's the only reason they are through to the final,' one female was simpering to him. Neville was doing nothing to dissuade her of the fact.

'Where's Hattie?' Rafe asked Ho.

'I don't know.'

'Well, she would have been invited, wouldn't she?'

'I don't think so. It's only crew and design.'

Rafe stared at him, dismayed. 'But I just presumed that . . . '

'I know. It doesn't seem right after all she's done for the syndicate but I suppose that they can't invite just anybody.' Ho shrugged.

But Hattie isn't just anybody, Rafe thought to himself.

*   *   *

He wasn't the only one looking out for somebody.

'Has anyone seen Mack?' asked Bee. 'He is coming, isn't he?'

'They're flying all the skippers and syndicate heads in by heli-copter,' said Milly. 'I should think they'll be here in a bit. Did you see one of the papers nicknamed him Atlas this morning? Because he has the weight of the world on his shoulders. Such wide shoulders too; he must have been devastatingly attractive when he was younger.' Milly eyed Bee with interest. Bee was feigning attention in some proffered canapés of Bailey's-filled strawberries.

Bee wanted to say that she thought Mack was devastatingly attractive now but instead she said, 'I do miss English straw-berries, don't you?'

All the skippers and syndicate chiefs and their partners had been afforded the luxury of coming in black tie and their stark dress stood out amongst the glittering colours and fabrics.

Mack and his date strode in through the hordes causing a stir. The beauty on his arm was a stunner.

Custard – Buttons – stared open-mouthed at Mack's companion. 'Hattie!' he exclaimed. 'You look . . . ' He was almost lost for words. 'You look gorgeous.' Hattie was the Queen of Hearts in a sumptuous satin, tightly fish-tailed, strapless red dress. Her hair, newly highlighted with soft blondes and caramels, was pulled up with soft, curly tendrils escaping on to her beautiful, toned shoulders, her make-up decisive and dark, pulling out the depths of her eyes, all accompanied by her trademark red lipstick.

'I thought I couldn't possibly leave her at home,' said Mack, 'after all she has done for us.'

Hattie smiled brilliantly at Custard, but her eyes were searching the crowd. This effect had been created for the benefit of one person only. The admiring looks from everywhere counted for nothing.

Suddenly, she saw him coming towards them, a big bad wolf in a white dinner jacket. He looked flabbergasted, she hoped for the right reasons. 'Hattie!' Rafe exclaimed. 'You look . . . ' He looked her up and down in awe. 'Stunning. I was worried you weren't going to come.'

'Mack invited me.'

Rafe felt a shot of guilt. It should have been him. 'I'm pleased you're here. It wouldn't be the same without you.'

Hattie smiled back at him and wondered if he really meant it.

'Where's Bee?' Mack asked.

'Just over there.'

No wonder that Mack hadn't recognised her. She had her back to him and her normally relaxed tresses were done up in a stiff chignon. When she turned around he saw that she was wearing a tight, corseted black dress and holding an apple. Her face was made up in pale colours with dramatic black eyeliner and a slash of red lipstick. 'The wicked witch from *Snow White*,' she explained as she came over. 'Doesn't everyone look marvellous? Milly has worked so hard.'

'You look fabulous.'

'I make a good witch, don't I?'

'Where's Tom?' Mack asked Bee.

'Have you two met? Gosh,' she said as Mack shook his head. 'How remiss of me. He's been here for such a while that I presumed you had.' She beckoned him over and Mack gripped his hand. Probably a little too hard.

'So nice to meet you,' he enthused, as Tom tried not to wince.

'You too, and many congratulations on your win. Can I get you a drink?'

'Thank you. Beer if there is one and champagne if I must.'

'Bee?'

'Champagne for me and beer only if I must.'

'Nice for Rafe to have Tom around,' said Mack awkwardly. Normally conversation came so easily to them but the presence of Tom made him slightly uneasy. He felt a bit of a gooseberry around them.

'Lovely.'

'I suppose you two know each other quite well?' Mack was aware that he was fishing but they seemed so easy together. Oh, who was he kidding? Certainly not himself. He knew perfectly well what Bee meant to him, he just didn't know what to do about it. Not with everything else that was going on.

Bee smiled. 'It's wonderful to have him back,' she enthused. 'I can't tell you how I missed both of them all those years they were away.'

Mack bit his lip. No, he couldn't possibly think about Bee and Tom right now. All he wanted was for Bee to be as wonderful as she ever was and he would think about her properly after the races. If Tom hadn't whisked her away by then, that is. He changed the subject.

'Beautiful place, isn't it?' he said as he took a moment to look around. They were on a large private estate in a dramatic house surrounded by a moat. Everywhere they looked were ice sculptures of the America's Cup filled to the brim with different fruits. Mack felt suddenly very proud to see that lining the walls were pictures of *Excalibur* from the various racing series. It was only at small, private moments like these that the full impact of their achievement hit him.

'I feel I haven't seen you for ages,' said Bee chattily.

'We'll have at least one more crew supper before the end, won't we?'

'Of course! God, how strange to hear you say "the end". I'll be very sad to leave here.'

'Me too.' They paused for a second. 'How's Salty?' asked Mack. 'I hate to admit it but I really have quite missed hauling him out of strange kitchens.'

'Salty is quite well. A little mad today but then he has been eating peanuts.'

'Aah, the peanut defence. A classic.'

Tom returned with their drinks. Bee gave him such a delighted smile that Mack excused himself as soon as it was polite to.

* * *

Two hours later the party was in full swing and they were sitting down to a lavish feast of stuffed courgette flowers over venison carpaccio and then snapper fillet with braised fennel and crayfish and caviar risotto. The tables were under a sheer crystal marquee so the guests could enjoy the fireworks raining down on them later without having to move. Excalibur and Phoenix were obviously the guests of honour and Custard was amazed to see the linen napkins had all been embroidered alternately with a picture of *Excalibur* and then *Phoenix*. Just like the Montagues and the Capulets which he had alluded to a lifetime ago, the room was split into two camps, with the supporters and friends of Phoenix to one side and Excalibur to the other. Custard anxiously looked over at Saffron. He hadn't seen her properly since that brief meeting in the Casa America's Cup where she had told him about Luter's involvement with the illegal boat allegations. He thought he would feel better for seeing her tonight but in actual fact it was absolutely killing him to see her sitting with Luter and the rest of the Phoenix syndicate.

Jason Bryant stopped by their table.

'Excalibur,' he drawled, his eyes lingering on Inky a little longer than was comfortable for the rest of the crew. 'I'm looking forward to meeting you all on the start line. Especially you,' he looked directly at Rafe. 'Personally I think you must have a little help calling the shifts, maybe an illegal radio?'

Mack rose slightly to his feet. 'What exactly are you saying, Bryant?'

'Just that I find it hard to believe the things they are saying.'

'You don't need to believe them, Bryant. You'll see it in action soon enough.'

'We'll be scanning all the frequencies just the same.' He nodded curtly at them and took his leave.

Custard kept disappearing, ostensibly to go to the loo, pausing in front of the Luter table in the hope that Saffron would be able to follow him out. On the fourth attempt she was able to slip away, and once out in the vast hallway he pulled her behind a pillar. Saffron was looking pale but delicately beautiful in a silver Dior gown, weaved with ribbon stretched tightly across her torso. His heart twisted with the ribbon.

'Thank God,' he said. 'The whole crew think I have a bladder infection.'

She smiled. 'I've missed you.'

'Things will be better when the racing starts,' whispered Custard. 'We'll be able to see more of each other.'

Saffron looked anxiously over her shoulder. It was amazing what risks you took for love.

'What happens after the racing?' she asked haltingly. Her eyes searched his. The question had been playing more and more on her mind as the two syndicates prepared to race. This time, one would win and one would lose. No second chances. *No habrá segundo*.

Custard faltered. He too had been thinking about their future. But how could he ask Saffron to leave *Corposant*, to leave the money, the clothes, the hair appointments, the luxury, to join him in an uncertain life – sailors never knew where their next job would lead them – with not much money (not much compared with Saffron's lifestyle certainly). He didn't even have a home to offer her. And what about Henry Luter? Custard could only imagine what his reaction would be. At the very least he'd probably try to ensure Custard never worked again. Then how would he earn enough money to keep them both? He had no other trade to fall back on. He had no fear of this himself, but he didn't feel he could put Saffron through it. After all, there was a reason (which seemed to stem from her childhood and was well buried, he knew) why she had married Henry Luter in the first place. She'd wanted the security of his money and position. She wanted to be looked after. He could do none of that.

'I don't know,' he said eventually. 'We'll figure something out. I promise.' Her eyes fell a little. 'It will take some time to pack up the bases afterwards. We'll have time.'

Saffron didn't like to say that if Henry lost then she knew they would leave Valencia immediately. It didn't seem fair to pressurise Custard with so much else going on. Besides it didn't look likely that Phoenix would lose. In the battle of the syndicate purses, Phoenix won hands down. No one particularly rated Excalibur's chances.

'Won't you tell me how you got hold of that information for the trial?' he asked again. 'I'm worried for you.'

Saffron shook her head and smiled. 'It was nothing.' She would never tell Custard what a risk she took to obtain that information.

'But isn't he furious?'

'He's certainly that.' Nor did she tell Custard that when Henry found out that the Excalibur allegations had fallen through, she had never seen such fury. She was truly scared for what she had done. He had embarked on an extensive mole hunt. If he ever found out that it was she who had betrayed him then he would put his hands around her neck and squeeze until she couldn't breathe any more.

But she knew she would do it again. Not only because she would do anything for Custard, especially after the lifeline he had thrown her over the last few months, but because what Henry was doing was immoral and wrong. Saffron had some scruples left. Henry couldn't eradicate them all. Her act was almost one of defiance. Henry hadn't broken her. No one had.

'Can you come and see me on Tuesday night?'

'But that's the night before your first race.'

'I know. So that will be the first night you'll be available.'

'I don't want to distract you.'

'Too late for that.'

Saffron closed her eyes. She was weak with love. 'Very well. I really have to go now.'

Custard reluctantly let go of her hand and watched her lithe, light figure as she ran across the hall. The light bounced off her hair. He knew he would have to do something soon. It was getting harder and harder to watch her go back.

Inky and Dougie sat together. Now that he was part of a winning crew, all manner of women seemed to be interested in him.

'What about her?' said Inky pointing out a stunning blonde in a short dress who had been shooting the whole of the *Excalibur* crew looks of longing all night.

'No.'

'Her?'

'No.'

'Her then?'

'No.'

'Dougie!' said Inky in exasperation. 'One minute you're gagging to go out with any girl and now you're getting picky.'

'I'm not sure I want to go out with a racer chaser.'

Pudding arrived, all in pink as a tribute to Excalibur as the official challenger of the Cup. Cherry jelly with a vincotto berry tart and rose-petal ice cream, accompanied by pink champagne.

Milly had noticed Fabian texting and then he tried to hide his mobile phone under his napkin when she returned from the loos.

'Who are you texting?' she asked, gesturing her head towards the phone. She wanted to make it quite clear that she wasn't fooled by him.

'No one.'

'No one?' she said lightly. 'It must be someone.'

'My mum.'

'Does your mum know how to text?' She stared at him defiantly. She wanted to have an almighty row. How dare he treat her so. Then, once again, she relented. She couldn't ruin tonight, after they had all worked so hard to get here. She bit her lip. Her scene could wait a few more days. Just a few more days.

The band started up for dancing. Inky dragged Mack on to the floor, leaving Bee looking rather wistful until Tom asked her to dance. Slowly everyone got up either to go to the bar or to dance, until Hattie was the only female left. Hattie took a gulp of champagne for consolation.

Rafe was about to ask Hattie if she would like to dance when there was a little tap on his shoulder. Ho, Sparky and the newly returned Custard went absolutely quiet. Rafe turned round to see Ava, looking fabulous in the very same Gucci dress which she wore when he first met her. 'Who are you supposed to be?' was all he could think to say.

'I don't know,' she said slightly mockingly. Typical of Ava not to actually bother coming as anything. 'Rumpelstiltskin? I just came over to say good luck. I'll be rooting for you.'

'You promised you would never wear that dress again,' he couldn't help remarking.

She looked puzzled. 'Did I?'

He looked at her and suddenly all he could see was a selfish, egocentric woman, whose beauty would last no longer than her promises. Suddenly she seemed insubstantial, overlaid in his mind by the image of Hattie. Hattie planning his birthday, loading her iPod for him, giving him the *Book of Winds*. Hattie standing in her too-big swimsuit and laughing in the sun. Hattie doing her best for everyone and not expecting anything in return. He was about to say that it didn't matter any more. None of it mattered any more when he saw a flash of red from the corner of his eye.

'Oh dear,' said Ava, watching Hattie trying to escape through the throng of people gathered on the dance floor. 'It would seem your little friend is upset.'

Rafe sprang up and set off after Hattie when Jason Bryant appeared before him, huge, powerful, overbearing. He poked him, his face bulging with fury. 'I want you to stay away from my girlfriend.'

'I'm trying to,' said Rafe and dodged round him. He could still see the brilliant red of Hattie's dress in front of him. She wasn't making much headway.

'Hattie! Wait!' called Rafe, desperately trying to push his way through.

'Well done, Excalibur!' someone called. Someone else patted him on the back. Everyone seemed intent on holding him back. He struggled on, feeling terrible. He had to get to Hattie. He pushed harder and eventually managed to grab hold of her elbow.

'Wait!' he repeated.

Hattie didn't look at him. 'Whatever you have to say, Rafe, I am simply not interested.'

'Hattie, it's just that—'

'Please don't patronise me. I'm not stupid. I know that you and Ava will be getting back together.'

'But—'

'I will happily handle all the press if that's what you want to ask me but only because—'

'Hattie,' said Rafe gently. 'Would you please shut up?'

At that she finally looked at him and opened her mouth to hurl a torrent of abuse at him but the next moment she was forced to shut up as he swiftly bent down to kiss her. He kissed her hard and she was aware of the whole world melting away.

She eventually surfaced and gasped, 'But I don't understand. You and Ava . . . ?'

'Me and Ava are nothing. She was just a mirage. An illusionist's trick. I'm sorry I took so long to realise it. She confused me. I just couldn't remember the reasons why I came to Valencia any more, which should have told me that I was actually over her.'

She looked up at him in pure, undiluted happiness. 'Do you want to go somewhere more private?' she asked, suddenly acutely aware that the whole of the America's Cup fraternity were surrounding them open-mouthed.

'No, I don't.'

'You know there'll be lots of gossip?'

'I know just the girl who will handle it for me.'

As his lips came down on hers Hattie caught a glimpse of Ava through the crowds. She looked as though her whole world had fallen down and was lying in pieces around her.

Chapter 50

The de-skirting of the boats was like Salome's dance of the seven veils.

This official unveiling of all the keels allowed every syndicate to look at each other's designs which had been so well hidden for most of the competition. All this technology was no use to anyone now (as soon as a boat crossed the final finish line, it all became obsolete) but it was a big occasion, well attended by the public. Everyone was particularly looking forward to *Excalibur*'s unveiling. She had been the mystery boat in this Cup and her performance had been extraordinary. Everyone was quite sure the key to this lay under her skirt.

Long before the appointed time, a crowd had gathered outside the Excalibur base and were yelling 'STRIP! STRIP! STRIP!' Inside the base, Mack, Sir Edward, Colin Montague, Hattie and various members of the design team were trying to decide how best to manage the press.

'It was your idea, Neville,' said one of the designers. 'You have to take all the credit.'

'I . . . I . . . I don't know if I want to.' Neville gulped nervously and looked pale. Hattie wasn't certain whether this was due to nerves or to his excesses at the ball.

'You were certainly the toast of the town last night,' commented another of the team rather nastily. 'I think you should take full responsibility.' It hadn't escaped their notice that Neville had spent most of the evening draped around different blondes and letting the full glamour of the Cup go to his head.

Hattie took matters into her own hands. 'I know that *Excalibur* is generally regarded as Neville's brainchild but I don't think he needs to feature in all this. I think we should just stick to the plan and have Colin make a short speech after the unveiling.'

Excalibur was waiting for them in her cradle, complete with full skirt, as they all walked out to the pontoon with the crew following behind them in uniform. Rafe managed to squeeze Hattie's hand as she walked past. She smiled at him gratefully.

'Custard, you're looking amazingly pristine,' whispered Inky. Custard's pink *Excalibur* shirt was freshly pressed, as were his beige chinos.

'Bee came and ironed them for me this morning. Please don't talk to me. It hurts to move anything in my head.'

'Did you sleep OK?'

'I dozed off occasionally between Alka Seltzers.'

The crowds had since been allowed in, with the press and photographers being given a separate area from which to view. Neville gave a small wave to some of his blondes who had turned up. 'That's the designer,' some of the press whispered to one another. They muttered within their groups that there was surely nothing new to be found, all parameters had been exhausted. But their designer was a new whizz kid, wasn't he, recruited fresh from design school before his thoughts could be tamed and schooled and before his eyes started to see boundaries. The buzz of anticipation grew.

There was a short ceremony, for most of which Custard kept his eyes closed, and then, to a great fanfare, Colin pulled a cord and *Excalibur*'s skirt dropped to the floor. People gasped and stared at the huge leaden keel weighing over twenty tonnes and painted with the Union flag.

It wasn't long before the yachting journalists who knew what they should be looking at started to look at each other too with slightly perplexed expressions. Neville tried to sidle behind one of the other designers. Slowly a small hum of chatter started up.

Colin Montague went forward to the small platform and microphone which Hattie had set up for him.

'Colin!' called one of the reporters. 'Can you tell us what exactly is different with the keel?'

Colin took a deep breath. 'There is nothing different about our keel.'

The hum of chatter became more insistent. 'But you were supposed to have a mystery keel!' called out someone else.

'We never actually *said* we had a mystery keel. I'm afraid people presumed.'

'What about your new young, brilliant designer?'

'It was actually Neville Stanley's idea. Quite ingenious, I think you'll agree . . . '

Hattie read the headlines the next day with one eye closed and the other only just open. 'EMPEROR'S NEW CLOTHES' one of them read.

The design team of *Excalibur* must be laughing today. The levels of security and extraordinary advancement of the crew through the stages led all to believe that their skirt hid an incredible design. But the unveiling of their secret weapon showed nothing more than a standard keel. The syndicate head, Colin Montague, admits that they did nothing to deter this belief which possibly gave them a psychological advantage over the other crews. Mr Montague said rather than spend their money on a revolutionary design, they spent it wisely on sail technology and making *Excalibur* as light as possible. 'The crew won the races, not the boat,' he said.

Hattie sighed with relief. When the press realised that it was they themselves who had perpetuated the rumour, most of them had taken it in good part. Some of them, however, still wanted to believe that there was some mystical power surrounding *Excalibur*'s success and were now citing Rafe Louvel as the source. Hattie's heart swelled slightly every time she read his name.

On and off the water the countdown had begun. Both the crews of *Excalibur* and *Phoenix* could be seen out on the water, day after day, slogging up and down an imaginary course for hour after hour, retesting sails and combinations, practising their starts and tactics. No one on the crew of *Excalibur* had time for anything else. They fell into bed after long hours at the end of the day, hoping for a dreamless sleep, but usually waking with a jolt at the sight of a black and orange boat crossing the line before them.

Since the hype for the last round had grown everyone was starting to become concerned about security around *Excalibur*. They became especially jumpy when for two consecutive practice days something had gone wrong with her. Once their boom had broken and then a chronic gear failure. Mack wasn't leaving anything to chance and got on the phone to the security firm. He changed all the security guards and then doubled them up. 'No one touches *Excalibur* without my permission,' he instructed them.

It was not only around *Excalibur* that extra security measures were being taken. After one of the shore crew had a very near miss with a car on a syndicate bicycle, Colin Montague suddenly decided that the bicycles were far too visible ('he means too pink,' said Fabian) for it to have been an accident and he didn't want any members of the crew riding them. They were thenceforth instructed to walk everywhere in pairs and not to let each other out of their sight. 'God, don't tell me you're going to make me come and buy underwear and other woman's things with you,' moaned Custard to Inky.

'I don't think you can talk. What are you going to do about meeting your racer chaser?'

'I'll think of something,' said Custard darkly.

* * *

The night before the first race, Mack sent everyone home early. All their families were out in Valencia and he wanted them to have a relaxing night at home. He stayed at the base and watched over the final preparations for *Excalibur*.

This was a difficult situation for Mack. For him the shore crew were an extended arm of the sailing crew so he hated to suggest that he didn't trust them. What else could he do? America's Cup yachts were precision instruments. The shore crew had to check over eight thousand winch components alone. Every single screw on the boat had a line painted on it which matched a line on the fitting so minute movements could be seen. Each of those must be checked.

Mack watched one of the shore crew being hoisted up the mast going over every inch whilst Ho's sewer was being washed down with fresh water. Someone would then put in a dehumidifier to make sure it was dry by the morning. The hull was being cleaned, sanded and repainted. 'And all of this happens twice a day, every day,' he murmured to himself. There didn't seem any way to take enough measures to stop any potential tampering.

Mack stood and looked up at the vast shape of *Excalibur* before him. Even though the secret of her keel was out, she was more alluring to him than ever before. Such extraordinary power combined with great beauty. Sir Edward came up beside him. 'I'll check it all personally when we're finished,' he said nodding towards the men who were swarming all over her like locusts. 'Why don't you go home and get some rest?'

'I can't rest.'

'You need to relax. Why don't you go and see what Bee is up to?'

Mack opened his mouth to say no, and then paused. 'Yes,' he said. 'Yes, I think I might do that.'

Bee was just popping a huge cake in the oven ready for visiting Excalibur families whilst crying over a baby elephant who had just died in the nature documentary she had been watching, oblivious to Salty and Pipgin licking out the mixing bowl.

She answered the door wiping away the tears with her apron.

'Am I disturbing . . . God, are you OK? What's happened?' Mack followed her through to the kitchen.

'Yes, I'm fine. A baby elephant has just died. David Attenborough said they thought it was dehydrated but it turned out to be really ill.'

'Bloody nature documentaries. What have I told you about these things?' He grabbed the remote control and turned the TV off. 'Don't watch them. Are you alone?'

'Yes. Why?'

Because I get to have you to myself, he thought. He didn't voice it but said instead, 'Just wondered. Where are Rafe and Tom?'

'Gone down to their boat to drink some beer.'

'But they are together?'

'Oh, yes. Is that OK?'

'I'm just worried about Rafe's safety. I wouldn't put anything beyond Henry Luter, especially now he's found out that there is nothing special about our keel design. He might realise how good Rafe and the rest of the crew are.'

'No, they are definitely together. Mind the grapes everywhere, Salty has developed a penchant for them. I popped to the loo in the middle of the night and about three of them squiggled between my toes. Would you like a drink?'

'What have you got?'

'I bought some of that beer you and Rafe seem so fond of.'

'Great. I'll get it. Do you want one?'

Bee glanced up at the clock whose hands were pointing well after seven. 'No, I'll have a gin and tonic please.'

Mack got out the ice which was next to several packets of tights and stockings and a bottle of vodka in the freezer and found a wizened old lemon in the fruit basket. He peered out of the window and then lowered a little pick-your-own basket

515

down into the garden which was the Excalibur system for telling anyone in the garden that they needed more oranges and lemons from the resident trees. Bee was attempting to wash up. 'No hot water.'

'I should think Custard has taken it all again.' Each floor shared a hot-water tank.

'He keeps on falling asleep in the bath. You don't think he'll drown, do you?'

'No, I don't. Leave that, we'll do it later. Come and sit on the balcony.'

Bee took off her apron to reveal a light embroidered linen skirt and top. Mack didn't like to mention the smudge of flour running across her forehead.

'Hot, isn't it?'

'Very.'

'When Sir Edward popped in this morning he said that Henry Luter's huge Phoenix balloon on the top of their building was shot down last night.'

'Yeah, I know. Good thing too. It was bloody irritating. He's slapped that emblem all over town. They keep putting stickers all over the cars, it's bugging everyone.'

'Well, I saw Dougie creeping in at midnight last night with a *flare gun*. Very furtive he was looking too.'

'Dougie? He shot the Phoenix balloon down with a flare gun? He could have set the whole compound on fire. I'm amazed we've made it to the final without one of them being arrested.'

They started to laugh. Bee decided not to tell him about the three jailbirds. Instead she looked at the creased face of the usually inscrutable man before her and thought how much she liked him.

'I was very pleased to hear about Rafe and Hattie,' he commented.

Bee beamed. 'I *know*. I'm thrilled. I have to stop myself from smiling at Rafe all the time, I think he's getting quite irritated with me.'

'I expected him and Hattie to be together tonight.'

'She wanted him to get an early night.'

'So he's gone to have a beer with his dad instead.'

'I know. Not quite the idea. I just think he needed to relax. It's easy with his dad.'

'Tom seems nice,' delved Mack, his voice thickening.

'Tom's great. It's been so wonderful to see him again. Have you eaten? Can I make you some food?' she asked. Mack shook his head. 'Would you like a piece of cake?'

'I thought you made that for the families?'

'Oh, I can always make another one. It's only an excuse for me to eat it anyway. Besides, who would complain about a slice being given to the great John MacGregor?'

'Not so great, more bloody knackered.'

When she went through to get him some cake, she found herself muttering all the way, 'Please don't let them lose, please don't let them lose, please don't let them lose . . .'

Chapter 51

'Well, the good news is that the prime minister can't come out to watch us . . .' Mack waved a congratulatory telegram in front of the crew. 'But the bad news is that most of our yacht club can.' Mack grinned. He'd actually managed to elicit a very grovelling apology from the chairman of the yacht club who had been so insistent last year that he throw Rafe off the team. It had given him an inordinate amount of pleasure. 'As you know the King of Spain will be riding in the eighteenth man position of *Phoenix* and Prince Andrew will be riding with us on *Excalibur*. So no fucking swearing.'

The *Excalibur* crew walked out on to their pontoon to scenes of mayhem. Hundred and hundreds of people lined the compound fence, pressing against the wire, their sheer weight buckling the perimeter fence. Armed guards, placed at intervals, were pushing them back. It was the biggest crowd they had ever seen. There was a roar when the crew finally appeared.

'You can do it, Excalibur!' someone yelled. 'Go and get that Luter bastard!'

'God, it's like we're going to war. It's like we're never coming back,' whispered Dougie who was quite green. 'I think I'm going to be sick.'

'Well, it won't look terribly good if you're sick here,' said Inky bossily. 'Come and be sick over the side.'

'Why is the crowd so big suddenly?' asked Custard in puzzlement.

It was actually due to all the good work which Hattie had been putting in, spreading the word back at home. People had flocked out to support their little patch of England called *Excalibur*.

Inky waved at their old favourites; the lady dressed in tweed was at the front as was the man with the bagpipes who was having difficulty playing with all the people round him. Inky pointed him out to Custard. 'God, do you remember at the start when there were so few people he could swing his bagpipes and not hit anyone?' she giggled.

Fabian surprised everyone by rushing to the fence. 'Oh my God, you're here!' he exclaimed. A well-dressed middle-aged couple were standing on the other side. It was Rob's parents. Fabian sobered suddenly as he realised that just because they were here didn't necessarily mean they'd forgiven him. He stood in front of them in his bright pink shirt and short blond hair looking rather dejected.

'Thanks for the postcards, Fabian,' said Mr Thornton stiffly.

'We just came to say good luck,' said Mrs Thornton. Her tone was more kindly.

Fabian smiled his brilliant smile. 'Thank you. Thank you very much.'

Colin Montague followed behind them wearing a new T-shirt which said UNDERDOGS TO SEADOGS and elicited a round of camera clicking. He waved graciously to the crowd. There weren't many people there who didn't feel a slight lump in their throat as the beautiful white phantom of *Excalibur* eased away from the docks. The British support boats were waiting out in the harbour, ready to follow *Excalibur* on her tow and as the crew cast off, they all sounded their foghorns in support.

With the security for the prince and all the extra press attention, the tow out to the race course seemed to take for ever. There were press boats, police escorts, the umpires, the committee boat. Small RIBs zoomed in and out of the traffic not to mention spectator boats of every size and description, from the towering presence of *Corposant* to a tiny fisherman's tug. On puffed this elite little band, up the canal and out to the open sea.

Out on the starting line more scenes of mayhem waited for them. As the crew emerged blinking into the sunlight, there seemed to be nothing but boats bobbing around on the surface and helicopters buzzing overhead.

Mack swung the crew into action quickly, giving them no time to get distracted. The tension on board *Excalibur* seemed explosive, which worried him. There were too many undercurrents. Some of the *Excalibur* crew knew the *Phoenix* crew from when Henry Luter had managed their challenge. Rafe wanted to take out Jason Bryant. Mack wanted to take out Henry Luter. And Ho just wanted to take out everyone. Even Custard seemed jumpy. By contrast the crew of *Phoenix* were in a bumptious mood. They were pumped up by the energy of the strongly Spanish crowd. 'Don't look at them,' ordered Mack. 'Let's just get *Excalibur* ready.'

The radio was buzzing with weather reports. 'The left-hand side is an absolute must-have,' buzzed Laura's voice over the radio. Mack looked at Rafe who had been looking at the sky, in particular a little cirrus streak; he nodded sharply in agreement with Laura. 'It's non-negotiable,' he said. He looked over to the committee boat which was flying the course flag. 'Course set,' he said. 'Ten minutes until the pre-start gun.'

With a few minutes to go an eerie silence pervaded the yacht. Everyone was still and watchful, as though in the trenches and waiting for the first sounds of enemy fire. Golly turned his winch slowly. The staccato clicking was the only sound on the yacht. Rafe watched the seconds tick down. 'Here we go,' he murmured.

The five-minute gun fired and Dougie instantly sheeted the genoa in hard. *Excalibur* leapt forward into the starting box, her bow jetting spray. *Phoenix*, menacing in black and orange, came thundering towards them but seemed uninterested in a close-up fight and she bore away before Mack could properly engage her, leading them a merry dance. It didn't feel as though *Excalibur* was hunting them down but more as though *Phoenix* was beckoning them on.

'What the hell are they playing at?' said Mack.

Time was ticking on and just as Mack was starting to judge his time on distance run into the start, *Phoenix* dived suddenly into the spectator fleet, taking a sharp turn around one of the coastguard boats. Inky hesitated for a millisecond – if they kept on their current course, *Phoenix* could come up behind them and herd them away from the left hand side of the start.

'Follow them,' she said.

Mack cut in closely by the coastguard's boat but just as he did one of the spectator boats, clearly getting panicky at being so close to the action, reversed back into the fleet closing the gap for *Excalibur* and Mack had to dodge round a whole group.

'FUCK IT!' he roared, oblivious to any royal presence.

'Kill time,' ordered Inky as they emerged from the fleet. 'If we take an extra circle, we'll give *Phoenix* the left-hand side of the line.'

'We're going to be dead in the water,' commented Rafe. They were having to go so slowly that *Excalibur* would have no momentum by the time they crossed the line.

Rafe started the vital countdown and eyed the start line nervously. Still twenty seconds to go and only a boat length from the line. 'Twenty . . . nineteen . . . '

In order to give them some momentum, Mack didn't order Custard to tighten the mainsail until the count hit twelve. Everyone was poised, almost frozen into their positions ready for action. 'Ten . . . nine . . . eight . . . ' 'We're too close, Mack. Head her up.' 'Seven . . . six . . . five . . . ' 'We're going to hit the fucking buoy,' cried Fabian. 'Head her down.' 'Four . . . three . . . two . . . ' 'We're over! We're over early!' The crew stared at each other in horror.

In the whole competition, Mack had never been early over the line. He had just oozed over the line in the last second.

'Sheet in the mainsail, Custard! Give me some speed!' cried Mack, furious with himself, as he prepared to circle the buoy for the start again. *Phoenix* crossed the line in front of them. On the left-hand side.

All on board the *Mucky Ducky* watched in absolute horror. This was a monumental setback. Everyone on *Phoenix* must be rejoicing. Colin and Sir Edward couldn't help but see a smug glance back from Henry Luter as *Phoenix* rocketed on ahead. Sir Edward looked down to see that he was clenching his fists so hard that his nails had drawn blood. Colin lay a hand on his shoulder. 'Mack will catch them up,' he said with more confidence than he felt.

Back on the water, a lesser crew would have been overwhelmed but all on *Excalibur* set their teeth and chased after *Phoenix*. Sammy's priceless monologue of information started up and it was business as usual. Rafe seemed completely unperturbed by the encounter.

'There's a header coming, Mack. We have the first knock. It's on five degrees.'

'Tack now!' said Inky.

They all looked towards *Phoenix*, expecting her to follow their tack and keep a loose cover on them. But Jason Bryant must have thought he could do better than Rafe because he declined to follow them, clearly looking for a shift still on the left and stayed on his original tack whilst *Excalibur* peeled away.

Sir Edward was peering through his binoculars at them whilst Colin was at the bar because he couldn't bear to watch. 'They're tacking away. Rafe must have found them some wind. *Phoenix* isn't following.'

'I just hope to God that they catch her,' murmured Colin into his glass.

Another painful few minutes passed before Sir Edward suddenly said, 'Would you look at that?'

'What?' said Colin spinning round and sprinting from the bar. 'What?' He snatched the binoculars from Sir Edward, nearly throttling him in the process, to focus on *Excalibur*.

'They caught their wind shift. That boy is a genius,' said Sir Edward and calmly disengaged himself from the binocular strap. '*Phoenix* should have followed them.'

He pushed Colin gently towards the languishing shape of *Phoenix*. It was as though someone from the English boat had gone over there, snatched away their breeze, popped it in their pocket and marched it back to *Excalibur*.

'Another header, Mack. Let's tack back and join *Phoenix*,' said Rafe.

The two boats were now headed on a collision course towards the top mark together. It was hard to tell who exactly was in front but *Excalibur* had caught up most of the distance she had lost. Closer and closer they converged.

'Standby to tack,' said Inky quietly, intending to take them to the mark with the right of way. Mack would have to slam the wheel around and park *Excalibur* next to *Phoenix* in a sort of giant skidding motion which would leave them running parallel up to the mark but give them right of way.

Fabian started to call the distance to *Phoenix*. 'Four boat lengths, Mack.'

'Ten point two, ten point two, ten point one . . . ' said Sammy.

'More boat speed if you want right of way,' said Inky.

'Custard!' yelled Mack.

'I heard!'

'Two boat lengths . . . '

'Ready to tack . . . '

'TACKING!' yelled Mack. He wrenched the boat hard round, Fabian hung on for dear life at the bow and *Excalibur* punched directly on top of *Phoenix* with her bow just edging ahead and rounded the mark first.

* * *

For the following legs the lead changed over eight times. Jason Bryant didn't make the same mistake again and refused to leave *Excalibur*'s side for the whole match which was infuriating. *Excalibur* was leading at the start of the last leg. 'We need to put some distance between us,' said Inky. 'They're faster than us downwind.'

Mack looked worriedly up at the spinnaker. 'Should we change it?'

'No, it's fine,' said Rafe.

But there was nothing they could do. *Phoenix* stole their wind and pulled up alongside them. The finish was one of the closest in Cup history. Everyone on board *Mucky Ducky* breathed in but *Phoenix* eased out her spinnaker gently at the last minute which meant she was across the line first.

No one could bear to look at the exalted faces of *Phoenix* and especially Henry Luter, who jumped up and down until he was puce in the face, punching his fist into the air. Mack broke out the protest flag regardless.

As soon as the crew was back at the dock, they all gathered in the common room to discuss protesting against *Phoenix*. Letting out your sails as you cross the line was strictly illegal. They waited for official tape of the incident which showed that *Phoenix* did indeed let out their spinnaker just before they crossed the line but also showed that their bow was a few inches in front of *Excalibur*'s when it happened.

There was no more discussion. They were 0–1 down.

Chapter 52

Custard had picked up a handful of stones from one of the palm pots outside Casa Fortuna and now nervously rattled them in his pocket. He said a cheery good evening to the security guards on duty at the super-yacht marina who recognised him and then walked on down the pontoon. *Corposant*, by far the largest of the super-yachts, sat in calm majesty at the end. Custard kept nervously looking over his shoulder, to see if anyone had been hiding behind one of the vast potted palms, which ran the length of the pontoon, to catch him out.

He had meant to be in bed by now. He had had supper with Bee and his parents, taken a shower and then got into bed and tried to listen to a relaxation tape which Hattie had given to everyone. No one was sleeping and because sleeping pills jigger the reactions, alternative sleeping techniques were having to be found. Unfortunately the only sleeping technique that worked for Custard was Saffron.

He had desperately tried to concentrate on fluffy white clouds and fields of wheat but the narrator's voice was annoying him and such was the extent of his longing that he found himself getting dressed and cycling down to the America's Cup village.

Tentatively he gently threw some pebbles at the window of Saffron's cabin. Luckily he knew the exact location of this room on *Corposant* since Saffron had often told him which window to look out for on the race course. The light was on and eventually, after the fifth stone, the curtain twitched and Saffron's pale face appeared at the window. Custard was craning his neck looking up at her.

After a second, she managed to get the window open.

'What are you doing?' she whispered down, unable to keep the delight out of her voice.

'I had to see you. Just for a few minutes. How can I get up?'

She looked anxiously over her shoulder. 'You can't!'

'I have to – please.'

'Oh God . . . walk along,' she hissed and pointed right. Shortly she appeared at the boat's railings and opened a little gate. 'I can't get the gangplank down, it will make too much noise. It's too dangerous to jump.'

Custard didn't answer. He backed up and made a running jump, grabbing on to the bottom railing, hanging there for a second before hauling himself up, hand over hand.

Saffron gasped, caught between horror and laughter. 'I can't believe you did that! You could have been killed.' She looked over the side, down into the gloomy waters, where, if Custard had fallen, he would have either been crushed by the boat or drowned underneath the pontoon.

'Come here.' He kissed her hard on the mouth and then she led him by the hand, round the corner, into the relative gloom of the stern of the boat. The night was heavy and lay on them like black velvet. The harbour was relatively enclosed and not even a breath of sea air ruffled the water's surface. The rich could pay even to keep the wind out.

'I thought we weren't going to see each other tonight?' she asked.

'I know. But I just couldn't sleep without seeing you.'

'I was just thinking about you when I heard the stones. I thought I was imagining things at first. How did you know that Henry wasn't here?'

'I peeked over the top of their compound fence on the way

down.' He grinned. 'I couldn't see him but I could hear him yelling at someone. Things getting stressful?'

'I've never seen him so stressed.'

Her face told a different story and Custard's grin faded. 'Is he taking it out on you?'

'A bit. The Coke tins are feeling it more than me. He lines them up at least ten times a day. They're exhausted,' she joked.

Custard hugged her tightly, knowing from the little she had told him that things must be getting bad.

'He constantly keeps his office door shut. I wonder sometimes whether he suspects me of giving that information to you.'

Custard looked worried, so she added hastily, 'I'm sure he doesn't though.' Because he would have killed me by now, she added silently to herself. 'How about you?' she asked, changing the subject. 'Still not sleeping?'

Custard made a face. 'Hattie is making us all drink that disgusting chamomile tea. She sits over us and none of us is allowed to leave the compound until we've drunk it, which is quite stressful in itself. Honestly, it tastes like weed killer.'

'Do you want a drink? Will that help you sleep?' Saffron gestured towards the small bar and, for the first time, Custard looked around him properly. He had never actually been on *Corposant* before. The stern of the boat had a bar built into the back of it and one enormous sofa spanned the width of the deck.

'Just a quick one. I don't want to stay long and put you at risk.'

'All the staff are in bed and Henry will be at least another hour. Please stay a little while. It's so wonderful to see you,' she begged.

Custard sat hesitantly down on the sofa as though he expected alarm bells to go off whilst Saffron went to the bar to get him a drink. She came back with two small brandies.

'So this is your home?'

Saffron opened her mouth to say, 'My prison,' but then closed it. She never wanted Custard to feel any pressure from her.

'Yes,' she said simply instead.

'A little shabby.'

'I know, but one tries one's best.'

They smiled at each other.

'You are all taking care, aren't you?' Saffron asked. 'I don't know what he might be capable of.'

'We're all taking extra care,' Custard reassured her. 'We have to go everywhere in pairs and we have security on at Casa Fortuna now. Don't worry, no one is going to hurt us. There would be too much publicity.'

'How are Rafe and Hattie getting on?' Saffron had been avidly following their romance.

'They're sweet. He carries her things for her.'

'Do you think they'll stay together?'

'I don't know. We're all under so much pressure at the moment, it's hard to say what will survive at the end of it . . . ' He trailed uncomfortably off, suddenly aware that he might be talking about their situation too.

Saffron, to cover the embarrassment, awkwardly lunged for her glass and on the way her charm bracelet caught Custard's glass. It rang out like the chime of the bell. Custard dived forward to stop it.

He looked over to Saffron who was watching him quizzically. 'Sorry. Old superstition of my grandfather.'

'What is it?'

'Nothing. It's nothing.'

'What is it?' she persisted.

'It's just an old superstition. It's nonsense. They say if a glass rings like that it sounds like the death knell they ring on a ship's bell. It brings bad luck and . . . '

'And?' Saffron prompted.

'Injury. Or death.'

The next day, the same crowd was present outside, albeit a little quieter and more watchful. Custard was distracted by the sight of a small figure in a hat and sunglasses who stood very quietly at the fence almost without moving. He instantly recognised her.

'Just be a second,' he called to the rest of the crew's backs. He hurried over to her.

'Saffron!' he whispered. 'What on earth are you doing here? Someone will recognise you.'

'Please don't go. Please don't race today.'

'Why on earth not?'

'I'm sorry but I had to come. I've been awake all night. I've got a bad feeling about today. I'm worried.'

'I'll be fine. Look, I've got to go.'

'Please, Will.'

'I have to race.' He touched her hand briefly through the wire and then hurried after his teammates.

Jason Bryant chose to helm *Phoenix* on the tow out and Inky saw him waving and nodding at all his supporters, absorbing their good wishes and the press attention. If the finish line had been painful yesterday then the press conference had been even more so with Jason determined to undermine and criticise Mack in any way. Mack looked so mad that Hattie was sure he was going to hit him.

Nobody on *Excalibur* wanted to helm her on the tow out and the lot often fell to either Custard or Fabian, both of whom seemed to have some sort of fascination for the spectator fleet, or Sir Edward. The rest of the crew had their unseemly race into the sewer. They all tried not to look at the handsome black and orange boat being towed in front of them, but the impression of her lay behind their eyelids as they lay on the sails below trying to will themselves into unconsciousness.

'What's up with Custard?'

Inky looked over to him, lying on his back just staring at the ceiling. She shrugged. 'Nerves, maybe.'

'He doesn't usually suffer though.'

'We're all starting to suffer.'

* * *

In the pre-start warm up with *Slayer*, Custard looked out for *Corposant*. For a while he didn't think she was coming but, possibly due to Saffron's pre-race movements, *Corposant* suddenly appeared at the back of the spectator fleet later than usual. He heaved a sigh of relief and got back to his preparations.

When the starting gun went, Saffron was sitting up at the bow of the boat, nervously clutching a drink which she hadn't touched yet. A small group of corporate clients were being royally entertained with champagne and canapés followed later by a sumptuous buffet. Henry Luter's personal assistant, Jane, on whom the burden of organising these little trips fell, was firing around making sure everyone was fed and watered. She had arranged for a live commentator, an ex-match racer himself, to explain the race as it went on. She was privately furious at Saffron Luter for making them late leaving the pontoon, but Saffron had explained that she was delayed because she was performing a personal errand for her husband, and hoped that she would never check up on it. The PA was quite sure this wasn't true as there couldn't possibly be anything that Henry Luter didn't make her do. But she smiled sweetly and said it wasn't a problem.

BANG! The commentator swung into action. 'And that's the pre-start gun which signals the competitors have to enter the start box from opposite sides. It's five minutes until the actual start. That's *Phoenix* on the left and *Excalibur* on the right. *Excalibur* will have the initial advantage because she is on a star-board tack and therefore has right of way. Whoaa!! That's a beautiful move by John MacGregor, the helmsman of *Excalibur*. He paused in the middle of his tack, forcing *Phoenix* to guess which way he was going to go – like a goalkeeper saving goals on a penalty shootout – and they guessed the wrong way. *Excalibur* has *Phoenix* pinned now and is trying to herd her away from the start line. John MacGregor is a master of these pre-starts. Just his very name strikes fear into the sturdiest hearts. Everyone wondered whether his crew would have enough expe-rience to pull off something like this but it's looking . . . ' He trailed off as Henry Luter's PA gave him a very stern look. She hadn't paid him an inordinate amount of money to give *Excalibur* any good press. She knew he shouldn't have had that glass of champagne.

The commentator hastily started again. 'But Jason Bryant, the enormously talented helmsman of *Phoenix*, learnt from the master himself so it is fascinating to watch master and student come head to head like this . . . '

Saffron listened to the commentator prattle on and gripped her glass convulsively. She really ought to be circulating and making everyone feel comfortable but she couldn't take her eyes off the boats. Eventually they were off the start line with *Excalibur* across first and steaming towards the first mark. She tried to relax. Surely they would be OK now.

'OH MY GOD!' the commentator yelled. 'It looks like there is trouble on board *Excalibur*! The crew are running up and down the boat. 'It looks . . . yes, it looks like something is wrong with the mainsail. That is one of the joys and anguishes of match racing. Something can always go wrong on these boats. They are sending someone up the mast. Who, I do not know. I can't quite see. It's not the bowman, I can still see his blond hair at the base of the mast. It must be one of the trimmers . . . '

Saffron rushed to the side of the boat and peered at *Excalibur*. Grabbing one of the pairs of binoculars which Jane had strategically placed around the sides of the boat, she looked again. He said it was a trimmer. It was Custard they were sending up. It must be. The commentator's voice filtered through again. 'And in fifteen knots of wind, it is a dangerous thing to be up that mast. At a giddy thirty metres above the deck, every movement on the deck is amplified up the mast into a stomach-churning swoop.'

Saffron couldn't quite make out the figure who was precariously being hauled to the very top of the one-hundred-foot mast but she pinned the binoculars on him. 'Please make it, please make it . . . ' she repeated to herself. There seemed to be a gust of wind and the figure must have lost his grip on the mast because he flew way out over the waves like a pendulum. He crashed back in with arms and legs braced and then flopped. There he hung, like a rag doll on a rope, tangled up and being smashed against the main sail.

There was a stunned silence on *Corposant*. The commentator was lost for words. Just as he opened his mouth to say something, a disjointed screaming started up and Saffron belatedly realised it was coming from her. She tried to close her mouth.

'Get some water,' said Jane sharply. 'She's fainted.'

Chapter 53

Excalibur lost the race. The injured crew member was taken by stretcher off the boat after Rafe heroically went to get him down. He had to free-climb the mast after the last sixty feet and he was the only one with enough experience to do it. Hattie found herself unconsciously echoing Saffron, 'Please make it, please make it,' as every eye was on the dark wind caller, the ones from *Phoenix* possibly quite hoping he would break his neck. When Rafe reached his crew mate, he found blood was gushing out of a wound on his head. He couldn't tell if he had broken any limbs but the main thing was that he was alive.

They paused to get him off the boat and then pushed on with the race but the delays and the fact that they still had a crippled mainsail meant they limped home, a full six minutes and thirty-six seconds after *Phoenix*. Mack thought Bryant and Luter's overexuberant celebrations were a little tasteless considering the circumstances they had just won under. *Excalibur* was towed back with a very subdued crew on board and that beautiful boat crawled into harbour like a bird with a broken wing.

The shore crew immediately started work on her whilst the crew made their way to the common room. They were free to go home but none of them wanted to be anywhere else.

A shocked set of families had greeted the crew when they had arrived back.

'God, how awful. I'm so sorry,' said Bee to Mack. 'Tim Jenkins has run his folks over to the hospital. What are you going to do now?'

'We'll wait.'

The crew filed silently into the common room, leaving the families all hanging around outside the hangar very unsure what to do with themselves. Milly peeped through the window of the common room. 'Shall I go in?' she asked Bee, who was with her.

'No. Leave them. They need to be by themselves. Just them.'

An hour later, Mack called the hospital for what seemed like the hundredth time. This time there was news.

'He's just regained consciousness. He has a large gash to the head which they've stitched up and they're sending him for a CAT scan but he's going to be all right. Dougie is going to be all right.'

Colin Montague had requested a lay day for the next day so the crew went about their normal business, waiting impatiently for their teammate to be discharged from hospital. At about half past one Dougie came into the makeshift canteen where everyone was still having lunch. They all crowded round him, absolutely thrilled to see him.

'Dougie!' yelled Custard who was the first to see him and had leapt up. 'How are you feeling?'

One by one they all came up to him. Inky gave him a huge hug and a kiss and then was immediately concerned she might have hurt him. 'No, I'm good,' he reassured her. 'The CAT scan was fine. Just a few bruises and this of course.' He pointed up at his head. They all had a good look. Half his head had been shaved so they could stitch the wound up properly.

'Looks nasty,' commented Fabian.

'It's OK. Bit of a headache. I think I must have hit one of the halyards on the mast when I swung back in.'

He saw Rafe standing reticently at the back and pushed forward to shake his hand. 'I heard you came to get me down. Thank you.'

'It was my privilege,' Rafe said. He meant it. 'Everyone volunteered but I was the best at free climbing.' He didn't say that the only thing which did frighten him was the prospect of what he might find. When he'd seen that Dougie, hanging by his harness, was unconscious but alive, the relief was indescribable.

For a while they just stood around, thrilled to be all back together. This feeling of solidarity took Rafe especially by surprise. He wouldn't have thought he would notice the absence of one crew member when there were seventeen of them but they had all been wandering about that morning feeling completely lost without the full contingent.

Carla, wiping her eyes, brought over a batch of her '*special English buns*'.

'I make for your return from hospital,' she said to Dougie.

'Gosh, Carla, thanks.'

'God help us, what's special about them?' whispered Custard to Inky. 'Do you think she's cooked them specially for an extra half an hour?' Despite his manner he said it very, very quietly because they were all inordinately fond of Carla.

Mack, hearing the commotion, had come in and was now adding his relief at seeing Dougie back amongst them.

'Do we race tomorrow?' asked Dougie. 'I'm fit enough.'

At 2–0 down, the crew were desperate to maintain some momentum. There was a palpable silence as all eyes turned to Mack. He had had a long discussion with Sir Edward and Colin Montague about this last night and they'd decided that if Dougie was fit enough to race, even if he would be fifty per cent less effective, then they would let him rather than risk the team solidarity by putting someone from the second crew on the boat.

'Colin Montague asked his physician to fly out last night. If he says you're fit enough then you can race.' There was a great cheer and slapping of backs. Mack raised his voice. 'Now you go back to Casa Fortuna and get some rest, Dougie. I'll send the doctor up there when he arrives.'

'I just have to do one thing before I go back.'

'What's that?'

'Go and get my head shaved properly. I look ridiculous with just one half done.'

Throughout the afternoon all of the crew disappeared one by one on a secret errand, only to reappear half an hour later without another word. Eventually Inky stood up with a sigh. Most of them were in the sail loft.

'Where are you going, Inky?' asked Custard who had just returned.

'Where do you think?'

'Inky, you don't have to. No one will think any worse of you.'

'I know I don't *have* to, Custard. But there's only us, isn't there? That's all there is to rely on. So I will all the same.'

Custard grinned at her and watched her disappearing back. Only then did he take his mobile phone out of his pocket and frown at it again for what felt like the millionth time. He hadn't heard from Saffron since yesterday and he was concerned. No messages, no texts, nothing. He was racking his brains how to get in contact with her. They had a rule that only she could initiate contact when it was safe and they had never been so long without it. He hoped nothing had happened to her.

Saffron woke fully dressed, lying on their bed, and then sat bolt upright. Henry was sitting in a chair opposite her, staring at her. He was fingering a mobile phone in his hand and her eyes darted to it.

'How long have you been there?' was all she could think to say.

'All night.'

There was a silence as she stared at him, suddenly absolutely petrified.

'Who's Will?' he asked quietly a few moments later.

After Saffron had fainted on *Corposant*, Jane had her carried

536

inside and sent for a private physician from shore. She instructed a member of staff to watch over her whilst she explained to the rest of the guests that Mrs Luter had found the racing rather harrowing, probably got *Phoenix* and *Excalibur* mixed up and was concerned that her husband might have been injured.

After they had all returned to shore and the guests had been safely seen off the boat, including the physician who visited Saffron, Jane hurried down to Saffron's cabin to search it thoroughly until she found the item she was looking for.

When a jubilant and gloating Henry had returned to the boat, she had grimly showed him the item she had found. A mobile phone full of messages.

'Who is he?' he'd asked grimly.

'I only have a number and a name. Will.'

'I hope he's enjoyed his life so far because I'm going to fucking kill him.'

'What do you want to do now?'

Henry Luter had thought for a second. 'I'll wait for her to wake up. I want the full story.'

He sat there the whole night. The doctor, finding Saffron almost hysterical, was insistent he gave her a sedative. It was what she dreaded most: to be so deeply asleep that someone could do anything to her without her knowing so she became more hysterical and the doctor promptly increased the dosage.

'Who is Will?' Henry repeated again.

'Will? I . . . I don't know.'

'You look different,' he commented. It was the first time he had noticed the slowly evolving miracle in front of his eyes. Despite her fear at the moment, he could see where her face had filled out as she had put on some weight; her eyes had gained some light and her skin some colour. He felt stupid for not noticing. Henry Luter did not like to be made to feel stupid. 'Who is he?' he repeated. 'Don't deny it any more. We found your phone.' He held it out. 'Went out and got yourself one, did you? How very enterprising. I have been reading the messages all night. Couldn't face getting rid of them, I suppose? All very intimate. The man supposes himself in love with you. Well, you duped him well and truly. How could anyone fall in love with you?'

'Don't,' she said quickly.

He rose from the chair. 'Don't? Don't what? You're a lying, thieving little bitch.'

'I . . . I haven't stolen . . . ' Had he found out about the Frenchman?

'Haven't stolen? You steal all of this.' He waved his hand around the ornate cabin. 'Every day you are here. This is not yours, this is mine.'

She said with relief, 'I don't want it.'

'Only want lover boy?' he said sneeringly. 'Well, too bad, because you belong to me. How long have you known him?'

'Not long.'

'HOW LONG?' he yelled at her.

'A few months.'

He shoved the phone at her. 'Call him. Call him and tell him it's off.'

'I won't.'

His voice lowered down to a more threatening pitch. 'Saffron, I know things about you,' he said softly, almost beguilingly.

Saffron's head started to swim. 'H . . . h . . . how do you mean?'

'Did you really think I would marry someone whom I knew absolutely nothing about? I used private investigators. I know all about your dirty little secret. I know why the doors are always locked. I know what he used to do to you. Your father. Did you enjoy it? Did you ask for it?'

Saffron closed her eyes.

'You haven't told him, have you?' His voice was gloating. He was enjoying this. 'Dear Will won't want to know you when he finds out. He won't want to touch you. You're damaged goods.'

'You'd tell him?'

'Not just him. I'll tell the whole world. I'll tell them how I

538

rescued you from a life of abuse. You stay here with me. You belong to me.'

'You can't make me,' said Saffron in a trembling voice. She sounded braver than she felt.

'Oh, can't I? The doctor who just left – I'm sure he would be interested in some long-term private business. Maybe you're getting into such a nervous state that more sedation would be the answer. And I don't think you want to be sedated, do you? Who can say what can happen to you when you're half groggy with sleep?'

'NO!'

'Then call him.'

She stared at him, her eyes wide with fright and her mind racing. She knew what Henry was capable of with her, but what about Custard? Henry would kill him. She couldn't betray him. 'No.'

'Saffron, I have a name and a mobile phone number. I can trace him with the same investigators I used on you. If you want him to live and the little matter of your father to remain between ourselves, call him and tell him it's all off. That you want to stay with your husband. That I can give you things he can't. After all, Saffron, if you leave me, then where are you going to go? He won't want you. He won't want you and your disgusting little secret. He would recoil every time he laid a hand on you.'

He was holding the mobile phone out to her and she looked at it hesitantly. The next moment he had swung his arm and smashed her round the head with it.

She tripped and crashed down on to the bed. A warm trickle of blood fell down her temple. She was so petrified that she couldn't think. She desperately tried to force her brain to work. Henry would hurt Custard, she knew that. Maybe it would be better for Custard to think that she had just decided to call it off and think of her fondly occasionally rather than be revolted by her. She would make the call to placate Henry and then think about what to do later. She sat up groggily. 'I'll call him, I'll call him,' she said, starting to sob as he came towards her again. But this time only possession was on his mind.

Chapter 54

The crowd fell silent with wonder as the crew filed out the next day. Every single one of them had had their head shaved. All eyes whipped to Inky the minute she appeared at the back of the crew. She was wearing a bandanna. She had meant to take it off just before they left the docks but she'd forgotten about this crowd. She whipped it off quickly to reveal a completely shaven head and kept her eyes down. Dougie could hear her muttering behind him and thought for a moment that she was praying until he could just make out the mantra. 'It will grow, it will grow, it will grow.' He dropped back and put his arm round her. 'You've still got gorgeous legs,' he whispered. She gave his arm a grateful squeeze. A slow clap started up from the crowd.

Yesterday they had all trooped out one by one to get their heads shaved at the local barber without even mentioning it and Inky knew that, for the sake of the team, she would have to as well. Even Mack had walked in, seen everyone with their new haircut, said 'Oh bugger,' very loudly and then disappeared himself. Outwardly Inky had shown no reaction to her new appearance but when she got back to Casa Fortuna that night, she cried even harder than the day, over ten years ago, when she had decided that match racers didn't have long hair and she should have it cut short. Her mother was so alarmed with her hysterics that she ran downstairs to get some help from Bee, who was absolutely speechless when she saw her. But then the two of them rallied and sat on the bed to dole out the sort of comfort that only two mothers were capable of. First thing in the morning, Bee ran out to buy a bandanna and Mary went to the largest department store and bought the most beautiful La Perla bra that she could find, which Inky was now wearing underneath her Excalibur T-shirt. It was all cobwebbed black lace and turquoise ribbons and made Inky feel inordinately better.

Since one early-bird journalist had spotted them as they arrived at the base that morning, Hattie had most of the female journalists in Valencia squawking down the phone to her about the crew's new look. They were especially interested in Fabian and Rafe – generally considered the two most handsome crew members – and whilst Hattie felt confident enough to comment on Rafe, she didn't really know what to say about Fabian's reaction.

He'd certainly elicited one from Milly and Rosie. Rosie had stared at him with her big, blue eyes and then burst into tears. Fabian picked her up and hugged her whilst looking over her shoulder at Milly and explaining. He waited for her reaction; she looked at him for a second and then nodded slightly and got on with clearing the tea things. He looked strange without his trademark blond hair and whilst he wasn't particularly vain he was used to generating attention, particularly of the female variety. Milly wondered what Daphne would think about it and if she had already seen it.

Inky was so ensconced in her own problems that morning that she didn't notice Custard wasn't his usual self. He was very withdrawn and everyone missed the usual jokes as they pulled away from the docks but simply put it down to nerves. After all, as Mack had said earlier at the crew meeting, 'We lost yesterday. I didn't like it. Let's not do it again. We *have* to put a score on the board today.' He didn't mention the fact (although most of the crew probably knew it) that no one had ever come back from a 0–3 position in an America's Cup.

Custard elected to stay out on deck today for the tow and

ignored the usual unsightly tumble into the sewer and fight over the best sails to sleep on. Anyone watching him would have noticed that he held a mobile phone and kept staring at it as though willing it to ring, or kept watching the spectator fleet where *Corposant* was noticeably absent. Yet *Corposant* was always out to watch the racing. Something was wrong. Custard simply didn't understand. Saffron had called him yesterday.

'I don't want to see you again,' were her opening words.

'Why?' he managed to stammer out.

'I want to stay with Henry . . . He has more to offer me.'

'Meet me,' he urged. 'Let's talk about it.'

'No! Just accept it, Will. I don't want to see you again.'

'Please, Saffron. You can't just—'

Fear made her vicious. 'Yes. I can. You have nothing to give me. Don't even try to call me.' The phone went dead.

He stayed awake all night. He had no idea what to do. None of it had rung true – and yet neither of them had ever spoken of the future. He simply couldn't think beyond the America's Cup – but as he lay in his bed that night, all he knew was that he couldn't live without her. It wasn't just her beauty, it was the million and other things that he loved. He loved her interest in all the other members of the crew. She wanted to know all about them. And as he talked, she would match all his clean socks together, which never made it back into the sock drawer, or brush Pipgin until his coat shone. He would often find that she had made him a sandwich and left it in the fridge whilst he'd been in the shower. The other day she admitted that she longed to take up knitting, which made him smile for ages after she had left. To think of this stunning girl bent over a pair of knitting needles! She never talked about her life with Henry in poor-me terms but he had pieced an awful lot together and admired her bravery when she returned. But maybe she needed the security of Henry's money more than he knew. There was a reason that a woman like that married Henry Luter in the first place. He had begun to hope that it was something they could sort out together but maybe he was being naïve.

As he sat, lost in his thoughts, the world's press snapped away at the one, lone *Excalibur* sailor, sitting on deck and surrounded by his habitual seagulls.

The starting gun fired and *Excalibur*, snarling with aggression, pushed forward into battle. The crew made a formidable sight with their shaven heads. They were so wound up that for one ridiculous moment Mack wondered if any of them would actually try to board *Phoenix* like pirates. After a couple of circles, Mack got on to an unnerved Jason Bryant's tail and as Bryant led the way into the spectator fleet ('A trick I taught you, you arrogant little prick,' muttered Mack) he took a turn too tight and clipped the side of a spectator boat as he went round it.

Mack chased him back out on to open water and proceeded to mercilessly drive him away from the starting line.

'Rafe, do you still think the right-hand side to start?'

'Definitely.'

'Today, it's ours.'

He zealously shoved *Phoenix* away. He never gave her an inch. At forty seconds before the start, Mack broke for the line. *Phoenix* crossed seventeen seconds behind him.

The commentator on the press boat was having a dreadful time trying to identify any of the *Excalibur* crew, even Inky. Dougie, by virtue of his gash, was the only one they could pick out. Luckily the crew didn't struggle at all. Just as you can pick out your lover blindfolded, they could tell immediately from the shape of the shoulders and the particular way they moved even if they were at the far end of the boat with their backs turned. The commentator stopped squinting at different team members and got on with his job. '*Phoenix* seemed wrong-footed at every turn today. Everyone is delighted to see the port trimmer of *Excalibur*, Dougie, back in action even though his head must be still very sore. But I think it is their team cohesion that is upsetting *Phoenix*. Not only do they look extremely menacing with their shaven heads but it is that show of unanimity which is the strongest message. It says you will not break this crew. Even John MacGregor and Inky Pencarrow have followed suit.'

There was no doubt that Henry Luter's investment of millions had paid off in terms of superior boat speed and on that first leg *Phoenix* had all but regained the distance. They were barely a boat length behind after rounding the first mark. After a perfect set, *Excalibur*'s white spinnaker clouded into the sky; her crew were starting to display that combination of nerve and aggression which spelt out confidence. Mack could see that *Phoenix*'s trimmers preferred different sail shapes to Custard. Their sails were fuller whereas Custard's were more angular and flatter.

Custard read his mind. 'Like I prefer my women, Mack,' he yelled briefly, thinking of Saffron.

The sea was short and choppy today and with a strange feel about it which kept Rafe's eyes pinned to the waves. *Phoenix* was hunting them down, attempting to place them in their wind shadow, in fact they were so concerned about the boat in front that their afterguard had failed to notice a vital detail behind. Rafe saw it first and murmured to Mack, 'There's a surfing wave coming up. *Phoenix* hasn't seen it.'

Mack looked back. A surfing wave would lift them a few vital boat lengths in front.

'Tell me when to gybe.' Mack didn't need to say anything more than that. He had to gybe at exactly the right moment, forcing *Phoenix* to gybe in order to keep *Excalibur* in their wind shadow and thereby missing the full force of the wave.

Phoenix was hot on their tail now, within seconds of punching all the wind from their sails; already the trimmers could feel the slight slack in the sails as their air supply was beginning to be cut off.

'Gybe now,' said Rafe quietly.

'GYBE!' Mack yelled out.

Immediately Fabian swung along the spinnaker pole, hanging upside down like a monkey, and punched out the pin, before dropping back on the deck and moving the pole the other side of the spinnaker and clipping the sail back on.

'SET!' he yelled as he reset the pole.

Back on *Phoenix*, Jason Bryant smiled to himself. 'GYBE!' he yelled to his crew. 'Can't escape me that easily, Mack.'

But just as his bowman had reset the pole, Mack swung back through another gybe. Jason Bryant was just about to follow Mack when he felt *Phoenix* lift up on a surfing wave. 'What the fuck . . . ?' he glanced over his shoulder in confusion. But *Phoenix* was angled completely wrong and after surfing for a second the wave rolled on underneath them and lifted *Excalibur* a clear two boat lengths in front and out of the threat of *Phoenix*'s wind shadow.

'Didn't you see it?' Jason Bryant yelled at Henry Luter in exasperation. It was Jason's job only to drive the boat. Had it been anyone else, he would been spitting expletives.

'Don't fucking talk to me like that, I thought they were watching *us*, not the wave,' Luter said sharply, annoyed at being questioned.

'Shame Jason missed that wave. I taught him that too but he clearly wasn't listening,' Mack commented to Inky.

'Maybe he took more notice this time.' They smiled at each other.

Excalibur rounded the mark ahead.

'They're faster down these legs,' said Inky to Mack. 'We're going to have to duel to keep them from passing unless Rafe can see some wind.'

Rafe was watching a wind shift travelling across the water, darkening the surface like a rain cloud. 'A lift is coming but let *Phoenix* take it. There is better wind coming to the left.'

Inky looked over, alarmed. 'You mean, let them pass?'

'Let them pass. Then we can dodge over to the left and take the other shift. It's bigger.'

Inky gritted her teeth and as *Phoenix* called a dummy tack she pretended not to see them and *Excalibur* tacked over to the left whilst they stayed on the right and took the shift. Immediately *Phoenix* overtook *Excalibur* and pulled briefly alongside her.

'Women drivers!' one of the *Phoenix* crew yelled. 'Did your brain cells go with your hair?'

Inky bit the inside of her lip so hard that she could taste blood. That idiot must have left his behind because she had proved herself time and time again. *Excalibur* peeled off to the left whilst *Phoenix* seemingly sped on ahead. Rafe was absolutely unaffected by the encounter, his eyes firmly focused on the oncoming shift. 'Lift is coming in nine . . . eight . . . seven . . . '

Inky felt as though her blood was boiling but she had to admit she felt a lot better when she saw the astonishment on their faces as they reconverged at the mark with *Excalibur* a decisive five boat lengths in front. 'Men drivers,' she remarked looking back over her shoulder. 'Fucking useless. Never can judge a distance.'

Phoenix never recovered. To the jubilant blaring of horns from the British spectator boats, they slid across the finish line, nine seconds in front of *Phoenix*.

'And that,' Mack remarked to no one in particular, 'is how it's done.'

Chapter 55

They returned to shore with the chanting of a five thousand-strong crowd. 'EX-CAL-I-BUR! EX-CAL-I-BUR! EX-CAL-I-BUR!' ringing in their ears. It was the most magical sound any of them had ever heard.

Hattie bustled them all off for the customary press conference where the questions kicked off inevitably about the crew's shaven heads. Custard wasn't usually involved in this question time as Hattie considered it best that he be left out. He was utterly absorbed in worrying about Saffron anyway. He scanned the crowd for her anxiously but couldn't see any sight of her pale, beautiful face. He was convinced something was wrong. Maybe he could try and visit *Corposant* again tonight and see her. He positioned himself so he could stare at Henry Luter, desperate for some sort of clue to her whereabouts.

Henry Luter glanced over and Custard hastily looked away, only to look back a second later. Henry Luter's curiosity was piqued and he started to think. That's the man they call Custard. He was with me in Auckland. What was his real name? Stanmore, of course. Will Stanmore. It was only when Custard took a step forward to put himself out of view that Luter realised. Will. Of course. It was a piece of information that his private detective was a mere few hours from discovering anyway.

*   *   *

As soon as the press conference was over, Custard pushed his way through the crowds of people. He glanced briefly back towards Luter. But as the head of the syndicate he would have further interviews to deal with. As soon as he was free, he ran down towards the super-yacht marina. He didn't like the look in Henry Luter's eyes.

'Saffron!' he yelled as soon as he reached the yacht. 'SAFFRON! WHERE ARE YOU? SAFFRON!'

Eventually one of the staff popped an annoyed head out. 'What do you want?'

'I need to see Saffron Luter. I need to see her now.'

'Is it urgent? Mr Luter left instructions that she wasn't to be disturbed.'

'It's more than urgent, mate. Get her now.'

Custard's desperate tone convinced the man that there might have been an accident. He disappeared. Custard looked nervously up the pontoon. Within minutes, Saffron appeared on the top deck. She looked pale and wan. Custard could see a purple bruise on her temple. He came to the top of the gangplank.

'What are you doing here?'

'I've come to get you. Come with me.'

Saffron hesitated. 'I can't.'

'He's found out, hasn't he? Come with me. Now. Just walk away.'

'I can't,' she repeated helplessly.

'Whatever he has threatened you with, Saffron, we'll sort it out. I promise. I'm not afraid of him.'

Saffron wavered. Her hair was pulled back tightly, emphasising the paleness and lucidity of her skin. The blackness of the bruise stood out in a stark contrast. Her beauty had been a trophy to Luter and it was at his hand that it had been defaced.

But that was something Custard didn't see. He could only see Saffron was frightened and needed looking after. 'I'm afraid of him,' she whispered.

'You don't need to be. I'll be with you.'

She looked at him and knew that she needed to make a huge leap of faith. Did she trust him enough with her past to give him her future?

It was as though Custard read her thoughts. 'I know there is something you're not telling me and I promise that whatever it is, it'll be OK. We'll be OK. I promise.' He held his hand out to her. His eyes held hers, and the strength in them gave her courage. It would be OK. *They* would be OK. He had said so.

She stepped forward.

When Henry Luter found out that Saffron had simply walked off *Corposant*, his fury nearly blinded him. He just couldn't understand it. He always covered off every exit route for his adversaries. But there was one factor that he hadn't actually built into the situation. He hadn't realised that Custard truly loved her.

Custard couldn't get much out of Saffron on the way back to Casa Fortuna and presumed that she was slightly in shock. Once they reached his flat he went to hug her but she shied away from his touch. Puzzled, Custard led her to her favourite armchair and pulled a chair close to her, putting two hands either side of her face and anxiously examining her. He nodded at the bruise and cut where Henry had hit her with the mobile.

'Did he do that?' he asked.

She nodded.

'Anything else?'

Saffron hesitated and then shook her head. She couldn't tell him.

'How did he find out? He did find out, didn't he?'

Saffron nodded and then explained ' . . . and then he found my mobile phone. He said . . . he said he'd kill you and made me call you.'

Saffron dropped her head and when Custard went to take her hand she pulled it away. 'Is there something else?' he asked gently.

Tears started down her face and fell gently on her knee.

'Tell me,' he said.

She shook her head. 'No, Will. I can't tell you. I'm going to take a shower.' She got up abruptly and went to the bathroom, locking the door behind her. She leant her head back against the door, letting the tears soak her neck and hair. She couldn't bear to take any of Will's love even though it was the only thing she wanted. Henry would tell the world about her and then Will wouldn't even be able to look in her direction.

Feeling bemused and in need of some advice, Custard went upstairs to see Mack. The skipper could fix anything.

'So let me get this straight . . . ' said Mack an incredulous twenty minutes later. 'You and Saffron Luter were having an affair, you thought Henry Luter had found out and so you boarded his boat, demanded that his wife return with you and she's in your apartment right now.'

'That's right.'

'Could we ship her back before he notices she's gone?' he asked weakly.

'Mack, this is no laughing matter.'

'Oh, I'm not laughing. Believe me, I'm not. Dear God, boy, you have fucking awful timing, you know that, don't you?' Mack stared at him intently for a second. 'You love her, don't you?'

'Yes. Yes, I do.'

'If this comes out, that one of the *Excalibur* crew has been shagging his wife – pardon the expression – then the press coverage will be enormous and he will be made to look an utter fool, which is something he will absolutely hate . . . You'd better bring her up here,' said Mack. 'If Henry Luter knows who you are then he'll certainly know where you live. I only hope you know who you've made an enemy of.' If he wasn't determined before, then Henry Luter would do everything in his power to crush *Excalibur* now. It wasn't simply a matter of the Cup any more. It was personal.

*   *   *

Saffron was out of the shower and wrapped in a towel when Custard got back. Custard had collected Pipgin on the way down and he was noisily glad to see her.

'Darling!' he said, walking straight over to her. 'Are you feeling better?'

She nodded. She had made up her mind that she simply had to tell him. He hadn't let her down so far, had he? She clung to that fact and had chanted it to herself in the shower.

'Please tell me.'

'You'll hate me.'

'I promise I won't. Whatever it is.'

'When I was young . . . ' She hung her head slightly. The words were difficult to say. Custard took hold of her hand and squeezed tightly. 'My father,' she mumbled.

'Yes?' whispered Custard.

'My father used to touch me. Sometimes more than that. He used to come into my bedroom when he was drunk, and . . . Abuse is the official term.' Her eyes were brimming with tears. Custard scooped her into a tight hug and buried his face into her hair. He felt appalled. Appalled that she obviously thought it was somehow her fault, appalled that she could have thought he would love her any less. Not much could disturb Custard's usual sangfroid but this shook him to his roots.

'Henry is going to tell everyone. He said if I left him he would make sure the whole world knew,' she haltingly continued. 'You might not want to stand by me. It will be awful for you.'

'Do you honestly think I care about that? The only thing which would be awful for me is to have a life without you. I was wishing I'd insisted you left him before all this. It was just getting harder and harder to ask you to leave all the money. You know, the clothes, jewellery, the hair and beauty appointments . . . '

'I do it because it's expected of me,' said Saffron quickly. 'It doesn't mean anything.'

'Did you tell Luter about your father?'

'He found out. He put private detectives on to me.'

'And you married Henry to get away from your father?'

Saffron nodded. 'I thought Henry was an escape route. With his money, nothing would be able to touch me and I would never have to set eyes on my home town again. But I just swapped one controlling man for another.' She laughed, but there was a catch in her voice. 'Classic mistake.'

'I can't offer you money but Pipgin and I can give you lots of other things if you'll have us. Babies too if you want them.'

Saffron laughed and wiped her tears away. 'I would like that. I don't think I'm going to take showers any more. Only baths.'

'Baths?' said Custard slightly puzzled.

'That's right. Only baths.'

'OK, my love. I will make sure there are only baths. Marble ones, if you will.'

Saffron laughed. After the burden of the last few days, she felt light enough to float.

He held her tight. 'I can't believe that I'm never going to have to let you go again. I must be the luckiest man alive,' he whispered into her hair. He suddenly pulled away from her and looked at her. 'Could you start wearing your hair down? I hate it up.'

Saffron started to pull out the pins which held it.

'What have you done to yours, by the way?' she said looking at his bald head.

'Darling, I didn't wish to upstage you. Looks awful, doesn't it? My head is so white I look like I'm wearing a skullcap.'

Through her laughter and tears, he kissed her. Saffron closed her eyes and sank into his embrace. He held her tight, but she felt safe, not suffocated. All he knew was that he never wanted anything to hurt her again.

Saffron, Custard and Pipgin appeared together the next day for the racing. Mack had warned the crew (Sir Edward was so amazed that he kept saying 'Saffron Luter?' very loudly and tweaking his ears just in case he had misheard the name) but the common room still went completely quiet as they entered. No one knew what to say. They had all been so united and now they learnt that one of them had been having an affair with the enemy. It felt as though they, as the crew, had been cheated on. Custard looked from one member to another for some support. No one would look at him; each of them turned away. Even Inky didn't know what to say. Custard wasn't about to try and placate them by telling them that Saffron was the one who saved them with her information about the French hydrodynamics man. The silence stretched out, until mercifully Carla came bustling over. 'You must come out with Bee and me on the *Mucky Ducky* today. Help with the serving,' she said firmly to Saffron, planting her hands on her hips.

'Th . . . thank you,' stuttered Saffron. 'That would be nice.'

'Come now,' she held out a hand. 'The crew must prepare to race. You safe with me.'

Custard, who felt as though he had TRAITOR emblazoned across his forehead gave Carla a grateful smile as she led Saffron away. But the damage was done.

The crew work was sloppy and communication was bad. They lost. They were 3–1 down and the smell of defeat was in the air.

Saffron had stayed behind at the syndicate to help Carla and Bee clear up but at the press conference after the race the air was still filled with tension and animosity. Hattie had a distinct impression of wild animals all locked into a room together. The press all thought that they were watching a crew in their death throes.

Henry Luter was poisonous in his victory. He didn't even cast a look at Custard as he danced into the room, to make the point that he didn't care that his wife had left him.

'Tell us about the race today?' was the first question.

'We won. I don't know what happened to their so-called wind

caller with his supposed spooky premonitions . . . ' He made little ghost noises to the shouts of laughter from his supporters. Hattie gripped her pen convulsively, quite wishing that she could stab it through his heart. 'But we made perfect weather calls, I got our tactics absolutely spot on and we out-sailed them with greater speed and better tacking. I think *Excalibur* and her crew have had their day.'

'Those shaven heads didn't overawe you like the last race?'

'They didn't even then. They got lucky in the last race, that's all. Shaving their heads was some sort of childish trick because they were obviously getting desperate . . . '

'At least ours will grow back!' yelled a voice from the back of Excalibur. The reporters laughed. Mack thought it must be either Golly or Dougie.

'And now,' continued Luter, 'they're resorting to petty insults because they can't take losing to the better crew.' He made the mistake of smugly looking over to the crew of *Excalibur* and staring straight into the infuriated eyes of Custard. The frustration of the day, guilt at the loss and the crew's reaction to him and Saffron, and his fury at what Luter had done to her all came bubbling over.

Custard stood up so violently that his chair flew backwards. 'COME ON THEN!' he roared, striding towards him. He bent low over the table which Luter had sat behind. 'I know this is all about you and me. Don't take it out on my crew. So do you want to fucking tell everyone what this is all really about or shall I?' He spat out the words in a low voice which quivered with menace. The surrounding microphones picked up every word and they resonated around the room.

The silence which followed was heavy with apprehension. Everyone held their breath. No one apart from Excalibur knew what Custard was talking about.

Although Luter stared back at him, he resolutely shut his mouth and Custard knew at that moment that he would never breathe a word about Saffron and her past. He cared too much about his reputation on the sailing circuit. He would protect himself and his very delicate ego. The press would never find out what that particular exchange meant.

Inky came up slowly behind Custard and put a hand on his arm, gently pulling him away and towards the exit. One by one, the crew got up and followed them.

Back at the base, no one breathed a word about what had just happened but all of the crew came over to say hello and meet Saffron properly. Inky immediately offered to lend Saffron some clothes for the next few days until she could go out and buy some. 'Thanks, Inky,' Custard muttered.

'Well, she has to have some clothes,' stated Inky.

'I don't mean thanks for the clothes.'

Carla came in. 'Saffron is too thin,' she announced to them all. 'I insist that she have hot chocolate and one of my special buns. You like it, yes?' she said to Saffron.

There was a silence as the crew waited for her reaction. 'Yes, very much,' Saffron said. 'It was delicious,' she added bravely.

Bee made some excuse why the crew supper had to be held that evening and not wait until Thursday. The excuse was terribly lame but everyone pretended to believe it because they were privately relieved that they could spend the night together and properly regroup. Being at 3–1 down, tomorrow might be the last race they would ever sail together. The thought hung consciously in the air but no one mentioned it. Because of Saffron and Custard, Sir Edward had increased security measures at the base. No one could fail to notice a stranger sweeping for bugs or that *Mucky Ducky* was having emergency repairs performed on her because she was having unexpected engine trouble. Colin had even ordered a complete sweep of *Excalibur*'s part of the harbour (and found several plastic bags suspended on fishing lines in the hope they might wrap themselves round a keel or propeller). Everyone was trying to take their minds off it by gossiping about Custard and Saffron.

Mack had invited Hattie along so he could talk over the implications of any press coverage if any of this story were to leak out. Hattie closed her eyes as the headlines crowded into her head (WIFE JUMPS SHIP! SEXCALIBUR! CUSTARD CREAM!).

'Actually Mack, would it be very awful if any of this did leak out?'

'Ha-ttie,' said Mack warningly.

'Well, it's tremendously exciting. Imagine Custard and Saffron Luter . . . '

'You'll be making things much worse for us and put the crew under tremendous pressure. Imagine how much more angry that sort of press coverage will make Henry Luter?'

'I suppose,' Hattie muttered, looking over at Custard.

Saffron went to help Bee in the kitchen. 'Bloody hell, mate!' exclaimed Dougie. 'She's absolutely gorgeous! How did you manage that?'

'Dougie, this is not helpful,' interjected Mack wearily.

'No, really. Have you any tips?'

'Why didn't you tell me?' demanded Inky, punching Custard on the arm.

'I'm sorry. I couldn't tell anyone. I didn't dare. I thought you would try and talk me out of it.'

'Of course I would have done!' said Inky staunchly. 'It's what any good friend would have done!'

'Well, there you are.'

'And I am doubly cross because you have cheated me out of all that time to take the piss out of you! I'll never fall in love indeed!'

'Being in love is very bad for the stomach,' said Sir Edward.

Bee, Inky, Hattie and Milly were very fastidious that night about clearing away the plates, merely so they could all congregate in the kitchen and have a good chat.

'Mack is insisting on them staying in his flat because he's

worried what Henry Luter might do when he finds out she's run off with Custard,' said Inky.

'Where's Mack going to sleep?' asked Bee with a frown, thinking of his small one-bedroom flat.

Inky shrugged. 'I don't know, he's only just said. On the sofa, I guess. That's where he slept last night.'

Bee stared at her in horror. 'He can't possibly do that! The helmsman sleeping on the sofa, the night before a big race! He will have to come and stay here. *I'll* sleep on the sofa.'

'He can sleep in Rafe's bed and Rafe can stay with me,' said Hattie and then blushed when all three women turned to look at her.

'Are you two . . . ?' asked Inky with a grin.

Hattie bit her lip, briefly nodded and then, still blushing, disappeared to clear away more plates.

'I don't know what's got into Mack,' grumbled Sir Edward to his wife as they got into bed that night. 'I was absolutely insisting that he come and stay with us whilst Custard and this Saffron were in his flat because of course he absolutely needs his sleep. Then Bee comes in and says he must stay with her and he pretends he hasn't heard me at all and accepts graciously.'

Mack did get a good night's sleep and the following morning led out a strange but strangely upbeat crew. Their usual supporters were on the docks refusing to give up on them just yet. Their faith was justified because *Excalibur* went on to sail a textbook race and came home the winners. They weren't finished yet.

Chapter 56

The strain of the Cup was particularly telling in the Beaufort/
Dantry household.

Fabian had just been reliving the race to Milly when Elizabeth
walked in, demanding supper.

'But it isn't pork, is it? You know I'm not terribly fond of
pork.'

Milly resisted the urge to rush down and slaughter the first
pig she could find simply so she could give it to Elizabeth and
gritted her teeth instead. 'No, it's chicken and pasta. Fabian is
racing again tomorrow,' she said pointedly. 'He needs lots of
carbohydrates.' Elizabeth didn't seem to grasp the gravity of the
occasion.

She should have been leaving us all alone, thought Milly.

To add insult to injury, Elizabeth kept asking Fabian all
through supper if he had met up with the Rochesters who were
also out in Valencia.

'But I know Alicia would simply adore to see you again,
darling. You really should give her a call.'

'I think Fabian has other things on his mind right now,
Elizabeth,' said Milly firmly. She couldn't help but stick up for
him – it infuriated her that Elizabeth was all but trying to match-
make in front of her and Rosie. How could she be so crass? She
had nearly winked at Fabian, before she remembered how cross
she was with him. Then she relented. He looked terrible, under

desperate strain and hadn't eaten a thing. She put a hand on his arm.

'I'm so glad, darling, that you are finally lifting the Beaufort name back to where it belongs.' Elizabeth was off again.

Fabian finally snapped. 'And I suppose you wish that Rosie was a boy, so she could carry on the fine tradition?'

Elizabeth stared at him in surprise. How did he know what she'd been thinking . . . ?

'And I think it's bloody rude to come round here and then not eat Milly's food that she's made for you.' He gestured towards his mother's plate where she had pointedly left most of her food.

'Darling, I can't help it if pasta isn't quite my thing . . . '

'Then don't turn up and demand supper. In fact, I don't think you should turn up at all until you learn some manners.'

Elizabeth was dumbfounded. Fabian glared at her, still very upset.

Ironically it was Milly who came to the rescue. 'Why don't you go to bed,' she interjected quickly. 'And I'll bring you some hot milk? I'll sleep here on the sofa tonight and give you some extra space.'

'No,' he said. 'No, don't do that. I want you with me.'

Milly took some consolation from the look on Elizabeth's face.

Fabian was feeling terrible. In a supreme effort of will, he had forced himself to focus on the America's Cup despite everything that was happening with him, but he couldn't always control his thoughts. The odd one would pop into his head and then his mind would be racing again, fretting about his father. He lay in bed with the sweetness of the milk lying on his tongue and remembered the last time he had seen David. He also felt terrible that he still hadn't told Milly about him. He was using the America's Cup as an excuse at the moment, he knew that. What he also knew, but found almost impossible to admit, was that he was terribly ashamed, not only of his father but his mother too. He'd known she was a bitch but hadn't realised how particularly spiteful she was to Milly. And Milly deserved better. He must make it right with Milly. He must, he thought as he drifted off to sleep. The one thing that his father had made clear to him over the last few weeks was that he didn't know how lucky he was to have found someone like Milly.

When he woke in the night with a start feeling that he was falling from the spinnaker pole, he was comforted to find Milly lying beside him. He turned over and pulled her to him. She didn't wake but murmured softly and automatically melded herself into his shape.

When they filed out of the morning meeting, the families and shore crew were there as usual to greet them. Milly and Rosie immediately ran forward to Fabian. Fabian bent down to his daughter with a smile. 'Are you watching Daddy today?'

Rosie solemnly nodded. 'Telly,' she said. Milly had elected to watch the race in front of the huge mounted plasma screen in the middle of the America's Cup village with her father.

'Can Daddy have a kiss for luck?'

She flung her arms around him and he hugged her close. Then he stood up to face Milly. 'Good luck,' she said and kissed him. She waited with the other families on the pontoon and waved goodbye as *Excalibur* prepared to let slip her moorings. She wondered if this was the last time she would ever do this. Not only as it might be the last race of the America's Cup but also maybe for the last time as a family. The sadness was underlain by the certain knowledge that she and Rosie would be perfectly all right by themselves. Valencia had given her something too. She knew now that she could make money in the fashion business. She also knew that she couldn't put up with these half measures any more. She had friends – old and new. Amy had already said that she and Rosie could stay with her until she had found a house, and Bee had repeated the offer. She was going to be just fine. A broken heart wouldn't kill her.

She was still lost in these sad thoughts when Fabian, standing at the bow, started to shout something to her. The cheering increased as the boat pulled away and Milly couldn't hear him.

'What did you say?' she shouted back. She could see him frantically mouthing, and pushed her way to the front of the crowd, moving along the pontoon.

'Say again?' she yelled. She was now at the end of the pontoon.

'I SAID, WILL YOU MARRY ME?' Fabian yelled from the bow.

The words hit Milly like a slap in the face. Slowly they registered. How dare he ask her in public? She had been a sucker for that twice before. She stamped her foot and bellowed back, 'NO, I WON'T, YOU SELFISH BUGGER! YOU'VE BEEN HAVING AN AFFAIR!'

Unable to face his shock and embarrassment, she tossed her hair and pushed her way back through the throng to Rosie who didn't appear to have heard any of that little interchange between her parents as she was being fed lollipops by Milly's father.

'Everything all right?' asked Bill Dantry with his eyebrows raised very high.

'Yes, fine, thank you,' said Milly and burst into tears.

Fabian was forced to concentrate on the job in hand because the wind was blowing at twenty knots, the strongest it had been for the whole competition, as they set off from the docks and the ride out was as bumpy as could be. Sparky looked at his closest working crew mate with concern. He had witnessed the little interchange on the docks. He would take up any slack he could from Fabian but he didn't know how much would be possible in these conditions. Water poured over the bow of the boat and, donning their wet-weather gear, most of the crew came up on deck, looking up at *Excalibur*'s mast as they came and willing her to stay together.

'All right, Fabian?' shouted Sparky above the noise.

Fabian nodded. Initially his mind had been in freefall. An affair? How could she think he was having an affair? It was something he could put right, he determined, when they returned. But now he must put Milly out of his mind. The whole crew was depending on him. 'I'm not sure she's built for this,' Fabian yelled back, indicating *Excalibur*. For all her power, she was a delicate boat, built with a minimum of tolerance to make her as light as possible. They simply didn't know how much stress she would be able to take – it was like running towards the end of a cliff blindfolded and guessing where to stop.

'Are you ready for this?' yelled Sparky. Today they would prove themselves as they would be the most brutally unprotected out of all the crew.

Back on shore, all eyes were on the bowmen of the boats. The television cameras swapped from one to the other as the bows of the boats crashed through the waves and buried the men headfirst. Fabian had thrown off most of his wet-weather gear so it was easier to move in a permanent flow of water. Wave after wave washed over him, leaving him gasping for breath. Milly's heart was in her mouth as she waited for the bow to come out of the waves with a bedraggled Fabian still clinging on. It didn't seem possible that he could, but each time it rose Fabian was still there. 'Oh God,' she murmured to her father. 'They're behind.' They miserably watched *Phoenix* cross the starting line first with *Excalibur* four boat lengths behind them.

The Spanish had already rounded the first mark when the camera focused on him and *Excalibur* at the mark as he hung upside down from the spinnaker pole to clip the sail on and then dropped back on the moving, pitching deck. Milly heard the admiring murmurs around her as all eyes were pinned on the handsome bowman of the underdog British team who were capturing the world's imagination. As he leapt from the pole to the knife edge of the boat, she heard the spectators gasp with pleasure and didn't think there was a female heart there which wasn't beating a little faster. Her own felt as though it might break into two. 'Daddy!' proclaimed Rosie loudly.

On board *Excalibur*, Fabian was so focused that he barely noticed the weather. He was as sure-footed as a cat and was exalting in the challenge of performing at this level. He was more than capable of it. The more that was thrown at him, the more he wanted of it. It was a sheer adrenalin rush. He yelled 'POLE!' as he clipped the sail on to the spinnaker pole and then rushed to raise the sail. Squinting his eyes against the spray, he watched as the huge white chute raised itself and prayed it would release properly. Thankfully her restraints pinged open one by one.

'Good set, Fabian,' came Mack's voice across his earpiece. 'We're going to run these bastards down now.'

Excalibur hadn't fared too badly up that first leg. They had managed to regain a boat length on *Phoenix*. Mack was determined to catch them in a wind shadow. 'Breeze is slightly better to the left,' said Rafe. 'Take it.'

'How does the spinnaker look? Shall we change it?'

'No. It's looking good.'

Slowly and surely they were gaining on *Phoenix*. The sea pounded the boat as *Excalibur* determinedly hunted *Phoenix* down and their sails impotently collapsed, announcing that *Excalibur* had come up close enough to steal their wind.

'Got them,' said Mack. 'I want to know every single shift coming our way, Rafe. We're going to roll right past them.'

For the moment though, *Excalibur* controlled *Phoenix* and every time *Excalibur* gybed, they had to gybe with her to stop her overtaking them.

'A lift is coming,' said Rafe suddenly. 'In ten . . . nine . . . eight . . .'

Just as Rafe was counting down Mack heard the rumble of a slack sail. The genoa was sagging. Dougie, whose job it was to trim the sail, had already run forward. *Excalibur* was losing speed.

'The lashing is broken,' yelled Dougie. 'Halyard's gone.'

Mack knew this weather was too much for *Excalibur*. Fabian

was at the foot of the mast as Mack handed over the wheel to Inky and sprinted down the length of the boat. 'Drop the jib!' ordered Mack. 'We'll have to go up the mast to get the halyard.'

Fabian was already clipping his harness on. 'Are you all right to go up?' asked Mack in a low voice. Should he let Fabian or not? He might not have to go all the way to the top to get the halyard and besides Fabian was all ready. 'It's pretty rough.'

Fabian nodded briskly. He didn't even think about what happened to Dougie.

'Just hold on.'

The conditions were awful. The mast was shuddering on the deck so God only knew what it was like nearly a hundred feet up.

The crowd on the shore could see that something was wrong with *Excalibur* and that she was now dropping behind *Phoenix* but the first they could see of the problem was when Fabian was hoisted those first initial few metres in the air.

'They're sending him up the mast,' Milly whispered to herself in horror. 'He's going to die and I've just screamed at him and refused to marry him.'

He could barely get a grip on the mast which was swaying uncontrollably. Every time they paused in their hoist, the mast would be wrenched away from his fingers and he would swing out over the waves for about fifteen feet before swinging back and meeting it again with a sickening thud. He tried desperately to stop himself spinning round so that his legs could take the impact on the return. The pain seared through his cold, numb limbs. He gestured down to the grinders to raise him up quicker. He kept trying to shout down to them but the wind whipped away his words. The halyard was luckily within reach about halfway up and he grabbed it quickly. They let him down as speedily as they dared.

'Is he all right?' whispered Milly. They couldn't see properly. She felt like crying but didn't want Rosie to see how distressed she was. Her father took hold of her hand. 'He looks fine. Look, they're unclipping him now. He's fine.'

Dougie and Ho were already reattaching the halyard to a new jib. Mack put a hand on Fabian's shoulder. He felt awful that he had put his life in such jeopardy. 'Are you all right?'

'Fine.'

'I'm sorry. You could have been killed. But you've saved our bacon.'

Fabian glanced up. 'I was just worried I would break my arm and not be able to win the America's Cup with you.' They grinned at each other. For a single moment they turned back the clock to a time when they raced around the world together.

It took them another three minutes to hoist the new jib.

They chased *Phoenix* all the way down to the mark and dropped their spinnaker in record time. Once round the mark, they started to edge up behind them and before *Phoenix* knew it the British boat had seized their wind and their bow was nudging up alongside them with a grinning bald bowman waving at them as they passed. *Excalibur* never relinquished the lead. One hour and thirty-nine minutes later the score was levelled at three all.

Back at the dock, Milly sagged against her father in relief. Fabian had survived. Never had she been so fearful for him before. She didn't know whether to be upset or proud that Fabian had pulled himself so visibly together. His performance hadn't been affected at all but when *Excalibur* docked, he immediately jumped off the bow, ignoring the shouts of his teammates. He grabbed hold of Milly's elbow with just a cursory, 'Excuse us, Bill. Would you mind looking after Rosie for a minute?' to her father and dragged her into the base.

'What the hell do you mean by that?' he asked as though they had merely had the conversation a few seconds earlier. 'Me having an affair?'

Milly blinked. Suddenly she felt a lot less certain. 'Well, you are,' she said. 'With Daphne. You keep texting all the time and then I found her name on a piece of paper and then you told me that ridiculous story about falling asleep in the park and . . . and . . . and you come back smelling of mints!' she added triumphantly.

'Mints?' he asked in confusion. 'But I like mints.'

'Well, it wasn't just that. There were lots of things.' Milly felt her conviction return. She knew something was going on. Fabian stared at her; she did not flinch. Then suddenly he sighed, and in that sigh he released emotions that had been pent up for too agonisingly long.

'I was actually out with someone,' he finally admitted.

'Ha!' said Milly feeling triumphant and yet utterly crushed at the same time.

'I was out with my father. Well, not out exactly. On his boat with him. His boat's called *Daphne*.'

Milly opened her mouth to say something but nothing came out. Eventually she tried again. 'Your father?' she said weakly. 'Your father? You mean, your dad? Why didn't you tell me?'

'I don't know,' he mumbled. 'I was worried what you might think of him. I wasn't sure if you were better off thinking he really was dead. You'd think he was a bit of a bastard. You might think I would be a bad father too.'

Milly felt a huge smile spread over her face – of relief or happiness, she wasn't sure which. 'But I'm thrilled for you. Truly I am.'

'Of course you are,' he mumbled. 'You're always so kind . . . Did you really think I was having an affair? How long have you thought that for?'

'Four weeks. Since the night you were out with Dougie.'

'Four weeks? And you didn't say anything?'

'I was going to let you finish racing. Well, I was more concerned for the crew actually.'

'And then?'

'Then I was going to take Rosie and go back to Whitstable.' She tilted her chin defiantly. Fabian could see she meant it and he was flooded with panic at the thought of how close he had been to losing her – and he hadn't even known. 'How long have you kept your father from me? Which is almost as bad as having an affair, by the way. The deception is the same.'

'Five weeks.'

'Five weeks is a long time.'

'Will you marry me?'

'I don't know. You've been an absolute shit. I should walk out of here and take Rosie with me for everything you've put me through. I'm bloody livid with you.'

'I'm sorry,' said Fabian humbly. 'I didn't realise. I didn't know you thought I was having an affair.'

'Well, you must be stupid then,' said Milly briskly. 'God help you if you ever did have one. You would be absolutely useless.'

'I know. I haven't really got any excuses apart from the fact that the pressure has been extreme.'

'Things will have to change.'

'They will.'

'I want another child.'

'I would insist upon it.'

'I also want to go home and do my fashion course.'

'Absolutely.'

'And I want you to put your mother right on a few things.'

'I was going to. After the America's Cup.'

'Nanny is not provincial or common. She's lucky that I don't teach Rosie to call her "old bag".'

'I've always considered nanny to be positively grand.'

'If we do get married – and it's still an "if" – then the wedding will be organised my way.'

'I promise.'

Milly nodded. 'Then I'll think about it.'

He wriggled his signet ring off his little finger. 'Will you take this? Wear it on the other hand or something until you've decided.' He proffered it to her in the palm of his hand.

'I can't take that,' she said. 'It was, I mean *is*, your father's.'

'And you mean more to me. Please take it. I want you to have it whatever happens.'

Wordlessly Milly took it and put it on the finger of her right hand. 'Just until I've decided,' she said firmly. 'Now tell me all about your father. When can I meet him . . . ?'

'Tomorrow will be the last time we will ever race together,' said Mack sadly to Bee. They were sitting out on her balcony at Casa Fortuna, having a late coffee (decaffeinated of course). Rafe was with Tom who had made himself scarce down at his boat. Only Salty remained, somewhat annoyed that his playmate Pipgin was now refusing to leave Saffron's side. 'Just one more time. We only need to win one more time.'

Bee was desperate to ask what might happen after that. Where Mack might go and what he might do. But she knew that for the crew of *Excalibur* there was only tomorrow and then there was nothing else.

It was difficult to know what to talk about when chatting was usually so easy for them. Bee didn't want to stress Mack with anything to do with the syndicate so she couldn't talk about that. She knew he wouldn't actually be able to think about anything beyond tomorrow, so that also wiped out another avenue of conversation. So she waffled blithely on about how happy Rafe seemed and what a relief it was, miserably aware that not only was it the crew's last race tomorrow but it might also be the last time she and Mack would spend any time together. She bit her lip when Mack said that he was going to try and go to bed.

They said goodnight and she cleared up a bit, but, feeling desperately depressed, decided to leave the rest until morning. She thought she would take a glass of wine (which she hadn't felt she could have earlier as Mack wasn't drinking), go to bed and try to perhaps read a book.

Feeling like a proper old soak, she and Salty climbed into bed and, propped against many pillows, she tried to concentrate but the words kept blurring as her mind focussed on some distant thought. Her head jerked up at a knock at the door.

Putting on her Japanese robe, she opened the door tentatively.

'I can't sleep,' said Mack.

'Neither can I.'

'You're distracting me.'

'I am?'

'I wondered if I might sleep better if I knew you would come home with me after the Cup.'

'Come home with you?'

'Yes. I thought we might get married. What do you think?'

'I think that would be nice.' Bee stared at him in surprise. He really was the most baffling man sometimes.

'I kept thinking Tom might get to you before me.'

Bee frowned. 'Tom? No, not Tom.'

He nodded. 'I'm going to try and sleep now.'

She smiled gently. 'It's a big race tomorrow.'

'Goodnight, Bee.'

'Goodnight, Mack.'

He turned on his heel and left her. She closed the door with a gentle click. Yes, he really was the most baffling man. And that was precisely what Bee liked about him.

Chapter 57

Whilst the crew of *Excalibur* tried their best to sleep, preparations were being made for the final race of the America's Cup. Down at the Excalibur compound Griff Dow and his sailmakers were recutting the engines of *Excalibur*.

Hattie was sitting upstairs in her office. She was still fielding press calls and requests for interviews up until midnight from a nation now transfixed with the America's Cup.

The heightened security surrounding her was busy with reports of a break-in and chased two intruders around the perimeter fence but failed to catch them.

Breakfast for the crew was a quiet affair with Carla silently dripping tears into the rice pudding at the prospect of their last day together. She had done the full British breakfast for the crew that morning and many of them looked on horrified as Golly and Ho blithely chucked back two plates of sausage, egg and bacon each. Inky had to rush to the loo when it looked as though Golly might go up for his third. Fabian managed a glass of orange juice and some muesli and Custard did at least keep some toast down but kept staring into his coffee mug as though it might hold the secrets of the universe. Mack and Rafe quietly discussed some starting tactics (with Inky in between her loo visits) whilst Carla replenished their coffee mugs. This being their last day she had relented and gave them coffee 'with enough water to boil pasta in'. After eighteen months at the compound the fridge still stood out in the centre of the floor trailing wires. No one had ever thought to question it.

At the crew meeting, Mack stood up and wished everyone a good morning. He paused for a second. 'Today is the last race we will ever sail together. It has been a privilege to sail with every one of you. If I never set foot in another match race boat again it won't be because of anything you've done but simply because any other crew will disappoint me.'

The crew looked at each other, then back at Mack. Just at that moment, they would have done anything for him. They would have swum round the course ten times for him if they thought it could help.

For one last time, they kissed their families goodbye. Hattie threw her arms around Rafe, thanking God it was their last race – she had been so worried for his safety in this series against Luter. Fabian, Milly and Rosie kissed each other goodbye. Bee had brought Salty with a huge pink bow on. She and Mack paused together and he kissed her roughly on the cheek, squeezing her hands before he left. Both Inky's parents were there murmuring words of encouragement. Saffron and Carla stood together and it was hard to tell who was crying the harder.

Mack asked Dougie's dad, who was in full regalia, to lead the way out to *Excalibur* and they deliberately delayed walking out on to the pontoon until the last possible moment. The crowds were too enormous to contemplate. As the door from the compound opened and the first sight of a pink shirt glimpsed, a roar went up from the crowd. The crew filed out, led by Dougie's dad and an armed security guard, to *Excalibur* who was waiting in the water for them. Everywhere they looked there were eager, excited faces. A huge gantry had been erected at the end of the pontoon for the television cameras to capture every moment; there were even cameras hanging out of helicopters buzzing overhead. There was a persistent hum of powerboats and RIBs as they darted hither and thither across the harbour and over two thousand boats waited patiently for them at the end of the canal.

'God, if my mum knew it was going to be like this, she would never have let me come,' Custard whispered to Inky.

They could just about pick out their usual supporters: the old lady in the green tweed and the man playing the bagpipes. 'Godspeed, John MacGregor!' the old lady called. 'Godspeed!'

Much to the panic of the security guard, Mack went up to shake the hands of both of them. 'Thank you,' he said. He touched *Excalibur* briefly as he stepped on board, willing her to stay together for one last time, to win for just one last time and knowing that Valencia would for ever remember her name if she did.

The tow out to the race course felt unbearable. Everyone sat in stony silence below the deck whilst Sir Edward steered the boat out. No one could speak. Rafe listened to Hattie's iPod. Fabian occasionally wiped his sweating palms on his shorts. Inky picked all the skin off her lips until they were red raw.

When they filed out to the deck, the black and orange boat loomed in front of them. Mack could see Jason Bryant at the helm and Henry Luter's familiar baseball cap. Bryant looked over briefly towards them but didn't even acknowledge their presence.

'Course posted,' said Inky seeing the flag raise on the committee boat. 'Let's get *Excalibur* ready.'

They waited for the ten-minute pre-start gun in complete silence. The seven thousand-strong crowd back at the America's Cup village waited in silence. The millions of viewers watching their televisions around the world waited in silence.

The starting gun went on the final race of the 2007 America's Cup.

Mack decided that he didn't want to have to hold *Phoenix* for more than four minutes – both boats seemed to be equally matched on the start line – so he held back from his attack and made slow looping circles, swiftly moving out of the way of trouble until Inky called the four-minute mark. He didn't need to go looking for them because there they were, waiting for him. There was a flurry of activity as the two helmsmen played chicken with three-million-pound boats, driving at each other again and again and then feigning away and missing each other by just a few feet. The sea was just a churning maelstrom as the boats tore over the surface, cutting grooves and ruts of white water. The crowd gasped and exclaimed as Mack used one of the press boats who had ventured in too near as an obstacle to get *Phoenix* off his tail. He was close enough to see the whites of their terrified eyes as he turned the twenty-five-tonne monster on a sixpence around them, *Phoenix* in close pursuit. The manoeuvre shook them off until Mack regained right of way again and lunged at them, trying to force them into a penalty, but they were too quick for him. They hit the line together, two seconds behind the gun with *Phoenix* edging slightly ahead.

Unbeknown to Excalibur, the whole of the Phoenix syndicate had been up most of the night. Still convinced there must be something in *Excalibur*'s design to aid her advancement through the series, they had had spies on her all week. Although it was strictly illegal, they'd had weight removed from the keel of *Phoenix* and the sail team had been working all night to imitate the shape of Griff Dow's sails.

Jason Bryant and Henry Luter looked at each other triumphantly as *Phoenix* started to ease away from *Excalibur*. 'They're falling behind,' said their navigator. 'We're faster and lower.' Luter smiled to himself and wondered how long it would take for them to realise that they were racing a different boat.

Back on *Excalibur*, Mack and Inky looked at each other in puzzlement. 'Have we the wrong genoa up?' he questioned.

'I don't think so.'

Mack looked over to Rafe, hoping for some miraculous wind

shift which might save them but he merely shook his head. 'Stay on this bearing.'

'Let's just keep going,' said Mack to himself. 'Let's get these numbers up. Talk to me, Sammy.'

'Ten point six, ten point six, ten point seven . . . '

Custard eased the mainsheet a touch.

'Up point one, Mack,' said Sammy. 'Ten point seven, ten point seven . . . '

Despite their best efforts all the way up to the first mark, *Phoenix* kept edging ahead of *Excalibur* until they were leading by a decisive twenty-one seconds at the mark. 'We can still catch them,' Mack called out to the crew as they came up to the mark. *Phoenix* had already rounded it, their spinnaker puffing out in front of them as they sped away. 'Give me a perfect set now. Code two spinnaker,' Mack shouted down to Ho.

Bellowing with aggression, Ho heaved the spinnaker out on deck by himself. Fabian leapt to clip the spinnaker pole, yelling 'POLE!' as he did so and then, dropping the sopping wet genoa, Ho and Fabian hauled it in hand over hand, puffing with its weight, desperately trying to keep it from touching the water, their arms just a blur.

Mack spun the wheel of *Excalibur*, a pain buried deep in his side from throwing himself at the wheel again and again, blinded to a developing drama by the sails.

Dougie had leapt forward to kick a jammed sheet free. They went over a sudden wave and, staggering slightly with the motion, he stepped back into a coil of lines just as Golly and Flipper started to grind up the spinnaker. It all happened so quickly. Dougie's foot started to be pulled towards one of the winches so fast that he fell, smashing his shoulder against the hull of the boat as he toppled overboard. It took less than a second. He yelled just before his head went under the waves. Miraculously Fabian had seen the swoop of colour out of the corner of his eye as Dougie was swept over.

Fabian leant down, grabbed hold of Dougie's waistband and with the adrenalin rush given to him with such a situation, managed to haul him back on board, ironically aided by the grinding motion of Golly and Flipper who were still slowly but surely pulling Dougie's foot towards the winch. Fabian pulled out the knife which was permanently strapped to his leg, ready to cut the sail away. If he did, they would lose the race. If he didn't Dougie would lose his foot. The pain was excruciating but for a wild moment Dougie actually contemplated making the sacrifice. Both of them were yelling, Dougie almost screaming in agony, but it was nigh on impossible for anyone to hear anything above the shriek of sails. Fabian and Dougie's eyes met. Dougie shook his head, agony hissing through his teeth. Fabian had no choice. He was about to cut the lines when Custard poked his head round the headsail. He'd heard something above the boat noise. 'EASE THE FUCKING SAIL!' yelled Fabian at him.

Custard couldn't see what had happened but in two strides he leapt across the deck and eased the sheet, giving Fabian a split-second window to release Dougie's foot. He and Fabian sat panting for a second, Dougie's head still cradled in Fabian's lap. 'Thank you,' murmured Dougie, briefly closing his eyes before hauling himself up and returning to his station.

Since the incident was completely hidden from all eyes apart from those involved, *Phoenix* could only see that they had gained some more vital seconds. Their lead now extended to thirty-five seconds. 'We're whipping them,' said Jason Bryant. 'They're on the ropes now.'

Over three thousand miles away, the British people who were watching their television sets slumped in despair as they witnessed *Excalibur* floundering around the mark and *Phoenix* pull into a significant lead. 'So close,' they all murmured. 'We were so close.'

Back in Rock, everyone from the sailing school was transfixed. There was hardly any traffic out on the water; there was no sound of lawnmowers despite the bright summer sun. Only foreign tourists boarded the ferry to Padstow. The village shops had closed for the afternoon and Rafe's old boss from the sailing school and his wife looked on in horror as *Excalibur* lost ground. A few comforting pats came their way from the people crowded into their small sitting room to watch the match. One of them sighed and went through to the kitchen to start putting away the celebratory feast and to hide the surprise sign which they had optimistically prepared saying 'CONGRATULATIONS RAFE AND EXCALIBUR!'

On board *Mucky Ducky*, Sir Edward rested his head in his hands, almost not bearing to watch. 'It can't end like this,' he said to himself. 'It can't.'

Back on *Excalibur*, Mack gritted his teeth. 'WE ARE NOT LOSING TODAY!' he roared. 'DO YOU HEAR ME? WE ARE NOT LOSING!'

They set off down their run together. The trimmers were concentrating so hard on the shapes of the sails, they managed to forget their very existence. Nothing mattered other than extracting the very last ounce of speed from *Excalibur*. 'Rafe, find me some wind,' implored Mack. 'Your one purpose in life is to find me some wind.'

'Their spinnaker isn't looking good,' said Inky, who hadn't taken her eyes off *Phoenix*. 'Their breeze is dropping.'

'The breeze looks better to the left,' confirmed Rafe in the same breath.

Mack cut over left with Sammy's words singing in his ears.

'Ease her up a touch, Custard!' called Mack but Custard's hands had already been busy.

'Head her down, Mack!' called Custard. 'Head her down a fraction. Just right.'

Inky looked at *Phoenix*'s sails again against the perfection of *Excalibur*'s beautiful curves. They were starting to flop a little. '*Phoenix* is losing speed. They're looking at us. We're worrying them.'

* * *

On *Phoenix*, they were indeed turning their heads. 'What the fuck's going on?' hissed Luter. 'How is she faster after all we've done to *Phoenix*?'

Jason Bryant looked round desperately for answers. Panic started up his throat. He couldn't see what to do. How the fuck could this happen to him? A wave of anger threatened to engulf him. He *couldn't* lose. He wouldn't let them. The crew started to look to him for answers and he tried to think of some rash move which might just heave him out of this predicament.

The gap was slowly and surely closing. It took another two marks before *Excalibur* truly had them in their sights. The two boats ran in parallel, with *Excalibur* closer to the wind.

'We need more speed, Mack. We need to cover them completely,' said Inky. As it stood, *Excalibur* was a few seconds ahead of them but hadn't caught them in a true wind shadow.

'Breeze is coming,' said Rafe. 'In six . . . five . . . four . . . '

It took just a couple of seconds for *Excalibur* to feel the benefit of the wind and catch the black and orange boat in their vacuum.

Inky knew that a boat caught in another's wind shadow would instigate a fierce tacking duel until the leading boat hopefully made an error and their opponent could move into some clean air. She frowned. '*Phoenix* don't seem very keen to be going anywhere,' she commented to Mack.

'They don't want to duel,' said Mack.

Then to Rafe. 'What's it looking like? Where's the breeze?'

'We need to tack soon; the wind will start to die off if we stay on this bearing.'

Mack looked to Inky; as the tactician it was her call to either stay and cover *Phoenix* or move off and trust in the fact that they would find the breeze sooner than *Phoenix* and sail the boat better.

She took a moment and then decided. 'Tack. Rafe will find the wind.'

'TACKING!' yelled Mack. The grinders' arms flailed away, driving the huge sails, and Pond's arms grabbed and grabbed at the loose lines.

'They're watching us, Mack,' said Inky quietly. Mack took a glance back to see the heads bobbing up and down, all turning towards them and then towards their own afterguard. Rafe had established a fearsome reputation. They didn't like the thought that the British boat might be in search of some breeze they didn't know about.

Rafe didn't find any miraculous wind because, as he knew, there was none to be found, but *Phoenix* soon followed their tack (Mack never knew whether it was because of them or because their wind started to die off) and Rafe continued to call the small lifts perfectly so Mack could sail the boat to the best of his abilities. For once there was silence from Custard. He couldn't tell Mack to bear up or bear down. Mack was sailing on a knife edge of perfection.

As they ran up to the first mark, Sammy shouted out 'CODE TWO SPINNAKER!' and Ho immediately heaved the sail on to the deck. Fabian clipped it into position and Ho dived for the halyard, desperate to get that sail up. He heaved the beautiful white chute into place all by himself. The sail opened her wings within eight seconds of her call-up.

'Beautiful set!' called Mack down to the crew. 'Well done!'

Phoenix rounded the mark twenty seconds after *Excalibur*. Mack looked over his shoulder. *Excalibur* was never very fast down these legs. Even so they just about managed to hold them off until the next mark but the margin was cut down to just a few seconds.

'They're going to start a tacking duel,' snapped Rafe, watching *Phoenix*.

'We're going start tacking,' Mack called to the grinders, intimating that they had better get ready because this was going to get painful. Inky's glance shot across to *Excalibur*'s grinders, Golly, Flipper and Rump. They looked as though they would tear *Phoenix* apart with their teeth if they needed to. They knew what was coming. They crouched over their pedestals, muscles tensed and hungry for battle.

'TACK!' yelled Mack in order to stop *Phoenix* from passing.

They leant into the winches, their arms a mere blur, perfectly in rhythm as the huge one-hundred-foot sail swung across the deck.

'TACKING!' yelled Mack again. And the grinders went hard at it – these guys didn't bench-press 120kg for nothing. By the time *Excalibur* and *Phoenix* had tacked ten times, the sweat was running off them and their lungs were gasping for breath, the pain so intense they felt as though they were going to cave in and dissolve in the acid.

Again and again Mack asked them to tack the boat. Custard and Dougie were shaking with adrenalin as they prepared to trim the sails from each tack. Fabian and Ho came up from the foredeck to give the boys a break for one tack. Inky noticed that *Phoenix* had already been using their bowman and sewer man to help them out for the last five tacks. Fabian, particularly, wasn't built for tacking and the strain on him must have been enormous but they egged each other on.

The Spanish boat came back again and Mack noticed that there wasn't any gain for them out of that tack. Their crew work must be getting sloppy. Henry Luter seemed to be screaming at the top of his lungs at them. 'TACK!' Mack yelled, and again they pounded away in the blistering heat of the day. By now their lungs were collapsing and their hearts about to burst but they still kept going. Rafe ran down to take a tack for Fabian.

Then Bryant started the age-old trick of throwing in dummy tacks and Mack handed the responsibility of calling the tacks over to Inky so the crew could respond quicker. Her eyes never shifted from *Phoenix* but she was starting to get a little anxious as they approached the twenty-fifth tack.

'Find me some fucking wind, Rafe, and get them off us,' she muttered as the huge sail thundered over the deck again.

'TACK! . . . TACK . . . NO, DON'T GO, IT'S A DUMMY . . . TACK!'

'Just waiting for the right shift.'

'TACK! Sod the right shift, find me any shift. *Excalibur* is losing speed with this many tacks. We'll be dead in the water soon.'

Phoenix was nipping at their heels. An arrogant American drawl came from their bow. 'Get out of our way, *Excalibur*, you're too fucking slow!'

It was just the impetus that Golly needed; he turned round from his pedestal with sweat pouring off him. 'I'll be pissing in the wind when you cross the finish line, you little shit!' he roared, shaking his fist in the air. He turned back and went at his winch like a man possessed.

Rafe hadn't found any wind by the time they came up to the mark but they had still managed to hold *Phoenix* off. The grinders flopped back from their pedestals, their chests still heaving as Ho dived below for the spinnaker. They had decided to use the same spinnaker as the last time and Fabian and Ho worked their magic as she cracked into place perfectly. The Spanish weren't quite as efficient and lost a couple of seconds in their spinnaker change. Even so these downwind legs were their strongest and there was nothing Mack could do about it. *Excalibur*'s spinnaker was as full and as stable as it could be, he even changed it but none of it did any good: the Spanish super-boat stole their wind and steamed passed them.

'Find me some breeze, Rafe,' Mack muttered to his strategist.

'A shift is coming in from the left but it's only going to be a few more knots than this. Not enough to justify the change in direction. We won't make any gains.'

'How long?'

'Two minutes.'

Mack thought hard. *Excalibur* couldn't beat them on a power reach like this. Not unless they had a breeze that *Phoenix* didn't know about.

'Let me know when it's coming, Rafe. We're going to take it.'

'But it's not enough.'

'They might think otherwise.'

'It's coming in thirty . . . fifteen . . . ten . . . nine . . . eight . . . seven . . .'

Mack swung *Excalibur* around thirty degrees and caught the breeze like an express train thundering through. Immediately the boat sped ahead.

Custard looked up from his station. 'Marvellous if we were going in the right sodding direction,' he muttered to himself.

'Look ahead, everyone. Concentrate,' ordered Mack. 'Just Inky look back and tell us what they're doing.'

'They're watching us,' she murmured. 'They're discussing.'

Back in the press lounge, watching the television screen with all the power of perspective and all the respect for Mack's helming skills, the Spanish journalists were jumping up and down yelling at the television screen. 'Don't look at his eyes, don't look at them!' they shouted, knowing that their boat would be pulled into Mack's devilish strategy. They could clearly see that *Phoenix* was ahead and should stay where they were. But it was to no avail. The Spanish boat altered its course and gave chase.

'They're coming after us. They've decided to stay with us,' said Inky quietly.

Mack let out a small stream of breath he'd been holding.

'We're right back in this. Rafe, tell me every single puff of air which is going to hit this boat. We need to catch every single shift. We just have to stay ahead of them on this leg. What about the chute? Do we need to change it?'

'No,' said Inky. 'It's looking good.'

'Sammy?'

'They're forty seconds behind us and we're just about holding them on speed.'

The tantalising and unspoken thought hung in the air that

they actually might win the America's Cup. Everyone was thinking it but no one dared to mention it.

'Flipper,' said Custard suddenly. 'You're not humming. Please start humming.'

Let the boat hold out, Mack prayed to himself and gripped the wheel even harder. They needed *Excalibur* to stay together.

They were the first around the last mark with *Phoenix* hot on their heels but Mack knew that these legs were their strongest. It was the final leg to the finish.

Jason Bryant was indeed getting desperate. He threw gybe after gybe at them, hoping something on *Excalibur* would break. You could nearly smell the blood on the grinders' handles and sense the tension as everyone knew that one mistake, one early or late cast off the winch could change the course of history.

Gradually *Phoenix* was gaining on them as they came closer and closer to the line with Fabian calling the distance.

'Fuck, this is going to be close,' murmured Inky. 'Six boat lengths . . . five . . . ' Fabian carried on calling. Up ahead Inky could see the entirety of the Valencia Yacht Club standing on their boat. She even thought she could hear her mother screaming her on from one of the spectator boats. 'Four . . . three . . . two . . . one . . . '

And there was the gun.

Chapter 58

'Excalibur wins, Excalibur wins!' yelled an overenthusiastic commentator and a triumphant blare of spectator horns rang out as *Excalibur* crossed the line. They had won. A disbelieving Mack relaxed his grip on the wheel and stared around him. An enormous sense of relief settled on him, not euphoria or triumph but pure, undiluted relief. Atlas felt his shoulders rise as the load was lifted. He blew a kiss to Bee on *Mucky Ducky* who had tears streaming down her face.

The rest of the crew were going absolutely berserk. The most delighted person was an almost demented Colin Montague who had risen from his eighteenth man position with a roar, unveiling his T-shirt underneath which said 'Excalibur pull the sword from the stone' and then promptly leapt into the water. On *Mucky Ducky* there was a scramble to fish him out. Hattie was wailing, 'I did not ask him to do that,' at Mack.

Over on *Phoenix*, Mack could see a similar sort of ruckus going on but this one involved a lot of ugly yelling. Henry Luter was letting loose his temper and berating every single member of the crew. Saffron, with her loose hair blowing in the breeze, didn't look at him once. She only had eyes for Custard, who she thought was the most handsome man on the boat, anyway, even without hair.

The tow home felt equally chaotic with two thousand boats accompanying them, each jostling to come alongside the crew to take their pictures and to shout their congratulations. Two coastguard boats were flanking *Excalibur* with their lights flashing and trying rather ineffectually to keep control. Inky's parents who had been on a different spectator boat came alongside briefly. They were absolutely bursting with pride. 'Well done, my darling!' called her mother. 'What a wonderful, wonderful race!'

'We're so proud of you!' called her father. Inky thought her face would split, she was grinning so hard at them both. Mack came up to hug his god-daughter, smiling and waving at his old friends as he went. Their boat started to pull away.

'We'll see you on shore!' called her mum blowing effusive kisses.

'Well done, Inky,' Mack whispered in her ear. 'You showed them all.'

Inky knew he wasn't generalising. She cast a glance at her father, and nodded. 'Thanks to you.'

'No thanks to me. I simply gave you the opportunity. Make sure they clear that bloody wall of trophies for you back home.'

'If it was up to my mother . . . ' said Inky. 'I don't particularly care about that any more anyway.'

'Good,' said Mack. 'Good for you.'

As they were towed down the canal which led into the America's Cup village the bank was lined with the staggering sight of thousands and thousands of people. Champagne was being popped all round, people were even letting off fireworks into the sunny sky. 'What are all these people doing here?' Rafe kept asking in wonderment.

It took at least half an hour for *Excalibur* to dock as she fought her way through all the boats. A band was very creakily playing 'God Save the Queen'. Eventually Mack and his crew stepped ashore and were reunited with a bedraggled, sodden Colin Montague. The presentation ceremony didn't take very long. The commodore of the Valencia Yacht Club made a small, gracious speech, presented Mack with a huge jeroboam of Moët champagne and then handed over the America's Cup to Colin. There was a huge cheer as Colin held the trophy over his head, accompanied by hundreds of camera clicks. After a moment, he handed the Cup over to Mack who had been busy spraying the crew with the champagne. He looked disbelievingly at it for a minute. Whenever he had seen it in the past he'd only been allowed to look at it from behind a cordon and two armed guards, and now he was actually touching and holding it. He stared at it for another brief second before handing it on to the crew.

Somehow the crew of *Phoenix* had fought their way through. Henry Luter wasn't with them. He couldn't face the humiliation of defeat and had already retired to *Corposant* despite his PA's pleadings that he would look like a bad loser.

Jason Bryant shook Mack's hand. 'Congratulations,' he said, trying to smile. 'I did do my best.'

'I know,' said Mack quietly. 'You sailed some good races.'

'You're the only person who that means anything from.' He looked quite hollow. His *Phoenix* crew behind him, he went slowly down the line, dutifully shaking hands with Pond, Sparky, Ho and the others as tradition dictated. He came to Inky. 'Well done,' he said stiffly.

'Thank you,' she replied and smiled at him.

Even with the stench of defeat under his nose, he still wanted her. He didn't want her pity though.

He almost couldn't distract Rafe from kissing Hattie to shake his hand. 'Congratulations,' Jason said stiffly. 'I guess all the things they were saying about you must have been true.'

'Thanks,' said Rafe.

Bryant wondered fleetingly whether Rafe was the reason that Ava had finished with him three nights ago, but his monumental ego wouldn't let him believe it. 'I hope you're going to stick around in match racing.'

'Maybe.'

'I'll enjoy beating you next time.'

'I look forward to it.'

Rafe went back to kissing Hattie. Hattie caught a glimpse of Ava. She looked stricken, her luminous beauty dulled. She was making no progress through the throng. For once Hattie felt a little sorry for her.

After the America's Cup had been kissed by all, the crew completed one very important aspect of a winning race. The dunking of the skipper. Pond and Custard both seized a foot, with Sparky and Dougie at the head. Mack flew off the side of the docks into the water and emerged spluttering. Bee sincerely hoped that she wouldn't have to follow suit. That would be taking wifely duties a little too far. Soon pretty well all of them had thrown themselves off the docks and were joyfully paddling around in the water.

'You know,' said Milly's dad thoughtfully to Elizabeth as they stood and watched, 'this is something I've always wanted to do.' With a terrifying Mohawk yell, he grabbed Elizabeth around the waist and both of them flew into the water. Milly was horrified. 'Can she swim?' she yelled after them.

Eventually Hattie got them all out of the water and along to the press conference. En route, soaking and limping, Dougie, who had been staring enraptured at a beautiful long-haired, brunette reporter, had been calling and calling home to try and speak to his mum, without success. He kept thinking, surely she wouldn't have gone out? He couldn't know that she was being carried on her gardener's shoulders down the high street of his village with the church bells ringing in her ears.

At the press conference, security was desperately trying to impose order. They were only letting the press and families of Excalibur in. Dozens of microphones had been arranged at the table. Everyone in the world wanted to hear what Mack had to say.

'Mack! Mack!' clamoured about a hundred voices. 'What does it feel like?'

'I'm inordinately proud to be the first skipper to take the America's Cup back to England. Back home. Back to where it all began.'

'Tell us about the race?'

'The crew were bloody marvellous, as they have always been.

We had a few dramas.' He peered down the table to the stitched and scarred Dougie. He and Fabian then proceeded to re-enact the whole scene including the swearing and the gritted teeth. The press thought they were hilarious. Inky noticed Dougie's brunette reporter was looking particularly intoxicated and was staring at him with a sort of trance-like adoration. She smiled to herself and wondered fleetingly whether Luca was watching. He might not have been able to stand it.

'Fabian!' one of the reporters called. 'As the bowman you were the first across the finishing line. How did that feel?'

Fabian smiled into the TV camera. He hoped that someone sitting in a bar somewhere might know that the smile was for him.

'It was one of the best moments of my life. I've been lucky to have a few lately.'

'What were the other ones?'

Fabian was about to open his mouth to say they were private when a small kerfuffle with the security guards distracted him. He squinted and recognised the small, wiry figure.

'No!' he called out suddenly. 'Let him in! He's family. He's my family.'

The security guards looked over and then reluctantly released the figure. Milly's dad emerged triumphantly into the press conference. Fabian continued to answer the question whilst Milly looked on in amazement at such a public admission from Fabian. She contemplated the signet ring on her right hand. A moment later, she swapped it over to her left.

The questions kept firing and firing, until the organisers, trying to wind it up, asked for one last question from a man at the front with the red tie.

'Mack! Have you thought anything about your defence of the America's Cup? Where is it going to be held? When's it going to happen?'

'Ah,' said Mack gravely. 'Now that is something I am really looking forward to. That promises to be a *real* battle.'

Bee sighed and lifted her eyes to heaven.

Epilogue

Inky Pencarrow took a year out of match racing to helm an all-female crew in the Volvo Ocean Race to see what all the fuss was about. It was an arena she had felt closed off to her before because of her brothers but now things had changed. After all, as she said to the papers, 'Who better to beat Mother Nature at her own game than a woman?' Her mother flew out to meet her at every stopover. Not only does Mary Pencarrow eat chocolate digestives on the beach for supper now but she has also started to plant tulips in her salt-encrusted garden.

Fabian and Milly got married. Just how Milly wanted, and in a dress designed by her and sold under her new label. They still travel all over the world for Fabian to race in regattas with their two little girls Rosie and Poppy, Rosie carrying her pet plastic rat and looking for the ghost of a boat named *Daphne*. Fabian still stares at Milly and wonders if she realises how hard he would fight to keep her.

Mack and Bee decided to take the long way home. They bought a boat in Valencia, took Salty, and Bee's spotty Cath Kidston china, and sailed around the Mediterranean, only pausing to get married in Nice. He still wakes up occasionally breathless at the sight of a black and orange boat overtaking him and grabbing for an imaginary wheel but Salty is always there for a comforting lick before he returns to sleep.

Saffron always sleeps well now; in fact Custard has great trouble waking her sometimes. They meet up with Fabian and Milly at regattas and spoil their girls stupid.

Custard's fears that Luter would damage his career were unfounded: Luter decided to turn his hand to offshore racing, and Custard had made many friends over the years anyway and their loyalty to him would always be greater than their fear of Luter. Despite the damage inflicted on Saffron in her childhood, the doctors are optimistic that she will be able to have children. Until they come along, though, they have Pipgin and a little Westie called Holly. They would consider adoption as a happy option.

The crew only hear about Rafe through Hattie, who is a vigorous correspondent. They know what he's like and don't take it personally. Rafe returned to his life of wandering with Hattie happy to accompany him but, restless for challenge, which is one of the many things that *Excalibur* left in his bloodstream, he rather thinks he will return to the competitive life he once so despised.

Despite the agonies and the glories, they are all looking forward to England's defence of the America's Cup.

Technical notes

Whilst I tried to be as accurate and true to life as possible, there were some technical issues which I had to fudge in order not to detract from the glories of the racing and the idea of the Cup. The America's Cup is splendidly complicated, which can be daunting for a novice. For the purists, I list the inaccuracies below:

- There is only one challenger for the America's Cup. The actual America's Cup consists only of a series of races between the official challenger and the defender. In order to determine that challenger, all the syndicates take part in the Louis Vuitton Cup. To avoid confusion, I dispensed with the Louis Vuitton Cup and simply referred to it all as the America's Cup with the 'final' between the challenger and the holder of the Cup.
- During the 2007 Cup in Valencia there was a rule change where, for the first time, the defender of the Cup was able to race with other challengers during a series of 'acts' leading up to the Louis Vuitton Cup.
- I missed out one round robin in the preliminary rounds.
- The actual America's Cup consists of the best of nine races, not seven.
- Until recently, in order to compete for a syndicate you had to take their nationality.

- If a sailor leaves a syndicate they are banned from working for another syndicate during the lifetime of that Cup.
- The timings for the Volvo Ocean Race and the World Match Tour may be slightly out of synchronisation with the timings of the book.
- I have referred to the Volvo Ocean Race throughout as the Volvo, even if the character in question sailed when it was still the Whitbread.
- The skirts of the boats in 2007 America's Cup were dropped before the Louis Vuitton Cup.

The Crew

BOWMAN; *Fabian*. Takes care of the forward sails, relays information to the helm during the start. Climbs out on the spinnaker pole. Must connect the sheets and halyards to the headsails and spinnakers when they're changed, including attaching sheets to the outboard end of the spinnaker pole, which means dangling above and in front of the boat. Works on a surface area no bigger than a footprint with no safety rails. Climbs the mast to deal with any problems.

MIDBOWMAN; *Sparky*. Also climbs the mast and helps bowman and sewer man.

SEWER; *Ho*. Looks after all the sails in the sewer (the only below-deck portion of the boat, called the sewer because of the large quantities of water which rush through the hatches), packs them away and takes them out. Helps with the sails during hoists and drops. Must have a strong stomach to avoid sea sickness.

PITMAN; *Pond*. Controls the ropes, the boom and the fine tuning of the mast. Orchestrates the sails and other control lines.

MASTMAN; *Jonny Rocket*. He is positioned at the foot of the mast, hoists the sails, helps the grinders and assists in sail drops.

GRINDERS x2; *Flipper. Rump*. The engine rooms of the boat. They use winches to power the sails up and down. The rest of the crew rely on their speed and efficiency during tacking. Substantial amounts of speed can be lost if they are too slow. Periods of rest and then explosive power.

TRIMMERS x2; *Dougie. Germ.* Trim the forward sails, the spinnaker and the genoa by fine tuning the sail to the wind to extract as much speed from the boat as possible. On-board computers are there to help them but the best trimmers rely more on instinct.

MAINSAIL GRINDER; *Golly.* Controls the mainsail with one huge winch. Exhausting work, particularly in the pre-start and rounding the mark when the mainsail can go from fully in to completely out within a matter of seconds.

MAINSAIL TRIMMER; *Custard.* Trims the mainsail and thus steers the boat. Works very closely with the helmsman. A huge responsibility as he has many tonnes at his fingertips.

RUNNER; *Bandit.* Controls the running backstay. The backstay is an important sail trim control and has a direct effect on the shape of the mainsail. If he misses his cue in a gybe then the rig (mast and sails) tumbles over the bow. If he delays his release then the helm loses control of the rudder.

TRAVELLER; *Cherry.* Works the mainsail traveller which helps to control the speed upwind.

HELM; *Mack.* Steers the boat and concentrates on driving it as fast as possible. He must be able to respond quickly to developing tactical situations.

NAVIGATOR; *Sammy.* Uses on-board computers and electronics to relay info to afterguard. Precision is tantamount and his main role on an America's Cup boat is to feed back vital statistics to the helmsman.

TACTICIAN; *Inky.* Acts as eyes of the boat and must have specific trust of the helmsman. Responsible for positioning of the boat on the course, taking into effect the wind, tide, sea conditions and state of the race.

STRATEGIST; *Rafe.* The wind caller – constantly looking out for changes in wind speed and direction and new shifts. Also acts as extra pair of hands during manoeuvres.

18TH MAN; *Colin Montague.* The joy rider at the back of the boat and strictly spectator only. He is allowed no participation whatsoever.

Glossary

BOW	Front of the boat.
DOWNWIND	Sailing with the wind behind you.
FOREDECK	The area of the boat's deck which is in front of the mast.
GENOA	The sail between the mast and the bow of the boat.
GYBE	To alter the boat's course so the stern travels through the wind.
HALYARD	A rope used to hoist a sail.
HULL	The body of the boat.
KEEL	This projects down into the water. The size and shape can enable the boat to go faster and turn quicker. It helps to prevent capsize.
LEEWARD	Opposite of windward or upwind. A leeward boat has another boat between it and the wind.
MAINSAIL	The largest sail behind the mast.
PORT	Left.
STARBOARD	Right.
STERN	The back of the boat.
TACK	Turning the bow of the boat through the wind and changing the side of the sails. A port tack is when the

wind is from the left-hand side of the boat and a starboard tack is when the wind is from the right.

UPWIND/WINDWARD   Sailing towards or into the wind.